ODD BILLY TODD
by N.C. REED
Published by Creative Texts Publishers
PO Box 50
Barto, PA 19504
www.creativetexts.com

Copyright 2017-2019 by N.C. REED
All rights reserved

Cover photos used by license.
Design copyright 2017-2019 Creative Texts Publishers, LLC

This book or parts thereof may not be reproduced in any form, stored in a retrieval system, or transmitted in any form by any means—electronic, mechanical, photocopy, recording, or otherwise—without prior written permission of the publisher, except as provided by United States of America copyright law.

The following is a work of fiction. Any resemblance to actual names, persons, businesses, and incidents is strictly coincidental. Locations are used only in the general sense and do not represent the real place in actuality.

ISBN: 978-0692544044

odd BILLY TODD

N.C. REED

For those who believed,
For those who encouraged,
For those who inspired,
For the Billy's I have known.
And finally, for Bad Karma00 fans.
Thank you, each and every one.

Table of Contents

CHAPTER ONE	1
CHAPTER TWO	10
CHAPTER THREE	14
CHAPTER FOUR	19
CHAPTER FIVE	23
CHAPTER SIX	27
CHAPTER SEVEN	34
CHAPTER EIGHT	38
CHAPTER NINE	43
CHAPTER TEN	49
CHAPTER ELEVEN	54
CHAPTER TWELVE	60
CHAPTER THIRTEEN	66
CHAPTER FOURTEEN	72
CHAPTER FIFTEEN	77
CHAPTER SIXTEEN	82
CHAPTER SEVENTEEN	88
CHAPTER EIGHTEEN	96
CHAPTER NINETEEN	107
CHAPTER TWENTY	113
CHAPTER TWENTY-ONE	120
CHAPTER TWENTY-TWO	127
CHAPTER TWENTY-THREE	134
CHAPTER TWENTY-FOUR	140
CHAPTER TWENTY-FIVE	145
CHAPTER TWENTY-SIX	151
CHAPTER TWENTY-SEVEN	156
CHAPTER TWENTY-EIGHT	161

- CHAPTER TWENTY-NINE ... 166
- CHAPTER THIRTY ... 172
- CHAPTER THIRTY-ONE ... 176
- CHAPTER THIRTY-TWO ... 183
- CHAPTER THIRTY-THREE ... 194
- CHAPTER THIRTY-FOUR ... 203
- CHAPTER THIRTY-FIVE ... 209
- CHAPTER THIRTY-SIX ... 215
- CHAPTER THIRTY-SEVEN ... 221
- CHAPTER THIRTY-EIGHT ... 227
- CHAPTER THIRTY-NINE ... 232
- CHAPTER FORTY ... 236
- CHAPTER FORTY-ONE ... 242
- CHAPTER FORTY-TWO ... 247
- CHAPTER FORTY-THREE ... 253
- CHAPTER FORTY-FOUR ... 258
- CHAPTER FORTY-FIVE ... 264
- CHAPTER FORTY-SIX ... 271
- CHAPTER FORTY-SEVEN ... 277
- CHAPTER FORTY-EIGHT ... 283
- CHAPTER FORTY-NINE ... 289
- CHAPTER FIFTY ... 297
- CHAPTER FIFTY-ONE ... 303
- CHAPTER FIFTY-TWO ... 309
- CHAPTER FIFTY-THREE ... 315
- CHAPTER FIFTY-FOUR ... 320
- CHAPTER FIFTY-FIVE ... 326
- CHAPTER FIFTY-SIX ... 332
- CHAPTER FIFTY-SEVEN ... 339

CHAPTER FIFTY-EIGHT	342
CHAPTER FIFTY-NINE	344
CHAPTER SIXTY	347
CHAPTER SIXTY-ONE	353
CHAPTER SIXTY-TWO	357
CHAPTER SIXTY-THREE	365
CHAPTER SIXTY-FOUR	373
CHAPTER SIXTY-FIVE	381
CHAPTER SIXTY-SIX	389
CHAPTER SIXTY-SEVEN	398
CHAPTER SIXTY-EIGHT	404
CHAPTER SIXTY-NINE	410
CHAPTER SEVENTY	416
CHAPTER SEVENTY-ONE	425
CHAPTER SEVENTY-TWO	434
CHAPTER SEVENTY-THREE	440
CHAPTER SEVENTY-FOUR	446
CHAPTER SEVENTY-FIVE	453
CHAPTER SEVENTY-SIX	461
CHAPTER SEVENTY-SEVEN	469
CHAPTER SEVENTY-EIGHT	480
CHAPTER SEVENTY-NINE	486
CHAPTER EIGHTY	490

CHAPTER ONE

Billy Todd looked at the world around him, feeling as if he were on the outside of a glass menagerie, looking in. Smoke still rose from several places around the small town, but he knew no one was going to be putting out any fires. There was no one left to put them out.

Clutching his rifle, Billy walked across the street, careful to keep his eyes open for feral dogs. Funny, he thought, how it took centuries to domesticate the dog, and only a few weeks for him to revert to wild animal.

Of course, not being fed would do that to you, he allowed.

The virus had swept across the globe like a whirlwind. It had happened so fast that no one had ever bothered to name it. There hadn't been time, Billy figured. One minute everything was fine, then it wasn't.

Plague.

That had been the word most people had used, in the few short days where anyone had been talking about it. In what had seemed like a few short hours, the power had gone out, and other utilities, such as water and gas, had quickly followed.

Television stations kept broadcasting for a few more hours, gradually falling silent as the people running them fell sick and died. Radio stations had stayed on the air using generators for another day or so, being more closed, more isolated, but they too, in the end, had gone silent.

Billy had hid in his small apartment, using carefully hoarded food and water, waiting for help to come. None had come. For anyone. The last reports he had heard had claimed the death toll worldwide had climbed into the *billions*. Billy could scarcely credit that number. It was hard for him to imagine. Impossible to imagine.

William Conrad 'Billy' Todd was a small-town mechanic. Born and raised in Cedar Bend, he'd never been further than Nashville in his entire twenty-five years. His world revolved around cars, and the small farm he had inherited when his parents had passed away two years before.

He'd never really done anything with the farm, being too occupied with his job as a mechanic. He had made good money fixing cars for people. With the economy in the tank, more and more people were fixing the problems with their older vehicles, driving them longer. *And* Billy was the top mechanic in the whole county. Everyone said so.

Had said so.

There was no one left in Cedar Bend to say anything, now, so far as Billy knew. This was the fourth day he had dared venture outside the small apartment in the rear of his shop. The fourth day in a row that he had prowled the area around his garage, seeing no sign of life outside of animals. Apparently, only humans were affected by the virus. But for some reason that Billy simply could not credit, he had not fallen ill. He couldn't imagine why. There had to be a reason, he figured. Things just didn't happen for no reason. One of the silliest things people told him when they brought their cars in for repair was 'it stopped for no reason'.

There was always a reason. Billy was very good at finding those reasons, and fixing them, but he couldn't find the reason for his still being alive, when everyone else was dead. Billy knew he wasn't anything special. Never had been. He wasn't the smartest, or the strongest, the fastest, wasn't the best looking. In fact, he wasn't the best at anything, except fixing cars.

Somehow, he didn't think he'd be fixing many cars for a while.

Clanging metal startled him and he swung around to confront the noise. A dog looked at him from the overturned garbage can, studied him for a second, then turned his attention back to the garbage can. Billy watched the dog sift carefully through the can's contents for a moment, then resumed his walking. He'd have to watch for that dog on the way back, Billy knew. If he didn't find anything worthwhile in the can, he might decide some raw Billy would go mighty good about then.

Billy had found several bodies out and about, and most of them had been eaten at to some degree or another. Even the dogs that ate the dead didn't seem to get sick, though. Apparently, the plague really was only deadly to humans. Today would be the last day, he decided. The last day that he would search through town for anyone still living. Tomorrow, he would pack up and head to the farm. He had been in town when things got bad, and hadn't realized what was happening until it was late. Fearing the sickness, Billy had elected to stay in his small apartment rather than risk going to the farm.

In a way, he was glad he had, since he would have wanted to drive into town from the farm to see what had happened. Being the only living person in town for four days had cured him for the need to see it anymore. Once he reached the farm, he'd decided, he would stay there. He knew, now, that no one was coming. There was no one *to* come. Even the government radio, the NOAA channel, had gone silent three days ago. If they weren't on, then no one was left to do anything.

He hated to leave everyone lying about. He knew everyone in the small town. Had known them all his life. Now they were dead. He didn't know them anymore. And they didn't know him.

He would need food, he knew. Water he had in plenty at the farm, but food not so much. Oh, he had food, right enough, and he could grow his own food, when the season came again, but it was almost winter now. No chance to grow anything now. He would have to have enough food to get him through the winter.

Albert's grocery would have what he needed, he figured. Well, he hoped. There was no telling what folks had done in the few days before everyone died. Billy hadn't ventured out during those days, even when folks had come by, banging on his shop door. He had kept the lights off at night, hoping that no one would want to break in. No one had.

Billy decided that he would check the grocery, and Mister Wickam's hardware store, too. He needed a generator. There was a large one at the farm but he wanted a smaller one for times when he only needed a little bit of power, which meant he'd need fuel. As the list grew in his mind, Billy started to get a headache, which made him think of going by the Rex-all. He'd need medicines in case he got sick, and bandages in case he got hurt. He had a first aid kit in his garage, of course, but he needed more than a few Band-aids, or a small tube of antibiotic ointment. He

Odd Billy Todd

needed get more and better stuff.

Realizing that he needed a lot more stuff than he'd first thought, Billy knew he'd need a trailer. No way could his pick-up haul everything. He sighed. His headache was getting worse. That always happened when Billy got flustered. He got a headache. The doctor had called them migraines. Billy's mother had suffered from them, too. Sometimes, she'd have to lie down for hours with a cloth over her eyes, and earplugs in her ears. Light and sound, she had said, made the migraine hurt worse.

Making his way up the Alberts' front door, Billy carefully looked through the window. He was glad he couldn't see anyone. He didn't want to see anyone else he had known lying dead. Or worse, eat by dogs. Billy tried the front door, finding it unlocked. He was a little surprised at that but glad he didn't have to break in. He had never broken into anything. He didn't want to start now, even though he knew it didn't matter anymore. Billy had always been a good boy. Everyone said so.

Had said so.

No one was around to notice if he was good now. But his mom and dad had raised him to be a good boy, and he knew they were in heaven watching him. The preacher had said so. He wondered if the preacher would say Billy was a thief for taking things from Albert's. 'Thou shalt not steal', the preacher always said. He said it every time someone stole something. Well, he used to. He wasn't saying anything anymore. Billy decided that meant the preacher wouldn't say he was stealing.

After looking around for a minute, Billy took a cart, and started down the aisles. The store was in good shape. He had expected everything to be all torn up, lying on the floor, like one of those movies or stories where the world ended.

Had the world ended? Billy wondered. This part of it was pretty ended, he decided. But maybe, somewhere, there was people like him. People that found themselves all alone. He wondered if they wondered if they were alone in the world, like he did.

Billy took dozens of cans of his favorite vegetables from the shelves, and placed them into his cart. He also took the Treet, and the Spam, and all of the canned hams he could find, as well as any other canned meats he came across, and the tuna. Three country hams hung near the meat department. The smell told Billy that the rest of the meat was ruined, but the country hams would be okay, so he took them.

When the cart was filled, he pushed it to the front, and took another. He walked down another aisle, taking toilet paper, and paper towels. A man just didn't want to be out of toilet paper if he could help it, Billy knew. He also threw in some plastic cups, paper plates, and plastic eating utensils. This cart filled quicker, so it was back the front for yet another. This one was cleaning supplies. Billy liked to keep a clean house. His mother had taught him that. Cleanliness was next to Godliness. Billy figured right now only he and God were around, so he wanted to be clean.

After three more carts, Billy decided he had everything worth saving at the front. He stood there looking at the carts, deciding what he should do. He peered outside, and noticed there was still plenty of light. He decided that he would get his truck, and Mister Nelson's trailer from next door, and come get the carts now.

He walked back to the garage fairly quickly, though always making sure to watch for the dogs. Billy wished he had a dog. He'd been afraid to have one at the garage, because his insurance wouldn't pay if the dog bit anyone. His father had told him it wasn't good business to have a dog if he couldn't get insurance because of it.

Well, Billy decided, he didn't need insurance no more, that was for sure. And he really wanted a dog. Maybe he could feed one of the wild dogs and make friends with it? He didn't know. And dogs needed shots. He didn't know how to give them shots, and Doc Hayes, the town vet, wasn't going to be taking any new patients anymore, Billy knew.

Reaching the garage, Billy fired up his truck, which he'd kept parked inside while he was closed. Pulling out of the garage, he got out and closed the garage door, then climbed back inside. Mister Nelson's Lawn and Garden Center was right next to Billy's Garage. Billy had worked on Mister Nelson's truck, a beautiful old Ford that he'd restored with his son. Billy had asked Mister Nelson once why he didn't do the work himself, since he'd restored the truck. Mister Nelson had smiled sadly, saying that he and his son, Donnie, had worked on the truck together as a father/son project, but that had been before Donnie had gone off to war in the Far East. *Or was it Middle East?* Billy couldn't remember.

Donnie hadn't come back from whichever one it was he had gone to. Or he had, but in a box. With a flag on it. Mister Nelson was very proud of that flag, and of his son. He kept the flag on display in his store, with a picture of his son above it, in a uniform.

The trailer was one that Mister Nelson used to deliver the small tractors he sold. It was small enough that Billy could pull it with his truck, but big enough to carry most everything he needed to take with him. In no time, Billy had the trailer hitched up. He thought about leaving Mister Nelson a note, then remembered why he needed the trailer. Mister Nelson wouldn't ever read the note, so Billy decided not to leave it.

Billy drove carefully down to Albert's, parking in the fire lane. Billy grinned a little at that. He'd always been afraid to park there, even to load his groceries. He'd been afraid his truck might get towed. That wouldn't happen today, so Billy parked there, even though he wasn't supposed to.

Once the carts were loaded, and tied down, (his father had taught him it was always important to tie down a load, so nothing broke), Billy drove back to the garage. He backed the trailer into one bay of the garage, unhooked it, then placed the truck in the other bay. By now, Billy was hungry. He wanted to walk down to Loretta's Diner and get a cheeseburger. Loretta made the best cheeseburger in three counties. Everyone said so.

Had said so.

Billy remembered that Loretta wasn't making cheeseburgers anymore. Not ever. Sadly, he decided that he wouldn't get a cheeseburger. Shaking his head at his misfortune, Billy went into his small apartment, and made himself a sandwich. He was almost out of chips, he realized.

He hadn't gotten any chips! How could he have forgotten potato chips? He'd have to go back and get chips. And pickles. Billy loved pickles. Billy ate in silence, washing his meal down with a Coke. Greatest drink ever, Coke. Billy had always thought so. He'd have to enjoy what was left carefully, he decided. Once he drank all the Coke left in town, there wouldn't be anymore. Probably wasn't anyone left to make it, anyway.

Billy finished his meal, and carefully put everything away, just as his momma had taught him. He missed his mamma. He missed his dad as well. Billy took stock of his situation. That was something his dad had taught him. "Never rush off in a blind panic", he'd always said. "Make sure you know what you're doing". Billy had always found that had worked for him.

Billy knew he wasn't very smart. Plenty of people had told him that. Never about cars, of course. When they need their cars fixed, they all told Billy how smart he was. But any other time, he was dumb. Or odd. 'Odd Billy Todd', he'd heard more than once. He'd grown up hearing all these things, so once he was grown, they hadn't really bothered him anymore. His parents had never called him that. They had taught him how to do things, how to take care of himself, and how to protect himself.

"We won't always be here, son", Billy's dad would say as he showed Billy something or another. "You'll have to know how to do this alone when we're gone." Billy hadn't always understood why they would leave. He had learned, though, that people always left. Some went to heaven. Some went somewhere else. Somewhere that Billy didn't want to go. But Billy's mamma and daddy had made sure that he could look after himself just fine. He still remembered the day that his dad had led him out to the barn. He had just turned twenty-one, and his garage had been open for a year. Was doing real well. Daddy had decided that if Billy could handle that responsibility, then he could handle other responsibilities as well.

Once in the barn, the elder Todd had closed the doors, then led Billy to the far back corner, where all the junk lay. Odd bits of farm equipment, old bits of leather and metal, stuff that was broken, but might be used to fix something else. Only daddy never got around to using it. His father had started clearing away all that junk, and Billy helped. When it was all moved, Billy was surprised to see a door, but lying on the ground, instead of standing up.

"You can't ever tell anyone about this, Billy", his father cautioned before opening the door. "If people know it's here, they might try and take it from us. Understand?" Billy didn't, not exactly, but if wasn't supposed to tell, then he wouldn't. He knew how to keep a secret. Daddy had opened the door then, and Billy could see steps under the door. His father had walked down about three steps, then stopped, motioning Billy over to him. He showed Billy a switch, then turned it. Lights came on down in the hole. "Runs off sunlight, his father told him. I'll show you how to care for it." He walked further down, and Billy followed.

Below, under the barn, was a room, Billy was shocked to discover. He wished he had known about this growing up was his first thought. What a great place to play! But this wasn't a play room. There were buckets stacked along the far wall, each labeled and dated. All the buckets, he learned, were food of one kind or another.

Along another wall were two gun racks. Guns the likes of which Billy had ever only seen on TV. A row of rifles, shotguns, and on the wall behind them, pistols and revolvers. Billy already knew how to shoot, of course, and had guns of his own. But...

"These aren't like your guns, son," his father had said. "These are different.

I'll explain each one. These crates are ammunition", he said, pointing to the back wall, where several large boxes sat.

"Why do we need all this daddy"? Billy had asked. It wasn't that he didn't like all this, but he couldn't see a need for it.

"Sometimes, things happen", was all his father said. "When they do, we need to be prepared for them."

It took Billy and his father almost two months to get through everything. His father had made several notebooks, which were copied several times. Inside them were instructions and advice for every possible scenario that Billy's father and mother could come up with. Everything from house fires to atomic bombs.

But there wasn't nothing about being the last man alive. Billy thought on that as he finished his Coke. Was he the last man on earth? Surely not. There had to be more than just him. Didn't there?

His train of thought was broken then by a clanging noise from outside. Billy took his rifle, the one his father had always kept hidden for him here at the garage, and walked carefully to his small office. There was a window there, and from the doorway, where he couldn't be seen, he peered outside.

It wasn't quite dark yet, he noted. He could see several dogs outside, milling around. The can he had been using for his trash was overturned, and three of the biggest dogs seemed to be in a standoff over the contents of the can. Billy watched in fascination as the three huge animals looked each other over. One was a Rottweiler, he could see, but the other two he didn't recognize.

Even as he watched, the Rottweiler lunged at one dog, then actually attacked the other. Swiftly, and seemingly without effort, the Rottweiler seized the large dog by the throat, and shook him. The other dog, recovering from his dodge, instantly fell on the second dog as well, and the two killed it in seconds. That left two.

The two dogs circled each other warily, neither able to gain an advantage. It was the dog Billy didn't recognize that struck first, lunging at the Rottweiler, trying to grab his throat. But the Rottweiler seemed to have been waiting for this, and side-stepped the rush. As the larger dog extended himself, the Rottweiler clamped his massive jaws on the back of his adversary's neck, and bit down. Hard.

The other dog yelped briefly, struggling to free himself. His struggles simply made the Rottweiler's job easier. The massive jaws clamped down tighter, and Billy thought he heard the bones breaking from inside the building. Shaking the other dog violently one last time, the Rottweiler dropped him. As Billy watched, the victor looked around at the other dogs in the pack, as if asking if any of them wanting to dispute his dominance. None did, and the pack slowly moved off, leaving the spoils of Billy's trash can to the giant Rottweiler.

Billy watched as the massive dog claimed his bounty, wishing he had a dog like that. The Rottweiler lifted its head suddenly, looking around him, sniffing the air. His gaze came to rest on Billy, and stayed there. Billy was shocked. There was no way for the dog to know he was there. But he did! Billy did something then that he never did, but he wouldn't regret it. He made a snap decision.

With no uncertainty at all, Billy ran to his little kitchenette, grabbed the last of his sandwich meat, and ran back to the door. He opened it slowly, eyeing the Rottweiler, who was still looking at him. The dog didn't move, but did growl deep in its chest.

Odd Billy Todd

"It's okay, buddy", Billy called, holding some of the meat out to the dog. The smell of the meat enticed the large hound, and soon he began to shift on his feet, just a bit. He didn't offer to come closer, but Billy kept working. He sat down on the ground, cross legged, having read once that dogs found this nonthreatening. It seemed to work. The monstrous dog began to inch closer, still wary for any tricks. Billy held himself as still as possible, just holding the meat out before himself.

The Rottweiler sniffed the air, took another cautious step. Billy took one slice of the meat free, and simply laid it down. The Rottweiler eyed the meat with suspicion, slowly coming forward. He sniffed carefully, always with a wary eye on Billy. Billy remained motionless, studying the dog even as the dog studied him.

The dog's collar had a tag in it, and suddenly, as the dog lifted its great head, Billy could, for just an instant, read his name; Rommel.

"Rommel", Billy said the name softly, and the dog instantly locked eyes with Billy. Billy held out the meat again, and spoke softly; "Take it Rommel. I won't hurt ya boy." Rommel's great head tilted to one side, eyeing the man-thing that had called his name. He hadn't heard his name in a long time. A week was a long time in dog time.

"It's okay Rommel", Billy repeated, still in a soft, friendly voice. "It's yours if you want it."

Rommel had, until recently, been a pet. He remembered a man giving him food. It was a good memory. He cautiously leaned forward, sniffing the meat in the man-thing's hand. It smelled okay, not like some of the things he'd eaten recently. He nibbled softly on the edge of the meat, and it tasted good. Suddenly, he grabbed the meat, running off a few steps, then stopping.

The man-thing had never moved. It showed no fear. Rommel could smell no fear from him, nor sense any danger. This man-thing wanted to be friends. He gulped the meat down in three massive bites. He hadn't eaten this good in a while. He looked at the piece still on the ground, and quickly added it to his meal. Billy watched as the big dog looked up from the last piece of meat, as if wanting more.

"There's no more", Billy admitted. Carefully he stood. If he could find Rommel another meal, a good one, then maybe the dog would stay with him. Billy estimated that the dog was well over one hundred pounds, though he'd lost weight in the last few days. Billy remembered that Albert's had many bags of dog food. On an impulse, Billy started that way, then stopped, looking back.

"Come, Rommel. Dinner Time."

The dog remembered "Dinner Time". It meant food. He wagged his tail once, which Billy thought was encouraging. Calling the dog again, Billy turned and started for Albert's. It would be dark soon. Billy had a flashlight, but he didn't relish being in town after dark. He needed to hurry. But he could only go as fast as the dog and the dog was being cautious. Billy could understand that. He was cautious himself. It took several minutes, but finally they were back at Albert's. Billy opened the door, and stood waiting for Rommel. The big dog eyed him with suspicion, but Billy made no move. He spoke to the dog, low and friendly.

"Come on, Rommel. I'll feed you. C'mon, boy, it's Dinner Time."

That seemed to convince the dog. He eased through the door, careful to stay as far from Billy as possible. Once inside, Billy allowed the door to close. That didn't set well with the giant Rottweiler, but Billy simply stood very still, waiting for Rommel to calm down again. As he did, Billy moved toward the dog food aisle.

Rommel lifted his massive head, sniffing cautiously. He could, of course, smell the spoiled meat, which made him salivate. But Billy took down a bag of IAMS dog food, lamb and rice formula, and opened it. Rommel's ears perked up at that, remembering the sound of food in a bag. He trotted over toward Billy.

Billy had taken a large bowl from the shelf nearby, and filled it to overflowing. Rommel hesitated for less than a second before burying his head in the bowl, eating greedily. Billy watched him eat, careful to make no sudden moves. He really wanted Rommel to see him as a friend. Billy had a feeling that the large dog would be good company to him.

For his part, Rommel seemed to be completely fixated on the food bowl. Vague stirrings of memory came to him in flits and flashes. Chasing a ball. Lying by the door. Shaking of a food sack. Walking on a leash. Being groomed. He stopped eating suddenly, looking up directly at Billy.

The man watched him, friendly, unafraid. To Rommel that was important. He had learned that afraid people tried to hurt him. Threw things at him. He didn't like that. But this man wasn't afraid. Almost nodding, as if making up his mind, Rommel decided that this man-thing was his new friend. That decision made, Rommel returned to the food bowl.

Billy watched the dog eat, smiling to himself. He thought Rommel might stay with him now, which meant he'd have to come back to Albert's tomorrow and get all the dog feed. Well, he shrugged. He was coming to get chips and pickles anyway, so no problem.

Billy let Rommel eat until he was full. As the dog finished his meal, Billy gathered up some dog shampoo, a brush, and a flea collar. If Rommel was going to live with him, he'd need a bath, and grooming. Rommel, seeing the brush, actually wagged his tail, which Billy took as a good sign.

Billy led Rommel to the back of the store, where there was a large tub. Billy set his things down, and patted the tub with his hand. Rommel jumped inside it, remembering this as well from before. Billy brought three jugs of water over to where Rommel sat waiting. The first one he poured on the large dog in its entirety, making sure to cover as much as he could. The second, he set beside the tub. Taking a handful of the shampoo, Billy began to wash the dog.

Rommel stood still, knowing that the bath would make him feel better. As Billy rubbed his head, and then his back, belly and legs, Rommel whined just a little, happy. Billy noted the fleas that Rommel carried were dying rapidly, and used the second jug to wash him down after the time was up. He quickly brushed the dog down, getting the excess water from him.

Rommel enjoyed that exercise more than the bath. Rommel had always loved to be brushed, and eagerly pushed himself into the brush. It felt good against his skin. Finished, Billy took the last jug of water, and poured a bowl full, allowing Rommel to drink his fill. Once he was done, Billy called him to follow, and walked to the front of the store.

It was dark now, Billy saw. For a moment, he was worried. He hadn't been out after dark since IT had happened. There were no lights in town. He had his flashlight, and now he switched it on. Looking back, he called for Rommel to follow, then opened the door. Rommel followed.

Odd Billy Todd

Billy made his way carefully back to the garage, looking down at Rommel on occasion to see if the mighty dog was still there. He was. Once Rommel stopped, growling deep in his chest. Billy stopped as well. Suddenly, several large dogs, at least five, ran into the street in front of them, barking and snarling.

Rommel made as if to attack, but Billy laid his hand on the dog's head; "Stay", he ordered, and Rommel did. "Good boy", Billy soothed. The other dogs, wary, started around them. Billy and Rommel turned to keep facing them, and Billy leveled his rifle at the nearest one.

The dogs had seen a rifle before, and knew it was danger. As soon as Billy hefted it to his shoulder, they broke and ran. Billy watched them out of sight, sighing with relief as he lowered the rifle. He looked at Rommel, who was still watching where the dogs had gone, but had not offered to follow.

"Let's go home, boy", Billy said. Rommel recognized "Home", and followed.

That night, Rommel slept in the bed, curled up at Billy's feet, making himself at home. Billy went to sleep smiling. He had a dog.

CHAPTER TWO

Billy awoke the next morning with Rommel whining in his face.

"Okay buddy," Billy mumbled. "I guess you gotta go, too." Rising from his small bed, Billy stumbled to the door and let Rommel out into the small fenced yard behind the garage. He went to the bathroom, then washed his face and hands. He would have liked a shower, but had to conserve his water. Once he was at the farm, water wouldn't be a problem, though.

First thing I'm gonna do is take me a long shower. No, he decided, a hot soaking tub bath. Yeah, that's the ticket. He went to the back door, where Rommel was waiting patiently to be let back in. Billy smiled, ruffing the big dog's head. Rommel *wroffed* lightly, and licked Billy's hand in return.

"We going home today, boy," Billy told him. Rommel looked at him quizzically, almost as if asking 'isn't this home'.

"No, it ain't," Billy answered the dog's supposed question with a smile. "We get to the farm, you'll have all the room you want to run in. And a big ole bed to sleep on, too," he added. Wagging his stub of a tail, Rommel seemed to say, 'suits me'.

Billy began looking through his garage, packing the tools he knew he might need at home. He would lock up when he left, of course, but if there *was* anyone else still alive, the lock probably wouldn't stop them.

"Don't matter, I guess," he spoke aloud. "I just don't wanna have to come back." He loaded his tools and other equipment quickly, wanting to get on his way. For some reason he couldn't quite grasp, he wanted away from the town. Quick as he could get. He didn't know why. He just knew that he did.

Soon, he was ready to go. He pulled his truck out of the shop, then hooked it to the trailer. Once it was outside, he called to Rommel. Making one more look through his shop and apartment, he decided he had everything he wanted or needed.

"Let's go boy!" he whistled. Rommel jumped into the open truck door without hesitation. Billy grinned, and got behind the wheel.

"We gotta get ya some more food, boy," he grinned, once more rubbing the dog's large head. "We git that, and me some tater chips and pickles, and we're outta here." They pulled to the front of Alberts, and Billy soon had three more carts filled to overflowing with dog food. After a second, he went back and got all the cat food, too. Dog could eat it, he knew. He also decided to get all the little treats and such, since no one else would likely be needing them anymore.

He finally had everything loaded, and looked around him once more.

"Hardware store," he murmured. He'd forgotten that yesterday in his excitement over finding Rommel. He took four more carts and headed across the street to the hardware store. Once there, he went carefully up and down the aisles, getting the things he knew he'd need. His daddy had always been careful to keep plenty, and Billy knew just what things daddy had said were on the NEED list.

That was list of things that daddy and mamma had told him it would be hard to make or find, and just plain hard to do without. He took nails, screws, silicone sealant, glue, a complete set of hand tools, saw blades, the list went on. He finished just as his last cart was full. He tugged the carts over, and managed, barely, to get all of them into the trailer.

At the last minute, he went back. He gathered up as much pipe as he could find, with connectors, fittings, glue, everything he'd need to plumb the house over again. He managed to get that into the back of his truck, but it took some doing.

"We just can't carry no more, Rommel," he said at last. Hearing his name, the dog perked up.

"Let's go," Billy ordered. Rommel once again leaped into the truck, and Billy set off for home.

It was only a few miles to the farm, taking no longer than thirty minutes to travel. It took longer today. There were cars all along the road. Billy didn't understand that at first, until he looked down into one as he passed by. There were people in the cars. Dead people. They had driven until they had died, he realized. And that was where they stayed. There was no one to move them. Not anymore.

For some reason, the dead people in the cars scared him more than the prospect of being all alone. Billy didn't really believe in ghosts, at least he didn't think he did. Suddenly he was wondering. All these people had died in a horrible manner, and close together. Would that make a difference? Would the town be haunted? The whole world?

He just didn't know, and not knowing scared him. He unconsciously rubbed the bridge of his nose, right between his eyes, as he felt his head start to ache.

No, no, no, not now! he thought to himself, on the edge of panic. He had too much to do to have one of his headaches. If he took the medicine the doctor had given him, it would knock him out for…

He stomped on the brakes so hard that Rommel lost his footing and fell into the floor board. The massive dog shook himself, and jumped back onto the seat, giving Billy a look that clearly said 'what was that for?'

My meds! I forgot my meds!

He looked frantically for a way to turn the truck around. Nearly in a panic, he couldn't focus on where he was, what he needed to do. All he could think about was his meds.

As if sensing that his new person was in danger, Rommel looked around him in confusion, seeking a threat. Seeing none, he looked back to Billy, and suddenly head butted him in the arm. When he didn't get a response, Rommel repeated the action, and then a third time.

Suddenly Billy looked at the dog, still slightly wide-eyed. Rommel ran his head under Billy's hand, encouraging him to scratch. Billy did so without thought, rubbing and scratching the giant head for a full five minutes as he calmed down. The motion brought him back to clarity.

"Thanks, boy," Billy gave the dog's head a final ruffing. Realizing that the truck was still in gear, he placed in park, easing his now aching foot off the brake pedal. He took a few deep breaths, and then shook his head.

"I gotta keep calm," he said to himself. "Gotta keep calm," he repeated three more times. It became almost a mantra as he put the truck back in gear and started down the road. He remembered, now that his panic was gone, that he had a year's supply of all his medicines at the house. Something else his mom and dad had managed to get for him. He kept buying his prescriptions regularly, adding them to the stocks, and then using the oldest of the stockpiled medicine.

"We can always go back and get the medicine after we get settled," he told Rommel. The dog looked at him, head cocked to the side, then wagged his stump of a tail, as if saying 'sounds good to me'.

The rest of the trip was uneventful. Billy eased onto the small road that led to the farmhouse, stopping half-a-mile off the main road to open the gate. He drove through, locked the gate behind him, and then drove the truck and trailer the rest of the way up to the house.

As the truck pulled in front of the two-story white frame house, Billy looked it over carefully. He hadn't been here in almost three weeks. The fact that the gate had still been locked was a good sign, but he was always careful. Daddy had taught him that.

He and Rommel got out, the dog sniffing the air. Billy watched him for a moment. The dog didn't react to anything, so Billy decided to go on inside. He led the dog up the steps to the porch, and unlocked the front door. Rommel hesitated slightly, but when Billy walked in, the big dog followed.

After checking the house, both Billy and Rommel were satisfied that all was well. Billy checked to make sure that the power from the PV cells was still working, and then checked the batteries in the basement. The charge meter was right where it was supposed to be. Happy with that, Billy headed back upstairs.

He got back in the truck, and backed the rig to the barn. Rommel ran alongside, barking furiously, as if worried he was being left behind.

"Relax, buddy," Billy laughed. "I ain't goin' anywhere without ya." For some reason, this seemed to appease the dog, and he trotted alongside the rest of the way, quietly. It took a while, but Billy got everything squared away where it belonged. He put half the food away in the 'hole' as he thought of it, checking on the batteries there as well, just as his father had taught him. Finding everything there to be okay, he secured the barn, and once more got into the truck.

He drove to a smaller barn well behind the house, where he off loaded the other half of his supplies, including the other half of the dog food he'd gotten from Albert's. His father had taught him never to put all of his eggs in one basket, and practiced what he preached. Fully half of the stores that Billy's parents had amassed were in a much smaller 'hole', beneath this barn. While it didn't have its own PV system, a line ran from the house to allow a lighted interior.

"I'm glad that's done," Billy said to himself, wiping sweat from his brow. Doing so made him aware of his odor.

"I stink, Rommel!" he said with a laugh. "I need a bath worse'n you did!" Again, Rommel looked at his person, head cocked to the side. He'd heard his name, but no command, so his confusion was understandable.

"You're the only one I got to talk to, now, boy," Billy explained to him. "Better get used to it. Now I aim to have a bath, and then I'm gonna cook the both of us a good steak!"

The steak had been good, Billy decided. He'd used a marinade that his mother had taught him to make, one that she had said really brought out the flavors of beef. Rommel had seemed to enjoy it too.

"How'd you like that, boy," he asked, grinning at the enormous dog. "Good stuff, yeah?" Rommel wagged his stump of a tail in agreement. Or at least what Billy decided to take as agreement.

Billy cleaned the dishes, and the table, making sure that all was where it was supposed to be. Something his mother had taught him. If you put things back where they belong, you won't have to look for them next time you need them.

Billy walked out onto the front porch after that, taking a seat in his favorite rocker. Rommel followed, and sat down beside him. Billy absently scratched the big dog's head as he looked out over the farm.

The cattle looked good, he thought. There was good grazing this time of year, and the vet had been out to see them just three months ago. Billy didn't figure there' would be another visit from the vet anytime soon. He'd have to do what he could. He knew the cattle were important, as were the horses. There were eleven cows, one bull, and four horses on the farm. Billy knew them all by name. They were good animals.

He decided that tomorrow he'd get the Ranger out, and ride over the farm. He needed to check the fences. And the water holes. Had to keep them clean, his father had taught him. Billy didn't mind hard work. He'd always enjoyed it, in fact. It seemed to help him keep his mind centered.

Billy knew he had to be careful, now that he was all alone. The people who had helped him since his parents had died were gone, now. Of course, so were the ones who often caused him problems, too.

His spell earlier in the day, with the medicine, scared him more, now, as he looked back on it. If Rommel hadn't been there, and snapped him out of the mess he'd been in, Billy knew he would probably be still sitting there. Frozen. Unable to make a decision.

When Billy was calm, and not under stress, it was easy for him to see where his shortcomings were. He could see things clearly, then. But if panic ever gripped him, or if he ever felt like he'd made a wrong move, or a bad decision, it could cripple him for hours. With things like they were now, he couldn't let that happen. He might not have the time to recover.

Frowning, Billy sat further back, easing the rocking chair into motion. He would need a plan. For everything. His parents had taught him that making a plan was a good way to make sure that everything that needed to be done, got done. He needed a plan for making sure that he didn't have any more episodes like on the road today.

So long as he made his decisions carefully, like his mamma and daddy had taught him, he shouldn't have any panic attacks. If he was sure of his plan, then he would know he had made the right choice, even when it felt like he hadn't.

"I need a plan," he said aloud. "Yeah, that's what I need. I need a plan."

He took the small notebook he always carried with him from his pocket. Something else he'd learned from his parents. You don't write it down, it didn't happen. You don't write it down, you won't remember it. It didn't happen.

"Plan," he mumbled to himself again. He wrote PLAN in large letters atop the first empty page, then sat back, rocking and thinking.

This might take a while.

CHAPTER THREE

The next morning dawned bright and sunny. As he stood on the porch, looking out at the bright new day, Billy was almost able to forget that the whole world had died. That he was alone, save for Rommel, at least for now.

True, there might be other folks somewhere. But everyone he knew of in and around Cedar Bend was gone. He shuddered at the memory of all the bodies, especially the ones in the cars between his home and town. For some reason those in the cars bothered him more than anything else. He didn't know why, but they did.

He still couldn't figure why he was still alive, and everyone else was dead. What had he done, or not done, that everyone else had or hadn't? He had spent a lot of time figuring on that, but he just didn't know. He just didn't. And that bothered him too. If he had time to think over long on that, he knew it would bother him worse and worse until he couldn't think of anything else.

But he had plenty to do, today. Picking up his rifle, he whistled loudly. After a few seconds, Rommel came racing up from where he'd been running around the yard, marking the trees. Billy started for the barn.

"C'mon, boy. Daylight's a wastin'." The big dog followed him faithfully, right at his side.

Once in the barn, Billy walked to the four wheel drive side-by-side his father had always used to check the farm over. Billy hit the key, and was pleased to hear the engine turn right over. He hadn't used the Ranger in a long time, over a month he figured. Which reminded him of something else.

Whipping out his trusty note pad, Billy made a note that he needed to get parts, filters, oil and the like for the Ranger. Heck, he decided, he might even get a whole new one. Be nice if he could find one with a cab. And a heater.

Rommel had backed away from the noise the small 'truck' made when it started. He now stood several feet away, evaluating this new development. Billy noted that, and called to him.

"C'mon, boy. She won't bite," he laughed. Rommel cocked his head to the side, but remained rooted where he was. Billy frowned at that.

"Rommel, come on," he repeated. "We ain't got all day, you know." Rommel cocked his head in the other direction, but moved no closer. Billy began to feel frustrated.

What am I going to do if he won't get in? he thought to himself. *I want him to go along. And I can't use the horses yet, with him along. They need time to get used to one another.*

Repeated calls to the dog had no effect, and Billy's frustration grew. He felt himself slipping away, and caught it.

"Gotta keep calm," he told himself. "Gotta keep calm." He thought for a minute, remembering how Rommel had ran alongside his truck the day before. Of course! If Rommel could follow the truck, he could follow the Ranger! Smiling at himself for solving an unexpected problem, Billy stopped trying to urge Rommel into the small utility vehicle, and instead put the Ranger in gear. Easing it into motion so as not to spook the dog any further, Billy moved the Ranger toward the barn door. Rommel started barking immediately, but Billy, for once, ignored him. He pulled the Ranger outside, and stopped long enough to secure the barn door. Rommel ran outside, still barking some, though not as much as before. He circled the Ranger warily, barking at it on occasion, as if testing the new beast.

When the Ranger didn't react, Rommel promptly hiked his leg, and urinated on the rear passenger tire, then immediately jumped back. Still no reaction. Rommel snorted, confused. Why wouldn't this thing react? Billy watched in amusement as the large dog continued to circle the utility truck, sniffing, growling, and lightly biting in sequence, trying to get a sense of the beast in front of him, or at least provoke a response. Nothing.

"Satisfied?" Billy finally asked, moving to take his seat again. Rommel looked at him in confusion, as if to say, 'what is this thing?'. Billy laughed, and called him again, motioning to the passenger seat. Rommel circled to the passenger side, still cautious. He approached slowly, and Billy again patted the seat beside him.

Rommel recognized the motion, knowing that was what Billy did when he was ready to ride. Ride. Rommel finally connected the two things. Billy was going for a ride! Tentatively, Rommel raised one foot, placing it on the seat. The shaking of the vehicle caused him to withdraw it at once, but then he did it again, and waited. No reaction. He slowly placed his other fore paw on the seat, and again waited. Still nothing.

As if suddenly satisfied, since Billy wasn't afraid, Rommel leaped into the seat.

"Good boy!" Billy praised him, rubbing and scratching his great head. Rommel preened under the attention, and Billy put the Ranger in gear. He was careful to start out slow, so as not to spook the dog. Rommel was a little nervous as the vehicle started moving, but soon got the rhythm of the bouncing utility, and began to relax.

His first hurdle of the day completed, Billy started on his rounds.

-

Billy found the cows going about their business as usual. They were long accustomed to the Ranger, and paid it no mind at all. Rommel, however, was another matter.

Billy's father was a farmer, not a rancher. He kept a few cows as a hedge against lean years, and to put beef in his own freezer. Sometimes he bartered the beef for services he needed rather than having to pay with cash. As a result, Mister Todd had never used a stock dog. The cows were not used to seeing a dog in such close proximity. Two small donkeys, adopted through the Wild Burro Adoption program, kept dogs, coyotes, and the like away from the cows.

Rommel started barking as soon as he saw the first cow. Billy laughed at him at first, thinking it funny to watch the city raised dog reacting to farm animals. He didn't notice at first the commotion Rommel's presence or actions were causing among the small herd.

Cows bellowed, both in fear and annoyance. The burros, hearing the dog, looked up from their normal laconic existence, ears pricked. Rommel noticed that, and tensed. That was when Billy finally began to wake up to what was happening, and it was almost too late.

Odd Billy Todd

He just managed to grab Rommel's collar as the big dog went to bolt from the Ranger and run after the fleeing cows. The dog struggled briefly, trying to go after his fleeing prey.

"Rommel, NO!" Billy commanded, trying to make his voice as authoritative as possible. The dog didn't quite ignore him, but he didn't stop struggling, either.

"No!" Billy commanded again, this time with a soft rap to the head. That seemed to get Rommel's attention, finally, and he turned to look at Billy.

"No," Billy repeated, this time more quietly, but just as firm. Rommel finally calmed down, shifting in the seat. He was still eager to run after the cows, but understood, now, that he wasn't allowed to.

The cows, though, weren't aware of Rommel's new-found knowledge, and were still heading away. Billy watched as they gathered speed, suddenly very concerned. Where were they going?

Maybe I shouldn't have brought him along, after all, Billy thought. *Now what have I done?*

Panic began to set in, despite all he could do. His 'keep calm' mantra wasn't working, at least not yet. He breathed deeper, still keeping an eye on the cows. Just as he was sure they would run themselves to death, of impale themselves on the barbed wire fence, the small herd turned, and dove instead into a small pool of water about one hundred yards from where Billy sat. Immersing themselves in the cool water seemed to calm the cows, and Billy watched from where he sat as the animals got control of their ragged breathing, and began to act more normally.

The burros, having seen that the dog presented no threat to them, had simply gone back to eating, though they did wander slowly over to the water hole themselves. Their presence provided the final bit of calming that the cows needed. After ten minutes or so of watching, Billy saw the first cow emerge from the water, and begin cropping the grass around the hole. Others followed suit, and soon the small herd was back to normal, as if nothing had happened.

Billy breathed a sigh of relief, calming down himself. He looked at the dog.

"I think we'll ride the fences from the outside, Rommel."

-

With the Ranger on the outside, there were no more disruptions. Billy rode the entire fence, stopping at the other two gates to make sure their locks were undisturbed. They were, of course. There was no one left to bother them that Billy knew of.

Rommel had settled down at last, and seemed to actually be enjoying the ride. Billy figured that the next time he went to use the Ranger, Rommel would hop aboard with no problems.

It still nagged at him that Rommel had almost started a stampede. The dog wasn't used to cattle, and the cattle certainly weren't used to an aggressive dog like Rommel. Billy was bothered by the fact that he had recognized that using horses around the dog wasn't a good idea until they were used to one another, yet he had completely overlooked the possible problems of taking Rommel into the pastures.

I gotta start thinking about things more carefully, he chastised himself. *That could have been a lot worse.*

He sighed, realizing that despite his P L A N, things just weren't that cut and dried. This was a whole new world, and he would have to be more careful in the

16

future. He didn't want to leave the dog behind, but until he figured a way to make sure there wasn't a repeat of today's experience, he realized he just might have to leave Rommel at the house when working the cattle.

Just until they get used to him, that's all, he promised himself. That decision led to another problem.

And how do I get them used to him being there? Not to mention, how do I train him not to take out after the cattle like that again.

Billy grunted in exasperation. It seemed every time he solved a problem, another one, or two, cropped up in its place. At that rate, he'd have more problems that he'd started with, and soon. Shaking his head, as if that would rid him of the problems, or at least the thought of them, Billy started the Ranger moving back toward the house. He still had a lot to do today.

He needed to go back into town, as bad as the thought bothered him. Every time he turned around, there was something that he needed, and didn't have. Or at least, didn't have enough of. Using the Ranger today had reminded him that he would need more gas than the farm tank was likely to have in it. The tank held five hundred gallons when full, but Billy knew it wasn't full. What he *didn't* know was exactly how much gas was in the tank.

And he knew he should know. That was something his father had taught him. *Knowing what you have also let's you know what you don't have*, his father had always said. Billy stopped the Ranger and took out his notebook. He carefully wrote that saying on the inside cover. He figured that way he'd see it almost every day. As a reminder.

I need to know what I have. I gotta do better. I got to make a plan, and I gotta stick to it. Returning the notebook to his pocket, he started on toward the house.

Something else was still nagging him. There was just no way, none that he could figure anyway, that he could be the only person left alive in the world. His own world extended very little beyond Cedar Bend. He hadn't seen anyone else alive in Cedar Bend. He was smart enough to know that this didn't necessarily mean *there was* no one else. Just that he hadn't *seen* anyone.

And what about folk who lived outside of town, like he did? Were some of them still alive? There were a lot of people that Billy knew, people that knew him, that lived on farms just like his. Or even bigger. His farm wasn't that big compared to someone like, say, Mister Silvers. Jeremiah Silvers was the next farm down from his. He hadn't seen Mister Silvers in some time. Could be he was still alive, him and his family. He could go over and check on them.

That idea warmed him a little, until he thought of something else. What *if they're all dead? What if I go over there and Mister Silvers and his family are dead, just like all those people in town? Like all those people on the road?* That thought took the warmth he was starting to feel away again.

Another thing was, what if Mister Silvers didn't recognize him? Would the old man shoot him? Would his family? Billy just didn't know. He'd known Mister Silvers his whole life. Had worked on his truck. On his wife's car, and on his daughter's truck, too. The son wasn't old enough to have a car. Or, maybe he was, Billy thought, and it just never needed any work done on it. Yeah, that might be it.

There was also Widow George, who lived a few miles across a country lane from Billy. You could almost see her house without binoculars when the leaves were off. Was she alive? Was she okay? Maybe he should go check on her, and see if she needed anything. She was gettin' on in years, he remembered. Might need a hand or two. He liked Widow George. She kept her car clean, and always had him change the oil right on time. He liked that. People who took care of their cars, and their animals, were usually good people. Smart people.

Of course, Billy knew he wasn't smart, but he always took good care of his truck. Okay, so maybe people who took good care of their cars weren't *always* good people. But Widow George was good people. He knew that for a fact. Maybe her keeping her car took care of was just a coincidence. But Mister Silvers always took good care of all of his cars. And Billy was *pretty* sure that Mister Silvers was okay. He stopped the Ranger again, this time in sight of the house, and slapped his leg. How was he supposed to figure out who he could trust? If it wasn't people who took good care of their cars, then who? It came to him all at once.

The List! Daddy's List of People Who You Can Trust! How had he forgotten the List? It was one of the things Daddy had said was most important. People to check with if anything ever happened. Of course, he didn't think Daddy had ever counted on something like this. In fact, Billy knew he hadn't, because there wasn't a notebook for *When You Might Be The Last Person Alive.* Daddy had been plenty smart, but there was no way he could have seen this coming.

He started toward the house once more, feeling better now that he had remembered the List. The List would tell him who to go check on. Who to trust. Who to help, and who to ask for help, if he needed it. He didn't think he would need it, but you never knew.

He'd get The List out as soon as he got home. He stopped again, and took out his notebook. In block letters, he wrote *If they ain't on the list, don't trust them.*

There. He'd remember that, now.

CHAPTER FOUR

Billy parked the Ranger in the barn and went straight to the house. He wanted to take a look at The List before he forgot it. He knew he'd remember it again, since it was in his notebook, but he wanted to see it *now*. The idea that he just might not be all alone in the world had chased away some of his fear, at least for the moment.

Billy almost ran the final few steps, taking the porch steps themselves two at a time. Rommel bounced along behind, sensing that his person was excited. Billy went to his father's study, and looked at the shelf of notebooks and research material there. He quickly found what he was looking for, and pulled the notebook down. It was dusty, he noted, and felt a momentary twinge at that. His mother would not have approved. He took his notebook out, made a note to dust the house, then put it away and grabbed the large three ring binder from the desk. Sitting in what had been his father's favorite chair, Billy opened the book.

Dear Son,
I have made a list for you of the people you should be able to count on if there is ever a problem. Being able to count on someone, or trust them, doesn't mean they get to know all your business. If they ask something I've told you should be kept secret, you don't have to lie. Nor should you be rude by saying 'none of your business'. Just smile, and say 'I'm okay for now. I'll have to let the future take care of itself'.
Doing this let's them know that you are okay, and that they don't need to worry.
One last thing. Remember that hard times sometimes changes people. Just because someone is on this list, doesn't necessarily mean that you should automatically trust them. Think of it as a car problem. You think you know what's wrong, but until you check under the hood, you can't be sure.
Always check under the hood, son.
Love, Dad

"Yeah, always check under the hood," Billy repeated aloud. He could remember that. He took out his notebook again, and added '*always check under the hood*' to his note about trusting people on the list. Once that was done, he turned to the next page. There was The List. His father had organized the list by distance. The closer someone was to him, the higher on the list. Sure enough, Mister Silvers and Widow George were right there at the top.

The Widow George was first, Mister Silvers and his family second.

Ignoring the rest of the list for now, Billy set the book on the desk, and looked at Rommel.

"Let's go check on the neighbors, boy."

Billy eased his truck into the Widow George's driveway, careful to make sure she had plenty of time to see him coming. As he parked the car, he remembered again how Rommel had spooked the cattle. Turning to the dog, he pointed at him.

19

"Stay." Rommel looked at him, almost as if he was hurt Billy noted, but lay down in the seat. Billy ruffed his massive head lightly.

"Good boy." He got out of his truck, debating on whether or not to take his rifle. He was wearing his pistol all the time, now, and the rifle might spook the elderly woman. He left it laying on the seat.

Walking slowly, looking around him carefully as he went, Billy made his way to the Widow George's carport door. Her car was still here. He always used the carport door, because the Widow George always used it. She didn't like people tramping through her living room, she said. Billy respected that. He didn't like people snooping around his shop. Never had.

He rang the bell, and waited. And waited. Then he waited some more, before ringing the bell again. Nothing. He was about to turn away when he noticed that the interior door was slightly ajar.

Billy froze, not knowing what to do. Should he go inside, and check on Widow George? What if she was dead? What would he do then? What if she was *alive?* was his next thought. And needed help. What if she needed help he couldn't give her? She might be hurt, or sick, she might have fallen...

Billy took a deep breath, realizing that he was about to panic.

I can't just concentrate on what if, he chided himself. *I'm panicking over things that might not even be. Gotta keep calm. Check under the hood.* He took another deep breath, and opened the door.

The stench was overwhelming. Billy immediately gagged, and ran back out of the house. He ran to the edge of the carport, and stopped, stomach heaving as he tried to get his breath back, and get that stench from his nostrils. Nothing he had encountered in town had prepared him for this.

Gasping for air almost made him panic. The idea of suffocating was actually trying to suffocate him with fear of suffocating. He fought to clear his head as well as his lungs.

Gotta keep calm, gotta keep calm, gotta keep calm...

He felt a bump at his leg, and almost jumped. He looked down to see Rommel looking up at him. When the dog had seen Billy run from the house, he had leapt out the window of the truck to protect his person from whatever was chasing him.

But nothing was chasing me except fear, Billy's mind registered in slow motion. That realization helped him to finally get his breathing under control. *Calm, calm, calm...*

"Thanks, Rommel," he finally managed to say, rubbing the dog's head. "Good boy." Rommel's tail stub wagged as if to say, 'of course'. Billy looked back at the house, and immediately felt the gag reflex again.

I need to bury the poor soul, I guess, he thought to himself. *But I just can't go back in there, not right now. I'll come back, maybe, with a mask and gloves, and maybe some Lysol to disinfect....* He stopped right there.

What if he *wasn't* really immune? What if the virus had killed poor Widow George, and Billy was still alive by pure luck? If he went in there, he might get sick, and die. *What if breathing that foul air, even for a second, was all it had took to make him sick? Would he die, now? If he did, would there be anyone left?*

Who would take care of Rommel? Who would feed the horses and the cows? Billy's only thought at the idea of his own death was who would care for the things he left behind. He had no idea how odd, how very rare, that was. He fought off the re-emerging panic attack, breathing deep, clean air as he moved toward his truck.

I'm sorry Widow George, I just can't take the chance, he thought to himself. As if she might hear him. He looked at Rommel, walking right by his side.

"We can't take the chance, boy," he explained. "Let's go and see if Mister Silvers is alive."

-

Billy felt his dread building as he approached Mister Silver's farm. His experience at the Widow George's house had not yet left him, and probably wouldn't for while. There was nothing he could do for her, though, and he was smart enough to recognize that. So, he was doing the only thing he could do, under the circumstances.

Something else.

He turned onto the small road that led to Mister Silver's house, only to find that the gate was closed and locked. Was that a good sign? Billy didn't know. He did know that he wouldn't trespass. He thought about leaving a note for Mister Silvers, but decided against it. He didn't know who might read it. He *wasn't sure* he wasn't the only one left alive, but he wasn't sure he was, either.

Billy didn't want any trouble. Not from anywhere. He decided that he'd check on Mister Silvers and his family another time. He started back for his truck.

"Stop where you are!" he heard someone shout. Billy turned to see where the voice had come from.

"I said stop!" the voice called again, this time more frantic. Billy thought the voice was coming from his left-hand side, from inside the woods along the roadway to Mister Silvers.

"It's just me, Billy Todd!" Billy called out. "I wanted to see if Mister Silvers was okay!"

"Oh great, the dummy from down the road," he heard a female voice full of scorn from the other side of the drive. Billy frowned at that. That wasn't really called for, was it? He was just being neighborly, trying to check up on people.

"We don't have whatever it is you need, so get moving!" the female voice shouted.

"I don't need anything," Billy replied, puzzled. "I was just tryin' to see if Mister Silvers and his family were okay. I checked on the Widow George, and then. . . ."

"What about the Widow George?" the male voice called. "What did you do?"

"I didn't *do* anything," Billy was starting to get mad, now. "I went to check on her, just like I was here. Only. . .only she wasn't okay," he finished, his voice dropping some, and his anger abating as he thought about what he'd experienced at the George house.

"You take her things?" the female voice demanded. "Kill her for them, maybe?" That was it.

"You know what?" Billy shouted. "I don't seem to care no more if you're okay or not. I came up here hopin' to find out I wasn't the only person left alive in the world. Now, I wish I was." With that he started back to his truck, stomping the whole way.

"We didn't say you could leave!" the female voice shrilled.

"Last time I checked, I don't need your permission," he yelled back. He grabbed the door, and got into the truck. He did something then he'd never done before. He slammed the truck into gear, and spun his tires in anger as he peeled out, heading back home. He could still hear the two voices yelling, but he was so mad now that he wouldn't have stopped if they had stepped in front of him.

Well, I guess I can cross Old Man Silvers off the list, too.

He just couldn't understand. He would be glad to see someone he knew. True, he might not just invite them in for tea, but he wouldn't be rude to them. He was pretty sure, now, that he had been dealing with Mister Silvers' son and daughter. They had no call to be so rude, or so mean. The very idea that he would hurt Widow George!

If Billy had one failing, it was his anger. Billy was slow to anger. He always had been. His mother had told him that even as a baby he had never really been fussy, and rarely cried out. He was even tempered, almost to a fault. But that even temper and slow boiling point had a drawback.

When Billy got mad, he was mad all over. And he didn't, as a rule, get over it. Ever.

And right now, Billy was *mad*.

"Dummy from down the road, huh?" Billy said to himself. "Accusing me of doing something bad to Widow George! Of all the things! I've known that kind old woman my whole life!" Rommel looked at his person in confusion, but read Billy's anger correctly and sat still and silent on the seat beside him.

Billy was so mad that he drove right passed his driveway. He was half way to town before he realized it, too. He slowed his truck, and tried to simmer down. A few deep breaths and he began to center himself again. Now he was starting to get angry at himself for getting angry in the first place. Which reminded him why he was mad in the first place. Which made him mad all over again.

"I got to quit thinkin' on this," he murmured to himself. "I can't get mad. I can't stay mad. I got too much to do." He looked at Rommel.

"I have known Widow George my whole life, you know," he said to the dog. "I can't leave her there like that. It ain't Christian. Mamma an' Daddy wouldn't like me to do that. I gotta take care of her." Having said it aloud, Billy knew what he had to do.

"I guess we'll go into town, boy," he said finally. "Since we're already half way there anyway. I'll get what I need for the Widow George, and the stuff on my list, and then we'll go and bury her proper. I can't do no less than that for someone who was so nice to me all my life."

CHAPTER FIVE

Billy had forgotten his trepidation about the cars along the road into town. Those fears came rolling back as he started to see them again. He drove very carefully around them, as if afraid he could somehow disturb them.

Remembering that he was coming to town in part to get the things he would need to bury the Widow George, Billy was again reminded of all the people who had died in town, and now these on the road. Who would bury them? Say words over them?

"I can't do it all," he said to himself, shaking his head. "I can't do it all. I'm going to take care of the Widow, and then I'm going home, and I'm going to stay there." Seeking out people who might still be alive just wasn't working out, he decided. He could make it just fine on his own, and he knew it. It would be nice to have other people to talk to, but he didn't need it. He just wanted it.

And Mamma always said that needful things came before wantful things, he thought to himself. *I might want to have neighbors again, have friends again, but I don't* need them. And that was the end of it, so far as Billy was concerned.

Billy was in town by now, still driving carefully, although the streets in town weren't nearly as bad as the road leading into it. He eased to a stop when he neared the center of town, looking at the sky. Frowning, he looked at his watch.

"Wow!" he exclaimed out loud. "It's almost four!" It had been a full day. He looked at Rommel.

"I didn't know how late it was, boy. I think we need to hurry." He started looking at his list. As he read things off, a flurry of ideas started coming to him. Things he needed, things he should learn more about, things he should look for. Frantically, lest the ideas get away, Billy started scratching them down on his notebook.

- Library; encyclopedia, animal care, sickness, solar,
- Co-Op; hand tools, seeds, fertilize, wire, cattle, chicken and horse feed,
- Pharmacy; my meds, first aid stuff, regular meds for colds and such
- Hardware store; whatever I didn't get before
- Mister Traywick's Filling' station; gas,
- Manes' Auto Parts; parts for everything, oil, filters, spark plugs, wires, tires for everything

Billy sighed in frustration as things begin to slip away from him. Fleeting bits of information he had not been able to get down on paper nagged at him, but he couldn't recall them all.

"Dang it," he slapped his leg in more frustration. "Rommel, we need to think more on this. I need to make a plan about the town, that's what. And stick to it. Yeah, that's what. I need a plan to get everything I need, and get it. Once I'm done, we won't never have to come back here no more. Sound good to you?" Rommel wagged his tail stump, though of course he had no idea what Billy was saying.

Billy didn't care, just glad for the company.

"We can either go back home and think on it, or we can stay here, at the shop," Billy said, this time more to himself than anything. He looked at his fuel gauge. He still had a half tank of gas in one tank. He switched over, and saw the needle rise to three-quarters in the passenger tank.

"We'll get what we need for right now, and head home," he decided.

Billy went to the Co-Op and grabbed some gloves and a mask like people used to spray chemicals with. He hoped it would keep the smell from getting to him at the George house. He grabbed a large bag of lime, as well, and a shovel from the rack. He finally grabbed a roll of heavy plastic. Taking these to the truck, he placed them in the back. It was getting late, he realized.

"Let's go, Rommel!" he called. "I don't wanna have to be buryin' no body in the dark!" Rommel dutifully jumped into the truck and the two started back out of town. Billy noted that there were several U-Haul trailers at Mister Traywick's, and nodded to himself. He'd use one of them when he came back.

Billy forcefully ignored the cars on the road, this time, and drove with purpose to the Widow George's house. Once there, he put on the mask, donned the gloves, and rolled out enough of the plastic to place poor Widow George's body in. He went straight to the carport door again, but hesitated once he got there.

What am I going to find in here?

Taking a deep, calming breath, he shook of that thought, and went into the house.

The mask kept the odor away, but the house was awash in flies. Huge, ugly, biting, black flies. Billy went first and opened the windows and doors, allowing some air in, and many of the flies out. That done, he looked at the mass on the kitchen floor.

The Widow George had died on her kitchen floor. Her body was the most horrible thing Billy had ever seen. Black and blue, bloated and swollen, covered in fly larva, just the sight was enough to turn his stomach. He looked away for a moment, unable to recognize the kind old woman. She had always been very nice to Billy. Treated as well as she would have treated her family. It was hard to see her like this.

Shaking his fear off, Billy turned to his work. He poured a bit of the lime on Widow George's body, helping get rid of the last of the flies. Next, he carefully laid the plastic out on the floor next to her, making sure it was straight. Thinking of what was next, Billy hesitated again. Knowing he had no choice, he was still reluctant to touch the body. Carefully, he reached down and gently took her ankles in his hands, pulling her toward...

Her body came apart.

Billy stood frozen in horror for a full second, and then the room began to spin around him. In seconds he was hyper-ventilating, gasping for air through the mask's filters, panic filling his mind and preventing any form of rational thought. He backed away from the body, fighting the urge to retch, eyes locked on the horrid scene. He stumbled slightly as his foot hit the back of a chair from the kitchen table, and then he was running blindly out of the door.

When Billy hit the carport door he was still in a panic, and running was the only thing he could seem to do. So, he kept running. Rommel's head came up when Billy came running out of the strange house, and he instantly looked to see what might be chasing his person. To Rommel, the house smelled like death, and he didn't like that. It reminded him too much of his last person.

When nothing came out of the house, Rommel took off chasing Billy down. His person was almost fifty yards away from the house when Rommel tackled him, bring them both to the ground. Stunned, Billy ripped off the mask, still gasping for air. He lay there on his back, looking at the sky, for a long time, his breath coming in ragged gulps.

Ohmigod, ohmigod, ohmigod... His mind echoed that one phrase for a very long time. He didn't know how long he had lain there when he finally got himself under control. He rolled over to his hands and knees, his breath calmer if still a little ragged, and pushed himself to his feet.

"I ain't goin' back in there," he declared for anyone near by to hear. Of course, there was no one. Billy was simply talking aloud, trying to allay his fears in any way he could.

"C'mon, Rommel," he ordered. The dog fell in beside him as he walked to his truck. He threw the mask to the ground, followed by the gloves, which he would never have used again, anyway.

With tears in his eyes, both at his failure, and at the horror he had seen, Billy backed his truck away from the house, and headed home.

He swore right then and there that he wouldn't come back. He couldn't do no more for Widow George.

He had to look after himself now.

-

Once home, Billy went immediately and took a long, hot shower. As he stood beneath the shower head, the image at Widow George's house played over and over in his mind, terrorizing him all over again.

Billy had never had an encounter like that. When his parents had died, he had been distraught, but their bodies had been cleaned and dressed at the funeral home before Billy ever saw them. He had not had to endure the trauma of seeing them immediately after the accident.

Both of Billy's parents had been only children. He had no close relatives that he knew of anywhere. As a result, the loss of his parents had been his first real world loss, other than favorite pets as a boy, and one horse that had been injured in a fall and had to be put down.

The first weeks after his parents had died had been very hard for Billy. He was used to having them around, depended on them to help him see things clearly. Fortunately, his parents had prepared him well for the time when they would no longer be with him. They hadn't anticipated him losing both at once, nor so early, but both his mother and father were realists. They knew that anything could happen, at any time, and had worked hard to ensure that Billy would be able to survive on his own, without them. Had they not done so, Billy would have been in dire straits after the plague.

Billy shut off the hot water, allowing the cold to keep pouring over him. The water helped to calm him, as he fought to get the horrible images out of his mind. This had been a very long day, and it had been trying for him in many ways. He breathed deeply as the water flowed, feeling his calm slowly returning to him.

Calm was always Billy's watchword. He knew that he was easily frustrated, and easily distracted. He couldn't allow that. Not anymore. He shut the water off, finally. Leaving the shower, he dressed in clean clothes. He looked at the clothes he had discarded, and decided to dispose of them. Right away.

He gathered them up, careful to wear gloves, and took them outside. The waning light was just enough for him to see the burning barrel he kept a good distance from the house, and he walked straight to it, and dumped the clothes without a thought as soon as he made sure the pockets were empty.

It was supper time, but Billy didn't have an appetite, and something told him he wouldn't keep the food down regardless. So, he fixed himself some lemonade, and sat on the front porch for a long while that evening, listening to the crickets and the night birds, watching fireflies in the distance. He breathed long and deep, enjoying the cooler air now that night was upon him.

Finally, when he was so very tired that he could barely keep his eyes open, Billy went to bed. Rommel trotted into the bedroom behind him, jumping onto the large bed. The dog watched Billy closely, as if he knew something was bothering his person. He didn't know what it was, but it was enough that he could sense Billy's unease.

Billy was asleep almost as soon as his head hit the pillow, but rest was elusive that night. His dreams were haunted by images of Widow George, asking him why he hadn't buried her proper, of bodies in cars, along the road, crying in anguish that they were not moved, and of blind panic and sheer terror at the images.

CHAPTER SIX

Billy was awakened the next morning by the constant honking of a car horn. It was unfortunate that it came during a part of his nightmare about the cars along the roadway. He sat bolt upright in his bed, sweating profusely, looking around him in panic.

It took him a minute to realize that he had been dreaming. Then he heard the car horn again, and realized that all of it hadn't been a dream. Someone close by was laying on their car horn. From the sound, Billy thought it was coming from his gate. Frowning at that, he dressed quickly, and hurried down the stairs. Almost as an afterthought, he put on his pistol, and then grabbed his rifle. Calling Rommel, the two started off for the gate.

Billy decided to walk to the gate, being careful to stay out of sight. He didn't know who was there, or what they might want. After the rough time he'd had the day before, he decided that caution was the order of the day. He would have been cautious anyway, since daddy had taught him that it was better to go slow, and be careful.

An ounce of prevention is far better than any cure, his father had said. When Billy hadn't understood, his father had explained.

Think about a car, son. If you don't keep the oil changed, and the car serviced, what happens?

It won't run, daddy. Something will break.

That's right, son. Something will break. Approach everything like you would a car. Preventive maintenance can keep a car running a long time without trouble. Preventive action in life can keep you from making a mistake that might get you hurt, or even killed. It's not a crime to be slower than someone else. It isn't a sign of weakness, either. It's a sign of a cautious and careful man, who thinks before he acts. Preventive maintenance, son. Always do your preventive maintenance.

Billy's parents had recognized early on that Billy had a fascination with automobiles and machinery of almost every kind. He was able to absorb and maintain knowledge about cars, trucks, tractors, and other kinds of moving equipment far easier than most 'normal' men. And much more readily than he could grasp most other things. Seeing that, they had developed ways of transferring things Billy needed to learn into automotive terms. Things that Billy could not only understand, but would remember.

Billy eased through the woods, rather than going down the drive. He was able to get to a spot not more than twenty-five yards of the gate without being spotted. When he was there, he peered through the trees at the gate.

Mister Silvers' truck was at the gate, and Mister Silvers himself was leaning on the horn. His son was with him, Billy noted, and felt his anger flash slightly, remembering yesterday.

"We're wasting our time, dad," the son said just then. "He ain't here, or he's scared to come out. Let's go home."

"Shut up," Jeremiah Silvers said sternly. "He's probably watchin' us right now. And no wonder, after what you two did yesterday." Billy frowned at that. What had the 'two' done yesterday, he wondered? Deciding it didn't matter, Billy stepped out of the woods just as Mister Silvers was about to hit the horn again.

The son saw him first, and his eyes grew overlarge in his head. Seeing Billy with a rifle, the younger Silvers started to raise his own rifle. Billy didn't hesitate. Long hours of training kicked in automatically, and in less than a second, Toby Silvers was looking down the barrel of Billy's rifle.

"Stop!" Jeremiah yelled, running to Toby's side. He pushed the boy's rifle down, and then smacked him on top of the head.

"You idiot," his father scolded him. "If he was going to shoot, he would have done it from the trees." The older Silvers turned to look at Billy.

"Billy, it's Jeremiah Silvers!" he called.

"I can see that for myself," Billy replied, his rifle still leveled at Toby Silvers. "What can I do you for, Mister Silvers?"

"Toby and Michelle said you came to the house, yesterday," Jeremiah called. "I wanted to make sure you were okay."

"I'm fine," Billy assured him. "And I didn't come to the house, just to the gate. Where I was threatened, accused o' doin' somethin' bad to the Widow George, and called the 'dummy down the road'. Decided we wasn't bein' sociable no more, and left." Billy heard the older man swear again, and saw him turn to glare at his son.

"I'm right sorry about that, Billy," Jeremiah told him. "They're a mite scared. Try and understand that, and overlook it."

"I ain't scared o' that. . . ." Toby began, only to wilt once more under his father's glare.

"I don't usually hold no grudge," Billy called, lowering his rifle slightly. "What can I do for you?" he asked again.

"I just wanted to try and clear up this. . .misunderstanding'," Silvers called back.

"Oh, I understood just fine," Billy shot back, his anger swelling in spite of his best efforts. "Don't worry, none. I wasn't aimin' on comin' back." *Ever*, he didn't add, but with the tone of voice he used, it wasn't necessary.

"Now Billy," Silvers called back, "ain't no need to take that route. Your folks asked me to look after you, should anything happen. I'm just trying' to do like I promised."

"That's what I was doin' yesterday," Billy told him flatly. "Mamma and Daddy always said I was to make sure you and yours were okay, if anything happened. You and the Widow George. And I did."

"What about Henri?" Silvers called. "Was she okay?"

"No, she ain't," Billy shook his head, his anger replaced by the terror of the day before. "She's dead. Looks to have been that way a while. I tried to bury her proper, but. . .but she. . . ." Billy trailed off, unsure of how to describe what he had seen. Of if he wanted to, for that matter.

"I can imagine," Jeremiah Silvers nodded in sympathy. "It was good of you to try, Billy. Whether you could manage or not, it was good of you to go and check on her, and try to do right for her."

"Just figured it was what my folks would want," Billy shrugged.

"Billy, we need to work together, now days," Silvers said. "We need to help look after one another. You'll need help with your place, and I'll need help with mine. We can help look after one another too. I don't know how many folks around besides us has survived. We ain't seen nobody but you in over a week."

"I don't reckon I need to be workin' with your young'uns, Mister Silvers," Billy was able to say calmly. "I don't think that would do at all. They don't like me at all, and after yesterday the feeling' is mutual. But you need me to help you, just you, mind, and I'm glad to do it. Just give me a day or two's notice, and I'll be along when you need me." Silvers nodded in understanding.

"That's right decent of you, Billy, after what happened. And I am sorry about that. I didn't think to say anything to the kids about our. . .arrangements, if you know what I mean. And I honestly didn't know you'd be here. I just figured you'd be in town."

"I was in town," Billy surprised the older man. "Ain't no one left there, that I could see. So, I packed up and came on home. I went back yesterday, to get the stuff to bury Widow George. Still ain't nobody there."

"You been in town?" Silvers was astonished. "Land sakes, Billy, you could have taken sick!"

"I was in town when everyone else *did* take sick," Billy shrugged. "Don't know why I didn't, but I never did."

"Well, I'm glad of that, Billy, I am," Silvers replied to this news warily. "But what if you're carrying' the virus? Just cause it didn't kill ya don't mean you ain't got it in ya somewhere."

Billy hadn't thought about that. He didn't know what to think of it now, anyway. He still didn't know why he was alive, and everyone else in town was dead.

"Well, we best be gettin' back," Silvers said finally. "I just wanted to see how you were faring."

"You need anything, Mister Silvers?" Billy called. He didn't know why he did, considering that he was still pretty mad about yesterday.

"Could use some gas," Silvers shrugged. "Other than that, just a few odds and ends. Ain't never got too many nails and screws, or lumber for that matter."

"I'll see what I can come up with," Billy told him. He didn't mention that he was planning a trip into town to gather the things he needed himself. For some reason, he was uneasy. It might have been the younger Silvers presence, he didn't know. But he knew he didn't like it, and decided to be cautious. At least until he'd checked under the hood.

"Kind of you," Silvers waved. "We'll be seein' you." With that the two men got into the truck and headed back down the drive. Billy watched them go, not moving until they were out of sight. He headed back to the house, his mind full of questions he couldn't answer.

This would need some thinking on. He took out his notebook an scribbled a hasty note to himself;

Don't know can I trust Silvers yet. No, I can't trust his kids. Ain't seen his wife. He needs gas, and lumber, screws and nails. See what I can do. Keep eye on them kids. Can't see under the hood.

He put his notebook back in his pocket. Something was still nagging at him, something he had meant to do, before the terror of Widow George's house. Something he'd thought of in a fleeting moment while in town. He chewed his lip slightly as he walked, trying to remember. Finally, he shrugged.

"If it was important, it'll come to me," he murmured. Meanwhile, he had work to do.

It was still early in the day. Not even nine o'clock. He decided to see if he could get his P L A N for town together, and go on in. Something was telling him not to wait. He didn't know why that was, he just knew it was. There was some reason he needed to hurry a bit.

He sat on the front porch with his breakfast, the last of his fresh fruit for now. The orchards on the farm would give him apples, pears and peaches soon enough, but Billy figured these two oranges were the last he'd ever see, barring a miracle. Oranges wouldn't grow here for some reason. Daddy had said it was because the winters were too cold, and Billy figured his daddy knew. Whatever the reason, he took his time, and enjoyed the oranges, with some dry toast, a couple of scrambled eggs, and some lemonade.

Eggs he would have, he figured. The farm had a dozen chickens, for just that reason. He had made sure the coop was secure as soon as he got home. He hadn't been giving them laying mash, so there weren't so many eggs, and he knew not to eat the ones that had been laid while he hadn't been here on the farm. He had disposed of them, and would now gather his eggs every morning.

He figured next year he'd let one or two brood, and then he'd have fresh chickens. He could eat the older ones as the younger ones started laying eggs.

As soon as he was done with his breakfast, Billy took out is notebook again. He looked over his notes so he'd remember what he'd thought about yeste...

Suddenly he remembered that nagging thought. He hastily turned to a new page, and made another note for himself.

Need to keep a journal. Get some notebooks and pencils, pens, in town. I need to write down stuff that I do, and stuff that happens, so I don't forget.

Satisfied that he had finally remembered that nagging thought, he turned to his list for town. It took him over an hour of hard thinking, and not a little of going and looking for stuff, before he thought the list was finished. He looked at the list, feeling another nagging thought. There was something he had meant to add. What was it? Oh, yeah.

Remember to look around. Never know what you might find that will come in handy later on. Another lesson his daddy and his mamma had taught him. Sometimes just looking will make you realize something you forgot. Sometimes, when working on a car, Billy would get that same odd nagging, like he'd missed something. When that happened, he would stop and study the car carefully, until he found the problem. Once he had left the oil pan plug out of Mister Jamieson's truck and had been about to pour the new oil into the engine. Boy, that would have made a mess. Billy had learned to trust those nagging pressures he sometimes felt. They had kept him from making mistakes more than once.

Finally satisfied with his list, Billy gathered his things, and called Rommel, who had been running around the yard, chasing and barking at squirrels.

"What would you do if you caught one?" Billy asked, laughing. "You ain't a huntin' dog, Rommel. That squirrel might wind up treeing' *you*." Rommel looked mildly offended at the tone, almost as if he could understand what Billy was saying.

Odd Billy Todd

"C'mon, then," he called again, opening the truck door. His hurt feelings forgotten at the prospect of a truck ride, Rommel ran to the truck and jumped in. Together the two of them headed into town.

-

Somehow, the trip into town was easier today. Billy didn't know if he was just getting used to seeing the cars with dead people in them, or if he was learning to ignore it. Either way, he was grateful.

His first stop in town this time was Mister Traywick's. Billy attached the largest U-Haul trailer on the lot to his truck. He opened his notebook to check the trailer off the list, and saw his note to himself to look around. Putting the notebook away, he started looking around.

Inside Mister Traywick's car bay, Billy found an truck tank like those used by farm owners to carry fuel to their tractors in the field. This was a large one, and would hold two hundred gallons. Billy looked at it, wondering. If he put that thing in his truck, and filled it up, how would he get it unloaded? It would be too heavy, full.

Why couldn't I empty it into the tank at the farm? he thought suddenly. Well, there wasn't no reason, not really. He could just pump it out of the tank and into his own.

Then I could refill it and take that to Mister Silvers, he decided.

"Not that I owe him nothin', I guess," he added out loud. Despite his best efforts, he couldn't get over his mad. And there was just something about those two kids that outright bothered him. It wasn't their insults, either. Billy had a pretty good sense of when he could trust people or not. And right now, he just didn't think he could trust those two.

"But I reckon that ain't the issue, today," he decided. He went and unhitched the trailer, and pulled his truck over to the shop. It took him half an hour to wrestle the large empty tank onto his truck, and secure it. He stopped at last, winded. Wiping the sweat from his brow, he took a pull from the water jug he'd brought with him. The cool water helped him recover from the effort. He set a bowl for Rommel on the ground and filled it, calling the big dog over. Rommel readily drank the water.

Meanwhile, Billy pulled the truck over to the pump. He started to insert the pump into the tank, then shook his head.

"No power, no pump," he chastised himself. He knew Mister Traywick had a generator and went to start it. The small generator was right where Billy remember it being, set far back into the shop, in a corner. Billy checked the fuel and the oil, grateful to find both okay. He started the generator, and flipped the switch on the wall that activated the pumps.

It took a while to fill the tank. Once it was topped off, Billy filled the truck tanks to the top. With that took care of, he pulled his truck back to the trailer, and hitched it to the truck once more. Easing onto the street, Billy headed for his next stop.

He'd just been to the Co-Op yesterday, but he preferred not to think about that right now. He pulled around to the loading gate, and got out, with Rommel trailing right along with him. The feral cats that lived here, taking advantage of the natural draw of a feed store to mice, yowled and hissed at Rommel, and Billy didn't try to stop him chasing the cats. He wouldn't catch them, he knew.

While Rommel entertained himself, Billy set about loading all the things on his list. It was a long, hard and dirty job, but Billy didn't mind. The mind-numbing labor helped him forget the horrors of the last few days. He worked steadily, stopping twice briefly to rest and drink water. It took two hours, but he managed to get everything on his list. The long trailer was over half full, and that half was crammed to the roof.

Once finished with his list, Billy walked through the store, looking around carefully. He picked up a chainsaw, with extra chains and oil, which he placed in the bed of his truck. He also took the time to look up the parts he would need, should the saw break down. He added a set of tires for his truck, and for the Ranger as well. Various odds and ends were added as he walked, always trying to think of how he could use each item he found. He walked to the Carhart selection and picked out three pairs of insulated coveralls in his size, and four pairs of rugged pants as well. Six shirts and a heavy jacket finished his shopping.

He loaded his plunder up and called Rommel, who came running at once. The two of them got into the truck, headed this time to the hardware store. Once there, Billy quickly gathered several tubs of nails and screws for Mister Silvers, things he'd left or overlooked on the day he'd left town. Billy wouldn't need them, he figured, and he had told Mister Silvers he'd see what he could do.

Billy looked in the back of the store this time, and found something he'd never thought about. A tiller. He could use it. He would need to plant a garden, and since his father had owned a tractor, he'd never bothered with a tiller. Billy didn't plan on farming like his father had. With no one to sell to, he didn't see the point. And he wasn't that good a farmer, anyway, he admitted.

Once he was finished, Billy looked into the lumber shed. There was a pretty good selection for a small-town hardware store, and Billy picked through things fairly carefully. He loaded some wood for himself, in case he needed to make any repairs, or add on to anything, and then finished the trailer off with wood for Mister Silvers.

Next stop was the auto parts store. Billy took his time here, making sure he looked up each and every part he might need for his truck, the Ranger, and even the tractor, though he figured he probably wouldn't use it. Better to have and not need, his daddy had always said.

Satisfied that there was nothing else here that he needed, Billy headed for the pharmacy next. He had a list of his meds, and went through the pharmacy very carefully, making sure that the stuff he took from there matched the words on his bottles exactly. As he walked out, he went down the aisles and took the things he needed to make a very good first aid kit. His parents had one, but he hadn't kept it up to date like they had, since he hadn't lived everyday at the farm. He knew he should have, and frowned to himself at what his parents would have said about that.

While he wouldn't have thought it when making his plans, his last stop took the longest. Maybe it was because he was tired, but going through the library looking for books that would help him took longer than he thought it rightly should have. But, he admitted, it was worth it, looking at one book he'd found. In it was everything he needed to know about taking care of Rommel. With this, he could go to the vet's office, and get everything he needed to give Rommel his shots, and make sure he was healthy.

Billy made that his actual last stop. He wished he hadn't.

He was glad he'd left Rommel in the truck. Billy had never thought about Doc Danvers having had animals in his office. Once more Billy was assailed by the stench of rotting flesh, and he wondered if he would ever be free of it. He couldn't run away, this time, however. He chose not to look for the animals, knowing they would be in the cages in back of the building. Instead he went straight to the treatment room, and carefully read from the book he'd found, taking everything he'd need to see to Rommel's health. He had gotten medicines for the cattle and horses from the Co-Op.

In hindsight, he realized that he could probably have gotten Rommel's meds there too, but he hadn't known what they were. He wished he had known. It would have spared him being in here, with the stench.

Billy felt a moment of sadness, and twinge of guilt. He should have thought about that, that animals might have been here. He could have come and let them go. But he hadn't. Tears filled his eyes at the thought that these poor animals had died for lack of care, food and water, when he was just across town, hiding. He dropped his head for a moment, as the guilt threatened to overwhelm him.

But how could I have known that no one would think to let them out? he thought after a minute. *I wasn't responsible for them. It wasn't my responsibility to care for them. And I didn't know they were here.*

Straightening up, he put the thoughts of guilt and sadness away.

So long as the problem's in the barn, son, leave it there. Don't bring it into the house. That's what daddy had said. When Billy hadn't understood, daddy had tried again.

When you stop work for the day, son, don't bring car problems home with you, even if you're staying in your apartment right there in your shop. As long as the problem is in the shop, it has no place in your home. Billy had understood that. Don't bring trouble on your own house.

With that thought, and the memory of his Father's voice comforting him, Billy lifted his head, and left.

He wanted to get home before dark. He still had a lot of work to do.

CHAPTER SEVEN

-

It was nearly dark when Billy finally pulled into his yard. Between the fuel tank, the trailer, and the stuff in the bed of his truck, it had been a slow trip. Billy's truck was plenty strong enough to pull the load, but it was difficult to stop, and to keep steady. Fortunately, Billy had always been a good driver. His father had taught him to drive on the farm, and he had taken to it with relish.

Billy opened the barn doors, then backed the trailer into the barn. He decided at the last minute to leave the entire rig there, for the night. He was tired, and dirty, and hungry. Closing and securing the barn door, Billy went to the house.

He didn't realize how tired he was until after a hot shower and a quick meal. He could barely keep his eyes open.

Deciding that unloading the truck and trailer could wait, Billy went to bed.

-

The next morning Billy arose to the sound of thunder. As he lay motionless in the bed, he could hear rain pounding on the tin roof of the farm house. The sound made him drowsy. He was almost back to sleep when he felt a *thud* on his belly. Looking down, he saw Rommel staring intently at him.

"Awright," Billy grumbled, throwing the covers off. He went to the front door and opened it. Rommel walked out onto the porch, stopping at the sight of the rain. He paused, and looked back at Billy expectantly.

"Oh for. . .c'mon," Billy grumbled again and led the dog to the back door. He opened the door that led out onto the patio. The roof covered not only the patio, but all of the area immediately behind the house, so the ground there was relatively dry. Rommel went out quickly and did his business, then hurried back in at *crack* of a nearby lightning strike and the followup roll of thunder.

"Happy now?" Billy asked him. As if in reply Rommel trotted over to his empty food bowl, and looked at Billy expectantly. Again.

"You sure are bossy this mornin'," Billy mumbled, pouring the bowl full of food. As soon as he had touched the sack of feed, Rommel's tail stub was wagging frantically. Billy couldn't help but laugh a bit at the dog.

With Rommel attended to, Billy did something he almost never did.

He went back to bed.

The sound of rain hitting the roof soon lulled him back to sleep.

-

The rain lasted for three days. Hard at times, gentle at others, it continued without ever stopping completely. For the first day, Billy stayed in the house. He read some, he made notes to himself, and he rested.

He hadn't realized how tired he was. He had slept off and on for most of the day. Usually just for a half hour or so at the time, once for almost two hours. He had fixed a light lunch, having forgone breakfast to return to bed. Supper was also just a light meal, as Billy didn't have much of an appetite.

He tried to stay busy, though. Idle time was Billy's biggest problem, he knew. If he didn't keep busy at something, then his mind would wander, and latch onto some imagined problem. One he couldn't let go of. He couldn't afford that.

He had placed notes all over the house to remind him that he had to focus. This was something he'd learned from his folks, as they tried to help him get his business started. He had notes to help organize his supplies, keep his books, tend to daily chores.

He spent part of the rain filled first day making a list of all the things he should check on each day, another for things that needed checking at least twice a week, and than one for weekly items that needed looking after. The lists were part of the instructions left in the many notebooks his parents had assembled for him in the event he found himself alone, just like now.

Billy knew he wasn't 'dumb'. His parents had taken great pains to ensure that. But he was aware of his limitations, and his weaknesses. His parents had taken steps to ensure that as well. His father had translated that into car jargon, as he did most other things.

If you know your car is burning or leaking oil, you keep a check on it, right? Add oil when the car needs it. When you know that your clutch is slipping, and you can't get it fixed right away, you baby it, until you can fix it. So, when you know something will cause you problems, you baby it. Never approach it head on, like dumping the clutch under a load. Never run the engine's rpm so high that losing some oil will hurt it.

When you know what your weakness is, just like the clutch, or the oil leak, you can work around that weakness.

One of Billy's weaknesses was remembering things. So, he made notes. He made lists.

- Check PV cells and batteries
- Check fuel tank
- Check house for leaks
- Check water pump on well

And on and on. Billy wrote out four copies of each list. One for the front door, one for the back door, one for the barn, and one for the truck. He would always have a list somewhere nearby, reminding him of things that needed to be done.

Billy went to bed that night, satisfied that he'd done a good day's work.

-

When Billy awoke the next morning, the rain was falling heavy again. He sighed, torn between being frustrated and a little bit glad. He was frustrated because he knew there was a lot he needed to do, and the rain really kept him from doing that.

But he was a little bit glad because he really wanted to take the day off. The day before had been a wake up call for how tired he had been.

He decided that he would remain indoors. He could let the eggs go one day, he figured, and the cattle had grass and hay available to them, as did the horses. His truck and trailer were locked securely in the barn so they were in no danger.

Yep, he'd just rest today, and take it easy. Billy loved to read. Despite his struggles in school at times, he'd always been a good reader. Billy found that he could get lost in a book. Almost as if the book drew him in, and took him away to

Odd Billy Todd

wherever the book led. It had been a great escape during tough times when he as younger.

He walked to the study and browsed for a few minutes. His mother and father had, over the years, amassed a large library for farm folks. His mother had always watched for good books for sale at the town library, and yard sales.

He came across one of his father's older books, called the *Ranger Handbook*. Billy wasn't sure what it was about, but it looked interesting. And, it *felt* right. Billy trusted that intuition in almost everything, and saw no reason not to trust it now. He took the book down, settled into his father's old chair, and started reading.

At first, he found the going difficult. The book was very detailed, and often the writing was so technical that Billy just couldn't get it. But as he continued to read, the book began to flow to him much better. The instructions began to simplify, and accompanying diagrams and drawing helped him better understand what he was reading.

By the time he was a fourth of the way through it, Billy found himself immersed into the book. So engrossed was he, that he didn't realize how long he'd been reading until Rommel came to him, insistently wanting 'out'. Looking at the clock on the wall, Billy realized he had been reading for over three hours. It was nearly lunch time.

"Wow, boy. Sorry about that," he told the dog, laying the book aside, and rising. He took Rommel to the back door and let him out, then decided he'd fix a light lunch. Rommel was finished by the time Billy had mixed some tuna, so he let the big dog back inside, fixed himself two sandwiches and a glass of water, and continued to read over lunch.

Billy realized that his father must have read this book. There were notes in many of the margins, and some of those notes were addressed to him. To Billy.

The notes explained several items in the book in terms that Billy found easier to read and retain. Facts began to squirrel themselves away in his mind, mingling with other things his father had taught him over the years. Tactical solutions to problems he encountered. Ideas to improve his security at the farm. Billy began scratching notes to himself as he read, making sure to take note of the most important things. Or at least, what his father seemed to have thought were the most important things.

He paid extra close attention to those notes, knowing that his father had made them for him. As he read those notes, Billy began to think about the things he'd done the last few days. Now, looking back, he could see that he hadn't been nearly as careful as he should have been. He'd gone into more than one place without his rifle. He wasn't carrying extra ammunition for the rifle or his pistol. He wasn't carrying his shoulder bag, but rather leaving it in his truck.

I got to pay more attention, he told himself, shaking his head. *Stupid, stupid mistakes. Mistakes that could get me hurt, or killed. I need to be more careful.*

As these thoughts started bouncing around in his head, Billy started re-thinking everything he'd done in the last few days. Was someone watching? Had they seen him? Did they know him? Know where he lived? Every question just brought up more questions, and with them more uncertainty. He had thought, at least some of the time, that he might be the only person left alive anywhere around. Thinking that had made him careless.

I knew better. I know better. Dumb, dumb, dumb!

Billy was starting to get what his mother had called 'worked up'. His mind was racing, playing over all the mistakes he had made, the things he had done wrong, the chances he had taken, all in an endless loop. Finally, he couldn't stand it anymore, and stood up. He paced all over the house, walking back and forth. He didn't know how long he did that.

Rommel followed Billy every step of the way. He could tell that his person was upset, but the dog could see no threat. This wasn't the first time his person had become like this, even when there was nothing to be afraid of. Rommel was becoming used to it, but he still didn't like it. Finally, after a long time, (thirty minutes is a long time in doggy time) Rommel had had enough.

WOOF!

Billy stopped in his tracks, jolted from the circle his mind was thinking in. Startled, he looked at the dog, who was simply looking back at him. Billy stared at him blankly for several seconds, then grinned.

"Thanks, boy," he said, rubbing the big dog's head. Rommel leaned into his hand, encouraging Billy to scratch between his ears.

"Sorry about that," Billy told him. "Sometimes I get that way," he shrugged. Rommel licked him then, as if to say 'apology accepted'.

"C'mon. I'll get ya a treat. Seems I owe ya one, don't I?"

-

Billy woke up on the third day with rain still hitting the roof. It didn't matter, he decided. He had work to do. He rose quickly and dressed. He let Rommel take care of his business, then left the dog in the house while he ventured outside. There was no sense in letting him get all muddy, he decided.

Firstly, he gathered the eggs, an threw out some mash for the chickens. He hadn't been out yesterday, so there were several eggs. The chickens were glad to have the mash, it seemed, running everywhere trying to get as much of it as possible.

"Bad as Rommel," Billy muttered. Despite his raincoat he was already soaked, and his mood was equally bad.

Next, he checked on the horses. They weren't in the stalls, and weren't all that hungry, though the sound of grain hitting the covered trough did convince them to amble over and check it out.

With that out of the way, he walked down to the cow pasture, where the cows were starting to amble about as they were inclined. All looked healthy and whole, so he didn't bother them further. He made sure they still had plenty of hay in the pole barn, and decided to call it a day. He wasn't going to bother with the truck and trailer in the rain, he decided. He might slip and fall.

Billy knew he had made a lot of mistakes. He'd spent a long time the day before with those mistakes, those errors, playing through his mind again and again. He walked back toward the house, trying to clear his mind of that loop, and replace it with how he would make sure not to be so careless in the future.

CHAPTER EIGHT

It was four days before the ground was dry enough for Billy to decide he could be out, working. He had unloaded the truck and trailer, leaving only what he planned to give Mister Silvers. He had also drained the truck tank into the farm tank, emptying it so he could refill it for Mister Silvers. He frowned to himself at the thought of having the deal with the Silvers' kids again, but Mister Silvers was okay, so far as Billy knew.

He'd just have to make allowances, and be careful.

Billy and Rommel climbed into the truck just as the sun was peeping over the trees. Billy wanted to be in and out of town as soon as possible. He had a short list of things he still needed, things he had forgotten. Once he got those things, and refilled the truck tank, he didn't want to go back into town again if he could help it.

Billy frowned again. During the self-imposed isolation during the rain, and the mud, Billy was reminded of how alone he was. When he had his shop, there were always people coming and going, and he had the whole town to roam in, visiting and talking. He knew who his friends were, and who to leave alone.

Now, the only living people he knew were the Silvers and their rotten kids. Sighing, he shook his head.

Just have to get used to it, I reckon, he told himself. *Be awful lonely, though.* He looked at Rommel.

"Reckon you're the only friend I got, anymore, boy," he smiled, ruffing the dog's large head. Glad for the attention, Rommel leaned into the contact.

"Let's get this done."

Filling the tank took the longest, Billy decided, so he did that first. He was tempted to wander about and get the things he still needed while the pump was working, but decided against it. Leaving that pump running was an invitation to disaster, and even Billy knew that. He'd also wondered why so many 'smart' people would leave such things unattended. If he, Billy, was supposed to be dumb, and he knew better, then they certainly should.

It was thoughts like these that kept Billy from thinking he was dumb. He might not know everything, and he might not be as smart as some, but he knew what he knew, and that was enough. His mamma and daddy had made sure he wasn't 'dumb'. They had worked with him all his life, finding ways to educate him, teach him things, and make sure he could care for himself. Thanks to them, Billy wasn't dependent on anyone else.

When the tank was finally full, Billy topped off the truck tanks again, just to be sure, then secured the pump, and the generator.

Might need what's left, one day, he told himself.

His next stop was the library again. He walked the aisles more carefully, this time, finding instructional books that he could use to help make himself more comfortable, and more prepared, in the new world he found himself living in. The next stop was the pharmacy, again.

Billy had read a great deal while waiting for the rain and the mud to go. He had a list of drugs that might be needed, and he hurriedly took them from the shelves. He also added to his stocks of bandages and OTC meds. When these were gone, there probably wouldn't be any more. Braces, splints, hygiene supplies, his list was better organized this time. He also added 'feminine' supplies to his cache, having read that they would be in demand. The only women he knew of were Mrs. Silvers and her. . .daughter. He'd give some to them, and store the rest. Might be handy at some point.

He also took every roll of toilet paper and paper towels he could find in town, placing them in the trailer. He'd have to unload what he wanted before he went to Mister Silvers. No sense in letting them know anything about what he had.

Next came the Co-Op. Billy hadn't thought about the animal medicines the Co-Op kept the last time he was here. He *wasn't ever* going back to the vet's office, could he help it. His reading had given him a better list of things he needed for his animals, however, and he decided that he should get what he could from the Co-Op while he was here.

As he moved about town, Billy noticed something he'd never really seen in Cedar Bend.

Rats. Lots and lots of them. Rats were something Billy had never thought of, and now he wished he had. Where had they came from? Why were they here, now?

The answer presented itself when he saw a pile of the things feasting on a corpse lying on the sidewalk.

They're eating the dead people!

Billy stopped in the street right there, horrified at the sight. He could suddenly see himself, in his mind's eye, being consumed by the rats. He sat there for several minutes, just staring, that scene playing over and over again in his mind.

Rommel's barking finally brought him out of his trance, and Billy shook his head as if to throw the horrible thought out of it completely.

"I ain't gettin' eat by rats," he said to the air around him. "Ain't gonna happen. I'm gettin' what else I need, and I'm gittin'. Ain't coming back here, *ever*."

With that he went quickly to the Co-Op. He ordered Rommel to stay in the truck. He didn't want the dog chasing after the rats, and getting bit.

Billy worked as quick as he could, grabbing everything in his carefully prepared list. He also picked up what ammunition the Co-Op had, mostly hunting rounds. At the last minute, he went looking for rat poison. He found it, and took all the Co-Op had.

"That's it," he told himself, loading the last of his things. Whatever he didn't have, it wasn't worth staying any longer, or coming back for. More than almost anything he'd seen since the sickness started, the rats scared Billy. Rats carried disease. Everyone knew that, including Billy. Rats made people sick. Made people die. Then they ate the people.

Billy hadn't known that last. He'd never once imagined rats in such large number in a place like Cedar Bend, either. What looked like thousands. Enough to over run the town in just two weeks.

What would they look like in two months? Two *years*?

That thought scared Billy even more, as the idea of rats invading his farm, over running his home, killing him and Rommel, and all the animals, almost overwhelmed him.

"Gotta keep calm," Billy whispered to himself. "Calm, calm, calm. Can't stop now. Might not start again. Can't let the rats get me." Ironically, the fear of the rats, which had caused his panic, now helped him overcome it. His fear of what could happen to him if he froze made him move past the paralyzing panic that so often disabled him.

He moved quickly to the door of his truck, and jumped inside.

"We're outta here, boy," he told Rommel, firing the engine. "And we ain't coming back."

-

Billy stopped once more at the Silvers' gate. He wasn't happy about being here, but he meant to keep his word.

He had unloaded his own supplies at home, before coming here. Billy was more determined than ever that the Silvers, especially their kids, not know what he had, or where it was. There was something about those two that just didn't set well with him. He couldn't see under the hood, where they were concerned.

Billy honked his horn three times, waited a minute, and then honked it again. He almost hoped no one would come to the gate. He could go home, safe in the knowledge that he'd tried.

He waited for ten minutes, according to his watch, with no response. Just as he was getting ready to leave, Mister Silvers' truck came bouncing down the drive. Mister Silvers was alone, Billy was relieved to see, as he stepped out of his truck.

"Afternoon, Mister Silvers," Billy called.

"Hello Billy!" Silvers called back, walking to the gate. "What brings you out?"

"Got some stuff for you," Billy told him. "What you asked for, and a little more. And some gas," he added, pointing to the truck tank. Silvers just stared.

"Where'd you get all that?" he asked.

"Town," Billy shrugged. "You said you had need, so I went and got this stuff for you."

"Billy, you hadn't oughta be doing' that," the older man said softly.

"Won't no more," Billy assured him. "Scared me. Towns full o' rats. Great big ones. I ain't never going back again. Probably won't never leave my farm again, to be honest. I ain't been so scared anytime I can remember."

"I was afraid o' that," Silvers nodded. "I'd read it could happen, but I just. . .I guess I just didn't want to believe it." The older man looked much older for a minute, then shook it off.

"Billy, I can't thank you enough for doing this for us," he extended his hand. "Come on up, and I'll get it unloaded." Billy got back in his truck as Silvers opened the gate. Billy waited for him to close it, then followed the older man's truck up the drive.

He'd been here, before, of course, but Billy was impressed with Mr. Silvers' place. Good strong house, two barns, equipment shed. All laid out well, and in good repair. Silvers led him to one of the barns. As the older man opened the doors, Billy backed his trailer up to where the doorway opened into the barn.

"Stay," Billy ordered Rommel. He left the windows low enough that Rommel wouldn't get hot, but not low enough the dog could get out. He grabbed his gloves and exited the truck.

"There's lumber, screws and nails, and some rat poison," Billy told him. "Few other things, as well, and some stuff for your women folk. What I could find," he added. Silvers looked at him with affection.

"That's right. . .that's very thoughtful of you, Billy."

"Trying to help," Billy shrugged.

"What's going on?" Billy turned to see the Silvers' children, trailed by their mother, walking toward them. Toby and his sister looked like they wanted to kill him. Mrs. Silvers didn't.

"Ma'am," he nodded to Mrs. Silvers, who smiled warmly.

"Hello, Billy," she said kindly. "I'm glad to see you well."

"Thank you kindly, ma'am," Billy nodded. "Good to see you, too."

"What is all this, doofus?" the daughter asked in disdain. Billy saw red almost instantly, but it was Mr. Silvers who replied.

"You know what? Just for that, you two can unload all this by yourself," he ordered.

"I ain't said nothin'!" Toby exclaimed.

"You did the other day, and me tellin' ya to keep quiet, now get on with it!" Silvers ordered.

"Thanks a lot, Shelly!" Toby growled.

"It's Michelle, not Shelly!" the girl shot back.

"It'll be 'cold' and 'hungry' you don't get to work," Silvers interrupted. "Now get working." The two teens grumbled, but went to work. They hadn't been working long before there was a delighted shriek from the trailer, and Shelly came out with a large box of feminine napkins.

"Are these for us?" she asked, her voice much nicer than before.

"And this?" Toby asked, trailing her with a large box of toilet paper.

"It's all for you," Billy nodded. "For all of you, I mean," he added.

"Thank you, Billy Todd," Mrs. Silvers said earnestly. "I'm afraid we were caught short by all this."

"Well, there's a good bit in the trailer," Billy assured her. "All I could find, anyway."

There was less grumbling now as the two teenagers went about unloading the trailer. Billy helped, wanting to get home before dark. Billy fished out a small box that he handed to Mr. Silver.

"Twenty-two long rifle, and four-ten shot shells," he told the older man. "Found'em at the Co-Op. Though you might could use'em. Ain't got no need for'em, myself."

"Thanks son," Silvers looked at the ammunition. "Body can't have too much hunting ammunition." Billy nodded, and checked the trailer.

"Well, that looks like it," he announced. "I'm gonna head home, Mr. Silvers. Ma'am," this to Mrs. Silvers, "was good to see you again."

"Won't you stay for supper?" Mrs. Silvers asked.

"Would ma'am, but it's been a long day. And I got chores still to see to at home. Maybe another time."

Billy piled into his truck and followed Mr. Silver to the gate. Waving back to the older man as he hit the road, Billy went straight home. Parking the truck in the barn, and locking it, Billy led Rommel inside. It had been along day. He decided to take a quick shower, fix a bite to eat, and then go through some of the books he'd gotten.

And try not to think about the rats.

CHAPTER NINE

Billy stopped his work for a few minutes and looked up at the sky.

"Be snowin' 'fore long, I guess," he said to the air around him.

It had been two months since Billy's last trip into town. His final trip. Nightmares about the rats in Cedar Bend still haunted him to that very day, though not as bad as the first week. Dreams of giant rats invading the farm, attacking him, Rommel, the horses, the cows, eating everything they could find.

Billy's fear had driven him during that first week or so. He'd fixed several rat traps along the edge of the farm, small covered boxes with rat poison and bits of cheese. He'd used cheese puffs, too. Meat scraps. Anything he'd thought might entice the rats into eating the poison. He'd also made sure that all of his storage areas were sealed against rats. He'd barely stopped to sleep and eat until he was certain that his home, his storage, and his feed rooms were as rat proof as he could make them.

Now, two months later, he hadn't seen sign of that first rat. He wondered, sometimes, if he'd gone a little overboard. But the material left for him by his parents had covered rats. Detailing the dangers, and telling him what he could do to keep them at a distance.

Once, during that first week, Billy had been almost overwhelmed by the desire to drive back to the edge of town and start shooting every rat he could find. Common sense had finally stopped that idea, since he didn't have nearly enough .22 ammo for that sort of thing.

Oh, he had plenty, for anything else. But there were so many rats. Thousands of them. Maybe tens of thousands. And there would be more in other places. He couldn't shoot them all.

So, he stayed on the farm, and he worked. He read. He prepared. It would be winter soon, and he'd cut wood for almost two weeks now. The outdoor furnace that heated his water also heated the house in winter. He could fill it once or twice a week, with everything from tree stumps to railroad ties, and it would burn it all.

Today was the last day he'd planned to cut. There had been a good supply of wood already, probably enough for this winter and the next, but Billy wasn't taking chances. Some of his reading, both from his parents' books and those from the library, had provided some detail of what could be expected in situations like these. With a mass die off of the world's population, there would be less heat being generated on the earth. That meant cooler temperatures. Weather patterns would slowly move back toward the days before cars and factories covered the world. Without all that heat, the planet would cool some, and be more like in the 'old days' of the 1800's and before.

That was fine with Billy, since the 1800's seemed like a better time when he read about them. Simpler. Not easier, by any means. Billy knew he'd have to work ever harder. He already was working as hard as he ever had. But he'd read about how eventually modern conveniences would wear out, or resources would be gone, or parts would become impossible to get, or...

Or, or, or. It never stops. Might be slow, but it's always moving.

Billy thought about these things for a minute, wiping his brow. He knew he had it easier than someone like Mister Silvers. He had a family to care for, provide for. Billy didn't. All he had to worry about was himself.

Billy knew that he would eventually die. That didn't scare him. Everyone died. His mamma and daddy had died. So would he. It was as natural as being born in the first place. So, Billy didn't worry about it.

That didn't mean he *wanted* to die, of course. So, he worked. He planned. He prepared.

There was certainly plenty to keep him busy. He'd already cut the hay field, and stored the hay in the pole barn. The cattle and the horses would need it come winter. Billy had paid to have the hay cut before, when he was still working in his shop, but those days were gone. There was hay a plenty for now, since he had just bought some before the Plague hit. But he would need more.

And that meant cutting it himself.

He'd been very careful, operating the tractor. He'd never been good at it, despite all his father's attempts to teach him. But he could use it. Without it, cutting and storing the hay would be more of a chore than just one man might could manage. He'd worry about that when the time came.

He'd cut wood, of course. He'd tended to the cattle, and the horses. He had thought about planting a garden, but knew it was too late for it to make much. Better to save the seeds, and plant a good garden next year, he decided. He wished he had a green house. He knew how to build one, thanks to his books, but he didn't have the materials. Maybe if the rats ever went away, he could ease back into town and find what he needed.

But he wasn't going to fight the rats for it. Thinking about them left Billy right back where he'd started this long thought process.

Scared of rats. Of a rat invasion.

He sunk his ax into the cutting block and picked up his rifle.

He needed to check the traps. Again.

-

Billy had made his rounds and was back to the house when he heard the horn. He was startled at first, it had been so long since he'd heard such a sound. As the horn sounded again, he realized it was coming from his gate. Frowning, he picked up his rifle and motioned for Rommel to follow him. Over the past two months, Billy had worked with Rommel a good bit, and the two had developed a good relationship. Rommel would follow hand gestures, and he would signal Billy with his actions, rather than barks and growls.

It wasn't the same as having another person with him, but maybe it was even better, Billy had decided. Rommel was loyal to a fault. People weren't always loyal. The two of them started for the gate, taking the trail through the woods that allowed them to reach the gate unseen.

The horn blew three more times before they could make it down. Whoever it was wasn't being patient, that was for sure. Billy didn't feel any danger signals, and Rommel didn't appear to either, but he decided they'd be careful anyway.

When he reached the little spot where he could see the gate, Billy was surprised to see the Silvers' daughter there. As he watched she honked the horn again, her face worried looking rather than angry.

Odd Billy Todd

Now what would she be doing here?

Deciding that the only way to find out was to go see, Billy stepped out of the woods.

"There you are!" she spotted him at once. She started to walk toward him, but stopped cold at a warning growl from Rommel, who stepped between them.

Good dog, Billy couldn't help thinking. *You don't like her either, do ya boy?*

"What can we do for you?" Billy asked, his voice low, but carrying.

"My papa sent me to give you some news!" Michelle told him excitedly. "He was able to talk to someone on the radio a little while ago! Over toward Franklin, he said!"

"No kiddin'!" Billy was enthused. "Any idea who it was? Did they have any news?" She nodded.

"They built a little settlement over there. Got nearly a hundred people so far, the guy on the radio said. Lively trading, and even a doctor!"

"Well, that is good news," Billy said. "Body needs a doc, now and again."

"Ain't it great!" the girl enthused. "We ain't all alone!"

"Sounds like great news," Billy nodded again. "You pa didn't tell'em where we are, I'm guessing'?" he asked. She looked at him.

"He's a little smarter than. . .than that," she managed to catch herself. Billy snorted.

"I know that," he surprised her. "You note that I said he *didn't*, I was guessing. Your pa's a bit too smart to give away where he is."

Michelle didn't know how to respond to that, so she just nodded. Maybe the 'doofus' wasn't as dumb as she'd thought. And he had been nice to them, even when they hadn't been so nice to him.

"Well, I need to get back," she said suddenly. "But pa wanted you to know. He tried calling' you on the radio."

"Never use it," Billy shrugged. "Guess I'll need to start, now," he added.

"Well, see you later," the girl waved, getting back into her truck. "Mamma says she's still expecting you for supper some night," she added. He nodded.

"We'll see," he was non-committal, but thought it would be nice.

"Okay, then. Bye."

Billy watched her go, then looked down at Rommel. He was still watching the truck as it disappeared.

"Well, what about that?" Billy asked. Then the two started on their way back to the house.

Billy realized as he walked back to the house that he had ignored the radio. He shouldn't ought to have done that. He didn't need to talk on the radio to just listen and get news. As he walked up on the porch, he decided he'd turn it on and see what was being said.

His father had been an avid 'ham', and had set up what he called his radio 'shack' in an unused downstairs bedroom. Billy sat down in front of the radio and went through the power-up check list carefully, not having used the radio much at all. He knew how, his daddy had seen to that. He'd just never felt the need to use one like his father had. The news from Mister Silvers' was making Billy second guess that choice.

As he spun the dials, he heard bits and pieces of signals playing in and out. He

45

tried to tune in to several of them, but distance, weather, or some other form of interference prevented him from locking onto the sporadic signals. Billy was patient, however, and kept turning the dials.

"...*storm hit way too early for this time o' year...*"

"...*get some rain, we'll be hurtin' for water...*"

"...*there must be twenty or thirty of them! They just came in shootin' and grabbin' what they wanted. Killed ol' Clem and his boy, right there in the street! We tried to...*"

Billy frowned as the last signal faded, and worked to try and get it back, but it was gone. It sounded like someone had attacked someone else. *Ain't there enough trouble*, Billy thought, *without we turn on one another? I wonder where they are?*

Leaving the radio on, Billy went to his father's study, looking for a book he'd seen, but never really imagined he'd need. He peered through the titles until he found what he was looking for.

Defensive Preparations for Farm and Surrounding Area

Billy took the loose-leaf binder down, and opened it up. There was, as usual, a note from his dad.

Billy, I hope you never need this. But it's better to be safe than sorry. I've tried to think of every possible need, but remember to use your imagination. If you can think of it, someone else can too.

Dad

Going back to the radio, Billy sat down and started reading. Even as he read, his hand absently moved the tuner on the radio slowly back and forth, listening for anything else. He heard more about the weather in other places, talk of several 'trade days', requests and offers for certain hard to find items, people searching for news of friends and family.

Billy listened to all this with only one ear, as he continued to read, and study not just the notes and instructions, but the maps that showed where certain things should be done if the farm, and the surrounding area, found itself in a hostile environment. Billy's father had been a meticulous man, and far smarter than he had felt the need to let on to his friends or neighbors.

As he continued to read, Billy got a notebook, and started making notes of his own. There were several things he was going to have to do, and a list of materials he would need.

This was going to be a lot of work.

-

Billy looked down at his notes with a sigh. He'd been working far into the night, going over his father's preparations for something like this. Raiders or outlaws who had survived whatever troubles had come this way, and were now prowling and preying on others instead of working for what they needed or wanted.

It was a long list. Billy wasn't worried about an attack on the farm so much. The house was built to withstand anything short of a tank, thanks to the forethought of his parents. But there were problems he'd have to deal with. Things he should already have done, had he given any thought to such gangs having survived the plague.

He would have to go back into town, too.

Dammit, dammit, dammit all! Billy almost threw the clipboard he'd been making his notes on he was so angry at himself. And scared.

I did not *want to go back into town!* His thoughts were savage as he felt his anger swell. If not for these raiders, he could have set here on his farm and been safe and secure. Now, in order to be safe, and keep the others safe as well, he had to go back.

He shoved his chair back and stood, walking around the house, trying to work his anger off. Rommel looked at him, but read his person's mood well, and simply lay his head back down. He knew Billy was upset, but could sense the anger as well. Rommel had no help for that, and he knew it was better to let Billy work it off.

And work it off he did. After about twenty minutes of pacing, Billy had decided what he had to do. He looked at the clock, seeing that it was just nine in the evening. He had thought it much later. Billy thought about his situation.

There was a lot he didn't know. He didn't know where the raiders were, or where the man talking about them were. The signal hadn't been strong enough to tune it in tight, but Billy knew there were many reasons that could be so. His father had explained that 'atmospherics' could often carry a wave far further than it would normally carry, while at the same time preventing people who normally spoke to each other regularly from communicating at all.

Were there any of these 'raiders' in his own area? No way to know for now. If there *were*, had they attacked anyone yet? Again, no way to know. How much time did he have to take care of things before it was too late?

No way to know.

"Dammit!" he muttered. There was just no way to make a good plan, with so little information. He looked over at Rommel.

"Looks like we got a trip to make, boy."

Twenty minutes later, Billy started his truck, trailer hooked up behind. There wasn't much choice as far as he could see. This had to be done. Should already have been done.

Sighing in angry frustration again, Billy headed for town.

-

There were rats, of course. Billy had expected them. But at night, there were a lot *more* rats. And they looked *huge* in his head lights.

"It don't matter," Billy sighed. "This has to get done."

His father's instructions had been clear. Leave nothing that raiders could use against the people in the area. Nothing that would help them. Especially weapons and ammunition. Everything had to go, or be destroyed.

Billy's first stop was one of the few places he'd never even considered going to. Lem Higgins' gun shop. In his defense, Billy hadn't thought about it because he had his own guns, and plenty of ammunition. He didn't need anymore. Never once had he considered the need to take it before it could be used against him. Still shaking his head at his own stupidity, he pulled into the front of Higgins' and shut off the truck. He placed a head lamp on his head, put another light in his coat pocket, then checked his pistol and rifle. And then his extra mags. He wasn't making the same old mistakes, at least.

"No, just a whole bunch o' new ones," he muttered to himself as he got out of the truck. There were no rats in the immediate area, so Billy motioned for Rommel to follow. The dog leapt out, looking around. He woofed lightly at a gaggle of rats across the street, but Billy stopped him with a motion. Rommel still wanted to go, but followed orders.

The steel cage that usually blocked the door when the shop was closed was quick work for a crow bar and a strong back. Billy had both and was soon standing in front of the more traditional glass door of a storefront. He gently rapped on the door with a hammer, and knocked enough glass loose to get his hand inside and open the door. He reached inside, careful not to cut himself, and unlocked the door. He eased inside, Rommel following, and closed the door.

Casting the light around the shop, Billy saw that the place was largely undisturbed. It did look as if some things had been taken in a great hurry, but for the most part, the store was still like it normally was. There was a large rack on the floor, holding shotguns and rifles, while another large rack adorned the wall behind the counter with more expensive weaponry.

Glass cases that made the counter were filled with handguns and some accessory items. Shelves behind that counter held countless boxes of ammunition, while others, in cases, were stacked neatly about the floor. Billy expected to find more such cases in the storeroom behind the counter.

"Well, at least I remembered the two-wheeler," Billy shook his head. The dolly would at least make loading the heavier pieces easier. "Let's get started, boy. We got a lot o' work to do before..."

Rommel suddenly tensed, growling deep in his chest. Billy shut his head lamp off at once, having come to trust Rommel's instincts. He took two steps to the left just as he heard a pump shotgun rack a shell into its chamber.

"Whatever you got in mind, it had better be peaceable," the female voice warned. "Else you ain't long for this world. 'Least what's left of it."

CHAPTER TEN

Billy was dumbfounded. There was someone still alive in town!

"Uh, ma'am, I... that is, I'm, uh..."

"I ain't got all night," the voice told him flatly. "And tell that dog to stop movin', you want to keep him alive." Rommel was following the voice as it moved.

"Rommel, come," Billy ordered. Rommel looked at him, then back to the dark.

"Now, Rommel," Billy snapped. Rommel walked slowly to Billy's side, and placed himself between Billy and the unseen speaker.

"Now, why are you breakin' into my place?" the speaker demanded.

"Well, I didn't think no one was still alive," Billy replied honestly. "There's been some trouble out and about, and I didn't want to leave all this stuff to the raiders that are poppin' up all over. I thought to take it and hide it somewhere, so they couldn't use it against the rest of us."

"Not takin' it for yourself, then," the mocking voice floated through the dark.

"Well, no," Billy answered. "Don't rightly need it, I reckon. I got plenty for me. But I surely don't wanna be facin' a bunch o' criminals and such after they clear this place out. They'd be right well armed."

"Billy Todd, is that you?" the woman surprised him suddenly.

"Uh, yes'm, it is," he didn't even think of lying. Billy wasn't much on lying anyway.

"Why in hell didn't ya say so, ya idiot!" a lantern flared to life, and Billy shielded his eyes in the glare, seeing Rhonda Higgins standing in the light, now holding her shotgun up and away from him.

"Rhonda?" Billy blinked. "What are you doing here?"

"My daddy owns this place, I'll thank you to remember," she shot back, laughing just a little. She placed her shotgun on the counter. "So why are you really here?"

"Told ya," Billy shrugged. "Read one o' daddy's books about this kinda stuff. Says to make sure not to leave anything laying around that can be used against you. I hadn't thought about that. So, here I am."

"Where you aim to take all this stuff?" Rhonda demanded.

"Out to the farm, I guess," Billy shrugged. "Ain't got nowhere else any safer to hide it. I don't want nobody getting hold to it, then using against other folks."

"And you know that folks is doing just that?" she asked.

"Heard tell of it on the shortwave," Billy nodded. "Just this afternoon, in fact. Group of 'bout thirty or so, sounded like. Killed two folk right in the street somewhere."

"Somewhere?"

"Couldn't rightly get the where," Billy admitted. "Was havin' a hard time holding' the signal. Ain't right as good at it as my daddy was."

"You don't need that 'dumb' act with me, Billy," Rhonda giggled slightly. "I been knowin' you all my life. I know you ain't maybe smart as some, but I also know you ain't all that dumb, neither." Billy didn't know what to say to that, exactly.

Rhonda Higgins was two years younger than he was, about. He didn't know exactly, but he knew she was two grades behind him in school. She was pretty, but a tomboy from head to heel. Her father had raised her since she'd been three, when her mother had died in a car wreck. Billy had heard his father say more than once that Rhonda probably knew more about guns than Lem did.

"Well, I ain't much on acting'," Billy finally replied. "But I can follow directions. What are you doin' still here, anyways? How come you didn't leave?"

"And go where?" Rhonda snorted. "This is my home, Billy, remember? We live upstairs. Or I do, anyway. Daddy, he didn't. . .daddy. . .didn't make it." He could hear the pain in her voice, but there was strength there, too.

"I'm sorry, Rhonda," Billy said, and meant it. "If I'd known you was here, alone, I'd have helped you any way I could." Rhonda smiled at him.

"I know that. I seen you taking stuff from town. Started to call out a time or two, but..." She trailed off with a shrug.

"Well, why don't you come out to the farm with me?" Billy blurted. "I mean I got a big house, plenty o' room, and plenty to eat. Got horses and the like. Plenty o' room. Got electricity and hot water too," he added, and saw her eyes shine at that.

"Really? Flush toilets, and showers and such?" her voice was sounding like a little girl's, now.

"And such," he nodded. "You know you're welcome. You family and mine been friends for a hundred years or so, at least," he laughed, causing her to giggle again.

"I have to admit, it sounds like heaven, after all this time living here without," she agreed, her voice taking on a dreamy quality. "But would folks think?" she added, giggling.

"Well, there ain't no one else I know of around, save for Mister Silvers and his family."

"Shelly made it huh?" Rhonda almost growled.

Guess she don't think no more o' 'Shelly' than I do, Billy grinned to himself.

"'Fraid so," he nodded. "But we don't see her much. Once in the last two months. Today, in fact, when she came to tell me about Mister Silvers hearing folks on the radio. What got me to listenin'."

"Billy are you sure it's okay?" Rhonda asked, her voice very serious now. "I mean, I'd love to not be alone, and be somewhere safe, and with some modern conveniences, but I don't want to put you out." Her voice was sincere. And worried.

"You won't be puttin' us out," he promised. "We'd be glad for the company."

"We?" Rhonda's voice was wary now. "There's more than you?"

"Sure," Billy grinned, and looked down. "Rommel, this here is Rhonda Higgins. Friend," he added, pointing to her. "Rhonda, this here is Rommel. Done saved me more than once."

"So, it's just you and the dog?" she brightened again.

"Well, and the horses, cows and chickens," Billy added. "But yeah, just me and Rommel in the house. Course you'll have to work your way onto Rommel's good side. I'd go with food. It's his weakness," Billy whispered conspiratorially.

"Oh, I have an idea that I got something that will make me Rommel's new best friend," Rhonda smiled mischievously. "Okay, I'm sold. You start loading. I'll get my things, and then I'll help you when they're loaded. Deal?"

"Deal!"

-

Billy was huffing slightly as he maneuvered another dolly fully of ammunition up the ramp and into the trailer. He'd loaded the weapons first, using every gun case in the store, and then falling back on the manufacturer's boxes when they ran out. He'd loaded the handguns and magazines into plastic totes, which stacked nicely inside the trailer. He'd then started packing reloading supplies, including all the presses and dies Lem had kept in inventory. He grabbed some of the packs, and gun socks as well, adding them to the padding around the guns.

He looked up at Rommel's *woof* and saw Rhonda coming from the store, backpack and two suitcases in hand, her shotgun over her shoulder, and a pistol on her belt. Rommel went straight for her, and Billy panicked.

"Rommel, no!" he shouted, almost tripping in his haste to get out of the trailer and stop Rommel from attacking Rhonda. Rhonda's laughing brought him up short.

Rommel hadn't given Rhonda Higgins a second thought. At her feet was another Rottie, a *female* Rottie, about two-thirds Rommel's size. The female was hesitant as Rommel sniffed at her, but then the two began to make introductions to each other as dogs are known to do. Rhonda laughed.

"I told you I had something that would make me and old Rommel friends right off. Rommel, this here is Dottie."

-

With Rhonda helping, the loading went much faster. She also knew where some of her father's more interesting 'goodies' were hidden, and brought them out to the trailer as well. Billy didn't ask what they were, deciding that if Rhonda wanted him to know, she'd tell him.

Rhonda also took the clothing that Lem had in stock. Most of it was camouflage hunting clothes. Even if they couldn't wear it, they could trade it to those who could. Billy had told her about the trading going on in Franklin.

"We can do pretty well at that, at least for a while," she told him. "There's all sorts of things still here that we can take and use for trade items. And I can trade for empty casings, and reload them. Daddy had a lot of powder. It won't last forever, of course, but it will last a while. And there's the black powder, and the Pyrodex, and..." She stopped, blushing a bit.

"Sorry," she apologized. "I do rattle on sometimes."

"Ain't botherin' me," Billy shook his head. "I ain't thought o' none o' that myself. I had decided I was just gonna stick to the farm and never come out no more. You done got me wanting' to see the trade day, now," he laughed.

"Well, your trailer's almost full, now," she frowned. "We can empty it, and come back."

"I still need to check Ralph's Trading Post," Billy told her. "Then we can go."

"Okay," Rhonda deflated a bit. "But after that, I'm gonna want to see that shower you promised me!"

-

Emptying the Trading Post wasn't as much work as the Higgins' place had been. Billy did find some very interesting items hidden in the storeroom there though.

"Daddy always thought old Ralph was dealing' dirty," Rhonda said musingly as Billy showed her what he'd found. "That's Class Three stuff. And he ain't a Class Three dealer."

"Ain't no kinda dealer, no more," Billy reminded her. "This look familiar to you?"

"They're H&K MP5's," Rhonda said at once. "Nice weapons, but strictly illegal without the Class Three stamp. Not that I think anyone's checking' on that stuff nowadays," she added with snort. "Looks like a dozen of'em, with mags."

"Well, we ain't leavin'em to be used against us," Billy declared. He loaded them with the rest. Rhonda continued to snoop and found a half dozen M-4's hidden in a crate as well.

"Select fire," she told Billy. "I'd say these were stolen from some armory, somewhere. See here? They still got military markings on them." She moved to another box, and let out a gasp.

"Hand grenades," she almost whispered. "Where did that old' crook get hold o' *grenades*?" Billy looked to see two small cased of cylindrical devices. "He ain't allow. . .*son-of-a-bitch*, this is *C-4*!" She dropped to her knees in front of a small box and held up something. To Billy it looked like a gray stick of butter. "And all the trimmings," she added.

"I'll take your word for it," Billy grunted as he heaved another box onto the dolly. "I think this is it. Make another round and make sure. I'll be back with the dolly and get them," he nodded his head at the newly discovered hardware.

Their last look revealed that they had taken it all. Billy took the time to grab whatever chips and food stuffs hadn't gone bad, including some soda. He hadn't had any soda in a while. Once this was gone, it would be a lot longer, he figured. Rhonda took the time to get some beer. Billy shook his head in amusement at her look.

"What? It'll all be gone bad by the time I can legally drink. I think I'm entitled."

"Get all you want," Billy told her. "It'll keep pretty well in the basement. Or the refrigerator." Rhonda goggled a minute.

"I forgot you have power!" she squealed, and went on a shopping spree. Billy just laughed again, and hauled the last dolly load to the truck.

By the time they had gotten back to the house, Billy was tired. He backed the trailer into the barn, explaining that the barn could be locked.

"We'll unload tomorrow," he told her. "Or the day after," he groaned, getting out of the truck.

"Tomorrow," Rhonda told him firmly. "We need to get back to town as soon as we can. There's a treasure trove there for trading. We need to get as much as we can save right now. Cloth, thread, needles, shoes and boots. Those are all things that aren't being made anymore, Billy. We need them for ourselves, and for trading."

"All right, all right," Billy raised his hands in surrender. "Tomorrow."

Despite his groaning, Billy couldn't help but smile as he made his way tiredly to the house. He liked Rhonda. She was smart, and thought of things he didn't.

Together, they'd get by pretty good, he figured.

He laughed once more at the squeal from the bathroom when Rhonda Higgins

Odd Billy Todd

got her first hot shower in months.

CHAPTER ELEVEN

Billy had never thought of himself as lazy. He was a hard worker, or had always thought so. Sure, he had time when he sloughed off, like when his work at the shop was slow. Didn't everybody?

Everybody except Rhonda Higgins he had learned. That woman was *on go* every minute of the day.

In the week since Billy had 'found' her, the two had made a trip into town every day. Things that Billy would have left behind or looked over, she took. Bolts of cloth, rolls of thread, sewing needles, every new pair of boots and shoes in town, the list was never ending.

And Billy had never seen a list. It was like Rhonda had the list in her head, and never forgot what was on it. She also never ran out of things for him to do.

Ever.

Billy had thought of a few things too, he reminded himself proudly. Firstly, he had found two nearly new fuel tanks, each capable of holding three hundred gallons of fuel. He had refueled the truck tank every day they went into town, first taking enough gas to top off his old tank, and one of the new ones. Then, after cleaning the tank out, he had proceeded to get the old diesel tank topped off, and finally the other new tank as well.

Their second day in town, Billy had found them another truck. This one had belonged to Mister Johnson, who owned the Motor Parts store. An F-250 crew cab, with a diesel engine, duel tanks, and four-wheel drive. There was also a Warn winch on the front rated for 8,000 pounds. Since they had two drivers, now, he saw no reason they couldn't haul with two trucks. It was the work of a few minutes to appropriate another trailer, and hook it to the Ford.

This had cut down on the trips to town, for which he was grateful. His fear of the rats hadn't diminished much. Rhonda just ignored them. All Billy could do was shake his head.

"Well, I think we got everything from the stores worth saving," Rhonda announced, as they finally finished emptying the last trailer load. The hidden room under the barn was now absolutely full, bulging with the additional firearms and ammunition. In truth, this wasn't the *last* trailer, since five more sat around the barn. There simply wasn't anywhere to put that stuff. He'd have to see about putting up some storage buildings.

"Thank goodness," Billy groaned. His back hurt like never before.

"Oh, stop being' a wuss," Rhonda slapped him on the shoulder. "It ain't that bad."

"I guess not, when you ain't the one doin' the heavy lifting'," Billy shot back. Rhonda was a red headed spitfire, but she was a *small* spitfire. At five-one, and a hundred and ten pounds, she would never tip the scales as a heavy weight. Or a light-weight either. But she was like a Banty hen. What she lacked in size, she made up for in spunk.

"That's what men are for, sweetie," she smiled at him. "At least that's what my Granny Higgins taught me."

"Taught you pretty good, then," Billy replied.

"Tomorrow we can start going through houses," Rhonda announced. Billy froze.

"What?" she demanded.

"I. . .I can't. . .I ain't goin' through no houses, Rhonda," he told her. "Not after Widow George."

"Billy, there's no tellin' what's in them houses," Rhonda told him. "Including weapons and ammunition. I promise you, anyone else would do it.""I ain't anyone else," Billy shook his head. "And I ain't doin' it." Rhonda studied the set look on Billy's face, and knew she faced an uphill battle. She softened her stance a little.

"Look, Billy, I know what you must have went through," she placed a hand on his arm. "It wasn't all that easy for me, either," she admitted. "But there's things in those houses we'll need, or that we can trade. And, trust me, there's a whole bunch of guns and ammo in them houses. My daddy sold most of'em. Anyone of them gangs you heard about goes through'em, they're gonna be mighty well armed."

Billy continued to look at her, his face telling her he was flatly refusing to consider it. She tried another track.

"Billy, if we don't do it, someone else will come along and do it anyway. Eventually, someone will, no matter what we do. Do you want to leave anything useful for them what might mean us harm?"

Billy looked away, weighing her words against his fear. He didn't want to go through that again. And now there were the rats to consider.

"We'll get sick," he told her. "Bein' around all them dead people and them rats eatin' on'em. We'll get sick."

"No, we won't," Rhonda shook her head. "We'll wear protective gear, and masks. And we've got a little something for them rats, too," she added, hefting a small rifle.

"This here is an air rifle. Not like one of them cheap kind you get at Wal-Mart, neither. This here is strong enough to kill a squirrel or a rabbit at forty yards. Imagine what it'll do to them rats. And we got pellets and bbs aplenty. Won't make no noise, won't draw no attention, and we'll make a hefty dent in the rat population. I got three of'em," she added. He looked at the gun, then sighed.

"I don't want to," he repeated, "but if you think it's needful, then we will. But not today," he added. "Not today." Rhonda nodded.

"Okay. Let's just rest today, then. Get a good start in the morning."

"Fine," Billy nodded, and started for the house. Rhonda watched him go, wishing she could cheer him up. She knew what she was asking was ghoulish, at the very least. But she also knew it was necessary. The only reason she hadn't already started was because she had been alone. And afraid.

Rhonda didn't like showing fear, but she had been terrified the night Billy had broke into her place. The relief she had felt when she found out it was him was so palpable that she could have almost touched it. She wasn't afraid of Billy. She'd known him, as she'd said, all her life, give or take. He was about the nicest person she'd ever known, outside her father and grandmother. He was kind, and gentle, almost to a fault.

He had a temper, too. She'd seen him beat a football player to a bloody pulp for pulling her hair once in school. She doubted he even remembered it, but she did. Billy had seen it, and suddenly he wasn't the nicest guy in school anymore.

Unfortunately for Billy, the thrashing had just made everyone pick on him more. 'Freak' and 'weirdo' had been some of the nicer names. She had talked to her father about Billy more than once.

"'Ronnie,' he'd said, "Billy Todd is a good boy, from a fine family. Raised proper, and taught his manners. But there's something about Billy that ain't normal. I can't rightly put it to words, but it ain't what people say about him, I can tell you that. That boy was born outta time. He ain't supposed to be here, with the likes of us.'"

She's asked what her father had meant by that.

"'He's a throwback to an earlier age, baby,' he father had replied. "'I know he's a bit slow minded, but only where certain things are concerned. When he's in one of his 'cycles', as his daddy calls'em, he's struggling to make a decision. He knows right from wrong, Bob and Robbie seen to that. But his instincts are tellin' him something' else, sometimes. And he has a hard time fighting' them instincts.'"

Rhonda thought back to that conversation as she watched Billy trudge toward the house.

"'Is he dangerous, daddy?',", she'd asked her father.

"'Only to them what do him or his wrong, baby,'" her father assured her. "Only to them what would do someone harm that can't defend themselves. To them, he's a man to be reckoned with. I've seen him shoot, and it's as natural to him as breathin'. I've seen him pull a fence post outta the ground with no more than a grunt. I'd not want to be the one that hurt something or someone he loved.'"

Her father rarely spoke like that about anyone, let alone a man Billy's age. She's thought about that over and over for the last week. She hadn't hesitated to go with Billy when he'd offered, in part because of her father, and in part because Billy had defended her in school.

No, she didn't have to be afraid. And she would try to make sure Billy didn't have so many 'cycles' either. She could be a good influence on him, she decided.

Her mind made up, she followed Billy to the house.

-

Going through the houses *was* gruesome.

They had been at it for almost a week. So far, they had cleared sixty-nine houses. Billy had been nervous at first, and though she wouldn't admit it, so had Rhonda. She had made sure they took extra precautions. Both were armed, and she carried a pellet rifle with her every time they entered a house.

Both had discussed the possibility of finding someone else alive. Both hoped to do so, believing that if the two of them had survived, someone else had as well.

So far, it was a wasted hope. What they had found were bodies. Horribly decomposed bodies of friends and neighbors who had died in agony. Some were in beds, some were in easy chairs, and more than a few were lying in the floor, having died where they'd fallen. Each house, it seemed, was a new nightmare, waiting to be opened.

The rats were everywhere.

They had just come from the latest house, a truly awful scene where a family of five, including a new born, were lying dead.

"That's it, Rhonda," Billy told her, gasping as he pulled off his mask. "I'm done with this. I can't keep seein' all this." Rhonda sighed, nodding.

"I know. Here's what we can do. We'll get daddy's files, see who had the weapons, and just get them. We need to round them up. Can you stick with me that long?" Billy looked at her for a long time, then nodded.

"But that's it," he warned, his face telling her that this time he meant it.

"We should have started sooner," she told him. "Or waited for winter, either one. I'm like you, Billy. If I see one more baby, I think I'll scream." She had thought she knew how hard this would be. She hadn't.

They went to her father's store, now empty of anything useful, and Rhonda wasted no time in opening the transfer files. She gave some to Billy and kept the rest for herself.

"We're only interested in the one's that have Cedar Bend's zip code," she showed him where to look. "If it's out of town, we skip it." He nodded, and quietly began to sift through the papers. She watched Billy carefully for a few minutes. Satisfied that he was okay, she started on her own pile.

It took the better part of two hours to go through all the papers. He father had owned a popular and successful shop, and the size of his store belied the sheer volume of trade he had done. Finally, they were through the list.

"Still a lot of'em," Billy noted. She nodded.

"I know. But these are either here in town, or just outside. We can get them, whatever ammo we find, and then call it done."

"We'll need to be careful," Billy warned. "Someone still alive might shoot us with them guns we want to find." Rhonda started, not having considered that.

"I hadn't thought about that," she admitted. "What can we do?"

"We can forget this, and go home," Billy told her flatly. "That's what we can do."

"What if someone comes and finds all this stuff?" she asked, waving the papers.

"Then they're welcome to them," Billy replied. "If they want to wade through all those bodies, and rats, to get them, more power to them."

"You were the one who said we needed to get them," Rhonda pointed out. "That we needed to secure them so no one could use them against us." Billy started at that one. He had forgotten how all this had started.

Had that really only been two weeks ago? Almost two weeks, anyway. Since he'd come to town under cover of darkness to take everything from Lem Higgins' store? He looked out the window for a moment, all this running through his head. His father's instructions had been pretty clear. Finally, he nodded, turning back to Rhonda.

"You're right," he told her, his voice soft. "I did. Let's go." Decision made, Billy was no longer hesitant. Rhonda nodded her agreement, and the two of them left the store, on their way to try and secure anything that could be used against them.

Rhonda hadn't told Billy how bad she felt in going through homes that had once belonged to neighbors, friends, and even a few distant relatives. She felt like a grave robber. Intellectually she knew that wasn't quite right. The rules had changed, and now their survival was more important than society's niceties and rules. Her father had always favored a saying from the Bible, 'Let the dead bury the dead'. She didn't really understand what it meant, since it was obvious that dead people couldn't bury other dead people.

But she had applied it in her own way. There was simply no way she and Billy could bury everyone. And by this time the bodies were so decomposed that not only would handling them be dangerous, it would prove difficult. Billy had told her what he had encountered when trying to bury the Widow George. Rhonda didn't want to go through anything like that herself.

They parked in a spot where several of the addresses were easy to get to on foot, and the truck was out of the way a bit. Billy had decided that they needed to keep out of sight while they were 'scavenging', in case some of the raiders he had heard about happened upon Cedar Bend while they were out.

In truth he didn't expect it, not yet. Having read his father's books, he thought he had a better idea what to expect. This wasn't a societal break down. Not too many people had survived. Those that had would need time to get organized. When they did, it was only natural they would head to the larger cities first, to pick them clean of anything they could find. There was simply more to be had in a city like Nashville, Memphis, or any of the other larger cities, than could be found in an out of the way map dot like Cedar Bend.

That didn't mean that they wouldn't make their way here, eventually. Sooner or later, they'd use up what they found, and start looting the smaller towns. And there was one other thing that his father's notes had mentioned.

They'd likely be looking for women as well. He cast a quick glance at Rhonda at this thought. He had read that in a society like this one, women would often be considered possessions, rather than anything else. Billy had no intention of letting that happen to Rhonda, or to Mrs, Silvers and her daughter. He didn't like Michelle Silvers, but that didn't mean he wanted to see her treated like that.

"Maybe if we split up..." Rhonda started.

"No," Billy's reply was flat, and final. "We stick together, or we go home. Period." Rhonda looked at him strangely at that, but nodded.

The two of them reached the first house, took a deep breath, and got started.

-

"I think that's the last one, Billy," Rhonda told him softly. She was looking at the 4473's from her father's shop, and each one had the tell tale mark she'd used to signify that they had checked the address. It was well after dark. They had hurried through the afternoon, wanting to get done and get home, for good.

Now, it seemed they could do so.

"All right," Billy nodded, almost smiling. "Let's get this stuff loaded, and get outta here. I always loved this town, but nowadays, it gives me the willies."

Rhonda nodded. She had lived here for two months alone. She knew all about that feeling.

It was the work of only a few minutes to finish loading, and then Billy had the truck running, heater working full blast. It was cold, now that the sun had gone down. Rhonda huddled next to the vent, grateful for the heat.

"We're not coming back," Billy told her, still looking out the windshield at the ghost town they'd called home once. "Is there anything else you want? Now's the time to get it."

"No, Billy," Rhonda shook her head. "I brought everything that meant anything with me when I came. I'm ready to go home."

Home. Billy was inordinately pleased to hear her call the farm home for some reason. Putting the truck into gear, he started them both toward home.

CHAPTER TWELVE

The next week was a whirlwind for Billy and Rhonda. The two spent almost every spare minute listing and separating the goods they had recovered from town. Fortunately, the large farm house had plenty of room because it seemed that everything that Rhonda touched was something that 'didn't need to be outside'.

Cloth, consumer goods, boxes, Billy just shook his head as the list grew and grew. Finally, he pulled up short.

"I'd better start moving our stuff out here," he told her calmly. Rhonda looked at him in confusion.

"What?"

"At this rate, we're gonna be livin' in the barn," he pointed out. Rhonda flushed a bit, looking at the ground.

"I'm sorry, Billy. There's just so much stuff that can be damaged leaving it out here, that's all. I promise I'll cut it down."

"It ain't that I'm fussin'," Billy told her. "But there has got to be a tipping' point here, and we're beyond it already, way I'm lookin' at it. It's a big house, sure, but it ain't that big. There's gotta be a way to keep this stuff safe, out here, or in the back shed. Plastic tubs, I can build wooden boxes, something."

"Tubs would work," Rhonda chewed on her bottom lip for a minute. "How many do we have?"

"I don't know. We did use a lot of'em for the ammunition. And some other stuff. And I know we can't take that stuff out. But what we can do is this. We got both these trailers. And we got two more outside. We ain't never gonna need more than two at the time, 'cause we can't pull more than that, ever. I say we store that stuff in the same trailers we brought it here on. I think two of them will fit in here, with a little room to spare. We just keep'em locked in here." Rhonda brightened at once.

"That's a great idea, Billy!" she enthused. "You're very smart."

"No, I ain't," Billy muttered. Rhonda frowned again.

"Yes, you are," she insisted. "I know you may not know everything there is to know, but who does? And right now? In the situation we find ourselves in this very minute? You're very smart for this kind of thing." She paused, then rushed on.

"I'm glad you found me, and asked me to come here, Billy Todd." He looked at her for a minute, then grinned.

"Me too."

-

With the new plan in place, it was easier to work. By the end of the week, everything had been counted, tagged, and placed into a trailer. In the end, very little had to be taken into the house, after all. Rhonda did insist that all the cloth be taken in, and Billy agreed it was necessary. He had a good supply of moth balls, but as far as he knew, no one was making anymore. At least in the house, the cloth would have a better chance of surviving.

Box after box of detergent, soap, candles, wax and wicks, were left outside. The same went for hygiene supplies, paper goods, pencils, and so on. There were so many items, that Billy couldn't keep them straight. Or he didn't figure he could, so he didn't bother trying. That's what lists were for, he figured.

Two salvaged refrigerators, which Billy had cleaned liberally with bleach, were pressed into service to hold OTC meds in, the two thinking that the colder temperatures would extend their lifespan. All the prescription meds were kept in the house, in cool, dry places.

The guns we another matter.

"We can't keep everything here," Billy told Rhonda. "In fact, I figure we need to start caching this stuff, at least some of it anyway. In case we have to hit the road. Guns, ammo, water filters, first-aid kit, clothes and such. Maybe some long-term food, too."

"That's a good idea," Rhonda nodded. "How do we hide it? And keep it safe? Dry?"

"With this," Billy told her, holding up a piece of six-inch plastic pipe cut four-foot long. There was a cap on one end already. "We put our stuff in these, cap the other end, and bury them, along with maybe a saw blade, or something along them lines, so we can cut it open. Can use five-gallon buckets too, if we seal the lids."

"I'd never have thought of that," Rhonda shook her head. "See? I told you you were smart!"

"Just stuff my dad taught me, or I read in his notes," Billy murmured, shaking his head lightly.

"Well, you still know it now," Rhonda said flatly. "We'll get that done. I'm anxious to go see this trade day! I want to know what people are trading, and what for. I bet a lot of them are using gold and silver now, too," she added. Billy looked at her.

"Think so?"

"I'd bet on it," she nodded firmly. "Folks won't want paper money no more, since there ain't really no government behind it now. They'll either want to barter, or take PM's. Precious metals," she added, when Billy frowned at the term.

"Well, that'll be okay," he nodded. She looked at him.

"You have any? Gold and silver coins, I mean?"

"I might," Billy tried to evade the direct question.

"I have some," Rhonda surprised him. "Daddy kept it all the time. He dealt in coins a little, on the side. Kinda like he pawned stuff, once in a while. I got a good bit."

"I might have a good bit, too," Billy finally told her. "Ain't never had no need for it. But I reckon if some folks will take it, then we can use it."

"We really don't need anything, Billy," Rhonda shrugged. "But that ain't no reason not to be trading. My daddy always said there was no such thing as a bad trade day, just bad trades." Billy nodded. He liked the way that sounded.

"Well, we can head over to the Silvers'," Billy told her. "See what Mister Silvers found out about Franklin. It ain't that far, I guess. We can go there, check it out."

"You think we can?" Rhonda asked. "I mean, that it'll be safe?"

"I reckon it will," was all Billy said.

-

Michelle Silvers surprised them both by running to hug Rhonda as soon as they arrived. The two had decided to walk through the woods to the Silvers' place, leaving Rommel and Dottie to guard the farm, so to speak.

"Oh my God, Rhonda! I am *so* glad to see you!" Michelle almost squealed. "Where have you been? What have you been doing?"

"I been livin'," Rhonda shrugged, not overly impressed with the contact. "Billy came to town one day, and there I was. So, he up and asked me to come out to his farm. And here I am."

"You're staying with *him*?" Michelle was almost aghast. "You can't do that! You *have* to move in here! We'll go and get your things right now!" Billy frowned at that, but said nothing. He didn't want Rhonda to leave, but she was grown, and could make up her own mind. The two had talked on the way over, and decided that they wouldn't share the things they'd done, or collected, however.

"Michelle, I'm not moving in here," Rhonda told her, laughing the suggestion off. "I'm settled in perfectly well at Billy's, thank you very much. But it's great to have another girl to talk to," she added, trying not to bring Michelle down too much. She didn't really like Shelly Silvers, but then that was going around these days. In fact, no one had ever really liked her *before* the world had more or less ended.

"Why, that's ridiculous," Shelly told her. "You can't possibly stay over there with. . .with him," she changed her words slightly when a dangerous light appeared in Rhonda's eyes.

"I can and will," Rhonda told her flatly. "Anyway, we came over to say hi, and talk to your folks. They about?"

"They're at the barn, right now," she pointed. "I'm sure they'll be glad to see you. And insist, *insist*, that you come here to live," she added, her nose raising slightly.

"Shelly," Rhonda smiled sweetly, "I'm all grown up, and haired over. Nobody *insists* to me. Not anymore. Understand?" Shelly frowned at Rhonda's words, but nodded.

"Well, come on, anyway. They'll at least want the two of you to stay for dinner."

"Hello, Billy!" Mister Silvers called, when he saw the trio coming. "Who's that stray you found," he added, laughing.

"I heard that, you old fuddy!" Rhonda called back, laughing. "I ain't no stray. I was perfectly fine, but Billy was worried to death over me, and made me come stay with him!" Billy was about to object when he heard Emma Silvers speak.

"Good for you, Billy," the older woman nodded firmly. "Folks got to cling together nowadays. And you two will be good for each other."

"Emmaline, don't go tryin' to do no matchmakin'," Jeremiah warned, making both Billy and Rhonda blush and Michelle snort in amusement.

"And just what's so funny about that?" Emma Silvers demanded. Michelle wisely made no reply, just looked at the ground. "You two gonna stay for supper?" she all but demanded.

"Long as we can get back 'fore dark, ma'am," Billy agreed, after looking at Rhonda, and getting her nod. "We walked over here, through the woods. Decided it'd be best to get a good trail blazed and started. Be smarter'n usin' the roads all the time."

"Good idea, son," Jeremiah nodded. "Fine idea, in fact. Less attention we draw to ourselves, better off we are." Billy caught Jeremiah's eye, and nodded.

"Why'nt you two girls help Emma get supper ready while Billy and I take a last look at this fool horse. Won't be a bit," Jeremiah spoke easily, and caught his wife's eye. She nodded.

"Come along, ladies," she smiled. "I am getting hungry, and Lord knows, Michelle, your brother is always hungry."

"I don't see how," the girl replied. "He don't do nothing."

"Pot and kettle, dear," Emma gave her a look. "Pot and kettle." As the three went out of ear shot, Jeremiah turned to Billy.

"You been monitoring your radio lately, son?" he asked.

"Not the last few days, to speak of," Billy admitted. "Been working' to get Rhonda settled and tryin' to keep up my chores. Did hear a bit a couple weeks ago that bothered me a might. About raiders hittin' a place, killing' some folk." Silvers nodded.

"Bit more o' that going' now," the older man told him quietly. "Been several families hit on one level or another. From gas siphoned to stock going missing to outright killing' and burning'. One group in particular seems to be might well organized no longer'n things has been like they are."

"Anywhere around here?" Billy asked, leaning against a fence post, adjusting his rifle.

"Not right on top of us, no," Jeremiah shook his head. "But they've been within a hundred miles of us in the last week or so. Hit a little settlement down Beaver Lodge way six days ago. Know where that is?"

"'Bout to the interstate?" Billy asked.

"That's it," Jeremiah nodded. "Had about twenty folks set up down that way, trying to make a go of it. They had some cattle, and were planning on harvesting as much of the corn crop around there as they were able. Been a boring winter food wise, but they'd have stayed fed."

"Would have?" Billy asked.

"All dead and gone, save a handful. Five people left, one o' them hurt bad two more just little'uns. They're in a right bad way, to hear it on the radio. Less mouths to feed, but almost no hands to do the work. They asked that bunch at Franklin to give a hand, but they aren't much better off for manpower. Afraid to leave their own places for fear they'd get hit while too many was gone."

"Anyone offer to help?" Billy wanted to know.

"Three fellas offered to come help get corn up and gather the stock. Help the survivors get better hid, and ready for the winter best they can. Want food and gas as payment."

"Reckon food's about the new money, right now," Billy said quietly. "You folks set okay?" he asked.

"We'll get by, don't nothin' bad befall us," Jeremiah said carefully. Billy grinned.

"Yeah, us too. I hadn't planned on feeding' two people, but I was set to do it, anyway, thanks to the Lord."

"How'd that come to be, anyhow?" Silvers smiled. The two had just told each other the same thing without telling each other anything. They would help each other if needed.

"Well, I went to town..."

"...and that's when I realized who I was talking' to," Rhonda finished up. Emma shook her head.

"That boy is a plumb caution, he is," she laughed. "He's a good boy, Rhonda Higgins."

"You ain't got to tell me, Misses Silvers," Rhonda grinned sheepishly.

"Are you two actually talking about Billy Todd?" Michelle looked incredulous. Rhonda turned flinty green eyes on her 'friend'.

"We are," she said quietly.

"Billy Todd's a fine young man, missy," Emma told her daughter flatly. "Pity that you can't recognize things like that. If you're lucky, you'll find someone like him to take care of you. You certainly aren't able to take care of yourself. Or at least you aren't very willing."

"I can *too* take care of myself!" Michelle shot back.

"When was the last time you built a fire, or brought in fire wood, or cooked a meal?" Emma challenged. "Can you make bread, Michelle? Kill a chicken, clean and cook it?"

"You and daddy do all that!" Michelle protested.

"And what, pray tell, are you going to do when we're gone?" her mother asked calmly.

"What?" Michelle was brought up short by the question.

"You heard me," Emma bore in. "Your father and I aren't spring chickens by any means. And with things so much harder now, we're like as not to die much younger than we might have. When we're gone, who's going to look after you? Certainly not Tobias. He can't look after himself either."

Michelle Silvers opened her mouth to retort, but stopped as her mother's words hit her.

"Things will be back to normal by then," she finally said, although her voice was far from confident.

"Shelly, I think this is the new normal," Rhonda told her softly. "Normal like we used to have, well, it just ain't coming' back, I think. Not for a very long time, anyway."

"Don't be ridiculous!" Michelle bit out. "Things will be back to normal some day. Probably sooner than you think, too. Once the government gets things straightened out, we'll be fine, and back to good in no time."

"The government?" Rhonda goggled. "Michelle, you do realize that most of the government died just like everyone else did, yeah?"

"They've got those bunkers!" Michelle was almost yelling now. "Once they come out, they'll make things right! You'll see!" With that she stormed out of the kitchen. Rhonda looked at Emma Silvers apologetically.

"I'm sorry, ma'am," the girl said softly. "Maybe we oughta just go? I don't want to stir nothing' up."

"Hush, child," Emma scolded softly, wiping a single tear from her cheek. "She's been that way, off and on, since things started. One minute she's fine, the next...well, you saw." Rhonda nodded. "She can't seem to wrap her head around

64

how bad things are."

"One reason, I guess, is because we haven't left the farm since things started. She hasn't *seen*. Hasn't been out there, like you have. I haven't either, but I know what's happened. I don't have to see it."

"Toby is almost as bad, but in a different way. He just doesn't seem to *care*. He does his chores, does everything we ask of him, but shows no interest in learning how to take care of himself, how to make the farm work once we're gone. I... sometimes I don't know what to do. I always thought I'd raised my children better than that. I knew they didn't want the life we have, and I accepted that. But now, there doesn't seem to be a choice. And neither of them seem to realize it." She looked up suddenly.

"Don't mind me, sweetie," she told Rhonda. "Let me get a friendly ear, and I'll talk it to death. I'm sorry about that."

"Don't be," Rhonda told her. "Heck, I'm glad I was here for you. You ain't had no one to talk to about your troubles. I doubt you want to talk to Mister Silvers on it overmuch, on account o' he has so much on him, the way things are. I spent a long time alone, except for my dog. I know all about how nice it is to have a ear to bend. I been talkin' Billy's head of for nigh on to two weeks!" They both shared a laugh, and both needed it.

"So, what about you and Billy?" Emma asked coyly, once she'd gotten her laughter out. "Is there a story there?" Rhonda blushed furiously at that, but smiled.

"I don't know, just yet," she admitted. "I gotta be honest, I always did like him. I mean, I know he ain't maybe so smart as some, but like I told him, he ain't near as dumb as he sometimes let's on, neither. I know that for a fact, cause I done seen it, the last two weeks. And he's got a good heart, too."

"That he does, dear," Emma smiled. "That he does. His mother and father taught him well, I'll have to say. Oh, I *do* miss Robbie so, sometimes," she added wistfully. "I miss Robert as well, don't get me wrong, but Robbie and I were very close. She was a dear friend."

"I knew Mister Todd a lot better'n I did Misses Todd," Rhonda admitted. "Mister Todd was always stoppin' by to see Daddy. But I know they was well thought of."

"Yes, they were," Emma nodded firmly. "Well, if you'll check the bread, I think we're about ready to eat, here."

CHAPTER THIRTEEN

"I've been thinking," Jeremiah said, after the blessing had been given and the plates filled. "There's a lot of stock around, Billy. Cattle, hogs, horses. They're probably okay for the short run, but time's running out for some. Especially the hogs. We should try and save what we can. No telling where we'll ever find more. The problem is, where do we put them?"

Billy used the time he was chewing his food to form an answer.

"Mister Franklin's place runs along behind ours," he said after thought. "He's got about two hundred acres in grass, but he wasn't runnin' stock when things got bad, I don't think. We could drive the cows there. Be hard to spot back there, and there's a gap in the tree line that'd let us get to'em without using' the road."

"Hey, I'd forgot that!" Jeremiah nodded enthusiastically. "We could squeeze maybe two hundred head in there. A few more, if we can find hay for the winter."

"Mister Franklin had a good pole barn. Be a good place for the hay. Might have to do a little work on it, but it's doable," Billy added. "This is right good eatin', ma'am," he told Emma.

"Thank you, Billy," she smiled.

"What do you say, then, Billy?" Jeremiah guided the discussion back to the stock. "Maybe we can saddle up and take a look see tomorrow?"

"Can I go?" both Toby and Michelle asked at once. Emma looked startled, while Jeremiah just looked doubtful.

"Ain't nare one o' you two can sit a horse all day without complaining and bellyachin'," he grumbled. Both looked a bit shamefaced at that, but were undeterred.

"We won't complain, Pa," Toby said earnestly, and Michelle nodded her enthusiastic agreement. Jeremiah looked at Billy, recalling the younger man's words. Billy just shrugged.

"Okay by me," was all he said.

"I'll go too," Rhonda added, grinning. Billy looked at her.

"You ride a horse?"

"Yes, I can ride a horse!" Rhonda feigned indignance at that question. Billy wasn't sure it was fake, so he just nodded, and filled his mouth again. The cornbread was really good, he decided.

"Well then," Jeremiah stated, "what say we ride over to your place around eight? We'll take a look up the hill at Franklin's, and then scout around to see what's what elsewhere. Sound good?"

"Like a plan," Billy agreed.

"We also want to go over to Franklin," Rhonda added. "We'd like to see the trade day. Or post, if it's everyday."

"Oh, can we go too daddy?" Michelle asked quickly. "I'd love to go and see it!"

"I wouldn't mind that, myself," Emma threw her oar in. "I'm interested to see what they have, and what they expect for it." Jeremiah eyed the table warily.

"I reckon we can go over there," he finally agreed. "But not knowing' what they're in need of would be a bit o' difficulty in takin' the right goods."

"Could ask on the radio," Billy spoke up. Everyone looked at him.

"What?" he asked.

"That's a mighty fine idea," Jeremiah laughed. "And the easiest thing to do. I been talkin' to a fella over that way for the last month or so. I'll give him a yell tonight if I can, and see what they got and what's sellin'. We might be able to take a few things and barter."

"Yay!" Michelle and Toby both exuded. Rhonda resisted the urge to shake her head, while Billy just took another bite of his meal. He'd already known he and Rhonda were going, anyway.

"We should go together," Rhonda stated firmly. "Even if we take two vehicles, we should travel together, and stay together."

"Need to go and come back same day, too," Jeremiah added. "I don't relish being' away from here overnight. Way things are, I'd be worried over it."

"Good idea," Billy managed around a mouthful of green beans.

"Don't talk with your mouth full," Rhonda told him, nudging him with her elbow. He nodded, but didn't repeat it. Eating took precedence for Billy.

"Well, I'll find out tonight, if I can, and let you know in the morning," Jeremiah said. Billy looked at the window, and drowned his last bite with tea.

"Reckon we better be gettin' back," he said easily. "Be gettin' dark soon."

"We'll see you in the morning, Billy," Jeremiah promised. Rhonda hugged Emma, and sort of hugged Michelle, then patted Toby on the shoulder. He was clearly expecting a 'hug' of his own, but Rhonda easily sidestepped it. Toby frowned at her, then realized that Billy Todd was watching him *very* closely. Swallowing his pride, and any comment he was about to make, Toby decided that a shoulder pat was okay after all.

"You kids come back," Emma smiled at them. Jeremiah nodded.

"It's right nice to have comp'ny."

"Maybe we can start swapping back and forth," Rhonda suggested. "We can have you all over, too, that way."

"We can work it out," Billy agreed. "But tomorrow. It's coming on to dark, and I want to be home when it gets here."

"All right, all right," Rhonda waved him down. "We're going."

As they entered the woods, Rhonda could better understand why Billy wanted to be home.

"Lot darker in the trees," she commented.

"Yep," Billy replied. "We got lights, though, so we're okay. But I don't want to make a habit of being out like this after dark. No way o' tellin' what's liable to be out and about these days."

"Say what?" Rhonda pulled up short at that.

"There's all kinds of critters out here, Rhonda," Billy explained. "When there was folks about, and noise everywhere, they stayed away, deeper in the woods. Now, after all this time, and most all of the people gone, they'll be more likely to be around."

"What kind of 'critters'?" Rhonda wanted to know, looking around her.

"Coyotes, for sure," Billy told her, guiding her by the arm through the trees. "There's a few cats around, too."

Odd Billy Todd

"Bobcats?"

"Them too, but I meant *big* cats. Cougars. Ain't all that many, but even one is too many, if he's hungry, and we're out here in his way. And that don't even take into account wild dogs. Lot o' dogs ain't got people no more, they'll be turnin' feral, huntin' in packs, and they ain't scared o' people. Been around'em all their life."

"How come you didn't say nothing' 'bout this 'fore we went over there!" Rhonda wanted to know. Her red hair hid a fiery temper. And a sharp tongue.

"Didn't want to scare ya," Billy shrugged.

"How 'bout next time you scare me a little! Instead o' lettin' me wander around out here with. . .with dogs, and coyotes, and lions, and who know what all!"

"You ain't wandering around," Billy told her. "I know exactly where we are, and where we're going. I just don't believe in takin' extra chances, especially not now."

"What's that mean? Especially not now?" Rhonda demanded.

"Know where the nearest doctor is?" Billy asked, starting to get exasperated. "Nurse? How 'bout a paramedic? No? Nearest one I know of is in Franklin. Little over two hours drive from here, *if* the road ain't blocked. Now days ain't no time to get hurt like that cause you wasn't thinking about what you was doing."

Rhonda didn't reply as they continued to walk along. She was impressed with what Billy had just said. Everyone always underestimated him, and yet, here he was, going over so many reasons for his decisions. Just more proof that her opinion of Billy wasn't off. He might not be a genius, but he was smarter than people thought. And much smarter than he let on, despite whatever confidence issues he might have. She'd just have to work on that confidence.

If the cougars, dogs, or coyotes didn't get her, anyway.

-

Billy was up early the next morning. He was already outside when Rhonda woke. By the time she was outside, he was leading the horses out of the barn.

"Which one's mine?" she asked brightly.

"The mare," he nodded to a gray mare with white socks. "Name's Mabel. My mom's old horse. She's gentle, but got plenty of bottom. Sure footed, too."

"She's nice," Rhonda noted, patting the mare gently on the neck, after stroking her nose. She watched Billy clean the hooves of the mare, then check those on the gelding he was going to ride.

"He got a name?" she asked.

"Samson," Billy replied, still working. "Good horse. Had him a while. Ain't rode him much till late. Been using' him to ride the fences when it was good weather. Was using' the Ranger, but decided it wasn't fair not to get the horses some work, since we'll probably be depending on them more and more. Gas won't last forever."

"You have a stallion?" Rhonda asked. "Gonna need to raise some more horses eventually."

"We don't, no," he shook his head. "But there's a few around. Maybe we can find one." He looked up.

"I hadn't thought about that," he told her. "We will need to raise horses. Might even be a good business, down the road. People will have to learn to use them, once the gas is gone."

"Yep," Rhonda smiled. Billy was thinking ahead, now. With only a little prompting. They heard the dogs barking, and turned to see the three Silvers coming through the woods on horseback.

"Rommel!" Billy called.

"Dottie!" Rhonda called at the same time. Both dogs immediately stopped barking, and came to their owners. Dottie had had time to get used to horses being around in the last two weeks, and Rommel, finally, had adjusted to the fact that he wasn't the only animal around.

"Mornin' folks," Jeremiah called.

"Mister Silvers," Billy nodded. "We're about ready to go, I reckon," he added, placing the two kits he'd made for himself and Rhonda on their horses. Water, food, first aid, and ammunition. Both were wearing pistols, and Rhonda slid her shotgun into the scabbard Billy had mounted on Mabel. She was also carry a Bushmaster Carbon-15, a lightweight AR model that she could handle easier than the heavier rifles.

Billy placed a Remington 700 model bolt action in his own saddle scabbard. The rifle was chambered for .308 Winchester, and sported a 4-12x40 scope. He was carrying an M-4 rifle from Bushmaster as well.

"You folks expecting trouble?" Jeremiah asked in amusement. Toby was staring at the rifles, especially seeing Rhonda with one. Michelle looked disinterested.

"Better to have and not need, Sir," Rhonda shrugged, mounting Mabel.

"I carry mine everywhere," Billy shrugged, also mounting up. "Rommel, Dottie, lead!" He pointed to the hills, toward the gap they would be using. The two dogs started off at once, Dottie basically following Rommel's lead. She was still a pup, basically, just over a year old. Billy didn't know how old Rommel was, but he guessed he was about three. He was mature enough to follow orders, but still had some play in him.

"Dogs get along with horses?" Jeremiah asked.

"Pretty good," Billy nodded. "And they're good at spottin' trouble."

"Sounds good."

Not much was said for the next few minutes. It wasn't long before they were on the hill top, looking over the valley behind them.

"Well, that's encouraging." Jeremiah came to a stop beside Billy. The latter nodded.

"Yeah. I can't believe I didn't think to come up here before now. We could have cut this field. Baled the hay."

"Don't worry over it," Jeremiah shook his head. "This field will cover feed for a good while, and we'll find somewhere else to get hay."

"Yeah," Billy sighed. "Well, let's take a closer look, I guess. If we're gonna think about driving cows today, we need all the light we can get."

-

Drive cows indeed.

The Franklin place was in good stead. The house was empty, Billy was relieved to see. He had half expected the find the old couple dead inside. He really didn't want to go through any of that, anymore.

Odd Billy Todd

The barn was in fine condition, as was the larger pole barn used for storing hay out of the weather. Jeremiah and Billy looked the place over, and deemed it sufficient for their needs.

The five of them were in the saddle again right after, heading down the roads and trails, looking over stock. To their delight, the animals had not suffered much in the two months of neglect. Only two barns had had animals stalled. They had died, of course, after their water had run out. No one bothered to go inside, since the smell was enough to tell the story. Jeremiah noted that they could burn the barns if needed, come winter.

They managed to find several hogs, as well. They weren't fairing as well as the horses and cattle. The latter two were grazing on still green grass, while the hogs were milling around for what was left in the pens. Although many had perished, enough remained to start a decent swine herd. They fed and watered all the hogs still alive, leaving them until they could come for them in a stock trailer. Having a 'swine drive' just didn't sound like anyone's idea of a good time,

Horses and cattle were another story. They began gathering them on the way back. Rommel and Dottie helped keep the cattle in line, running along side of the small but growing herd. Neither were stock dogs, and didn't have a clue how to herd or manage cattle, but the cattle didn't know that. All they knew was that two very large and ferocious animals were along their flank, and so the cattle tended to stay huddled together for safety.

"We might make good cow dogs out of them yet," Rhonda beamed at Billy.

"I'd soon not," Billy laughed. He related the story of how he'd first introduced Rommel to his own small herd. Rhonda's laughter was heard over the bellowing of the cows.

Sooner than Billy would have thought possible, the cattle were safely settled on the Franklin acreage. Billy had done a count, and there were one hundred and seventy-two cows, nine bulls, and thirty-two horses, three of which were stallions.

"Nice haul," he showed the numbers to Jeremiah. The older man nodded.

"Reckon we can rest up a day or so, then take the truck and trailer to get the hogs. Need to scavenge what feed and tack we can as well. I don't know how to make a saddle. You?" Billy shook his head.

"No sir. Bit much for me, I reckon." Jeremiah frowned at his young neighbor. "Billy, you really don't give yourself enough credit. I reckon you can do 'bout anything you set your mind to, myself." Billy didn't frown, but it reminded him an awful lot of what his parents used to say to him.

Maybe he wasn't giving himself enough credit, but Billy had always liked to believe he knew what his limitations were. He knew he wasn't overly smart, at least in books. But maybe Rhonda had a point. Maybe the things he did know, the things he could do, were well suited to a life like this.

I wish I could talk to daddy for just a few minutes, he thought to himself. *Daddy would know what to tell me. He'd know how to tell me, too.* It was one of the rare moments that Billy allowed himself any self pity. He'd been raised to view such things as worse than useless. Wasteful at best. He sighed.

"Reckon all I can do is what I can do," he said to Silvers by way of an answer. He looked up at the sky. Where had the day gone?

"Be gettin' dark soon," he noted. "Guess we oughta pack it in for today."

"Yeah, we need to be headed home," Jeremiah nodded. "Have to get these horses rubbed and put away. Like as not I'll have to do all three."

The Silvers' kids hadn't been useless today, for the most part, and true to their word they hadn't complained. They did look haggard, however. Neither was accustomed to doing serious labor for any length of time, and it was showing. Billy had to admit, however, that Toby had seemed to come into his own on horseback, working the cattle. Despite how tired he was, he still looked eager and excited.

"You know, Toby," Billy called out, "you make a pretty fair cowhand." The boy lit up at that, smiling.

"Really?"

"Yep," Billy nodded. "Just don't forget, caring for your horse is just as important as riding it. Horses need good care so they don't let you down when you need them the most."

"Okay," Toby nodded eagerly. Jeremiah looked at Billy questioningly, but grinned just a little when Billy winked at him.

"Well, we better be gettin' home," Jeremiah said again. "Billy, talk to you tomorrow, I reckon."

"We'll be here," Billy agreed, as he and Rhonda turned toward home.

-

Billy and Rhonda worked their horses down, finishing with a good rubdown. Samson and Mabel had worked hard today, and Billy rewarded them with an apple apiece, and a few cubes of sugar.

"That was really slick, what you did with Toby," Rhonda said casually.

"What?" Billy asked, not having been paying attention.

"The way you talked to Toby, about caring for his horse," Rhonda said. "That was pretty good thinking." Billy shrugged.

"He did a pretty good days work, considering. He might not be a total loss. I guess if you can find something to interest him, he'll give a better effort."

"Maybe," Rhonda mused. "But the way you tied him caring for the horse to his working the cattle got him thinking, I think."

"Mister Silvers needs some help," Billy shrugged. "Toby oughta be helpin' his dad. He ain't. Maybe gettin' a hint from someone else will nudge him a little."

"Misses Silvers said something about that," Rhonda nodded as the two headed for the house. "She laid into Shelly pretty good about how she don't know how to do nothing', and Toby don't seem to care one way or 'nother. Shelly didn't take it too well. She seems to think that the 'government' is gonna fix everything back the way it was." Billy snorted.

"I know, but that's what she thinks," Rhonda continued. "Emma says she might be in denial cause she ain't been out and seen how bad things is."

"Today should have cured her o' that," Billy commented. They'd seen several homes that obviously had dead people inside. They hadn't bothered to enter them.

"I think it woke her up some," Rhonda agreed. "She wasn't so talky, that's for sure."

"Don't look a gift horse in the mouth," Billy told her.

Rhonda was still laughing when Billy walked inside.

CHAPTER FOURTEEN

"Where have you been?" Rhonda asked as Billy walked into the house, Rommel and Dottie close on his heels. It was two days since the cattle drive.

"Been workin'," Billy told her. "With all the other stuff last two weeks, ain't got a lot done. Been catchin' up."

"You should have said something!" Rhonda scolded lightly. "I could o' helped."

"Don't need it," Billy shrugged. "Stuff I'd have to do was you here or not. Ain't nothin'," he shrugged again.

"Are you finished?" she asked.

"More or less," Billy nodded. "What you been doing?" he asked, nodding to all the papers on the table.

"Oh," Rhonda started gathering the papers up. "I've been going over all the lists we made when we sorted through the stuff from town. Trying to get a better idea what all we have, and what we can spare, and what we can trade, and so on."

"Okay," Billy nodded. He opened the refrigerator and took out a cup of tuna salad to make him a sandwich.

"I can make you something to eat," Rhonda told him. He just looked at her.

"I don't mind," she added. Billy's brow furrowed a bit.

"Is something wrong?" he asked. Rhonda had never been very hesitant in the days since he'd found her hiding in her dad's store. Why was she so hesitant now?

"No! Nothing!" Rhonda said quickly.

"Rhonda, what's going on," Billy asked, setting the tuna on the counter. "You're acting a little squirrely. You sure ain't nothing wrong?"

"I. . .I just don't know what to. . .I mean, we ain't never really talked about how. . .*dang it* Billy! You ain't makin' this easy for me at all!"

"Huh?" Billy was really confused now.

"I'm trying to talk to you about us!" Rhonda almost yelled.

"What about us?" Billy asked. "Are we. . .did we do something wrong? Can we fix it? As far as I know I ain't done nothin' different the last few days, but if I. . ."

"That's not what I mean!" Rhonda was almost in tears now, and that just made Billy feel more disoriented, and confused.

"Rhonda, how 'bout we just settle on down, and you tell me what it is, okay?" Billy asked cautiously. He tried to guide her to a chair, but she wrenched her arm away.

"Billy Todd, dammit, I'm trying' to tell you I like you!" she almost wailed.

"Uh, okay?" Billy tried. "I like you, too, Rhonda."

"You do?" the change was instant. Rhonda looked at him with wide eyes, her expression gone from anger to hopeful.

"Well, of course I do!" Billy exclaimed. "Why would I. . .I mean I wouldn't ask someone to come out here and live here if I didn't like you. I like you." Rhonda's face fell.

"You mean like a friend," she said sadly, sitting down heavily.

"What?" Billy was lost again, poor thing.

Rommel had come into the room when he heard the commotion, sat down, and was watching the two of them. Dottie sat down at the hallway entrance, looking between the two of them.

"You like me like you like Mister Silvers," Rhonda explained. "Like a friend."

"Well, I wouldn't compare you to Mister Silvers," Billy told her. "And I don't know what he's got to do with this nohow. I'm just not. . .Rhonda, I ain't all that smart. I know you and Mister Silvers been trying' to tell me I am but I'm really not, at least not on some things. I do know some stuff, but I ain't real good at others. If you got something to tell me, please just tell me right out."

"Are you wanting' to leave? Is that it? Cause if it is, I'll take you anywhere you want to go. Heck, you can have the other truck, for that matter, but I'll help you haul all this stuff to wherever you. . . ."

"I don't want to leave you dope!" Rhonda shouted before she thought. She knew as soon as she said it, it was the wrong thing. But it was too late.

"Dope, huh?" Billy's voice wasn't angry, but sad. "I ain't heard that one in a while, anyway," he shrugged.

"Billy that wasn't what I meant!" Rhonda rushed out of her chair, wanting so desperately to hug him. "It's just that. . .you are so clueless!"

"Yeah, that's me," Billy nodded, easing away from her.

"Dammit Billy Todd!" she almost screamed. "I'm trying to tell you that I love you! And you're a dope because you can't see it!"

Billy froze.

He had never heard anyone but his parents tell him that. He didn't know what to do. Or what to say. He was having trouble processing.

"Well, say something!" Rhonda demanded. "Don't just stand there!"

But he did just stand there. That was all he could think of to do. He looked at Rhonda, and she could tell he was struggling to decide what to do.

"Billy, it's okay," she said, her voice softer. "If you don't lo. . .like me back, it's okay."

"I. . .but I. . .I mean I d. . .I do," he said haltingly. "I just. . .I mean I never imagined anyone telling me that," he admitted. "Especially not someone so pretty as you," he added, his voice completely subdued and sincere. Rhonda blushed prettily at that.

"You do, what?" she asked him. "Like me? Or love me?"

"Lo. . .Li. . .er, both?" he stammered. Rhonda screeched in delight, and threw her arm around him. Before Billy knew it, they were kissing, square on the mouth. Billy didn't know what to do, so he just. . .did something, anyway.

When Rhonda came up for air, her face was as red as his.

"I wanted to do that for nearly two weeks," she breathed. "It was worth the wait."

"It was?"

"Definitely." She kissed him again, slower this time, with more care. Billy responded nicely, she decided. Without a thought, she began to steer him toward the stairs.

Billy didn't really notice that, still caught up in this sudden change of things. He didn't mind it, he decided. It was just so sudden that he was caught off guard.

Odd Billy Todd

It wasn't until he fell backwards on his own bed, with Rhonda atop him, that he realized where they were. And what she intended.

"Rhonda, wait," he managed to get out between kisses. She stopped, and looked down at him.

"I… I ain't. . .I mean, that is, I never..." She stopped him by pressing her fingers over his lips.

"Shhhh," she told him softly. "Me neither. We'll figure it out."

Jeremiah Silvers rode over the next afternoon. Billy was outside, working in his father's small shop building. He heard Rommel's bark, and went out to say hello.

"Afternoon Billy," Silvers nodded, stepping off his horse. "Sorry about not getting back to you sooner. Been a little busy."

"Everything okay?" Billy asked.

"Better than okay," the older man smiled, and it was a genuine smile. "I want to thank you, Billy. When we got home the other night, after the cattle drive, Toby had me show him how to care for the horses, and did all three of them, with a little help from me. Last three days, he's kept me jumping, showing him everything he can think of on the farm."

"Well, that's good," Billy nodded. "I hoped it might."

"Even Shelly is doing better," Jeremiah told him. "Not like Toby, mind, but still, she's gotten her mother showing her how to cook more, and been helping around the house more. It ain't perfect, but it's a start, and a damn sight better than it has been."

"I'm glad to hear it, Mister Silvers," Billy nodded.

"Expect it's about time you called me Jerry," Silvers told him. "You're a man grown, Billy. Time you was treated like one." Billy looked at him for a moment, then nodded.

"I'll try, Mist. . .Jerry."

"Good deal, then," Jerry smiled again. "You 'bout ready to round up some hogs?"

"Hey Mister Silvers!" Rhonda said, coming outside just then. She walked up to Billy, and kissed him on the cheek. Billy blushed a bit, but Jerry smiled.

"Wondered when that might happen," he chuckled. "Plain as day you two belong together."

"He just needed convincin'," Rhonda winked, grinning from ear to ear. "What you two talkin' about?"

"Gettin' the hogs gathered," Billy managed not to stammer. He wasn't used to being the center of attention. Anywhere.

"Where we gonna put'em?" Rhonda asked, frowning. "We ain't really got a suitable pen around here."

"I was thinking' on that," Jerry nodded. "Reckon we can get into town? Maybe see can we grab some wire and posts at the Co-Op?" Billy looked hesitant at the thought of going into Cedar Bend again, but Rhonda nodded.

"We can. We can take the red truck," she pointed to the Ford. "Might need to get a trailer, though," she added.

"Can we use one of them?" Jerry asked, pointing to the three trailers in the

74

yard.

"We can take that one," Billy pointed to the one empty trailer. "Others got stuff stored inside."

"Well, then we got a plan, then," Jerry declared. "I thought we could put the pen up in the woods, say about halfway between your place and mine?" he asked/suggested.

"Sounds good," Billy nodded. "There's a little clearing along the path we been using. Should be a good place. We'll need to look about building a shelter for'em, too, I reckon."

"Thought we'd see if we couldn't scavenge some tin whilst we was in town," Jerry replied. "Use that and a few posts I got, and build a good little lean to barn for'em. Time might come when we can trade some o' the hogs for other things we want or need, you know."

"And eat'em if we can't," Billy grinned. "Well, I guess we better get going. Wasting daylight."

"I'll go and get Toby, and be back in a few," Jerry nodded. "Need to tell Emma where I'm going, anyway."

"We'll hook up and be ready," Rhonda smiled. As Jerry rode away, she turned to look at Billy.

"I know you didn't want to go back," she said softly.

"Ain't got a choice, I think," he shrugged. "He's right. We should have done this a month ago. Maybe 'fore that. We already lost a lot o' stock, waitin' so long. Sooner we get it done, sooner we'll *be* done, my dad used to say."

"I like that," Rhonda giggled.

By the time Jerry returned, the trailer was hooked up, and the truck already pointed out. Rhonda was surprised to see Michelle along with Toby and Jerry.

"I haven't been to town since. . .well, since," she explained. "I want to see."

"Ain't pretty," Billy warned gently. "And the town's over run with rats, so be watchful."

"Rats?" Shelly looked wide eyed.

"They won't bother you, if you don't bother them," Rhonda told her, half glaring at Billy for bringing it up.

"Better she knew up front," he shrugged, reading her glare perfectly. The five of them loaded into the crew cab truck, and were soon headed for town.

The Silvers hadn't been to town since the trouble had started, so seeing all the cars along the road, most with bodies in them, was a shock to the system. No one spoke as they eased into the ghost town that had once been their home town.

"My Lord," Jerry finally broke the silence. "I. . .I mean I knew, of course. You told me, Billy. But. . .this is way beyond what I'd imagined."

"It's rough, I know," Rhonda nodded, as Billy drove. "And it's spooky, too. So quiet at night. I mean there's almost nothing to hear. So, everything is louder. No air conditioners and cars to drown out the sounds."

"I don't. . .I want to go home," Shelly said suddenly, her eyes filling with tears.

"We ain't going home till we get what we came for," Jerry said roughly, but kindly. "I told you this wasn't a sight seeing trip, girl. You can sit in the truck, if you want, but we need to get what we came after."

"The rats are eating the people!" Toby exclaimed suddenly, looking out the

Odd Billy Todd

window.

"Stop!" Shelly almost screamed. "Stop the truck, I'm going to be sick!" Billy hit the brakes, and ordered Toby to let her out. No sooner had Shelly's feet hit the pavement than they could hear her retching. Toby turned a little green, but managed to keep his lunch down. Billy and Rhonda had seen far worse, and just ignored it. Jerry looked on with concern, and seemed a little pale, himself, but managed.

Finally Shelly's stomach was empty. Rhonda had gotten out of the truck, and handed Shelly a baby wipe. The other girl used it to clean her face, then gladly accepted the small bottle of soda Rhonda offered her.

"Oh, I haven't had a Coke in ages!" she exclaimed, draining the small bottle in seconds.

"Ain't many left," Rhonda agreed. Shelly blushed at that.

"I'm sorry, Rhonda," she said quietly. "I. . .I shouldn't have. . . ."

"That's what it was for, honey," Rhonda told her, grinning. "Now, if you're able, climb back aboard, and let's get this done. I don't like being here any more than you do, I promise you that."

The rest of the trip was, thankfully, uneventful. Fencing and posts were stacked at the Co-Op, and willing hands grabbed the rolls and bundles and placed them in the trailer. Billy grabbed three new post drivers, and another pair of post hole diggers, laying them in the back of the truck. They were about to leave when Billy spotted something.

"Wait," he told the others, walking to where a carport was standing near the building, with a sign that said '*Installed $590*'. He looked over at Jerry, who had walked up with him.

"Reckon that would make a fine little hog barn," he said softly. Jerry just chuckled.

"Boy, you're a caution, you surely are. I should o' thought o' that. Toby!"

The three of them wasted little time, locating the stash of small buildings, and taking four of them. All they could manage to get into the truck with the parts and frames.

"These will do just fine," Jerry nodded. "Maybe we can come back and find more, later on, if we need them. Meantime, we got work to do, and we've already got what we need. Let's go." They piled back into the truck and headed home.

It was very late in the afternoon when they finally got back. It was decided that work would start on the pen and barns first thing in the morning. Jerry and Toby would be over to help move everything to where they would build the pen, and hopefully they could be ready in the next two to three days.

As the Silvers rode away, Rhonda put her arm around Billy's waist.

"Hungry?" she asked.

"Starving," he agreed, smiling down at her. The events of the previous night were still on his mind, as he looked at her. He swore he'd never seen a prettier girl in his whole life than Rhonda Higgins.

"You finish putting your tools and such away, and I'll start us some supper, then," she smiled, kissing him lightly, then bounding off to the house. Billy watcher her go, then went back to work. Smiling.

CHAPTER FIFTEEN

-

Building the hog pen went pretty well, Billy decided. It took two full days, but they managed to get the fence up in its entirety and two of the pre-fab carports were in place. The third was framed, and ready to be skinned.

"I'd say we're ready to haul some pigs," Jerry declared as the work wound down on the second day. "This will do nicely I think."

"Looks good to me," Billy nodded. "Think them carports will be just fine for what we want'em for, too."

"I agree," Jerry nodded. "Time to go and get them piggies, yeah?"

"First thing in the morning?"

"Sounds good. We still need some kind of livestock trailer."

"I got a four-horse trailer," Billy mentioned. "Ain't used it in a while, but it oughta do the job well enough, I'd guess."

"Hey! That would do it!" Jerry grinned. "We've got a two-horse trailer. Between them, we can make a pretty good haul."

"Well, we got a plan then," Billy decided. "See you early on?"

"Be here by eight," Jerry nodded. "We'll get what we can, and bring them back here." The two men shook hands, and Billy bumped fists with Toby, who grinned at being treated like a man. At seventeen he was a man, at least physically, but the last three or four days he had begun to act like one as well. Billy figured he was deserving of being treated that way.

The two Silvers walked toward their own home, as Billy turned toward his. He walked slowly, pondering events of recent weeks. He remembered how it had felt that he was basically all alone, despite his neighbors having survived. He remembered the urgency of finding and stocking supplies, knowing that some things would become harder to get in the months, perhaps years, ahead. He remembered finding Rommel, and grinned down at the dog, who had walked with him to the pen site.

"Been a pretty busy time, huh boy?" he asked. He reached down to ruff Rommel's head, and the big dog leaned into it, directing Billy's hand where he wanted it to go. Billy stopped, kneeling, and spent several minutes lavishing the great dog with attention. Rommel enjoyed every minute of it.

"You're a good pal, Rommel, you know that?" he said finally. With one more vigorous rub, Billy stood, and resumed his walk.

"We're doing pretty good, boy," he spoke to the dog as he walked. "Things are lookin' better, now. Much better."

Billy contemplated on his relationship with Rhonda. He'd always figured he'd be alone in the world, and the thought had held no real fear for him. The fact that he wasn't alone, now, gave Billy a whole new set of things to think on, and worry over.

He felt responsible for Rhonda now. He had to think about what might happen to her if some misfortune befell him. He also realized that he would need to be more careful now. If he were hurt, laid up, even temporarily, then Rhonda's life would be much harder. She would have to take care of him, along with everything else.

He didn't like the thought of that.

Rhonda Higgins wasn't a fragile, timid being by any stretch of the imagination, and would probably 'huff and puff' if she knew he was thinking in those terms. He could almost hear her;

I can take care of my own self just fine, Billy Todd, thank you very much, her voice rang in his ear. *I ain't no wall flower, or debutante.*

Billy didn't know what a debutante was, exactly, but he did know that Rhonda wasn't one, so he figured a debutante must be a bad thing. She worked hard, and didn't shirk from anything that needed doing. As for the rest...

Billy blushed at the thought of their physical intimacy, even though he was alone. Rhonda had been right again. They had 'figured it out'.

As he pondered on all these things, Billy stopped short suddenly, realizing something for the first time.

He and Rhonda were, for all intents and purposes, married.

"Huh," he grunted, as the full import of his circle of thinking hit him.

Billy had never counted on that. Ever. He knew he wasn't the kind of man that most women would find desirable. He wasn't smart, he wasn't rich. He wasn't good looking, at least not to his eyes.

Of course, in this new world, Billy was far more wealthy than he realized. He had land, livestock, even electricity. He took those things at face value, because he'd always known he had them. His parents had been prepared for almost any eventuality, and thus, so had he. He knew how to live in these times. He knew how to survive. More than that, he would *thrive*.

Billy hadn't taken those things for granted, and had learned from his parents. Rhonda had added a whole new level of thinking to what he knew, or what he found in his father's notes. Between the two of them, they had managed to think of a good many things, and they had amassed a great deal of property. Things that would last for a long while, and be worthy trade goods in the days ahead.

Billy had cut out three solid mares from the horses the group had collected, and brought them home, along with the stallion he judged to be the strongest of the three. Soon, they would be raising horses. They had his own small herd of cattle, and now part interest in what Billy thought of as the 'community herd'.

Tomorrow, they would be in the hog business as well.

Thanks to Rhonda's father, their own good thinking, and his parent's efforts, they had more firearms and ammunition than they should ever need, which meant that some of them could be used in trade. They would be very careful about that, Billy decided. He didn't want to wind up looking down the barrel of one of those guns later on.

Which led him to another concern. They had to make sure that the farm remained undetected. His place and Mister Silvers' were well off the road, almost three quarters of a mile. They were on a small back road as well, an old county road that most would simply look past when driving by. But if anyone found them...

Billy resolved right then that any 'trading' they did would done somewhere else, far from the farm. Like that place in Franklin. He didn't want anyone within five miles of the farm, if he could prevent it. The further they could keep people, the safer they would be. Even potential friends could give them away, either not meaning to, or being forced into it. It would be hard to trust anyone at this rate, he feared.

Billy rubbed his temples. He was getting a headache. The first one he'd had in almost a month. Having time to think about the problems they still faced, the potential dangers that lurked just outside their insulated world, was going to make him have a migraine.

He couldn't have that. He didn't have time. And, he admitted, he didn't want Rhonda to see him as weak, either.

But this time, he didn't have much of a choice. His head was pounding, and his eyesight was starting to blur, just a bit.

"Boy, we need to get home," Billy told Rommel. The dog wagged his tail stump, recognizing 'home', and started that way. He stopped after a few steps when he realized that Billy wasn't behind or beside him. Looking back, he saw Billy stagger just a bit, and loped back to his side.

"Just take it easy, boy," Billy almost whispered. "Take it easy." Holding Rommel's collar, Billy began making his painful way home once more.

-

Rhonda was on the porch, reading about canning, when she saw Billy and Rommel come out of the woods. She waved at them, then frowned as she saw Billy staggering along, holding to Rommel. Fearing he was injured, she was off the porch in a flash, running toward them.

Rommel was accustomed to Rhonda being part of their family, now, and didn't object as she ran to them. In fact, he whined slightly as she ran up, his worry over his person plain.

"Billy! Are you okay? What's wrong?" she asked, placing herself under his arm, and wrapping an arm around his waist.

"M... Migraine," he gasped. "Need pi...pill," was about the best he could do.

"Okay, baby," Rhonda soothed. "No problem, let's just get you up to the house. Can you make it?" Billy nodded, then gasped as the movement made stars flash before his eyes, and the pounding behind his eyes intensified.

"Easy, baby," Rhonda almost cooed. "Just a little bit, then I'll get you fixed right up. C'mon, honey, it ain't far." Led on by Rhonda, with Rommel just inches from his side, Billy staggered on toward the house.

Getting up the steps was a chore, but Billy was able to grasp the rail on one side, and pull himself, as Rhonda helped from the other side. Once inside, she didn't even bother with trying to get him up the stairs. Instead, she gently laid him out on the couch, and ran to get his meds. He had shown her what he needed not long after she'd moved in, 'just in case'.

She grabbed one of the pills, and a glass of water, hurrying back. She pushed the pill into his mouth, then held the water up to his lips. Billy drank gratefully, swallowing the tablet.

"Pill, knocks me out," he warned. "Sleep for a while," he added in a gasp. "Sorry 'bout this, Rhonda. Didn't want you to see me like this. Weak. Helpless."

"You ain't weak, Billy Todd," she scorned lightly. "Or helpless by any means. Just sick. And this will fix you right up, won't it?"

"Yeah," he gasped. "It'll fix it..." Exhausted, Billy lay back on the couch.

Rhonda stuffed a pillow under his head, then removed his boots and his pistol. She covered him with a bed sheet, and elevated his feet with a folded blanket, trying to make him as comfortable as possible. Finally, she stood back.

"Well," she looked at Rommel, "looks like it's a good thing I'm here. And you too, boy," she knelt and rubbed the great dog's head. "Thank you so much, Rommel, for bringing him home to me." Rommel licked her face lightly, then went and laid down near Billy's feet. Rhonda had to smile at that.

"I'm glad you were here with him, when he didn't have anyone else, Rommel," she spoke softly. She went and wet a bath rag, laying it gently on Billy's forehead. She then took a seat in the easy chair next to the couch, and sat vigil as Billy's medicine did its work.

Soon, Dottie was curled up at her feet, and the four of them spent the rest of the day in silence.

-

Billy awoke suddenly, disoriented. He sat up abruptly, startling Rommel, who had still been lying at his feet. This in turn startled Dottie, who had stretched out beside the chair Rhonda was sleeping in, and she *woofed*, looking around for whatever had startled her canine companion. That in turn jarred Rhonda awake.

"What?" she muttered, still half asleep.

"Rhonda?" Billy said softly, finally realizing where he was. "How did I get here?" The last thing Billy could remember was walking toward home with Rommel.

"Well, Rommel brought you home," Rhonda yawned, getting up to come sit next to him. "I saw the two of you coming out of the woods, and ran to help. Got you in here, and gave you your pill. You were out in less than a minute," she explained, then kissed him, wrapping her arms around him.

"I was so worried," she whispered.

"I'm sorry," Billy told her, hugging her to him tightly. "I didn't want you to see me like that." Rhonda slapped his shoulder.

"I wasn't worried once I found out it was a migraine, you dolt!" she told him sternly. "I was worried because I thought you'd been hurt!"

"Oh," Billy said, not knowing what else to say.

"I don't want you going anywhere without him from now on," she pointed to Rommel. "He brought you home. I don't think you would have made it without him. What caused your headache, anyway?" she asked, snuggling into his embrace.

"Thanks, Rommel," he ruffed the big dogs head, and received a lick in return. "I was just thinkin' too much," he told Rhonda. "That happens sometimes," he admitted, shamefaced.

"Yeah, right," Rhonda slapped him playfully again. "Seriously, Billy, what caused it?" Billy looked at her.

"Thinking too much," he repeated, leaning back. "*I was* serious. Sometimes I get caught in a loop, sorta, thinking about one thing, makes me think about another thing, which makes me think about something else, which. . .well, you get the picture. Sometimes it just overwhelms me, hits me all at once like, and it leads to a migraine. I'm usually more careful about it, but there were so many things the last three weeks or so that it kind of snuck up on me."

"What things?" Rhonda wanted to know. "You should share that stuff with me,

Odd Billy Todd

Billy, not try and go it all alone."

"It isn't like that," Billy shook his head. "Not at all. It started out fine, me thinking about what all we've got done, and how you came to be here, and how. . .well, you know," he looked at her, and Rhonda blushed slightly.

"Yeah," she smiled shyly. "I know."

"Well," Billy continued, "that led me to thinking about how we got the cattle now, and the horses, and now tomorrow the pigs, and what we could do, and how to do it. Which lead me to thinking' about how we need to keep people away from here no matter what, so that the farms are safe."

"That led me to thinking that something could happen to me, leaving you all alone, maybe even having to take care of me, if I was laid up. Plus, havin' to do all the work around here. I didn't like that. Made me think that I need to be more careful, so nothing happens to me, which made me think about the way I do things, going over the stuff I do, trying to make sure it was as safe as possible, which made me think about keeping you safe, which made me..." He stopped suddenly, looking at her.

"I'm doing it again," he said sadly. "That's always been my worst weakness, I guess. I can't control that kind of thinking once it starts."

"Oh, baby," Rhonda stroked his head, then kissed him softly. She snuggled closer to him, hugging him tightly.

"We'll work on it," she promised. "We'll find a way, together, to help you not obsess over this stuff. And the first thing is for you not to worry about me. I can take care of myself just fine, thank you." She was startled when Billy started to laugh. She pulled away from him, frowning.

"And that's funny in what kind o' way?" she demanded.

"It ain't funny by itself," he told her, still laughing. "It's just, when I was thinking about all this, I could hear you in my head, saying almost that exact same thing. Almost word for word, even," he added, still laughing.

"Oh," Rhonda's near anger left in a hurry, her face turning just a little red.

"So, I guess you know me pretty well, then," she added, grinning.

"Yeah, I guess I do," he agreed, kissing her lightly. She liked the way Billy had loosened up since . . . well, *since*. He was even more fun to be around now than he had been before.

"Well, I think it's time we get you cleaned up, and then get some food in you," she ordered. "Do you need help cleaning up?"

"I think I can manage," Billy said dryly. "Give me a few minutes." He headed off to the shower.

He had let the water run until it was warm, and had just picked up the soap when the curtain moved slightly, and a now naked Rhonda stepped into the shower with him.

"I just thought I'm make sure," she murmured, kissing him.

CHAPTER SIXTEEN

The next day dawned bright and clear, with just a hint of a chill. It was the middle of fall, now, almost Halloween. There was a great deal still to be done before winter sat in, and Billy was anxious to get it done.

There was one thing in particular that he wanted to do. He had discussed it with Rhonda, and had gotten her opinion. She had readily agreed, saying that it was a good idea.

When Jerry and Toby arrived, Billy had pulled the older man aside, and explained what he had in mind. Jerry wasn't opposed, and was even eager to help. Billy and Jerry decided that would be the next thing on the list, and they would do it tomorrow.

With that decided, they had headed out, two trucks pulling the two stock trailers. With some feed corn, it hadn't proved too difficult to convince the hungry hogs to enter the trailers. It took a while to get everything done, and it took three trips, but by early afternoon, the 'Farms', as Billy now thought of them, were in the swine business. Thirty-one sows, eleven of which already had piglets, and nine grown boars, all fat and healthy looking. Those they couldn't care for had been turned into the wild.

Billy and Jerry had discussed that one at length, going over the pro's and cons. It was cruel to leave the others to die of starvation. They considered trying to maintain them where they were, riding over once in a while to feed them, and check their water. That idea had finally been rejected. So had gathering them all in one place off the farm. The work and materials involved seemed a bit more than they could take on, with work on their own places, plus their combined efforts.

Turning them loose meant some of them would certainly die, killed by dogs, or even the few larger cats around. Even coyotes might try and take down a domestic hog.

And feral pigs weren't something to sneeze at either, the two men agreed. They were hard on crops, and were often as likely to attack a man as they were anything else. In the end, however, they felt that the risks were worthwhile. In a few years, those domestic pigs that survived might lead to herds of wild pigs that could be hunted for meat. And so the decision was made.

The last thing on the pig business list was the movement of a small silo. It wasn't huge by any means, but would hold a good bit of corn. Enough, they judged, to feed the hogs through the winter. When spring came again, they hoped to have a better place for them, a larger pen, separated into smaller ones, where they would get more sun, and more air. For now, they were satisfied with what they had. If nothing else, they could always trim away the trees around the clearing, enlarging it.

The silo proved to be easier to load than unload, however. It was sturdily made, and quite heavy. Billy wondered more than once how they had ever managed to load it, considering how hard it was to get it off the trailer. But finally they had managed. It took a bit of shovel work to get the silo standing upright, but once it was done, they were satisfied with it.

"Now we gotta fill it," Jerry said at last, rubbing his back.

"There's some corn still in the fields," Billy commented. "Might harvest that."

"Take a good bit o' fuel," Jerry warned.

"There's some left in town," Billy sighed. "Might as well use it, I guess. Even Pri-D won't make it last forever."

"Makes sense," Jerry finally nodded. "We'll see can we get someone's combine runnin', and gather what we can. At least fill this up. Might store some more off site, too, you know," he added, thinking.

"Yeah. Any extra can go to stretch the horse feed, or the cattle's hay, come winter," Billy nodded. "Any idea how long stored corn will last?" he asked the older man.

"I ain't never had enough left after the winter to know," Jerry shrugged. "I guess we'll find out, if there's enough."

"Reckon," Billy nodded. "Well, let's get over to the house. Rhonda will have us something ready to eat and we can take the time to lay things out for tomorrow."

"What are we doing tomorrow?" Toby asked.

"You'll see," Billy grinned at him. "C'mon. We can start today, so we're ready for tomorrow. Rhonda should have things laid out, by now." Jerry and Toby drove home, parking the truck and unhitching the trailer. They were soon back, having walked through the woods. Billy had already put his trailer up, and was sitting outside, with some objects on a folding table, covered by a sheet.

"Toby," Billy looked at the teenager closely. "I figure you been doing a man's work. I'm glad to see it. Your pa is a good man, and he deserves it."

"I know," Toby said, somewhat shamefaced. "I… I already told him I'm sorry for not helping more sooner. I just figured this would all go away. I done seen, now, that ain't gonna be." Jerry nodded, backing the boy's statement.

"Back in settler days," Billy went on, "boy your age'd most like already be married, and be counted a man. Be doing a man's work. I aim to treat you like a man, from now on. That means when you do something unmanly, you get treated like any other man. Get that?" Toby nodded.

"I aim to be good, Billy," he said, his voice sincere. "And I... I'm right sorry how I treated you, before. It ain't just that it wasn't right, but you ain't. . .I mean, everything people say ain't always true, y'know?" Billy smiled.

"Yeah, Toby, I do. And don't worry over it. Let's say that all that's behind us, startin' today. I *judge* you from now on, on what you *do* from now on. You do me the same way. You live with that?"

"I sure can!" Toby smiled.

"Good, then," Billy nodded, and pulled the sheet off the table.

Toby gasped at the hardware sitting in front of him.

"Holy smokes!" Jerry and Billy both laughed at his expression.

"Toby, I know you got a rifle," Billy said. "But it's a hunting rifle. Bolt action, I believe?" Toby nodded.

"Well, these ain't huntin' rifles," Billy pointed to the table. "We're gonna get you checked out on these, and then take you shooting tomorrow, so you know what you're doing."

"Toby, son," Jerry looked at his son. "There's bad people about. I know you know that, and you know that's why we been tryin' to keep still, and not bring attention to ourselves. But once we get out, like we did today, and like we'll have to goin' over to Franklin, then people will see us. And some will want to hurt us. Take from us."

"Some will want to hurt your mother, or sister, or Miss Rhonda, in ways we've talked about since all this started. You recall?" Toby's eyes narrowed at that. He did recall, and he didn't like it. He and his sister almost never agreed on anything. But she was *his* sister, and he'd been damned if any low life was going to hurt her if he could stop it. As for his mother, Toby figured he could kill a man who *spoke* to his mother wrong, let alone touched her in a harmful manner.

"Well, you're gonna have to help us protect them," Jerry continued. "That means you need the tools to do it with. And, comes to it, so do I," he admitted. "I got them, honestly, just ain't bothered to bring them out. And I had a small carbine for you to use. Billy suggested this, though, and I took him up on it. Figure your sister can use that carbine, she ever comes out of her shell," he grinned.

"Okay!" Toby grinned, suddenly realizing that he was going to get one of these beautiful rifles.

"Toby, Miss Rhonda and I talked this over, and decided to give you a rifle, a shotgun, and two handguns. We'll go over each one today, talking about safety and care, letting you handle each one. Tomorrow morning, we'll saddle up, and ride away a ways, so we won't spook the animals, and let you shoot until you're sure you know what you're doing. After that, we'll practice when and if we can, but never, *ever* close to home. Understand?"

"Why not?" Toby asked. It wasn't a challenge, but rather just simple curiosity. And perhaps the chance to learn something.

"Gunfire is loud, and carries a long way," Jerry told him. "If someone was about, and heard, they could use it to try and find us. We don't want that. If you have to shoot, here at home, it needs to be to protect yourself, or others. Understand, now?"

"Yes, sir," Toby nodded. Billy was pleased. The boy had come a long way in a short time.

"One last thing, while I'm thinking about it," Billy said. "Don't ever, *ever*, say anything to Miss Rhonda about needin' any protection, okay?"

"Why not?" Toby asked, again just wondering.

"Because it'll make my life much harder than it needs to be," Billy answered. "And I won't like that. Got it?"

"I got it," Toby grinned. And he did, too, it was plain.

"Okay, Toby," Billy said finally. "These came from Miss Rhonda's daddy's place. There wasn't much left," he lied a little, "but these are among the best that he had still in stock. So, let's get started. This here, is an AR-15..."

By the time they had finished letting Toby get used to his new weapons, Rhonda had food waiting. The three men sat down around the table, with Rhonda joining them.

"Miss Rhonda, I want to thank you for the guns," Toby said after the blessing had been made. "I really appreciate it, and I promise I'll take good care of them."

"I'm sure you will, sweetie," Rhonda smiled. "I wouldn't have given them to you, otherwise. Billy and your father think it's time you were treated like a grown up, and I know you've been doing a man's job these last weeks, cause I've seen it myself. Just remember that using a gun has consequences. Make sure before you act."

"I will," Toby nodded.

"And don't call me Miss Rhonda no more," she added. "I ain't but three, maybe four years older'n you. 'Miss' makes me sound a lot older, and I ain't sure I like it."

"Okay, Rhonda," Toby smiled around his sandwich. They ate then, talking about odds and ends, and the trip tomorrow, and the need to find a combine they could operate, and get the corn they could gathered. Finally, Jerry pushed his chair back.

"Reckon we better be gettin' home, folks," he declared. "Might good eatin' young'un," he winked at Rhonda.

"Thank you," she smiled. "Day after tomorrow, when we ain't shootin' and the like, I want the four o' ya'll to come over to supper. Reckon we can swap out, and visit back and forth. Sound good to you?"

"Sure does," Jerry nodded. "We'll see you two in the morning."

"Well, I have to say, Toby has changed an awful lot in the last week or two," Rhonda smiled at Billy. "Looks like you really did good on that one, dear."

"Hope so," Billy nodded. "He needs to learn all he can. And his pa needs the help. You aimin' to go with us tomorrow?" he asked.

"I'd like to, but I hate to you rob you three of your 'guy time'," Rhonda replied.

"Don't worry none 'bout that," Billy waved the idea away. "You want to go, you go."

"Do you want me to?" Rhonda asked, looking up at him.

"I wouldn't mind it," Billy replied.

"Well, then, I guess I'll just go," Rhonda smiled.

"Well, good then," Billy didn't seem to know the way out of this conversation.

"You got work still to do, as I recall," Rhonda helped him.

"Dangit!" Billy slapped his leg. "Forgot all about that!" He kissed her lightly, and then was out the door, heading for the barn, Rommel right behind.

Rhonda looked down at Dottie, who was still sitting beside her.

"Boys."

–

The next day was cloudy, and there was a definite chill in the air. Still, it wasn't that bad, and there was no reason to put off going to the range.

"Where you plannin' to take us, Billy?" Jerry asked, as they finished loading the horses. Jerry had brought his M-1 Garand, and was looking forward to a chance to shoot it.

"Me and daddy use to go to the gravel pit, over on Hancock Road. Ain't but a little ways, through the woods. We can be there in less'n an hour."

"That's a good spot, right enough," Jerry nodded.

"We ready?" Rhonda asked, as she stepped outside with a small basket. There were sandwiches inside, and everyone had plenty of water.

"I got us loaded," Billy nodded. "Waitin' on you," he teased.

"If you're waitin' on me, you're walkin' backwards," she shot back, poking her tongue out at him. Everyone mounted up, and they set off, with Rommel in the lead, and Dottie loping close behind him.

Billy led them down small trails in the woods, then a fire trail used by state forestry for fighting wild fires. Soon enough, they emerged onto Hancock Road. From where they left the woods, it was only a ten-minute ride to the gravel pit.

"Ain't been here in years," Jerry commented. "Used to come over here and shoot once in a while myself," he added.

"Yes, sir," Billy grinned. He knew that Jerry and his father had shot here in this pit together. Along with a few others that weren't around any more. Billy shook of that thought. *No more o' that,* he warned himself.

"Well, Toby, what you want to try first?" Predictably, the teen held up the AR he had just removed from his saddle scabbard.

"I'd really like to shoot this one," he grinned.

"Works for me," Billy nodded. "Be back in a minute." Billy went to set up the targets. They were old, now, and starting to rot around the edges, but were still serviceable. He set them up, and pasted a target on each one that he had brought from home. Rhonda walked along, and was helping him.

"This ain't a bad place to shoot," she commented idly.

"Nearest place to us, when we didn't want to shoot at home," Billy agreed. "Gunfire irritates the cows some," he added, grinning.

"I can imagine," Rhonda giggled. Their job done, the two walked back the thirty or so yards to where the Silvers were waiting. The horses had been picketed almost fifty yards away, near the entrance but out of sight of the road. Just in case.

"Okay, Toby," Billy told him, handing him a pair of safety glasses and ear muffs. "Remember what you learned yesterday," he cautioned. Then stepped back. Jerry was his father, it was his right to teach the boy.

"Toby, make sure the barrel ain't obstructed," he reminded.

"Already did, pa," Toby smiled. "I have shot a gun before, you know," he added jokingly. His father smiled at that.

"Just remember this ain't your rifle," he warned. "Every time you pull the trigger, it's gonna shoot." Toby nodded.

"Insert the magazine, and chamber a round," Jerry ordered. Toby deftly placed the magazine, then pulled and released the charging handle.

"Fire when you're ready, son," Jerry spoke loud enough Toby could hear through the muffs. Toby took two breaths, then flipped the safety to 'fire'. Sighting carefully, he squeezed the trigger.

The recoil was less than he was used to, but the flat crack of the small round surprised him. He took aim again, and fired. He repeated that process until the thirty-round magazine was empty. He flicked the rifle on safe, then removed his hearing protection.

"Well, let's go see how you did," Jerry patted his son's shoulder. Everyone walked down range to the target Toby had been using. Billy gave a low whistle when he saw the target.

"Nice shootin', Toby," he told the teen. "I see a few fliers, but they would still be hits on a man-sized target."

"Trigger surprised me a time or two," Toby admitted. "Take me a little to get used to it."

"That's what they call a combat trigger," Rhonda told him. "It will take a little time, as it's likely to be stiff at first. It'll get better, though, and then it'll be smooth as a baby's bottom." The men laughed at that, and she just waved them off.

"Let's have you run another magazine, and then we'll all join in," Jerry suggested. Toby was eager to shoot again, and nodded readily.

After his second magazine, the others all took a turn. Jerry Silvers' Garand was dead on, and the older man pitted the target twenty-four times out of twenty-four.

Rhonda used her Carbon 15, and cranked out twenty rounds in rapid fire. Toby almost goggled at the small target area of her shooting. Rhonda just smirked at all three before waltzing back to the line.

Billy went last. Lifting his M-4 style Bushmaster, he sighted, then let go of a thirty-round magazine in about the same time Rhonda had fired her twenty. His fire was methodical, for all that it was fast, and he instantly dropped the magazine when it clicked empty, and shoved a new one home.

"Pretty handy with that thing, ain't you," Jerry asked.

"Pa taught me," was all Billy had to say. When they reached the targets, everyone was stunned.

"Damn," Rhonda finally spoke. All of Billy's rounds were inside the space of a small saucer. Rhonda figured she could cover every hole with the opening of one of their larger tea glasses.

"Fine shootin' Billy," Jerry nodded. "Real fine."

"I want to shoot like that!" Toby enthused.

"Takes time," Billy told him. "And practice. Mostly it's up here," he pointed to his head. "Go over what you do in your head. Over and over again. Get so's it's second nature to you. It helps once you get on the range."

"How long have you been shooting that rifle," Rhonda asked.

"I ran a mag through it back when I got it," Billy shrugged. "Make sure it worked okay. It's pretty new, really."

"No kiddin'," Rhonda murmured. She had assumed that Billy had been using the rifle for some time, with shooting that accurate.

"Pa always said shootin' came natural to me," Billy shrugged. "I didn't have to work so hard at it as I did other things." Jerry caught himself before he said anything, but was thinking about what Bob had told him about Billy.

Never seen anything like it, he had told Jerry one evening, when Billy was about twelve. *Picks up a gun, any gun, and pings with it the first time. I've let him shoot everything I own, and borrowed a few to boot. Don't matter. Never fails.*

Jerry hadn't really doubted Robert Todd's word, but seeing for himself was something else. It was one thing to know someone could shoot well. Seeing it was another thing altogether.

Not for the first time he was glad he and Billy were friends as well as neighbors.

"Well, let's get on to your others, son," Jerry said, breaking the spell.

"Got a lot yet to do."

CHAPTER SEVENTEEN

It was the last week of October, when Jerry heard from one of his contacts in Franklin that there was a big trade day coming that weekend, likely the last one before bad weather sat in. He gave Jerry a list of what items he knew were in demand, and another of things that could usually be found for sale or barter. Most vendors would accept gold and silver coins for all but the rarest of commodities. Those would only be bartered, and the price tended to be high.

Jerry gave a copy of the list to Billy and Rhonda, and they went through it.

"I don't want to carry too much," Billy said thoughtfully. "We don't want to attract attention."

"I agree," Rhonda nodded. "I thought I'd take just a few things on this list, and use them as barter items. I don't want to be set up for business. The longer we wait, the more in demand our stuff will be. I might buy up any used brass I find, though," she added thoughtfully. "Maybe any primers that are in good condition."

"We can take a few coins," Billy said finally. "In case we find something we just really want to have."

"Well, I can't think of anything, right off hand," Rhonda mused. "But it doesn't hurt to be prepared. Let's start looking at this list, and decide what we want to take. The one thing I do want to find is a good supply of borax. I found a recipe in your mother's things to make our own laundry detergent. We have everything we need except the borax. I mean, we have some, but I'd like to have more."

"Okay, we'll add that to our list," Billy agreed. "I want to see about finding someone who does leather work, too. Hopefully we can trade a few cowhides for at least part of what we need."

"You have cowhides ready?" Rhonda asked.

"No, but we will have next spring, in all likelihood," Billy reminded her. "Even one or two, fixed properly, will go a long way for a good leather worker."

"What do we need?" Rhonda asked.

"Well, we can always use extra tack. I don't think we need saddles, since we found so many in other barns. We can use them, once we get them back in shape. But straps break, and leads fray. If we can find someone who can make them, and make good one's, we'd be smart to set up a deal with him or her."

"And there's always the chance they can make boots, or holsters," he added. "Plus, we can save the pigskins, when we slaughter the hogs, and they make tough leather. Especially good for gloves."

"Wow," Rhonda blinked. "I hadn't thought about how valuable the hides would be."

"In the old west, before they started driving herds to market, cows were sold just for their hides," Billy shrugged.

"Didn't know that either," Rhonda grinned. "Okay, so we stay on the lookout for a good leather worker. What else," she asked, scribbling a note.

"Someone who wants cows," Billy shrugged. "We can work on that with Mister Silvers. He's a good business man. But we have to be careful," he cautioned. "I don't want no one else around here knowing where we are, or what we have."

"I agree, and you know Jerry thinks the same way," Rhonda nodded. "We'll talk to him about the cattle. And the hogs," she added, making another note.

"Yeah," Billy had forgotten them. "They'll likely sell pretty well."

"Maybe," Rhonda was cautious now. "Don't forget, there'll almost certainly be other people doin' what we did. We'll have competition for sure."

"I don't want to get into it with anyone over sellin' hogs or cows," Billy was adamant. "We'll do what we can, but if push comes to shove, we don't need to sell any. We'll just keep'em for ourselves, or give a few to people in need, and let it go at that."

"Aww, you're so sweet," she rubbed him under his chin. Billy grunted, but didn't pull away. "Okay, what else?"

"I don't know," Billy shrugged. "We already have what we need, I guess. What do you want? Is there anything we don't have that you need?" Rhonda colored a bit.

"Well, I need some ah. . .some. . .well, lady stuff," she finished lamely.

"I got that covered," Billy told her. "There's plenty out in the shack behind the house."

"Really!" Rhonda exclaimed. "Oh, Billy that's great! I was almost out, and... well, you don't really want to hear that," she finished.

"I'll get them for you when we're done," he promised. "Anything else?"

"I really can't think of anything else," she shook her head. "But like you said, we can take a few trade goods, and a few coins, in case we find something we haven't thought of. I can't wait to go! I don't expect it to be like mall, but I love a flea market. That's what I'm really expecting, honestly, is an old-fashioned flea market."

"What it sounds like," Billy nodded, getting to his feet. "Be right back." He left the house, returning a few minutes with three large cases of. . .lady stuff.

"Oh!" Rhonda squealed. "That's plenty!" she told him.

"I'll put'em upstairs," Billy told her. "There's some more," he added.

"Good!" she grinned. "What about toilet paper?" she asked.

"More than there is of this," he promised. "I didn't over look *everything* before I met you, ya know," he winked. She laughed.

"That's my man. Smart."

Billy walked up the stairs smiling at that. Her man, indeed.

-

It was decided that everyone could squeeze into the Ford for the trip. Billy had checked the vehicle over, and it seemed in good shape to make the trip. He had put some tools, and parts most likely to go out, into the truck box behind the cab, just in case, along with enough water and coolant to refill the radiator twice. There were also two five-gallon cans of diesel, though he didn't expect to need them. The truck had twin tanks just like his own, and they were both full.

Billy just didn't like leaving things to chance.

The seating was done with forethought. Billy would drive, with Rhonda riding shotgun. Emma Silvers would sit between them. Jerry would ride behind Rhonda, with Toby behind Billy, and Michelle between them. That way there were shooters on both sides of the vehicle.

Toby had his rifle, and Jerry had decided to carry the M-1 .30 carbine he had originally bought for Toby. He had several magazines for it, and it was easier to carry than the Garand. Billy had his M-4, and Rhonda her Carbon 15. All four were carrying at least one pistol, and Billy had placed a shotgun under both the front and back seats, within easy reach.

"Seems like a lot," Rhonda commented.

"It *is* a lot," Billy agreed. "But we don't know what we'll find 'tween here and there. Or when we get there, for that matter." She nodded agreement, and said nothing else.

With the goods they were taking in the back, and the coins they had on their person, they were ready. They loaded quickly, and set off. It was early, not long after daylight, but both Jerry and Billy were adamant that they get there early, and leave so they could be home before dark. Jerry had another caution as well.

"We don't tell no one, and I mean *no one*, where we are," he told his children. "I don't care how cute, or how hot, or how *nice* they seem. You've got a radio frequency you can give them, and that's all they get. No mention of Cedar Bend, either. That's too close to home. If someone asks, you tell'em you're from out o' town a ways. And no tellin' how long the trip takes, either, while I'm thinkin' on it. That's just somethin' else someone can use to find us. No highway numbers, nothing. Got that?"

"Yes, sir," both children agreed. Shelly obviously didn't like being 'treated like a child', but she didn't object. Toby agreed because he knew it was smart. He had come a long way in a short time. Billy was glad to see it, since it took a lot of pressure off Jerry to have Toby on board.

Their trip would take them through or around several small towns. Billy had read his father's notes on traveling carefully before choosing the route, and had spoken to Jerry in depth about it. They would avoid the towns where possible, and get through those they couldn't avoid as quickly as possible. Any road blocks would be a problem, but Billy had a solution for that, he thought.

On the front of the Ford there was now a snow blade. He had attached it directly to the frame, and then strengthened both the plow and the frame of the truck. If they had to hit a car blocking the road, it should hold. If not, then they'd probably have to shoot their way through. They had two spare tires, so hopefully they had that covered.

The first town they came to was hardly more than a village. Billy knew the name, but couldn't think of it to save his life.

"Cottonwood," Jerry spoke softly as they drove through yet another ghost town. "Ain't been here in a while."

"Looks like they took it pretty hard," Billy added, looking at the road carefully, depending on Rhonda and the others to spot trouble.

"Slow down a little, once you cross the tracks, Billy," Rhonda asked. "I want to see something." He complied, easing the truck across the railroad tracks that cut through the middle of town.

"Hmm," Rhonda mused, looking at store fronts.

"What is it?" Billy asked.

"The fabric shop is still intact," she noted. "And Wally's Gun shop is too. I don't think anyone's been here. The town may be completely deserted."

"Might be," Billy shrugged.

"Best not to take chances, I'm thinkin'," Jerry added from the back.

"Oh, I ain't," Rhonda assured him. "Just thought it was a good way to see if anyone might be about." She wasn't being completely truthful, but that didn't matter. She and Billy could handle what she had in mind, if they decided it was worth the risk.

The truck went on, easing around cars that had stopped in the highway as their drivers succumbed to the Plague. Once Jerry and Toby had to get out, and push three cars that had wrecked off the road. Rhonda got out to keep watch, while Billy kept the truck running.

"Why ain't you helping?" Shelly demanded.

"Shelly, you're talking," Emma said firmly. "Might want to see to that." Shelly *hmphed* from her spot in the back, but said nothing else. Billy hid a grin. Once everyone was back inside, she broached the subject again. Her mother frowned at her in the mirror, but it was Toby who answered.

"Shelly, don't be stupid," he sighed in resignation. "Billy can't help cause he's drivin'. If someone started shootin', or tried to run up on us, he needs to be here, ready to get us out o' Dodge." Jerry looked out the window quickly to keep his smile from showing, and Rhonda had a suspicious coughing fit.

"You just *want* someone to 'run up on us' don't you," Shelly accused her brother. "So you can use that new gun of yours."

"No, I don't," Toby replied calmly. "I hope I never shoot this thing, except at a paper target for fun, or practice. I want to be peaceful, and live in peace. But not everyone else feels that way. I want to live, and survive. Some might not want to let me, and that's why I have this rifle."

Taken aback by her brother's grown up response, Shelly sat quietly for a good while, thinking on what Toby had said.

Billy judged they were no more than twenty miles from Franklin when they topped a hill, and saw the roadblock. Two pickups were parked nose to nose across a levee, and he could see at least three men standing there with long guns.

"I see four people, all together," Rhonda said, eyeing the roadblock with binoculars. She passed them back to Jerry, while Billy looked around them for any signs of an ambush.

"Yeah, me too," he agreed. He scanned around with the glasses for a bit.

"I don't see anyone else," he told them finally, passing the glasses back. Rhonda used them the same way, and agreed.

"Well, what do we want to do?" Billy asked. He was oddly calm.

"I didn't come this far to just go home," Jerry said quietly. "And if we try to run, they might chase us."

"Why don't we just see what they want?" Shelly asked. Everyone looked at her, and she made herself smaller in the seat.

"Because whatever they want, it's too much," her father informed her. "This is a public road, like it or not. We ain't closed our road, or any others, now have we? And that bunch looks plenty well fed."

"Well, let's go on up there, then," Billy shrugged. He looked at Rhonda, who nodded. She looked scared, but determined. Billy took one his pistols out of it's holster, and stuck it down between his legs, where he could grab it with either hand. His left hand went to this jacket pocket, removing something no one else could see,

Odd Billy Todd

and then into his lap, where he kept it. Everyone rolled their windows down, and got ready.

"Toby, lay your rifle up on the window seal," Billy ordered. "I want whoever walks up here to be lookin' at it, and not payin' me much mind." Toby nodded, and did as Billy had told him.

"This guy tries anything like going for his gun, you shoot him," Jerry ordered. The teen paled, but nodded again. He would do what he had too. Billy put the truck in gear, and headed for the roadblock.

There were four of them, Billy saw, as they slowed to a stop about twenty yards from the trucks. The man out front waved for them to come closer, but Billy shook his head, and waved for the man to come to him. After a brief conference with his confederates, he slowly walked up.

"Where you folks headed?" he demanded gruffly. The man was large, and badly needed a bath. He was carrying an older model M-16, which Billy noted looked military issue. It was dirty, and Billy doubted it would fire more than a few rounds without jamming. He didn't miss the way Big Dirty's eyes wandered over Rhonda, either.

"Can't see how that concerns you," Billy told him calmly. "Ya'll need to move 'em trucks outta the way, so's we can pass." The man laughed out right at that.

"This here is our road, friend," he replied. "You want to go through here, you pay us. Or you just turn around."

"You the man we deal with?" Billy asked, to the surprise of everyone in the vehicle. "I assume you're in charge?"

"That's right," Big Dirty nodded. "I'm the man in charge."

"Good," Billy said, and reached out of the window, grabbing the man by the throat.

"This here, is a grenade," Billy said, his voice still calm. "I done pulled the pin, as you can clearly see," he added, holding a pin up for Big Dirty to see. "Since you're in charge, I expect your friends there will do what you tell'em, yeah?" Big Dirty nodded.

"Then you best tell'em to lay them guns down on the ground," Billy warned. "I'm scared, mister. Real scared. So scared there ain't no tellin' what I might do. Like drop this here grenade in your pants. Know what I mean?" Billy didn't sound the least bit scared. That fact wasn't lost on Big Dirty, either.

"Put'em down!" he called. The others just looked at him.

"I said put'em down you idiots!" he repeated. "He's got. . . " he broke off as Billy tightened his grip.

"Let's just keep that between us, *friend*, huh?" Billy told him.

"Just put'em down, dammit!" Big Dirty yelled again. Still confused, they did as they were told. As soon as they had, Rhonda and Jerry were out of the truck, covering them.

"Tobe, why don't you get out, real easy like, and relieve our *friend* here of his rifle," Billy ordered. Toby did as ordered, then back away, making sure he could cover the man with his rifle.

"Back up," Billy ordered, releasing him. "That's good," Billy told him, taking his pistol in hand, and opening the door. "Now, get down, on your belly, and keep your hands well away from your body." Seething, Big Dirty did so.

"You're makin' a mistake, buddy," he tried to sound threatening.

"I'm famous for it," Billy nodded, searching the man quickly but thoroughly. He took two pistols, one a 1911 copy, the other a revolver, off him, as well as three knives, one which looked suspiciously blood stained.

"Crawl over there with your buddies," Billy ordered. When the man started to get up, Billy put his foot on his back, and placed his Kimber 1911 to the back of his head.

"I said crawl," Billy almost whispered. The man crawled.

"Toby, stay here, watch our backs, and your mom and sister," Billy ordered, never taking his eyes from Big Dirty.

"Yes, sir," Toby answered, and put himself where he could do as ordered. Billy walked to the front, where Jerry had similarly disarmed the other three.

"Now, you boys are bein' naughty," Billy said, his voice projecting an eerie calm. "This here, this is a public road, as I recall. That sort of trumps your claim to ownership, the way I see it."

"We're just trying to live!" one of the others snarled. "We gotta right to make a livin'!"

"You can work for what you want and need, same as ever body else does," Jerry snarled back. "You ain't nothin' but a pack of wild dogs!"

"You talk mighty tough behind that rifle, old man," a third shot back.

"Kinda how you aimed to talk to us, huh?" Rhonda smiled sweetly.

"When I get my hands on you, Red, you'll wish..." Big Dirty didn't get the chance to finish, as Billy's Kimber barked once. Big Dirty's head exploded on the road. Rhonda and Jerry looked on in shock as Billy walked up to the rest.

"Now, gimme one good reason I don't do for you what I just did for him."

"Hey, mister, we ain't like that..."

"He ain't nothin' but a fool! We only followed him cause he..."

"He would o' killed us, we didn't do what he..."

"Shut up," Billy ordered, and there was quiet. He looked them over, disgusted.

"All of you, strip off, right now," he ordered suddenly.

"What?"

"Now!" Billy ordered. All three reluctantly began to undress. Rhonda looked at Billy.

"Not now," he told her, and she nodded. Jerry was grinning.

"Now," he told them once they were naked, "you push them trucks outta the way. Try to start one, and you'll get what he got." They began to push the trucks, first one, then the other, until the road was clear.

"Now, get that dead slime off the road," he ordered, pointing to Big Dirty. Even more reluctantly, the three drug their former comrade to the side of the road, and rolled his body off the levee.

"Okay, you can go now," Billy told them.

"What about our clothes?" one had the courage to ask.

"You mean *my* clothes?" Billy asked. "See, that's my toll for you using my road. I take everything, and then you can move on. Which you need to start doin', before I change my mind. We're going that way," he pointed north, "so you can go that way," he pointed south this time. "And you should run, for a while, cause like I said, I might change my mind."

Odd Billy Todd

"We'll freeze without our clothes!" another protested.

"Want me to send you someplace warm?" Billy replied, lifting the Kimber again. "No? Then you start in to runnin'. Better keep at it a while. I might decide to follow you. Now *git*!"

They got. Fast. Billy watched them go, following them out of sight.

"Well, let's grab this stuff," he pointed to the weapons, "and get goin'."

"Billy," Rhonda's voice was soft, "why'd you shoot that man? He was already disarmed." Billy's eyes were flat as he looked at her.

"He threatened you," he said simply. "No man threatens you, and lives."

"Damn good policy," Jerry murmured, as he and Toby gathered the guns left behind. He didn't look up, not wanting to get between the two younger people, but he felt the need to voice his approval of Billy's actions.

"Okay," was all Rhonda could get out. She'd been prepared to shoot them if she had to. What Billy had done frightened her just a bit. Until she remembered her father's words;

I'd not want to be the one that hurt something or someone he loved.

Now, Rhonda finally understood what her father had meant. And it didn't bother her so much anymore.

She got back in the truck, ready to go.

Shelly, of course, was a bit more vocal.

"Why did you shoot that man!" she almost screeched. "He couldn't hurt you!"

"He was a thug," Billy shrugged. "He wasn't no good, and no good would come of leavin' him alive. His knife had blood on it, and so did his clothes. Ain't no tellin' who all he's hurt, and killed."

"You can't just kill someone like that!" Shelly shot back.

"I did, therefore I can," Billy shrugged. "He had it comin'."

"Shelly, shut up," Jerry told her before she could start again. "If Billy hadn't shot him for what he said, I would have. He threatened Rhonda. In a way that only a low-down animal can threaten a woman. Billy's right. I'd o' done the same thing, had he threatened you, or you ma, in such a way."

"What do *you* think, Rhonda?" Shelly just had to get one more dig in. "About what he did?" Rhonda looked back at her for a minute, then looked back front.

"I think I have a man who loves me, and won't let any harm come to me so long as he's alive to stop it," she replied truthfully. "And I'm proud to be his woman."

Emma squeezed her leg, and Rhonda looked over to see the older woman smiling at her in approval. Somehow, it made Rhonda even more glad of her answer.

"Next stop, Franklin," Billy said into the silence.

"Billy, one thing," Jerry spoke up. "I'd appreciate a warnin' next time you aim to pull the pin out of a grenade."

"You mean this pin?" Billy asked, holding up the pin he'd shown Big Dirty at the roadblock.

"You didn't put it back in?" Rhonda gasped.

"Never took it out," Billy grinned. "This come out of an old lighter my daddy had. It's sittin' on his desk in the study. I was thinkin' it might come in handy."

Everyone but Shelly was still laughing when they pulled into the market in

Franklin.

CHAPTER EIGHTEEN

The 'market' left a lot to be desired, at least as a true trading post, Billy decided. But it was a passable flea market, just as Rhonda had thought it might be. There were people inside, as well, in what had been the city convention center.

When they parked, they were met by two men wearing badges on their jackets, and wearing armbands that read *Constable*.

"You folks headin' to the market?" one asked, while the other stood back.

"We are," Jerry nodded.

"Your vehicle should be safe, but we can't guarantee it, understand," he told them. "If you're carrying items for trade, it might be best to leave someone to watch it. Carrying weapons is okay, so long as you stay peaceable."

"I'll stay peaceable so long as everyone else does," Billy shrugged.

"That's the idea," the constable nodded. "We don't have a problem with self defense around here. Be forewarned, however, that any sort of violence will have an inquiry to see that it was justified."

"Enjoy the market, folks," the other nodded, and the two were on their way.

"Well, who wants to take a turn with the truck, first?" Jerry looked around.

"We will," Rhonda smiled. "You guys go ahead. When you get back, me and Billy will go."

"Thank you, Rhonda," Emma smiled. "It'll be nice to get out as a family. We haven't done that in a while."

"Take this 'fore you go," Billy called, handing Jerry and Toby a small radio. "FRS. Won't work so well over long distances, but they should do okay somewhere like this. They're already set."

"Good idea," Jerry nodded, placing his in a shirt pocket. Toby studied the radio for a moment, then did likewise. Emma pointed out baskets she wanted taken, and the two teens picked them up.

"We'll be back in a bit," Jerry waved, and then the Silvers were gone, lost in the crowd.

Billy hopped up on the tailgate, taking a seat, and Rhonda joined him. The two were silent for a while, then Rhonda looked at Billy.

"Thank you, Billy," she said softly.

"Huh?" Billy was jolted out of his reverie. He hadn't seen so many people in a while.

"Thank you," Rhonda repeated. "For earlier. For not gettin' mad when I asked why. For doin' it in the first place. For. . .well, just for everything."

"You're welcome, sweetie," Billy said, trying to use endearments the way she did. He could tell by the way her face lit up, she liked it.

"I knew things would be different," she went on, laying her head over on him. "I really did. It was just, seeing it for myself, instead of hearing about it, or thinkin' 'bout it, was. . .well, it was different when you had to see it."

"I know," Billy placed his arm around her, and she snuggled into him. "I'm sorry you had to see it," he said truthfully. "I should have sent you back to the truck. But I didn't figure you'd go, for one. And, to be honest, I shot him 'fore I thought much about it."

"I know," she patted his chest gently. "Because of me," she added.

"Yes," was all Billy said. "But that don't make it your fault. He made his choice, and it was the wrong one."

"I know," she nodded. "Don't worry, I don't feel guilty. I seen him looking me over when you was talkin' to him. I knew what he meant to do, if he had the chance."

"I'll not let something like that happen, can I prevent it at all," Billy promised.

"I know that," was all she said.

The two of them fell silent after that, just enjoying each others company, and watching the people come and go. There were more people than Rhonda had expected, and she mentioned this to Billy.

"Well, they've had three months or so to get organized," Billy commented. "And, this is likely the last big trade day before winter sets in. And they advertised it, if you want to call it that, over the HAM. Lot o' people are probably makin' stuff to sell by now, or at least trade. And I'm sure there's scavengers about, just like us. This is the best place to try and buy, sell, or trade, without gettin' stole from, or maybe killed, I'd imagine."

"Yeah," Rhonda nodded. "Still, I'm surprised to see so many people. Not in a bad way. Kinda glad to see so many made it."

"Big change from the last little bit," Billy agreed. "I'd say a lot o' these folks, while they'll make a deal if they can, or want to, are here more for socializin' than anything else."

"You know, I was thinkin' that, too," Rhonda replied. "It must be nice to have a place like this, where so many are near enough to have a get together."

"Yeah, I doubt we'll be having anything like this anytime soon," Billy sighed. "It ain't that I don't want to, but I gotta admit I'm not unhappy with how things are at the moment. We may can get some neighbors, if we can get to know people a little better. There's plenty of room."

"That'd be nice," Rhonda smiled. "But I'm like you. I want to know people pretty well 'fore we invite 'em into the neighborhood."

"Where you folks from?" a voice broke in on their conversation. Both turned to see a less than savory man in a dirty suit looking at them.

"What's 'at?" Billy asked, though he'd heard the man just fine.

"Just wondering' where you folks is from," the man repeated. "I'm Nate Blaine, from here in Franklin." He extended his hand, which Billy looked at, but didn't take.

"No offense, mister," Billy told him. "But I ain't interested in givin' out my name, or my whereabouts." Blaine's smile slipped just a bit, but he caught it.

"Perfectly understandable," he nodded, using his best used car salesman demeanor. "I just don't recognize you. Thought you might be new in town."

"Maybe you just never saw us before," Billy shrugged.

"Oh, I'm sure I'd remember a fine couple such as yourselves," Blaine scoffed. "I try to get about and see everyone. And everything," he added. "For instance, I noticed your truck doesn't have a tag."

"Fell off, I guess," Billy didn't bother to look. He knew there wasn't a tag. He'd taken it off himself.

Odd Billy Todd

"Sure," Blaine grinned knowingly. "Mind if I ask what business you're in?"

"I do," Billy growled slightly. "We ain't botherin' you mister. You oughta return the favor." He was getting tired of dealing with the greasy looking Blaine.

"Ain't no call for unkindness, friend," Blaine raised both hands in supplication. "I was just thinking there might be a deal we could strike. I'll just be moving along."

"I think that's a fine idea," Billy agreed.

"Nice meeting you, ma'am," Blaine tipped an imaginary hat at Rhonda, and Billy stiffened. Her fingers dug into Billy's arm, stilling him.

"It ain't, really," she assured Blaine. He flushed slightly at that, but nodded, and turned away. They watched him go, although Billy kept a look all around them, as well, just in case Blaine had been a diversion.

"What a charming fella," Rhonda said dryly, when Blaine was far enough away. Billy grunted.

"Makes me feel like I need a bath, just talkin' to him," he noted, and Rhonda laughed at that. Billy had a dry sense of humor most times. And sometimes he just said what was on his mind, which was funny in it's own right. She loved that about him.

"He does look a little greasy, don't he?" she giggled.

"Wonder what his game is?" Billy mused, watching as Blaine tried another group.

"What ya mean?" Rhonda asked, rummaging through the basket of food she'd brought. She handed Billy a sandwich, and a bottle of water, and got one for herself.

"I mean, what's he up to," Billy said, opening his sandwich. He hadn't realized he was hungry. "He ain't just passin' the time o' day, he's up to something. He's either lookin' to rook somebody outta their stuff, or else he's workin' to find out where people are livin', and what they got, so's him, or someone else, can go and relieve'em of it. He might not go with'em, but get a finder's fee, like." Rhonda looked at Billy, almost dumbfounded.

"I didn't never think of anything like that," she admitted. "I just didn't like him."

"I don't neither," Billy grunted. "And I don't like how he looked at you."

"Men look Billy," Rhonda teased. "It's in your nature." Billy turned to look at her.

"I know men will look at you, darlin'," he grinned. "You're a right pretty girl, though some'd say you ain't got no sense, takin' up with the likes o' me. But he didn't look at you in an admirin' fashion," he added, turning back to keep an eye on Blaine. "He looked at you like a thing. Something to possess, or buy and sell. I don't like that."

"Billy, you can't go killin' ever man looks at me, or the Silvers women, like that," Rhonda chided gently.

"I can't?" Billy raised an eyebrow. It took her a minute to realize he was kidding.

"No, my He-Man, you can't," she giggled. "Ain't done in polite society."

"We ain't livin' in a polite society no more," Billy pointed out, but grinned, and winked at her to show he was still just being playful.

"Well, some, like that guy this morning, you probably saved someone else by gettin' rid of," Rhonda admitted. "But that greasy goof ain't a real threat, at least not by himself. And don't forget, I shoot pretty good myself," she grinned.

"So, you do," Billy nodded. "So, you do."

They ate the rest of their meal in silence, once more enjoying the day. It had warmed up enough that it was comfortable, and they soon stripped out of their jackets. Both were wearing long sleeve flannels, and they were warm enough.

The Silvers were gone perhaps an hour-and-a-half, returning with several things they had traded for.

"Well, it ain't Wal-Mart," Emma laughed, "but it is nice, considering. I managed to find some canning lids, and rings. Traded home-made jam and preserves for them. And I found some fleece that I traded for, too. I figure it will come in handy, this winter."

"There's a man set-up in there with ammunition, but he knows it's worth it's weight in gold," Jerry muttered. "Got a reloading' set-up too, trades live rounds for empty brass at the tune of five empties per the round."

"Don't do no business with no one about that," Rhonda told him quietly. "I got daddy's set up, and plenty of stuff to keep us going. I was thinking about running a business like that, but if there's a man already doing' it, I'll just wait a while. What he's got won't last forever."

"Go deal, Little Bit," Jerry grinned.

"And don't you go tradin' for no fabric, till I can show you what I have," she added to Emma. "I ain't got no fleece, as it happens, but I do have some other stuff. Ain't much," she lied slightly. "But if you have a need, you can have what I can spare."

"I can't just take your material, dear," Emma told her. "You might need it, too."

"I might," Rhonda nodded. "Might need something else, sometime, too," she pointed out. "We two families have to work together. 'Fore we come here again, we'll see what each other has that the other needs. Ain't no need to let these other people get our goods, or our money, if we ain't gotta."

"Well, that does make sense," Emma agreed. "All right, we'll work that out before we come back. Meanwhile, it's your turn to take a look around. We'll eat, and watch the truck."

"You two have fun," Jerry smiled.

"Reminds me," Billy said. "Was a greasy lookin' cuss named Blaine come by here whilst you were gone. Askin' where we was from, what business we was in, that sort o' thing. I put him on the road pretty quick, but you might be watchful for him, or others o' his kind."

"Good idea," Jerry nodded. "Thanks for lettin' us know."

"Well, let's go see what's what!" Rhonda exclaimed, taking Billy's hand. Billy handed Jerry the truck keys, and the two set off.

-

Billy had to admit, if only to himself, that the 'market' was a pretty good set-up. Signs warned people about stealing, and cheating, stating clearly that either would be punished quickly and severely. There were several more men inside the building, and all around it, wearing the Constable armbands, and they seemed to take the duty seriously. Anything that even looked like it might turn into something attracted their prompt attention.

Odd Billy Todd

"Seems pretty well run," he told Rhonda.

"Yeah, I thought so too," she nodded. "I like how everything has its own spot. Everyone who's selling food is in one spot, guns and ammo somewhere else, and so on. Keeps you from getting taken." Billy nodded. He hadn't noticed that himself.

They took their time, looking over everything they took interest in, Rhonda haggling on occasion to try and get a better price. Sometimes successful, sometimes not. She didn't begrudge anyone. That was the way of bartering. If you had what someone wanted bad enough, they'd trade. If not, then you might be out of luck.

They did pass one man who was hawking 'women's supplies'. He saw Rhonda and started in on her about 'stocking up'. She tried to wave him off, but this guy had obviously been a high-pressure salesman before the Plague. A stern look from Billy, however, was enough to make him retreat to his table.

"I knew you'd come in handy for something," she teased as they walked on by.

"I'm here to serve," Billy chuckled. He was enjoying himself, he admitted. He and Rhonda had no chance to get out and do things like this at home. Today was a nice break from their routine, the roadblock not withstanding.

Billy was looking at some holsters and leather goods, thinking he might see if the man selling them had made them himself, when his radio crackled. The noise startled Billy, as he had forgotten the thing until now.

"*Billy, can you hear me?*" Jerry's voice came through loud and clear.

"I hear ya," he replied.

"*Hate to ask, but I'm gonna need you out here at the truck. We're havin' an. . .issue, with your friend from earlier.*"

"We'll be right there," Billy said at once. He looked at the leather man. "I'll try and come back, if this ain't somethin' bad. You think you'll be here a little longer?"

"Sure," the man nodded, dealing with another customer. Billy grabbed Rhonda's arm.

"What's wrong?" she asked, not having heard the radio in all the commotion.

"Jerry needs us at the truck," he told her, making his way through the crowd. "Said he was havin' an issue with our friend from earlier. I guess he means Blaine, but we'll be careful, just in case."

Rhonda nodded, and the two made the trip back to the truck in silence. Billy slowed as he approached. It was Blaine, and he was squawking at two constables, a different pair than they had met earlier, while pointing at Jerry and his family. Billy frowned as he noted one of the constables was all but pointing a shotgun at his friends.

". . .and that nice young couple aren't anywhere around!" he heard Blaine finish as he drew near.

"You mean us?" he said softly. The Constable jerked at the sound of Billy speaking, and turned quickly.

"You hadn't oughta be sneaking up on people, Mister!" the Constable stammered.

"And you ought not be pointin' a gun at my friends, who are God fearin', law 'bidin' citizens, neither," Billy shot back. "What are *you* doin' here?" he asked

Blaine. "I thought I made it clear to you this mornin', whatever you're sellin', we ain't buyin'."

The Constable turned again, just as swiftly, his attitude toward Billy now directed at Blaine.

"That right, Blaine?" he demanded, angry.

"I... well, how could I have known. . .I mean, they were here..."

"We travel together for safety," Billy told him. "And I can't for the life o' me see how it's any of your business."

"Now see here!" Blaine blustered. "I was merely trying to do my duty as a...."

"Connivin', low down, snake," Billy finished for him. "You folks okay?" he asked Jerry.

"Reckon we are now," Jerry nodded. He was red faced from anger.

"Can I assume this it over with?" Billy demanded of the Constable who was doing the talking.

"Yes, sir," the man managed to stammer. He whirled about to face Blaine.

"If you start anymore ruckus, Blaine, I'll ask the Board to ban you from the market, understand me?"

"I was just..."

"Did you hear me?" the Constable grated.

"Yes, William, I heard you," Blaine grumbled. He shot a withering look at Billy, and it was all Rhonda could do to keep him from pummeling the man right there, with the Constable's watching.

"I better not see you 'round me or mine, no more," Billy satisfied himself with saying. Blaine didn't reply, but walked off in a huff. The Constable turned to Billy.

"We don't allow people to make threats, here, Mister...?"

"I wasn't makin' one," Billy assured him, not bothering to answer the almost question of what his name was. "I got here to see your partner holdin' a gun on the only family we got left," he indicated the Silvers. "I don't much like that."

"We have to do our job, sir," the one who had held the Silvers at gunpoint offered, though not in a confrontational way. "We get people from all over in here on a trade day."

"I take it you know that Blaine, fella, though?" Billy asked.

"We do," he agreed.

"And he don't never cause no trouble, I'm guessin'?"

"He is prone to..."

"That's beside the point," the first constable broke in. "We were just doing our duty."

"Well, the next time your 'duty' includes pointing a gun at a man and his family, on nothing more than that snake's word? It had *better* not be my family. Got that?"

"Sir, we could arrest you for creating a disturbance right now, and be within our rights!" the Constable blustered.

"Just the two o' ya?" Billy asked, his voice going very calm.

"Billy, that's enough," Rhonda said softly, taking his arm. "If you gentlemen are quite done pointing guns on the word of that. . .that, *creature*, then we have business to attend to."

"You folks go ahead," the second constable said as the first spluttered in rage.

Odd Billy Todd

"Sorry about that," he offered to Jerry. "Next time, I'll know who you are."

Jerry just nodded his thanks, not trusting himself to speak.

Billy watched until the two had moved away, then stormed up and down the sidewalk for three minutes. Rhonda walked with him the entire way, not saying a word. Finally, though, she reached out and took his hand. When she did, Billy stopped, and looked at her.

"Sorry," he murmured, as if a light had come on, and he realized what he'd been doing. "I just don't like that sort o' thing."

"I know, baby," Rhonda soothed. "And you handled it pretty good, I'd say. Now let's just see if the Silvers are okay, and then go back inside. I know you wanted to speak to that leather guy."

Billy nodded. The two walked back to the truck.

"Billy, I'm really sorry," Jerry started, but Rhonda cut him off.

"Ain't your fault, Mister Silvers," she smiled at him. "It was that slime ball Blaine. Trying to stir up trouble. Probably thought that he could get the truck, if he played his cards right. Or at least what he could get from the back."

"Probably," Jerry nodded.

"You did right," Billy sighed. "I'm the one should of shut up sooner. I'm sorry about that. I'll do better, happens there's a next time."

"Billy Todd, you hush that talk right now!" Emma Silvers scolded. "It's rolling over to that kind of behavior that kept us a prisoner in our own country for too long. *It needs* to be stood up to, and you did just fine. Don't you agree, Jerry?"

"I do," he nodded, not even seeing the glance from his wife that 'told' him he agreed. "Handled it mighty fine. I just wish it hadn't been needful. Ticked me off, being accused like that."

"Would me too," Billy nodded. "We need to see a man inside, then we'll be back. Maybe twenty minutes or so. That okay?"

"We'll be here," Jerry said firmly.

-

"So, you can bring me hides?"

"Some," Billy nodded. The leather man's name was Ralph Maness. "They'll be tanned, and what not. I just don't know how many at the time, so I'm hesitant to promise you anything."

"Well, a promise ain't worth much more'n a man's word now days, anyway," Maness shrugged. "Man might want to keep his word, and can't. Tell you what I can do, though. I can cut you a deal on the amount of stuff you want, based on what you do bring. In other words, you bring me three hides, tanned and ready to work, then you get three hide's worth of stuff for labor and materials other than the leather. Sound good to you?"

"That's exactly what I wanted to do," Billy nodded eagerly. "We might be able to find some of the other things you need, too, once in a while. You got a list of stuff you're needful of?" Maness grinned, and pulled out a handwritten note.

"Keep these all the time. Most of the traders here do. Never know where the next goldmine'll come from."

"Not bad thinking," Rhonda complimented. Maness looked at her.

"I'm takin' it you've been doing this for a while before the sickness hit?"

"A little," she smiled at him disarmingly. "Learned from my daddy," she

102

added. Maness groaned a little.

"Glad I already struck a deal with your mister, then," he laughed. "Got a feeling you'd drive a hard bargain."

"Only when it's something' I want *real* bad," she smiled again, hugging Billy's arm to her. Maness laughed outright at that.

"You got yourself a sure enough spitfire, there, boy," Maness told Billy. "Better take good care of her."

"He does," Rhonda sing songed brightly before Billy could answer. Billy handed the list to Rhonda. She looked at it, a smile tugging at her lips as she put it away.

"You make that saddle?" Billy asked, pointing to a beautiful black saddle sitting on a wooden horse.

"I did," Maness sighed. "Doubt I'll be able to make many more. Even though there's bound to be a demand for them, it takes a lot to make one."

"Not enough leather?" Rhonda asked.

"Not enough thread, oddly enough," Maness shook his head. "And that don't even get into the rings, rivets, and so forth. Folks don't realize how much stuff goes into a saddle. Not these days, anyway," he shrugged.

"What you askin' for that one?" Billy asked casually. He didn't need it, but this man might be a good trading partner, and possibly someone they might want as a neighbor someday. And it *was* a nice saddle.

"Three ounces of gold," Maness replied. "Know it seems high, but I like as not won't have another. Need to get some tradin' money outta that one." Billy did some not so quick arithmetic in his head.

"What about one ounce of gold, five ounces of silver, an M-16 that needs a good cleaning', with one hundred rounds and three magazines, and a Smith and Wesson .357 revolver. Got about thirty rounds for it, too," he added. Maness blinked at him.

"Well, let me see. . . ." He obviously was thinking about what he could do with the goods, and was it worth the ounce of gold it replaced.

"How about one-and-a-half ounces of gold, instead of one ounce," Maness countered.

"How about one-and-a-quarter ounces, eight ounces of silver, and the guns," Billy came back. Maness again had to figure.

"If you can add another fifty rounds for the rifle, it's a deal," he said finally. Billy seemed to ponder the offer, then extended his hand.

"Deal. I'll be back in a few minutes." Rhonda waited until they were out of earshot to speak.

"Billy, I thought we didn't need a saddle," she said softly.

"We don't, really," he replied. "But it's a nice saddle, and he's a nice guy. I think he'd make a good friend. Today has proved we need friends around here, wouldn't you say?"

"Well, yeah," Rhonda agreed. "And he does seem like a good guy. Wonder if he knows anything about country living?"

"Well, let's not get ahead of ourselves," Billy chuckled. "He may turn out to be a dick, for all we know."

"Billy Todd!" Rhonda almost squealed. "Such language!"

Odd Billy Todd

"What can I say, you're a bad influence on me," Billy laughed as they reached the truck.

"Make you a deal?" Jerry asked, as Billy started gathering.

"I did, and got rid o' this awful rifle," Billy chuckled.

"Was thinkin' on usin' that myself," Jerry said quietly. Billy scoffed.

"You want somethin' like this, I'll get you one when we get home," Billy told him flat out. "Way hell and gone better than this. I promise," he added.

"Okay," Jerry nodded, pleased. "I. . .today made me think that the Garand is good at the house, but maybe I'd be better off to have something. . .else."

"You and Toby can share ammo and mags, and it's lighter, and easier to reload. And you ain't got to grope around to find them en bloc clips, once you're done," Billy agreed.

"Yeah, that can be a hassle."

"We get home, I'll take care of ya," Billy winked. His goods in hand, including the coins already counted out, he and Rhonda went back inside. Maness grinned when he saw them coming.

"You know, I about half-way wondered if you'd come back."

"I make a deal, I stick to it," Billy frowned.

"No offense meant," Maness said easily. "But you'd be surprised at the people who stand and dicker, then tell me they'll be back, and ain't."

"I doubt it," Rhonda laughed. "I've dealt with the same kind o' people."

"I might have been wrong about him being easier to bargain with, too," he winked at Rhonda. She smiled, and glanced nervously at Billy, wondering what he'd think about that wink. Surprisingly, he just smiled.

"Don't fool yourself," he told Maness. "I ain't the sharpest tool in the shed by no means. She's smart."

"Well, I'd hate to have to barter with you if you was *smarter*," Maness laughed. Billy chuckled lightly, handing over the coins.

"Like I said, this thing is in desperate need of a good cleaning," he said, handing over the M-16. "I can't swear to you it's in good shape. Just got it this morning. But I think once it's clean, it'll be fine. If it ain't, I'll make it up to you on the next visit," he promised.

"Wow," Maness said, looking at the rifle. "This looks like the real deal."

"It's a 2-A," Rhonda offered helpfully. "Long on tooth for the military these days. . .well, before, anyway," she added. "But still a good rifle."

"Revolver looks good, too," Maness nodded. Billy handed over the ammo, in a small box he'd taken an alternator out of.

"I kinda feel bad, now," Maness admitted.

"Why?" Billy asked.

"This ammunition is worth a lot of money, here," he told Billy. "Fella over yonder kinda cornered the market, when everything went to hell. Pardon, ma'am," he added to Rhonda.

"I've heard worse," she giggled.

"You've *said* worse," Billy reminded her, and she stuck her tongue out at him.

"Look, Ralph," Billy said. "I'm looking to make friends. And business connections. I've got ammo aplenty right now. Can't say it'll stay that way, but I'm good. And it's worth it to me, anyway, to be in good with you." Maness looked at

Billy closely, and nodded.

"Spoken like a man," he replied seriously. "Ain't too much of that around here, these days, in spite of how bad off folks are getting."

"What's the problem?" Rhonda asked.

"Well, food is getting hard to come by, believe it or not," Maness admitted. "Seems a few folks banded together when things fell apart, and sort of cornered the market on some things. Including livestock, ammunition, and such. It's hard to be able to hunt, even. There ain't much in the way of canned goods left, either, the way I hear it."

"Ain't so bad for me," he admitted. "I was divorced long before the sickness, and we never had any children. But people who have kids are having to really dig to keep food on the table. I tried to tell them to use the summer to gather food, but they seemed to think that the stuff in the stores would last forever. Or at least longer than it did."

"There's a lot of people around here in for a rude awakening. And I'm afraid it won't be long coming, either."

"Do you live here in Franklin?" Billy asked. Maness shook his head.

"No, I live a few miles south of here. I only come in for the trade days."

"Are you set okay?" Rhonda asked.

"Yeah, I'm pretty good," Ralph smiled. "*I took* my advice," he laughed. "I've got enough put by for the winter, and seeds for the next season. I don't have all the heirlooms I'd like, but I'll stay fed."

"Good," Billy nodded. Rhonda handed him a slip of paper.

"This is a radio frequency we monitor," she said quietly, making sure no one could overhear. "If you get in a bind, call us. I can't promise we can help, but if we can, we'll try." Maness took the paper, and hid it away in his wallet.

"I... I really appreciate that," he said slowly. "You two show a lot of trust in someone you just met," he added, looking at them curiously.

"Well, we don't necessarily trust you *yet*," Billy grinned. "But like I said. I want to do business, if I can. And you seem like a straight shooter, as my daddy used to say. I'm willing to take a risk once in a while."

"Me too," Ralph nodded. "I'll be here next month, the weekend before Thanksgiving. After that, it'll depend on the weather, and how hard fuel is to come by."

"We'll try and be here then," Billy promised. "Say, I meant to ask. You make boots?"

"You mean cowboy boots?" Ralph asked, and Billy nodded.

"I can. At least for now. The heels are the hard thing to come by, these days. I'm thinking of starting to make moccasins. They're easier to make, and faster, too."

"If you take our sizes now, you think you can have us a pair each o' moccasins and boots by next time?" Billy asked.

"I don't see why not," Ralph nodded.

"What would the cost be?" Rhonda asked. "We may not have hides, that soon, so figure it like you would for anyone else. If we can bring hides, we'll work something else out."

Ralph quoted a price, which Rhonda readily agreed to, and Ralph quickly and

Odd Billy Todd

expertly took their measurements. As they were getting ready to leave, Billy asked one more thing.

"If you're gonna make moccasins and such, I assume you'd make use of deer hides, when you could get'em?"

"Sure!" Maness nodded excitedly. "They're much better for moccasins, in my opinion."

"I'll see what we can do, then," Billy promised. The two men shook hands.

"We'll see you next time," Rhonda said as they shook as well.

"You folks be careful, hear?" Ralph said as they left. "Man can't afford to lose any friends, these days."

"We'll mind it."

CHAPTER NINETEEN

The trip home was uneventful. Billy took a course that kept them clear of the roadblock, just in case. The way he chose was clear, and the group consensus was that they'd try and use that route next time as well.

Rhonda again looked closely as they drove through Cottonwood. She could still see no sign that anyone was around. That didn't mean there *was* no one, but it was a good indicator. There were plenty of decomposing remains, though. Just as had happened in Cedar Bend, some people had simply died wherever the fever had finally taken its harsh toll. At the end, there was no one to bury them.

They managed to arrive back home before dark, beating the sunset by half-an-hour or so. It was later than Billy had wanted, but considering the day's events, he couldn't complain.

Once they had dropped the Silvers off at their home, Billy and Rhonda headed to theirs. Pulling up into the yard, Billy could hear Rommel woofing at the door. Rhonda hurried up to the door, allowing both dogs to go outside. With a day of pent up energy, they quickly did their business, and then started romping in the yard. Billy took the new saddle to the tack room, while Rhonda unloaded the few items she had traded for.

All in all, Billy was pleased with the trip. They had hit some rough spots, to be sure. But they had made a new friend, or at least laid the foundation for friendship, and made a pretty good business deal for the future. And they had used less than three-quarters of a tank of diesel, which pleased Billy no end. He knew their fuel wouldn't last forever, but he wanted to stretch it as far as possible.

Once they had put everything away, the two sat down to a small meal.

"Billy, I want to go to Cottonwood," Rhonda said as they ate.

"Huh? Why?" Billy asked.

"I want what's in that gun store," Rhonda admitted. "And the fabric place. At least. There's a small hardware store there, too. We might find some of the things Ralph needs there."

"You think it's worth the risk?" Billy asked, after a minute of silent thought.

"I don't know," Rhonda admitted. "I wanted to know what you thought about it."

"Do we need it?" Billy asked directly. Rhonda thought before she answered.

"Not right now, no," she admitted, almost reluctantly. "But I didn't like the things Ralph told us. Wally's is. . .*was*, a pretty good store. He would have had a lot of reloading supplies, as well as ammunition. And guns."

"We got a room full, now," Billy pointed out.

"I know that," Rhonda nodded. "But what we have won't last forever. And no, if we get what's at Wally's it won't last forever, either. But I keep thinking about what Ralph said. Someone is bein' pretty systematic about their gathering. I'd like to be in a position to oppose them moving in our direction. If there's nothin' to take, then maybe they'll go on and go."

Billy thought about that. He hadn't liked what Ralph had to say about things either, but he didn't see how he could change it. If people were willing to live under someone else's rule, in exchange for relative safety, and comfort, then he couldn't do anything about that. In fact, why should he?

One of the main things his parents had hammered home to him was that once you gave up your independence, it was hard to get back. If you let someone get in a position where they controlled your life, then your life, in effect, became theirs. You lived how they wanted, instead of how *you* wanted.

Billy didn't aim to live like anyone else wanted. Well, except Rhonda. He had to start remembering that. He wasn't alone any more, and he had to start thinking on that. Not just when he thought of it, but all the time.

But other than her, Billy aimed to live his life as he seen fit. Period. He didn't look for trouble, and didn't want any. He was a simple man, by choice and by nature. He couldn't change the problems that had caused him to be the way he was. He had worked hard to overcome them, and he was almost certain that he was a lot better, now, than he had been just a few short weeks ago, when he'd found Rhonda Higgins.

As long as other people left him be, then Billy would leave them be. That made him think of people like Big Dirty. And Nate Blaine. And even that one smart mouthed constable at Franklin.

People like that weren't going to leave him be. Someone like Billy, and Rhonda, and the Silvers, were a challenge to the way they thought the world should be now. People like that couldn't have someone challenge them.

Like Big Dirty, Billy thought. *All he had to do was move them trucks, and let me pass. But did he? No. He couldn't let me challenge him. And then he had to look at Rhonda like she was a piece of meat.* Billy felt the blood rush to his ears, and his heartbeat echoing there. Just thinking about it made him angry all over again, and he had already killed the man!

Stop it, stop it! he chided himself. *You can't keep doin' this. It ain't the way you want to live. Calm, calm, calm. You already took care of it.*

But, deep down, Billy knew why it still made him mad. Big Dirty wasn't a one-time thing. There were others, too many others, just like him. Out there, waiting. If he wanted to avoid them, he'd have to just stay on the farm.

And even then, trouble might find them.

Rhonda's right, he told himself finally. *Them same people, or others just like'em, will come eventually, lookin' to keep others from havin' what they need. And if they find us, then they'll try to take from us. And I don't aim to have it.*

"If you want, we'll go," he said finally.

"Are you sure?" Rhonda asked.

"I'm sure," Billy's voice was firm. "I was wrong. We can't just sit here. I seen that today. We have to be part o' the world. We *need* to be. We had fun today. And we deserved it. I don't aim to just sit here, and let people force me to hide, and I sure ain't aimin' to let them tell me how I gotta live."

"So, we'll go."

"Okay," Rhonda nodded. She'd not seen Billy like this. He had obviously worked his way through a problem. But there was no pacing, no circles, no nothing. Was that a good sign? She didn't know, but she was hopeful.

"When do you want to go?" Billy asked.

"Sooner the better, I guess," Rhonda shrugged. "You want to see if Jerry want's in?"

"I'll leave that up to you. He didn't seem to cotton to it, today, though. Whatever you decide, I'll go with. We can go tomorrow, if you want," he surprised her by adding.

"Tomorrow?"

"Day's ain't gettin' any longer. It's up to you. Just tell me a day ahead o' time, so I can get things ready." Rhonda studied him for a minute. She hadn't seen him like this before. She knew that once Billy set his mind to something, that was it. But she'd never seen him make a decision like this. He was completely decisive.

I don't know what he thought of, she pondered to herself, *but whatever it was, it's got him worked up.*

"Tomorrow, then."

-

They were up early, long before dawn. It was cool, but clear, stars still twinkling in the sky. They dressed, ate a simple breakfast, and gathered their gear. Billy laid a crowbar and bolt cutters in the truck, and a bag with enough food, water, and gear to get him and Rhonda home, if something happened to the truck.

Rhonda had decided not to tell Jerry. He had been reluctant to consider it, the day before, and she knew that was not likely to have changed, after the problems they had incurred along the way to the market, and after they'd arrived. She had checked the phone book for businesses in Cottonwood. There was a small hardware store, just as she's suspected. She decided to try and limit their time by focusing solely on what they could make the most use of.

There was a small grocery store as well, and if there was time, they might check it for canned goods, and any long-term foods. Rhonda didn't hold much hope for things like rice and flour. The rats would have long since torn into such things. They didn't need the food themselves, but after hearing how things were in and around Franklin, she couldn't help think of the trade value of a truck full of canned foods.

Both were quiet as the set out. Rommel was in the rear seat. Rhonda had left Dottie in the farm house. She was a good dog, but still young, and her training wasn't nearly as good as Rommel's. She was working on that, but until Dottie was better, she'd have to miss trips like this.

Billy had hooked up their largest trailer, and made sure that the large appliance dolly was on board. He was nervous about the trip, though not hesitant. Once Billy made up his mind, then it was made up. That didn't make him immune to reality, though.

The two of them were going into a town that appeared deserted, but that didn't make it so. There had been no signs of life, but again, that didn't mean there was none.

We'll just have to see once we get there, I guess, Billy shook off his worries, and concentrated on his driving. Using the route they had taken before, he figured it should be no more than twenty minutes, half-an-hour at most, until they were in Cottonwood.

-

Billy stopped the truck on the small rise that overlooked Cottonwood. Rhonda, and then Billy, used a strong set of binoculars to scan the streets visible from the hillside, looking for anything that would be a reason to turn back. Neither saw anything. Finally, Billy looked at Rhonda.

"Ready?"

"Yeah," Rhonda nodded. She was scared, but determined. This was far riskier than what they had done in Cedar Bend. But it needed doing.

"We'll pull behind the building," Billy told her. "We should be able to access both stores from the back. Once we're done, we'll decide whether to press on to the hardware place. That okay?"

"Sounds workable," Rhonda agreed. "Let's get this done. I want to get it over with, and go home." She was tired. Both of them were. They'd worked almost non-stop for four weeks or a little better. Yesterday had been the first day they'd really taken 'off', but after the stresses of what all had happened, they might as well have worked double time.

Billy put the truck back in gear, and gently goosed it into motion, rolling slowly, and he hoped quietly, into yet another ghost town.

-

The crowbar made short work of the rear entrance to Wally's. Billy had expected it to be harder, but Wally had apparently depended on his alarm to keep thieves away. The alarm wasn't working anymore.

The store was small, but packed to the gills. Wally had less in the way of outdoor clothing and equipment than Rhonda's father had had in his store, but made up for it with other items. Most notable, at least for Rhonda, were cases and cases of powder and primers for her reloading.

To say she was pleased would have been an understatement. Billy got the dolly, and the two of them worked in tandem, Rhonda readying each stack of boxes, crates or cartons, and Billy hauling them outside, and up the ramp into the trailer. Rommel say by the back door, as ordered, watching their surroundings carefully. Billy was glad to have him along.

It took what seemed to Billy an inordinately long time to load the ammunition stocks. When he mentioned it, Rhonda had nodded.

"He must have just stocked up when the Plague hit," she whispered. Billy almost laughed at her attempt to be quiet. They had made enough noise coming into town to wake the dead. But he realized it was helping to remind her, and him, to use caution.

Finally, they had everything except the guns, and their accessories. Rhonda wasted no time in looking for boxes, instead just placing as many as possible into the shooting bags, storage crates and rifle cases that Wally had for sale. She worked far quicker than Billy could load, so once everything was packed, she started helping him load.

When the last load finally went on board, she was pleased to see that the trailer still had about a third of it's length available. The goods already aboard were stacked about three-fourths of the way to the top, leaving room on top for the fabric, or any other items that were small enough to fit.

Since the fabric store was next door, there was no need to move the truck. Billy simply forced the door, and the two entered. Rhonda 'oohed' and 'ahhed' so many times that Billy became frustrated.

"Reckon we can do all that at home?" he asked, but grinned as he said it.

"Sure," Rhonda smiled slightly, embarrassed. "Just. . . sure." She started hauling the bolts of cloth to the trailer, Billy following.

It took far less time to empty the fabric shop than it had the gun store, but Billy was shocked to see that it was close to eleven a.m.

Where did the morning get to? He wondered.

"I think we're ready for the hardware store," Rhonda whispered.

"Are you sure we need it?" Billy asked. "We won't be able to carry much, and its already nearly noon."

"We'll just check for things that Ralph needs, or things that jump out at us as needful at home," Rhonda assured him. "And maybe check the grocery store for canned goods," she added, looking away from Billy as she spoke.

"You didn't mention no grocery store to me earlier!" Billy almost hissed. Rhonda flinched, but held her ground.

"I just thought about it this mornin'," she told him. "I figured we might take it to the next trade day. Or, we could give it to the Silvers if they had need. Or stock the Franklin house if we find someone to live in it. Or. . . ." Billy held up a hand for her to stop. She could see he was. . .well, pissed probably wasn't too strong a word.

"We do that, and I mean that's *it*," Billy said forcefully. "This ain't Cedar Bend. We ain't got no real clue is anyone about or not. This is it. Get me?" Rhonda nodded, knowing he was right. Exasperated, Billy climbed into the truck after opening the door for Rommel to leap inside. Rhonda climbed into the passenger side, painfully aware that Billy wasn't looking at her.

He was right to be angry, Rhonda figured. She was pushing their luck, and his patience. She just had the feeling that they should get everything they could, while they could.

Billy followed her instructions to the hardware store, where they quickly went through the inventory. There wasn't much, but Rhonda did find what she'd hope to find. Rivets, rings, and the tools to use them. Items on Ralph's want list. Even better, this was horse country, even more so than Cedar Bend. On a small shelf in the back of the store she found five priceless rolls of leather thread, and numerous rolls of leather cordage and pigging strips. Everything was loaded hurriedly into the truck.

Billy paused long enough to grab the knife display, then thought better of it, and checked under the counter. The inventory was all in boxes, in a neat row. He swept everything off into a bag, then grabbed the display again, heading for the truck. Rhonda nodded in approval. Knives would be good trading material. If not now, then in the future.

Billy still hadn't spoken, and Rhonda didn't try to force conversation on him. She still felt guilty about springing the grocery stop on him. As they got into the truck, Billy spoke for the first time in several minutes.

"Where's this grocery at?" he demanded. His tone of voice brought a wince.

"We don't have to go, Billy. . . ." she started.

"Where is it?" Billy grated. Rhonda gave him the directions. Billy drove there in silence, parking behind the store. The two got out, Billy telling Rommel to 'stay', and 'guard'. The big dog wagged his tail stub in agreement, and sat down near the truck.

N.C. Reed

Billy and Rhonda entered the store, and Rhonda started to do inventory. Since it was a small store, there wasn't a great deal of inventory, but there were some things she desperately needed. Canning ingredients, salt, sugar, and other baking needs were unmolested, rats not having made it into the store. She hastily started pointing out items she wanted, and Billy started hauling them.

It took almost as long as the gun store had, not least because Billy had to work to find room for everything. Finally, though, they had everything Rhonda wanted. She had even loaded three cases of Billy's favorite; Coca Cola. It was a peace offering, and Billy recognized it as such, grinning at her, and shaking his head. She returned the grin, and wrapped him in a hug, which Billy was glad to return.

They were about to mount up for the trip home, when Rommel stirred suddenly, growling deep in his massive chest. Billy froze, his head tilted to the side, straining to hear.

"Listen!" he hissed when Rhonda tried to ask what he heard.

"Hear that?" he asked. Rhonda tried, but couldn't hear anything. Billy suddenly dropped to his hands and knees, and placed his ear to the ground.

He looked up suddenly, shock evident on his face.

"It's a train!"

CHAPTER TWENTY

Billy grabbed his rifle and went back inside. From the front windows of the store, you could see a section of the track. Rhonda followed him, along with Rommel. She was afraid to leave the dog outside on his own.

Billy watched in silence until the train engine came into view. He noted it was a diesel electric, and also that two more followed. The cars started coming into view, and the first one was a flatbed carrying a tank! The next two were Bradley Fighting Vehicles. The train began to slow, and people appeared. Some were in uniform, but others were not.

As the train slowed to a stop, a boxcar just coming into view opened its doors, and a ramp fell down. Billy could see dirt bikes going down the ramp, and could see others going out the other side as well.

Men and women began to appear, all armed, and pulling game carts or other wheeled baskets. One was pushing a large wheel barrel. Something about the scene struck a chord in Billy's mind, but he couldn't quite put his finger on it. His frustration didn't prevent him from making a decision, though.

"We need to get outside," he told Rhonda, going back through the store. "We need to be able to see and hear. I don't like this."

"But if it's the Army, wouldn't that be a good thing?" Rhonda asked, confused.

"I don't think that's the Army," Billy shook his head. "Not no more. Some of'em probably used to be, but if they were still Army, they'd all be in uniform. They ain't. This ain't. . .somethin' 'bout this ain't right."

He couldn't quite put his finger on it, but something wasn't right. There was something nagging at the back of his brain, something he just couldn't quite put his finger on, but he knew it was there.

Once they were outside, Billy made a quick decision.

"They'll scout the town," he told Rhonda. "They're. . .*locusts*!" he cut himself off as the nagging thought finally took shape. "They're using the train, moving like locusts! They strip everything they can near the tracks, and then move on!" He looked at her.

"They won't be happy with us, either," he told her flatly. "We need to get moving." Rhonda nodded dumbly, her mind not able to keep up with Billy's thinking. But she trusted him. Even if he couldn't make her see it, she knew that *he* knew something she couldn't see. That was enough.

Billy jumped into the truck, and started it, while Rhonda let Rommel in, then got in beside Billy.

"We need the noise of the train to cover the sound of the truck," he explained quickly. "We need a way out of town, too. One where they hopefully don't see us."

"We can go that way," Rhonda pointed to a side street. "Go down a block or two, then start movin' away from town. Billy, they're blocking' the tracks! We can't get home!"

"Yes, we can," Billy told her. "There's more than one way back, Rhonda. There's a map in that glove box. Get it out, and open to where we are, while I get us out of here." Billy backed the truck around expertly, then headed down the street

Rhonda had pointed out.

Billy had the front windows down, so he could hear. He eased the truck along, despite the desire to go tearing off in the opposite direction of the train. He needed to keep the noise down until they were well away.

There was no apparent reason for his fear, yet he couldn't escape the feeling that he needed to be afraid. Something was just wrong about it.

I wish I could figure out what it was that made me think that, he thought as he guided the truck down the street. A few cars were in the street here and there, but he was able to get around them.

The problem was that he couldn't find a way back to the other side of town. Every little side street was marked as a dead end.

What kinda town ain't got nothin' but dead ends? he thought furiously. Then, suddenly, he could see why. The side streets all ended at a chain link fence that bordered the Cottonwood High School.

As he was muttering, he became conscious of a buzzing sound, similar to a chainsaw, but stronger. He looked into his mirror, and saw two dirt bikes screaming down the street behind them.

"We got company," he told Rhonda, his voice far more calm than he felt. Rhonda looked in the mirror on her side, and could see one of the bikes.

"What do we do?" she asked, scared but still in control.

"We run," Billy replied, tromping on the gas. The big truck shot forward. The acceleration wasn't as good as his own truck, but the big diesel had power to spare, and would run as long as there was fuel. As the truck picked up speed, Billy could hear gunfire behind them.

"They're shooting!" Rhonda exclaimed.

"Really?" Billy shot back, trying to concentrate on the road. "I thought it was just a really hard rain."

"Smart ass," Rhonda muttered, bringing her rifle up to her own window. "With the trailer behind us, I can't get a shot."

"Don't worry about it," Billy told her. "Just get down, a little." Rhonda was about to object when she saw Billy had a grenade in his hand. He also had a small glass jar that he pulled from under the seat.

"Tape the grenade to this," he ordered, showing her a roll of electrical tape. "Make sure the tape goes under the spoon."

"Teach your grandmother," Rhonda muttered again, working fast.

"What's in the jar?" she asked, as she worked.

"Surprise," Billy grunted, as he fought the wheel around, narrowly missing a car that sat sideways in the street. The truck and trailer were bouncing around pretty good, but he couldn't slow down. He'd just have to hope they'd packed well. He could hear firing again, as the motor bikes gained ground, always being careful not to get too close. Billy realized they were shooting at the tires.

They want the trailer, and maybe the truck, he realized. And *maybe her, too,* he thought, glancing at Rhonda. *That ain't gonna happen.*

"You 'bout done over there?" he asked, whipping the wheel to the side as one of the biker's tried another shot. Billy could see tufts of pavement flying up where the shots hit. That would have been close.

Billy counted over and over, gauging the distance between him, and the bikers.

Odd Billy Todd

He only had once chance at this, and it had to be right. Too late, and the bikers would speed by what he had in mind. Too slow and...well, he didn't need to be slow.

"Ready!" Rhonda told him, holding out the jar. Billy took it, transferring it to his left hand.

"Reach over here, and when I say, yank the pin out."

"What!" Rhonda almost screamed.

"Hey! I can teach, or I can do. Your call!" Billy retorted. They wouldn't even be in this mess if not for that stupid grocery store. He didn't say that, but then he didn't have to. He could see in her eyes she was thinking the same thing.

"Okay," she nodded, almost breathless. Billy started counting again, and had to swerve sharply once more to avoid a truck in the road. This also happened to throw the aim off from the second biker, who had been lining up for a shot.

"Now," he said calmly, and Rhonda pulled the pin. Billy started counting.

"Throw it for God's sake!" Rhonda shouted. Billy ignored her, and kept counting. Suddenly he heaved the jar, with the grenade attached, out the window, throwing it as high as he could manage, and angling the throw a little to the rear. As soon as he released it, he floored the truck.

"Might want to get down," Billy told her calmly. Before she could react, there was a huge explosion behind them. She could see the flash in the mirror.

What she couldn't see was the fireball that blossomed when the grenade went off, igniting the mixture of gasoline and gelatin inside the jar. The jellied gasoline went everywhere, clinging to anything it touched.

Including the bikers.

Rhonda couldn't hear the screams of the most unfortunate of the two, who burned alive as the concoction immolated him. The lucky one was killed out-right by the grenade blast.

Billy never slowed down.

Thanks, dad.

—

"They just started shooting at us for no reason!" Rhonda exclaimed. She was over her fear now, and was just mad. And maybe still a little chagrined that it was her desire to loot the grocery that had led them to be there when the train had cut them off from home.

"Well, no matter how nice you phrase it, we are looters," Billy shrugged. "Even if the former owner is dead, I think it's still looting."

"But they just assumed. . . ." Rhonda retorted.

"Look, I told you that something' wasn't right about them," Billy shrugged. "They were lookin' to do the same thing we just did this morning. Which means we need to watch real close when towns have a set of tracks going through them. We might run up on that bunch, or another like'em, again.

"I hope not," Rhonda said.

They were on their way home, by a round about route that wouldn't require them to go back through Cottonwood. It wasn't far out of the way, and much safer than trying to wait, hoping the train moved on.

"Think they'll be mad about them two?" Rhonda asked. Billy shrugged.

"Imagine they'll be madder 'bout them bikes, than they are about the men,"

115

he told her. "Kind o' people like that, they'll figure them two was stupid to get killed."

"You seem to know a lot about this, Billy," Rhonda said evenly.

"I been readin' my daddy's books," Billy shrugged. "Where I learned that trick with the jar. 'Sposed to be a road flare, but I figured since I had that grenade, it'd work too."

"I'll say it did," Rhonda nodded. "We probably ought to think about diggin' out some o' them autos we found at the tradin' post," she added.

"We'll see," Billy nodded. "But this kind o' thing, we ain't doing' it again. At least not where they got train tracks going' through town," he added. Rhonda nodded, knowing that was as close as Billy would get to blaming her for what had happened.

"Where's the nearest track to us?" Rhonda asked. "I know there's not one in Cedar Bend."

"There's an old spur line up on the north part of the county," Billy told her. "They built it for the car parts plant, so they could ship to the car factory by rail. As far as I know, that's the only one. We ain't too near the river, so we shouldn't have trouble with 'pirates' either."

"I hadn't thought about that."

"Well, the river ain't really navigable, so I doubt we have much trouble anyway," he chuckled. "But the Tennessee is, and so is the Cumberland. I'd imagine there's boats out there right now, with people who took to 'em tryin' to avoid the sickness."

"You know," Rhonda mused, "I had thought we had it pretty bad, here. But when I think about the stuff you talked about, we got it pretty good, don't we?"

"We do," Billy nodded. "We're not near a major highway, and most thugs and thieves won't 'waste' the time to check little back roads like ours. Course, them that do are likely to be more organized. Smarter."

"Well, the house is pretty well concealed," Rhonda pointed out.

"Yep," was all Billy said. "But like I said yesterday, we can't just sit there. Well, we *can*," he amended, "but if we do, what's the point? Before we met up, I was content to just sit on the farm. And I would have kept sittin' there after emptying your pa's place, and the trading post," he admitted. "I wouldn't have gathered all that stuff you suggested we get."

"I might have gone to that trade day once in a while, with Jerry and his family, but that would have been about it. After we went yesterday, though," he continued, still keeping his eyes on the unfamiliar road, "I don't want to do that no more. We had a good time. It was nice to be around folks again, even though we had to deal with that roadblock, and that Blaine guy. Bein' able to go and do stuff like that gives us something' to look forward to."

"I kinda like that," he finished, looking at Rhonda and smiling.

"I did too," she admitted. "And I'm sorry I got us into this mess, today," she went on, wanting to apologize, even though she knew, deep down, that it wasn't necessary. "I. . .I just didn't think about something like that happening, Billy. I'm sorry," she repeated. He shrugged.

"I. . .It wasn't a bad idea," he admitted. "But we should o' planned for it. One thing I know, is that *we always* need a plan, and we need to *stick to it*. Makin' changes on the fly just ain't a good way to do business." He was falling back on the way he'd ran his garage with that statement, but he saw nothing wrong with that. His business had been successful as long as he kept to his plans. So had his life after the plague.

"You're right," she nodded. "I tried to do today by the seat of my pants. We won't do anything like that again."

"Nothin' wrong with the seat o' your pants," he snickered, and she punched him lightly on the shoulder, blushing.

"Pervert," she teased, and he shrugged.

"From now on, if, and I do mean *if*, we do anything like that, we make a plan, we stick to it," Billy said. "We'll take a day and watch the place, and if there's people about, or signs of people about, then we move on. Today was okay, really. There was no way for us to know about something' like that train."

'That train' was still nagging at Billy, though, and he didn't know why. There was something important about it, he decided, but he just couldn't figure it out.

"That train bothers me," he shared his worry with Rhonda. She needed to know, he reasoned. One, she could help him figure it out maybe. Two, she just deserved to know. They couldn't keep things from each other if they wanted to make it, both as a couple, and as a team.

"Well, I can see why," Rhonda admitted. "I mean, they had at least one tank, and a couple of AFV's. I'd say they got more than that, too, that we didn't see."

"Did you see the way they came off that train?" Billy noted. "That wasn't the first time, or even the second or third that they've done something like that. They got a plan."

"And a pretty good one, it looked like," Rhonda nodded in agreement. "I'd say whoever is in charge is pretty smart, and spent a little bit of time working on that idea."

"It ain't a bad notion," Billy shrugged. "I hate to say it, but it ain't. Stay mobile, well protected, and just take everything you can find along the tracks. The main question is, to me, are they heading somewhere, and just strippin' all they can as they go? Or are they making a livin' at stripping towns along the tracks. If it's the second, then they're probably changing tracks along the line. Which means they'll be moving all over the country."

"That could lead them to Franklin," Rhonda said softly. "There's a lot of people in Franklin."

"Lot of goods, too," Billy agreed. "We need to tell Jerry about this. He can maybe warn that guy he talks to over there, and he can warn the others."

"We could call Ralph," Rhonda offered. Billy thought about that.

"Probably a good idea," he nodded after a minute. "We owe him that, anyway. I don't know if he's near any tracks, but if he is, he'll want to look like he ain't got nothin'."

They spent the rest of the trip home discussing their options, and formulating a plan for future salvaging runs.

-

"A train?" Jerry asked, surprise evident in his face.

"Yep," Billy nodded. The two men were at the hog pen, looking over their project, and eyeing what trees they might cut to enlarge the pen area.

"And they had a tank, of all things?"

"Yeah, at least one, and a couple of those Bradley's, too," Billy nodded again. "And they were well prepared. They swept off that train with dirt bikes, and people swarmin' through town pullin' game carts and such. They'd done it before."

"You said they chased you?"

"Two of them did," Billy confirmed. "But they're gone. No one else was around. We took another way home, and sat and watched a couple times, just to make sure no one was following. I don't think they would have, anyway. I think, from lookin' at them, they're just takin' what they can find along the tracks."

"What were you two doin' there, anyway?" Jerry demanded. Billy looked at the older man, face set.

"Lookin' around," he said evenly. "Lookin' for things we could use. That sort o' thing."

"You hadn't oughta be doin' that!" Jerry exclaimed. "At least not without lettin' me know!"

"How you figure that?" Billy asked calmly, looking Jerry right in the eye.

"Billy, if someone follows you, they'll find *us*!"

"*If* they do," Billy nodded. "Believe it or not, I figured that out on my own," he added. Billy didn't like Jerry's attitude. No sir, he didn't.

"I made plans to keep that from happening," Billy told him. "Not just for you, but for us too. I don't want *nobody* knowin' where we are, Jerry. Period. There's safety in stayin' hidden, and unknown."

"But that don't mean we can just sit here, neither. We can't just sit here, hidden, and let the world pass us by. Just like goin' to Franklin. Everything is a calculated risk. We want stuff to trade, we have to sometimes go out and get it. Did you know that every trader up there has a list they hand out? Of things they need, and are willing to barter for?"

"No. No, I didn't," Jerry admitted, his stance softening some.

"Well, they do. And we ain't just doing all this for the two of us, Jerry," Billy added, trying to keep his voice more friendly. "We're thinkin' o' ya'll, too. Like yesterday, in Cottonwood, Rhonda went to the fabric place, and got Emma a whole bolt of fleece material." Jerry didn't know what to say.

"I. . .Billy that was. . .that was mighty thoughtful," he stammered. "But you hadn't ought to take such risks. Not for that."

"I thought that way, too, at first," Billy admitted. "But, there's things out there, ain't bein' made no more, Jerry. Things we need, or things we can trade for other things we need. Way I see it, we got two choices. We can sit here, and let people like them on that train, or at the roadblock, or that Blaine character get everything, and have us at their mercy, or we can get up and go get our share."

"Ralph told us that several people in Franklin had cornered the market early on, there, scooping up everything of value and basically selling it or trading it for anything they wanted. Some people havin' it hard to just keep food on the table. Ammunition is scarce, and higher'n a cat's back, cause that one guy has got almost everything took up. And he charge's all he can, and a bit more, for every round he sells, or reloads."

"I don't aim for us, and that includes you and yours, to be in that shape. Not if I can help it." Jerry studied him for a while, then looked away, lost in his own thoughts about what Billy had just shared. Billy gave him time, knowing he'd have to work through it the same as he had.

Finally, Jerry nodded at some unspoken idea. He turned back to Billy.

"You're right," he said simply. ". . .I reckon I been livin' in a dream world. Things are bad, Billy, and like to get a lot worse before they get better. If they ever get better. You're right. We gotta look after ourselves, prepare ourselves. What can we do to help?" It was Billy's turn to be surprised.

"Help?"

"Yeah, me and Toby. We can go with you on these trips, at least some of them. With us helping, things might go faster."

That was true, Billy thought. *But then Jerry and Toby know what we get. And they'd get a share, as well. How do we divide things? We can split everything even, that's how,* he answered his own question.

"That's probably a good idea," Billy mused out loud. "We can split what we find down the middle, like. We each get trade goods, and useful things of our own, and the work goes faster. And," he added, "with more of us, someone can stand guard." Jerry nodded.

"I like it," he agreed. "Any idea when you'll go again?"

"No, have to find a place, first," Billy admitted. "We ain't really done this, but once," he lied slightly. "Have to learn as we go. But we avoid places with train tracks," he laughed lightly.

"Yeah, I can see where that'd be good," Jerry chuckled.

"You know," the older man mused aloud, "we really oughta think about some security here. Maybe we can find some cameras, and the like. Even some microphones. Have them where we can turn them on and off at random."

"We should have enough solar power to do that," Billy nodded. "Might even find some o' those smaller sets that are self contained. Could power the stuff independent like, from nearby."

"Yeah!" Jerry nodded. "You know what, let me work on that for a day or so. We may can find what we need somewhere. Like a Radio Shack or something."

"Okay," Billy readily agreed. "I best be gettin' back, I reckon. But I thought you might want to warn your friend in Franklin about the train. There's several tracks in and out of there."

"You really think they'd hit somewhere that big?" Jerry asked.

"They got a tank," Billy shrugged. "I expect they figure they can hit anywhere they take a notion."

CHAPTER TWENTY-ONE

"What'cha doin'?"

Billy looked up from his work bench to see Rhonda watching him from the doorway. He was in his father's small work shop. In front of him was a 'pile o' stuff' that he was working on, trying to figure out what should go into the cache's they'd planned. He wanted to put some of them out on their way back to Franklin.

"Workin' on the cache tubes," he told her. "Wanna make sure that each one has everything we might need, was we to get in trouble."

"Cool," Rhonda nodded, walking over and taking the stool next to him. "What you got so far?"

"Well, I got a map, compass, fire-starter, and tender. A machete, two knives, belts, and small day packs. Got four Mountain House pouches, with two GI mess kits. Two water bottles with filters, and purification tablets. Belt pouches. Tarp, line, and a few stakes. Hatchet. Two ponchos. Two of those emergency blankets, and two real ones."

"I need a suit o' clothes for each of us, a handgun and a long gun, and the ammunition. Maybe a pair o' boots. I wish I had told Ralph to make us a half dozen pair o' them moccasins. They'd be ideal for this."

"We can call him on the radio," Rhonda shrugged. "He already knows our sizes. See if he can make a few more pairs. We got another two weeks, almost." They hadn't been away from the farm since Cottonwood, almost two weeks ago. The two had needed rest, and there was a lot of work to do around the farm. The only time they'd come close to leaving was to walk over to the Silvers', twice, for supper. They had entertained the Silvers once as well. Their turn was up again in a few days.

"That's a good idea," Billy looked thoughtful. "That would make this a lot easier."

"Want me to call him?" Rhonda asked, eager to help.

"Yeah, go ahead," Billy nodded absently. Rhonda studied him a minute.

"Billy are we okay? You and me, I mean?" she asked tentatively.

"Huh?" Billy shook of his thoughts and looked at her. "What do you mean?"

"Well, I know you were mad about Cottonwood," Rhonda said softly, looking at the floor. "And you really ain't had a lot to say to me, last few days. And we ain't. . .well, *ain't*. . .you know. I was just wondering' if you was still mad at me?" She looked at him with lidded eyes.

"No!" Billy exclaimed. "I ain't mad at you. I told you right then that it wasn't a bad idea, we just needed to plan better. And I didn't know I hadn't said much to you, neither," he admitted. Now it was his turn to look at the floor.

"I just sometimes don't think to say nothin', even was there somethin' to say," he told her honestly. "That don't mean nothin', though. Just how I am, I guess. And," he reminded her, "I been hustlin' pretty good around here, ya know. Be winter soon. Work ain't done 'fore snow flies, have to wait for spring, or at least a thaw."

"And so far as the. . .the. . .well, the *ain't*, uh. . .thing, well, I just. . .I mean, that is. . .see, I figured if you wanted to, uh. . ..." He finally trailed off, as Rhonda smiled, trying vainly to suppress a giggle.

"Billy Todd, you have *got* to get over that shyness!" she told him, throwing her arms around his neck, and kissing him soundly.

"See, the way this works," she told him sagely, "is that I tell you when I *don't* want to."

"And how would you be doin' that?" Billy asked, grinning. "I mean, just so I know. You know, for reference and all."

"Well, I might say I have a headache," Rhonda batted her eyes coyly. "Or I could just ignore you. Or give you *The Look*."

"Which look is that, exactly?" Billy frowned. "You got a few looks, you know. Sometimes I have a hard time tellin'em apart."

"See, we were havin' a moment, and you had to go and ruin it," Rhonda sighed theatrically.

"I did?" Billy's eyebrows rose. "All I was doin' was gatherin' information."

"See, you don't *gather* information by *asking*' me," Rhonda poked him in the chest. "You learn it the hard way."

"I don't see the attraction in that," Billy frowned.

"But *I* do," Rhonda informed him, tossing her hair. "So figure this out, Billy Todd." With that she turned and walked away, making sure that her hips caught his eye.

"Okay, that one was easy," Billy murmured. He hurriedly shut off the light, closing the door on his way out, following Rhonda to the house.

I might get the hang o' this yet.

-

"So, you're aimin' to go back to Franklin?" Emma asked. The Silvers had come over for dinner the following night. Rhonda had cooked a beef roast, with potatoes, carrots, and cornbread. She had also made a gravy with the leavings from the roast. Desert was apple pie, and there was tea and lemonade.

"Yeah," Rhonda nodded. "We got us some stuff to pick up, and a little bit to deliver. Made a trade with that leather worker for some moccasins." Ralph had assured her that making the extra moccasins wouldn't be a problem, and he'd have them ready on trade day.

"Ya'll wanna go with us?" Billy asked, dodging an elbow from Rhonda for 'talking with his mouth full'.

"I don't know," Jerry hedged. "That last trip was kinda an eye-opener, if ya know what I mean. Lot o' trouble just to go to a trade day."

"Jerry, if we want to keep being part of the world, we have to get out in it," Emma reminded him.

"I'd sure like to go," Toby put forth, and his sister agreed.

"Me too," Shelly nodded. "I know it ain't much, compared to what used to be, but it's nice to be around other people some. Even if you don't know them," she shrugged.

Jerry looked torn, but finally nodded.

"All right," he said. "We'll give it another try. Emmaline is right. We can't just sit here. We'll go stir crazy eventually."

"I figure now that we know the route, we can leave a little earlier," Billy told them. "There may be new problems since we went last, but we'll have to deal with them anyhow. We leave early, we can maybe get back early. Day's are gettin' shorter all the time."

"Good idea," Jerry looked relieved at the notion. "That's the biggest worry I have, anyway, is bein' out after dark. Can't see nothin', and we know, for sure, there's people out there ain't nice to be around."

"Then I reckon it's a date," Rhonda smiled, getting to her feet. "Who wants pie?"

-

Billy spent the next three days preparing the cache tubes. They were ready, all but the moccasins. They had selected inexpensive but reliable arms for the tubes, and placed ammunition, magazines, and cleaning kits in each tube.

There was a first aid kit, featuring a small selection of OTC meds for several different problems, and one gallon of distilled water.

"Why distilled?" Rhonda asked, when Billy had waved away the bottled 'filtered' water.

"Distilled water is boiled," he told her. "Heat kills any germs, helps prevent any bacteria growth. It'll keep longer."

They had selected clothes for each one. Not knowing what the weather would be if or when they had need, they had chosen carefully. Jeans, long handles, long sleeved shirts and t-shirts, two pairs of socks, and clean underwear.

There were also hygiene supplies for each, along with body powder, and ointments.

"I can't believe we got all that in there," Rhonda shook her head.

"Well, it's packed careful," Billy nodded. "Still, it's a tight fit, with the other stuff. There's room for the moccasins, but that's about it."

"We gonna take'em along this time?" Rhonda asked.

"Don't think so," Billy shook his head after a minute. "We'll make a trip later on. We'll need to use the hand auger to bury these things. It makes noise, and it's time consuming. Plus, we want to study real careful where we leave these things. Want to make sure there's one handy, no matter where we happen to be."

"Makes sense," Rhonda nodded. "Might want to put a few coins in there," she added. "Junk silver, anyway. If we're hard up, a little money might make things go easier if we needed help." Billy thought that over, and agreed.

"Good idea. We can add that before we start settin'em out. I'm gonna go ahead and close'em up, but not seal'em. We can leave'em out here until we're ready. I oiled the guns good with collector oil, so they'll be fine. I wrapped'em in plastic, too. Should protect them from anything that happens to get inside. In fact, everything is in plastic or zipper bags. Just in case."

"Well, I think you covered it all," Rhonda smiled.

"*We* covered it all," Billy corrected. "You had as much input as I did. And some o' your ideas were better, too."

"Ah," Rhonda waved the compliment away. "Point is, I think they're good. It's still early on. Want to go ridin'?"

"Sure," Billy nodded. "Need to check on the herd at the Franklin place anyway. And ride the fences. I'd say we got time for that," he decided, studying the sky.

"Billy, do you even own a watch?" Rhonda asked in amusement.

"Sure," he nodded. "Why?"

"I never seen you use it," she pointed out.

"Oh. Well, I never need it," he shrugged.

"Then how do you know what time it is?" she demanded.

"Well, I look at the sky," Billy replied. "See how much day there is left."

"And you just know," Rhonda almost challenged.

"Well, yeah," Billy looked confused. "Don't everbody?"

"No, my wonderfully capable man, they do not," Rhonda hugged him. "They do not. C'mon, let's saddle up."

-

They rode their own fence lines before heading up the ridge to the Franklin farm. The fences were fine, and Billy was pleased with his own small herd. The cattle looked healthy, and were fattened good against the coming winter.

"Be ready for calves come spring, I guess," he noted absently.

"Well, least we'll have beef," Rhonda grinned.

"We got plenty o' beef on the hoof," Billy corrected. "Problem we'll have is slaughtering. I need to talk to Jerry. We'll have to kill any we want to put up while it's cold. That's gonna suck, too."

"How come?" Rhonda asked.

"We ain't got no cold room to slaughter in," Billy replied. "Butcher's use a cold room to hold beef and hogs they've slaughtered in while they work the meat up. We ain't set up here to slaughter, and I'm fair certain Jerry ain't neither. So, we'll have to do it while it's cool."

"Huh," Rhonda grunted. She was learning something new everyday it seemed.

They headed up the ridge, taking it slow. Rommel and Dottie were in the lead, though Dottie was staying closer to them. Rommel strayed out far ahead, sniffing cautiously. Billy was more grateful than ever that he'd found the big dog. He was more than a pet. He'd become a friend.

Billy drew his horse up short. Rommel had reached the top of the ridge, and stopped, stiff legged. Billy was certain he could hear the large Rottie growling.

"Hold up," he ordered Rhonda. She reined in her horse beside him.

"What's wrong?" she asked quietly.

"Rommel see's something he don't like," Billy replied. Handing her the reins of his own horse, he stepped down, taking his rifle from the scabbard.

"Wait here, and keep a look out," he told her. "Somethin' happens, you high tail it for Jerry's and get him and Toby."

"You don't know what's up there!" Rhonda hissed.

"And there ain't but one way to find out," he nodded. "I'll be back." With that he started making his way stealthily up to the crest of the hill where Rommel still stood. He reached a spot by Rommel's side, and softly patted the dogs side.

"What'cha got, boy?"

Rommel looked at him for a second, then turned his eyes back to whatever he had seen. Billy took a small but powerful pair of binoculars from a pouch on his belt, and held them to his eyes.

"Damn," Billy swore softly. He could see all too well, now, what had Rommel stirred up.

Below them, in a corner of the pasture they were using, a pack of feral dogs, at least seven of them, had manage to cut a cow and calf away from the herd. Had this been Billy's own herd, the jacks would have long since stomped the dogs to death in all likelihood. But they didn't have any here, yet.

Turning, he waved Rhonda up to him. Aware that Rommel was quivering with the desire to run down and rip into the dogs, he ordered the dog to stay, thankful now for all the time he'd spent training his wonderful companion. That made him think of Dottie. He turned back to Rhonda, and signaled for her to stop. He hurried down to her.

"Send Dottie home," he ordered.

"What? Why?" she demanded.

"Wild dogs, down below," Billy said hurriedly. "Rommel won't attack unless I let him. She ain't so well trained yet. There's too many. She won't stand a chance. Send her home, and bring your rifle."

Realizing the wisdom in his orders, Rhonda pointed Dottie toward the farm. The female slunk away, head down, thinking she was being punished. Rhonda hated for her to think that, but promised herself she'd make it up later. Grabbing her own rifle, she headed up the ridge, where Billy had already taken up a prone position. He was using his Remington 700. She had one as well, but in the .243 caliber, easier for her to use with her small stature.

"The big Husky, I think, is the pack leader," Billy whispered. "I'll take him. You get that Doberman. See him? The red one?" Rhonda looked down the hill through her scope, and nodded.

"Got him."

"On three then. Get set," Billy told her. He nestled his rifle to his shoulder, and drew a bead on the Husky. It was too bad, he thought. The dog was beautiful. But wild dogs would kill cattle, and even people. It had to go.

"Ready," Rhonda breathed.

"One. Two. *Three!*" Billy pulled the trigger even as he spoke.

Both rifles spoke in near unison. The Husky fell dead, shot through and through in the heart. The Doberman yelped, and fell to his haunches. Rhonda worked the bolt quickly, and shot again, just behind Billy. This time the Doberman stayed down, while another dog, this one a shepherd mix of some kind, fell dying, shot through the front quarter.

The other dogs hesitated for just a second, and Billy dropped another, this one looked like a pit bull, but from that distance he wasn't sure. Rhonda winged another pit bull type, catching him in mid jump, the bullet taking him in the hindquarter.

With four down, and another hurt, the remaining two healthy dogs fled, the wounded pit bull trying to follow.

"Finish him!" Billy ordered, trying to get a shot at the other two. Rhonda watched the injured dog through her scope, almost crying when she saw the dog struggling to follow its fellows. As she watched, a red mist exploded from it's side, and the dog fell flat, no longer moving. She looked up, startled, to see Billy standing, his rifle at his shoulder.

He said nothing, opening the bolt to reload the rifle. Rhonda followed suit, unwilling to face Billy for the moment.

"Don't worry over it," he said gently. "It's hard to do, I know. You did good."

"Wasn't hard for you," Rhonda's voice was almost accusing. He shrugged.

"Had to be done," he said simply. "Sooner or later, they'd have attacked one of us. And they'd have killed a lot of cows 'fore then."

"Maybe we could have caught them," Rhonda said softly. "Re-trained them." Billy shook his head.

"Once a dog goes feral, it's hard to get one back. They been runnin' alone for three months. Maybe longer. And they done tasted blood. Been on the hunt. Be hard to get them off that. Maybe impossible."

"Still. . . ."

"Rhonda, you want to go out to gather the eggs one day, and find them dogs waitin' for you?" Billy's voice wasn't challenging. In fact it was the opposite. Patient, kind, and understanding. She shook her head.

"Well, that's just what would have happened, sooner or later. I'd wager they already had a taste o' long pig. Once that happens, that's it. They got to go."

"Long pig?" Rhonda looked confused.

"People," Billy informed her, not looking at her. She shivered. She hadn't considered that. But there were a lot of bodies around. The odds were all of them had tasted human flesh at least once.

"Let's go check that cow and calf," Billy told her. They went to their horses, and started down into the valley.

-

The calf had a bite on his left hind leg, but it wasn't much. As near as Billy could tell, the bite hadn't done much more than broke the skin. He couldn't get near enough to touch the calf, and the cow was starting to bellow. Billy backed off, and remounted.

"We need to cut him out," Billy told Rhonda. "I don't think he's hurt, but if one o' them dogs had somethin', then the calf could get it. Ain't worried about much, but rabies is a real threat."

"Where can we put him?" Rhonda asked.

"Holding pen yonder," Billy pointed to a movable corral. "For horses, but it'll work for this. I'll get the mother," he said, shaking out a rope. "He should follow along, but if he doesn't, I'll need you to latch on to him."

"Billy, I ain't never roped no cow!" Rhonda exclaimed.

"He ain't a cow, he's a bull," Billy laughed. "And he ain't nothin' but a baby, yet. He won't be much trouble." Rhonda eyed the calf warily, but took her rope in her hand, acting like she knew what to do with it.

Billy had the cow in just the work of a minute. She fought, at first, but Samson was stronger, and hadn't just been attacked by wild dogs. The big gelding held his ground, and soon the defeated cow was following him to the pen.

The calf watched his mamma being led away. He stood rooted to the ground for a few seconds, then bolted after the only meal source he knew. Rhonda laughed in spite of the situation, seeing the little cow run to his mamma.

Billy handily guided the cow inside, then made room for the calf, who hesitated for perhaps a second before following. Billy closed the gate, then tossed over some hay. There was water available, and the hay would hold them overnight.

"He'll be calmed down by mornin'," Billy told Rhonda as he remounted. "Be easier to check him, then. Meanwhile, he's separated from the herd. If he does get somethin' from the bite, he can't spread it." He looked back to where the dog bodies laid.

"Why don't you head on back," he suggested. "I can handle that, and be right on."

"No," Rhonda shook her head. "I got to learn, and you learn by doin'. I. . .I shouldn't have hesitated. And I did kill one of'em."

"That you did," Billy nodded. He had studied her closely, but she seemed okay. "Let's get it over with."

It was nearly full on dark when they got home. The dogs had been drug by rope off the pasture and into the woods. Both horses were rubbed down, fed and watered, and then the two went into the house. Dottie was glad to see Rhonda, and Rhonda was careful to lavish attention on her, and gave her a treat.

This seemed to appease her, and Dottie was soon annoying Rommel.

"Well, I guess her feelings ain't that hurt," Billy chuckled.

"I need to work more with her," Rhonda admitted. "She was supposed to be a pet, and maybe protection. I was gonna send her to obedience school, but that's out, now."

"We'll get it done," Billy promised. "She's already learning from Rommel, just by watching what he does when I speak to him. That'll help."

"Let's get cleaned up and I'll cook us some supper," Rhonda sighed.

It had been that kind of day.

CHAPTER TWENTY-TWO

The calf had to be put down four days later. Despite Billy and Jerry's best efforts, the bite became infected. The two decided, after three unsuccessful days of treatment that they wouldn't be able to keep the infection down, and decided there was no reason to waste their meager supply of animal meds trying. Whatever the dog that had bitten the calf had, it was bad. The infection had taken root, and spread, quickly.

The meat was lost, but Billy skinned the calf out after killing it, and began working the hide. There was no way it would be ready in time for their trip to Franklin, but once it was cured, it could be stored.

Billy staked the hide out and began to scrape it clean, using an Ulu knife. The knife was flat, with a broad blade that angled up to a stag handle. The blade had originated in the Arctic, among the native tribes. Called a 'woman's knife', as it was used primarily by women for everything from preparing food to skinning, it was an ideal tool for this kind of work.

Billy had learned the basics of tanning from his father, and had, as a boy growing up, practiced it on deer and small game he had shot or trapped. This was his first cow hide, but figured he could apply the same basic principles. He had cut the hide as close as possible when skinning the calf, but there was still a good deal of meat and fat in places.

Using the Ulu, Billy scraped the proteins clean of the hide, careful to avoid damaging the hide itself. Once that was done, he would lime the hide, essentially soaking the hide in a mixture of slack lime and distilled water. That process would help remove the hair from the hide, and soften it slightly to help with working the leather. It would also remove most of the remaining fat, protein, and other substance found naturally in any living tissue.

Once *that* was done, he would have to remove the remaining hair by hand, de-lime the hide, and began salt curing it.

Basically, it was a lot of work. And it was time intensive, doing it by hand. But the end result, if he did it correctly, would be a beautiful tanned cowhide, of soft leather. The calfskin would be especially soft. *If* he did it right.

As he started to work, he decided that making mistake on the calf hide would, at least, keep him from ruining a larger hide. But he wanted to try and not make mistakes. The calf hide was almost perfect for something he really wanted to do.

"Ewww!" Rhonda's nose wrinkled as she walked into the barn. Billy had moved the trailers out, for now, so that he had somewhere to work.

"What in the *world* is that smell?" she demanded, holding a hand to her nose.

"Money," Billy grinned, looking up from where he was working on the calf skin.

"Argh!"

"Yeah, well, you won't think that when it's done," Billy told her. "It should make a good piece, if I don't screw up."

"How much money?" Rhonda asked, the trader in her blood wanted to know, despite the smell.

"Don't know, these days," Billy admitted. "Depends on what the market will bear. At the least, it should be good for tradin' for something we want." He didn't tell her that he had plans for this hide.

"Well, just make sure you clean up before you come in the house!" she ordered.

"I'll have to come in the house to clean up," he pointed out.

"Then you better burn those clothes," she warned. "You ain't washin'em in my washing machine."

"Uh, technically. . . ." Billy started, but trailed off when he got *The Look*.

"Never mind," he muttered.

"That's what I thought," Rhonda nodded. Flipping her hair, she walked out, leaving Billy to shake his head. He looked at Rommel, who snorted almost in amusement.

"Women."

-

After the long wait, Trade Day was upon them. Everyone had loaded the items they wanted to carry the night before, save for some home-made jellies and jams that Emma had made, in case the cold affected them.

"We'll need to find some canning jars, soon," Emma laughed. "Unless I can start getting some back."

"We've got some," Rhonda told her. "But maybe we should start trying to buy back all we can. You may can offer discounts to people who provide their own jars."

"You know, you have a mind like a steel trap, young lady," Emma laughed. "I hadn't even thought of that."

"Hey, my daddy taught me never to pass up the chance to make a dollar, or a good trade either one," Rhonda grinned. "Just business."

"Maybe we should be partners," Emma decided. "I think you're a much better 'trader' than I'll ever be."

"I can do that," Rhonda said seriously. "If you want, I'll do your bartering for you. Better yet, we should find someone who'll simply take all you can make, and sell it themselves. Let them be responsible for getting the jars back, if they want more."

"A steel trap," Emma repeated, shaking her head. "I was thinking about sewing, too. Maybe making clothes to order." Rhonda nodded eagerly.

"That's something that will come into it's own, especially in another year or so. Stuff people bought, or took, will start to wear out. And there won't be anymore going to the mall for clothes. Not for a long time, anyway."

"I think this might be the beginning of a beautiful partnership," Emma sighed, settling into the front seat of the Ford. Everyone took the same positions they'd had the last time. This time, though, Jerry was holding an AR-15 identical to Toby's. Billy had made good on his promise. Jerry had also swapped his older model .38 revolver for a .45 Smith & Wesson. Toby carried the same. The two Silvers were able to share magazines and ammo now.

Billy headed down the road, using a set of low light goggles rather than the head lights. Rhonda had a pair as well, and used them to help watch the road. This way they would avoid attracting any attention to themselves.

The trip went well, if a bit slower, due in part to their traveling so early, and in part for the need to avoid Cottonwood. Billy was near certain that the train would have moved on within hours, but he didn't *know*. And someone, or several someone's, could have decided to stay behind.

By full day, they were almost there. Billy was pleased to see his time estimate had been correct. If things went smoothly, they would be home long before dark, this way.

As they pulled in, it was evident something was amiss. There were only a few people, and those were running around aimlessly. Billy frowned. He knew they were early, but he'd expected people to be out, and about. Then he saw the bodies.

Laid out in a row, no, two rows, were more than twenty still forms, all covered with sheets or some other form of material. Several had blood seeping through them.

"Toby, wait here," Billy ordered, as he stopped the truck. "Rhonda, take the wheel. Jerry, let's go see what's happening." No one thought to question Billy's orders. Emma moved to the back seat, and Toby climbed up front with Rhonda. Once they were secure, she locked the doors, just in case.

Billy and Jerry advanced slowly, rifles ready, but not raised. It was obvious some sort of violence had occurred, but until they knew what it had been, they figured better safe than sorry.

"Billy?"

Billy turned at the sound of his name and saw Ralph Maness walking toward him. The leather man was carrying the M-16 he'd traded from Billy, and was wearing the .357 as well.

"What happened here, Ralph?" Billy asked.

"Raiders," the older man shook his head. "I guess advertising on the HAM and CB radios wasn't all that great of an idea. They hit right after dawn, and went through here like a dose o' salts." He looked at Jerry.

"Ralph, this is Jerry Silvers," Billy introduced. "Jerry, this here is Ralph Maness. He's the leather man I was telling you about."

"Saddle maker," Jerry nodded. "Fine piece o' work."

"Thanks," Ralph nodded. "Anyway, they had several vehicles. Rolled in here, shot the constables and anyone else around, and started loading up. Took all the food they could find, as well as ammunition, guns, and tools, hell, *anything* they seemed to think was useful."

"They get you?" Billy asked. Ralph shook his head.

"Wasn't even set-up, yet," he replied. "I engaged a couple of'em, know I hit one. Seen him fall. But they took their wounded and dead with them, looks like."

"Was it the train?" Billy asked warily. Ralph shrugged.

"Didn't see or hear one," he admitted. "But the tracks are maybe ten minutes from here. They could have unloaded and drove this far without anyone even seein'em, this time of the morning."

"Wonder can we help in some way?" Jerry mused, looking around.

"Who are you?" All three men jumped, turning to the sound of the voice. There were four men standing there, all more or less pointing their weapons at them.

"We were comin' in for the trade day," Billy said calmly. These men were jumpy, and he didn't blame them. "Just got here about five minutes ago."

"Yeah?" one of the men almost sneered. "I didn't see you come up!"

"I can't be helpin' that," Billy shrugged. "Like I said, we just got here."

"It's true, Kelvey," Maness cut in. "I saw them drive up. They was here to do business with me. Ordered stuff last Trade Day. Was to take delivery today."

"Didn't see you come up, either, Maness!" Kelvey spat back. "How do we know you ain't part o' this?"

"Mister, I don't know you," Billy said softly. "But you aim to accuse me o' somethin', you do it. Flat out. And you better start pointin' that gun in another direction, now that I think on it," he added. Billy was patient. And forgiving to a point. Kelvey had reached that point.

"You threatening' me?" Kelvey demanded, taking a step closer. Billy grabbed the barrel of the pump shotgun, jerked the weapon from Kelvey's hand, and smashed the butt into his jaw. As soon as he did, he threw the gun to one of his friends, who somehow managed to catch it, despite being startled by Billy's sudden move.

"Don't make threats," Billy kept his voice soft. "Don't take to'em, neither," he added, looking around at the rest. "We came to do business. Like ever'one else. Just got here. Don't blame you fellas for bein' on edge. I would be too. But we ain't the ones what did this. Don't suggest it again."

"Now, can we help, some kinda way?" he surprised them by asking. "Got a first aid kit in the truck. And some food and water. Ain't but sandwiches and such, for our lunch, but we can get by."

"We could use a hand movin' the injured," one man spoke up. He figured if the stranger was going to do any harm, he'd have done it when he took Kelvey's shotgun.

"We can do that," Jerry nodded. "Where you want us?"

"We're still searching the area," the man replied. "We haven't checked the other side of the building yet. Why don't you three cover that? Stay together, though. And be watchful. We've already found two that we left behind. Cost us a man killed and two more wounded."

"We'll get over there," Ralph nodded. As the three walked away, Billy called Rhonda on the radio, and told her what had happened.

"*What do want us to do?*" she asked.

"Follow along behind, I guess," Billy told her. "We can load any injured into the truck, and take'em to the clinic."

"*Will do.*"

The three started at the Civic Center, and began clearing the east side from there. They found one man right away, but he was dead. Shot through the chest, he had bled out. They found a woman behind a row of cars, her clothes ripped, a vacant look in her eyes. Billy didn't need to be a doctor or nurse to know what had happened to her.

"Rhonda, send Emma up here." Billy called. Emma got out, and headed that way. When she saw the woman, really just a girl about her own daughter's age, she gasped. Kneeling beside the young woman, she spoke softly.

"What's your name, dear?" she asked softly. The girl looked at her, but made no reply.

"I'm Emma," the older woman spoke gently. "This is my husband, my neighbor, and our friend," she pointed to the three men in turn. The girl looked, and her eyes filled with fear. She struggled to back away, but the cars stopped her.

"They won't hurt you, honey," Emma soothed. She motioned for the men to back away, and they did so, quickly. Emma spoke to the girl too low for them to hear, and they concentrated of protecting the area. Finally Emma got up, and walked over to Jerry.

"Rhonda, Shelly and I will take her to the doctor," she told them. "She needs to be around women, right now, and not men, if you know what I mean."

"I. . .all right," Jerry agreed reluctantly. "Take Toby. . . ." He broke off as Emma shook her head.

"No. Not even Toby. We girls will handle this."

"Take the truck," Billy ordered. "Toby can stay with us." Emma looked at Billy and smiled, then nodded.

"Rhonda, bring the truck up," Billy called. Soon the big Ford was there. Emma quickly explained the situation, and Shelly got out to help at once. Jerry had wondered how she would react, but Shelly didn't panic. She did have an odd look on her face, though. As if something had clicked into place. He could only hope that was a good thing.

The women got the girl loaded, and left, Rhonda promising to stay in touch by radio. Once they were gone, the men looked at each other.

"Something's gonna have to be done 'bout these people," Billy said softly. The others nodded.

"For another day, though," he shook his head. "Right now, we offered to help. That's what we'll do. Toby, we'll move in a diamond. You're the back corner. We'll watch front and sides, you cover the rear. Ready?" Everyone nodded.

"Let's go then."

-

The four of them found three other people, all wounded. One was serious enough that Billy called Rhonda to see if she could bring the truck. Satisfied that Emma and Shelly were safe in the clinic, she was there in minutes.

The men quickly loaded the injured onto the truck, and then Rhonda drove them to the clinic. Billy and Toby, who had taken First-Aid as a Scout, were working on the injured man when they stopped at the clinic.

"We need a stretcher!" Toby called. Someone came running out with a collapsible stretcher, already stained with blood. He quickly examined the wounded man.

"Good work," the EMT nodded. "Just might have saved his life. Lift!" he ordered, and Billy lifted the end off the truck as the EMT got the back. Together the two of them walked the stretcher inside, while the others helped the remaining wounded out of the truck bed.

The clinic was a mad house. People scurrying everywhere, crying, screaming, impatient demands that their son/daughter/wife/husband be treated *right now*. Another EMT was doing triage assessments.

"Low chest wound," the EMT that had helped Billy informed his colleague. "No sucking, doubt the lung is hit. Heavy blood loss, but appears stable."

"Right. Get him over there," he pointed to a line of litters. "Check between four and five. Place him between, if I recall right. Head wound ahead of him, gunshot to the leg behind." They moved the man to the ordered place.

"Appreciate your help, friend," the EMT told Billy.

"Boy did all the work," Billy shrugged. "Good kid."

"We need all the help we can get. I gotta go. Thanks again!" The man hurried off. Billy looked at Jerry, who was searching for Emma and Shelly.

"Talk to you?" Billy asked. Jerry frowned.

"I was lookin' for Emma and Shelly," he replied. Billy nodded.

"When you find'em, and see to them, we really need to talk." Jerry nodded, and Billy walked outside. Toby was standing by the truck, rifle ready. Rhonda was sitting on the hood, rifle in hand, while Ralph leaned against the fender. He looked tired. Billy saw the man who had given them their search area, and went to report.

"Found three wounded, and brought them in. One dead, just other side of the building. One woman, girl really, who'd. . .she'd been. . .look, you know. . . .."

"I'm afraid I do," the man nodded. "I'm Norman Riggs, by the way. Head of what's left of our emergency services."

"Billy Todd," the men shook hands. "Our women folk brought the girl in. Two of'em are inside there with her, now. We. . .I mean there just ain't much can be done for that, I reckon."

"No," the man sighed sadly. "There isn't."

"Well, we made a five-block sweep, one over, two up and two down. Anything else?" The man shook his head.

"No, I think we've covered it all. Listen, about earlier."

"I don't take no offense," Billy shrugged.

"Well, Kelvey does," the man informed him. "He'll be lookin' for you with blood in his eye. Might be best if you leave."

"Can't leave till the women folk are done tending to the girl," Billy shrugged. "I'll stay outta his way. Suggest to him he stay outta mine."

"He's not normally that way," Riggs told him. "He. . .he lost his wife to the plague, and then these raiders this morning shot his brother. We still don't know if the brother will make it. He wants to hit back at someone."

"I can understand that," Billy nodded. "But I ain't the one responsible, and I don't aim to be hit on. Just so's we're clear," he added. Riggs nodded.

"We really don't need any more trouble," he said softly.

"Won't be none, unless he starts it. You got my word. If he confronts me, I'll walk away, if he'll let me."

"That'll have to do, then," Riggs nodded. "Thanks for your help."

"You're welcome." Billy walked back to the truck.

"What now, Billy?" Toby asked. He wasn't eager. None of them were. Billy was pleased that he was willing, though.

"Nothin' right now, Tobe," Billy shrugged. "Good work, by the way. You'll do to ride with, I reckon." Toby swelled slightly at that, and grinned.

"So, we just sit here?" Rhonda asked. Billy shrugged.

"Jerry, Emma, and Shelly are still inside," he reminded her. "And we need to stick together if we can. If they ain't out soon, I'll go look for'em."

-

Jerry emerged a half hour later, with Emma and Shelly in tow. Ralph had left to go see to his own things, and had agreed to meet up later. Jerry came up to Billy, looking pensive.

"It's a right mess in there," he said softly. "I think we oughta just head home, Billy. Ain't gonna be no tradin' today."

"Got some tradin' already done. Just need to take delivery." Billy looked around. "We'll be a little bit, but not long."

"What'd you want to talk about?" Jerry asked.

"Was thinkin' this might be a good time to see about recruitin' some neighbors, so to speak," Billy shrugged. "Be a sure bet that some o' these folks won't want to stay. Not after something' like this."

"Well, I ain't against the idea," Jerry replied thoughtfully, rubbing the back of his neck. "But we don't really know any o' these folks. We don't want the wrong kind o' people movin' in on top of us, I'm thinking."

"Me neither," Billy nodded his agreement. "We don't have to take no one with us. Today or any other day. We can keep gettin' by the way we are right now. But if we can get a few hardy folks, people that'll work, and fight when need be, we might be a mite better off."

"Hell of a choice to make, ain't it?" Jerry almost spit in disgust. "I guess ain't no harm in talkin'. Where you aimin' for'em to live?" he asked.

"Well, the Franklin place is a good start," Billy shrugged. "Havin' someone up there, all the time, might keep another dog pack from gettin' to the herd. We need to try and find some jacks, by the way," he added. "If we had a couple, or even three, runnin' with the cows, they'd be handy to drive the dogs off."

"If we can find some we can afford," Jerry nodded. "Be a good idea. Well, I ain't against someone using the old Franklin place, myself. What kinda folks we thinkin' on looking for?"

"Well, if we could find a nurse, or even a paramedic, it'd be a help. And I was thinking about asking Ralph if he was interested," Billy added, looking at Jerry.

"I like him," Jerry said at once. "Seems like a solid sort. Not to mention, someone who can work leather would be a fine addition."

"I thought that too," Billy nodded. "If we can get a few artisans, we might just build a good, solid community that can support itself, and do business with other folks on a regular basis."

"I like that idea," Jerry agreed. "And, you made a good point about maybe finding a nurse, or at least a paramedic. Okay, let's keep our eyes and ears open, so to speak. And we should talk to Maness. Today, even, if you want."

"We can sound him out a little better," Billy nodded. "But he seems pretty good on face value."

Decision made, the two men decided they would head over to talk to Ralph first. He might know others who'd be interested himself.

CHAPTER TWENTY-THREE

"I don't know," Ralph mused. "I'd sure be interested, depending on the set up. But I'd need room to work in," he added thoughtfully. "I've got my shop, at home. I'd need something like that where ever I wound up."

"How big is your shop?" Jerry asked thoughtfully. "We can probably put something together. What do you do for power?"

"My shop is twenty-four feet by twelve feet, right now," Ralph told them. "I'd really need to stay that size, if possible. I don't need much power, to be honest. I've got a fairly simple solar set up that provides all I need."

"We can probably find a building that size, and move it onto the property we're thinking about," Jerry mused, thinking about places he'd seen such buildings. There was one in Cedar Bend, in fact. "And I think we can provide some solar for the house, which mean you can use yours just for the shop."

"That'd be ideal," Ralph was enthusiastic. "Gotta warn you, though. It'll take three, maybe four trucks, or at least some trailers, to get me moved."

"We can do that," Billy assured him. "Meanwhile, the Franklin place has four bedrooms, a den, living room, and a full kitchen, plus a two-car garage. In fact," he brightened, "I don't see why the garage couldn't be used as a shop for you."

"Hadn't thought o' that," Jerry nodded. "Be ideal, really."

"I like the sound of that," Ralph agreed. "These days, ain't never no tellin' when someone will try and take what you have."

"We've been careful not to advertise our presence," Jerry promised him. "That don't mean someone won't just stumble across us, though," he added.

"I got a pretty good guard dog," Ralph grinned. "In fact, I've got three of them. Anatolian Shepherd dogs. Used to raise'em, in fact. Got a male and two females."

"Is that a fact?" Billy asked, now really interested. "We could sure use a good set of stock dogs. Might be you could raise a litter for us to use keeping watch on the stock. Or help drive them, if there was a need?"

"Sure," Ralph nodded. "They're great stock dogs. It's in their blood, really. All three of mine will herd anything. Even ducks, if they can," he laughed. "It's just their nature to be protective."

"Like I said, the Franklin place is good sized," Billy got back to his point. "Do you know of anyone with skills we might need that you would want to share the house with? Somebody with some medical training would be great. But there's other things, too."

"Well, ah. . .I was going to mention it," Ralph said with a sly grin. "I've been, ah, seeing, I guess, one of my neighbors. She's a. . .well, she *was*, a nurse, at the hospital in Murfreesboro. She's been trying to help people on the sly, so to speak, and not call attention to herself. Seems some 'groups' are looking for anyone with medical expertise, and they don't really care if you want to join their little group or not. She's kinda been staying with me," he added, red faced. "For protection," he added.

"Uh-huh," Jerry grinned. Ralph sputtered a bit, then laughed.

"Aw, hell, you know," he shrugged. "What can I say? She's cute. And smart.

And capable."

"Sounds like a good combination," Jerry smiled. "I take it she's why you'd be interested, but 'don't know', just yet?"

"Well, yeah," Ralph admitted. "I mean, I think she'd go for it. But I don't want to answer for her. She's got a teenage daughter, too," Ralph added. "Fourteen years old. She's as cute as her mamma, and that's another reason she's so worried. Now days, women are more like to be victims than not."

"We can understand that," Billy nodded.

"And sympathize as well," Jerry chuckled.

"Well, so long as we're decided before the weather gets bad," Billy pointed out. "We don't want to be moving you in bad weather. And we really want to get everything in one trip, too. Someone see's you moving, and leaving something, might not be there when you get back."

"Good point," Jerry nodded. "Anyone else, Ralph?"

"Not right off hand," Ralph shook his head. "Amy, that's her name, Amy Shands, she might know someone. Her daughter's name is Amanda. Just have to ask her."

"Well, I think we can take Amy and her daughter just on your word alone," Jerry told him. "Anyone else, we'll want to meet."

"Don't blame you," Ralph nodded. "What say I call you tomorrow, or so, and let you know?"

"We can work with that," Billy nodded. "And we'll need a day or two to work out what we need to bring to get you moved. You have a truck, or trailer?"

"Yes to both, but I don't have a lot of fuel."

"We can bring enough fuel, I think, for your truck," Billy told him. "I've got a farm tank that should be enough. If we bring two trucks, with say sixteen-foot trailers, do you think that'll get it all?"

"I. . .I think so, yeah," Ralph nodded, caught off guard. "I can get all of my leather tools and supplies into my own trailer. Will we need furniture?"

"House is still furnished," Billy shrugged. "Might want your own bed, or favorite chair, but that's up to you. We can probably scrounge up some other furniture from around. Maybe even new," he shrugged again. "Just so we can get everything you need on the one trip. We'll have the backs of the two trucks, plus the trailers."

"Sounds good to me," Ralph nodded. "If we can think of anyone else that might do for what you want, we can have them meet us at my place, so you can talk to them."

"That sounds like a plan," Jerry agreed. "Well, I guess we need to think about getting home," he spoke to Billy.

"Yeah, 'spose so. Ralph, Rhonda has some things you'll want. And we'll need to settle up for the other stuff."

"Really?" Ralph was pleased. "That girl o' yours is really something."

"You don't know the half of it," Billy grinned. "Let's get things sorted."

-

Ralph was very pleased with the thread, rings and rivets that Rhonda had collected.

"This will keep me in business for a good while!" he enthused.

Odd Billy Todd

"Thought it might help," Rhonda grinned. "And here's the money for the other moccasins," she added, giving Ralph a handful of silver coins.

"Surely you want some o' this back for the thread and stuff," he argued.

"You know what? I don't," Rhonda surprised him. And Billy. "You need this stuff to stay in business. I need you to stay in business. Call it an investment."

"I can do that," Ralph nodded. "What will it cost me," he asked with mock wariness. Everyone laughed.

"Just your good will," Rhonda assured him. "And a high spot on your list, if I need something done in a hurry."

"That's doable," Ralph assured her, laughing. "You're the best customers I have, anyway."

"Well," Billy looked up at the sky. "I don't think there's gonna be a market today, and it's gettin' on past noon."

"How do you do that?" Toby asked, looking up at the sky.

"Do what?" Billy asked.

"How do you know what time it is, just lookin' at the sky?" he asked, pointing to his watch. It was ten minutes after noon.

"I just do," Billy shrugged, and Rhonda laughed.

"I asked the same thing, Toby," she told the boy. "Got the same answer."

"I want to learn to do that," Toby said. "Can you teach me?" Billy looked flummoxed at that.

"Well, I. . .I don't really know. Reckon I can try," he shrugged. "We'll work on it," he promised, wondering how in the hell he could teach something that he just knew without thinking about it.

"Thanks!" the teenager was appreciative.

"Anyway, reckon Jerry's right. Time we was headin' home. Ralph, we'll be waitin' on your call."

"Let you know in a couple days, at the latest," he promised.

Everyone started piling into the truck. Billy was about to get inside when he heard someone yell.

"*Hey you!*"

-

Billy turned to see Kelvey standing about thirty feet away, gun in hand.

"I aim to settle things with you!" the man called.

"Mister, ain't there been enough blood shed here, today?" Billy asked calmly, stepping away from the truck slightly. He was wearing his pistol, but his rifle was inside the truck. Billy could hear the others getting out on the other side.

"For all I know, you was a part of it!" Kelvey shouted, his face red. And swollen where Billy had smashed him with his own shotgun.

"I think you know better than that, Kelvey," Maness said evenly from behind the truck. "The man was here to trade, just like the rest of us."

"Shut up, Ralph!" Kelvey snarled. "I didn't ask your opinion."

"Mister, I promised a man named Riggs that I wouldn't cause any trouble," Billy said evenly. "That I wouldn't say anything to you, and I would walk away if you'd let me. We helped as much as we can, and now we're goin' home. Tryin' to get there before dark."

"You ain't goin' nowhere!" Kelvey shouted, raising his shotgun.

136

"Kelvey!"

The other man started at hearing his name called. He turned slightly to see Riggs and two other men covering him with their rifles.

"You aim to shoot me, Riggs? Instead o' these outsiders?" Kelvey challenged.

"They're here for the trade day, Ben," Riggs said calmly. "They aren't the enemy. You shot your mouth off, and got it mashed for the trouble. The man's telling you the truth. They worked all morning helping look for wounded, and bringing them to the clinic. Including Howie Rickman. Probably saved his life, according to Benton."

"What?" Kelvey looked stunned. Howie Rickman was his nephew. One of his few remaining family since the plague.

"Looks like he tried to protect Beth," Riggs nodded. "Beth is okay, but doc says. . .well, she was. . .you need to be at the clinic, Ben, instead of over here, starting trouble with good people." Kelvey looked stricken. He looked back to Billy.

"You saved my nephew?" he asked. Billy shook his head.

"If he was saved, was Toby that did it," he nodded to where Toby was aiming his rifle right at Kelvey's chest. "He did the first aid. I just did what he told me." Kelvey let his gun drop. He looked at Toby.

"I'm right grateful to you, son," he spoke quietly. "I. . .Howie and his girl are about all the family we got left."

"You're welcome," Toby said evenly. "Was the Christian thing to do, but I'm glad we helped save some o' your folks."

"I'm sorry, Mister," Kelvey told Billy. "I'm. . .I'm just a jackass, I guess," the man looked as if he was going to break down.

"Don't think so," Billy shook his head. "Look more like a man love's his family to me. Ain't nothin' wrong with that, in my book." Kelvey's eyes watered slightly.

"Thanks," he said quietly. "Reckon I'll go on over to the clinic."

"I hope they're all okay," Billy nodded. "Good luck."

Everyone breathed a sigh of relief as Ben Kelvey walked away toward the clinic, the two men with Riggs accompanying him. Riggs sighed, and looked at Billy.

"Appreciate you not shooting him," he said. "We really do need him."

"Wasn't no call to shoot him," Billy shrugged. "We ain't exactly crazed killers, ya know."

"I know," Riggs colored a bit. "Didn't mean it that way. You could have shot him, and been justified in doing it. Fact that you didn't means a lot. Thanks."

"Reckon we'll be goin'," Billy nodded, and the others started piling back into the truck.

It was time to go home.

-

"Reckon we can't go nowhere 'thout some excitement," Jerry sighed as they pulled up into the Silvers' yard.

"Looks that way sometimes," Billy nodded. "Spect it'll be a while 'fore there's another trade day at Franklin."

"If ever," Jerry agreed. "They took a hard hit. Hope they can recover."

"So do I," Rhonda sighed. "Just as things looked like they might be lookin' up, too."

"Things are looking up, dear," Emma smiled. "We're alive, healthy, and fed. The rest will sort itself out, sooner or later."

"Reckon you're right, Miss Emma," Rhonda smiled, hugging the older woman. "See ya'll tomorrow."

Ten minutes later, the two of them were in their own yard, unloading.

"I'm tired," Rhonda sighed, sitting down on the porch. "And I ain't done nothin', either."

"Long trip, hard day," Billy shrugged, sitting next to her. "Do it ever time."

"Billy," Rhonda sighed gently, laying her head on his shoulder, "I wish you wouldn't take so many chances."

"Huh? What chances?"

"Oh, Billy," Rhonda groaned. "Like yankin' that damn shotgun outta Kelvey's hand like that. What if it had gone off on you?"

"Couldn't," Billy replied. "He had the safety on. And his finger wasn't on the trigger, neither." Rhonda sat up sharply.

"What?!?" she almost screeched. "You *knew that?*"

"Well, yeah," Billy shifted a little, nervous. "I mean, I ain't gonna go grabbin' a gun what could shoot me. Not if I gotta choice, no way."

"Argh!!!" Rhonda punched him in the arm. Hard.

"Ow!" Billy complained. "That hurt, girl!"

"I oughta do more than that!" she let loose again. "Scarin' me that way! And then facing him down later on, when we was gettin' ready to leave!"

"That was different," Billy objected. "He wanted somethin' specific then. He wanted to get even. He couldn't get at the one's that hurt him, so he was lookin' for anyone else. I don't think he's so bad a guy, to be honest. He was just mad, and wanted some payback. You was to get hurt, I know I'd want some payback," he added.

"Billy, you are the strangest man I have ever known," Rhonda sighed in exasperation, laying her head against him again.

"Is that. . .I mean is that a compliment? Or should I be mad?"

"It's a compliment," Rhonda sighed again. "Let's get finished and get inside. Talking to you just wears me out, sometimes."

-

They heard from Ralph two days later. Billy was in the field when his radio crackled, the mike keying three times. They had agreed to use the FRS radios only sparingly at home. Keying the mike three times meant that Rhonda needed him to come to the house, but it wasn't an emergency.

"Ralph wants to come," Rhonda said as soon as Billy walked in. "He said there's a family near him that are interested. Husband, wife, and son, eight years old. The husband is a farrier in his spare time. Well, it's a hobby is what he said," she amended.

"Well, that sounds good," Billy mused. "I can cold shoe, but I can't make no new ones."

"His wife was a school teacher," Rhonda added.

"Well, that'd be useful," Billy admitted. "We'll likely have to make at least two trips, if we bring them on."

"True," Rhonda nodded. "I wonder. . . ."

"What?" Billy asked.

"Well, if we can find a big truck, like a big U-Haul, that might make it easier. We'd still be able to pull a trailer. And we'd still need to take another truck. But we could carry a lot more, too."

"That ain't a bad plan," Billy nodded, thinking. "Wonder where we can get one?"

"I don't think there were any in town," Rhonda admitted. "But we might find something comparable. Maybe a delivery truck, or something like that."

"Why not a big rig?" Billy asked suddenly. "You know, an eighteen-wheeler? Get everything in one go, then."

"Billy, can you drive one of those?" Rhonda asked. "I sure can't."

"Don't know till I try," Billy shrugged. "And if we get one rollin', sure would be easier to transport cattle or hogs, if we ever get to where we can find a market."

"It would at that," Rhonda agreed, her mind already working on costs opposed to price. "I guess we better look for a big truck, then."

"I guess we had."

CHAPTER TWENTY-FOUR

"Well, that oughta do it, all right."

Billy, Rhonda, and Jerry Silvers were just outside Cedar Bend, on the Main Highway that ran through town south to north. Sitting in front of them was a nearly new Freightliner tractor, with a box trailer behind it. The truck and trailer had once belonged to the Ingall Trucking Company.

Now, it sat empty, and abandoned.

"Wonder if it still runs," Jerry mused.

"One way to find out," Billy shrugged. He climbed into the cab, and inserted the key he'd found in the office. He had already attached a portable jump pack, one that he'd used in his shop. It was fully charged, and more than capable of lifting a dead battery back to life, even on this rig.

Letting the plugs warm for a minute, Billy hit the key. The truck turned slowly, almost reluctantly, at first. Gradually it began to spin faster, and finally caught. Sputtered. Died.

"Try it again!" Rhonda called. Billy glared at her through the window. He was gonna do that anyway.

Once more the truck engine turned, faster this time, and caught again. Sputtered. Died.

Billy waited a full minute, then tried again. This time the truck kept running, although the engine was ragged. Billy allowed the big truck to idle, getting down out of the cab.

"We'll need to let it idle a few minutes," he told them. "Let the cleaner and the Pri-D circulate through the fuel system. Once it clears out, we should be good to go."

"Don't like sittin' here, out in the open like this," Jerry commented, looking around as if he expected an attack at any moment.

"Me either," Billy shrugged. "Is what it is, though."

After five minutes, Billy climbed back into the cab, and applied pressure to the throttle. The big engine raced slightly, with little sign of it's earlier sputtering or hesitation. He gave the others a thumb's up.

"We can go, I think," he told them. "Let's see can we get this big ol' truck back to the house!" Jerry and Rhonda went to the pickup, while Billy found the air brake, and released it. There couldn't have been much air left, anyway.

He tested the air for the truck brakes, and heard the hiss of release. Good. The fuel tank was almost three quarters full. With Pri-D, that fuel would be usable. Releasing the brake, he eased the truck into second gear.

Easing carefully off the clutch, Billy put the Freightliner in motion. He wasn't used to driving these rigs, though he had worked on a few in the past. He'd never driven one on the road. This would be a learning experience.

"Here goes nothin'," he told himself as the truck moved up onto the road. Billy watched the mirrors carefully, remembering that he was pulling a fifty-three-foot trailer. He couldn't forget that. He'd made a hasty sign, and put it on the wheel.

Remember Trailer!!!!!

That should remind him.

He didn't have a note to remind him to shift gears, and soon the truck was screaming. In second gear, the big Freightliner wound up quickly. Working the clutch, Billy shifted into third gear. This time he watched the tachometer, and shifted into fourth gear when the red line neared.

"I just might be able to do this," Billy had decided, just as the trailer brakes locked up, and the smell of burning rubber and brakes assaulted his nose.

"Or not!" he added, standing on the truck brakes.

-

"I hit the trailer brakes by accident," Billy said, red faced, after checking things over. Jerry grinned at him, while Rhonda just *hrmpphed.*

"Hey, I told you I ain't never did this before!" Billy objected. "Anyways, now that I know what I did, I can keep from doin' it again. Let's get movin'."

True to his word, Billy was able to keep from doing it again. Once he had the shift timing worked out, he was able to move the truck fairly well. He worried, though, about maneuvering the big rig onto his drive. He wasn't sure it would fit.

"I'm gonna take the rig around behind," he called over the radio.

"*Roger that,*" Jerry's voice came back. "*We'll watch the rear.*"

Satisfied that the others knew where he was going, Billy made a wide turn, taking the big rig toward the Franklin place. It was even more off the path than his own, and had a large area for him to turn into, and even turn the truck around.

He was pretty sure he'd need it.

-

"I'm pretty sure she'll do just fine," Billy told them, after getting a look under the cab. "Belts and hoses all seem fine. Generator is turning good. Coolant levels are good. Compressor is workin'. Ain't nothin' like a new truck," he sighed. Rhonda laughed.

"Boys and their toys," she shook her head.

"Well, least these 'toys' can get the job done," Jerry chuckled. "Okay then. Guess that's outta the way. When you aim to go? And who all's going?"

"We can go tomorrow, you want," Billy shrugged. "As to who, I dunno. Need to have someone from both families, I guess."

"You two should go," Rhonda said at once. "And take Toby. You may need the help."

"Hate to leave you women all alone," Jerry said at once. Billy winced, and stepped back a little.

"Excuse me?" Rhonda asked sweetly.

"I said I hate to. . . ." Jerry started to repeat.

"*I heard what you said*!" Rhonda flared back. "I'll have you know I'm perfectly capable of takin' care o' myself, thank you very much!" Jerry looked at Billy in bewilderment, but the younger man just shook his head sadly.

"And we *women*, as you put it, will be just fine while the three of you *men*, are out gallivantin' all over the country side in your *toys*, I'll have you know!"

"I'm sorry," Jerry held up his hands in supplication. "I didn't mean it like that!"

"And just how *did* you *mean it*?" Rhonda shot back. "That we're weak, and frail, and need you to look after us?" Her voice was mild. Deceptively mild.

"That. . .well, look. . . .Now see here!" Jerry spluttered. "All I was doing was voicing' my concern!"

"I know that," Rhonda's voice dropped a decibel. "But we can look after ourselves for one day. The three of you will need to help load. Don't forget, there may be another family coming. You'll be late gettin' in, if you don't wind up out for two days rather than one. We'll be fine," she finished.

"Okay, you've convinced me," Jerry nodded, feeling like he'd stuck his head in a badger hole.

"Oh, good," Rhonda smiled that too sweet smile, and Jerry braced himself for another explosion.

"I think you made your point," Billy said quietly, but firmly. Rhonda looked at him for a moment, then nodded.

"'Spose I have, at that," she agreed. Jerry was almost goggle-eyed now. How in the hell had Billy ever learned to tame that girl?

"Well, want to go tomorrow?" Billy asked. Jerry thought for a moment, and nodded.

"Might's well. Sooner we go, sooner we're done."

"Figure we can leave out at daylight, or a little sooner," Billy said, as the three climbed into the Ford. "Have to allow a few minutes for the Freightliner to warm up. After that, we're good to go."

"Works for me," Jerry nodded.

-

"Billy, promise me you'll be careful tomorrow."

Rhonda was lying draped over Billy in their bed, her hand tracing a pattern only she could see across his stomach. Her voice was quiet. Soft.

"I will," Billy promised. "We ain't goin' to market, just goin' to pick up some folks. And, once we get there, we'll have others to help on the way back. No problem."

"There's always problems," Rhonda sighed.

"Do you want to go?" Billy asked, knowing what was really on her mind.

"You know I do," Rhonda slapped him on the stomach. "But we agreed. . . ."

"We agreed that someone from both families needed to go," Billy cut her off. "Jerry don't want Emma and Shelly to go, that's his look out. He don't make decisions for us. You want to go, you go. Period."

Rhonda raised her head, looking at Billy. His face was calm, and his eyes were looking right into hers.

"You wouldn't mind?" she asked, almost hesitantly.

"Nope," Billy shook his head. "Not a bit. Be glad for the company."

"What will Jerry say?" Rhonda wondered aloud.

"Don't care," Billy shrugged. "Can say what he wants. Free country." Rhonda almost giggled at that.

"You don't think it'll cause a problem?"

"If it does, then it's his problem," Billy told her flatly. "I like Jerry, and I'm startin' to like Toby. Miss Emma I've always liked. Shelly, I can take or leave. But much as I might like Jerry, and respect his opinion, he ain't in charge o' this place. This here, this farm? It's ours. Yours and mine. He don't call the shots over here, or over us. I'm fair certain I made that clear when he and I talked about what happened in Cottonwood."

"What?" Rhonda asked. Billy sighed.

"He allowed how we shouldn't have 'gone off' like that without tellin' him," Billy replied. "I disagreed."

"Uh, disagreed how?" Rhonda asked, with some concern.

"Just told him we had to go and look for things we needed, and things we could use to trade for other things. He offered to help, next time."

"We'll have to share," Rhonda mused aloud.

"Thought o' that," Billy nodded. "Figure it's a good thing, though. That way, we ain't gotta carry'em, later on. They get their own, they're on their own."

"I couldn't do that to Emma," Rhonda protested.

"I ain't sayin' we can't swap back and forth," Billy sighed in exasperation. "Just that we ain't got to go and get them stuff so they can trade and what not. They go with us, they help, they get a share. Simple."

"So, it is," Rhonda smiled, lying her head on his chest again.

"You goin' or not?" Billy asked.

"We'll see."

-

"I thought we had settled this yesterday!"

Jerry wasn't exactly mad, but he didn't like changes at the last minute.

"We settled that someone from both families should go," Billy explained patiently. "And they are. Truth is, I need someone in the truck with me. I ain't drove this thing but the one time, ya know. I can't be takin' my eye off the road for even a second in this thing. I need another set of eyes."

"And she wants to go," he added, shrugging. As far as he was concerned, the discussion was over.

"And I'm supposed to just head off and leave Em and Shelly alone?" Jerry demanded.

"That's up to you," Billy replied calmly. "We left Miss Em alone when the rest of us went into town. Was gone all day," he pointed out.

"That was different!" Jerry exclaimed. "We could have got back in a hurry, if there was need!"

"That's true," Billy nodded. "They could still go with us," he added.

"I. . .dangit, Billy, this is just what I was talkin' about! We can't just keep changing things from one minute to the next!"

"Facts is facts," Billy shrugged. "Need someone in the truck with me. You need someone with you. And we're burnin' time arguing' over this. Are we goin' or not?"

"Well, since you've made up your mind, I guess we are!" Jerry shot back at him. Billy's eyes flashed just a bit, and Jerry noticed it.

"I don't aim to make decisions for no one 'cept us," he said quietly, indicating himself and Rhonda. "Your family has to make their own decisions too. I ain't made up my mind about nothin' to do with you and yours. Rhonda wants to go, she goes. That's what I decided." He leaned in just a little.

"Are we havin' a problem about this, or are we going' to get these other folks. Once we got more people, then they'll always be someone about. That was sorta the point, if you'll recall."

Jerry looked at Billy for a minute then looked away. Finally, he sighed in exasperation.

"Yeah, we're going. That was the plan," he agreed. "But. . .Billy you gotta stop surprising' me with stuff like this. I'm an old man, and I'm set in my ways. I need some warnin' 'bout these changes. Don't just spring'em on me all at once like." Jerry's voice was more pleading than demanding.

"Yeah," Billy nodded after a minute of thought. "I see what you mean. I'm kinda set in my own ways, I guess. Helps me think clear. I'll do that. No more surprises from now on," he promised, and offered his hand.

"Thanks," Jerry took the hand with a sigh of relief. For a minute there, he'd been thinking maybe he'd pushed his young neighbor too far.

"Okay, now that all that's settled, we need to make with the leaving part of the plan," Billy suggested.

"I need to tell Em and Shelly that Rhonda won't be here," Jerry nodded. "Won't take but a minute."

"We'll be waitin'." Jerry moved away to use the radio. Rhonda leaned down from the big truck. She'd heard everything, but hadn't interfered.

"That went well," she remarked, just a hint of sarcasm in her voice.

"Yep," Billy nodded, stepping up onto the truck. Rhonda straightened up, giving Billy his seat. She snuggled into her own.

"I was being sarcastic," she rolled her eyes.

"Yeah, I got that," Billy nodded, checking the dials. He'd had the truck running for almost fifteen minutes. The idle had smoothed out, and the Freightliner seemed ready to go.

He saw Jerry waving in the mirror, and put the truck in gear.

"Here we go."

-

The trip was long. Everyone was pretty much bored except for Billy, who was in a constant state of near panic as he concentrated on driving the truck. He wanted to have the basics under control at least, before he reached the Maness place. His confidence was growing slowly, but he was constantly aware that he was only one error away from disaster.

"I don't know how these guys did this," he muttered once.

"What?" Rhonda looked over at him.

"I don't know how drivers did this job," Billy repeated. "I mean, the road ain't got a soul on it, and I'm still nervous as a long-tailed cat in a rockin' chair factory. This thing is huge!"

"They just trained for it," Rhonda shrugged. "Same way you learned to drive a truck."

"I learned to drive on a dirt road," Billy told her.

"You know what I mean," she replied.

The two rode in companionable silence, each comfortable in the presence of the other. It took a little longer than Billy figured, but by ten o'clock they were where they were supposed to be.

CHAPTER TWENTY-FIVE

Ralph Maness goggled a bit as Billy brought the Freightliner to a halt in front of him.

"Wow," he managed as Billy and Rhonda climbed down. "Now that's a truck."

"Like it?" Rhonda asked. "We got a good deal on it," she grinned. Maness just laughed and shook his head.

"Please tell me you live somewhere I can turn this thing around," Billy almost pleaded.

"I live on a circle drive," Ralph nodded. "You can make the whole circuit, come right back out on the highway."

Billy sighed in relief. That was the best news he'd had all day.

"Well, let's get goin'," he said after a minute of small talk. "We don't want to burn too much daylight. You folks all packed?"

"Yep," Ralph nodded. "Purdy's are packed too, just in case," he added. "I think you'll like'em. Good people. Known'em a good while."

"Ain't gonna be a problem sharin' the house with'em, I expect?" Billy asked. "Ain't got but the one place nearby, and it's the only one suitable to live in, right now."

"No, should be fine," Ralph shook his head. "You said it was four bedroom?"

"Yeah, pretty big place," Rhonda nodded. "Two couples and two kids oughta be able to make a good home there, and not get on one another's nerves too much."

"We'll get by," Ralph assured her. "The main thing, we'll be together, and closer to others. Things are gettin' a bit hinky anymore."

"Had trouble?" Billy asked.

"We ain't. Not yet, anyway," Ralph shook his head. "But there's trouble coming', looks like. That hit on Franklin hurt. People are just now seeing' how bad. Raiders took every bite o' food they could find, and stripped the place of anything usable."

"Seems like folks didn't really notice at first, what with all the killed and wounded. They're noticing' now. Already had several working' their way out into the country side, lookin' for food. Some ain't choosy how they get it, neither," he added.

"Well, that's sounds like a reason to get a move on," Billy suggested. "So let's get at it. Like to be close to home 'fore dark."

He and Rhonda climbed aboard, and Ralph got into his own truck. They followed carefully. There was only one bad moment, when it came time to turn onto Ralph's road. The road looked a little narrow.

Billy swung out as wide as he could, and Rhonda watched her own mirror carefully as the trailer made the turn behind the Freightliner. Billy cleared the culvert with barely a foot to spare.

"I hope it's easier to get back out," Billy muttered through gritted teeth. Rhonda nodded, knowing Billy was worried about driving the big rig.

Five minutes later, they were sitting in front of Ralph's place. It was a small house, with a very neat yard. A garden plot to the side of the house stretched around behind. His shop was visible from the road.

There were five people in the yard, waiting. A tall, trim woman, with athletic good looks embraced Ralph as he got out of his truck, which told them this was Amy. Her daughter was, indeed, almost a mirror image of her mother.

Nearby was a large, heavily muscled man with short cropped hair. Next to him stood a much smaller woman, with long dark hair, and a friendly, fresh-faced look. The boy between them favored his father. It was apparent that he would rival his father in size, once he grew to manhood.

"Billy, Rhonda, Jerry, and Toby," Ralph pointed to each, "this is Amy Thomas, and her daughter Amanda. And this is George Purdy, his wife Debbie, and their son Georgie." Ralph pointed to each in turn.

"Please to meet you folks," Rhonda smiled, talking each hand in turn.

"Same here," Debbie Purdy smiled.

"Heard a lot about you folks," George nodded.

"Sure have," Amy smiled. "Course, knowin' Ralph, I'm sure it was all lies, and you folks are actually good people," she added, chuckling. Rhonda laughed. She decided right away that she and Amy at least would get along.

"Well, it's prob'ly not all lies," Jerry dead panned, drawing another round of laughter.

"Reckon we need to get down to business," Billy said quietly as the chatter died down. "You folks know the deal, I'm takin' it?" he asked George and Debbie.

"We'll share a house with Ralph and Amy," George nodded. "I've got my rig ready to move. I can shoe, of course, but I can also smith. My forge is mobile, but I can set it off. And, if we can get the materials, I can build a larger, more permanent one, too."

"I'm a school teacher," Debbie said. "I know that's not a skill that's in immediate demand, but I think it will be important in years to come. Meanwhile, I know how to ride, and how to shoot. I grew up on a farm, and can deal with animals without a problem."

"Well, I'm an RN," Amy spoke next. "But I started out as an EMT. Worked my way through nursing school that way. And. . .well. . .okay, I grabbed everything I could get my hands on when I ran," she admitted sheepishly. "I've got meds, bandages, books, IV's, everything. It's not an endless supply, but I've got a good bit of everything. It'll last a while," she shrugged. "And I've got five years of ER experience on top of the EMT work," she added.

"Wow," Rhonda managed. Jerry gave a low whistle.

"How're you folks set for food, and weapons?" Billy asked, ever practical.

"Well, 'sides what I got off you," Ralph said, "I've got a Remington 870, and 700 chambered for .30-06."

"I've got a 870, and a side by side," George added. "Also got a Savage .308. Got a couple Ruger 10-22's as well, and a .22 pistol, and an old Colt 1911 I got when I was in service."

"You were in service?" Jerry asked, interested.

"Yes, sir," the younger man nodded. "Served eight years in the Army. Infantry," he added quietly. Billy was pleased to hear that.

"As for food, we got about three months worth of dry goods," Ralph added. "Rice, flour, what not."

Odd Billy Todd

"We've got more, since I can," Debbie put in. "Probably go four, six months, if we stretch it."

"Well, we can add to that, with beef, pork, and fresh eggs," Rhonda told them, and all smiled at that.

"Sounds like we can get by okay until we can get some planting done in the spring," Billy nodded. In fact, they could get by for probably two years, but he didn't see the need to say that.

"George, Debbie, we all share in the work," Jerry said. "You'll be over to the old Franklin place, and that's where we're runnin' the majority of the cattle. You'll need to look after them. We've got horses and tack aplenty. I understand all of you ride?"

"Even Georgie," George nodded. "We've got horses, and tack, too. And I've got a six-horse trailer, so we can pull it behind my truck. I think I've got enough fuel to make the trip."

"We brought some," Billy told him. "Gas and diesel too."

"Well, we can make it, then," Ralph nodded. Billy looked at Rhonda, who nodded ever so slightly. He looked at Jerry, and saw that the older man was looking at him expectantly. When Billy raised his eyebrows in question, Jerry nodded at him. Billy turned back to the Purdy's.

"Looks like you're in," he said simply. The relief on the couple's face was palpable.

"You folks all packed?" Jerry asked.

"We are," George nodded. "Just in case. All I need to do is load the horses, and we're good to go."

"Then I guess we better get loadin' stuff," Jerry smiled. "We got a lot of work to do, I'm guessin'."

-

There was indeed a lot of work to do.

Ralph had already loaded his own trailer, so there wasn't as much of his shop to load. Amy and Amanda had packed, but everything had to be loaded on the truck. Seeing the big rig, instead of two pickups with trailers, made both women rethink their strategy. As a result, several pieces of cherished furniture were added to the load.

Billy thanked the stars that George and Debbie Purdy lived on the same road that Ralph did. That same wonderful, wide, gently curving, *circular* road.

It took a while, but with so many adults working, the truck was finally loaded.

"Make sure anything you might need tonight is in your personal rigs," Billy warned. "I can't see us unpackin' this thing tonight."

"Or tomorrow, either," George added, chuckling.

"Works for me," Billy agreed. He was tired, and it was still a long way home.

At long last, with the sun threatening to fall behind the trees soon, their task was done. A small convoy was formed along the road in front of the Purdy house.

"Ya'll made sure you ain't left nothin' you want behind, right?" Billy asked. "Still room in the truck. I don't relish makin' this trip again. Takes a lot o' fuel."

The others consulted among themselves, and decided they had everything.

"I think we're ready to go," George said quietly, looking at his home, now mostly empty.

"It's just a house," Debbie told him softly.

"No, it ain't," he shook his head. "Been my home, my family's home, for near three generations. Hate to leave it."

"We can still stay," Debbie told him, her voice still soft, but tinged with a hint of fear.

"No, we can't," George shook his head again, then looked down at his wife. "Home's where you and Georgie are, I reckon. And we know we can't stay here, all alone. We've been lucky so far. Luck won't hold forever."

Debbie stood on her toes to kiss George's rough cheek. The two had only been married ten years. Georgie had been born while George was overseas.

"Well, I guess we best be goin'," Billy said quietly. He hated to intrude, but there was still a long trip to make. And at least some of it would be after dark.

As everyone headed for their respective vehicles, Billy heard something. At first, he thought it was thunder, but there wasn't a cloud to be seen anywhere. As the rumble continued without letup, it grew gradually louder.

"Vehicles," Rhonda said from beside him. "Loud, too. Maybe motorcycles."

"That's all we need," Billy sighed, and reached into the truck. He pulled his rifle from behind the seat, and then Rhonda's, passing it to her.

"What's goin' on?" Jerry asked, as he and Toby came up to the truck, carrying their own rifles.

"I think we're about to have company," Billy said calmly. Ralph was running toward them.

"I think that's the group that's been runnin' around here last week or so," he told them, keeping his voice down. "May be they decided to come callin' on us today."

"Let's get the women folk and the kids into the truck," Billy ordered calmly. "Rhonda, get them squared away in the sleeper, and keep a watch over'em. Maybe we can just run away."

"Maybe," Jerry looked doubtful. "Depends on whether they come this far or not. Reckon they'll stop at your place first, Ralph?"

"Might, but you can bet they'll be sending some around from this side," George had joined them. "Cut us off, like."

"Well, we need to make a decision," Billy told them flat out. "We either stand here, or we run. Which is it?"

"How many of them are there?" Jerry asked, looking at the other two men.

"At least a dozen," George replied. "Might be one or two more or less, but I'd count on at least that many."

"That ain't bad odds, we surprise'em," Billy mused. "Reckon we could get five or six right off, we played it right. Reckon they'd run, we was to hit'em that hard?"

"Prob'ly," George grinned. He was going to like Billy Todd, he decided right then. "They ain't really used to being opposed. Losing a bunch right off, like that, might break the rest."

"Any idea how they're armed?" Ralph asked. "I ain't never seen'em."

"Me either," George admitted. "But they're sloppy. Leave sign behind. I found shell casings for .223, .308, and .243, but the most was .22. I'd say they got three, maybe five guys that's heavy armed, and the rest is just carrying' what they can find, or get ammo for."

"Well, I don't wanna get shot, even with a .22," Billy said dryly. "Still, we need a plan, and we need it right quick from the sound of it."

"Well, we got two choices," George said. "We either make a stand here, and try to fight them off, or else we high tail it, and hope we can blow through the one's we think are coming in the other way."

"I say we run," Billy said suddenly. "We can bowl our way through'em with the rig, probably. If we stay here, then they might be able to just wait us out."

"Agreed," George said at once.

"Me too," Ralph nodded.

"Works for me," Jerry agreed. "Toby, drive our truck, and stay right on Billy's rear end. George, I'll ride with you, actually I'll drive, an you can shoot."

"Okay by me."

"Wait a minute," Billy said suddenly. He looked up into the truck. "Hand me that bag, honey." Rhonda grabbed the bag in question and passed it down to him. Billy took the bag, handing it to George.

"M-4, select fire," he said as he passed the bag over. "Ten mags. Suppose you know how to drive that?"

"I sure do!" George breathed. "Where did you. . . ."

"I 'spect we can jaw on that later," Billy told him. "Two grenades in there, too," he added. "Let's mount up. "All these rigs got a CB, so I suggest we use, say, channel 30. No names, and no word at all about where we're headin'."

"Let's move!" Ralph nodded, running for his truck. Jerry gave Toby a brief hug, then hurried off with George. Billy looked at Toby, and held out his fist.

"Time to cowboy up," he grinned. Toby returned the grin, bumped fists, and ran to the Ford. Billy climbed up into the cab. The two women, and their children, were in the sleeper, with Rhonda sitting in the passenger seat.

"You heard?" he asked, strapping himself in and checking the truck.

"We did," Rhonda nodded curtly. She was afraid, but hiding it very well.

"Wish you'd stayed home now?" Billy asked, grinning. That made Rhonda smile.

"Nope!"

"Ladies, you may want to hunker down," Billy told the women in the sleeper. "If we see someone on the road, we're gonna run right over'em."

"I can shoot," Debbie told him flatly.

"Me too," Amy added, surprising them.

"Rhonda, hand out whatever extra we brought," Billy shrugged. "Don't chamber a round until and unless we have to fight, though," he added. "Don't want to get shot by accident. Gonna be a bumpy ride."

With that, he put the truck into gear, and started the Freightliner moving.

"We're leading, so if anyone is coming this way, we'll see them first," Billy warned Rhonda. "Help me be watching. If someone's in the way, and they look hostile, I'm gonna bowl right over'em, so ya'll be prepared for a rough ride," he added for the sleeper passengers.

"We know how many there might be?" Rhonda asked.

"Least a dozen, maybe a couple more, if they brung'em all," Billy told her. "What worries me is they might try to follow us. George and Jerry are takin' the rear, so they should be able to stop'em."

"Hope so," Rhonda said quietly, he eyes on the road ahead.

"Good thing we came on today, I'm thinkin'," he added, grinning.

"I'm glad you did, too," Amy said quietly. "They would have gotten us alone, and separated, if you hadn't."

"Well, they ain't got nothin' yet," Billy told her over his shoulder. "Maybe we're a mite more'n they bargained for. We'll see." He looked at Rhonda.

"Think that little toy o' yours might come in handy, 'bout now," he said. She nodded, and reached for a small bag at her feet. She withdrew one of the MP-5's, and slotted a magazine into it.

"Ain't never really used one o' these before, ya know," she said casually.

"Reckon the noise might be enough to make'em keep their heads down a mite," Billy chuckled. "I know it would me."

"What about you?" Rhonda asked, indicating the bag. Billy shook his head.

"Can't. Need both hands for the wheel." Rhonda nodded, her eyes back on the road.

They were, according to Ralph, about three road miles from the highway. Billy hoped that was right. He'd already logged a mile since leaving the Purdy farm. If they could get on the highway, they would stand a better chance, especially of the raiders attacked piecemeal. They could damage one group, and then hopefully either evade or damage the second.

Doing so, he hoped, without any damage to the vehicles, or the people inside them.

If they could just make it to the hig. . . .

"There they are!"

CHAPTER TWENTY-SIX

There they were indeed. Four motorcycles, followed by a pickup truck with two men in the back, leaning their weapons over the truck's roll bar.

Billy hadn't slowed. When the lead motorcycle drew a shotgun from somewhere around his handlebars, Billy stomped the accelerator. He'd deliberately avoided shifting too high, wanting the rig wound out in case he needed speed. It was slow going on the back road anyway.

Now, the Freightliner responded. Although the trailer was pretty loaded, it was a much lighter load than the truck was accustomed to pulling. The truck had no problem gaining speed.

"Hold on!" Billy called, right before he smashed into the very surprised motorcyclist with the shotgun. Billy could see the man's eyes go wide as he realized Billy wasn't stopping. Then, both the bike and the rider were gone.

"We've made contact!" Rhonda yelled into the radio. "Four bikes and a truck. One bike down!"

The other bikers managed to swerve away from the oncoming semi, two of them choosing Rhonda's side. She took the opportunity to spray them with the MP-5. She knew she hit at least one of the bikers, but she also trashed both bikes in the process.

"Bike on your side, Toby!" she yelled into the radio. Billy could hear Toby's rifle, *crack crack crack crack,* behind them. He didn't care if the teenager had hit anything or not, so long as Toby was okay. He didn't hear any return fire.

The driver of the pickup had braked hard, seeing the semi coming. That in turn had thrown the two men in the back around violently, preventing them from shooting for a few seconds. Now, they were back up, and started shooting wildly in the direction of the big truck. The windshield starred, but held.

"Get down!" Billy ordered Rhonda, just as he hit the pickup.

The pickup's driver was trying to get out of Billy's way, backing away to Billy's left, but Billy wasn't having that. If he allowed them to just sit there, then the two shooters would have a clear shot at Toby, and then at the others. Aiming the nose of the big rig right at the front left wheel of the pickup, he hit the truck square in the side.

The pickup, a short bed 4x4 model that had been raised significantly, tipped dangerously onto it's side, and Billy wrenched his wheel back to the right, careful not to over-correct. The resulting turn let the semi break free, but allowed the trailer to sideswipe the already teetering pickup, sending it over on it's side.

"Road's clear, truck down, maybe one cycle still up!" Rhonda advised the others. "Watch for passengers. We took fire, but I think we're okay!"

"*Left side cycle rider's down,*" Toby called.

"Good job, kid," Billy nodded grimly.

"*Got two on foot on the left!*" Ralph called out. "*Rifles!*"

Crack crack, crack crack.

"*They're down,*" George said calmly. "*I think we're clear.*"

Billy was having to fight the truck a little, but the gauges all said the truck was okay. He figured they might have damaged a tire, or a support. Whatever it was, he wasn't going to stop as long as the truck would run. It didn't matter if it ever ran again, so long as they made it home.

"Highway coming up!" Amy told him. "Just over that rise."

"How wide is the turn?" Billy asked.

"Remember there's a passing lane?" Amy said. "Heading up a hill?" Billy nodded.

"You're going to hit the road right where the passing lane starts. You'll be going up hill as soon as you hit the highway." Billy grimaced at that, but there was nothing he could do about it now.

"What's wrong?" Rhonda asked.

"Truck took some damage," he told her. "I can hold it, but goin' up hill might be slow. Slow is bad."

"Slow is bad," Rhonda agreed. She picked up the radio.

"We're almost to the highway. The truck's damaged, but still going. We aren't stopping, but it'll be slow going, trying to get up that hill. T. . .second truck, you may want to drop back a little, and give us room."

"*Got it,*" Toby replied at once. He sounded as sure of himself as he ever had. Rhonda looked over at Billy.

"You can do this," she said simply. He snorted.

"You can," she insisted. "If I didn't think that, I wouldn't be in here." Billy nodded, never taking his eyes from the road. They topped the rise, and Billy could see the highway, about one hundred fifty yards away. He was grateful to have a little time to study the road.

He noted that the road he was on didn't have much rise on it, for which he was thankful. The highway had only the barest hint of an incline at the intersection, which should make the turn easier. He hoped. He down shifted, and started angling the wheel for the right hand side of the road, wanting as much turning clearance as he could get. As he steered back left, straightening the truck, there was a loud crash from underneath, and the truck jolted like it had hit a speed bump. Billy had to fight the wheel for a second, but then, suddenly, the truck was handling much better.

"*Bi. . .uh, Big Rig,*" Toby's voice came over the radio, "*truck handling any better?*" When Rhonda looked at him, Billy nodded. She keyed the radio.

"Yeah, why?" she replied.

"*Well, you just kicked out a used Harley,*" Toby told them. "*And, uh, a used Harley rider, too,*" he added. Billy shook his head.

"Thanks," was all Rhonda could think to say.

Billy hit the turn still going about twenty miles an hour. In his own truck, he would have been going much faster. But Billy was scared. He didn't want to stop the rig, since it would take forever to get it going again, especially uphill.

At the same time, he was afraid to go very fast, because the trailer might tip over, taking the rig with it. He hoped that he was going slow enough that something like that wouldn't happen.

It didn't.

The Freightliner made the turn well, all things considered. As soon as Billy straightened out, he downshifted, and hit the accelerator. The truck surged forward, slowly but steadily gaining speed.

"We're clear!" Rhonda announced over the radio.

"*Everyone's on the road, behind you. Let's hit it,*" George replied a few seconds later.

"Anyone damaged besides us?" Rhonda asked. "Anyone hurt?"

Everyone checked in okay. Apparently, no one had been shot at other than the semi.

"Everyone okay back there?" Billy asked over his shoulder.

"I think we're fine," Amy told him, having already checked everyone over out of habit. "Just a little rattled."

"Yeah, that happens to us a lot," Rhonda sighed.

Nervous laughter filled the cab as Billy pointed the rig toward home.

-

The mini convoy stopped after ten miles with no pursuit. The passengers in the semi rejoined their own vehicles, and Jerry came back to the Ford, with Toby standing there.

"I'm real proud o' you, son," Jerry said quietly. Toby smiled, his face showing the pleasure the words brought him.

"I am too," Billy nodded. "Good work. Like I said, you'll do to ride with."

"Thanks, Billy," Toby grinned.

"Okay, if ever-body's where they want to be, we need to be movin'," Billy ordered. "We still got a way's to paddle, and it's near on dark."

"What time is it, Billy?" Toby challenged, looking at his watch. Billy looked at the sky, frowning.

"Say, five. . .fifteen, or so, I'm guessin'," he told the teen. Toby shook his head, and showed Rhonda and Jerry the watch.

"Five twenty-two on the nose," Jerry shook his own head. Billy just shrugged.

"What's that all about?" Ralph asked, as Billy headed for the semi.

"No one can figure out how Billy always knows what time it is," Rhonda grinned. "And 'fore you ask, no, I don't know either," she teased Toby. "You'll just have to weasel it out of him on your own." Toby laughed as he went to the Ford.

"Better go, little bit," Jerry nodded to where Billy was looking back. "Think he's ready to go."

"This has been a rough day for him," Rhonda nodded. "Driving that truck has made him nervous all day."

"And gettin' shot at didn't?" Jerry asked.

"Oddly, no," Rhonda frowned. "He was actually much calmer when they were shooting at us. Hmm."

"Well, he won't be calm long, we keep him waitin'," Jerry chuckled. "And I'm as ready to get home as he is, to be honest."

"Me too," Rhonda sighed. "I ain't doin' nothin' tomorrow I ain't gotta," she said over her shoulder, heading for the semi.

"You and me both, little'un," Jerry laughed. "You and me both."

-

"It's a lot nicer than I had hoped for," Amy said at once, as Rhonda took her, Debbie, Amanda and Georgie into the house.

"Wow," Debbie agreed. "I. . .I admit, I didn't know what to expect. This is nice."

"Yeah, it's a great place," Rhonda agreed. "There's three bathrooms, and a large family room, with a separate dining room. Mister Franklin had a large family years ago. This house was in his family for a long time."

"I know how that is," Debbie nodded sadly. "George's family have owned the place we lived in for almost ninety years. His granddaddy bought it right after World War One, I think."

"Well, the beds are all made," Rhonda informed them. "And the house was sprayed for bugs just a few days ago. Water works, but I'd let it run a few minutes before I drank it. Make sure the pipes are clear. Well's out back. We can cover all that tomorrow, though, I guess."

"Long as we can make some kind of supper, we'll be fine," Amy nodded.

"Ya'll come over the hill in the morning, for breakfast," Rhonda told them. "Miss Emma, that's Jerry's wife, and their daughter Shelly will want to meet you, I'm sure. We'll have a good old-fashioned country breakfast, but not too early. See you about nine?"

"Make it ten," Amy chuckled. "I think I'm gonna sleep for a while, tonight, but it'll be a while before I sleep, if you know what I mean." Rhonda laughed.

"Yeah. It ain't always like it was today. So far, we haven't had any trouble here," she immediately rapped her knuckles on the wooden door frame. "It's always been when we were out, somewhere."

"I hope we haven't brought trouble to you from today," Debbie said quietly.

"We weren't being followed," Rhonda shrugged. "If they didn't follow us here, they'll have to hunt for us. Someone may find us, eventually. But, tomorrow you'll get a better idea of how isolated we really are, here."

"Thank you, Rhonda," said Amy, and Debbie joined her.

"For everything."

"Hey, no problem," Rhonda assured them. "Good night."

The men were all gathered around the front, talking quietly when Rhonda came outside.

"I think they've about got your night planned out," she told Ralph and George primly. "And we'll see you all over at the house at ten, tomorrow morning for breakfast. I thought I'd give you a big feed, since you ain't set up yet. After that, you're on your own, though," she laughed.

"I'll tell Emma, soon's we get home," Jerry nodded.

"Good," Rhonda smiled. "I told them I was sure Miss Emma and Shelly would both want to meet them all."

"Well, I figure I'm headin' home, right about now," Billy told the crowd. "I'm give plumb out."

"Wait a minute, Billy, and I'll get your rifle," George told him.

"Nope, you keep it," Billy surprised the man. "You know how to use it, and I got a rifle, anyway. I ain't no soldier, and ain't ever been. Be like to shoot my foot off with that thing. I figure you can make good use of it."

"I. . .I don't know what to say," George admitted.

"How 'bout you take a look at our horses, after you settle in," Billy told him, including Jerry in that wave. "Be good to have your opinion. Might need some work done, too."

"Sure!" George agreed happily. "Be glad to!"

Odd Billy Todd

"Then I reckon we'll see you folks in the mornin'," Billy shook hands all around. Jerry and the others did the same, then all four piled into the Ford. Billy dropped the Silvers' off at their house, then he and Rhonda went home.

The dogs were elated to see them, and they spent a few minutes playing with them. But soon the two were eating a small meal, and contemplating a warm shower and sleep.

"Long day," Rhonda said, as they cleared their supper mess.

"Sure was," Billy sighed. "I don't recall bein' this tired in along time."

"Tomorrow will be a down day," she declared. "We'll do only what has to be done. Take it easy the rest o' the day." Billy almost objected, but then seemed to have second thoughts.

"You know, that sounds pretty good."

"Thought so," Rhonda smiled coyly. "Now, how 'bout a shower, big boy?"

CHAPTER TWENTY-SEVEN

By the time the 'new folks' had found their way to Billy's, Rhonda, Emma and Shelly had a huge breakfast ready for them all. Billy's table wasn't really big enough for them all, so the crowd divided, as if on cue. Women to one table, men to another spot, with Georgie and Amanda sitting in the living room, watching a DVD.

Toby was about to be sent to the living room, but Billy himself stopped that.

"Sorry, Miss Em, your boy's all grown up," he said, leading Toby out to the patio table where the men were congregating. Soon everyone was digging in, getting to know one another, and reliving the prior days events.

Despite the fact that the newly arrived Maness and Purdy families hadn't even begun to unload their belongings, the four families spent the majority of the morning, and on into the early afternoon, simply discussing plans for the future. There would be plenty of time, everyone seemed to have decided, to unload. It was more important that the people involved get to know one another, and that plans for the days to come be hammered out, or at least sketched out, in some cases.

Division of labor, work that still needed to be done, problems that needed to be solved, everything and anything that could affect their ability to survive was laid on the table, with options and ideas from all sides. After the meal, the adults had all gathered outside in the agreeably comfortable fall afternoon. Amy got a notebook and pen from Rhonda and began taking notes.

Partway through the discussion, Shelly had approached Rhonda quietly, asking to talk to her alone. Rhonda was surprised, but nodded her agreement. The two young women found themselves on the front porch, sitting in the afternoon sun.

"I need a favor," Shelly told Rhonda, looking down at the floor of the porch.

"Sure," Rhonda said at once. "If I can do it, I will."

"I need to learn to shoot," Shelly said firmly. Nothing could have shocked Rhonda more.

"I've been an idiot," Shelly admitted, looking up at Rhonda. "I. . .I don't have any real excuse, other than I just. . .all of this has just overwhelmed me, I guess," she held up her hands in a palms-up gesture. "After that first night, when you and mamma tried to tell me what was what, I guess I started opening my eyes a bit more. And then the trip into town. . . ." She trailed off, shaking her head.

"And then, seeing what happened in Franklin, seeing that poor girl. . . ." She trailed off again, but her eyes hardened as she looked Rhonda in the eye.

"I don't want to be like her. I don't want to be a victim. I need to learn to protect myself, and help my family. I'm already learning all I can from mamma. How to cook, sew, can, about gardening. I mean, we can't garden this time of year, but there are books galore, and I think mamma has most of them," she laughed. "I'll be ready come spring time."

"But I can't just sit back and depend on Daddy and Toby, and you and Billy for that matter, to protect me. I need to be able to do it myself. More than that, I'm tired of being dead weight. I want to do something. To *help*," she emphasized. "I want to be able to defend my home, and my family. Daddy told us what happened yesterday. He said Toby 'manned up' when he had to, and did what he had to."

"He did," Rhonda nodded firmly. "He was calm, cool, and dependable."

"He hasn't said anything about it," Shelly admitted. "I tried to talk to him about it, but just shrugged it away. Said he didn't do much of anything except help load the trailer, and drive the Ford. Daddy says different, though. And daddy don't stretch the truth for nobody."

"Toby acted like a man, that's for sure," Rhonda agreed. "Don't push him too much about, Shelly. I'm sure he's working' through the fact that he probably killed at least one man yesterday. Maybe more. It's not an easy thing."

"Did you?" Shelly asked. "I don't. . .I shouldn't have asked that," she said, shaking her head. "I'm sorry."

"Don't be," Rhonda held up a hand. "It's an honest question, especially considering what you want. And the answer is I don't know," she shrugged. "I didn't stop to look. I shot at two men, and I'm certain I hit at least one. Did it kill him? No idea. Considerin' they were shootin' at me at the time, I won't lose any sleep over it, though."

"I'm pretty sure I wouldn't either," Shelly admitted, almost reluctantly. "Especially after what I seen in Franklin. That was. . .that was bad."

"Yeah, it was," Rhonda agreed. "Well, I guess if you want to learn to shoot, we need to figure out what kind of guns you need."

"Daddy said I could have that little carbine that he has," Shelly offered. "The one he had for Toby to use."

"If you want too, sure," Rhonda nodded. "But I've got what was left in daddy's shop. Granted, it wasn't much," Rhonda fibbed a little. "But it's what we let Toby choose from. And your dad," she added. "I don't mind letting you do the same thing. We'll need to get you a good kit together. I have pretty much anything you'll need. When do you want to start?"

"Can we do it tomorrow?" Shelly asked. "Or even start today, if you want. I'll do it whenever you have time."

"Well, let's do this," Rhonda offered, after pausing to think. "Let's get you fixed up with what you need today. You can see what fits you best, and we'll get you geared up. After that, we'll spend the rest of today goin' over what you pick out, and fittin' your gear to you."

"Then, tomorrow, we'll head out to the gravel pit. We'll start with something light, a .22. Once you've got the shooting part down pretty good, then we'll get you set up on the rifle and pistol you pick out, and you can practice with them. I guess we all need to practice a little, anyway. Would it bother you if Toby and Billy go along? I'm sure Toby will want to practice some more, and we need to have someone else along, just in case."

"In case. . . .?" Shelly asked.

"Well, we don't think anyone else is around," Rhonda told her. "But if they are, I'm sure they'd love to run up on two girls, all alone in the country side. See what I mean?"

"Oh," Shelly said softly. "Yeah. No, it won't bother me. Long as they don't make fun."

"Billy would never make fun of anyone," Rhonda told her flatly, and Shelly had the good grace to blush at the rebuke, reminded of all the times *she'd* poked fun at *him*.

"And I don't think Toby will either, after yesterday," Rhonda continued. "He see's things more seriously now."

"Okay, then," Shelly stood. "I guess we ought to get started."

—

". . .but I had just sold off my little herd right before the virus," George finished. "So yeah, I think I can look after the herd pretty good. Won't be able to move'em alone, of course," he added.

"Wouldn't expect you too," Jerry shook his head. "Just work'em and keep an eye on'em day-to-day like. We'll be gettin' a better fix for'em soon. Likely split'em up between there, my place, and Billy's, I guess," he looked at Billy.

"Yeah, good idea," Billy nodded. "That way, if one group get's infected, it maybe won't spread to the others. The cattle will be important for us, time's to come. I think it'll be one of our better chances to trade or sell off things."

"Probably," Ralph nodded. "I mean, there's plenty of other things, too, but food will be a big deal, especially by next year. All the canned stuff will be long gone. In fact, there'll be some lean wintering' for most people, 'fore it's done."

"Figure you're right," Jerry nodded. "We can get a good crop in next year. Likely gather all we can eat, and then some. We can always trade off or sell what we can't eat."

"You know once folks realize you got a good food supply, some'll be like to try and take it, right?" George asked.

"We do," Jerry nodded. "That's why we're going' to such great pains to keep our location hid. That won't work forever, o' course, but it gives us time to prepare."

"We'll eventually need more folks," George said, albeit reluctantly. "There's good land here. But eventually we'll need more than just us to take care of it. And to protect it," he added.

"Thought about that too," Billy nodded. "One reason we were so pleased about Ralph knowing' you all," he grinned. "We'll just have to take things as they come, right now. If we happen on some good folk, then we can always ask'em to join us, if they're of a mind to."

"I. . .I know a couple guys might can help," George said, with a little hesitation. "They were. . .well, we served together. Good guys, and able. One's married, and got two young'uns. Other one's still single, kinda young guy, but a good boy. I talked to them up in Franklin not long after the plague, so unless something else has hit'em, they're still around."

"Both from the Army, then," Jerry mused.

"Yes, sir," George nodded. "Like I said, good guys, and capable."

"Think they'd want to?" Billy asked. "Join us, I mean. If they've got it good where they are, they might not," he pointed out.

"Pete may not," George admitted. "He's the young one. Livin' alone, like he does, he can take care of himself fine. Might not want the responsibility. Terry, though, he's got two kids, boy and a girl. Him and his wife might well welcome a chance to be in a place like this. Security, neighbors, what have you."

"Well, we can feel them out, comes time," Jerry offered. "I'd say, for now, we got about all we can do, for the moment. But that means we need to take a look at some of the nearest houses, I reckon. Make sure they're livable."

Rhonda entered just then, and whispered in Billy's ear. He looked up at here, and nodded.

"Be right back," he said, getting to his feet and following Rhonda off to the side.

"So, what about Billy?" George asked Jerry, when Billy was gone. "He seems like good people."

"He's *fine* people," Jerry corrected. "Good boy, good raisin'. Man couldn't have a better friend, or neighbor."

"Every once in a while, he seems, I don't know, unsure of himself, I guess," Ralph put in. "Don't see it often. And when the pressure's on, he always seems to be confident enough."

"Billy has some issues," Jerry spoke slowly, weighing what he should say. "Had a learnin' disability as a boy. He's pretty much licked it, thanks to his folks, hard work, and his own plain stubborn refusal to give up. He's smart as a whip in some things, but others, especially social situations, he sometimes trips up. He's more practical than anything, I think. He can see the simplest solution to any problem, when most try to make it complicated."

"He's strong as bull, and I mean that near literal. Shoot the wings off a fly, too. He's a kind and gentle soul, most times. When he's riled, though, he's a force o' nature. And anything that even looks like it might threaten the little'un there," he nodded to Rhonda, "probably won't live too long." He briefly explained what had happened at the road block.

"I like him," Amy said firmly. "When we were in that truck yesterday, he was as cool as ice. We were all scared silly, but he just went and did what had to be done, cool as you please."

"I agree," Debbie said at once.

"Well, he was a bit nervous, himself," Jerry chuckled. "Mostly about drivin' that semi, though. I don't reckon I ever seen, or heard tell, of Billy actually being afraid of man nor beast. Take that dog o' his," he nodded to Rommel, who was laying off to the side, watching the 'new people' warily.

"That dog was livin' wild, in town. Had been for a week or two. Billy made friends with him, and that dog hardly leaves his side, now. If Billy had been afraid, I figure Rommel would have tried to tear him to pieces."

"Probably," Ralph was studying Rommel. "That's some dog. He must weigh a good one thirty. Maybe closer to one fifty."

"That little one, the gyp," he pointed at Dottie, "that's Rhonda's dog. Ain't near as old, still just a pup, really, but comin' along nicely, I think. They're pretty lucky. Wouldn't mind havin' a dog o' my own, nowadays. Always seemed more trouble'n they was worth, before," he admitted.

"Well, one of my female Anatolian's will be coming in season, soon," Ralph offered. "I already decided to let her bear a litter. Figure we'll need the dog's to help with the cattle. Annie's are great stock dogs. And good against almost any kind of predator."

"I'd sure like one, happens you have a good litter," Jerry admitted.

"You'll have one," Ralph promised. "I think dogs, especially good ones, are going to be very useful from now on. Way more than just pets, too," he added. Billy came back about then.

"We was talkin' 'bout seein' houses," he told the others. "Why don't you take'em to see some o' the ones around here tomorrow, Jerry? I got somethin' I gotta do tomorrow," he added.

"Orders from headquarters?" Jerry grinned.

"Somethin' like that," Billy agreed, grinning himself.

"I don't see why we can't," Jerry shrugged. "Horseback okay with you folks?" he asked. Everyone agreed that it was.

"Well, sounds like a deal, then."

"I think we'd better be going," George got to his feet. "We got a load o' work to do, still."

"Got some catchin' up to do myself," Billy nodded, and so did Jerry.

"I'll be around about eight or so, tomorrow, then," Jerry told them. Good-byes were said all around, and soon Billy and Jerry were alone, watching the others walk back over the hill to their new home.

"So, what you got to do tomorrow?" Jerry asked, teasing. He didn't expect an answer, since he was playing. He *really* didn't expect the answer he got.

"Teaching your daughter to shoot, looks like."

"What?" Jerry was stunned.

"Well, not me," Billy admitted. "She asked Rhonda to teach her. Said he wanted to learn how to defend herself. I think seein' that girl in Franklin, the one we found? I think that opened her eyes. Rhonda agreed to do it, and I figure me and Toby will trail along. Toby can use a little practice, I'm sure, and I'll just sorta watch over everything."

"Well. . ." Jerry looked thunderstruck. "I guess miracles do still happen."

"Might go easy on 'er,' Billy cautioned. "I think Shelly's had what some folks call a 'moment o' clarity'. Her eyes is open, now, and she ain't really likin' what she see's. She want's to be able to take care o' herself, and help you and Toby protect the farm."

"Her and Rhonda want a greenhouse, too," he added with a grimace. "We'll have to see can we come up with somethin'. Seems your girl has been readin' up on gardenin'. She was resigned to wait til spring, but o' course Rhonda had to go and mention a greenhouse," he groused a little. "Now they're all up in a hullabaloo about gettin' one, and startin' in on growin' right now."

"Well, I can't say I'm sorry to hear that," Jerry had to admit. "And even though it's a bit o' work, I don't mind it, seein' as how Shelly is startin' to come around."

"Figured you'd feel that way," Billy nodded. "Told'em we'd see about it, maybe later on this week, or next for sure. Ain't really got no idea where to look, though, to be honest."

"Well, I don't know about findin' an actual greenhouse," Jerry admitted. "But I do have an idea how we can make one outta scratch, so to speak."

"I'm listenin'."

160

CHAPTER TWENTY-EIGHT

-

The next day was clear, but a bit cool. There was no wind, for which Billy was thankful.

Shelly had chosen a light weight AR model like Rhonda's. She had also chosen herself a nice S&W 6906, a small, but capable handgun with a good mag capacity. She liked the feel of it, she had said.

Rhonda had also showed her a small revolver, a S&W model 60. A stainless five shot, the little gun was about a fine a hideout gun ever made, Billy figured. He had one in his safe that had belonged to his mother.

Billy had added a shotgun to the mix, wanting Toby to be familiar with the 870. He had several, thanks to his and Rhonda's 'foraging', and he wanted to give Toby one, if he didn't already have one. Sometimes, Billy figured, a good twelve gauge was just plain nice to have around. There was also a 10/22, along with a Ruger Mk II pistol, both for Shelly to practice her form on, before trying the heavier stuff.

"We all ready?" he asked, as Rhonda came bouncing out of the house. She had packed a lunch for the both of them. Shelly was bringing one for her and Toby as well.

"Reckon," Billy nodded. "Sure, you got everything?"

"Yep," Rhonda smiled. "You know, I think this is great. Shelly really seemed to be waking up. She might be changing for the better."

"You say so," Billy murmured. He wasn't convinced.

"You know, you gave Toby a chance," Rhonda reminded him.

"He earned it," Billy corrected. "Didn't give him nothin'. Reckon she can earn her's too." Shaking her head in amusement, Rhonda finished packing.

By the time the two of them had mounted up, Shelly and Toby were riding up, having come through the woods. Jerry was with them, and waved from a distance as he started up the hill to the Franklin place.

"All ready to go?" Rhonda asked Shelly as the two rode up.

"Yeah," Shelly nodded, casting a glance at the stone-faced Billy. "Little scared, I guess, but I'm ready."

"Well, let's go, then," Rhonda smiled. With Rommel and Dottie leading, the four made their way down the trail to the gravel pit. Billy sat looking at the pit, frowning.

"Wait," he ordered, dismounting.

"What is it?" Rhonda asked, frowning.

"Just wait," Billy told her, looking at the range. Rhonda waited for a minute, then asked again;

"What's wrong?"

"Somethin' ain't right," Billy said softly. "I just. . .I can't put my finger on it, but. . .it just ain't." He continued looking, and suddenly his he realized what it was.

"The target's up," he said softly, un-slinging his rifle.

"What?" Rhonda asked. Toby hadn't said anything. Instead he dismounted, handing his reigns to his sister, and turned to watch their backs. He unlimbered his own rifle as he did so.

"The target," Billy nodded, still looking around. "We left them all down. One's back up, now."

"Huh," Rhonda grunted, seeing it now that Billy had pointed it out.

How the hell does he do that? she wondered, not for the first time.

Billy was walking slowly toward the shooting area, looking at the ground. She saw him squat down, and pick up something shiny. He held the shell casing to his nose, then examined it. He rose, walking back to her.

"We policed all our brass, right?" he asked, handing her the round.

"Yeah, so I could reload it," Rhonda nodded, taking the case.

"Did we count it?"

"I did, yeah," Rhonda was studying the casing. "This ain't ours, anyway. It's the wrong brand."

"It's not recent," Billy told her. "And there aren't many. Looks like someone fired off about twenty rounds, and quit. Just makin' sure the gun would work, or sightin' it in, most like."

"Who could it be?" Rhonda asked, looking around.

"Anybody," Billy shrugged. "Rommel," he spoke to the big dog. "Search," he ordered when Rommel looked at him, waving toward the trees around the pit. Rommel set off at once.

"He does anything you tell him, like that?" Shelly asked.

"Anything I trained him to do," Billy nodded, eyes never leaving the dog.

Rommel made a complete round of the pit, then returned to Billy's side. Billy leaned down and ruffed his head.

"He didn't find nothin'," Billy told them. "I say we go on about our business."

"How do you know?" Shelly asked. It wasn't a challenge, just curiosity.

"He would have stayed where ever he found something," Billy told her. "Let's unload, and get started," he told Rhonda. "One of us can keep watch. Fact, that's why you brought me along, as I recall," he added, grinning.

"So, it was," Rhonda smiled. "Have to get something out of ya, all the food you eat," she teased.

Billy watched as the two of them started, Rhonda going over the safety routine again, and showing Shelly how to load the 10/22, and get a sight picture.

Toby walked up to where Billy was watching, still keeping a careful watch on their back.

"Reckon we need to worry?" he asked.

"Don't think so," Billy shrugged. "But it pays to be careful. Could be somebody we ain't seen yet survived. This place ain't no secret. Lot's o' people used to come here to shoot. Sight in scopes for deer season, plink, what have you."

"Someone could o' just wanted to see if their rifle worked, or if the site was on."

"But it could have been someone else, yeah?" Toby prodded.

"Sure," Billy nodded. "Ain't no way o' knowin', though, unless we just happen on'em when they're here. If they was just checkin' the rifle, then I doubt they'll be back," he added.

"Okay," Toby nodded, and fell silent.

The two of them split their time between watching Rhonda teach Shelly to shoot, and watching the area around them.

Billy was fairly confident that no one would bother them, but then he'd been fairly confident that he wouldn't wind up in the position he was in now, too. He figured that anything was possible, now days.

Shelly was hesitant at first, but Rhonda was patient. The hours she had spent the day before were also paying off. Shelly knew a good deal already thanks to that, and she eagerly applied it to the task of learning to handle the weapon.

After almost two hours, and two hundred rounds of .22, Rhonda decided it was time to try the bigger weapons.

Following instructions carefully, Shelly loaded the Carbon-15, and raised it to her shoulder.

"Remember," Rhonda told her. "Squeeze the trigger, just like before. Don't forget there'll be recoil this time, too. It'll kick a little."

She forgot.

The rifle held too loosely in her hands, it flew up, and the rear sight popped her lightly in the head.

"Ow!"

"Told you," Rhonda was unsympathetic. "There's recoil. I explained recoil. Hold the rifle firmly, and pull it into your shoulder. That will minimize it. Try it again.

Shelly reluctantly raised the rifle again, sighted, and squeezed the trigger. This time she held onto the rifle. And was delighted to see she had hit the target.

"Cool!" she exclaimed.

"Be cooler when you do it again," Rhonda grinned. "Go on, shoot it!"

Shelly willingly cranked the whole magazine out, concentrating on being accurate. Now that she had hit the target once, she wanted to do it every time.

Billy was walking around the entrance to the pit, having ordered Toby to stay put, and keep an eye out. Billy was looking for anything that would give him an idea as to who had been here since their last visit.

Look though he did, however, there was nothing to find. No boot tracks, tire tracks, and the only horseshoe prints were their own.

Maybe they walked in through the woods, he decided, after a minute. He wasn't about to go looking though, not with Shelly blasting away at the targets. Shrugging, he walked back to Toby's side, and watched the 'lessons'.

-

Shelly turned out to be a pretty fair shot. She wasn't as good as Toby, and nowhere near Rhonda or Billy, but for someone who hadn't really ever shot a gun before, she did well.

Watching her use the 9mm was a little funny, as she took longer to get the hang of it. Her wrist was weak, and that caused the little semi-auto to stovepipe a good bit.

She finally worked it out, however, and was looking overly pleased with herself by the time she'd finished.

"We get back, you'll have to strip it down and clean it. Oil it, and put it back together," Rhonda informed her.

"Okay," Shelly nodded. She'd learned to disassemble and reassemble both weapons the day before.

"What now?" Rhonda asked, looking at Billy.

For the next few minutes, Billy worked with Toby on the shotgun. He didn't need much instruction, but, as Billy had feared, the youngster had no experience with buckshot.

"Man, that would tear a man clear in half," Toby whistled lowly, seeing the damage that 'double-ought' had done to the wooden target frame.

"Always a buryin' with buckshot," Billy nodded. "What my pa used to say, anyhow. Ain't good at much distance, but say, twenty, twenty-five yards, it's pretty good."

"Yeah, I can see that," Toby nodded. The two walked back to where the women were standing.

"You want to shoot any?" Rhonda asked. Billy shook his head.

"Nah."

"We ready to go, then?"

"'Spect so," Billy nodded. Rhonda and Shelly had policed their brass while Billy had shown Toby the shotgun. They put away their stuff, and mounted up.

With Rommel again leading, they set out on the return trip. At the last minute, Billy stopped them.

"Let's do something else," he said suddenly. He led them down another trail.

"What we doin' this for?" Rhonda asked, pulling alongside him.

"Ain't smart to use the same trail all the time," he shrugged. "Just bein' careful." She nodded in understanding. Things were different now.

"This won't take no longer, anyway," he offered.

They rode in silence the rest of the way. Rommel ranged a little, but not as much on the unfamiliar ground. Dottie stayed in front of the horses, but much closer. She did keep her eyes on Rommel, always taking her cues from him.

They left the woods almost straight across the road from the house.

"Well, I'll be danged," Toby chuckled. "I never even knew this was here."

"Ain't used much," Billy shrugged. "Old fire trail, but the Forestry Service quit keepin' it up long time ago. Comes in handy, now'n again."

They eased up to the house, and dismounted. Everyone unsaddled their horse, though Toby and Shelly picketed theirs while Billy and Rhonda led theirs into the stables.

"Want to grain'em?" Billy asked Toby, indicating the Silvers' horses.

"Nah, I'll do it when I get home," Toby shook his head. "They get a belly full o' grain, they'll be salty when we head back." Billy nodded, pleased that the boy knew that.

Shelly broke her rifle and handgun down under Rhonda's watchful eye. Rhonda quizzed her all during the process, with questions about safety, mechanics, and other details.

"She's pickin' things up pretty good," Toby admitted grudgingly, watching.

"She's had a eye openin' experience," Billy nodded, his voice quiet. "That deal in Franklin made her think about things, I reckon."

"Yeah," Toby looked at the ground. "That. . .that was a bad business."

"It was," Billy nodded again. "Could happen anywhere. Always could, o' course, but these days I'd say it's way more likely than before."

Toby nodded, thinking about that. There was no more law. Not anymore.

"Reckon how dad and them are makin' out?" he asked, wanting to talk about something else.

"Was just wonderin' that myself."

CHAPTER TWENTY-NINE

"Mornin' folks," Jerry called, as he rode up to the Franklin house.
Have to start callin' it something else now, I guess, he told himself.
"Morning Jerry!" Ralph greeted enthusiastically.
"You're awful bright and shiny this mornin'," Jerry chuckled.
"Yeah. We got the truck unloaded, finally. Took til near dark to do, but we're about half settled in. Makes us feel more at home."
"I 'spect so," Jerry nodded.
"We'll be ready in a just a sec," George told him. "Reckon it's just us two goin'. Women want to finish settin' up house. Now we got the heavy liftin' done, we're just under foot, it seems."
"Know that feelin' well," Jerry laughed. "Reckon we'll ride up yonder a bit," he pointed down the road, opposite of the direction they had entered. "Couple houses up there. We ain't looked at 'em, so I got no idea what we'll find."
"Suits us," Ralph replied, and George nodded. The two quickly finished checking their horses, and climbed aboard. Ralph whistled sharply, and a large male Anatolian came bounding around the house. The dog drew up sharply seeing Jerry and his horse.
"Is this gonna be a problem?" Jerry asked warily, as his horse stamped nervously.
"Nope," Ralph shook his head. "Reb, friends!" he ordered, pointing. The dog relaxed slightly, and walked slowly to his master's side.
"Annie's are great dogs, but they're protective as all get out," Ralph said, as they started for the road. "Reb likes to check things out for himself, but I did train him to recognize friend when I said it. He'll still want to keep an eye on you, til he knows you better, but he won't bother you now."
"Billy's got Rommel doin' that."
"Yeah, I figured," Ralph nodded. "He must o' worked long and hard with that dog, get him trained that well so fast. And with him already grown when he picked him up."
"Billy's a caution," Jerry agreed. "The Smith family used to live up here," he pointed to a nice brick home on the right. They were about three hundred yards down the road.
"Older couple, passed on last year. Kids had it for sale when the plague hit. It's been empty for a while now."
"Looks like it," George nodded. The house wasn't in bad condition, but it was clearly unkept.
"Yeah, shame they didn't keep it up no better," Jerry nodded. "They hired my boy to keep it mowed for a while, but then stopped when the place didn't sell right away. Reckon they let the real estate agent deal with it."
They rode into the yard, not bothering to dismount. Reb took the time to urinate everywhere he could, while the men looked things over.
"This would probably be a good candidate to fix up for a new family," George announced finally. "It'll need some work, but not too much. Imagine a good

cleanin', maybe some bug spray and mouse traps for a little while, she'd be good to go."

"Probably," Ralph nodded. "Close by, too."

"Yeah, nearest house to you for about a mile," Jerry nodded. "Wanted you to see this one first, since we'll like as not turn around. Ain't another house on this road for about two miles or so."

"Where does this road come out at?" Ralph asked.

"Well, it don't, really," Jerry scratched his neck. "Kinda dead ends at the Clifton place. Big outfit, back in the day. Kinda fell off as the young'uns moved on, and Mister Clifton got on up in years. I ain't even been up there since all this started," he admitted a bit shame faced. "Not very neighborly I guess," he shrugged.

"We can check it out later," George shrugged. "Ralph and I will ride up with you sometime, you want to go."

"I'm almost afraid to," Jerry admitted. "But, can't hurt. You wanna go on up there today, then?"

"Nah," Ralph shook his head. "Too far, for just a look see. We'd rather get the lay o' the land around here, if that's okay."

"Sure," Jerry nodded, reigning his horse around. "Makes more sense, anyway. Let's head back down."

The three men rode slowly, discussing different subjects as they went. Ralph was confident that Reb would alert them to any danger.

Twenty minutes later, they were sitting in front of a large two story white frame house, with a horse barn sitting in the distance behind.

"Nice," George whistled.

"Barn's a loss," Jerry shook his head. "Had three cows and six horses boarded inside. Ain't nice at all."

"Aw, *maaan*!" Ralph exclaimed in sympathy.

"Yeah, it was rough," Jerry nodded. "Probably still is. And the house like as not ain't no better. We took a peek inside the front windows, and the rear door. There's a body lying on the dining room floor. Looks to have been there a while."

"Be hard to clean up, I guess," George said sadly.

"Need formaldehyde I'd say, at least," Ralph agreed.

"If it could be cleaned up, and the odor got rid of, the house ain't very old," Jerry allowed. "And it's a nice place. Hate to lose that barn, but I just don't see no help for that. Probably needs to be burned."

"I imagine," Ralph nodded. "Place got a well?"

"Two of 'em," Jerry nodded. "If I remember right, there's solar pumps on 'em too. House is electric, so if you could find some solar panels, wouldn't be too hard to set it up. But, like I say, there's at least one body inside."

"Yeah," George nodded. "That's a shame. But we ain't really needin' to move ourselves. House is comfortable."

"Sure is," Ralph agreed. "And there's safety in numbers, too."

The three moved on, looking at place after place. Jerry pointed out local features they could use as land marks, showed them reliable water sources, and explained the pros and cons of each house they came to. After three hours, the men were ready to head back.

Odd Billy Todd

"My ass is asleep," George joked.

"Wish mine was," Ralph frowned, shifting in his saddle.

"Takes a few days to get used to this as a full-time thing," Jerry nodded. "We done seen a good bit o' what I wanted to show you anyway. There's a few other places, but we can get to them later."

"Well, there's a lot that's been lost, or will be," George allowed as they ambled toward home. "But overall, this is a great area. Land looks good. I see there's a lot of unharvested crops in the fields. That's a shame, too."

"We took as much corn as we could," Jerry nodded. "Put it up for the hogs, and the cattle, too, if needs be. Thing is, fuel's gonna become a problem sooner or later. Just don't see no way around that."

"Need bio-diesel," Ralph suggested.

"Well, I thought on that," Jerry agreed. "Thing is, I ain't gotta clue how to make it. I mean I know roughly how it's done, just from readin'. But never did it. And ain't got the equipment for it neither."

"We may can salvage what we need," George mused. "It's not that uncommon anymore. Need a few chemicals, too, but they can be found. We'll just have to take a look around, that's all."

"Well, I'm all for it, happens we can do it," Jerry agreed. "If we can make some, and keep the tractors and combines running, then we can produce a lot more food than we can eat. And that means we can sell or trade the balance away."

"Absolutely," George nodded firmly. "We'll grab a phone book tonight, look through the yellow pages, and see what we come up with."

"Good deal."

The discussion fell away then to more talk on division of labor, responsibility, and other mundane items. While they were 'mundane', they were also important. Despite their far-reaching goals, the three of them didn't over look the fact that there were more immediate goals to consider.

Like surviving what was almost sure to be a hard winter.

George and Ralph would have to harvest a good deal of wood. Jerry assured them they wouldn't have to do it alone, but even so, he, Toby, and Billy had work of their own to do. The other two men would have to do the majority of their own wood cutting. Neither minded, but they were also aware of the time constraints. The nights were already getting cold, and that cold would creep into the day time more and more with each passing day.

"Reckon we'll start cuttin' wood tomorrow," Ralph said, as the three of them arrived back at the house.

"May be we can help, but not tomorrow," Jerry told them. "Got too much to see to, after so long doin' other things," he chuckled.

"We'll make out," George assured him. "Help's always nice to have, but we can make a start without it. And you guys have done a whole bunch for us already," he added sincerely.

"Well, I'll give you fellas a chance to rest your backsides, then," Jerry laughed. "Time I was gettin' home. See you fellas later." With goodbyes said, Jerry headed over the hill.

"We got awful lucky, you know," George said, as he and Ralph stripped off their saddles, and cared for their horses.

"Sure did," Ralph agreed. "Seems like a miracle, at times. I knew we were in a tight spot, but. . .I had no idea how tight."

"Me neither," George admitted. "And I thought I'd scoped things out pretty fair, too."

"Well, this is a good place," Ralph said firmly. "Good people around us, and plenty to provide for us. I don't aim to let nobody scare us off, anymore."

"Me either," George nodded. "Me either."

-

Jerry rode into the yard at Billy's to find his daughter working diligently to clean and reassemble her new guns.

"Hi, daddy!" she smiled, waving with an oil covered hand.

"Shelly, you look like you've been hard at it," he smiled, dismounting.

"I have!" she enthused. "And I did pretty good, too! Didn't I Rhonda?"

"She sure did," Rhonda smiled broadly. "I think she's squared away fine."

"Well, I'm right proud of you, girl, I surely am," Jerry told her sincerely. "Never been more proud, way you've come around last few weeks."

"Thank you, daddy," Shelly blushed a little at the praise.

"Billy, how you gettin' on?" Jerry asked, seeing Billy and Toby talking quietly.

"Found some sign at the range," Billy told him flatly. "Someone cranked off at least one mag from an AR, or maybe a Mini-14."

"What?"

"Found their brass, and they left the target up," Billy explained. "Ain't recent, but it's since our last visit. Ain't much sign. I'm almost sure whoever it was was afoot. Can't be sure, o' course, but that's how it looked."

"Well," Jerry scratched his head. "That could be good or bad. Reckon someone around here besides us has made it?"

"Could be," Billy shrugged. "Or could be someone on the road, found that rifle in a house, and wanted to make sure it worked for they took the trouble to pack it along."

"I'm inclined to think it's somebody 'round here, though," Billy went on. "That gravel pit's kinda off the beaten path. Unless somebody just lucked up on it, they'd near 'bout have to know where it was to find it."

"That's true," Jerry nodded. "Guess we'll need to be extra careful, next little while." Billy nodded.

"What'd you think about those two friends of George's?"

"Don't know'em, can't think much about'em," Billy shrugged. "Be nice to have a couple more grown men around, especially if they know how to handle themselves." He looked at Jerry intently.

"We seen a couple days ago how bad things may get. It's comin' winter time, and folks that ain't prepared is gonna be scared. Scared people do dumb things. We got it pretty good, here. Anyone finds or figures that out, we're gonna have company callin'. Worries me, some, what might happen."

"Yeah, me too," Jerry sighed. "I. . .I don't know, sometimes, Billy," he admitted after a pause. "I'm pretty sure we won't regret askin' George and Ralph to come here. But others? I just don't know."

"Well, we can always go meet'em, like we did George," Billy shrugged. "Don't see no other way to find out if we think we can trust them, or anyone else, for that matter. Thing is," he added, gesturing skyward, "I don't fancy being' out and about in hard winter, can it be helped. That means, we got to go soon, or wait for spring."

"Some folks we'd like to maybe have might not make spring," he finished with another shrug, this one more questioning.

"Hadn't thought about it like that," Jerry admitted. "I guess I figured everyone would make plans for the winter."

"Remember what Ralph said about Franklin," Billy cautioned. "Ever body acting' like the canned and dried stuff in the groceries would last'em a good long while. They'll be people out on their own, like us, that'll be fine, if they take precautions. Places like Franklin are what bother me. Lot o' people there. Cold, hungry, *angry* people. Decide that us country folks got a plenty, and they only want their 'fair share'."

"Fair share is it?" Jerry snorted, angry. "Funny, I didn't see them out here workin' to get the food in."

"Won't matter none to them," Billy shook his head. "All they gonna see is that we got what they need, and it's only 'right' that we give it to'em."

"That ain't happenin'," Jerry said forcefully.

"I agree," Billy assured him. "And that means we'll have to fight, sooner or later, to keep what's ours. Better be ready for it, all I'm sayin'."

The three of them stood there, soaking in that last statement. They'd already fought more than they'd expected. There was sure to be more to come.

Shrugging it off, they decided to join the girls. Soon there was talk of supper, and Toby saddled his horse to go and get his mother. They'd make a good meal tonight at Billy and Rhonda's, and celebrate the good things.

That was all they could do for the moment.

-

After the Silvers had gone, Billy sat up late. Rhonda had already taken a bath and gone to bed, warning Billy not to be up too late. He promised he wouldn't if he could help it.

But he couldn't help it.

Finding that the 'range' had been used bothered him. Not in an 'I'm scared' kinda way, but in a 'who was it' kind of way. He wanted to know who it was, and where they had gone.

The more he chewed on it, the more certain he was that it had to be someone local. There just wasn't much chance that a casual passer by would find that gravel pit. It was in back of beyond.

Unless, he decided, someone was deliberately following rural roads, and keeping off any main roads. Staying out of sight, moving from place to place, just scavenging what he or she could to get by, and then moving on again.

Billy had to admit that for someone who wasn't prepared, that wasn't a bad way to get along, things being what they were. It was a lot like the train, really, at least on theory. He hoped that whoever it was didn't share the train people's way of thinking about every one else.

If someone was out there, have they moved on? Or have they decided to stay, with winter coming on? If they decided to stay, did they know about the folks already living here? Was that *the reason they'd decided to stay?*

Too many questions and not enough answers. Billy shook his head and got to his feet.

He had work to do tomorrow. He'd need rest.

He headed up the stairs to Rhonda, leaving the problem behind for tonight.

CHAPTER THIRTY

"Hey, Billy!" Ralph called as he and George rode into the yard. Rommel was instantly on guard, but since he knew the two men, he waited to see if he'd have to attack or not.

"Fellas," Billy nodded, laying aside the hammer he'd been using. He was beefing up the 'shack' as he called it, where his secondary storage was. "What's goin' on?"

"You got a minute?" George asked. "We need to talk to someone with some local flavor."

"Well, I guess that's me, okay," Billy grinned. "Ya'll wanna come in? Rhonda's got some coffee on."

"Sure!" the two men chorused. Coffee was hard to come by.

Once seated, with Rhonda joining them, the two men got down to business.

"We talked to Jerry yesterday about maybe making some bio-diesel," Ralph said. "We've not ever done it, but we know how it's done. Thing is, there's some stuff we'll need in order to make a start. And," he added, "we'll need some specific seeds to grow the best crops for the process."

"Well, what kinda 'quipment do ya need?" Billy asked, frowning a little.

The talk turned technical after that. George and Ralph went over the plan they had worked out over the last evening, and Billy tried to follow. Finally, though, he gave up.

"Look, guys," he said, sighing, "this is lost on me. I can't follow half what you're sayin'. Tell me what you need to make it work."

"Oh, uh, yeah," Ralph looked a little embarrassed. "Sorry, we kinda get carried away."

"No problem," Billy nodded. "But I can't really follow all that technical stuff. And anyway, I ain't gotta. I just need to know what you need. Then we'll see if I know where it is, or if we gotta go lookin' for it."

George produced a list, which he handed over. Billy read it, frowning at times, nodding at others.

"Okay, I know, roughly, where we can get about half this stuff," he told them. "Some of the others, I don't even know what they are. You need to decide what you need first, to get started. And you need to list alternatives we can all be lookin' for, in case we can't find what you want, or there ain't enough of it."

Both men looked at him for a moment, the looks on their faces indicating they hadn't thought about any of that. Rhonda didn't quite smirk as she refilled their coffee cups.

"Uh, yeah, we can do that," George nodded. "You think we can get the stuff in the town nearby?"

"Some of it," Billy nodded. "The hardware for almost certain. Some o' them chemicals, I don't know. Maybe. That oil, cookin' oil and the like, we can scavenge from restaurants at first, to get you started. After that?" Billy shrugged.

"Best bet would be if we could find a warehouse that had a lot of it."

"Well, the oil is just for now, and to help us get the project going, and perfect our. . .well, methods. To make diesel in any significant amount, we'll have to plant a lot of acreage in something we can extract oil from."

"Such as?" Rhonda asked.

"Probably rapeseed," George replied. "It's what they make canola oil from, and it's about the best oil for making bio-diesel, at least so far as I know of. There's plenty of others, too, but if we can generate canola oil on a big scale, we're on our way to makin' bio-diesel."

"Sunflower oil is about the next best thing," Ralph opined. "It's not quite as good as canola, but it's still pretty good."

"Can you mix the two?" Billy asked. He got owl blinks in reply.

"I have no idea," Ralph admitted. "None at all."

"Well, 'spect we can worry on that later," Billy shrugged. "You guys get your lists straight, and then we'll head into town. What we can't get there, we'll have to go further out for."

"That could be risky, too," Rhonda spoke up. "Don't forget the train."

"You really think they're still around?" Ralph asked, frowning.

"No idea," Billy held his hands up, palm up. "But I ain't takin' no chances. We'll be extra careful. But still, this is somethin' we need. Without it, we're back to a mule and a plow. We can stay fed, but you can forget anything extra."

"If we can keep machinery going, we can grow wheat, too," Ralph nodded. "Be nice to still be able to bake bread a year or two from now."

"Sure would!" Rhonda enthused. Mostly to cover her near slip of revealing that she and Billy would have bread in a year or two. No sense sharing that, as Billy liked to say.

"What about these two other fellas ya'll was talkin' about?" Billy asked. "Tell me more about them. Or anyone you've thought of besides."

"Well, Terry Blaine is about forty-two, maybe forty-three, I can't recall exactly now. He's married, wife's name is Maria. They got two kids, a boy who's twelve, I think, and the girl is nine. He's a gunsmith. Got to doing that work in the Army, and kept it up afterward." he broke off as Billy rolled his eyes.

"He's also a pretty fair mechanic, or was when we were in service together. Maria was a veterinarian assistant. Well, I guess she still is."

"Pete Two Bears is an Apache Indian. By now he's got to be, oh, twenty-six, maybe twenty-seven. He joined up at seventeen, to get off the reservation. He settled in Tennessee because his last duty post was Fort Campbell."

"Paratrooper?" Ralph asked.

"Nah, they don't do the paratroop thing anymore," Billy shook his head.

"Right," George nodded. "They use helicopters. Air Assault they call it, now. Anyway, Pete was a designated marksman, what they used to call a sniper. Hell of a tracker. Several NCO's tried to get him to go SF, but he was determined to get out. Said he'd done his thing."

"Sounds reasonable," Ralph nodded.

"Anyway, they're sorta hangin' together at the moment, I think. At least they were together when I saw them at Franklin. That was. . .two, no, more like three months ago now."

"They're good people, you think?" Ralph asked.

"I think so," George nodded. "Served with them in Iraq, and Afghanistan. We were in the same squad, in fact, in Iraq. Same platoon in 'stan. Took fire with'em," he added solemnly.

"Always a resume booster," Ralph agreed. "Any down side?

"Terry can be short tempered," George nodded. "His wife, o' course, takes some o' that starch outta him. She wasn't with us in theater, mind, but when she's around, he's better behaved."

"That short temper be a problem?" Billy asked.

"I really don't think so," George shook his head. "Like I said, it was while we were in country. Man acts different, times like that."

"What about. . .Two Bears, did you call him?" Billy asked.

"Pete's kind of a loner," George said. "Quiet, unassuming. But he is lightning fast, and as dangerous as a rattlesnake. If you hear him rattle, it's too late."

"I take it he'd not be inclined to act such upon us?" Ralph asked.

"Nah, he ain't like that," George assured his friend. "And he's a hard worker. Man, he could go all day, seemed like, and never stop. He works slow but steady, and just keeps right on until the job's done."

"I like that," Billy nodded. "I tend to do that some."

"He's a lot like you, Billy," George nodded. "Lot o' the same ways about you. Slow, deliberate thinking, but once the actions starts, he never hesitates." Billy murmured something the others couldn't hear, his ears reddening at the implied compliment. Rhonda snickered, but held her tongue.

"Well, I guess if we're gonna contact them, or anyone else, we need to do it soon," Billy sighed. "I gotta feelin' we ain't gonna be too mobile once winter sets in. I figure this'll be a cold one, and likely wet, too. Travel might get pretty dangerous."

"Well, I can call Terry on the HAM," George offered. "See if he's interested. He'll know how to contact Pete, if he thinks Pete might be interested."

"Ralph, what about you?" Rhonda asked. "Anyone else you can think of, that might make a go of it here? Especially someone with skills we need?"

Ralph pursed his lips together, thinking. He snorted, finally, and grinned a bit lop-sided.

"Well, yeah, there's one," he answered finally. "One outfit, actually, but I don't much think you'll want him around here."

"Who?" Billy asked warily.

"Ben Kelvey and his bunch," Ralph admitted.

"Oh, *hell no!*" Rhonda snapped out before Billy could even reply. "I ought to whack you upside the head for even suggestin' it!"

"Hold on gal," Ralph held his arms up in appeasement. "I said you're not likely to want him around, but hear me out, okay?" Rhonda folded her arms, her face set into a look that said *it's not happening,* but she didn't object.

"Ben really ain't a bad sort," Ralph told her. "You saw him on a very bad day, don't forget. Man loves his family. Can't fault him for that. Ain't sayin' what he did was right by any means, I'm just sayin' you caught him on a bad day."

"Ben is good fella, just got a mite o' temper. You should know how that is," he risked a grin at the flame haired Rhonda, who snorted. She was not amused.

"Anyway, if his brother, Jonathon, and their nephew Howie survived, they'd make a good addition around here. Ben is a carpenter. I don't mean a shade tree one, neither. A master carpenter. Can build a whole house from scratch, you give him the goods for it."

"Jon used to drive a log truck. Big woodsman. Knows how to hunt, track, and the like. So good that people hire him as a guide during huntin' season, you know?"

"Howie is an electrician. Rebuilds electric engines, appliance repairs, wires houses from the box on. In fact, when Ben built a house, it was usually Howie who wired it, unless he was busy somewhere else. They're all pretty handy."

"I. . .I don't know about Beth," he admitted. "After what happened, I got no idea what frame of mind she'll be in, or whether her and Howie are even still together."

"Anyway, like I said, they're pretty good stock, all things considered. And I'm fair sure Ben is sorry for what he did and said," he added. "I mean, that crunch to the jaw didn't hurt him, none, either," Ralph grinned, nodding to Billy. "But honestly, he's not bad people."

"I have to agree," George nodded. "No one ever had anything bad to say about Ben, or any of the rest, either. Stick to their own knittin', and take care o' each other. And," he added thoughtfully, "right now, they'd be likely to react pretty well to becoming part o' this set-up. Things ain't good in Franklin. And if Jon and Howie ain't able to work, Ben will work enough for all of them. That's just the way he is. He don't want charity. He works for everything he gets. They're all like that."

Rhonda looked at Billy, clearly expecting him to say no.

"We can talk to him," Billy said evenly.

"*What?*" Rhonda all but screeched.

"Rhonda, I told you before I didn't think he was a bad man," Billy said calmly. "And he ain't like to forget that jaw, neither," he admitted. "If he's as good as these guys think he is, then we can at least talk to him. And his family."

Rhonda spluttered, looking for a coherent thought.

"We can always say no," Billy reminded her.

Rhonda *harrumphed* loudly.

"We *can*," Billy stressed.

"Fine," she waved the subject away.

"Rhonda, I swear," George said earnestly. "If I thought, even for a second, that he would cause trouble, I wouldn't even mention him. I like Ben, but I love my family. This place is a paradise in the time's we're livin' in right now. My family is safe, sheltered, and well fed. I won't risk that for *anyone*."

"Same here," Ralph agreed with an emphatic nod. "And if I get even a hint of a suspicion of a *thought* that he might make trouble, I'll tell you straight out. Like George said, I don't like *nobody* that much."

"We can talk to him," Rhonda muttered. "Ain't no harm in talkin', I reckon."

CHAPTER THIRTY-ONE

The next day, despite any misgivings, Billy took George and Ralph into Cedar Bend. All were armed, of course, and Billy pulled one of his empty trailers.

"Be careful," Rhonda whispered as she adjusted Billy's collar against the morning cold.

"You know I will," he grinned at her. "Always careful."

"No, Billy, you're not," Rhonda sighed. "Go on, and get, now. Sooner you're done, sooner you're back." She kissed him lightly, and stood on the porch as he walked to the truck. She waved at George and Ralph, then walked into the house.

"You're a lucky man, Billy, if they ain't nobody told you already," George told him. "She's got sand. Like my Debbie. Man got a woman that'll stick by him in times like this, he's blessed."

"I know," Billy said quietly.

They drove to town amid talk of what they could do, and what they could do it with. It was a chance for them to see some more of the available farm land, and to get a look at the grimness of what was left of Cedar Bend, Tennessee. Population now zero. And holding.

"Damn," Ralph murmured to himself, seeing the carnage still everywhere.

"Yeah," George agreed, though he wasn't as shocked. He's seen worse in Iraq and Afghanistan. But this was America. This didn't happen here.

Don't be a fool, George, the former soldier shook himself mentally. *It can happen anywhere. Anytime.*

"Let's see what's on this list at the Co-Op, first," Billy said, taking them that way. "Watch out for the rats."

The two men had already been warned about the rats, but seeing was believing as the saying went. Both were astounded.

"Man, this is bad," Ralph said softly.

"Happenin' like this in plenty o' other places, too," Billy told them soberly. "Won't be long 'fore anything worth usin' is gone. Ate up or chewed up. Rurnt."

"Maybe. . .well, that can wait," George waved it off. "We got other problems right now."

"What's in that head o' yours?" Ralph asked his friend.

"It'll keep," George smiled. "Let's get today behind us. Then we'll talk."

Satisfied, Ralph nodded.

"Here we be," Billy said brightly. "Let's start lookin' for the gas station."

-

"All we need now is some wire, sealant, a few electrical connectors, and some water heaters," George announced, looking at his list.

"What?" Billy asked. "Water heaters?"

"Yeah, that's what we'll use for tanks," Ralph nodded. "Easiest thing to use, according to what we've managed to read, so far."

"Well, there's the hardware store, and there's Mister Burke's furniture'n appliance store. Don't know that he'd have water heaters, though," Billy rubbed his neck. "Ain't really an appliance, I guess."

"We can check, if there's nothing at the hardware store," George shrugged.

"If there ain't, there's plenty o' houses," Billy shrugged. Both me looked at him.

"What?" he asked.

"Why in the hell didn't we think of that?" Ralph asked George, accusingly.

"Hey, you're the brains in this outfit," George protested.

"Is that why you insisted on making the list, then? On account of I'm the brains?"

"Reckon we can do this later?" Billy asked quietly, but firmly. "I really don't like it here." Both men looked chagrined. They had been joking, actually, but realized how hard it must be for Billy to see his home town in the shape it was in these days.

"Sure, Billy," Ralph nodded. "We was just funnin' anyway," he added.

"Figured that," Billy nodded. "Ain't against it. Just want to get done. I don't like it here," he repeated.

"We're on it," George said firmly, getting into the truck.

The hardware store held three water heaters, two of them thirty-five gallons, and one larger one at fifty-five gallons.

"Man, these will work great!" Ralph enthused, as they carted them out of the store. A hurried search found the other items they needed, including the wire. Willing hands seized them, and soon everything was loaded.

"Not a bad haul," George smiled. "We can probably get something going in a few days," he added, clearly thinking.

"Where you aim to set it up?" Billy asked.

"Probably need a barn, somewhere," Ralph offered, looking to George for confirmation.

"Yeah, that'd be good," the other nodded. "Somewhere we can get some power from a solar set-up, or even better, a generator. Something that will give us a good power source."

"Problem with solar is just in the batteries," Billy said. "Better the batteries, better the power source. All's the panels do is recharge the batteries."

"True, but we'll need a good, solid source for six hours or so at a time. That would take a lot of batteries."

"True," Billy nodded. "Well, I got a heavy generator I took from the hardware store when I left town," he told them. "Eight thousand watt. Runs on diesel, too," he grinned. "Guess the more you make, the more you can run the generator, huh?"

"Sounds like a plan," George nodded. Yes, sir, he liked Billy Todd. Liked him just fine.

Wouldn't o' minded havin' him in the Outfit, back in the day, he thought to himself. But he wouldn't wish that on anyone he really liked.

"Let's go home," he settled for saying.

-

George and Ralph picked a barn about two miles away to work in. It was on the Williamson farmstead, and was in good repair. They went to work right away, promising to get things going, and then get back with Billy on what else they would need.

Billy spent the next two days working on his own farm, checking over the community herd, and making sure that his and Rhonda's storage was in good shape for the winter. He still had a feeling that the winter would be a hard one. With so many people gone, factories and cars idled all over the world, the temperature was bound to drop some.

It wouldn't be unlivable, but it would be harsher than anyone now living had experienced, other than the occasional winter over the years. The house was set. He'd already checked the insulation, the window and door trim, and the flues to the chimneys.

They had plenty of wood, there was still nearly ten thousand pounds of propane under ground, and the above ground five-hundred-pound tank was three quarters full. Billy didn't want to use much more of that than he absolutely had to, since there was nowhere to get more.

He straightened up at that idea. Nowhere to get more? Sure, there was!

"Tanks are full of it!" he said aloud.

"What?" He started at Rhonda's voice from behind him. He hadn't known she was around.

"I was thinkin' out loud," he admitted. "About propane."

"You sound like Hank Hill," Rhonda giggled.

"Who?"

"Hank Hill? *King of the Hill*? It's a. . .never mind," she sighed. "What about propane?"

"Well, I been worryin' about not havin' more, once what we've got is gone," he told her. "Thing is, there's propane everywhere! It's in tanks in no tellin' how many yards, and it's in the big tanks at the gas places! We just gotta go and get it!"

"You know how to do that?" Rhonda asked.

"Well, I know how the transfer works on our tanks," Billy said thoughtfully. "Maybe one o' the other guys knows..."

"It's a thought," she nodded. "Still won't last forever, but it's better than not havin' it at all." She took his hand.

"But that's enough on that, for now," she smiled. "C'mon. It's supper time, and I'm hungry."

"Works for me."

Billy spent the next day making a plan. He hadn't made a new plan since everything had happened. He didn't like being without a plan. Not having a plan was an invitation to disaster in his view.

They needed to take a look at the propane situation. Each farm had a tank of it's own, though he doubted that the others had the reserves he did. And he wasn't telling them. That was his business, he figured. Well, his and Rhonda's.

Gotta get in the habit o' thinkin' like that, he chastised himself again. He and Rhonda were together now, and he had to stop thinking like he was still alone.

They needed the chemicals for the bio-diesel. Sure, they had what they needed for now, but that was just to get started. If they wanted to keep making the diesel, they needed more. Probably a lot more.

They needed to get prepared for winter. Billy was prepared at home, but it was coming time that everything on the Farms would need to be set for the winter. Did they have enough feed and hay for the cattle? Horses? Hogs? Where all the structures sound enough to hold a foot, or even two, of snow? Were their vehicles capable of winter travel if needed? Someone might need the doctor in Franklin. Long trip on snow and ice.

Billy spent a good deal of the morning studying the problems they faced, and trying to figure the best course of action to deal with them. Rhonda, seeing him so deep in thought, left him be, baking bread most of the day, and a pecan pie for after supper that night. She also took time to clean the house, and do their laundry, something that had been neglected over the last week's hectic work schedule.

By the time she was finished, Billy was up and moving.

"Get everything worked out?" she asked with a smile, as Billy walked into the kitchen.

"Some, maybe," Billy nodded. "Somethin' smells good!"

"Fresh bread," she told him, and handed him a slice of hot buttered bread. He bit into it hungrily, realizing that he was famished.

"Man, that's good!" he exclaimed, gobbling the bread down quickly.

"Easy, tiger," Rhonda teased, handing him another. "There's more where that came from." He ate the second piece more slowly.

"I made a list o' things we still need to get done," he told her while eating. "Not you and me us, but all of us," he clarified. "Reckon we need to have a meetin' o' some kind. Gonna take all hands, maybe, to lay all this in. And it's almost Thanksgivin'."

"It sure is," Rhonda realized. "Wow, I hadn't even thought that far ahead. I need to get together with everyone else and see about a Thanksgiving Dinner."

"Good idea," Billy nodded. "We can play host, I guess. Our house has got the most room." Rhonda smiled, not telling him how warm and comforting hearing him refer to the house as 'ours' made her feel.

She sometimes had to stop for a moment, and take stock of the flurry of things that had happened in the last few weeks. It seemed like things had always been the way they were right now, sometimes. Like the two of them had always been together.

Time has a funny way of making that happen.

"Anyway," Billy was saying when she broke free of her reverie, "there's a lot to do. We need to make a plan for all that, and then get on it. I think we'll see snow 'fore Christmas this year."

"Maybe a white Christmas?" Rhonda brightened, smiling hopefully at him.

"I dunno," Billy shrugged. "Be nice, though, wouldn't it," he added.

"Yeah, it would."

-

There was a meeting the next afternoon at the Todd place. Everyone was there, and Rhonda had made finger foods like cookies and muffins. There was no milk, but there was coffee and hot chocolate, and still some soft drinks. The adults all gathered around the big table, and listened attentively as Billy ran down his list.

"Wow," Ralph was the first to speak.

"Yeah," Jerry sighed heavily. "Reckon we got a load o' work to do, yet, 'fore winter. Normally wouldn't be a big deal, but we ain't normal no more."

"Well, I reckon this here is the new 'normal'," Billy pointed out.

"True enough," Jerry nodded. "Well, what's first on the agenda, then?" he

Odd Billy Todd

asked. Jerry had no problem letting Billy take the lead. Even when Billy didn't want to.

Jerry Silvers knew his limitations. And he knew how old he was. Children had come to him and Emma late in life, and they were not, as Emma had put it, spring chickens. Most mornings, in fact, Jerry felt more like a rooster from two years before.

He knew, even if Billy didn't, that Billy was the future. Billy shortchanged himself too much, the older man figured, and he understood Billy's reluctance. But the facts were there for all to see. Billy was the one who always found a way to get things done. Sometimes when everyone else had thrown up their hands.

There would, sooner or later, be trouble with others, and Jerry knew that. He would back any play that Billy made, but he knew that Billy would handle things better than he would.

He also knew that one day there'd be a community here again. Not in Cedar Bend itself, but here, on the farms around their neighborhood. And that community would need a strong leader, with a load of plain old-fashioned horse sense.

Jerry had decided that leader would have to be Billy Todd.

He had *not* shared that decision with his young neighbor, however. Or with anyone else, for that matter, including his wife.

He'd just have to see how things played out.

"Well, first off, we talked about some other folks being brought in, if they was willing and able," Billy replied. "We need to talk that out, and decide what we aim to do. Then do it. Once that's done, we'll have to tackle this list head on. If we get the others, then we'll have more hands for everything."

"Where would they live?" Jerry asked.

"Well, there's the Smith place, you showed us," Ralph offered. "We'd likely need to do some work in there, but I think we can make it habitable in a couple days. And it's a nice place," he added.

"True," Jerry mused. "How many people we talkin' about, anyway?"

"Well. . . ." Billy started.

When he mentioned Ben Kelvey, the room erupted.

"*Absolutely not!*" Jerry thundered, coming to his feet. Billy looked up at him calmly.

"Sit down, Jerry, and hear them out," he said softly. "I did, and I was the one he was pointin' a shotgun at."

"Well, that's true," Jerry replied, the wind leaving his sails. "I reckon if you can hear it, then I ought to."

Ralph and George repeated what they'd said earlier about the Kelvey family, or what remained of it. When they finished, Jerry pursed his lips, then turned to Billy.

"If everything is like they say," he spoke slowly, "and I mean *everything*, then I reckon it's up to you, Billy. Like you said, you're the one he pointed the gun at. If you can allow that to pass, then I reckon I have to, too."

"Fair enough," Billy said after a minute. "What about them two soldier friends o' yours, George? If they want to come in, we'll need another place."

"What about the Williamson place?" Ralph asked. "It ain't far away, about two miles is all. And since we got the bio-diesel set-up down there, it wouldn't hurt to have someone down there. Heck, I bet Howie could build a lot better rig than we can," he added to George, who nodded.

"That's a good house, too," he put in.

"Little small," Jerry mused. "I think it's got three bedrooms."

"Could be four, though, Daddy," Shelly said suddenly. "Remember how they added a family room on back, about three years ago?"

"Hey, that's right," Toby chimed in. "We used to hang out in there and play video games when I'd spend the night with Chuckie. . . ." His voice trailed off as he realized he was talking about one of his best friends. Before the plague, anyway.

"Sorry," he muttered, looking down.

"For what?" George asked. "For remembering your friend? Hell, son, don't never apologize for something like that. *Ever*."

"Absolutely," all the others added their encouragement.

"It ain't nothin', Toby," Billy whispered softly, and the boy looked up. "Let it go, little brother. All over and done with. Just remember the good times, and let them be what you keep with you."

No one spoke for a moment, as all of them drank in Billy's words. Everyone at that table had lost someone. Friends, family, neighbors, someone. There were empty holes in every life sitting at the table. Billy's words help fill some of them. Just a little.

"Anyway, it's a little bigger," Shelly opined after a minute, drawing attention away from her brother. "So really, you could call it four bedroom. And there's two baths, too."

"That would do pretty good," Amy said. "Sounds nice."

"Ya'll want it instead?" Jerry asked.

"Not a chance," George and Ralph said at the same time, which caused general laughter. "We ain't movin' that stuff again," George finished for them, with Ralph nodding in agreement.

"Well, sounds like we got a plan, then. Put who where, you think, assuming they all want to join up?" Billy got back to business. Had to stick to the plan, after all.

"I think the Kelvey's at the Smith place," Ralph said. "They're gonna need to be close by, since Howie ain't really recovered yet. Being that close will let Amy keep a close eye on him," he added, looking at her. Amy nodded.

"Yeah. If he's battling infection, I'll need to be where I can bathe his wound several times a day."

"That put's Terry and Pete at the Williamson's then," George nodded. "They'll be good security for the place. Though I don't like their kids being anywhere away from the rest of us."

"Straight as the crow'll fly, it ain't but less'n a mile," Billy shrugged. "We can get over there pretty quick, anything bad happens."

"That's true," George agreed after thinking it over. "And that place will give them plenty of room if Pete decides to stay with them."

"If he don't, I don't know where else we can put him," Jerry pointed out.

"Pete's an odd duck, sometimes," George shrugged. "He's as liable to build a lean-to in the woods as he is to live in a house."

"Sounds like an interesting guy," Shelly remarked, earning her a look from her father. She just shrugged.

"Okay, then. Ya'll contact'em if you can," Billy decided. "Me and Jerry, and I guess Rhonda and Em," he added, seeing a frown from Rhonda, "will go with you to talk to'em. Remind'em not to be sayin' nothin'. Don't want folks to be all eager." Everyone nodded at that, remembering the last two trips in that direction.

"Now, there's some other things. . . ."

CHAPTER THIRTY-TWO

The radio calls were positive all around. All parties were interested in at least talking to the 'Farms'. Jerry and Billy wanted to go as soon as possible, and a meet was scheduled for three days later.

In the meantime, there was much to do. Jerry and Billy had bailed as much hay as they could before the second trip to Franklin. The first day after the meeting was spent by all able hands moving that hay to storage. Some went to Billy's, some to Jerry's, but mostly it was placed in the large pole barn at the Franklin place.

The next day was spent in the gruesome task of making sure the Williamson place was ready for occupancy, just in case. No one wanted to do the job, but Billy was adamant that he wasn't going to go through another 'Widow George' incident. Rhonda and Jerry quietly explained what had happened to the others, who nodded in understanding. George and Ralph removed the house's sole occupant, which they were fairly sure was Mister Williamson himself.

The house was cleaned thoroughly, and the food stocks gone through. What was still good was left for the next occupant, the rest discarded. The freezer had kept running, thanks to the PV cells on the roof, and the contents were checked. Most looked okay, and only a few meat items were discarded. The refrigerator was also still running, although everything in there had long since ruined. With bleach and cleaners, the ladies managed to save it, while Ralph, George and Jerry buried Mister Williamson. Toby was elected to cart off the ruined refrigerator's contents.

Billy had checked the PV cells and batteries, while the others worked inside. One battery had burst, and he replaced it with one he'd taken in town. The others looked good, and with the others using power, the batteries were getting a good pull for the first time since the plague. He checked all the connections, and the inverters. He was pleasantly surprised to find them in good working order.

It took most of the day, and the group was exhausted afterward, but they were able to deem the property ready for habitation. The Williamson's personal effects were removed, although the furniture remained. Billy dutifully carted the boxes to the barn, storing them in the tack room, which Mister Williamson had made fairly rat and mouse proof over the years.

"Well, that was a day's work," Amy stated, wiping her brow. Despite the cool air, everyone had worked up a sweat today.

"Sure was," Debbie agreed, fanning her shirt. "Nice place, though. People who owned it put a lot of love and hard work into it."

"That they did," Jerry nodded sadly. Emma had agreed to stay at home and watch the two children in the group. She figured it wasn't a good thing for them to see the house.

"Well, I'd say we're done here," Rhonda came out of the house, carrying her cleaning equipment. "Looks good."

"Yeah," Amy agreed, picking up her own buckets. "We'll do the Smith place tomorrow. It doesn't look so bad."

"Don't forget that place has been empty a while," Jerry cautioned. "Don't take no chances, or go stickin' your hands in no dark places."

"I'll go and spray it, when I leave here," Billy offered. "Overnight should kill most of the bugs. Once we're done, we can bomb it, and burn a formaldehyde candle overnight. That'll kill anything in there."

"Never heard of the candle thing," Debbie was interested.

"Mamma used'em," Billy just shrugged. "Said it killed the germs and bugs and such not. I got some of'em still."

"Sounds like a plan," Amy nodded. "Tomorrow then?"

Everyone agreed, and all set off toward their respective homes. Billy and Rhonda stopped at the farm to pick up the spray.

"I can get this alone, you wanna stay here," he offered.

"Nah, I'll go with," she smiled. "Be nice for the two of us to do something. Like everybody, but not all at once. And not all day."

"Yeah," Billy agreed.

They pulled into the yard at the Smith place. There was still light, but it was fading. The Smith place didn't have PV power, so it was dark.

"Least it'll be empty," Billy said, as he prepared the sprayer.

"Might be snakes," Rhonda replied, hefting her little .410 shotgun.

"Just don't do no damage we'll have to fix," Billy teased. She snorted.

"Long as I kill any snakes, I'll fix the damage."

The went into the carport, intending to get inside through that door. Billy had just tested the door knob, when the door splintered as a bullet whizzed by. Both dropped to the ground, Billy drawing his pistol.

"Don't come in here or I'll shoot!"

"What the hell!" Billy exclaimed. "Whoever you are, you better not be shootin' at me no more! I don't like it!"

"Is that the best you can come up with?" Rhonda asked in disgust.

"I don't see you doin' no better!" Billy snapped back. "Damn near took my head off!"

"I mean it!" the voice cried again. "I gotta gun, and I ain't afraid to use it! Ya'll best just be gettin' on!" It was a girl's voice, maybe just into her teen years, Rhonda was almost sure. And she was scared, it sounded like.

"Who are you?" Rhonda asked.

"None o'yer business!" the voice screeched back. "Now I mean you best just take off, you hear!"

"I think we know now who was shooting at the gravel pit," Rhonda told Billy dryly. Billy looked at her with dawning comprehension. Then he frowned again.

"I still don't like bein' shot at," he said sullenly. Despite the situation, Rhonda had to stifle a giggle.

"Whoever you are, we don't mean you any harm," she called out. "Can we at least talk?"

"Yer talkin' right now!" the voice shot back. Rhonda noticed that she sounded a little unsure now.

"Look, I don't know who you was expectin', but we live just over the hill. There may be some folks comin' to live here in a few days, and we wanted to make sure the place was clean. That's all."

"Well, I'm livin' here, and I don't aim to leave!" came the defiant answer.

Odd Billy Todd

"I'm gonna tear a strip off o' her hide, we get in there," Billy muttered angrily. "Of all the fool notions. . . ."

"Hey!" Rhonda snapped at him. "She's alone, most like, and afraid. Until you been in her shoes, you don't get to decide how she get's judged. This ain't some bully, or jackass at the trade day. This is probably a scared little girl, protecting herself from stuff only another woman can imagine. Now shut it!"

Billy glared at her, which just bounced off of her. She turned back to the door.

"My name's Rhonda Higgins," she said, not as loudly. "What's yours?"

"Mary," the voice sounded a little less sure of herself now. "Not that that changes nothin'," she added.

"That's fine, Mary," Rhonda replied. "What's your last name? Are you from around here? I am. My daddy ran a gun shop in town, before. . .well, you know. Before."

"Jerrolds," Mary replied after a minute of silence. "My name's Mary Jerrolds."

"Jerrolds?" Billy frowned. "Hey, you ain't Dennis Jerrolds' kid are you?" he shouted.

"I. . .I might be," Mary answered, sounding a little less scared. Maybe.

"Hell, gal, I knowed your daddy! He worked at the car plant! I worked on his truck once in a while."

"What kinda truck?" the girl asked. Rhonda grinned. Cagey little minx.

"A ugly yellow Ford F-150," Billy told her, smiling.

"That truck wasn't ugly!" an indignant reply shot back. "That truck was beautiful!"

"Yeah, you're Dennis' girl alright," Billy laughed. "He told me he bought that thing cause his little girl liked the color. Said it looked like Tweety Bird."

"He painted Tweety on the hood!" Mary exclaimed.

"Mary, can we come in, now?" Rhonda asked, shooting Billy a smile. "We won't hurt you. We really did just come to clean this place up. And you don't need to be living here alone, any way." There was a long hesitation, and a longer minute of nothing. Then, the door opened hesitantly.

"I reckon you can come in."

-

"How long have you been here, Mary?" Rhonda asked, looking around the dimly lit house. There were empty cans on the counter, where the girl had apparently been about to prepare a meal. There were two gallon jugs of water there as well.

A sleeping bag was laid out in the far corner of the room, surrounded by mouse traps. Two large coolers were next to the bag, one of them with a battery powered lantern atop it. A bible lay beside the light.

"I don't know," she shrugged helplessly. "Long time. 'Least a month."

"Why in the world didn't you come down to the house and ask for help?" Billy all but demanded, and the girl shrunk back, grasping the heavy Mini-14 tighter.

"Shut up!" Rhonda scolded. "He has got a point, though," she added, turning back to Mary. "What didn't you just come down and see us?"

"Scared," Mary replied softly, still looking at Billy.

"Of what?" Billy asked, perplexed.

"Ever body," the little voice admitted.

"Honey, how old are you?" Rhonda asked, kneeling next to the girl.

"Twelve," Mary replied. "But I'll be thirteen soon!" she added, with just a hint of challenge.

"Really? How long?" Rhonda asked.

"Um," Mary bit her lip. "I. . .what day is it?" she asked.

"Oh sweetie," Rhonda said softly. She looked at Billy and saw with relief that he was finally 'getting it'.

"Girl. . .Mary," Billy said easily, "this here ain't no way to live."

"S'all I got," Mary replied stoically. "Gotta make do."

"No, you don't," Rhonda stood. "Billy, you start loading her things into the truck."

"Huh?" Billy asked.

"What?" Mary demanded at the same time, backing up a step.

"Listen," she told Mary. "You need to be somewhere safe, honey. And this ain't it. You need clean water, and better food than you can get from a can. You're comin' to live with us!"

"I am?" Mary asked, trying not to let her hopefulness show.

"She is?" Billy asked, again at the same time.

"She is," Rhonda told him firmly. "And you ain't gonna get this stuff loaded standing here talkin', neither."

Billy grunted at that, but dutifully went to get one of the coolers. He picked it up with little effort, and trekked out to the truck.

"Don't let him fool you," Rhonda smiled. "He would have been up here himself, if he'd known you was here all alone. Ain't a better man nowhere than Billy Todd."

"I don't think he like's me much," Mary said quietly.

"Well, you did almost shoot him," Rhonda chuckled. "Billy takes a dim view o' that sorta thing."

"Oh. I did, didn't I?" Mary asked, wincing a bit.

"He'll be fine in a while," Rhonda assured her. "Now, start getting your things together. When we get to the house, you're taking a nice hot bath, while I fix you something good to eat. Deal?"

"Deal!" Mary smiled.

Mary's few things were loaded quickly. Billy took the sprayer, and their flashlight.

"What are you doing?" Rhonda demanded.

"Gonna spray the house," Billy told her, as if it was a stupid question.

"I'm not keeping that child out here in the cold for you to spray that house!" Rhonda informed him.

"Don't 'spect you to," he told her calmly. "Take her on down to the house. 'magine she needs some time with just a woman for a bit. I'll be along once I'm done here, and unload her stuff."

Rhonda was taken aback by that. She smiled at him suddenly, and kissed him soundly.

"You are *so* getting lucky tonight," she whispered in his ear.

"Yeah, yeah," Billy shooed her off, laughing. "You're just tryin' to bribe me into lettin' her stay with us."

Odd Billy Todd

"Ain't you?" she demanded, surprised.

"Oh, for. . .of course I am!" he exclaimed. "Good Lord woman, what kinda man you take me for?"

"A really good one," she said softly, and kissed him. "Be careful coming home."

With that she loaded the girl into the truck, and headed for home. Billy watched her go, and then, shaking his head, went to work.

-

Rommel was instantly suspicious of the new person Rhonda brought home. Dottie, far more friendly, ran to the girl, and started sniffing and licking.

"Rommel," Rhonda warned. The big dog looked at her, but reluctantly backed down. He eased closer, and Mary watched him with trepidation.

"I don't think *he* like's me either," she whispered.

"Well, it's Billy's dog," Rhonda laughed lightly, and Mary had to giggle at that.

Rommel sniffed slightly. She smelled wrong, but not untrustworthy. He caught several different smells, all of which he could identify, yet he couldn't. He didn't like mysteries. He edged closer, nose out. Mary carefully lifted her hand, palm up, and let Rommel sniff her.

"Friend, Rommel," Rhonda told him sternly. Rommel looked at her, as if to say *are you sure*?

"Yes, I'm sure," Rhonda interpreted the look correctly. Rommel sniffed again, and then again.

"That's enough," Rhonda told him finally, and led the girl toward the house.

Where, true to her word, Rhonda drew Mary a steaming hot bath.

"These clothes need a serious washing," she declared. Mary blushed a little.

"I. . .I tried to clean them in the creek, but without soap, it just wasn't. . .I didn't do a good job. And I had. . .I mean. . .well, you know," she trailed off, blushing deeper.

"Don't worry," Rhonda told her. "I can help you with that. Now, settle in, and soak a while, and get clean. I got some clothes that should fit you fine. I'll dig them out, and then get started on fixing some supper. Okay?"

Rhonda went and rummaged through her things, finding the things she wanted. Pants, shirt, socks, and underwear. She frowned as she thought about a bra. The girl wasn't developed enough for one of her's, and the others were out in storage. She didn't want Mary to feel uncomfortable, so she grabbed a t-shirt, and a large sweater. As an after though, she also got one of Billy's shirts for the girl to sleep in.

After leaving these things for her, and making sure she was okay, Rhonda went to the kitchen.

She was just finishing up a pot of chili when Mary appeared in the kitchen, wearing the new clothes. Rhonda smiled at her.

"How do you feel?"

"I done forgot what it was to be clean," Mary admitted. "Thank you so. . .so much," her voice faltered. All at once the realization that she wouldn't spend tonight alone, cowering in the dark, hit her, and she almost collapsed. Rhonda grabbed her, and guided her into a chair. She held the girl while she cried.

187

Dottie edged into the mix, huddling between them. Rommel refused to do so, but did sit stoically near them, between them and the door, while Mary cried herself out.

"I'm. . .I'm sorry," she sniffed, raising her head finally. "I. . ."

"Don't be sorry, honey," Rhonda told her, stroking her hair gently. "You been all alone for a long time. I was too, but I'm a lot older'n you. I can't tell you how relieved, how happy, I was when Billy found me."

"He found you too?" Mary asked, eyes wide.

"He's got a habit o' picking up strays," Rhonda smiled. "Ain't he, boy?" she asked Rommel.

Woof!

The bark startled the girl, which startled Dottie, which of course made Rommel stand up, looking for what was wrong.

"Easy, big boy," Rhonda said, gently rubbing Dottie's coat. "Take it easy, girl," she soothed. Dottie responded well, and 'allowed' Mary to pet her as well.

Rommel wasn't so easy.

Rhonda fixed Mary a bowl of hot chili, with some bread and a soft drink.

"Hope you like Coke," Rhonda asked. "Only kinda soft drink we have."

"Oh, I haven't even seen a Coke in. . .well, forever!" Mary gushed.

"All yours," Rhonda smiled, handing the open can to her. Mary chugged on it, then returned to the chili. She was on her second bowl when Billy came in.

Rommel ran to him at once, turning to look at the girl, then back at Billy, as if to say *do you see that stranger in our house?*

"Yeah, I know, boy," Billy said easily, and ruffed the dog's massive head. Rommel accepted this attention with gusto, satisfied that he had done his job. If Billy wasn't worried about the girl being here, then neither was Rommel.

"Somethin' smells good!" Billy said, coming into the kitchen.

"Homemade chili, and fresh bread," Rhonda smiled, setting him a bowl on the table, then one for herself.

"You look better," he told Mary. "Ain't nothin' like a hot bath to make things better, I say," he added, sitting down. "That was how I conned Rhonda into comin' to live with me, ya'know," he winked. "Offered a hot shower."

"Billy Todd!" Rhonda slapped him on the arm. "Well, that was an enticement."

Mary couldn't help but laugh. Billy had put her at ease in just a minute.

"You're not so bad as I thought at the other house," she told him.

"Yeah, well, you didn't shoot at me when I came in, either," he grinned. Mary blushed, but knew that he wasn't serious. Billy had calmed down on the walk home. One of the reasons he'd wanted to walk.

"I put your stuff on the porch," he told her. "We can go through it in the morning."

"Thank you," Mary said quietly.

"Welcome," Billy nodded.

"Okay, let's eat!" Rhonda ordered.

Afterward, Rhonda led Mary to the bedroom near theirs, and made her comfortable.

"You can relax here, sweetie," Rhonda promised. "Nothing will hurt you here, I promise." Dottie jumped up on the bed, curling up on the foot of the bed.

Odd Billy Todd

"Traitor," Rhonda accused, and the sensitive Rottie looked down shamefully. Rhonda rubbed her head, and scratched behind her ears to let her know it was in play. Dottie licked her hand, then settled in.

"Looks like you got company for the night," Rhonda laughed. "Good night honey."

"Thank you," Mary said for at least the hundredth time.

"You're more than welcome. Sleep well." Rhonda went out, and eased the door closed. She turned to go back downstairs, and nearly tripped over Rommel, who had laid down just outside and to the side of Mary's door.

"You old faker," Rhonda chided. Rommel sniffed at that, but made no other response. He curled back up on the floor, just a step away.

"No monsters tonight, little one," Rhonda smiled, and went back downstairs.

-

Mary started awake. She lay perfectly still, looking at the ceiling over her. It was strange. She didn't recognize it. And she wasn't alone.

Warily she raised her head, an inch at the time, until she could see down near her feet. Laying alongside her leg was a dog. A large black dog, dozing comfortably, warming her as she lay in bed.

Bed. She didn't have a bed. All she had was. . . .

"It wasn't a dream," she said to herself. Hearing the girl speak, Dottie roused herself. Crawling up the bed, she licked the girl's hand, and then her face.

"Eww," Mary laughed, pushing Dottie gently away. "Doggy breath! But I'm so glad to see you," she hugged the dog tightly. "I thought it was all a dream!"

Her raised voice prompted another, much larger dog to enter the room, investigating. He sniffed the air, looking at the girl. Puzzled.

"Rommel!" Mary jumped from the bed, racing to the big dog and enveloping him as well. The normally ill-tempered dog allowed this hugging with a snort, sensing that the girl wasn't a threat. He remembered meeting her, last night. And, unlike the girl, he had the advantage of knowing that last night had not been a dream.

"Looks like someone's up early," Mary heard a voice say. She looked up to see Rhonda smiling down at her.

"Oh my God!" Mary leapt to her feet, bounding the few steps to where Rhonda stood and throwing her arms around the older girl.

"I thought it was a dream!" she exclaimed yet again, holding Rhonda tight. "I thought it was all a dream!"

"No, sweetie, it wasn't a dream," Rhonda promised her, returning the girl's hug with enthusiasm of her own. "You're safe."

"Oh my God," Mary repeated, her eyes brimming over with tears. She cried, then. Cried and cried, until Rhonda wondered how many tears her little body could hold. Or spare.

"What in the name o' tar-nation is all. . . ." Billy cut himself off as he saw the scene before him. Rhonda's glare didn't hurt.

"Sorry," Billy muttered, heading for the bathroom.

"Hi, Mister Billy, and I'm *sooo* sorry I almost shot you!" Mary cried, running now to hug Billy as well. Billy caught the girl, a stunned look on his face. But he returned her hug, more from not knowing what else to do than anything otherwise.

189

Rhonda managed to stifle a giggle at the look on his face.

"I'm really, *really* sorry, Mister Billy," Mary told him over and over.

"It's okay, gal," Billy assured her, patting her gently on the back. "Ain't no harm done. Miss is as good as a mile, my Pa used to say."

"I'm so sorry," the girl cried one more time, before stepping back, and wiping her eyes. Billy looked down at her, smiling.

"You said that already," he told her, and Mary laughed at that.

"I know, but I thought it was all a dream. That I had dreamed how you came and found me, and then Miss Rhonda brought me here, and I had a bath with *hot water*, and she cooked me a meal, and. . .and. . .and. . . ."

"It's all real, honey," Rhonda promised, her eyes watering slightly at how amazed the girl was over such simple things. How hard must she have had it? Not for the first time, Rhonda paused to reflect on how blessed they were on the farms, compared to so many others. Yes, they worked hard, and it wasn't easy to make things go, but they had food, clean water, really all the amenities they had enjoyed before the plague.

Not everyone was so fortunate.

"Thank you. Thank you," Mary said softly, sinking to the floor and starting to cry again. Rhonda sat down beside her. Billy looked at them for a minute, and started again for the bathroom.

"You need to go get Amy," Rhonda informed him.

"Uh, why?" Billy asked.

"To check Mary over," Rhonda told him. "She's been on her own, making do any way she can all this time. She needs a check up."

"Okay," Billy shrugged. "I'll go soon as I get dressed."

"Meanwhile, we'll start some breakfast."

-

"Well, other than her being very underweight, and malnourished, I think she's okay," Amy declared. "I can't be positive, of course, and bear in mind I'm only an RN. I can't really do a blood work up, but everything seems okay. Her skin is in bad shape, but a few good baths, with good soap and maybe some lotion or oil and that should clear up. She does have some sores, especially on her legs. She told me they're from walking, and falling, as she moved from place to place. Scrapes and bruises galore."

"Will they heal?" Rhonda asked, concerned. "Are they infected?"

"As she starts to get her health back they should. Her undernourishment is almost certainly playing a part in her slow healing. Her body just doesn't have the vitamins and minerals it needs to keep her immune system operating normally."

"None of them appear to be infected, but I can't tell you why, considering how she had to live," Amy shook her head. "Keep them washed with peroxide twice a day, and bandaged. Some antibiotic ointment wouldn't go amiss, either, just in case. Use it twice a day for three days. That should be enough. Use the peroxide for five, though. After that, she should be fine to go without the bandages. Is she. . .?" Amy gave Rhonda a look.

"Yes, but we dealt with that last night," Rhonda told her. "When her cycle happens again, we'll mark it. And she'll have. . .she'll have what she needs when it happens," she added.

"Then that's it, I'd say," Amy declared. "Unless a problem presents itself, she looks fine. She needs plenty of good food, and clean water. That's the only thing that bothers me, though if she'd developed dysentery it would likely have killed her by now. Still, if she has any problems, let me know right away."

"Thanks, Amy," Rhonda said. "Want to stay for some breakfast?"

"No, thanks," Amy smiled, putting her things away. "I need to get back, and help get our bunch fed. We'll be back over a little later, anyway, for the meeting."

Rhonda walked Amy to the door, then headed back to where Mary sat in the kitchen.

"What would you like for breakfast?" she asked. Mary looked at her.

"Whatever you have?" she replied hesitantly.

"We have about anything you might want," Rhonda told the girl. "Pancakes, bacon, eggs, sausage, biscuits. Name it, we might have it."

Mary's eyes had gotten progressively bigger as Rhonda had run down the menu options. Now she was goggling.

"Where did you get all that?" she asked, her voice nearly breathless.

"Well, some of it we had, some of it we got elsewhere, some we grew ourselves, and some we get fresh here on the farm," Rhonda explained. "Depends on what it is."

"And you still have all that?" Mary asked. "After all this time?"

"Well, we've eat some of it already," Rhonda replied in mock seriousness. "But there's plenty to eat, Mary. I promise. Remember last night?"

"But I. . .I thought that was just because. . .well, because you found me. You can't eat like that all the time! You can't waste food!"

"Honey, we aren't wasting it," Rhonda said kindly. "We have to eat. Around here, we work, and work hard at that. Got to have food when you're working hard."

Mary sat, staring. After three months of living literally hand to mouth, it was beyond her comprehension that she might be eating well, and regularly, once more. Silent tears begin to flow once more as the notion that she really was safe, at last, begin to impact on her.

Rhonda sat down at the table beside her, and took one of the girl's hands in her own.

"Want to talk it out?" she asked.

"I. . .I don't know what to say," Mary didn't quite sob. "I. . .I've been alone for so long, it seems like, and so scared, of everything. I can't. . .I don't. . . ."

"It's okay, honey," Rhonda soothed. "I know some of how you feel. I was all alone for a while myself, before Billy found me. And I'm all grown up. I was still scared. All the time."

"Daddy, he. . .he got sick, like most ever one else did," Mary said slowly. "I took as good o' care of him as I knew how, but nothin' worked. He. . .he died while I was asleep," she squalled. "I didn't *mean* to go to sleep! I was so tired, and I sat down in the chair I kept by his bed, and started readin', and the next thing I know, I'm awake, and he ain't breathin', and I panicked. I tried to wake him up, but he wouldn't wake up. Finally, I figured out he was passed on," she looked at the floor.

"If I hadn't went to sleep. . . ."

"Your daddy would still have died, sweetie," Rhonda told her gently, but firmly. "Not all of us got sick at all. But no one who did recovered. Not a one.

191

Anyone who got sick, died, Mary. Every single one. You going to sleep didn't make any difference." The girl looked up at her, tear filled eyes full of hope. She wanted, needed, to believe it.

"You sure?" she asked, hesitant.

"I swear it," Rhonda nodded. "Same thing happened to my daddy, too," she added, her own eyes misting over. "I took care of him, just like you took care of yours. I was awake when my daddy died, but there still wasn't anything to be done, honey. My daddy just went to sleep, and never woke up. I'd bet your daddy was asleep, too, wasn't he?" she asked, hoping he had been. Mary nodded.

"Yes."

"Now you can't blame yourself for this, Mary," Rhonda told her. "There's no blame here for anybody. And them that's gone, they're all likely better off than we are, right now. They're in a better place, sugar. We're the one's in a mess o' trouble," she added with a grin.

"I. . .I stayed at home for a while, but. . .food kept gettin' harder and harder to get. I finally had to just move on. I had daddy's rifle at first, but it was too much for me to shoot. I found the one I got now in a neighbor's house. It's heavy, but I knew how to use it, and it didn't kick so hard." She paused.

"There was dog's ever where. Seemed like every time I went out, I seen'em. Some didn't pay me no mind, but some did. I had to shoot at'em a few times, just to keep'em away from me. I think a time or two them dogs would have killed me, I hadn't had that rifle."

"We've had trouble with them, too," Rhonda nodded, thinking back to the day she and Billy had found the dog pack attacking the cattle.

"I. . .I never did see nobody alive," Mary said so softly that Rhonda had to strain to hear her. "Ever time I looked, all I found was dead folks. I. . .I knew so many of'em, and now they're all gone. Ever one."

"I know, honey," Rhonda laid a hand on Mary's shoulder. "I know."

"I walked a long way, over time," Mary went on. "I found a little food here and there, and started gathering stuff. I was using a little wagon to pull behind me with the stuff I found. When I found the house over there," she nodded toward the Smith place, "I decided since it was gettin' cold, I better make me a spot. I could hear all of you going around," she added.

"You should have said something," Rhonda told her.

"I was afraid," Mary shrugged. "I heard a bunch of shootin', and, well, I was just afraid. I didn't know who you were, and I was afraid you'd be bad. Mean," she clarified. "Bad people."

"I can imagine," Rhonda nodded. "Well, you don't have to be scared anymore. And you don't have to find a place to stay anymore either. You can stay right here, with us." Mary looked at her, eyes suddenly bright.

"Really? With you and Mister Billy, and Dottie and Rommel?" Rhonda laughed.

"I never thought about you wanting to live with Rommel, but yeah, right here with us. Rommel included."

"I'll. . .I'll work," the girl said firmly. "I can pay my. . . ."

"We all work, Mary," Rhonda stopped her. "And you can help. But you're not 'paying your way'. You're a girl yet, and you're going to have a chance to go back to being a girl for a little while longer. There'll be time enough for you to be a grown up in the years ahead. We'll teach you how to take care of yourself, but you won't be on your own anymore. Not until and unless you want to be. Understand?"

Her answer was to bury her head in Rhonda's shoulder and cry until her little body was wracked by sobs or relief, and joy.

"It'll be okay," Rhonda told her. "I promise."

CHAPTER THIRTY-THREE

"Well, I'll be damned."

Jerry's statement was the general consensus after hearing about Mary Jerrolds.

"That poor girl," Emma said sadly. "All alone for months."

"Thing is, she ain't like to be the only one," Billy noted. Everyone was gathered once again at the Todd household, discussing recent events. This was supposed to have been a meeting about work still to be done, but some time had to be devoted to the addition of Mary Jerrolds to the fold.

"I think we need to add looking for people like her to our 'to do' list," Debbie stated firmly. "We can't let these children face all this alone." The school teacher in her was both shocked and saddened by what had happened to Mary.

"I don't disagree," Rhonda nodded. "But we're going to have to make a place for them. We need to scout around, and find a safe, secure place for them. And someone to oversee it."

"I...I don't see why we couldn't at least help," Debbie said, looking at George for confirmation.

"Likely be others out there somewhere that can too," Jerry offered. "But we're gonna need to study this one. This is a big responsibility we're talkin' about takin' on. We can't just wade into this without some thought, and some plannin'."

"So we just leave them out in the cold while we 'plan'?" Emma demanded.

"I didn't say that," Jerry sighed with frustration. "I don't have a thing in the world against takin' in children. And you ought to be ashamed to suggest it," he added, face reddening.

"All I'm sayin', is we need to study on it, and come up with the best possible way o' handlin' the situation. As for waitin', we've all of us already waited too long. And I'm man enough to admit, the thought didn't occur to me. All I was studyin' on at first was keepin' my family safe."

"And there ain't nothin' wrong with that," Billy spoke up, almost as if daring someone to disagree. "There ain't no blame to be laid on nobody, here. This is just somethin' else we didn't think of. Now that we know, we can try to fix it. Make it right."

"True," Ralph nodded. "I...I'd like to think that people in general would have been open to the idea of caring for a child. But some people don't have enough for their own families right now. Be hard to question them for not wanting more burden when they can't handle what they've got."

"Since when are children *a burden*?" Amy asked scathingly.

"Anyone who has to be fed and can't do it themselves is a burden," Ralph defended himself. "I'm not saying that children in general are a burden. And to quote Jerry, you should be ashamed for thinking about me in such a way." Amy conceded the point, considering that Ralph had taken her and Amanda in to protect them. And care for them.

"Okay, this arguin' ain't gettin' us nowheres," Billy announced, standing. "We got work to do, and a schedule already laid out. Tomorrow we're goin' to meet up with them other folks. We'll have more help, and better safety, maybe. Meanwhile, there's a house to clean, and there's work gotta be done. Everybody can think on this whilst we're workin'."

Nodding, everyone got to their feet.

"Billy, we need to check on the Clifton place," Jerry said suddenly. "We should have done it already, mind. I don't know if there's anyone alive up there or not. Time to find out."

"All right," Billy nodded. "Let me saddle Samson, and I'll go with you."

"We'll ride along, you want," George offered. Ralph nodded.

"Well, ladies, I guess that leaves us cleaning up, as usual," Emma snorted, though it was good natured.

"House is empty," Billy shrugged. "And I sprayed it good last night. Ain't much to do, just some sweepin' and the like."

"You obviously don't know anything about keeping a house," Debbie snorted.

"I'll have you know I kept my own house for some time," Billy shot back. Rhonda nodded.

"When I moved in here, this place was clean as a pin," she told them. "Not even dusty," she added.

"Well, that's a first," Debbie said, casting a glare at George.

"Man done said there's work to be done," George replied, unperturbed. "Let's get at it."

Laughing, the group split up. The newer families had drove over from their place, and now loaded up for the drive back. Billy and Rhonda went to saddle their own horses.

The Silvers and the 'Todds' rode over together. Mary had, thankfully, ridden a horse before, so Billy had taken the most gentle mare he had, and put her on it. She and the horse, an old mare named Bessie, had hit it right off.

"She ain't no race horse," Billy told her, "but she's a gently soul, and sure footed. Just let her follow along, and giv'er her head. She'll take you safely where you want to go." Mary nodded, eager to ride.

"Rommel, Dottie, lead!" Billy ordered.

"Reckon he'll get on with Reb?" Jerry asked.

"Might as well see now, I reckon," Billy shrugged.

Reb was on patrol when the group came down the hill. He spotted the two Rotties at once, and went stiff legged. Billy stopped at that point, and ordered Rommel to stay. The dog quivered, but obeyed. Reb barked once in warning, but otherwise simply stood his ground.

Ralph came out at Reb's bark, and ordered the dog to 'heel'.

"Come on up," Ralph called. "Might as well get it over with!" Billy chuckled, and touched his boots to Samson.

"Rommel, trail," he ordered. Rommel looked at him in confusion, but dutifully fell into trail.

When they were about fifty feet from Reb and Ralph, Billy dismounted.

"Rommel, friend," Billy said forcefully. Rommel looked dubious.

"Friend!" Billy said again, and Rommel understood the authoritative voice.

Billy led Rommel to where Reb was standing, and the big Annie snorted once in warning.

"Friend, Reb," Ralph ordered, much as Billy had. Reb looked just as dubious.

Odd Billy Todd

The dogs squared off, and the owners allowed them to 'greet'. There was some pawing, and snorting, as well as sniffing. The two dogs circled each other, looking for a weakness.

After nearly five minutes, the two dogs abruptly broke apart, and returned to their respective masters.

"Huh," Ralph grunted.

"Okay, I didn't see that comin'," Billy looked surprised.

"Me neither," Ralph admitted. "Dare we assume it's just mutual respect?"

"I don't assume nothin' where this lug is concerned," Billy laughed, ruffing Rommel's head. "Good boy," he added. Ralph did much the same for Reb.

Apparently, the dogs had decided to view each other as equals. Their owners would take that, and gladly.

-

"Now that there is a house," George murmured, getting a look at the Clifton house for the first time. The house was a two story structure, large and solid looking. The windows all sported real shutters, and PV panels lined the roof.

"What ya'll got against electric meters?" Ralph asked, laughing.

"Storms roll through here ever year," Jerry shrugged. "Go three, four days 'thout power four or five times a year, you start into thinkin' you can do better."

"Makes sense," Ralph nodded.

"Save enough on buyin' power that you pay for it in a few years," Billy added. "It's a good investment, and it's payin' off now."

"Can't argue with that," George nodded.

"Any idea if there's still someone here?" Billy asked Jerry, dismounting.

"No," Jerry admitted. "And I should o' came up here and checked."

"Ain't no need in blame layin'," Billy told him flatly. "We all had plenty on our plates, of late." Jerry nodded, and got down.

"Reckon we can just go and knock, first," Billy noted. He walked up to the house, shouting as he did so.

"Mister Clifton! It's Billy Todd, from down the way! Ya'll about?"

Nothing stirred other than a few leaves blowing about in the wind. Billy turned to them.

"Be watchful. Even if the Clifton's ain't about, someone else may be." With that he went to the door, and knocked. He did so from the side, remembering the narrow miss from the night before. There was no response after five minutes of knocking.

"Reckon we can try to get in," Billy said. He found a window that wasn't locked, and forced it up. The smell hit them all at once.

"I'd say your neighbors are inside, all right," George noted sourly.

"Yeah," Billy sighed.

"I'll go," Ralph offered, but Billy shook his head.

"No. I skipped out yesterday. Reckon it's my turn." He pulled himself up to the window, and shimmied his way inside. He saw right away why the stench was so bad.

Mister and Misses Clifton were lying in their bed, side by side. Their withered, nearly mummified remains were still holding hands in the bed they had shared for over fifty years.

Billy removed his hat, gazing at them for a moment. Then he tore himself away and went to open the front door.

"C'mon in," he told the others. "That was their bedroom," he added. Jerry nodded.

"Let's search the rest o' the house, first," George suggested. The others agreed, and spent the next ten minutes doing so. There was no one else in the house, and nothing had been disturbed.

"Well, this place is huge," George said, coming down the stairs. "There must be like eight bedrooms."

"Full basement, too," Billy nodded, coming up from there.

"Was a big bunch, once upon a time," Jerry nodded mournfully.

"Let's get the Clifton's moved to a decent spot," Billy suggested. "Jerry, why don't you see if their tractor'll start. We can use that to bury them with." Grateful for the reprieve, Jerry nodded, and hurried outside.

"He was close to Mister Clifton, once upon a time," he said quietly to Ralph and George. "C'mon."

Together the three men carefully and respectfully wrapped the bodies in what Billy thought were their favorite quilts, and then with a sheet. One by one, they carried them carefully outside.

"Tractor had a trickle charger on the battery," Jerry announced, getting down from the tractor he'd brought up. There was a front scoop and a back hoe attachment hooked up.

"Why don't you pick a proper spot, Jerry," Billy said softly. The older man nodded, and climbed back aboard. He drove to a spot beneath a large oak tree, and started digging.

The job was finished in less than half an hour, as they laid the Clifton's to rest, still together, after all those years.

"We should all be so lucky," Ralph intoned quietly, as the bodies were being covered.

"Yeah."

-

"Needs a good dustin', but otherwise, I'd say it's a good deal, especially if we're thinkin' on little one's and what not."

"The house is as secure as we can ask," George agreed. "How far back to the next road?" he pointed toward the back of the Clifton property.

"At least five miles, I reckon," Billy nodded, looking at Jerry. The older man nodded his agreement.

"Then I'd say this is the place," Ralph said firmly. "I guess we can start with Mary."

"Um. . .yeah, 'bout that," Billy said hesitantly. "I. . .I wouldn't count on that, was I you."

"What? Why?" George asked.

"I'm fair certain that Rhonda aims for Mary to stay with us," Billy told them. "She ain't out an' out said so, yet. But I'd not bet a'gin it."

"Well, that's different," George chuckled. "Still, you guys can't take them all in, so this place will still serve, if and when we wind up with more people."

"I agree, and Hank would like that," Jerry smiled. "He loved a big family."

"Well, reckon that's settled then," Billy nodded. He took a key ring from the hanger by the door, and fiddled with the keys until he found the right one. Locking the door, he handed the keys to George.

"'Spect you'll be needin' them."

Rhonda had left Mary with Georgie and Amanda, not wanting to put her through being in the Smith house again. Mary had readily agreed, which just re-enforced Rhonda's sense of the situation. The girl was still shy, and hesitant, but she was improving. Only one day removed from her long ordeal, Rhonda thought Mary was doing wonderful.

"So, you want us to take Mary?" Debbie asked, smiling.

"No," Rhonda shook her head. "I promised her she could stay with us." Debbie looked shocked.

"But she. . .she really needs a family, Rhonda!" Rhonda stopped dead, looking at Debbie.

"You don't think Billy and I can give her that?" she challenged.

"I. . .I didn't say that," Debbie demurred. "I was just thinking about what's best for Mary."

"And you'd be better for her than we would, is that it?" Rhonda asked, her voice dangerously calm.

"Well, we do have children of our own," Debbie nodded, blissfully unaware of the dangerous ground she was treading on.

"All the more reason not to take on any more," Rhonda nodded firmly. "And we can take care of her just fine, I imagine."

"I wasn't saying that you couldn't, dear," Debbie said, reaching out to touch Rhonda's shoulder. Rhonda dodged away.

"Yeah, you were," the younger woman shot back. "Why is it so hard to believe that we could give her a good home, huh?"

"Rhonda, I don't think that's what she was getting at," Amy said, trying to gently break the discussion up.

"Then just what *was* she gettin' at?" Rhonda demanded, hands on her hips now, green eyes blazing.

"Rhonda, you two are so young," Debbie tried again. "And. . .well, inexperienced."

"And you was experienced, when your son came along?" Rhonda asked.

"Well, I've been teaching for. . . ."

"Teaching?" Rhonda scoffed. "And what does *teaching* do for your parenting skills? Besides, it ain't like Mary's a baby. She's almost a teenager. She don't need coddling, she needs people who can help her grow into a confident woman who can look after herself!"

"Rhonda," Emma said softly, and the young woman snapped her head around.

"That's enough, dear," Emma said kindly. "I don't think anyone objects to your and Billy raising Mary. Especially if that's what she wants. Right?"

"Suits me," Amy nodded, trying to calm the waters. She didn't know Debbie much better than she did Rhonda.

"Well, I still think she needs a stable family," Debbie had to add.

"What's unstable about us?" Rhonda demanded. "Wasn't for us, where would *you* be?" Debbie didn't have an answer for that, and wisely shut her mouth.

"I think I'll head home," Rhonda said suddenly. "I don't like the atmosphere around here," she added, looking at Debbie. The older woman wouldn't meet her eyes.

"Rhonda, I don't think that's necessary," Emma told her. "There's plenty of work to do, I'm sure." Rhonda looked at her for a moment, then nodded sullenly.

"Stay away from me," she told Debbie pointedly. Grabbing her cleaning gear, she stalked up the road, where the Smith house sat in sight. Emma waited until she was out of ear shot, then turned to look at Debbie.

"What is your problem with them raising that child?" she demanded. Her voice had lost the 'kind old lady' tone she usually adopted.

"I just think that it's best for the child to be raised in a proper home," Debbie replied, just a little defiant.

"And who defines proper?" Emma asked.

"Well, a mother and a father," Debbie answered. "What else?"

"So you think Billy and Rhonda can't function as a mother and father? Or maybe an older brother or sister?"

"That's hardly the point," Debbie waved her comment away. "I've had years of experience dealing with children, and have one of my own. I'm obviously the best. . . ."

"I have two children, myself, you might have noticed," Emma cut in icily. "As for your teaching skills, I hardly see where that qualifies you to be a parent. You have a son, and he deserves your attention. Bottom line, I think that Mary Jerrolds is more than able to decide who she wants to live with."

"Children can't just live where they want!" Debbie objected. "They have to have a safe and stable environment. One that has been certified by. . . ."

"By who?" Emma challenged. "By you? By some social worker? Politician? Let me tell you something, missy," Emma scolded. "Those two young people are as fine a couple as you'll ever meet, anywhere. Billy Todd has more moral character than any man twice his age. His parents raised him to be a good and honest man, and to care for those who can't care for themselves. To help those in need, and to protect those who can't protect themselves. And Rhonda Higgins had raisin' that was just as good, and she's as smart as a whip to boot. They're two of the finest people this county ever had the privilege to be home to."

"And that girl is from right here in our county," Emma added. "We're fresh out of social workers and regulations, in case you hadn't noticed. And I hardly think that you should be offending the very people who helped pull you out of a bad situation. Should I go on? Or are you getting my meaning?"

Debbie's face was red by the time Emma was through. She was preparing a retort when Amy interrupted.

"Debbie, what the hell is wrong with you?" Debbie looked at her house mate.

"With me?" she demanded. "Are you taking their side, now?"

"The only *side* here is Mary's," Amy told her flatly. "What is your problem with Billy and Rhonda."

"They aren't even married," Debbie said quietly.

"Neither are Ralph and I, but you're sharing a house with us."

"That's hardly the same thing!" Debbie retorted. "Children need a good, stable home environment. Those two are fine people, but hardly parenting material."

"And who the hell put you in charge of deciding that?" Amy huffed. "Am I bad parenting material because Ralph and I aren't married?" Amy was starting to get mad now.

"Debbie, dear," Emma said. "I think there's an old saying you should acquaint yourself with."

"What?" Debbie demanded.

"When you see you're in a hole, stop digging." Amy guffawed at that.

"Lord, I ain't heard that in *years*!" she exclaimed, laughing. Debbie looked between the two women, at a loss for words.

"She's right, Debbie," Amy told her, when she stopped laughing. "You're dead wrong, and deep down I think you know it. Now, let this go, and let's go clean a house. And you might want to start thinking about how you're going to apologize to Rhonda."

"For what?" Debbie demanded.

"For being a pompous ass, dear," Emma smiled sweetly. "Now, let's do go and clean a house. We have other things to do today."

-

"Well, of course I want to stay with Rhonda and Billy," Mary looked shocked at the question. "Where else would I stay?"

-

The house was clean, and the women were gathered back at the Maness/Purdy place. The men were there as well, and had each been told, by the women in their lives, of the 'discussion' on the road that day.

There was no real arguing, just a good bit of heated discussion. Billy listened quietly for a while, then stood.

"Let's ask her, and be done with it."

"She can't make such a decision herself!" Debbie had objected.

"She lived all alone for near three months, maybe more," Billy replied flatly. "Reckon she's earned the consideration to choose for herself." With that he'd called Mary into the room.

"Girl, we need to know something. Ain't no one gonna mind, whatever you say. Some here don't think you can decide on your own, and some don't see as you should live with Rhonda and me. Thing is, you're near thirteen. Done lived on your own all this time, and done well. I figure you earned the right to choose where you want to live."

"Do you want to stay with Rhonda and Billy, dear?" Emma asked.

-

"I still say she can't make that decision herself!" Debbie exclaimed after Mary's declaration.

"And who are you again?" Mary asked, surprising them all. Debbie looked at her.

"I'm Debbie Purdy, dear," she smiled.

"And you think I ought to live here, with you, is that it?"

"Yes, honestly I think it's best," Debbie replied.

"And just why is that?" Mary wanted to know. Debbie blinked at that. Such a direct question from the girl startled her.

"Well. . .I mean, I just assumed you'd want to be here, with us. With the other children, and where I can teach you."

"Teach me what?" Mary asked. "How to spell, and do math? I know all that," she waved her hand away. "There won't be no college for me, and even if there was, what would I do with it?"

"My daddy always spoke high o' Mister Todd," she pointed at Billy. "My daddy didn't speak high o' many. But he said Mister Todd was the fairest, most honest man he'd ever dealt with in Cedar Bend. And trusted him to work on his truck, and no body else."

"And even after I near shot him to death, he and Rhonda took me in, and fed and clothed me. And. . .and after so long, all on my own, I slept last night feelin' safe for the first time in I can't even remember when." She looked at Billy and Rhonda.

"So long as they'll let me, I aim to stay with them."

"Well, I'd say that settles that," Emma declared. "Now, I need to get home. I've got to make sure that Shelly hasn't burned my kitchen up." She rose, and Jerry took her arm.

"See you boys in the mornin'," he said to Ralph and George. Both nodded.

"Guess we can head on, too," Billy rose. "Get your coat, little'un. Time to go home, I think."

"Okay," Mary smiled, and went to do as she was told.

"This is a mistake," Debbie told those still at the 'meeting'. "That child needs a good home."

"We've got a good home," Billy shrugged. "She wants to stay with us, she can. We got plenty o' room. We can take care of her."

"She needs a family," Debbie insisted.

"Reckon we can be a family," Billy said, starting to get just a little touchy. "And she made her choice. Reckon that's it."

"Me too," Rhonda said coldly. "Let's go," she said to Billy. "I want to be away from here." Billy nodded. They went to collect Mary, and left.

"This is wrong," Debbie told the others.

"Debs, the girl made her choice," George tried.

"She shouldn't have had a choice!" Debbie almost yelled. The others, George included, frowned at that.

"Debbie, what makes you the authority on that?" Amy asked.

"I know what's best for that child!"

"She knows what she wants," George told her, his voice soft but firm.

"I'd say this is settled," Ralph nodded. "I know you wanted her to stay here, but she wants to be there. And she's old enough to know what she wants, Debbie."

"I'm through talking about this," Amy said, standing. "I got better things to do." With that she departed, intending to start supper.

"Reckon we all do," George agreed. "Deb?"

"Fine," she snapped, seeing that even her husband wouldn't support her. She stood and stalked after Amy. Ralph watched her go, and turned to George.

"What was that all about?" he asked, puzzled. "Never seen her act so."

"We can't have no more children," George said sadly. "Deb always wanted a daughter."

CHAPTER THIRTY-FOUR

The next morning was colder than previous days. It was still almost three weeks until Thanksgiving, but it was already feeling like December. Billy had checked some of his father's books again concerning climate change after something like this. There was little in them about something like this, but most experts had agreed that a mass die off of people, which would be followed by a similar die off in domestic animals, would affect the temperature at least some.

As near as Billy could tell, they were just starting to see that now. Without so many cars, without so many people trying to heat their homes, the heat level was far lower than usual for these days. That meant cooler temperatures.

He thought, anyway. Some of the information frustrated him a little, since he couldn't really grasp all of it. Some of the so-called 'higher math' was just beyond what he knew. But his father had, as usual, made margin notes to himself, and Billy could follow those. He was convinced that the colder temperatures were probably a sign of more of their 'new normal'.

"Cold this mornin'," George noted.

"Sure is," Jerry agreed, rubbing his hands together. "Afraid we'll see more o' this."

"Prob'ly," Ralph nodded. "Ain't so many people no more. Or cars. Or factories. Gonna be colder."

"Everybody ready?" Billy asked, as he and Rhonda came outside. Rhonda handed out coffee to everyone, and placed a picnic basket inside the truck box, next to the one Emma had brought.

"Yep," Jerry nodded. "Thanks, lil bit," he gratefully accepted the coffee from Rhonda. Mary had gone to Emma's for the day, where Shelly and Toby had agreed to keep watch over her, and Toby would be watching over all the places while the others were away.

"Guys, I want to apologize for last night," George said, once they were in the truck and on their way. "I. . .I didn't see this coming. We can't have no more kids, and Debbie always wanted a girl. I should have been watching out for that, but I. . .there's so much other stuff going on, I just didn't think about it."

"She'll come around, I'm sure," he ended on what he hoped was a high note. No one spoke for a minute, until Rhonda finally turned to look at him.

"It's all right, George," she said softly. "Truth is, I could have handled it better, I imagine. I'm prone to be. . .touchy, about stuff."

"You?" Billy asked, in mock incredulity. "Touchy? Say it ain't so, baby!"

"Smart ass," Rhonda muttered, her face reddening. Everyone had a much need laugh over that.

"You don't think it's gonna be a problem while we're gone, do you George?" Jerry asked, thinking that Mary would be at his place.

"No, I don't, or I would have stayed home," he shook his head. "She's just. . .she just saw a chance to have a daughter, and grasped at it. She promised me last night, after we went to bed, that she wouldn't say anything else."

"And, if we happen to find more children, then I imagine she'll have her hands full," he chuckled.

After that, discussion fell to just normal business. They discussed how they would handle meeting the others, and then chores still needing to be done before true winter. As a result, the trip passed fairly quickly.

The selected meeting place had been a country store, five miles east of Franklin. It wasn't middle ground by any means, but it was a good place, and far enough from the Farms that no one could simply guess where they'd came from.

They arrived right on time, to find three vehicles waiting. George and Ralph had warned both parties that there would be others at the meeting, hoping to avoid any surprises. They were grateful to see the members of both parties talking to each other when they pulled in.

"George you old grave robber!" Terry Blaine bellowed, grabbing George into a bear hug. "Where you been hidin'?"

"Here and there," George grunted. He was a big man, but Terry Blaine was a monster, easily four inches and sixty pounds larger. Sixty pounds of muscle, George reminded himself as he mentally checked his skeleton for breaks.

"Good to see you, man," Peter Two Bears nodded, opting to shake hands rather than hug.

"You too, Pete," George grinned. "Guys, this is Jerry and Emma Silvers, and Billy and Rhonda Todd." he pointed to each in turn.

"Folks, this here is Terry Blaine, and his wife Maria," he pointed to a petite Hispanic woman. "And this is Pete Two Bears."

"Please to meet you folks," Terry said, shaking both Billy and Jerry's hands. Maria nodded her agreement.

"Heard a lot about you," Jerry said, smiling.

"All lies," Terry snorted at once.

"Gentlemen, ladies," Pete said from where he was. He wasn't unfriendly, but didn't offer to make contact.

"And I think we all know Ben, here," Ralph pointed to a red-faced Ben Kelvey. He nodded jerkily.

"I. . .let me just apologize for my jackassedness from earlier before I do anything else. I am so truly sorry for how I acted, and I hope there ain't no hard feelin's."

"Not on my part," Billy shrugged, and extended his hand. Kelvey took it, grateful.

"I really appreciate that," he said earnestly. "This here is my brother, Jon," he pointed to the man next to him. Jon gingerly extended his hand, obviously in pain.

"Nice to meet you," he said, smiling in pain. "Thanks for not shooting the jackass," he nodded to his brother. "He's been a life saver since *I* got shot."

"Welcome," Billy smiled.

"This is my nephew Howie, and his fiance Elizabeth," Ben introduced the young couple.

"I understand I owe you for more than just not shooting the jackass," Howie grinned, shaking hands.

"Toby did all that," Billy murmured. "I just helped. Glad to see you're okay," he added.

"Well, reckon I'm not okay, as yet," Howie shrugged. "But I'm well on my way."

"Ma'am," Billy nodded to Elizabeth. She nodded in return, but looked at Emma.

"I remember you," she said softly, smiling for the first time. "I. . .thank you so much," she added.

"You're welcome, dear," Emma smiled.

"Well, reckon now we met, we can talk!" Ralph said, grinning.

-

"I think we can say we're interested," Ben said for his family, after discussion had died down. "It'll be a job movin', that's for sure, but it sounds like it's more than worth it. Truth to tell, we was figuring we were gonna have to do something soon, anyways."

"Why's that?" Jerry asked. He had to admit, when Kelvey wasn't being an ass, he was a pretty good guy.

"Since what happened in Franklin, folks is startin' to get desperate," he admitted. "That bunch took every scrap o' food, and anything else they could lay hands to, and then headed off. People are hungry, and hungry people sometimes ain't nice people."

"That's a nice way of putting it," Emma said. Ben shrugged.

"Can't blame'em so much. They're in a tight spot. I don't like what they're doing, but I do understand it."

"Pretty charitable," Jerry added, surprised. Kelvey just shrugged.

"We've seen the same thing," Terry nodded. "Ain't nobody tried to take from us, yet, but they ain't sure just where we're at." He studied the others.

"I'm not against what you're doing, but I don't know that I want to just up an re-settle somewhere else. We've got a lot of stuff to move, and it would be a job of the first order, to be sure. And our place. . .well, let's just say it was built with something like this in mind," he settled for saying.

"I don't have a lot of stuff," Peter interjected. "But I've decided I'll stay with Terry and his family. Whatever they decide to do, that's how I'll go."

"Well, as to moving," George shrugged. "Billy brought a semi to move us."

"I'd need one, just for my own stuff," Terry nodded seriously. "And still would need my truck and trailer," he admitted.

"Well, we'd need something similar, I'd guess," George scratched his head. "I mean, we've got a lot o' tool's we'd have to move. Can't leave'em behind, cause we couldn't maybe replace'em."

Billy watched as these exchanges took place. Everyone weighed in, including Rhonda and Emma, but Billy stayed silent. He listened to the arguments for and against, listened to potential problems, and proposed solutions. In all that time, he said nothing.

Finally, he did.

"Look," he stood. "All this is great, but it ain't gettin' the cat skint. Bottom line is, do you guys want to go or not? Any kinda problems with gettin' you moved, we can deal with. If not one way, then another. That ain't an issue. We have to get another semi, we will. We need two, we'll get'em. All that hinges on what you guys want to do."

"I got a semi," Jon said, chuckling. "It's not an OTR rig, I just hauled logs with it. What I don't have is a trailer."

"Then let's go get one," Billy shrugged.

"Just like that?" Terry asked, appraising the up to now silent Billy again.

"Yep," Billy nodded. "Ya'll live around here, so where could we find a couple trailers?"

"Today?"

"Why not?" Billy shrugged. "We're here, you're here. Got light left. We can get trailers, move'em in where you can start loadin'. We'll help, or we can do it when we come back to help you guys move. Meantime, you can load what you can yourselves. I know ya'll ain't able," Billy waved in the Kelvey's general direction. "But we can lend a hand on that. Once it's done, we bring a truck, you can use yours," he nodded to Jon, "and we convoy you all back to the Farms."

"Simple, huh?" Pete Two Bears snorted.

"Most things are simple, when you get to the root," Billy nodded, looking right at the former soldier.

"And what if we don't *want* to live on your 'Farms'," Two Bears asked, not quite making it a challenge.

"Then you stay where ya are," Billy shrugged. "Simple," he added pointedly.

Two Bears stared at Billy for a long minute, and several onlookers began to look concerned. Billy simply returned the look with a calm air, waiting.

Suddenly Two Bears nodded, as if deciding something.

"I like you," he said. "I like a man looks me in the eye when he's talking."

Billy shrugged, nodding by way of a reply. Collective breaths were released around the group, held for very different reasons.

"Well, we're in, I think," Ben repeated. "And I'm ready to get started. Sooner we do this, sooner we're finished. I'd like to be settled in before winter hits full on."

"Well, let's us go find you a trailer, then," Billy smiled.

Terry Blaine looked at his wife, who had so far had nothing to say. She returned his look for a moment, then nodded abruptly. He raised an eyebrow in question, and she nodded again, more firmly.

"Well, looks like we're in," he announced. "Better go get two trailers, I guess."

-

Jon had gone with Billy and George to get his truck, and then to get a trailer.

"I know where some box trailers are," he told them. "Should still be there, anyway. And they're probably empty. I'll have to watch the fuel gauge though. Truck ain't got much fuel left."

"I got some in that tank," Billy pointed to the bed. "We'll be fine."

"Great!"

Billy followed Jon for almost ten miles, until the trucker pulled off the road into a gravel lot. There were five box trailers sitting in the lot, none of them hooked to trucks. There were, however, two trucks in the lot.

"We oughta look at one o' them," George said.

"Might do," Billy nodded.

The men all emerged from their vehicles, Jon having backed in to one of the trailers.

"Didn't think about them trucks bein' here," Jon told them. "Might have more fuel than mine."

"You game to leave yours here, though?" George asked.

"Well, there ain't no real sentimental value to it," Jon said dryly.

"We can see about gettin'em started, I guess."

"I'll take that Pete, if we can get it started," Jon offered. "Nice rig."

The men worked on the trucks for a few minutes, and used Billy's truck to jump start them. Both ran ragged for a few minutes, until the Pri-D that Billy had added to the tank started to help.

"Handy to have around," Jon grinned at him.

"Sometimes," Billy shrugged. "Well, I guess we can see about these trailers."

All of them turned out to be empty, just as Jon had suggested. He chose the best two, and he and Billy hooked up. Billy's truck was a Mack. He hated, *hated* the thought of driving one of these things again, but George had no experience in one, and for his sins, Billy had a little, now.

"Guess we'll follow you," Billy said over the radio.

"Works," Jon replied. They had already agreed to a radio protocol. Jon pulled out of the lot, with Billy following. George rode the drag. Billy wished now they had brought another vehicle, with a local to drive ahead. But it was too late for that now.

Prob'ly be all right, he told himself. Billy didn't like probably. Not one bit, he didn't.

The trip wasn't as nerve wracking as his first had been, but there were a few moments. In one close turn, the trailers rear wheels went off the culvert slightly, even though Billy had followed Jon's turn as closely as possible. With George coaching, however, Billy managed to get the trailer back on the road, no worse for wear.

That turn was the last one, he discovered, as they followed Jon to the Kelvey home. Everyone had gathered there, waiting for the trucks. Surprise was evident when they saw the two new trucks.

"I see you're driving again," Rhonda smirked, as Billy climbed down.

"And I still don't like it," he grumped, as Rhonda hugged him tightly.

"Did okay, though," George encouraged, coming up from behind.

"Had a little practice this time," Billy grinned sheepishly. "Anyway, we got two pretty good trucks, and trailers."

"Like my new rig?" Jon asked his brother, grinning.

"Always did want a Pete, didn't you," Ben chuckled. "Only took the end of the world to get one." Everyone had a good laugh at that one.

"We'll follow you to your place, now, I guess," Billy told Terry Blaine. "Drop this truck and trailer off. We need to decide when we want to do the move. We'll come back and help."

"Well, we been kinda talking that through," Terry told him. "I figure we can come help Ben, and he can come help us, and the three of us can get everything loaded in about a week. That's allowing for the unforeseen, mind you. Likely we can get it faster than that. Once we're ready, we'll give you a call. Ya'll come down, and lead us there, and maybe ride shotgun. Ralph told me what happened when they moved."

"Yeah, that was tight," Jerry nodded. "Good thing we went when we did, though, or. . .well," he shrugged.

"We'd have been corn-cobbed," George finished for him. "Plain and simple."

"All right, so a week, or so. That can work," Jerry mused. "We got work we need to do, anyway, so it ain't like the time will be wasted. Be nice to know what the weather would be like, week from now," he sighed.

"Yeah, I miss the Weather Service," Terry chuckled. "'Bout the *only* thing I miss, though. I swear, I hate to say it, and don't want no one thinking bad of me for it, but my life has been a lot better these last few months, in some ways."

"I think we've all had that thought a time or two," Jerry agreed. "Still, there's some comfort to be found in knowin' things."

"And in numbers," Ben put in. "I ain't gonna lie, I been on edge ever since what happened in Franklin. That town was doing pretty good until the raid."

"Ever figure out who they were, or where they came from?" Billy asked.

"Folks said they was usin' a train," Ben shrugged. "Unloaded like a swarm o' grasshoppers, and just started strippin' the town of anything useful." Billy and Rhonda exchanged glances.

"I think we need to look at a map," Billy said finally, and Rhonda went to get one from the truck. "We seen that train before, I'm thinking. Further we stay from the tracks, better off we're likely to be."

CHAPTER THIRTY-FIVE

"Did you have a good trip?" Mary asked, as the three of them left the Silvers' farm for home.

"Well, nobody shot at us," Billy told her, and Mary blushed.

"That ain't what I meant," Billy told her, seeing her reaction. "Seems ever time we leave here, someone wants to shoot at us, or take somethin' from us."

"Ain't that the truth," Rhonda murmured.

"So this time was different?" Mary asked.

"Smooth trip, little'un," Billy smiled. "We'll have some more neighbors in a week or so."

"Who?" Mary asked, a little concern in her voice.

"Folks from up around Franklin," Rhonda told her. "Two families, in fact. Five men, two women, and two kids."

"How old?"

"You know, I didn't ask," Rhonda admitted. "But the little girl looked like she was close to your age, and the boy maybe a year younger."

"Neat!" Mary grinned. Rhonda looked at the girl from the corner of her eye. Mary seemed to be recovering well from her ordeal. Rhonda shuddered every time she thought of her being alone for so long. Her lack of a good food supply, coupled with the inability to have proper hygiene had taken it's toll.

But a couple days of decent food and safe sleeping had helped her along. Rhonda was giving her vitamins every day as well, just as Amy had ordered. The wounds on her little body were looking better each time Rhonda washed and rebandaged them. Emotionally, Mary was still on a roller coaster. Sometimes talking and acting like a normal pre-teen girl, others she broke down into tears for no apparent reason. But Rhonda knew the reason. Everyone did.

"Well, home sweet home," Billy sighed tiredly. "I don't reckon you got the eggs, did you?" he asked Mary.

"Yep!" she smiled. "Toby brought me over here, and helped me feed the horses, and I got the eggs then."

"Well, good job," Billy told her. "And I 'ppreciate it."

"Me too," Rhonda smiled. "That was very thoughtful of you, Mary."

"Ah, I enjoyed it. Toby's nice." Billy looked at her for a moment, but didn't say anything. Rhonda's eyes danced just a bit, but she managed not to giggle.

"Well, I'm goin' in and takin' a load off," Billy announced. "I gotta see about hookin' up the PV cells at the old Smith place tomorrow, and gettin' the panels up."

"Anyone helping you?" Rhonda asked.

"Ralph and George are," Billy nodded. "Still take most of the day, though. I just hope there's enough to make do." They had scavenged all the panels, inverters and batteries they could find, but not everyone used solar, even in the far rural areas they lived in. Most places where people could afford them had at least a small system, for power outages, but it took more than a three or four panel set-up to power a house.

"Well, what time are you going up there?" Rhonda wanted to know.

"Not till after eight or so," Billy shrugged. "I'm sleepin' in tomorrow."

"Eight is sleeping in?" Mary looked aghast.

"Around here it is," Rhonda nodded. "Early to bed and all that," she grinned.

"Ohh-kay," Mary drew out the word. "That would explain certain people's grumpiness," she eyed Billy carefully. He snorted.

"So does gettin' shot at," he reminded her, and she blushed, but then grinned. "At least I didn't hit ya!"

"For which I am truly thankful," Billy said dryly. "You sit out here in the cold all you want. I'm goin' inside."

-

A week seemed like a long time, and it was in some cases. Waiting a week to see a doctor, for instance. That was a long time. But there was a lot of work to be done before winter, and a week didn't seem so long when it was stacked up against a list of things that had to get done.

The entire first day of that week, for Billy, George and Ralph, anyway, was spent on and off the roof of the Smith house. Installing PV cells, running lines, and hooking up inverters took up the entire day. Billy lost count of how many trips he made up and down the ladder. But, by the time they'd finished, the house was ready. The Kelvey's power needs would be met, although Billy didn't think they'd be able to run the microwave and the washer at that same time. Still, they'd eventually find more panels. Any type of solar equipment was high on their salvage list.

"Well, that's one thing off the list," Ralph sighed, as they gathered their tools and equipment.

"Yeah," George nodded. "Too bad there's umpteen more behind it."

"Won't take too long, on most of it," Billy said. "Biggest thing is just makin' sure we're good for winter. I'd love to have some more food put away for the stock, but most of what's out there is. . . ." he trailed off, thinking.

"What is it, Billy?" George asked.

"We been worryin' all this time about feedin' them hogs. There's corn and soy and milo all over this valley, just lyin' there. Folks that raise hogs in a big way just turn the pigs into the harvested fields and let'em glean the leavings."

"Huh," Ralph stopped, looking at him. "I. . .you know, I knew that, but it never occurred to me."

"Me either, and we used to do it with cows," George shook his head sadly. "Why in hell didn't I think o' that?"

"We'll have to see about which fields are fenced okay enough for it," Billy warned. "And we can't just leave'em out there, neither. On account o' the wild dogs, and coyotes. Not to mention any cougars around."

"I don't know that the dogs would be a serious problem, Billy," George replied. "Hogs are mean by nature. The boars alone would probably stomp any dogs that got inside. The cats, now, that's something else again," he said thoughtfully.

"Well, hadn't thought about that," Billy nodded, thinking. "We need to talk to Jerry about this, I reckon. But that can wait one more day, far as I'm concerned. I don't know 'bout you fellas, but I'm hungry."

"Me, too," the others chorused, then laughed.

"See ya'll in the mornin'."

-

Odd Billy Todd

"Yeah, that would work," Jerry nodded. "I should o' thought of it, too, Billy," he patted Billy's shoulder. "I raised hogs for years. Only got out of it cause the price fell out of'em. It was easier to buy than to raise, and it was a lot of work."

"Well, we maybe can look things over, once we get caught up," Billy offered. "Meanwhile, what you think we should do tomorrow?"

It was the bi-weekly 'meal' where the Todd's and the Silvers' got together for supper. Tonight, they were at the Silvers'. Billy was studiously ignoring Mary's blatant mooning over Toby. Toby was too.

Rhonda was watching the going's on with a definite sparkle in her eyes, both at Billy's wary glances, and Toby's discomfort. She was pretty sure that it was a harmless crush, and one that Mary would get over it soon, and that Toby wouldn't do or say anything bad in the mean time was a given.

But, in their greatly reduced world, the fact was there weren't many options for either one, and Toby was only four years older than Mary. That was a lot, right now, but in another three years it would mean nothing.

But we don't have to think about that tonight, she shook herself. *Tonight, we just enjoy.*

The week had gone by fast. In that time, the folks on the "Farms" had managed to get everything on the list finished, but at the cost of being completely exhausted.

So of course, that was when the Blaine and Kelvey families had called to announce they were ready to go. Hasty radio codes had been worked out so that eavesdroppers wouldn't realize what was being planned. After what had happened on the trip to reach the Maness and Purdy families, no one was taking any chances.

Terry had informed them that far ranging parties were increasing, taking food and other supplies from wherever they could find them. The group at the farm had postponed the trip for one day to rest, and outfit for the trip.

"Truck tank is full," Billy said, as everyone who was going had gathered around the table in his dining room. "We're only taking one truck, so we're good."

"There's three private vehicles, but they have drivers for all of them," Terry added. "All we need is people to help run security."

"I figure we take the Ford and run blocker with it," Billy continued. "We got three maps fixed up, with rally points, and two different routes, in case we get separated. None of'em show where we are," he added. "The last rally point is at Gauge's Grocery store." Jerry nodded at that. Gauge's had closed long before the plague, but was still a landmark used by locals, as it had been for years. He and Billy had even talked about using the building as a market, once they reached that point. But for now, it was a good meeting point, about eight miles distant from the Farms.

"We'll leave 'fore dawn," Billy told them. "Be nice to start headin' back this way by two hours after first light. If we can, that'd give us plenty o' light left to get folks settled."

"George will ride with Terry," Ralph said. "I'll ride with Ben. That way, someone is with each party who knows how to get where. That work?"

"Long as someone from their group rides with me," Billy nodded. "I wanna make sure we can bust up any roadblock we come across. I'll need an extra gun." He looked at Jerry.

211

"You, Toby, and Rhonda will secure the farm while we're gone. We can't keep leaving ourselves uncovered like we have been. If these 'parties' are going further and further out, then sooner or later they're liable to find us, even if it's by accident."

"We'll handle it," Jerry promised.

"About that," George spoke again. "I've been looking for a place for an observation post. I think I've got a good spot picked out. I thought once we get back, and settled, I'd let Pete take a look. We can build a small shed, maybe get a stove in there for some heat. We may want to think about manning that, at least during the day."

"That ain't no bad idea," Jerry mused, thinking about it. "If we had warning before someone just showed up, then we could have time to get things into position before any kinda trouble reached us. We need to see about that." "Soon's we get this done," Billy nodded, trying to get back on track. "As it stands, now, it's me, George, and Ralph going. We'll take supplies for staying overnight, and a little extra. Anybody got anything to add?"

"Seems like you're going shorthanded," Rhonda said, not happy that she was being left behind.

"Ain't no help for it," Billy said, shrugging. "We can't keep leaving this place unattended, and that's just a fact. We done took too many chances with that as it is." The others nodded in agreement. Except Rhonda. Of course.

"All right, then," Billy brought the meeting to a close. "We'll plan to leave here by four. I'll be by to get you fella's by then. Anything else?" No one had anything, and the meeting broke up.

"I think I should be going with you," Rhonda said firmly, once the meeting had ended, and everyone had gone.

"I'd like it, but we can't keep doin' that. Not now, anyway," he added, nodding toward Mary, who was watching a DVD. Rhonda looked at her, then back to Billy.

"You're blaming her?" Rhonda asked, eyes narrowing.

"I'm not *blamin'*, I'm *explainin'*," Billy emphasized. "Fact is, we're responsible for her now. And this here is the last time we're doin' this, at least for a while. I like these new folks pretty good, and I'm glad they're comin', but I don't want us goin' so fast with this."

"And she needs someone here with her," he added. "Not to mention the fact that if something happens here, Toby and Jerry will need your help. Once I get back, we'll see about cachin' our stuff, so that no matter where we are, we'll be near something we might need. Since what happened in Franklin, I don't think we need to worry about too many caches on that trip. Ain't likely we'll be going much," he admitted.

"Yeah, I'd thought about that," Rhonda nodded. She hadn't counted on how keeping Mary Jerrolds with them would impact their lives so much. She was used to going everywhere Billy went, and she didn't like not being able to. She looked at Mary again, however, and realized that she was willing to make those sacrifices in order to give the girl a good home.

Debbie hadn't said anything more about Mary living with them, just as George had promised. She didn't seem bitter about it, either. Rhonda was willing to forget it, so long as Debbie did. And, she figured she could have handled things better, herself.

"Anyway, I got a early mornin', so I'm gonna get cleaned up and hit the hay," Billy said. He kissed Rhonda lightly, and headed upstairs. She watched him go, still wanting to make the trip, but knowing that Billy had made good sense.

But then, he always did.

That didn't mean she had to like it.

-

The next morning was cold. Not the cool, chilled or 'nippy' they had been experiencing, but plain old, down right *cold*.

Billy went outside and started the truck, turning the heater full blast, before coming back inside. Rhonda had gotten up behind him, and he found her in the kitchen, fixing him something for breakfast, and a lunch to take with him. He stopped for a moment just to look at her, in her flannel sleeping shirt. It was one of his, and it caught her about mid thigh. Her hair was still askew from a fitful night of sleep, and her make-up free face was just about the most beautiful thing he'd ever seen.

Rhonda looked up.

"What?" she asked, seeing that he was looking at her.

"Just lookin' at ya," Billy smiled. "You're 'bout the prettiest thing I ever seen, ever. You know that?" She colored at that, her face going red, but she smiled, looking back down at what she was doing, and biting her lip.

"Thank you," she murmured. Billy walked the short steps to where she stood, and wrapped his arms around her from behind. She leaned back into the embrace, and the two of them just stood there for a moment.

There was just no way Billy could credit his being here, with her, like this. His life hadn't been supposed to include anything like this. He'd known it for as long as he could remember. Yet, here he was. Here she was.

He finally released her, and sat down to eat. She joined him, but just nibbled at a little pancake, not really hungry. Billy ate, both because he was hungry, and because it was cold. He expected a long day. Hunger would make it longer.

At last he had to go. He got reluctantly to his feet, taking the bag Rhonda had set out for him. It held some water, and, he chuckled, a Coke. He kissed her.

"I'll see you tonight."

"You had better," she warned. "Please be careful."

"Promise."

She followed him to the door, but didn't go outside. It was cold, and she didn't want to see him drive away, anyway. Once he started moving, she closed the door, bolting it tight. She looked down to where Rommel had gone to the window, watching as the truck left the yard.

"Bad luck to watch him out of sight," Rhonda said softly. Rommel looked up at her, his tongue running across his nose. When he looked back, the truck was gone.

He followed Rhonda upstairs to bed, and cuddled next to her as she tried to go back to sleep. She was grateful for his presence.

It was a long time before she finally got back to sleep.

-

"Damn, it's *cold!*" Ralph exclaimed as he climbed into the Ford.

"Sure is," Billy nodded. "You guys all right? Ready to go?"

"We're good," George nodded.

"Well, I guess it's time we went, then," Billy said, putting the truck in gear.

They were silent for several minutes, no one really saying anything. Billy used his NVG to drive, keeping the lights off. Car lights would carry a long way, with the leaves off. He didn't want any telltale signs like that to give them away.

Once they got on the main highway, Billy used his lights, and put the goggles away.

"Anyone else got a funny feeling about this?" Ralph asked.

"Funny how?" George asked.

"You know, like. . .well, odd," Ralph shrugged. "Like something ain't right."

"No, other than it's a long trip, for these days, and it's cold, and we're leaving our families alone, and going through what might be hostile territory, and . . . ."

"Okay, okay, I get it," Ralph groaned. "Yeah, I guess that's it. I really didn't want to leave this morning."

"Don't think any of us did," Billy said. "Fact is, with all that's goin' on, we're all uneasy about leavin' the Farm uncovered, even for somethin' like this. But this is it. Once we get this done, we're pretty much home for the winter, barring any unforeseen happening."

"Yeah, you're right," Ralph agreed. "I don't feel anything bad about the trip. I just didn't want to leave."

"Get used to it," George shrugged. He didn't want to leave either. But he'd done it over and over again when he'd been in the Army. He never had liked it.

"Well, we're on our way, anyway," Billy noted. "Sooner we get there, sooner we're home."

"Amen."

CHAPTER THIRTY-SIX

For a wonder, the trip up went smoothly. Of course, that just made everyone more jumpy. The feeling that things weren't right somehow just wouldn't leave Ralph alone, and it was contagious. More than once the three men debated turning the truck around and going back, postponing the trip for another day.

Eventually they decided against it. They needed to get this ordeal behind them, and get the newer families settled in. If this morning had been an indicator, their mild weather was coming to an end.

Billy pulled up into the Kelvey's drive to see Ben already outside, taking last minute boxes to his truck. He waved when he saw the Ford, and walked over to say hello.

"You boy's are a sight for sore eyes," he told them. "Thought sure we'd have some trouble, yesterday."

"What happened?" George asked, glancing at Ralph.

"Heard a good bit o' shootin' over to the east," Ben informed them. "Went on for some time. At first I thought someone was just out practicing, but the fire was sporadic, and more than one gun. Or even two."

"Heard any word about it?" Ralph asked.

"Not as yet," Ben admitted. "And I hope time any news gets here, we're long gone," he added.

"We will be," Billy nodded. "You guys ready?"

"Sure are," Ben nodded. "Got just what we kept out for the night in the house, and I just loaded some o' that. Everyone is up, dressed, fed, and ready to go."

"Outstanding," George complimented. "In that case, let's get you shook down, and on the road. Do you know the way to the Blaine's?" Even as he spoke, they could hear the sound of vehicles.

"Should be them, there," Ben told them, looking down the road. From the opposite way the three had come, they saw a Ford Bronco pulling a trailer coming up a hill, followed by the other semi that Billy, George and Jon had 'found'. Behind that came a Dodge Ram pickup, a crew cab 4x4 with a lot of attachments. It, too, was pulling a trailer, this time a U-Haul.

"Well, this is just too good," George nodded. "We can get on the road pretty quick like this."

Terry Blaine was driving the semi, and he stepped out, once he'd engaged the brake, leaving the truck idling. Two Bears was in the Dodge, which turned out to be his. No one was surprised.

"Ready to get this show on the road?" Blaine asked.

"Just about," Ben nodded. "Got a few little things, and then it's just to get loaded. We did a walk through last night, and everything's loaded except what we needed this morning."

"Outstanding," Blaine nodded. Some of the others chuckled at his echo of George's sentiment. Willing hands grabbed the few remaining articles and found places for them, while the injured Howie was made comfortable in his own Chevy diesel.

"Well, are we ready, then?" Billy asked, as the men gathered on last time.

"Looks like," Ben nodded.

"We're good," Blaine agreed.

"We'll use CB channel 14 on this trip," Billy told the others. "Ralph is drivin' Jon's truck, and he'll bring up the rear. George and me will take the Ford, and scout ahead. We didn't see any trouble on the way in, but that don't mean much these days. We had planned on splittin' up, so there would be someone with each outfit who knew the way, but I think this set-up is the best we're gonna get."

"No names on the radio, and no mention o' where we're goin'," he warned. "The idea is to get into the Farms without anyone the wiser. Once there, we don't have to worry so much, but it pays to be careful. Reckon no one ever died from an over abundance o' caution."

"Well said," Blaine nodded in approval. "Let's put my truck in front. I did some work on the front end, so we can use it as a ram if we need to. Maria and Howie should come next, with Ben and Pete. Then Jon, and Ralph."

"I don't like just one man on the rear guard," George stated. "But I can't see a way to do anything about it," he admitted.

"Agreed," Blaine said. "I thought about that, too. Thing is, we really need two men up front. Any attack that we encounter is likely to be met on the front of the convoy, while we're en route."

"Let's do it like this," Billy said. "If we come under attack from back, we'll slide over, and slow down. The rest of you floor it, and pass us by. We'll fall back with Ralph."

"I like that, but with one qualifier," Two Bears spoke up. "Let me ride drag. No offense, Ralph," he added.

"None taken," Ralph nodded. "I'll pull the trailer. Makes sense, anyway. I'm not a soldier. Never was," he shrugged.

"Well, alright then," Billy nodded. "Sounds like we got a plan. If we do, let's get goin'."

The changes were made quickly, and the trucks lined up. It took only ten minutes for everything to be ready, once the discussion ended.

"Ready to roll?" Billy asked, as George stepped into the truck.

"Yeah, everyone's set," George nodded, checking his M-4. "I'll be glad when we're there."

"Me too," Billy nodded. "I think this is the last time we do this for a while," he added. "We got too much to do as it is."

"I agree," George nodded. "And we can start checking for more like Mary. There's gotta be more in your area that survived."

"Maybe," Billy nodded. "We'll see, I guess."

Everyone checked in on the radio, ready to move out. Maria spoke for the first time that Billy had heard. She had a bit of an accent, which might explain why she was normally so quiet. He didn't know.

"Tell'em we're movin'," Billy ordered George, and started down the road.

—

The first few miles of the trip were used to 'shake down' their little convoy. Things were easier this time, Billy decided, with Terry and Jon doing the driving in the semi's. Both were much better at it than Billy, in his own opinion.

Odd Billy Todd

He and George were about a mile in front of the rest, with the convoy maintaining a steady forty miles an hour. They could have gone faster, but the consensus was that reaction time would be more valuable than speed. George and Billy were very cautious, constantly checking the roadway in front.

Pete Two Bears had dropped back almost half a mile, maintaining a watch on their rear. He was also ready to shoot to the front and help Billy and George, if needed. Considering their manpower shortage, they were covering things pretty well.

"Almost to the half way point," George informed Billy. They had been on the road a little over an hour.

"How far are we from the tracks?" Billy asked. George studied the map.

"I make it about four miles," he replied.

"Tell the others we're moving on ahead," Billy decided. "We need to get up there, and make sure it's clear." George nodded, and called the others. Billy sped up gradually, putting more distance between them and the rest of the vehicles. Two Bears called that he was closing up, just in case.

There was a small rise, and then a downgrade to the track crossing. Billy eased up on the rise, seeing that the track was clear. He started down the hill. They approached the tracks, and sat looking both ways. Billy pulled across, and shut the engine off. The two of them got out, listening for anything.

"I think we're clear," George finally said.

"Tell'em," Billy nodded, studying the area around the crossing. They waited until Terry's semi was in sight, coming down the hill to get back on the road.

"Don't bunch up," George ordered on the radio. "Things look clear, so we're heading back up front." The others acknowledged, and the Ford sped on down the road. Once they'd gone a mile or so, Billy slowed back down. He didn't want to get too far ahead.

"I don't want to jinx us, but things are looking pretty good, so far," George said, just before they heard it.

BOOOM!

-

"Of all the days to have a blowout," Jon swore, looking at the mangled truck tire. The big Peterbilt was sitting on the road, the outside rear driver's side tire in shreds.

"I don't even want to think how hard this will be to change," Ralph shook his head.

"It's a back breaker without a service center," Jon sighed. "We'll have to unhook the trailer, pull the truck out, and then jack it up. I...oh, hell," he groaned.

"What?" everyone asked at once.

"I don't have a spare," he told them, looking under the trailer, and then under the truck frame. "What kind of idiot takes a truck like this on the road without a spare?"

"Uh, you," Ben replied, grinning. Jon glared at his brother as the others laughed. Soon they were all laughing, Jon included. It was good tension release, and they needed it.

"Okay, we've had our fun," Terry broke up the laughter. "And there's a spare under the trailer I'm pulling," he added. "Let's get some local security up, and get to work. We're burnin' daylight."

"George, take about a hundred yards front," he ordered. "Pete, same to the rear. Rest of us will get the truck workin'."

Jon had told them true. It was a job, and then some. But with four of them working, it didn't take as long as they had feared. An hour later, they were ready to head out again.

"No sense takin' this with us," Jon shrugged, rolling the now warped wheel and the remains of the shredded tire off the road. "Hope that don't happen again. We'll be up a creek for sure without. . . ." He broke off with a frown as the Ford suddenly fired up, heading straight back to the group.

"What now?" Billy sighed. He *really* wanted to go home.

"Billy, there's trouble at the farm!"

-

The sun was well up when Rhonda and Mary went to do chores. The first order of business was to feed the chickens, and grab the eggs. One hen had gotten broody, which had surprised Billy, since normally they wouldn't do so in cooler weather. At least his never had. Still and all, she was sitting on eight eggs. Eight new chickens would be a good thing.

"How does she keep all of them under her?" Mary asked, shaking her head.

"Just does, I guess," Rhonda shrugged. She didn't know, either.

"Can I have a baby chicken?" Mary asked. "When they hatch, I mean?"

"As a pet?" Rhonda looked at her. "No, sweetie. That ain't a good idea."

"How come?"

Rhonda chewed on her lip for a minute, wondering how to explain that her 'pet' would likely wind up on the table, sooner or later. As the main course.

"Chickens don't make good pets, honey," she settled for saying. "And they can't live indoors. Better to just leave them with their own kind."

"Okay," Mary sighed. "I bet they'll be cute, though," she added.

"I'm sure they will," Rhonda nodded. *Right up until they hit the cooking oil,* she decided not to add. She'd find out soon enough.

"Take these eggs in the house, and then you can come out to the barn," Rhonda smiled. "We'll feed the horses, then go check on the cows. After that, we'll head over and look in on the hogs."

"Ew," Mary made a face.

"I don't hear you complaining when you're eating sausage. Or ham. Or bacon."

"I get it," Mary waved the comments away. "Be right back."

Mary took the basket of eggs into the house, and washed them at the sink. Once they were dried off, she added them to the carrier in the refrigerator. As she turned away, she had a view of the windows in the living room.

-

Rhonda was running before she realized it. Hearing Mary scream had galvanized her from the partial day dreaming she'd been doing while pouring a small bit of grain into the horse stalls, along with some hay.

Rommel loped at her side, head scanning everywhere. Dottie followed, and Rhonda heard the smaller dog growl. Something she rarely did.

Rhonda went into the kitchen door, pistol in hand, to see Mary still screaming.

Odd Billy Todd

Rommel barked, and Dottie followed suit. Mary jumped at the sound, and turned.

"Mary, what is it?" Rhonda demanded.

"There was a man in the window!" the teenager exclaimed. "Looking in the window!"

Rhonda ran to the front door, and jerked it open, careful to stand to the side. The moment the door was open, she heard Rommel growl deep in his chest, and like a flash the huge dog was outside. Rhonda followed, though slowly. Dottie streaked out behind her, following Rommel.

By the time Rhonda was out onto the porch, Rommel was perched atop a squirming figure in the yard. Dottie off to the side, watching the squirming figure closely.

"*Don't let him eat me I got the wrong house is all I thought this was Mister Billy's house I swear I don't mean no harm please don't let him eat me!*"

Rhonda almost laughed at the hysterical rant, the entire thing sounding like one very long word. She held her pistol at her side.

"Good boy!" she praised Rommel, who was looking at her as if to say *can I eat him?*

"How many of you are there?" she demanded of the still squirming figure.

"What? How many what?" The questioning tone took the place of the hysterics.

"How many people?" Rhonda asked. "How many of you are there!"

"Ain't but one o' me as I knows of Miss! Please don't let him eat me, my hand to *God* I got the wrong *house*, I thought this was Mister Billy Todd's place, I got the wrong house, that's *all*!" The last was said in a wail, accompanied by tears, it sounded like. Rhonda looked at the figure a bit closer.

With a start, she realized that it was a scrawny, filthy, terrified teenage boy.

"Who in the hell are you?"

—

"Danny Tatum?"

Billy paused, having heard the entire story over the radio. His first impulse had been to go streaking home, but Rhonda assured him that all was well. Rommel had tackled the boy, but hadn't hurt him.

"*You know him?*" Rhonda's voice came to him over the radio.

"Yeah, he worked for me some, after school, and during summer. Did odd jobs, ran for parts, cleaned up. What's he doin' at the house?"

"*Looking for you, he says,*" came Rhonda's reply. "*He's awful skinny, Billy. Ain't been eatin' good I'd say. And he's filthy. I don't know him. Never seen him before. Is he okay?*"

"Yeah, he's a good kid. Kinda like. . .me and him got some o' the same problems," he caught himself. He forced himself not to look at the others.

"His family lived on the other side of town from us," he went on. "Didn't come into town much. I used to give him a ride home o' the evenin', when we'd get done. Good folks. They didn't have much, but they was honest, God fearin' people."

"*He looks like he's about fourteen,*" Rhonda told him.

"Yeah, that'd be about right, I guess. And he said he came lookin' for me?"

"*Said he didn't know where else to go, and didn't know anyone else to look for. You were his last hope.*" Rhonda had calmed down some, by now, and her voice

219

sounded a little sad. She'd had time to talk to the pitiful boy, and couldn't help feel sorry for him.

"I'll talk to him when I get home," was all Billy could think of to say. "Meanwhile, give him something to eat, and keep him outside."

"*It's awful cold, Billy,*" Rhonda came back.

"Then give him a blanket," Billy shot back. "He's made it this long, he can make it a while longer. Until I see him, I ain't got no way o' knowin' he's who he says he is. We should be on in a bit," he added.

"*Okay, then. Out.*" Billy laid the mike down, and sat back in the seat.

"Everything okay?" George asked.

"I think so," Billy sighed. "Kid who used to work for me some showed up at the house this mornin'. Ain't got no idea why. Said I was his last hope, or words to that effect. Mary saw him lookin' in the window, and let out to screamin'. Rommel tackled the boy in the yard. Wonder he didn't eat'im." George nodded.

"Reckon I'll see to him when I get there," Billy shrugged. "Meanwhile, it's time we get this train back on the track, I'd say."

"Yeah, let's get home," George agreed. "Been a helluva day."

CHAPTER THIRTY-SEVEN

Billy looked down at Danny Tatum. He barely recognized him as the happy go lucky, slightly 'different' boy who had helped him out in his garage, what seemed like a thousand years ago now. The boy was rail thin, and his clothes were ragged and worn. And filthy. Danny wasn't any cleaner. His hair was filthy and wildly unkept.

"Danny, when'd you eat last?"

"Your misses gave me. . . ." the boy started.

"I mean 'sides that," Billy waved the boy's words away, irritated with himself.

"I. . .well, uh. . .I guess. . . ."

"That long, huh?" Billy asked, sitting down beside the boy.

"Been a few days, I reckon," Danny's eyes brimmed with tears, but they didn't flow.

"What happened, Danny?" Billy asked softly.

"Ma and Pa, they, they took sick," Danny sobbed a little. "I. . .I tried to help'em, but. . .I didn't know what to do, and there wasn't no answer for the nine-one-one." Billy nodded in understanding. As the virus had progressed, emergency services had broken down.

"They. . .when they died, I. . .I taken'em out to the back, and buried'em. I didn't know what else to do. I s. . .said words over'em from the Book, you know. From the Psalms. Pa, he. . .he always liked the Psalms. Said they soothed the troubled soul." Billy nodded, saying nothing. The boy needed to talk, and he, Billy, was probably the last living person Danny Tatum knew.

"After that, I just. . .I just tried to keep on," Danny went on. "I mean, that's all there was. But we didn't have a lotta food in the house, and daddy didn't have but a few shells to take game with. I. . .I did okay, though. Didn't waste a single shell, Mister Todd. Only they wasn't many."

"I looked at the neighbor's houses," he admitted, shame faced. "I know it maybe ain't right, but they was all dead, too. I. . .you know, I tried to bury them, too, but. . .Mister McAdams, and his misses, they. . .they. . .when I tried to move'em. . . ." Danny sobbed again, reliving a horror that Billy was all to familiar with himself.

"It's okay, kid," Billy said gently, wrapping an arm around Danny's shoulder. "Same thing happened to me, with one o' my neighbors."

"Anyway, finally I had to move further and further away, so it made me think, maybe I ought to just up and move closer to where I could find food. Found a little here and there, and a few shells, once in a while. I'm a pretty good shot, so I was able to take squirrels, and a few rabbits. Even got me one deer. But he rurnt 'fore I was able to get all of him ate," he added, a little sadly.

"Gotta smoke'em," Billy said seriously. "Only real way to make sure you can save the meat. Or you can jerk it. 'Bout the same thing, just a little different on how you get it done."

"Didn't think about jerky," the boy looked thoughtful. "I should have too. Pa, he always would. . . ." The boy stopped suddenly, the momentary relief gone at the thought of his parents.

"Ain't no thing, Danny," Billy told him. "Plenty o' time to learn how. I'll show you, when we get a chance." The boy looked up at him, eyes bright with hope.

"I can stay with you?"

"You bet."

-

"You're making a habit of taking in strays, Billy," Jerry told his young neighbor.

"Can't be helped, I reckon," Billy shrugged. "Boy ain't got nobody else, and he's a good kid. He's...me and him got a lot in common," he settled for saying.

"Then I'd say he'll grow into a fine man," Jerry Silvers said seriously. Billy might have blushed a little at that, but stayed silent.

"He gonna be okay?" Jerry asked, changing the subject.

"Amy says he's underweight," Billy sighed. "Sickly and poor, but otherwise okay. 'Bout the same as Mary. Good hot bath and some new clothes, few good meals and good night's o' sleep'll put'im right."

"Maybe," Jerry nodded. He looked at Billy.

"That's two young'uns you got now, Billy. Both of'em been through a rough time. You're gonna need to keep a close eye on'em for a while."

"Girl's doin' okay," Billy pointed out.

"She is," Jerry nodded his agreement. "Only she ain't yet had the chance to think on where she is, or how she got here. Like as not, she's still in a bit o' shock that her situation has improved so much overnight, after months alone and afraid. Liable to come back on'er. Might not, too," he admitted. "I'm just sayin' you need to be watchful, that's all."

"I'll mind it," Billy said thoughtful.

-

"I guess they'll keep *this* one, too," Debbie Purdy snorted, as George relayed the days events. He looked at his wife quizzically.

"The boy used to work for Billy, Deb," he said softly. "Came looking for him specifically."

"All that talk about setting up a home for kids, and we see what?" Debbie snorted again, ignoring George's statement. "The *Todds*! And they aren't even 'the Todds', you know. They're not married."

"Debs, I'm getting tired of hearing this," George told her. "I mean really tired. I don't know what it is that bothers you about this."

"Did we, or did we not, plan to use that place at the end of the road *specifically* to care for children we found who had been left orphaned by the plague?" she demanded. "Two children, so far, and the *Todds* keep them both."

"Debs, for God's sake, they aren't *keeping* them. They're aren't *things* to be possessed. They're *kids*!"

"All the more reason for them to be with a good family!" Debbie exclaimed. "There's not one good reason to let those two keep those children! And *plenty* of reasons not to!" George looked at his wife, incredulity on his face.

"Deb, there isn't a single reason I can think of for those kids *not* to stay with Rhonda and Billy. They're good people. Hard working, honest, and charitable to a fault. There's no reason, not a single one, to think that those two kids won't have the best possible life they can in the world we're living in today."

"They need to be with someone who understands children!" Debbie shot back. "Someone who can teach! They need an education, they need to be taught good values! How to function in society! Who is better qualified to do that than we are?"

"I'm starting to wonder if *we* are," George shook his head. "I'm trying to understand how you feel, Deb, but I can't. You're almost irrational about this. I've never seen you act this way."

"Maybe if you hadn't spent so many years running all over the world, you would have!" she retorted. As soon as the words left her mouth, she regretted them. The look on George's face was. . .heartbreaking.

"I'm sorry, George," she said hastily, as he stood abruptly. "I didn't mean. . .."

"Yeah, you did," he said sadly. "Suppose I had it coming. You knew what I was, what I did, before you married me. I never misled you in any way. And I left the service because you didn't like it. I gave up what I *was*, Debs, for you. Because that's what you wanted. I guess that wasn't enough for you, either." He moved toward the door.

"Where are you going?" Debbie asked, a hint of desperation in her voice.

"I'm going to see if I can help unload our new neighbor's things," he said stiffly. "I need some air. Kinda hard to breathe in here at the moment." With that he walked out the door, leaving his wife staring at his back.

-

Jerry Silvers looked up at the sound of footsteps. He was in his barn, looking over his horses.

"You got a minute?" George Purdy asked the older man.

"Sure," Jerry nodded, not missing the look on the younger man's face. Or the tone of his voice. There was only one thing that could cause that.

"I. . .I need to talk to someone, and I. . .I don't know what to. . . ."

"Just tell me what it is, son," Jerry said kindly. "I'll listen."

"Well. . . ." George started talking. Once he started, he couldn't stop. Jerry listened without comment, nodding on occasion, but remaining silent. George talked for a long time. Suddenly he stopped, and looked embarrassed.

"Sorry for rattling," he said, a bit shame faced.

"No need," Jerry assured him. "Sometimes it helps just to have someone to listen. Sounds like you've got a lot on you."

"It. . .it's not so bad as it seems, I guess," George shrugged. "Look, I know you and Billy are close. You'd know if he wasn't able to care for them, right? I mean, I think he and Rhonda are just fine for this, but I've been wrong before. If you thought they weren't up to it, you'd say so, right?"

"I would," Jerry nodded at once. "So would Emma. And you're right. They are up to it. Billy may have problems, but he's a fine young man. One of the best I've ever known, to be honest. His parents were fine people, George. And they raised that boy well."

"Rhonda is about the finest young woman I know, too, even before the world went plumb to hell in a handcart. His father was as honest a man as there was anywhere, and he taught that girl well. She's smart, resourceful, and about the shrewdest young business woman you'll ever meet. And both of them have got hearts that are a big as they are."

"Those two kids have a connection to Billy and Rhonda. Might not seem like much, but it's a site better than anything they'll have with the rest of us. And that's important for them both, right now. Those two young'uns have had it bad. Don't know which was worse off, and there ain't a nickel's worth o' difference in their two stories. They're in good hands, so far as I'm concerned. And the rest of us can pitch in as needed, I'm thinkin'."

"That was my thought," George nodded. "We. . .we've got to get back to the old ways, if we're going to survive. Children are going to have to be the whole community's children, no matter who their parents are. We have to work together to get by, Jerry, or we *won't* get by. I've seen too much of that in. . .well, in places far from here." Jerry studied the young man closely.

"I've seen what happens to children in times like these," George said softly. "I. . .one of the reasons I kept going back. Trying to help. I kept thinking if I could help save just one child, then whatever sacrifice I had made would have been worth it. Never thought to have that thrown in my face. Especially by Debbie. My own wife," he added, his tone not bitter, but hurt.

"Try and understand, son," Jerry told him kindly. "She ain't seen the things you have. You can tell someone all about that kind of thing, and they'll never understand completely. They can't. Not until they've seen it." George looked at the older man fondly.

"Thanks, Jerry. For lending me your ear. And for the advice. I. . .I don't know what to do, exactly."

"Have you thought about moving your family in to the Clifton place?" Jerry asked. "If you two are going to care for any other children we might find, you might as well be there, ready to go, when that happens. Might do the two of you some good to have your own place. Might go a long way toward easing some of the trouble."

"I hadn't thought about that," George admitted, his look thoughtful. "Might help, at that. Things have been. . .strained, I guess, between Debs and Amy since that ruckus over the girl."

"Just an idea," Jerry shrugged. George snorted.

"I knew there was a reason I came here."

-

"We're gonna run out of room," Rhonda joked lightly later that night, as she and Billy sat together in the kitchen.

"Could at that," Billy nodded absently, his gaze fixed on the window over looking the back yard.

"At this rate, we'll need to add on to the house, come summer time," Rhonda said, watching Billy closely.

"Might do," Billy nodded again, his gaze never wavering.

"Your hair's on fire," she tried one more time.

"Uh-huh," Billy nodded yet again. His eyes were fixed on something only he could see, it looked to Rhonda.

"Billy. Billy!"

"I heard you," he turned his gaze toward her finally. The look in his eyes made Rhonda hesitate.

Odd Billy Todd

"What's wrong?" she asked.

"Everything's wrong," he told her softly. "The whole world is wrong. And I'm the worst of it."

"What?" Rhonda demanded. "How in the *hell* do you figure that?"

"All that time I spent runnin' around, makin' sure I had ever thing I needed," he shook his head. "And them kids," he nodded toward the stairs, where both Danny Tatum and Mary Jerrolds had gone to bed earlier. "Them kids runnin' scared, doin' without. Starvin'," he murmured. "And I just sat here, feelin' all safe and secure. Didn't think a single time about anything like them. Not one time," he repeated, his voice full of scorn and self-loathing.

"How was you supposed to know?" Rhonda asked him.

"I *didn't* know," Billy shrugged. "And that ain't the point. Instead of lookin', I just sat here. And did nothin'. *Nothin'*!"

"What were you supposed to do?" Rhonda asked him, her voice gentle.

"Ain't got no idea, on account o' I didn't *do* it," he replied flatly. "I should o' looked. I knew Danny Tatum before all this. Why didn't I go check on him? His folks? What about all the other people I knew before? I didn't know Mary, but I knew her pa. Did I go and check to see if he was all right? No. I didn't check on nobody."

"You checked on your neighbors," Rhonda pointed out.

"I sure did," Billy told her. "And ran away from Widow George's house so fast, I near on forgot where I was goin'. Let it scare me so bad, I ran right over here, and stayed here for how long? At the moment, I can't even recall, 'xactly. How's that for manly?" He stood abruptly.

"Never really thought of myself as a brave man, Rhonda," he told her. "But I sure never figured myself for no coward, neither. But that's just what I am. Even when I found you," he looked at her closely, "I wasn't lookin' for you. I just wanted to make sure the stuff in your daddy's shop couldn't be used ag'in me. *Me!* Worried about me, and nobody else," he finished, his voice filled with disgust. He shook his head slowly as he went to get a glass of water. Taking it, he walked to the back door, looking out at the night. He drank from the glass, still looking at the dark.

"How many kids are out there, tonight, right here in this county, cold, hungry, alone. Hurt mebbe. And here I sit in my nice warm house, belly full, with you and them kids with me. Ain't right," he shook his head. "Ain't right."

Rhonda didn't answer at once. She didn't know what to say. She thought Billy Todd had done wonderfully, all things considered. It was obvious he didn't share that opinion.

"Billy, I don't see what you could have done any different," she settled for saying, her voice gentle. Concerned.

"I just told you two things," he replied, his own voice just as soft. Still full of self loathing. "And there was plenty more. I was so busy thinkin' o' myself, I never gave one thought to nothin' else." He turned finally, looking at her.

"It wasn't deliberate," he told her. "I. . .I didn't mean not to. I just. . .I followed daddy's teachin', and his notes. Only not even my daddy never thought about somethin' like all this," he admitted. He'd never once in his life said anything that might amount to even a suspicion that his parents might not have thought of everything. He'd never even *thought* it.

They had been the rock that he built his world around. The one solid, constant presence. He'd managed after their death by following the things they had taught him. He'd done well, and he knew it. He'd managed after the plague by following the same thing. And he'd done well, once again.

But not well enough.

"Billy, I know you're upset, but no one can think of everything."

"I ain't upset," Billy shook his head. "I'm *mad*. Mad at myself. Mad at the people on that train. Mad at them idiots at the road block. I ain't no better'n them. They ain't helpin' no one but themselves, and I ain't done no different."

"That is *bullshit*!" Rhonda's voice cracked across the room like a whip. "You've helped dozens of people, Billy Todd, me among'em. There's four families settled, or settling, here tonight, including *four kids*, that are here because you helped them! Because you were willing to risk exposing yourself to do the right thing! And I may not be all that, but I'm not *nothing*!" She walked up to him, then, embracing him.

"I was scared, and alone, and didn't have a clue what I was gonna do, where I was gonna go, how I was going to go on living. Or even what for. You came and changed all that. *You* did that Billy Todd. You may not have been looking for me, but when you found me, you didn't hesitate to take me in, give me a safe place to live, and even take care of me!"

"When we found Mary, you didn't hesitate to take her in, even after she almost blowed your fool head off! And today, you didn't hesitate to give the Tatum boy a place to live, and take care of him!"

"So this is the. Last. Time. I *ever* want to hear anything like that come out of your fool mouth ever again. You get me, Billy Todd?"

Billy looked at her for a long moment, until she could see the hint of a smile tugging at his lips. Finally, he grinned.

"You sure are pretty when you're riled up, you know that? *Owww!*"

He was still holding his arm when Rhonda stalked off to bed.

CHAPTER THIRTY-EIGHT

Snow came to the Farms without warning, two days later.

A lot had happened in those two days. Willing and eager hands had all pitched in to get the newly arrived people unloaded and moved in. The Blaine's, and Peter Two Bears, were very happy with the Williamson place, agreeing that it had plenty of room for their needs, and then some. The barn was a plus, allowing for extra storage even with the rudimentary bio-fuel set-up inside.

George and Ralph had been right about Howie Rickman. He had taken one look at the set-up and started explaining how it could be better, with work. He had experimented with the process himself, in years past, but as a hobby. Until something like this, he'd never had enough need for fuel to make something like it profitable.

"'I built something like this for the science fair, my junior year in high school,'" he told them. "'Looks like you guys did just fine. But I learned a lot about this last few years. If we can find what all we need, I can show you how to really get it cookin'. So to speak,'" he had added, grinning. Everyone was glad to hear that.

The Kelvey's had also been more than pleased with the Smith place. It wasn't as large, but with both Jon and Howie still not fully recovered, it would be more than enough. Amy had checked both over, and declared them to be doing nicely. Howie, it turned out, hadn't had a serious infection, after all, but rather a very raw wound that hadn't been kept cushioned. He had gotten back on his feet sooner than he should have. No one could fault him for that, but clothing rubbing against the wound, protected only by a thin bandage, had kept the area red and inflamed. Amy assured him that with proper care, he'd be ready for spring, no doubt. And he could be out and about before then so long as he took it easy.

Jon's wound had been more fleshy than anything, and while it still gave him trouble, it was in no danger of infection. It would continue to hurt, Amy told him, for a while. But he was able to work whenever he wanted. She cautioned him to stop when the pain flared too much, since pain often interfered with healing. Favoring a wounded limb while working made it harder on the other parts of the body.

With all hands on deck, it had taken one full day to get everyone unloaded. Unpacking would take longer, but everything that everyone needed was inside. Radio communication ensured that all could stay in contact.

The second day out, George and Peter had checked the spot that George had located for an OP. Two Bears looked it over, and agreed it was a likely spot. They sketched out how they would construct it, and started planning on how it would be equipped.

Debbie Purdy was sullenly quiet, but worked as hard as anyone else helping the new arrivals get set up. Her cold glances didn't go unnoticed, however, and Rhonda had been near boiling before the day was out. She had spent a lot of time talking to Emma, and the two women agreed that the problem was unlikely to be over. George had called that one wrong, perhaps. Time would tell.

Billy had spent the entire second day working his farm, catching up on things that had been neglected of late as they were helping the others. Danny Tatum, freshly outfitted with clothes and boots from the stores Billy and Rhonda had put away, was a constant shadow. It was almost as if the boy was afraid that if he let Billy out of his sight, then he'd lose Billy as well.

Danny and Mary got along fine, and Rhonda was glad to see it. The two teens would be good company for each other. Despite her deep accent, Mary was smart as a whip. She was very good at math, had extraordinary math skills for a girl her age, in fact. Rhonda was already allowing her to help do inventory on the food stuff's kept in the house, and plan meals, portions, etc.

Rhonda had found a meal planning guide at the library, and she and Mary spent a good deal of time going over it, planning meals that would be hardy and healthy, ensuring that the Todd 'family' got all they needed from their meals to keep them strong.

All in all, life was moving. Some things were bad. Some weren't.

Just like normal, almost.

-

"Well, you wanted a white Christmas," Billy told Rhonda, as they looked out the bedroom window at the snow-covered valley.

"It ain't Christmas, yet," she muttered. "Ain't even Thanksgiving. I had stuff I needed to get done today."

"Well, you can still do it," Billy shrugged. "But that looks like a heavy, wet snow to me. I didn't have to get out in it, I wouldn't."

"You're going out," Rhonda pointed out.

"*I* have to," he said pointedly. "You don't."

"You don't have to," she replied. "You could let things go one day."

"No, I can't," Billy shook his head. "That's how things start goin' bad on you. You don't follow your plan, and you get in trouble. Plan says I check the livestock. So, I'm checkin' the livestock."

"It's just one day," Rhonda rolled her eyes.

"To you, it is," Billy nodded seriously. "To me, it's fallin' away from my plan. I can't. . .I have to focus, Rhonda," he told her. "I can't just fly by my pants, and the like. I gotta have a plan, and I gotta stick to it. I don't, I start forgettin' things. I can't afford that. Not nowadays." He stood, having laced his boots. "And the plan says-"

"You check the livestock, I know," Rhonda snorted, holding her hand up. "I get it. I'll have breakfast ready when you get back."

"Okay," Billy nodded. He pecked Rhonda on the lips, and walked downstairs, when he found Danny Tatum ready to go.

"Ready when you are Mister Billy!" the boy said brightly. Amazing what a few good meals and good nights' sleep could do for a fourteen-year-old.

"You ain't got to go, Danny," Billy told him. "Your choice," he added when the boy looked slightly crestfallen.

"I want to help."

"Suits me," Billy grinned. "Let's go."

Rommel and Dottie followed them out, running and playing on the snow all the way to the barn. Billy showed Danny how to care for the horses, and watched as he did about half the work himself, nodding when the boy did the job correctly.

"Cows next," Billy told him, and the two walked over to where Billy's own small herd, grown now to twenty-five head, stood clustered together. They looked fit and well, and there was cover if they needed it. The hay was protected from the falling weather, and there was plenty of it.

They walked next to look in on the hogs, who were all gathered into the small make shift barns. They, too, looked fine, though they didn't seem to like the cold so much. They shifted some at the scent of the dogs, but the cold stopped them from doing much more than that.

Satisfied, Billy started back to the house, Danny in tow.

"Things look pretty good, Mister Billy?" Danny asked.

"Yep," Billy nodded. "Days like this, you just make sure the stock ain't in distress, and that they got access to feed and water. Ain't much else you can do."

"Them cows, they ain't got no barn," Danny said. "Where do they go when it's cold?"

"Cows is pretty much stupid by nature," Billy told him, sighing. "They'll all huddle under a tree durin' a lightnin' storm, where one bolt'll kill half of'em, you let'em. They can always get under the pole barn, if they're a mind," he reminded the boy. "But you see what they're doin'. Huddlin' together. That's just how cows is, Danny. O'nery and stubborn."

"To be fair, they don't really need cover, not for this little bit o' bad weather. Their coats are thick, and they'll stay warm huddled together like that. The jacks will stay with'em, and their coats are even thicker. Won't no harm come to'em," he assured the teen. Danny nodded, filing all this away.

Billy looked at the boy from the corner of his eye. Danny was bright eyed, and willing to work. Billy knew from experience he was a good worker. Always had been. His parents had been the same way. After Billy had talked to him, Danny had gotten his 'bundle' as he'd called it, from where he'd stashed it near the road. It had included two changes of clothes that he'd outgrown, and were in even worse shape that what he'd been wearing. His Bible, a gift from his parents, and pictures of both his mother and father. A Buck knife, which he was wearing right now, and not much else.

But there had been a rifle, and an over and under 20-gauge shotgun and .22 rifle combo. The rifle was a single shot .243 Handi Rifle. The shotgun was an H&R.

Billy would get the boy a better set of guns in a few days, when he had the time to check him out good, and take him to shoot them. Until then, he'd placed the boy's current armament in the downstairs safe. Danny hadn't objected.

"Danny, we might holler at Toby after while, maybe see can we scratch up a deer. Or even a turkey. Be Thanksgiving soon. Couple o' wild turkeys'd sure fit the bill for that, wouldn't they?"

"Sure would!" Danny nodded enthusiastically. "I like turkey!"

"You like ham?" Billy asked.

"You bet!"

"Well, expect we'll slaughter a hog, too," Billy told him. "Maybe slow cook it, weather allows."

"That'd be neat!"

"Thought you'd like that."

The weather didn't clear, though. In fact, the snow got heavier. And deeper. Billy checked the thermometer on the porch, and saw that the temperature was dropping, as well.

"This ain't just a snow," he murmured to himself, looking at the sky. Heavy gray clouds, seemingly pregnant with snow yet to fall, hung over them. The wind was from the north, and Billy judged it had picked up to around fifteen miles an hour.

"Makes the wind chill mighty frigid," he shook his head. He looked out over the land, wondering how many people, how many *kids*, were suffering through all of this with nothing. His eyes watered slightly at the thought, but he blamed it on the wind.

Shaking his head, he went back into the house. The house was warm, and inviting, with sounds of joy all over. Danny and Mary were playing a video game, laughing at and with each other. Billy had never really thought about whether they would get along or not, but they did. Both had lost everything, but had found a home here, with him and Rhonda. And perhaps they'd found a sibling, as well.

"Whatcha been doin'?" Rhonda asked, as Billy walked into the kitchen.

"Checkin' the weather," Billy told her, sitting down and taking the cup of hot chocolate Rhonda offered him. "Looks like we're headed for a full on blizzard, 'fore it's over." Rhonda frowned.

"Is that. . .I mean, are we okay?" she asked.

"We are, yeah," Billy nodded. "Everyone else here should be, too," he added, his wave indicating the Farms. "Was more thinkin' on them as are like those two," he nodded toward the living room, where a fresh shriek of laughter rolled through the house.

"Billy, there's nothing you can do about it right now," Rhonda told him, sitting down and placing a small hand atop his. "Please don't beat yourself up."

"I ain't," he assured her. "You was right, the other night. I. . .I can't do it all. And I can't be forgettin' how much we have done. We've helped a right smart o' people, you know? I wish. . .I wish I'd have thought about kids like them earlier, though. I do. Thing is, I was thinkin' about Danny on the way back. And Mary."

"Both o' them was armed. Had we just showed up, lookin' to help, might o' got shot for the trouble by a scared teenager. And that would suck," he chuckled. Rhonda laughed at that.

"You did *almost* get shot by a scared teenager," she told him.

"We can do what we can, and that's all we can do," Billy looked at her. "Thanks for makin' me see that, too."

"It's what I do," Rhonda smiled, and kissed him.

"*Billy, got your ears on?*" Jerry's voice came through the room from where the radio sat. Billy got up and went to answer.

"I'm here, Jerry. How ya'll doin'?"

"*We're fine, just fine. But I think this storm is still building. I ain't seen snow like this hardly at all in the last twenty years. And it's gettin' colder, too. And the wind's come up, last hour or so.*"

"I was noticin' that, myself, just a few minutes ago," Billy replied. "I think we're in the first stage of a real blizzard."

"*Me too,*" Jerry agreed. "*As far as I know, we're okay, all around. Still, it's a problem if we have to get out, any.*"

"Ain't plannin' on gettin' out," Billy told him. "Reckon somethin' might happen as would make us have to, but unless it does, I think we're gonna hole up tight, and wait for this to pass."

"*That's what I plan on doin', too. Still, it's a worry, not bein' able to move when we need to. Reckon we need to think on this a bit. We might need to find us a snow plow. You know, like them the highway department uses?*"

Billy thought that one over. Wasn't a bad idea. He keyed the mike.

"Ain't no bad idea, I'd reckon. Won't help this time, but if there was another time, it'd be here, was we to have a need."

"*What I was thinking, too. Well, I'm gonna go have a cup o' somethin', and relax. Reckon I can be lazy today, and not feel bad about it.*"

"Sounds like a plan," Billy echoed the older man's laughter. "Take care, and if you need us, we'll be listenin'."

"That ain't no bad idea," Rhonda nodded. "There's something else we might want to get too," she added, looking at the wood stove that was helping to heat the house.

"What's that?" Billy asked.

"A fire truck."

CHAPTER THIRTY-NINE

The storm lasted three days. Billy had never in his life time seen such a blizzard. It was like the storms he would see on TV from out west, or far to the north. Jerry agreed. He was by far the oldest person on the Farms, and never had he experienced this kind of storm.

Billy was more sure than ever, now, that the mass die off of people, accompanied by the untold numbers of cars gone idle, factories gone quiet, all of the things that had generated heat, now long still, would make their winters colder.

It could also, he thought, looking out the window at well over two feet of accumulated snow, make the summers less hot. He didn't know. Time would tell, he figured.

He had been thinking about what Rhonda had said, too. The one thing he'd never really considered was a fire. Why hadn't he? Fire was always a risk. Always. Especially in an area where so many had used wood to at least supplement their heating, if it wasn't their sole source of heat.

There was also the threat of a brush fire, and the winter was just as good a time for one as the summer. Everything was dead, or dormant, and dry as a tinderbox. Summer time brought thunderstorms, and lightning could touch off dead and dry woods and leaves, fires that wouldn't always be smothered by the rain such a storm might or might not drop.

And, how many houses still had some kind of power? It would all be solar, by now, he figured, but that would still provide power to things that had been on when the occupants passed on, or didn't return from where they might have been. And how many propane pilot lights were still on? Could they start a fire? Billy didn't know, but he wished, right now, that he did.

As he continued to look at the deep snow, he both admired the beauty of the snow-covered landscape, and cursed their inability to act on the new ideas that had come to them.

But right now, there was nothing he could do except sit, and wait.

-

It was a week before they were able to move. A week that Billy squirmed and fidgeted. He and Danny cleared a path to the barn, and then hooked the small blade to the Ranger, using it to slowly and carefully carve out a trail to the hog lot, and then to the pasture. They were able to feed, and make sure the stock was okay. The horses were becoming fidgety, having to stay cooped up in the barn. Billy cut their grain out, hoping that would keep them calm another day or so, until the weather was clear enough to get them out and ride.

Finally, six days after Billy had started worrying over fire, he was able to get out and move around. He and Rhonda saddled up their horses and rode the fence line. Danny wanted to go, but he wasn't a skilled rider, and Billy didn't have time to teach him, so the teenager had to settle for using the Ranger to clear the drive way. It wasn't the same as riding horses with Mister Billy, but as a consolation prize it wasn't bad.

The fences checked, the two of them headed to Jerry's. They found him doing pretty much the same thing they were, down to Toby using his four-wheeler to clear the Silvers' driveway.

"Hello, neighbor!" Jerry waved. "Climb on down!"

"Thought we'd see how ya'll was makin' it," Billy told him. "And we need to talk, too."

"Not a bad idea at all," Jerry nodded, after hearing Rhonda's idea. "One we should of already done, too," he admitted. "A fire anywhere would about wipe us out."

"That's what's got me worryin'," Billy nodded. "Hadn't thought about it at all, 'til she brought it up. Now, that's all I *can* think about," he said glumly.

"Well, there's a buncha trucks around," Jerry mused. "No idea how many, to be honest. All the volunteer outfits had'em, and they had three or four in town. And we need to try and get that plow, too."

"Yeah, 'bout forgot that, thinkin' 'bout the fire thing," Billy admitted.

"Well, let me tell Em what's doin', and then we can head out."

-

"Damn, I never thought of that!" Ralph looked stunned.

"Reckon none of us did," Billy said miserably. Now that the threat of fire had been brought to his attention, he simply could not let it go. It had driven him to distraction while he was cooped up in the house.

"Snow plow's a good idea, though," George added. "Especially after this."

"If we want to move in weather like this, we need it," Jerry nodded.

"Ain't 'specially *wantin'* to," Billy grimaced. "But we might *have* to."

"And we won't, without a plow."

"Well, we need to start lookin' for fire trucks and a snow plow, then, looks like," Ralph sat back. "Today?"

"Today," Billy nodded definitely.

"How many people we need?"

"I figure three, maybe four," Rhonda mused. "I'd say if we find more than one usable truck of each kind, we get it while we can. Anyone know how to operate a fire truck, by the way?"

-

"Actually, yeah. I can," Ben nodded. "Used to be a volunteer fireman. Jon, too."

"Ain't too hard, once you know what does what," Jon agreed. "We can work it out."

"Well, that's one problem solved," Jerry sighed. "Reckon we can figure out how to operate a snow plow, too," he added.

"How hard can it be?" George asked.

"Ain't no way o' knowin' 'til we get one," Billy said pointedly. "And we ain't gettin' one sittin' here."

-

"I've never ran one, but it's basically a dump truck with a blade on it, right?" Two Bears asked. Others nodded.

"Well, then once we figure out the blade, I'd say we'll have it down. I'm in."

"Well, we're set then," Jerry declared. He, George and Two Bears would accompany Billy and Rhonda in search of the needed equipment. Terry, Ralph, and

Ben would remain behind, in case anything happened.

The five of them piled into the Ford and set out for Cedar Bend.

"We'll hit the Five Forks Station on the way in," Jerry suggested. "Nearest volunteer station to us. They had a truck, and a rig for working brush fires and car wrecks, too." Billy nodded, and turned the Ford down the proper back road.

The Five Forks community fire station looked undamaged from the road. The Ford slid it's way into the lot, and the five of them got out.

"Reckon the door's locked?" Billy asked.

"Shouldn't be," Jerry shook his head. "If there was a fire, they'd need access to the truck in a hurry. Let's give it a try." The side personnel door opened without a fuss, and they walked inside.

The building was surprisingly warm.

"Well, this is a surprise," Rhonda said, feeling the heat inside.

"Not really," George said, pointing to two infrared heaters suspended from the ceiling. "I'd imagine the heaters are on a thermostat. Can't afford to let these trucks get too cold. The water would freeze. Might damage the pump."

"Lucky the fuel lasted so long," Pete remarked.

"Probably hasn't been running long," George pointed out. "Weather was pretty calm until about three, maybe four weeks ago, at most."

"Wonder if she'll turn over?" Jerry mused, looking at the truck.

"One way to find out," Billy shrugged. As he approached the truck he smiled.

"Looky here," he grinned, pointing to a long cable stretching to the engine. "This is a power couplin' for a trickle charger. If it's solar, then the battery should be hot."

It wasn't.

"Must've run off electricity," Billy murmured. "Ain't no way she'll turn over." Checking the brush truck, they found the same issue.

Billy pulled the Ford into the bay door, once they got it open, and they used it to jump start the engine. It ran rough, the fuel having soured some. Billy added some Lucas fuel treatment to the tank, with a bottle of Pri-G for good measure. Even with both chemicals, it took a half hour before the engine was running smoothly. As the men were working to make the engine road worthy, Rhonda inspected the smaller truck. It had been used for medical calls, vehicle accidents, and the occasional brush fire.

"Hey! You guys come look at this!" she called, having opened another hatch. The men hurried over.

"What is it?" Jerry asked.

"It's. . .damn," Two Bears gave a low whistle. "That's a defib machine. For heart attacks. Full trauma kit. . ., spine board. . . ." He trailed off as he started looking things over.

"We need to take this one, too," George declared firmly. "This stuff. . .Amy needs to see this."

It took them a while, but finally the smaller truck was running.

"Do we take them back now? Or wait and pick it up on our way in?" Rhonda wanted to know, as the two vehicles finally smoothed out.

"I say we take'em now," Jerry offered. "They're running, and we can keep'em running. We'll need a place to keep'em. One where we can keep the water from freezing."

"How 'bout the Clifton place?" Billy asked. "Got a big old barn there." Jerry nodded thoughtfully.

"And it's heated," he told Billy. "Nice call, Billy. George, can you get this thing up there? From here?"

"Sure," the soldier replied, grinning. "Can I run the lights and siren?"

"No siren," Billy said at once, not realizing George was kidding. "Noise carries too far on this snow." Peter Two Bears nodded, once more re-evaluating what he knew of Billy Todd. The more he saw, the more he liked him.

"He's right. Noise travels a long way on this stuff."

"Kidding, fellas," George rolled his eyes. "Kidding."

"Little'un, think you can drive the other one?" Jerry asked. Carefully.

"I imagine I can," the girl nodded, her eyes narrowing. Jerry winced.

Ten minutes later, George was on the road, carefully piloting the large fire truck back home, with Rhonda leading the way in the smaller truck. Billy followed them until the turn to town, and then the rest of them headed into Cedar Bend.

"County had a new truck," Jerry informed him. "Probably didn't have five thousand miles on it. Doubt the plow's hooked up, though."

"We oughta be able to get it," Billy said, never taking his eyes off the road.

"Yeah, be some work, though," Jerry pointed out.

"We need it, we'll get it done," Billy shrugged. He was already feeling better, now that they had a functioning fire truck. He pulled into the County Garage, and looked at the locked gate.

"Hold on," he announced, then eased the truck forward until the brush bumper was pushing the gate in. Slowly, he gave the truck more fuel until the gate gave way, and swung open.

"Nice," Two Bears grinned. Billy nodded.

"Beats tryin' to hammer it open, or riskin' a gun shot."

"There's the truck," Jerry said, pointing to where a bright green dump truck, less than a year old, sat under the shed.

"Well, that's. . .that's a green truck," Two Bears commented, his voice telling them what he thought about that particular shade.

"Don't care if it's purple, if we can get it runnin'," Billy muttered.

It took a little longer than the fire truck had, because the dump truck, while in the shed, was still exposed to the weather. But their persistence paid off, and the truck finally turned over. While they waited for the fuel additives to help restore the fuel, Billy and Jerry found the blade.

"This won't be too bad," Billy announced. "Ever thing's pretty much done with the hydraulics."

It took nearly an hour, but they managed to get the truck over to the blade, and the blade mounted.

"Now what?" Billy asked. "'Nother fire truck?"

"No," Jerry was looking at the sky. "I think we oughta call it a day, Billy. Be coming dark, soon enough. What say we call it a day's work, and head home?"

"Okay," Billy nodded. They had a fire truck. That was good enough for him.

CHAPTER FORTY

The weather began to clear during the week after the fire truck round up. Since the smaller truck carried a small tank of water for use in vehicle fires as well as brush fires, no one was itching to get out in the rough weather for more, just yet.

That suited Billy fine. He was happy, now, since they had a fire truck on hand. It was funny how much comfort that truck provided. Not just for him, but everyone.

When the weather broke for good, it was nice. The ground was still wet through and through, but the temperature came back up nicely, just in time for Thanksgiving.

Rhonda and Em had decided they would host the meal themselves, and that since the weather would allow them to dine outdoors, they'd host the meal at the Todd farm. Billy had no problem with that. He was always more comfortable at home.

He had taken Toby and Danny out hunting, and they had managed to bag three wild turkeys. Normally that would have been more turkey than anyone would need, but these days there were a lot of mouths to feed. As Billy and the younger men cleaned and prepared the turkeys, Jerry, Ralph and George had killed a large hog, and Amy, Emma, Michelle, and Debbie had worked the pig into various cuts of meat.

Billy had a large charcoal smoker that had belonged to his parents, so it was decided that the pork would be 'smoked' overnight. The turkeys would be cooked in various ovens the night before as well.

Jerry produced a nice surprise for the 'menfolk' the night before Thanksgiving, as they had assembled around the grill in traditional man fashion.

"This here is the real deal," he warned, producing a mason jar.

"Is that. . . ."

"Yep," Jerry grinned from ear to ear. "Gen-u-ine article. Made it myself."

"No kiddin'?" Billy asked. "I never knowed you had a still."

"And that's as it should be," Jerry nodded firmly. "Such nefarious items are a blight on society, and ought not exist at all. Except in secret," he winked. Laughter rang out all over the place at that one.

"Well, let's toast this valiant hog, who has given himself, that we might eat too much tomorrow, and give thanks that we're still alive, and still going." Ralph raised his small glass, once Jerry had poured everyone a round.

"Hear, hear!" Jerry praised, and raised his own glass. Billy sipped at his, never having been one for alcohol. It had a bite.

"Oh, that's good," Ben Kelvey smacked his lips. "Jerry, I do believe you make a mean shine, good sir."

"I thank you, good neighbor," Jerry nodded, pleased. He was glad to see that Kelvey was, indeed, a pretty good sort. The man had worked himself ragged nearly everyday at something. He didn't seem able to sit still, for long. Jerry admired a man willing to work.

"That is the hair o' the dog, sure enough," George chuckled.

"Best I've tasted," Terry Blaine agreed.

"None for you?" Jerry asked Two Bears.

"No fire water for red man," Two Bears managed with a straight face, but lost it at the look Jerry gave him.

"I don't drink," the younger man told him once his laughter was under control. "Thanks anyway, though. I appreciate it."

"I didn't mean no offense," Jerry said.

"None was taken," Two Bears assured him. "It's just that, in this case, the stereo type rings true. I don't do well at all on hard alcohol."

"That is true," Blaine nodded. "He turns as mean as a. . .well, Indian," he laughed. Two Bears chuckled.

"I pulled a drunk on R&R, once, in Kuwait. It. . .didn't end well," he shook his head sadly.

"Damn near an international incident," Blaine muttered, and George nodded in agreement.

"Had to get the State Department involved," he added.

"Must have been sooooome drunk," Ralph declared, already feeling the fire water.

"There was a woman involved," George told him sagely.

"Ain't there always?" Jerry laughed.

For a time, the gaggle of men were able to forget about the trials an tribulations of the recent weeks, and enjoy themselves. Long into the night, they drank, and talked, laughing often, crying once in a while, reliving memories of times passed, and friends and loved ones lost, both to the plague, and before.

For just one night, at least, life was almost normal.

-

Rhonda looked out at the feast and felt satisfaction. Everyone had helped. Well, all of the *women*, anyway. The men had cooked the hog, and that was about all they could manage. The only sober men in the bunch had been Billy, Two Bears, and Toby. Billy had shared his one drink with Toby, and the two of them had settled for sharing a sixpack of beer with Two Bears. Jerry had frowned for a moment, seeing his son with a beer, but then relaxed. His son had become a man. He was entitled to be treated like one.

The rest were useless, today.

"Get that other table set up, sometime today, fellas!" she ordered, as Billy, Toby and Danny worked to get things set up. Benches and tables were everywhere. In all, there would be twenty-three men, women and children at the meal.

"We're workin' on it," Billy didn't snarl, but he was getting tired of being ordered around.

"Just not fast enough!" Rhonda shot back. "It's almost time for everyone to be here!"

"Reckon if we ain't done, they can get their own chair!" Billy muttered. Low enough that Rhonda couldn't. . . .

"I heard that!" Billy could only shake his head as he headed back to the storage to get the last table, and some folding chairs.

"She sure is mean sometimes," Danny sighed, walking next to Billy.

"She ain't mean," Toby replied from Billy's other side. "She's just bossy. Like ever other woman in the world."

Odd Billy Todd

"Shut up, the both o' ya," Billy snorted. "She ain't. . .well, okay, she *is* bossy," he decided. "But she's usually *right*, too. So we do what she says. Get me?"

"We get you," both boys chorused.

"Good."

Two Bears was piling his plate high when he ran into someone else in the line.

"Excuse me," he said at once. "I wasn't watchi. . . ." he broke off as he got a look at who he had bumped into.

Michelle Silvers looked at the handsome man in front of her, and could not to save her life manage to speak. With everything else going on, there had been no meet and greet for the new families. She had never met Two Bears.

"Are you okay?" he asked, concerned. *Wow, but she's pretty!*

"Fuh. . .I mean *fine!*" she managed to stammer. "I'm fine, no problem."*OhmiGod he's handsome!*

"That was my fault, miss," Two Bears smiled easily. "I'm afraid all this food sort of blinded me." *Man, oh man, she's about the prettiest thing I've ever seen!*

"It's a good feed," Shelly nodded. "Made that cornbread myself," she added, proudly. *For heaven's sake, Shelly, is that the best you can come up with? Prattling about your cornbread?*

"I do love cornbread," Pete nodded. "Bet you're a good cook, too," he added slyly, and was rewarded with a blush of pleasure.

"Not really," she admitted, demurely. "But I am learning. My mom, she's a great cook. She's trying to teach me." *My God, Shelly, can you* possibly *sound any more like an airhead?*

"I'm sure you'll get it," Pete smiled again. "I think I'll just go grab me a seat, and sample this cornbread of yours." *Damn, that didn't come out like I meant it to. She'll get mad, and I don't blame her. I might as well of propositioned her.*

"If you like it, there's always more," Shelly managed to say, just a bit saucily. Peter Two Bears turned away grinning, until he saw Jerry Silvers looking at him. That wiped the grin right off, and he hurried to find a seat.

Shelly willfully ignored her father's stares, watching the man she'd just met walk to his seat with a grace she's only seen in cats. Every part of him seemed to ripple as he moved, almost like he didn't have a bone in his gorgeously muscled b. . . .

Argh! Stop it, stop it, stop it! She looked around quickly, only to see Rhonda across the table, grinning widely.

"Cute, ain't he?" the little redhead whispered loudly. Shelly almost snapped back at her, until she realized that Rhonda wasn't razzing her.

"Who is he?" she asked.

"Name's Pete Two Bears," Rhonda told her.

"Tw. . .what?"

"He's a Native American," Rhonda nodded. "Apache at that. Grew up on a reservation. Went into the Army when he was seventeen."

"Wow," Shelly eyes bulged at that. She fixed her own plate absent minded, and went to sit down with her family. Rhonda couldn't help herself, and snickered as she watched Shelly stumble along, still trying to catch a glimpse of Two Bears. It was obvious, to Rhonda, that the attraction was mutual. She was still laughing softly to herself as she took her seat next to Billy.

"So funny?" he asked.

"Nothing," she smiled. "Tell you later. Hush now, Jerry's speaking."

"Folks, reckon we got a lot to be thankful for today," Jerry said somberly. "I don't want to drag the day down, but I do think it's a good time to remember our blessings, and they are in good supply. I'll ask you to bow with me, and give thanks."

"*Almighty Lord, we thank you for this bountiful harvest, and for the fellowship of these good people, one with another. We're mindful of our sins, and ask forgiveness of them, that we might stand pleasing in your sight. We also pray you bless this food, Oh Lord, and the hands that prepared it, that it might nourish our body, just as Your Word nourishes our Soul. Let us enjoy this day in fellowship, food, and thanks. In Jesus' name, we pray, Amen.*"

"Amen," came a chorus of echoes, and then everyone was eating, talking laughing, and enjoying the day.

The meal lasted most of the day. After everyone had eaten, there were stories, tall tales, even singing. Music from a boom box encouraged dancing among the adults, with Mary coaxing Toby out onto the floor, and Amanda managing to get Danny out as well, despite his protests. Soon they swapped, with Mary dancing with Danny, and Toby with Amanda. All four were having a good time. The younger children danced alone, or with whatever adult was available, or with each other, much to the delight of all.

"Ain't been a bad day," Billy said, as he and Rhonda sat out for a while, sampling more of the food.

"It's been wonderful," Rhonda exclaimed. She nudged Billy suddenly, and nodded to where Michelle Silvers and Peter Two Bears stood, dancing together to a slow song.

"Jerry looks like he's gonna stroke out," Rhonda giggled. "He'll have to get over that. She's a year older than I am, even," she added, laughing.

"And you at the ripe old age of twenty?" Billy snorted. Rhonda nodded.

"Feel a lot older, these days," she admitted.

"Reckon that's true for most of us," Billy agreed. "Still, you're holdin' up pretty good," he added, mischievously. She answered with a punch to his arm.

"Why are you always hittin' me?" Billy exclaimed quietly, holding his arm.

"Cause you need it," Rhonda declared firmly, before kissing him.

Across the way, Terry and Maria sat watching for a while as well.

"Still glad we came?" he asked. Maria nodded.

"*Si*. These are good people, Terrence. It was the proper decision." Maria's English was heavily accented, but precise, as was common among those for whom English was not their first language. Maria had been born in a Latin Ghetto. Hard work had moved her away from it, where she'd met a young Army sergeant named Blaine.

"I think so, too," he agreed. "Hated to leave our place, though, after all the work we did to it."

"It will still be there, if we need it," she murmured. "We are not without options. And it is good for the *ninios*," she added, nodding to where their children

Odd Billy Todd

were now playing with the others.

"Yeah, I admit, I was worried about that," Terry nodded.

"*Dos Osos* appears to have found a playmate as well," she laughed, nodding to where Pete and Michelle were dancing. Terry took in the scene, and chuckled, but there was a note of worry as well.

"I hope he. . . ."

"New world, *mi gringo*," Maria said softly, taking his hand in her's. "Things have changed. He is no longer the *salvagito*. Leave it alone."

"*Si, mamacita*," Terry teased, hugging her close. "He'll have to look out for himself, now."

-

George and Debbie Purdy were watching as well, setting together.

"Your friend Two Bears seems rather happy," she said, nudging her husband to get him to look. George snorted when he saw the Apache and the Farmer's Daughter together.

"Never fails," he shook his head in mock sorrow.

"Well, she is pretty," Debbie told him. "And they're both healthy and single."

"And her father is the *defacto* leader of this outfit, too," George snorted. "Leave it to Pete to hit on the woman who would cause the most issues," he chuckled.

"Well, it could be worse," Debbie told him. "He might have 'hit' on Rhonda." George looked at her.

"He would never do that," George said quietly, his voice tinged with anger.

"Well, she's not married," Debbie said primly. "I'd say she's just as prime a candidate for his attention as the Farmer's Daughter." George sat silently for a few minutes, weighing his words. Finally, instead of speaking, he simply stood up.

"I'm going to take a walk," he announced. She looked up at him.

"I'll go with you."

"No, you won't," the slight edge in his voice made her wince. "I don't know why you keep saying and doing things like this Debbie. But I don't want it to happen again. Ever. If it does, there'll be consequences. Understand?"

"Are you threatening me?" Debbie asked, astonished.

"No, I'm telling you that I've had my fill. I'm finished. Starting today, if you can't say something nice, or at least constructive, about anyone, I don't want to hear it. Period. Understand?"

"So, I have to like everyone and everything, or else, is that it?" Debbie challenged.

"You don't have to like *anything*, or *anyone*," George sighed. "But you're going out of your way to make snide remarks about the people here, especially Billy and Rhonda. All because you can't get your way, all the time. I'm sick of it. You hear? *Sick*!" He took a deep breath, allowing some of his anger to ease out on the exhale, and mindful that some were looking over to see what the fuss was about.

"Maybe it's time. . .maybe we need to re-think things, Deb. Reckon I'll be doing that while I walk home." With that, George stuck his hands in his pockets and started for home.

Ralph watched his friend and house mate stalk off toward the house, and looked at Amy.

"Now what do you suppose that was all about?"

George had made up his mind by the time he arrived at the house. He needed time to think, and he couldn't do that in a house full of people. Reluctantly, he grabbed his duffle bag, and with long practiced ease packed his gear. He didn't take too much, just enough for a couple days, if it came to that. He didn't think it would, but in his frame of mind, he wasn't taking any chances.

He didn't know what else to do. His wife was apparently not the woman he thought he'd married. He'd never seen her like this. And he was sick at heart because of it.

He didn't understand her problem. He'd known she wanted another child, but she wasn't capable of having another. It was no one's fault, but simple fact. Had that been what had turned her so bitter, so suddenly? Seeing someone have something she couldn't have?

If so, then he had to rethink his life. The woman he'd fell in love with, the woman he had married, who had bore him his son, hadn't been like that. This was new.

And it was killing him.

With things the way they are right now, I don't need this, he thought to himself as he finished packing. *My God, the world is* dead, *and she's throwing snit fits over something like who's married and who's not, and the fact that two good people, out of the goodness of their hearts, gave a pair of orphans a good home.*

The woman I married would have praised that decision.

Looking around the house one more time, George picked up his rifle and started up the road to the Clifton place.

He didn't look back.

CHAPTER FORTY-ONE

"Did you hear?"

Rhonda looked at Michelle Silvers, who had practically ran through their yard to the back door.

"Hear what?" Rhonda asked. It was the day after the Thanksgiving dinner, and Rhonda was finishing her cleanup. Most of the work had been done before everyone left, but she had still needed to work in her own kitchen. She had barely finished when Shelly had appeared.

"George and Debbie!" Shelly exclaimed. "When the others got back last night, they found a note from George that he'd be spending a day or two at the Clifton place. I. . .I think he may leave her!"

"Wow," she was taken back by the news. Shelly didn't sound like she was gossiping, she sounded worried. That fact did not escape Rhonda's attention.

"Any idea why?"

"Nothing specific, but momma did say that she was unhappy about Mary," Shelly said, her voice sympathetic. "I know. . .I mean I was selfish when all this started, but. . .please, *please* tell me I wasn't this bad," she pleaded. Rhonda looked at her hope filled eyes, and smiled slightly.

"No, not quite," she winked, and Shelly looked relieved. And embarrassed.

"I was a bitch, and I know it," she murmured. "To everyone. But I was. . .you know what? It doesn't matter what I was. I was wrong, and that's all there is to it." The determination in her voice made Rhonda take another look at Shelly.

"Shelly, you came around, and more than made up for most anything you did or said," Rhonda said firmly. "Look at what you've done in the last few weeks. What you've learned. I'd say you're doing fine."

"Thanks, Rhonda,' Shelly colored a little at the praise. "I really appreciate that."

"Ah," Rhonda waved the comment away, and motioned for Shelly to sit.

"Now, does anyone have any idea what happened, and why?"

-

"I got no idea," Ralph shook his head. "None. When we got home, he was gone. The note was all there was."

"Mebbe he just decided on the way home," Billy shrugged. "Didn't say nothin' cause he hadn't made his mind up." Ralph considered that.

"Yeah, could be," he nodded finally. "I know they had words, him and Deb, right before he left the party."

"Reckon we oughta ride up and check on him," Billy sighed.

"No," Jerry Silvers said firmly. "I'll go. Just me," he added, when Billy was about to speak again. "Me and him talked a little, few days ago."

"What'd he say?" Ralph asked, interested.

"Nothin' I aim to repeat," Jerry told him abruptly. "He want's it told, reckon he can tell it." Ralph looked sheepish at the rebuke, but nodded his head.

"Wasn't meaning to pry," he promised. "He's. . .well, he's my friend, Jerry. If I can help him, I want to."

"And that's a fine notion," Jerry commended. "Keep it handy. He might need it. But let him ask for it. Even it's just coming to talk to you."

"Yes, sir," Ralph nodded.

"I can help, let me know," was all Billy had to say.

-

"Hey Jerry," George nodded, as Jerry rode up. The older man dismounted, and joined the former soldier on the porch.

"George," Jerry returned the greeting. "How you makin' it?"

"Gettin' by," came the drawled out reply.

"Lotta folks wonderin' about you this morning," Jerry noted, taking a seat.

"Sorry about that."

"Ain't no need o' being sorry," Jerry raised a hand. "They just wonder what's wrong, and can they help."

"Reckon not," George sighed. "Don't know that there is any help," he added with a shrug. "Just. . .I need some time to think on things."

"I take it your problem has grown?"

"Yeah, I think so," George nodded. "Or, at least, it ain't shrunk any. I thought maybe it had. But at the dinner she started in again. I. . .I don't know what to do, what to think. It's like the woman I married ain't here anymore, you know? She's like a different person, here of late. It's confusing, and I don't care for it, to be honest."

"Reckon we've all been changed in some way, after all that's happened," Jerry nodded.

"This is different," George shook his head. "There's. . .I don't know, there's something wrong," he shrugged. "She's so. . .so *bitter*," he almost spat. "Over nothing, too."

"Might be she don't see it as nothin'," Jerry replied. "Might be she see's it as a serious thing, and wonders why you don't."

"You think she's right?" George asked in concern.

"Nope," Jerry shook his head. "I'm talking about what she may think. I know she's wrong, and so do you. Just saying that, to her, she might seem right." George nodded absently.

"I got no way of convincing her otherwise," he said sadly. "It's to the point where I can't stand the idea of hearing her speak, Jerry. I'm always afraid of what might come out of her mouth, if she does."

"Ain't no way to have to live," Jerry agreed. "I guess you've tried talking all this through?"

"In a manner," George shrugged. "She agrees, won't do it again, and so forth and so on. But then she does. Every time."

"Well, I can see where that would frustrate you."

"I'm thinking of taking a road trip," George said suddenly. Jerry didn't hide his surprise.

"Where to?"

"Don't know, just yet," George admitted. "I want to see what's left. Who's left, I guess. Look around, some. See what there is still to scavenge. That kind of thing."

"Don't reckon we need anything, George."

"Maybe not now," the soldier replied. "But we will. And there's no point in letting things go to waste, can we help it."

"Well, 'spect there's some truth in that," Jerry allowed. "Still, not a good time to be off and away. Especially alone."

"Was thinking I'd see if Pete wanted to tag along," George shrugged. "He's usually up for a good adventure."

"Tell me about him," Jerry prompted, and George grinned.

"Got you worried, does he?" Jerry's face reddened a bit, but he nodded, hesitantly.

"Any man around my daughter worries me," he admitted.

"Pete's a good man, Jerry," George said seriously. "He's not so wild as he was just a couple years ago. Kinda grown up, of late. Proud of him, to be honest," he admitted.

"Pete won't do anything disrespectful, Jerry. I'd stake all I got on it. It just ain't his way." Jerry looked a little relieved at that.

"Wasn't passin' judgement," he told George after a minute. "Just. . .checking, so to speak."

"Any father worth his salt would," George nodded. "Though I'd say the attraction is mutual," he grinned.

"And that don't help me none at all," the older man grumbled. George laughed.

"One time, must be four, five years ago now, we was in Iraq. . . ."

-

Jerry was a while getting back, but Billy was waiting when the older man rode into the yard.

"Afternoon, neighbor," Billy nodded.

"Hey, Billy," Jerry nodded, stepping out of his saddle.

"How'd it go?"

"Man's got a lot on him," Jerry shrugged. "Seems Deborah still has some issues. Maybe relating to Mary," he added hesitantly. Billy's eyes narrowed just a bit.

"Ain't nothin' for you to worry on," Jerry added hastily. "Just saying, that seems to be what set her off. Got George terribly confused."

"Understandable," Billy agreed. "I thought all this was settled, though."

"Far as everyone else is concerned, it is," Jerry agreed. "She's the only one with the problem. She'll either get over it, or she won't," he shrugged. "Have to just see."

"So, what's George gonna do?"

"Says he's thinking on taking a road trip," Jerry told him. "Wants to go out and see what's left of things, and of the people. Scope things out, like, and maybe pick up usable stuff while he's at it."

"Sounds like a good plan," Billy said thoughtfully. "I've had that idea more'n once. Ain't had time to act on it, though."

"Well, he's of a mind to ask Two Bears about it," Jerry informed him. "See about the two of them making a trip."

"Wonder if he'd want some comp'ny?" Billy mused.

"Don't know," Jerry frowned. "You thinking of going with him?"

"Might do," Billy nodded. "Me and Toby both, if you can spare him."

"Toby?" Jerry looked surprised. "Why Toby?"

"Man grown, now days," Billy shrugged. "Do him good, I think."

"I don't know, Billy," Jerry sounded worried. "Might be dangerous."

"Ain't no more so that some of the other things we've had to do of late," Billy pointed out. "And the experience'd be good for him, too." Jerry thought that over, and finally nodded, though hesitant.

"Reckon if he wants to go, be wrong to try and prevent him," he said finally.

"Reckon I'll ask George, see what he says, 'fore I get Toby's hopes up," Billy said. "Might be fun, at that."

-

"More the merrier," George nodded, when Billy brought the idea up. "Don't bother me none at all, you two wanting in."

"I been wantin' to do the same thing," Billy told him. "Just ain't had the time. Figure now, maybe, we do."

"I got nothing but time at the moment," George nodded, glumly. "I got a hankering to see what's what, you know?" Billy nodded. He did know. Over time, he had lost the urge to sit at home, and let the world go by. He wanted to see what was left. Who was left. Seeing kids like Mary and Danny was still working on Billy's mind. If they had made it, maybe others had as well. He wanted to see. And help them, if they had.

"Tomorrow?" George asked, watching as his young friend worked through something. Billy looked at him for a long moment, then nodded.

"Tomorrow."

-

"And I'm supposed to just sit here, while you go out and 'see for yourself,'" Rhonda huffed. "Is that it?"

"Don't 'spect you'll do much sittin'," Billy shook his head as he finished putting his bag together. "Plenty o' work to do. Course, I 'spect you to have those two doin' as much as they can. They got to learn, in case somethin' happens to us. This place'll be theirs, if that was to happen. They need to know how to live."

"What?" Rhonda stammered.

"Well, we took 'em in, didn't we?" Billy shrugged. "Reckon we're responsible for 'em. Somethin' happens to us, they need to know how to get by without us."

"Then shouldn't you be here, teaching them too?" she demanded.

"Will be," Billy nodded. "I'll be back."

"And if you ain't?" she challenged, eyes watering.

"I will be," Billy said firmly.

"You're going, no matter what, ain't you?" Rhonda asked.

"Reckon so," he nodded. "It's got to be done. We ain't goin' far. Maybe fifty miles. See what we can find that's still usable. Might find people. Might find more kids, like those two," he nodded in the general direction of the living room, where Danny and Mary were reading. Rhonda's attitude softened at that.

"That's why you're really going, isn't it," she asked, her voice soft.

"Mostly, yeah," he admitted, turning to look at her. She took the three steps that separated them, and they embraced quietly.

"Promise you'll be careful."

"Always am."

CHAPTER FORTY-TWO

They had taken it slow, out of the gate. Billy was driving, since he was the most familiar with the territory they were traveling. Two Bears and George took the rear seat of the Ford, so they could provide fire on the flanks, and the rear, if it became necessary. They all hoped it wasn't necessary.

On the second day they made camp less than ten miles from Columbia. The snow was gone, now, and several days of sun and light wind had dried a good deal of the mud. Enough that Billy had found a small dirt road that had led them through a pasture, and into a copse of woods, near a small stream. The stream was clear, and swelled with run off, a good source of water, once it was filtered.

So far, their trip had not been that fruitful. A few smaller stores had yielded some items, including ammunition, canned goods, and some fuel. The fuel had been marked on the map for possible later use, the rest added to the back of the long wheel based truck.

They had seen horrible scenes of destruction, where fires had burned out of control, with no one left to contain them. They had seen cars on the side of the road with the bodies of occupants who had died on the road still inside. They had noted an abundance of wild game, and even some domestic animals, which they also noted on their map.

What they had not seen, anywhere, was people.

"Maybe they ain't none," Toby suggested as they sat around a small fire, eating their supper.

"Could be," George agreed. "Unlikely, though," he added. "We all made it. Imagine others did. Was a right smart o' folks in Franklin at one time, remember."

"And that train," Billy reminded them. They had been very careful about train tracks.

"Right," George nodded. "It's not unrealistic to think we'll find other people, Toby. The thing is, they might not want to be found."

"Huh? Why?" the teen asked, dumbfounded.

"They're scared," Peter shrugged. "They don't know us from the man on the moon, Tobe. They see us coming along, armed to the teeth, and their first reaction will be fear. It's natural," he added, seeing the boy frown. "Like I said, they don't know us. How are they to know we're peaceable, and don't mean them harm?"

"Yeah," the boy nodded, seeing the point. "I hadn't thought on that. I. . .heck, I just figured it they saw someone else, they'd at least want to talk."

"And they might," George told him. "But, think of this. If you were a woman, alone or with others, or maybe with kids, and you saw four armed men around, how likely would you be to want to talk to them?"

"Makes sense," Toby nodded. "Hadn't thought about that."

"Same goes for young'uns," Billy noted. "If Mary and Danny made it, some others may have too." Everyone nodded at that, not wanting to think of a child, alone, in this hard, new world.

"Let's get some rest," George ordered, standing. "I'll take first watch. Then Billy, then Toby, then Pete. We'll break camp at first light, and get on the road."

"Hey, look there!" Toby pointed. "Ya'll see that?"

'That' was a column of smoke to their front. Dark and angry looking against a clear morning sky. They had been on the road less than an hour.

"That's a house fire," George said softly. "See how that smoke is different shades of gray? Dark and light mixing together? House fire is almost the only thing that burns like that."

"Want to check on it?" Billy asked from behind the wheel. "We're still about three, maybe five miles from Columbia." George weighed the decision, then nodded.

"Let's get near, and then we can do some recon. Running up there in a truck, and jumping out armed and ready is asking to be shot." Billy nodded, and started easing the truck along. It took ten minutes to get within what Billy deemed earshot of the fire, and he found a seldom used trail, by the look of it anyway, nearby. He pulled the truck safely off the road, where it would be hard to spot, and the four of them dismounted.

"Me and Billy will go have a look," George ordered. "You two stand a watch. Keep your radios on," he added. "Quietly, though." With that, he headed into the woods, and Billy followed him, silent as a ghost. Two Bears watched Billy heading into the trees, and nodded in approval of Billy's skills.

"He get's ten feet in there, you won't never find him," Toby said softly, looking back toward the road. "Billy's a ghost in the woods."

"Looks like it," Pete nodded, glancing at the boy. When he looked back, Billy was nowhere to be seen. He grunted, scanning the woods.

"Told ya," Toby didn't gloat, just spoke. Pete looked at him.

"You like him a lot, don't you?"

"Used to didn't," the boy admitted, never taking his eyes off the road. "Didn't know him. Never bothered to. But yeah, I do. First one to treat me like a man."

"Means a lot," Pete agreed.

"So, what about you and my sister?"

George led the way. Billy watched their flanks, allowing George to concentrate on their trail. Every so often he stopped and made an arrow on a tree with a large white grease marker. It never pointed in the direction they took.

"Move it ninety degrees clockwise," George whispered. "Pete knows." Billy nodded. Smart.

They continued on. Some five minutes careful walk from the truck they began to hear indistinct voices. Some loud, others not as much. Moving more carefully, the two came to the tree line near the source of the smoke, and went prone, crawling the last few feet.

It was, as George predicted, a house fire. The house was engulfed in flames. Billy counted four women and seven children in the small group standing in the yard. And he counted three men holding guns, surrounding them.

"You had no right!" one of the women yelled, only to be back handed by one of the men. Billy growled deep in his throat, but George laid a hand on his arm, shaking his head. Billy looked at him, about to challenge, when two more men came stalking around the house, pulling small wagons.

Odd Billy Todd

"Look at all these goodies!" one crowed in triumph. Billy looked at George, and nodded his thanks. George winked at him, and pulled his radio.

"Leave Toby to watch the truck, and tell him to take a good hide. Then make your way up here. We got a little business here, it looks like." Two clicks answered him, and George put the small radio away.

"We'll wait for Pete. Meantime, let's see what we learn," he whispered.

Another woman in the group had gone to help the fallen one, while the two remaining tried to shield the children, especially the girls, from the other men.

"Figured you was out here," a wiry man armed with only a handgun grinned unpleasantly. "Been watching you for a spell, sneakin' into town, stealin' from us. Started once to take you, but I thought you was haulin' too much for one person. See now I was right." Billy frowned at that.

"We weren't taking anything you needed," the oldest woman in the group all but snarled. "Just enough to take care of these kids. And now you've burned up everything we've worked for!"

"You ain't gonna need it," the man sneered. "You're all comin' with us, back to the house. Figure ya'll can wait on us. And provide some much-needed entertainment."

"Hell will freeze, first!" the older woman snapped back.

"Well, then I'll just have to kill one o' these little ones, to convince you I mean business, then, won't I?" He aimed his pistol at the nearest boy.

"Don't you dare!" the woman moved to cover the child. "What you want is me. Harm these kids, and I'll kill both of us, first chance I get. Leave them be and. . ." she swallowed hard, "and I'll do what you want." Her voice was bitter with defeat. Billy admired her courage.

"See, you can be reasonable, now, can't you?" Billy heard a quiet whistle, and turned to see Pete crawling silently up to them.

"Well, what do we have here?" he asked.

"A pack of hyenas," George snarled. "You take the two on the right," he ordered without preamble. "Billy, the two center. I'll get the tough guy, and provide overwatch."

Both men nodded, and sighted their rifles. Billy's targets were armed with a shotgun, and an SKS. He decided the shotgun was the bigger threat to the women and children, and took aim at him.

"On three," George whispered. "One. . .two. . .three!"

The rifle sounded as one, and three of the five men fell. Billy and Peter looked their second shots, but their targets were already moving, and Billy had to hold his fire as his target took off, placing the women and children between them. Billy stood, and watched as the man ran for the woods. Sighting carefully, Billy led him just a little, and shot. The man tumbled to the ground, and stayed there.

Peter Two Bears took a snap shot at his second man, but missed. The man ran for the house, and escaped behind it as a round from George's rifle tore wood from the burning building near his head.

"Get'im!" George ordered, and Two Bears was on his feet. George grabbed his radio. "Toby, one of'em is moving! He may double back and come your way, so be alert!" Two clicks were his answer, and George nodded in approval. He moved out of the woods to where the women stood, still placing themselves

249

between the children and any threats. Billy took a flanking position, and watched in case the runner came back around.

"Ladies, my name is George Purdy. Can we be of assistance?"

The man Two Bears was chasing headed straight into the woods, once he got the house between him and his attackers. Glancing back over his shoulder, he saw the young Apache pursuing him, alone, and made a mistake. He stopped, turned, and raised his rifle.

Peter hit the ground rolling, bringing his rifle to bear as he did. A three-round burst from his M4 cut the legs from under his target, and left him screaming in agony on the ground. Two Bears walked carefully up to the man, and stood looking down at him.

"Now you, my friend, are in a pickle," he smiled nastily, and drew his knife.

"Pete, was that you?" George asked over the radio. "He dead?"

"*Not yet, but I'm about to fix that*," came the calm reply.

"You nick him?" George asked.

"*Yep. I'll be along after we talk a bit.*"

"No! I want him able to talk. I got questions I want answered."

"*Aw, George!*"

"Bring him around," George ordered.

"*On the way*," came the exasperated reply. George shook his head.

"Danged injun," he chuckled. Billy just looked at him, then went back to scanning the woods.

"Toby, you can bring the truck up. We're in the yard at the fire, all secure."

"*On the way*," Toby replied. George had to smile at that. The boy sounded as calm as he had the day they had all moved to the Farm. He turned his attention to the woman again.

"As I was saying, I'm George Purdy. This is Billy Todd," he pointed to Billy, who nodded. "Our young friend in back is Peter Two Bears, and the young one bringing up our truck," he nodded to where the Ford was making it's way into the drive, "is Toby Silvers. Can we help?"

"I'd say you already have," the older woman replied. She was in her late thirties, George decided. The others were younger, one looked like she might still be a teenager.

"I'm Regina Townsend," the woman told him. "This is, *was*, my home," she sighed, looking at the still burning house, tears welling in her eyes.

"These are my friends, Sissy and Barbara Pinson, and my niece, Ruth Townsend," she pointed first to the two older woman, and then to the teenager. "These children are orphans we've been trying to care for. This used to be a day care center," she sighed again. "No one came for them," she explained softly. George nodded.

"They were lucky to have you," he said. "All of you," he added, looking at the other women. "Is there anyone else?" She shook her head.

"Not here. Well, except the rest of these idiots," she pointed to the dead men in her yard. "There's plenty more of them, but I'm not sure how many."

"And he was the boss?" George pointed to the man he killed.

"Oh, no," Regina shook her head. "He was just a piss ant," she snorted. "No, I don't know who their boss is. I've seen him once, from a distance, when they attacked some townspeople, not long after things went to hell. He's huge. I mean, professional wrestler huge, at that. Never seen him around here."

"Are there any other children in town?" Billy asked. Regina looked at him closely.

"Why?"

"Because I'm lookin' for any kids that may need help," Billy told her. "We set up a house for just that purpose. Two kids wound up stumblin' on to us, all alone and needful. Starvin', and sick. I don't aim to leave no kids like that if I can help it." She studied Billy closely for a minute, apparently weighing his words to his actions. Finally, she nodded.

"There may be some children in town," she said slowly. "But. . .you can't help them," she added sadly.

"And why is that?" Billy asked.

"They'll have them," she pointed again to the men on the ground. Just then they heard a loud groan as the man Two Bears had captured came crawling around the house, dragging his useless legs behind him.

"Go on," Peter kicked him slightly, and the man screamed.

"Ain't so tough, now, is that it?" Peter kicked him again. "Funny, you looked like a real bad man while ago, when you was helping beat up the women and children, burn them out, and the like. What happened to all that?"

"Pete, that's enough," George ordered.

"Aw, I ain't hurtin'im," the younger man complained. Seeing George nod his head, Peter followed the nod, and saw all the children watching him.

"Sorry," he murmured. George walked over to the wounded man, and knelt down.

"So, how about this house of yours, yeah? And your boss? You just lie back, and tell me all about that, why don't you?"

-

It was a tight squeeze, but somehow, they managed to get all of them into the Ford, with Toby behind the wheel.

"You go straight back, hear?" George ordered. "You don't stop, no matter what. When you get there, put them in at the Clifton Place," he handed over the keys. "And then go get Terry, and bring him back with you. Tell him he needs his party favors. Got that? He'll know what it means."

"Yes, sir," Toby nodded.

"Toby, you go by the house," Billy said next. "Tell Rhonda I want the red box. You may have to help her get it, but let her ask for help. And bring Rommel with you. Oh, and tell her we need the green ammo crate, too."

"Okay, Billy," Toby nodded again. He looked at the three men. They had taken their own personal gear from the truck, and loaded the food and other items that the not so dearly departed thugs had taken from the house in the back.

"Get going," George ordered. Toby eased the truck down the drive, and was gone. George waited until the truck was out of sight, and they could no longer hear it, either. Then he looked at Two Bears.

"He's all yours."

The three of them walked two miles down the road, toward Columbia. George hadn't planned on this being part of the outing, but there was no way he was going to leave a pack of thugs like this anywhere he could help it. He looked over at Billy. In addition to his pack, Billy had a large soft case over his shoulder.

"You any good with that?" he asked. Billy looked at him, shrugging.

"Reckon," was all he said.

"When we make our move, I want you on over watch. Toby can spot for you, and we'll need him to feed us information. Think you can do that?"

"If you're askin' can I kill these people, I reckon I can," Billy nodded. "Reckon it needs doin'."

"It does," George nodded. "You can't hesitate, Billy," he added.

"Reckon I won't," Billy nodded, still watching his surroundings.

"It's important," George stressed. Billy stopped walking then, and looked at the older man.

"George, I done took your orders, seein' as how this was your trip. You fellas, you was soldiers, fought in the war together. I know that. Ain't never been a soldier. Army ain't got no room for such as me. But I reckon I done killed a man, and can do it again. Don't take no special pride in it, mind you, but it don't keep me up nights neither."

"I'll get it done."

"Damn, Billy," Pete grinned. "I think that's the most I've heard you say at one time since I've known you." Billy shrugged.

"Usually ain't got nothin' to say."

"Ain't no harm in silence," Pete nodded. He had been taught silence and stillness since before he'd been out of diapers. It was habit for him.

"All right, then," George nodded, satisfied. "Let's see what we can see."

CHAPTER FORTY-THREE

Toby didn't waste any time. He drove carefully, for all that he drove fast. His eyes were on the sun. It was already after noon, and he had a ways to go. Regina Townsend was sitting next to him, holding a two-year-old baby girl.

"Where is it we're going?"

"Place outside Cedar Bend," he said absently. "Just a farming community, really," he shrugged.

"And there's room for all of us?" she asked, not exactly suspicious, but far from sold.

"Yep," Toby nodded. "Clifton house is a big place. Reckon there's eight, maybe ten bedrooms, all told. And that ain't counting the basement. Probably room for two more down there. Nice place. Built back when they made houses big, ya know?"

"Sounds nice," she admitted.

"It is," he assured her. "We worked hard to get it cleaned up. Got electricity, hot water, all the comforts."

"Hot water?" the Pinson's asked in unison. They were fraternal, rather than identical twins, but they were still twins.

"Yeah," Toby nodded, glancing in the mirror at the women. "It's a good place. Plenty o' room. And you guys need it, looks like," he added.

"We do," Regina sighed. "We've been taking care of all of these children since the plague. My house is, *was*, fine for a day care center, but it was never meant to be home to so many."

"You'll like it fine at the Clifton's, then," Toby promised.

"Is it very far?"

"Not too much."

-

"Holy cow," Rhonda said softly as Toby drove into the yard. The truck was absolutely packed. Toby was out almost before the truck had stopped.

"Rhonda, I got a whole passel o' folks here. George said to take'em to the Clifton house. This here is Regina Townsend," he introduced, as the woman climbed out of the cab. "This is Rhonda Todd."

"Pleased to meet you," Regina offered her hand.

"Same," Rhonda smiled. "You look like you got your hands full."

"That we do," Regina managed to smile. She was still a bit overwhelmed by all that had happened today. And the day wasn't over, either.

"Miss Rhonda, I need. . .I mean Billy needs, the red box," Toby cut in. "And the green ammo crate, too, he said. Said you'd know what he meant. I got to carry them on to the house, then I'll come right back. And I got to take Rommel too. And go get Terry."

"Hold on, Toby," Rhonda held up a hand. "Let's see to them before. . ."

"No, ma'am," Toby shook his head. "I'll leave that to all o' ya'll. I need to get back 'fore dark." Rhonda frowned at that.

"I ain't got the time," Toby shook his head, heading back to the truck. "I'll be back in a few minutes, if you need help. I got to hurry." Regina sighed.

"It was nice to meet you," she told Rhonda.

"I'll be up there in a few minutes," Rhonda promised. "Soon as I've got Toby squared away. I'll bring our nurse up, too. Anything you need right away?"

"Diapers," Regina sighed. "And food for the children." Her voice made it plain she didn't expect Rhonda to have it.

"We'll bring it up," Rhonda surprised her. "You better hurry. I'll see you in a little bit." Regina had to hurry back to the cab, as Toby already had it in gear. As the truck pulled out of sight, Rhonda called for Mary and Danny. She had a lot of work to do, and not much time.

-

Toby left the women and children at the Clifton house, showing Regina quickly where the bathroom was, and turning the heat up.

"Rhonda and them'll get you squared away, ma'am," he promised, heading for the door. "I'm sorry, but I gotta go."

"Thank you, Toby," Regina said to his back.

"Welcome!" he threw over his shoulder. Then he was gone. Regina watched the truck for a moment, then turned around to examine her new home.

-

"Party favors, huh?" Terry grunted. "Run into a hornet's nest?"

"More like a skunk's nest," Toby snorted. "I got to go and pick up some stuff from Billy's place. Be back in just a few minutes. How long you need?"

"I'll be ready when you get here," Terry promised, already heading for the house.

-

"Man, this is heavy!" Danny exclaimed, as he, Rhonda, and Mary hauled a crate from the barn to where Toby would be able to get it into the truck.

"Yep," Rhonda nodded. She wanted to know what was going on, but there was no way Toby would wait around to explain. She'd have to get the story from the woman. What was her name? Regina. Yeah, that was it.

The last box Billy had wanted was just on the ground when Toby roared up in the yard again. He jumped out, and ran to the boxes. Danny helped him load, while Toby explained as quickly as possible what had happened.

"So, they're going to attack the town, now?" Rhonda asked.

"No idea," Toby admitted, short of breath. "But Billy don't aim to leave no young'uns in their hands. That much I do know." Rhonda nodded, sighing. He certainly wouldn't do that.

"That's it. Rommel!" Toby called. The big dog trotted up, looking at Toby in puzzlement.

"Rommel, you wanna go for a ride?" Toby asked hesitantly, opening the door. Rommel looked at Rhonda.

"Go on, boy," she encouraged. Rommel calmly walked to the truck, and hopped in.

"Whew," Toby sighed, closing the door. "Didn't know but what he wouldn't want to go. I got to go, Rhonda. You'll see to them, right?" he asked.

"Soon as you get gone, I'll head up there," she promised. Mary was already digging out diapers, powdered formula, and baby food, among other needs.

Odd Billy Todd

"Well, I got to go," Toby declared.

"Be careful!" Rhonda called. Toby waved, and then shot down the drive way. Rhonda shook her head. Twenty minutes, maybe, since Toby had pulled up, and he was already on the way back. She looked at Danny.

"Let's go help Mary. Looks like we got a bunch of new neighbors."

-

Rhonda and Mary left Danny looking out for the farm. They loaded diapers, formula, baby food, food for more adult needs, and clothing for all sizes and ages. She also added basic hygiene needs like soap, shampoo, and 'lady things', as Billy called it. Without knowing what else might be needed, it was all she could do, Rhonda decided.

They stopped briefly to get Amy, explaining what had happened. Debbie couldn't stop herself.

"You mean you aren't taking the children yourself?" she asked acidly. Rhonda looked at her, eyes narrowing dangerously.

"I've had about all from you I need or want," the little red head told her, voice low and dangerously calm. "Whatever your problem is, you need to get over it, before I break my foot off in your stuck-up ass."

"Are you threatening me?" Debbie asked, astonished. No one had really spoken to her so directly about her own future well being before, despite her spiteful bickering.

"I'm warning you, plain and simple," Rhonda corrected her. "I'm fed up with your bullshit. Come at me with it again, and you'll be sucking soup through a straw. You need to pull whatever it is out of your craw, and get with the program. The rest of us are trying to survive, and do what we can for others as we can. All you're doing is running your mouth. I don't aim to listen to it any more. And that's my last warning," she added. "Next time, it'll be my fist." With that, Rhonda stalked out of the house, leaving Amy to gather her kit and follow. Almost as an afterthought, she decided to take Amanda with her.

Debbie was still sitting there blinking like an owl, when the truck left the yard.

-

Toby had stopped for less than five minutes to get Terry Blaine before pointing the Ford back toward Columbia. Blaine had looked warily at Rommel, in the back seat, but the dog had merely looked at him, licked his own nose, and then took a seat where he could peer out the rear window behind Toby.

"Why is he here?" Blaine asked.

"Billy said bring him," Toby shrugged, watching the road. "All I know."

"So, tell me what happened."

Toby spent the trip explaining what had transpired. He had finished just as they rolled up to the still smoking house. He picked up his radio, set it to the pre-arranged frequency, and called for the others.

-

George, Billy and Pete had humped two miles in less than thirty minutes, careful to keep watch. They had frog-hopped, one always still and on the lookout while the other two moved, all the way, checking their back trail as often as they did what was in front of them. There was no way to know if the five men they had taken out at the Townsend home were the only group out and about.

255

They were nearing the city's edge, now. Technically they were inside the city limits, having passed the sign sometime back, but now they were getting into the city proper. That meant slowing down, and proceeding more carefully. They moved carefully into the shadow of a small store that had been ransacked, and nearly demolished. There was nothing of value left, but it provided them with cover.

"According to our friend," George told them, "we shouldn't be more than two, maybe two-and-a-half miles from this 'house' of theirs. We can't put too great a stock in what he said, though. He was as likely to lie, as he was to tell the truth. So, we find a place to hole up, set up camp, and start some recon. Once we find them, then we watch, and plan a way to take them out."

"Works for me," Pete nodded from where he was watching the front. Billy nodded, but then looked around him.

"I don't think this place is gonna do as a camp," he noted.

"No, it won't," George sighed. "We need to find a house that's empty, or, even better, a barn. Somewhere we can hide the truck, and where people aren't as likely to snoop around. I've seen a few places like that on the way in. We're still far enough out we may find what we need, but we'll have to start looking now. Closer in we get, less likely we are to find something useful."

"Need to get off this highway, too," Billy offered. "Get off on some of these side roads, might find a big old house, maybe with a garage. A two story place'd give us a good overlook. Make it easier to keep a watch." George looked at Billy for a moment.

"Are you sure you were never in the military?" he asked, grinning. Billy nodded.

"I read a lot," he shrugged. "And common sense tells me, the higher we are, the more we can see."

"Got you there, George," Peter called from the front. "Sounds like we got a plan. How about we see about putting it into action." George nodded.

"Always need a plan," Billy stood. "Got a plan, half o' the work's already done."

"Let's go," George agreed. "We want to be settled before dark."

-

It had taken less than an hour to find what they wanted. Less than a mile off the highway, near enough to the city to actually see into it, and empty. Completely empty. No furniture, nothing.

"Wonder if anyone ever even lived here," George said, looking around. There weren't even any light fixtures.

"Maybe not," Pete said from a side window. "There's a few more on down, some with construction materials still there. I think this was a development, maybe. A new one. No one ever had the chance to live here."

"Works for me," Billy said, shrugging out of his gear. "That means there ain't no bodies here, and ain't nobody hid out in the house, hopin' to get by. We need to check around before dark, though. Make sure we're alone."

"Pete and I will do that," George nodded. "I want you and that rifle upstairs. If we run into trouble, we'll need you to back us up."

"I can do that," Billy agreed. Taking his gear, he headed up the stairs.

"I don't know about you," Pete said, when Billy was out of sight, "but I'm always glad he's around. Funny, huh?" George shook his head.

"No, I agree. Billy's something else. I've never seen anyone see through the smoke as quick as he does. He doesn't give himself enough credit."

"Had a cousin like that," Two Bears commented, as the two stripped down for their patrol. "Had a birth defect. Mom was a drunk," he added. Drinking was a huge problem on most reservations. "He. . .he had some problems, but he could always find a way to get things done. He learned the old ways from our grandfather. Wish I'd paid more attention to the old man, now."

"Yeah," George nodded. "Well, Billy paid attention. I don't know anyone who could have done as well as he has in this new world of ours. No one." He checked his rifle, and his pistol.

"Let's go. We got a lot to do before dark."

They had just finished checking the last adjoining house, and clearing it, when Toby called.

"*Ya'll there?*" he asked, avoiding anything revealing.

"We're here, Toby. Come on up the road a ways. When you see a little store that's been hard used, wait for us there. We'll be a minute."

"*On the way.*"

"Let's head over there," he said. "At least we can ride on the way back."

-

"Look's like a good set-up," Terry commented, having looked around. The truck was unloaded, and now backed into the attached garage. The sun was gone, and the light was provided by a shielded lantern. Rommel was delighted to see Billy, and hadn't left his side. Billy was rubbing the dog's massive head absently.

"We can hoof it into town for recon," George nodded. "Nothing in the houses around us. We're clear, at least for now."

"No idea of the enemy numbers?" Blaine asked. The word hung heavy around the lantern for a moment. Terry sighed, and sat back.

"I guess we need to establish some Rules of Engagement," he said.

"What for?" Billy asked, looking at the three other men. "I don't see a need. We already know the kind o' men we're lookin' for. The kind that burns down a daycare center, and then threatens to kill the young'uns if the woman don't. . .*co-operate*." His tone made it plain he knew what he was saying.

"Ain't no kinda real man in that crowd. If they're holdin' a gun, we shoot'em. If they're hurtin' anybody, we shoot'em. If they're stealin', we shoot'em. If they threaten any women or kids, we shoot'em. If they're still alive, we shoot'em again. That 'bout covers it, don't it?"

No one spoke for a moment. All of them looked at Billy, surprise on their face. Not at him, but at themselves. Finally, George chuckled darkly.

"Billy, I really like having you around. You always make better sense than I do."

CHAPTER FORTY-FOUR

Rhonda took in the scene in front of her in silence.

Four women, seven children, aged one to seven years.

"Well, it looks like you've done an excellent job," Amy told her, re-packing her equipment. "You're all in good health for the most part. I do see signs of malnutrition, but very little. You've done well."

"Thank you," Regina sighed. "It's. . .it was a struggle, every day, but there wasn't anything else to be done," she looked at the children, all of whom were now sleeping. "No one came for them. I. . .I actually called HHS, asking what I should do. No one answered."

"If not for you, these kids would all be dead," Rhonda told her. "For them, it was a good thing no one answered. I don't know how you managed."

"It wasn't all me, I assure you," Regina replied. "If not for the others, I'd have gone mad. As it is. . . ." The older woman trailed off, her stamina about spent. She had been forced to be strong for so long, and she was so tired. Fatigue that had been held at bay for months had started creeping into her as the house warmed, and as she realized that she and the others were safe. Suddenly, she teetered just a bit.

"Maybe you better sit down," Amy said, concerned.

"I'm fine," Regina promised, but her pale features betrayed her.

"No, you're not," Rhonda told her, taking an arm and guiding her to a chair. "You're exhausted is what you are. Sit," she ordered. Regina sat.

"We're all tired," she murmured. "Always something to be done."

"Well, you need rest," Amy declared. "And we can see after the kids. All of you," she ordered, looking at the other women, who were almost dead on their feet from exhaustion. "Rest. The beds are made, I think. If not, I know there's bed clothes here. There's enough of us to watch over the children while you sleep."

"Absolutely," Amanda nodded. The teenager was sitting on the floor, next to the huge warm pallet where the children were currently dead to the world asleep. "I'll watch them. I haven't baby sat in a long time," she added, grinning.

"I can help," Mary added from where she was watching the one year old slumber after his first formula in three weeks. "I can stay. I can, right?" she added, looking at Rhonda.

"Of course, you can," Rhonda nodded. "I'll stay, too. Danny can watch the house. I'll go and tell him, and bring back some other things. You four get settled, and get some rest."

"Could we. . .could we shower, first?" one of the Pinsons asked. "I mean, with hot water?"

"Sure," Amy nodded. "See if any of the clothes Rhonda brought will fit. If not, we'll find something else for you. Somewhere."

The four women, relieved of their burden after so long, didn't know what to do with themselves at first. The mention of hot water showers sparked a bit of life into them.

"They need rest," Amy told Rhonda, as the four others went to clean up and change their grimy clothes. "And a lot of it, too. They're on the edge."

"I thought so too," Rhonda nodded. "Well, we can let the girls stay here for a day or two, and take turns with them, I guess. Shelly and Miss Em will help, I'm sure." She frowned.

"Thinking about Debbie?" Amy asked. Rhonda nodded.

"Yes," came the short answer. "She should be helping. But I don't want these women to have to put up with the crap she's gave me."

"I know," Amy sighed heavily. "On the bright side, maybe she will adopt one of these darling girls, and that will make her happy."

"Can we trust her with a baby?" Rhonda asked. "I mean, is she nuts, or does she just hate me? If it's me, then no problem. She can hate away."

"She's sane," Amy told her. "May not look like it, but she is. She just wants what she wants. No matter what. That's not insane. It's just selfish."

"No matter how much the world changes, people stay the same," Rhonda sighed. "Well, I don't want Mary around her until she's a bit more. . .unselfish. But if she's willing to take care of them, she needs to help. She don't seem to do much else."

"She works at home," Amy found herself defending her house mate, much to her own surprise. "I mean, she *works*, too. House is clean, meals cooked even when I don't have the time to help. Like I said. She just wants what she wants."

"Maybe helping here will do her good then," Rhonda nodded. "If not, I can always kick her ass."

-

The four women from Columbia all took their first warm showers in months. Soap and shampoo, even lotions, they hadn't seen so much in a very long time. By the time the last one was out, the first was already asleep.

Regina was the last, reluctant to be asleep when the other three were out. One of them had been awake at all times for so long, she couldn't seem to let go of the routine. Amanda and Mary both tried to persuade her to lie down, but Regina kept putting it off. Finally, Mary heard Rhonda pull up in Billy's truck. She went to the door, and helped Rhonda get things inside.

"I'll stay with you tonight, and probably tomorrow night," Rhonda told the older woman. "Amy will be here after that, unless Shelly or Miss Em decide to come over. You haven't met them yet," Rhonda said at Regina's look of confusion.

"And why aren't you in bed?" Rhonda demanded abruptly. Regina blinked at her.

"Ah, I don't know, exactly," she admitted. "I. . .that is. . .we always had someone awake. All the time. Just in case."

"Ain't no need o' that here," Rhonda assured her. "We can take care just fine. And if we need help, it's nothing more than a radio call or a truck ride away. So you get some sleep. You need it."

"We can take care of the kids for a few days, but after that, I'm afraid it'll be you four again, in all likelihood. We all got farms and chores to do and the like. But we can give you a few days help, to let you get rested."

"I. . .I don't know what to say," Regina said softly, a tear flowing from one eye. "We've been alone so long. . . ."

"I know," Rhonda told her kindly. "So was I. Not like you, I was completely alone."

"Me, too," Mary offered. Regina looked at her, and then back to Rhonda.

"She was living alone in the house down the street," Rhonda nodded. "We didn't know she was there until we went to clean the house up for some folks who moved into the house a few days ago. Nearly blowed poor Billy's head off," she chuckled.

"I didn't mean too!" Mary added, blushing a bit. "I was just scared!"

"I know, sweetie," Rhonda smiled at her.

"You had a gun?" Regina looked aghast.

"She *has* a gun," Rhonda corrected her. "All of us do. And carry it wherever we go, at all times," she added, pointing to where her rifle sat by the door. "We don't have much choice. According to what your story is, you should realize that by now."

"I just. . .I never owned a gun," Regina shook head. "I couldn't take the chance, with all the children in the house. And why would I ever need one?" she asked, the irony plain in her voice. "I never imagined anything like this happening, or I would have been better prepared for it."

"I'd say you did pretty good, considering," Rhonda told her. "I mean, you kept yourself, three other adults, and seven kids alive, and reasonably healthy in the worst possible circumstances. Can't do much better than that."

"Thank you," Regina smiled. "I guess we'll need to learn to use guns as well?"

"Won't force you," Rhonda shrugged. "Happens you're against it. But we can't always be lookin' out for you, either. Like I said, we all got things that have to be done. Every day. We're surviving, but it's hard work. And it ain't never done, seems like."

"We don't mind working," Regina assured her, stifling a yawn. "And, you're right. After today, I think learning to use a firearm should be high on our list. We lost. . .well, we lost pretty much everything," she sighed, tears again streaming.

"Don't worry over that right now," Rhonda patted her leg gently. "Just get some rest. We'll be here. No worries."

"I think I will," Regina nodded, rising from her chair. "I have no way of thanking you, you know. I mean, if not for those men, and now you, we'd be dead, or wishing we were. Or at the least, homeless and without anything."

"Don't think on that right now," Rhonda urged, smiling. "Rest, relax, and recover. We'll worry on replacing what you lost, or getting what you need, when that's done. Deal?"

"Deal," Regina smiled. With that she headed off to the bedroom she'd picked out for herself. After she had gone, Amanda looked at Rhonda.

"She's had it rough," the teenager said.

"They all have, but her most of all," Rhonda agreed. "She feels responsible for the adults, and the children all. Too much for one person alone."

"Well, we can help," Mary said, looking again at the tiny infant. "And things will be better for them."

"Yes, sweetie, they will," Rhonda nodded. "They will."

-

The sun was creeping over the trees as George, Terry and Peter prepared to depart. George looked at Billy.

"You see anything, you let us know. And be ready to support us if we come in running, or come get us if we need to scram."

"We'll take care of it," Billy assured him. "Ya'll be careful." George nodded, then looked to his friends.

"Let's boogie," he ordered.

"Keep the fires burning," Pete joked, and led off.

Billy and Toby watched them out of sight, then headed up stairs. They settled in by the window overlooking the street.

"One of us is here, all the time," Billy told Toby. "The other can make checks out the other windows, and make sure we stay clear. Got your radio?" Toby nodded, holding the small FRS radio up for Billy to see.

"Make sure it's on when you leave the room. Might not want to shout, if someone's close."

"Okay," Toby agreed. "If they find that bunch, what are we gonna do?"

"Reckon we'll see."

-

George watched as his two comrades leap-frogged down another street. They were three hours into their sweep. In another two hours, they would need to head back, if they wanted to be near the house before it was dark. Thanks to Billy, they had night vision equipment, almost as good as they had used in Iraq and Afghanistan. George didn't really want to know how or where Billy had managed to get them. He was just grateful to have them. If need be, they could stay out as long as their batteries held on.

He was about to move when Peter Two Bears' hand came up, balled into a fist. He opened his hand a second later, spread as far as his fingers would allow.

Spread out.

George and Terry immediately went to cover, each one moving to a different side of Two Bears' position. Peter ducked low, looking to see if he had their attention. Then his hand started signing.

Three Tangos. Armed. Moving across our path.

Both men signaled they understood, then hunkered down to watch. In less than a minute, three unsavory looking characters ambled past, talking among themselves, and making far too much noise. One was armed with a sawed off shotgun, another with a lever action rifle, and a third with an AR.

"Boss is some pissed about Shorty and them, sneaking off the way they did," Sawed Off remarked, walking along without a care in the world.

"Sure is," Lever Action nodded. He wasn't paying any more attention than the first man. "I sure wouldn't want to be in their shoes, they show back up. He'll probably shoot'em all."

"Shut up, and watch where you're goin'," AR ordered quietly. "We're supposed to be on patrol. Act like it."

"Aw, there ain't nothin' out here," Sawed Off responded. "We do this shit ever day, and don't see nothin'. Ain't nobody left. Not no more," he added, giggling. George was pretty sure Sawed Off was a meth head.

"Just because nothing was here yesterday don't make it so today," AR shot back. "And keep your damn voice down. Noise carries long way nowdays."

"Give it a rest," Lever Action snorted. "You always act like you're King Shit on Turd Mountain, playing like you know so much. You ain't no soldier, and

Odd Billy Todd

besides, no one died and put you in charge."

"Keep talking, lard ass," AR growled, fingering his rifle. "I'd as soon shoot you two as look at you. Tell the Boss you ran out when I wasn't looking. Or," he grinned evilly, "tell him you was talking about running off to join Shorty, and I shot you for that. Might get a reward for that."

The argument continued, but the three were moving away now, passed the three former soldiers' position. Two Bears watched them for bit longer, then looked to George. George nodded, and flashed a sign.

Follow them.

He could scarcely believe their luck. If what they had heard was accurate, they had just stumbled upon the perfect resource. A trio of idiots who would lead them exactly where they wanted to go.

Can't count on stupidity, though, he warned himself, getting ready to move. *Someone in there at least has enough sense to send out a patrol. And the one with the AR seems like a dedicated Mall Ninja. He might have some decent firepower. Even a blind squirrel finds an acorn now and then.*

He shook off those thoughts as Terry started moving. He was next. And he couldn't be distracted right now. One thing at a time.

Find the 'house', and then worry about what they would be facing. Terry went to cover then, and George was moving. Trying not to think about the last time the three of them had done something like this. Far, far from home.

-

Billy was starting to worry. It would be dark, soon, and they'd had no word at all from the others. Toby and he had shared the duty of checking the other windows, always careful to stay out of sight. They had lunched on MREs. Not exactly the quality of food they were used to, but they could heat them with the enclosed heat tabs, so they were at least hot.

Tasty wasn't a requirement for MREs, Billy knew.

"Hadn't they ought to be back, by now?" Toby asked, worry plain on his young face.

"Maybe," Billy tried not to let his own concern show. "But they might have found something. And they weren't on no set schedule, neither," he reminded the younger man. "We'll see'em when we see'em."

"They could at least call in, let us know they was all right," Toby observed.

"Maybe, maybe not," Billy shrugged. "If they found what they was lookin' for, then usin' the radio might not be a good idea. We'll just have to wait'n see. Don't forget, them three was soldiers. Done been to war and what not. Ain't likely they'll run into somethin' they can't deal with."

Toby nodded at that, and settled back in to wait. They didn't have long, as their radio chirped a few minutes later.

"*Coming in,*" George's voice was clear, but quiet.

"We copy," Toby answered, as Billy took up his rifle. Soon, three shadowy figured emerged from the trees opposite the house, making their way in. Billy watched behind them, making sure no one was following.

Ten minutes later, they were all seated downstairs, the three tired men gobbling MREs as they filled their friends in.

"They're in the damn Wal-Mart," George snorted. "All that talk about *The*

House, and we find them living in a Wal-Mart."

"Makes sense," Billy mused, thinking. "Plenty o' food, water, clothes and such. Guns, ammo, you name it. Pretty good idea." The three soldiers stopped eating as one, looking at him.

"Well, it is," Billy shrugged. Pete was the first one to speak.

"Son of a. . .I never thought about none of that," he admitted. Terry chuckled.

"Me either. Billy, I ever tell you how much I like it when you're around?"

"I. . .why?" Billy asked, cutting off his own answer.

"You always see through the smoke, that's why," George answered for all of them. "You see things plainer, easier, than we ever seem to." Billy shrugged at that, not knowing what to say. Or if it was a compliment or not.

"Told you," Toby smirked again at Two Bears, who threw the younger man a middle finger for his troubles, though smiling as he did so.

"Anyway," George went on, "we watched the place for about three hours. It's about an hour's walk from here, if we're humping good. We counted eleven men, in all. Just lounging around outside, sometimes, like they ain't got a care of no kind."

"They don't think they do," Terry shrugged. "No one's opposed them yet. And they have no reason to think anyone will."

"See any sign of people bein' held?" Billy asked. George nodded.

"Saw one man who was a prisoner for sure, and five women. One teenager. Probably more inside, especially if Regina was right and they're keeping kids in there. No way to see how many, though, from where we were. Or anywhere else. Not without getting inside."

"And I can't find a way to do that, without someone noticing," Pete added. "They may not be all that sharp, but someone knows at least enough to keep all the doors guarded. We can take'em easy enough, but if they get off an alarm, then we're looking at a gunfight. And the odds aren't on our side."

"So, we got a plan?" Billy asked, leaning forward.

"Well, we got the start of one," George nodded. "Let's see what you two think about it."

The talk lasted well into the night.

CHAPTER FORTY-FIVE

"Well, I think we're about ready to go," George announced.

It was roughly two hours until dawn. The plan was to be in place by sun-up. It appeared that this bunch liked to be up late at night, so they might just catch them still asleep.

They had a simple plan. Simpler was always better, in Billy's opinion. Less to go wrong. Less to remember. Less likely to mess up.

The 'red box' had contained a number of goodies that the three soldiers in the group hadn't counted on having, including three fragmentation grenades, and a half-dozen of Billy's homemade napalm bombs. All three had been impressed with them.

They also enjoyed the two MP-5's, complete with six mags each.

"Billy, where did you get this stuff?" Terry asked.

"Made them napalm jars."

"What about these?" Pete asked, holding up one of the sub guns.

"Found it," Billy shrugged, truthfully. All three snorted.

"Yeah, right," Pete snickered. "Anyways, I don't care. It's nice to have."

"True that," George nodded. He was still carrying the M-4 rifle Billy had given him. He hadn't bothered to ask again where it came from. He was just glad to have it.

"Okay, so we know what we're doing, right?" Terry asked, getting the discussion back on track. Everyone nodded.

"Toby, you need to be ready at a moment's notice," George told the teen. "If we can't handle this, we'll need to scram out of here in a hurry."

"I'll be ready," Toby promised.

"Billy, there's a nice tall building nearby, maybe two hundred yards distant. I'd counted on you having Toby as a spotter, but it's just you. Can do?"

"Reckon so," Billy nodded in agreement. "Two hunerd yards ain't no real shot," he added.

"Maybe not for you," Terry snorted. "Seen some couldn't shoot at two hundred *feet*."

"I can," was all Billy said.

"All right, then," George looked around once more. "Toby, you make a good check here, make sure everything's loaded, and we ain't left anything behind. Billy, you come with me, and I'll get you spotted. Terry, you and Pete go ahead and get in position, like we planned."

"We do this right, we'll be in and done before they know what hit them."

Billy settled in on the roof, putting the bi-pod of his rifle down. The Harris Bi-pod was a good platform. He made sure there was nothing underneath it, and then set a plastic cartridge box holding fifty rounds down near his right hand. He didn't think he'd need so many, but he wouldn't have time to dig more out if he needed them.

George had silently made his way down, and joined Terry and Pete.

The Wal-Mart was sitting among other stores in a large strip mall set-up. There were restaurants, convenience stores, and specialty shops. The Wal-Mart was one of the super-center type stores, and set alone among the other buildings. There was a Lowe's across the way, as well. Billy used his binoculars to quickly scope the Lowe's store. It looked intact. He filed that away for later, and turned his attention to the Wal-Mart. Using his rifle scope now, he looked over their target.

The parking lot had several vehicles in it, most appearing to have been long abandoned. Three four by fours sitting near the main entrances looked as if they were in use, the thin layer of dust, dirt, and leaves on the other vehicles being absent. Billy would have to watch those, he figured. If any of the gang inside tried to escape, that would likely be their first choice.

He continued scanning, locating a sleeping 'guard' in the entrance foyer. The man had a Ruger Mini-14 cradled in his arms. Billy decided he would probably have to be his first target, unless the others ran into trouble first.

During the night the decision had been made to enter through the garden center entrance. There had been no guard there the day before, and Billy couldn't see one now, either.

The plan was for Billy to engage the front of the store, while the other three used that distraction to enter the store from the side. In the confusion, the three soldiers felt like they could whittle the numbers down some before anyone realized they were in the store.

Billy looked at the roof, next, and saw a problem. There was a small 'knocked together' shack on the roof. Not much bigger than an old phone booth. And there was a man inside it. A man that was looking at Billy through a rifle scope!

There was no time to warn the others. Billy took a breath, let half of it out, and slowly squeezed the trigger.

-

"Okay, let's. . . ." George started, only to be cut off by the sound of a high-powered rifle.

"Damn it!" he swore. "Let's get going!" The three men moved.

Their plan had been to enter through the garden center, and there wasn't time to change that now. If Billy had fired, it was because he had too. They rushed the garden center door, hoping that the element of surprise wasn't totally lost.

Another rifle shot boomed as they reached the doorway, and George hoped that Billy was keeping the attention of the store occupants. He entered the store first, followed by Terry and then Peter covering their rear.

A man dressed in filthy biker leather was just coming awake where he'd been sleeping inside the door. George didn't hesitate, putting three rounds into him as the man struggled to escape his sleeping bag. The bag kept moving, and a woman's head and upper body popped out, a pistol in her hand. The shock of seeing her made George hesitate, even as she brought the gun to bear.

A three-round burst tore her and the sleeping bag to shreds. He turned to see Pete, MP-5 in his hands. George nodded his thanks, and Pete winked at him.

"Okay, so maybe all the women aren't prisoners," Terry interjected. "Let's keep that in mind, and get moving. They'll be getting organized soon."

The three men continued into the store.

-

Odd Billy Todd

Billy watched the front door as he fed two rounds into the open action on his Remington. He'd taken the man on the roof, then the man at the door, and made sure they stayed down. He rammed the bolt home, chambering a fresh round, and sighted in on the door once more.

A large man with a shotgun came running into the foyer, kneeling to check on the guard. Billy let him stop moving, laying the cross hairs of his scope on the man's chest. As soon as he was still, Billy squeezed the trigger. A second later, the man fell back onto the floor, a mist of blood spraying out behind him. Billy calmly worked the bolt again, and swept the rifle back and forth, watching for more movement.

He had to be careful at this distance. By now his three friends were inside. He didn't want to make a mistake.

-

The third rifle shot, muted this time, was obviously Billy again, the three decided.

"Sounds like he's cutting the odds some," Terry whispered. George nodded.

"Assuming one for one, we've still got at least seven targets," he replied. "We'll have to watch the women. Let's go."

Moving from the garden center, the three men worked their way through toys to the hardware section, and from there to sporting goods. As they worked to clear that area, another man jumped up in front of them. They recognized him as the man from yesterday with the AR, from the patrol they had followed.

The man opened fire with the rifle, shooting from the hip. George threw himself to the floor as the rounds chewed up the shelves around him. Terry Blaine raised his rifle, and three rounds tore through the 'mall ninja' in quick succession, putting him down for good.

Pete yelled a warning, and opened fire as two more men appeared, coming from the auto service area, one still in his skivvies. He liberally hosed the area with the MP-5 on full auto, cutting the two men down in a literal storm of bullets.

The noise of the gunshots, inside the store, was almost deafening. The three of them had worn electronic ear plugs that mitigated the sound, but it was still loud. Even the best hearing protection could only do so much, and still let them hear what they needed to in order to survive.

"Four to go, plus the women," Terry called. They kept moving.

-

Billy watched as two men exited the grocery side doors, heading for the Chevy Blazer sitting between the two main entrances. He sighted on the lead figure, and loosed a round. The target was moving, which made the shot more difficult. The round Billy had intended for the target's chest, struck him instead in the right arm. The blow put the man on the ground, and left the arm useless. Ignoring him for the moment, Billy sighted on the second man.

The second target had hesitated as the sight of his friend hitting the ground. Instead of seeking cover, he looked wildly around, firing his rifle in all directions.

That simply made it easier for Billy to put a .308 round into the center of his chest, which he did two seconds later. The man hit the ground as if he'd been de-boned. Billy turned his rifle back to the wounded man, to see nothing. The man had taken those few seconds to find cover.

And Billy had no idea where he was.

Inside, the three former soldiers were again moving, heading through the housewares section carefully. Their element of surprise was now gone. Worse, they had no way of knowing if any of the other women would be prisoners, or perpetrators. That made their work slower, and more difficult.

George looked down one aisle, only to see an armed man at the other end, looking the other way. George ducked back, signing to his friends. Peeking around the endcap again, he could see that the man was still there, obviously expecting them to be coming down the main aisle. He raised his rifle, taking aim. Before he could shoot, Terry shouted a warning.

"Action front!" George instinctively ducked, just as the man he was targeting turned, spraying round after round in his direction. George scrambled for cover as yet another man, the one who had prompted the warning from Terry, cut loose with a shotgun. George was showered with bits and pieces of plastic and rubber containers as the two men chewed through the items still on the shelves trying to hit him.

Terry Blaine brought his rifle to bear on the shotgun armed man, letting go with a pair of three round bursts. He didn't score a hit, but did make the man hunt cover, which was good enough for the moment.

Meanwhile, Peter Two Bears was working his way around the other side. He knew what aisle George had been looking down, and made his way to the opposite end of the same aisle. Going prone, he moved forward just far enough to see the man still crouched in the aisle. Moving the MP-5 forward along the floor, he triggered another burst down the aisle, and was rewarded with a scream of pain as the nine-millimeter rounds tore into his target's feet and legs. Satisfied, he scurried back behind the counters, and out of the line of fire.

There was still one active shooter, and at least three women, unaccounted for.

Billy searched the parking lot on row at the time, looking for the wounded man that had disappeared. He knew the man was hurt, and losing blood. Would probably lose the arm, if he didn't get medical attention, whether Billy found him or not.

But he was still a threat to the men inside the store, if they needed to exit through the front.

He kept looking.

Terry had ran down the aisle opposite of George as soon as he'd forced the man with the shotgun to seek cover. George was now in a position to keep the man occupied, and was shooting steadily to keep the man's attention. Terry eased around the shelving, making sure his way was clear, and moved slowly toward the shooter's back.

Suddenly a large woman with wildly unkept hair lunged out of the aisle, pointing another shotgun at him. Caught by surprise, Terry threw himself into the next aisle as buckshot rattled the shelves behind him.

"I got him!" he heard a woman's voice screech in delight.

"Shut up!" a man's voice demanded. "There's more than one!"

We should have watched longer, Terry decided. They had assumed the women were prisoners. Some of them might be, he allowed, but at least two were part of the 'gang'.

Know better than to make assumptions, Terry, he chided himself. He drew his pistol, and crawled back to the endcap. Using it for cover, he peered around the very bottom of the shelf, and saw the woman was still standing there. But looking back down the aisle at the man.

"I know I hit him. . . .*arggh*!" Her claim was cut short as Terry took advantage of her poor discipline to pump three .45 caliber rounds down range, striking her square in the chest with two of them.

"Damn you!" the man swore, seeing his partner fall. He erupted suddenly from his cover, shooting the shotgun from the hip as fast as he could work the pump action. George was forced to pull back under the hail of buckshot. At this range, the shotgun was far deadlier than his rifle.

He heard Pete's MP-5 rattle away on full auto, and heard the other man gurgle, then hit the floor. There was another short burst after that.

"Clear," Pete whispered, changing magazines.

"Clear," George agreed.

"Clear," Terry called, having checked the woman. She was dead.

The three reassembled. George took his radio out. He needed to know how Billy was making out.

-

"*Billy, what's your count?*"

Billy never took his eyes off the parking lot as he raised his radio.

"*I got four down hard, and another wounded, but hid in the parkin' lot somewhere. He's hit good, but made his way to cover. I'm lookin' for him. Ya'll come out the front, be a lookin'. I got no idea where he got to.*"

George did the math. All eleven men were accounted for. That left the women. Of the five they had seen, two had been part of the outfit, and were down. That left three, plus the teenage girl, and the man.

"Let's get looking," he ordered.

-

They found the others locked in a store room. All were malnourished, and showed signs of abuse. The teenage girl had a black eye, and her lips were swollen. Someone had worked her over pretty good, and recently.

The older women weren't in any better shape, and the man was favoring his side. Seeing the bruises and the swelling when the man raised his shirt, Terry announced that he likely had some cracked ribs. The man nodded.

His name was Robert Billings. He'd been traveling when the gang had caught him trying to siphon gas from a nearby filling station. Surrounded, and unarmed, he'd had no choice but to surrender.

"I was just trying to get home," he shook his head. "I'm from Lexington, Kentucky. Was working construction in Birmingham Alabama when things went south. Was trying to work my way home."

The women had similar tales.

"I'm Vivian Shell," the older of the three women told them. "This is my sister, Meredith, and our sister-in-law Katherine. We were in Biloxi at a real estate convention. We started back home when things started getting so bad. This is as far as we made it, I'm afraid. We're from Cleveland, Ohio. Or whatever's left of it," she sighed. "We have no idea if our families are even still alive."

The teenager was different.

"My name's Megan Johnson. I live here. These bums did too," she waved an arm to indicate the now deceased gang of misfits. "They caught up with me salvaging food from a grocery store, I guess three months ago, now." She didn't say more, but looked at the floor, hiding her face. The men gathered around her could guess the rest.

"Well, what do you folks want to do?" George asked. "You still want to try and get home?" All nodded. Megan just shrugged. She was home.

"Well, let's get you four set-up to travel, I guess," George told the adults. "Reckon you can travel together a ways, for safety."

"Can't you take us?" Katherine asked.

"Sorry, ma'am," Terry shook his head. "We got families of our own to see to. But we'll find you good vehicles, fuel, and supplies. Get you some good maps. You can find your way home okay, I imagine."

"But what if someone else, like them, attacks us?" Vivian asked. "I don't see why you can't take us!"

"Just told you, lady," Terry didn't quite growl. "We got families to take care of. We can't just up and go. Best we can do is set you up good for your trip. We'll make sure you're armed well enough to keep yourself safe."

"I've never touched a gun!"

"Ain't our problem," Terry shrugged. "We'll show you how. After that, it's up to you."

"Look, I ain't with them," Billings said. "You get me outfitted, and I'll get along toward home. I got a family too. Just hope they're okay."

That pretty much ended the conversation.

-

It took most of the day to get the former prisoners equipped. The women complained non-stop, to the point where George finally told them if they complained any more, they were on their own. That had shut them up.

No one had even approached the idea to let the women stay with them.

Billings had picked out a new truck at the local Chevrolet dealership, armed himself, packed supplies for his trip, and headed out long before sundown, thanking the men profusely for their assistance, and for rescuing him. The women, having chosen a large and comfortable luxury car, despite warnings about fuel economy, followed him. Billings had warned them he wouldn't be stopping at every opportunity, so keep up.

The five men watched them go, glad to be rid of the women, whose whining and complaining seemed to have no end. That left them with Megan Johnson.

Their remaining loose end had yet to be tied up when Toby had brought the truck up. He and Rommel had found the man Billy had wounded, or at least his body. Billy's round had pretty much mangled the man's right arm, and he had bled out shortly there after.

No one was really bothered by that.

"We need to get the big trucks, and come back here," George announced, having surveyed the area. "There's a lot of things here we could use."

"True enough," Terry nodded. "We can look for more trailers, and just use them for storage until we can do better. Plus, it'll make the job go faster, if all we have to do is drop the trailers and head back."

"There's a few things we'll want to do today, or tomorrow, before we go back,' George told them. "Or at least I do," he added, looking at Terry. "You okay with that?" Terry shrugged.

"As long as I can go back tomorrow, yeah," he agreed.

"We might as well get busy, I guess," George sighed.

"What about her?" Billy asked, pointing to where Megan sat, watching them.

"Damn," George swore softly. He hated to admit it, but he'd forgotten about her.

Billy looked over at the girl, and waved for her to join them. She did so, reluctantly.

"You want to come with us?" Billy asked her point blank. "There's other women back there, includin' some from here. Might be you know'em," he shrugged. Megan looked interested.

"Who?" she asked.

"Regina Townsend, for one," Toby answered. "Two twins named Pinson, and Miss Townsend's niece. Don't, ah, recall her name, exactly," he admitted sheepishly. "Sorry."

"I know Regina," Megan nodded eagerly. "She ran Little Tykes. Daycare?" she added, when the men didn't react.

"Yeah, she ran a day care," George nodded.

"Gone now, though," Billy told her. "We moved her and the rest down to a house in our community we'd set up for such as that, just in case. Reckon you can join'em, you want."

"I'd. . .I'd like that," Megan agreed. "I don't wanna stick around here alone, that's for sure. Didn't work out so well the first time. I would like to go and get my things, if they're still there, anyway."

"We'll see to it," George agreed. "Meanwhile, there's some things we want to do, right now, before we head home. Reckon you can help us out?"

"I guess," Megan nodded. "What you need me to do?"

"We're interested in finding any gun shops, sporting goods stores, that sort of thing. See what's left. . . ."

Soon, with new vehicles taken from the long-abandoned car lot, they were on their way, gathering useful and needful things.

There was a lot of work to be done, now.

CHAPTER FORTY-SIX

Rhonda saw the Ford coming, with four other trucks behind it, and frowned in concern. Then she relaxed, slightly. There was no chance that Billy would lead anyone back here who might be unfriendly.

Her confidence was confirmed five minutes later as the vehicles pulled into the yard at the Todd farm, being driven by George, Peter, Terry and Toby. Toby had a passenger.

"About time," Rhonda grumped, to hide how relieved she was to see Billy back safe. He snorted.

"What a fine welcome," he teased, then embraced her. She hugged him back for a second, then pushed him away.

"Ewww," her face contorted. "You need a bath, Billy Todd!" He nodded.

"Spect I do, at that," he agreed. "While I see to that, how 'bout you help this young lady here find her way up to the Clifton House. Megan, this is Rhonda. Rhonda, this here is Megan Johnson. She knows the women up there, and is gonna be stayin' with them."

"I can do that," Rhonda smiled. "I need to go up there anyway, and check on Mary, I guess. She and Amanda are helping Amy with the kids. We're swapping out for a few days to let them get some rest," she added.

"Sounds good," Billy nodded. He turned to the others.

"We heading back tomorrow?" he asked.

"The four of us will," George nodded. "We can scout out everything, get everything in order. Make it easier to get everything with one go, I should think."

"Okay by me," Billy nodded. "See ya'll then."

"You're going back?" Rhonda demanded. "What for?"

"Found a whole bunch o' stuff, that's why," Billy told her, already in the house. "The four of us are gonna get it all bundled, see can we find some semi-trailers, and then get Jon and Terry to start hauling it home. There's enough lumber, hardware, and even food to last a good long while. Not to mention some clothes and what not, especially at the Wal-Mart and a few other places. Ain't no need o' lettin' that go to waste. So, we're gonna go get it."

"And leave me here alone," Rhonda ground out. "Again." Billy stopped and looked at her.

"You make it sound like I don't want to be here with you, or want you with me," he frowned. "That ain't how it is. You oughta should know that, by now." Rhonda colored a bit at the dressing down. She had it coming. Maybe.

"And you ain't alone," he pointed out. "You wanted to take Mary in, and we did. Now we got Danny too. That makes us responsible. And besides, it ain't like I want to go. But George is right. This here is a big find, and we can't leave it go to waste. Rightly, should have some of us stayed there, and kept a look out. We decided if we went straight back, then we could all come home, rest, and be with our families, even was it for just one night."

"All right," Rhonda grumbled. "I. . .that does make sense. I just don't like not being able to go with you."

"What did you do when you stayed at the Clifton place?" Billy asked her.

"Well, I took Mary with me, and left Danny guarding the farm," she admitted.

"Well, reckon you can do it that way now, you want to go so back. We can ask Jerry to keep an eye on things. But it's rough goin'," he added. "Ain't no runnin' water nowhere. It's a rough camp all the way."

"Why don't you wait and come up with the trucks?" he reasoned. "See what you want, look around for things you want, and then come on back when the trucks make their next run?"

"I. . .you think that would be okay?" she asked.

"Can't see why not," Billy nodded. "Now, you need to get that girl settled, and I need a hot soakin' bath."

"Yeah, you do," she nodded.

"That ain't nice," Billy told her.

"You'll get over it, you big baby. I'll be back in a bit."

When she got back, almost two hours later, Billy was sound asleep on the couch, with Rommel tucked in at his feet. She covered them both with a blanket, and let them sleep.

After talking to Megan Johnson, she knew they'd earned it.

-

The group wasted no time. The four of them were back in Columbia by eight the next morning. Jon and Terry were waiting for the word, with Jerry and Ben watching the farms close. They were running short of people, that was for sure. Billy voiced a concern as they drove into town.

"I don't like this," he told them. "We ain't got enough people. We got to think on how them trucks is gonna look to anyone who spots'em. They might attack Jon and Terry. Or worse, just follow'em back to the Farms. We got to make sure that don't happen."

"Hadn't really given that any thought," George nodded, considering. "What have you come up with?"

"Think two of us need to go back with the trucks," Billy said at once. He had been thinking about it. "Way I see it, we take three, four days, make sure we've found most all we want or need, and get it loaded onto a trailer. Once all the trailers is loaded, then we call Jon and Terry, and start convoyin' this stuff home. Leave two here to guard the trailers, the other two ride shotgun."

"Me and you can ride shotgun," Two Bears said. "And that will give Toby some experience here that he might not get elsewhere," he looked over at Toby, who nodded.

"Works for me," the teen agreed.

"George?" Billy asked. "What you think?"

"I think it's the best plan we're going to get," he sighed. "You're right. We don't have enough people. But I don't relish the idea of adding any more to our group. At least not yet. We've pretty much exhausted all the people we know of that we can trust. At least, the one's that survived. Sure, there's others we know, but I got no idea where they are, or if they made it."

"We'll go with your idea, Billy. I think it's the best idea."

"Well, then we need a plan," Billy said as they entered town. "We need to make us a plan for all this, get it nailed down, and then stick to it."

The plan was pretty simple. They went store to store, marking things to take first, things to take if there was room, and things that would be worth an extra trip, if necessary. The entire first day was consumed with that. Lowe's, Wal-Mart, grocery stores, hardware stores, even the local fuel distributors.

"I like the idea of takin' one o' these tankers home," Billy told them, pointing to a truck normally used to deliver gas and diesel to service stations. "Small enough we can handle it, but it'll give us an edge on gas. And we need it."

They encountered some good fortune where gasoline was concerned. The distributor also stocked the highly valuable Pri-G, Pri-D, Stab-bil, and Lucas additives. It wouldn't last forever, but then neither would the gas. All of that material was considered high priority.

For three days, two of which it rained solid, the four of them went from store to store, using a forklift that operated on propane to load trailer after trailer. Fortunately, there were several trailers to choose from, and one trucking company had even had seven wonderfully empty trailers on their lot. They managed to coax a semi into life, which they used to haul the trailers, an extremely reluctant Billy Todd at the wheel.

On the fourth day, it snowed. The men had made camp in the Lowe's store, and stood looking out the front doors are the white flakes.

"Figures," Billy almost spat. He didn't like being away from home.

"Well, we were going to work in the Wal-Mart today, anyway," George sighed. They had left it for last, since the thugs they had eliminated had made it home for so long. There was some usable stuff left, to be sure, but the bunch had pretty well trashed the place.

"We did find that one pharmacy," Peter mentioned. "I don't know how that bunch missed it, but I'm glad they did." Everyone nodded. The medicines and equipment would come in handy.

"Well, let's get started."

-

After six days of hard, back breaking work, the four of them were satisfied they'd gotten everything they had need of.

They stood behind the Lowe's looking at thirteen box trailers.

"Bad luck," Billy muttered.

"What?" George asked, looking over at Billy.

"Thirteen. Bad luck," Billy repeated.

"Well, it's actually fifteen," George reminded him. "We've still got one trailer at the oil place loaded, plus the tanker." Billy brightened at that.

"Forgot that," he nodded eagerly. "Reckon it's time we called the cavalry?"

"I think so," George nodded. "Whatever else we want we can finish today."

-

Terry and Jon rolled in early the next morning. Rhonda had rode with Terry.

"Don't you dare," Rhonda ordered when Billy went to hug her. He frowned, then realized what she was worried about.

"We rigged us a poor man's shower. I'm all fresh and clean."

"Well," Rhonda hesitantly hugged him tight. He was right, she decided, kissing him.

"Would you really not o' hugged me?" Billy asked.

"Of course, I would," Rhonda replied at once. "Just. . .carefully," she added, grinning.

"Okay, let's get this done," George ordered. "How many runs can you guys make today, you think?" Jon and Terry conferred for a moment, then Jon answered.

"At least three," he said firmly. "Possibly four, but we'd get home after dark."

"That means, if all goes well, we can have this done in two days," George mused. Terry pointed to the truck they had used to move trailers about while loading.

"What's wrong with that truck?" he asked.

"Nothing," George asked. "Why?"

"Was just thinkin'," he shrugged. "Use that one too, and we can move almost all the trailers today."

"Who would drive it?" George asked. Everyone looked at Billy.

"No you don't!" Billy stepped back a few paces. "I ain't drivin' one o' them things no more if I can help it!"

"It would make things go faster," George told him.

"I ain't a doin' it," Billy shook his head firmly.

"It would get us out of here faster, Billy," Peter threw in.

"Not happenin'," Billy continued to shake his head.

"Be safe at home tomorrow night, work all done," Rhonda added. Billy shot her a look that practically *screamed* 'traitor'.

"C'mon, Billy," Toby pleaded. "Let's get this over with and go home." The teenager was proud to be treated like a man, especially among these men, but he was tired, too. He wanted to be home for a while.

Sighing in defeat, Billy ground out one word between clenched teeth.

"Fine."

Billy driving a third truck did put a monkey wrench into their plans.

"You gonna be here all by yourself, if Toby rides shotgun with Pete," Billy told him. George nodded.

"I'll make out. Ain't but one night," he said.

"I don't like you bein' here alone, though," Billy pressed. "Somethin' might happen."

"Well, someone might also steal these trailers we've worked so hard to load. I don't aim to let that happen."

"Trailers ain't worth losin' you, George," Billy told him bluntly. "Whatever we lose on them trailers won't even matter, we lose a friend." George smiled.

"I'm glad you think of me as a friend, Billy," he said earnestly. "You can't know how much that means to me. But I can take care of myself. I've done stuff just like this way more times than I can count."

"But not lately," Billy shot back, frowning.

"No, not lately," George agreed. "But it's a bit like riding a bike. It'll come back to me." Billy didn't seem convinced.

"Billy, I'll be fine. Now you guys need to get going. Got a lot of miles to cover today."

Billy finally gave up. George was right. There was a lot to do. The last snow hadn't stuck around, but the skies were threatening. They would be lucky to get everything hauled before the snow fell.

"Okay, let's get'em rollin'," he ordered. Rhonda joined him in the truck, as Toby got behind the wheel of the Ford, allowing Pete to ride hands free. The truck would lead, unless they picked up a follower.

Ten minutes later, the trucks were on their way, the first of a hopeful four trips.

-

George watched them go, sighing as they disappeared from sight. Truth be told, he wanted to go home, but he didn't.

He hadn't bothered to see Debbie while he'd been home. He was sure they would fight, and that was the last thing he needed. But sooner or later, they would have to address the problems between them. They couldn't let them fester much longer.

He thought of his son, then. He wished he could have seen little Georgie. The boy deserved better. But he also deserved better than for his parents to be fighting all the time.

He'd have to find a balance, George knew, if he was to ever make Georgie's life the best it could be. If he and Deb couldn't work out their problems, then he had to make that as easy on the boy as he could. He wouldn't let whatever life Georgie might find in this new world be screwed up by his and Deb's problems. His son would have a chance.

These days, that was all he could hope to give him.

Sighing again, this time in hopelessness, George turned and made his way back inside. He had at least four hours, he figured, before they were back.

He had a special project he wanted to work on.

-

Three times the trucks went back and forth to the farms. Each time the tension increased, as things went well. Each time Billy, as well as everyone else, expected something to go wrong.

By the time they returned for the fourth run, everyone was on edge. It was already dusk. They would be driving in the dark. Billy had enough NVG's, barely, for the drivers, and one each for Toby and Rhonda as lookouts.

"Take good care of'em," he warned. "Ain't got no more, and I couldn't even guess where to replace'em."

George didn't say anything, but he had an idea where to replace them. He'd been working on it most of the day.

"George, I really wish you'd come with us," Billy said, cutting into his train of thought. "I don't like you bein' here all alone, even for one night."

"Don't worry about me, Billy," George smiled. "I'll be fine."

"I still don't like it," Billy told him.

"I know," George nodded. "You've made that abundantly clear. But this was my trip, remember? You said you had taken my orders because this was my trip. And it still is. This is the way of it. Someone needs to keep a watch. And I slept some during the day." The lie came easily.

"I don't believe a word o' that," Billy told him bluntly. "But it is your trip," he sighed reluctantly. "Well, reckon we better go. Already gonna be drivin' in the dark as it is."

"Get going, then," George nodded, shaking hands with Billy. "See you at first light."

"Your lips to God's ear," Billy murmured, shaking hands.

"Don't worry so much, Billy. Everything will be fine."

Billy drove away shaking his head. He didn't know why, but he was sure things wouldn't be fine.

But they had moved twelve trailers, so far, and the gas tanker. Not a bad haul. He wished they could have moved more, but their manpower was stretched to the breaking point now. The Farms were almost bare of people, with Jerry, Ralph, and Ben making almost constant checks on things. Mary was still at the Clifton house, while Danny and the dogs guarded the Todd farm.

It was all they could do.

Billy just hoped it was enough.

CHAPTER FORTY-SEVEN

As soon as the others were gone, George took the truck he had appropriated, and drove to his special project.

The Tennessee National Guard Armory sat on Campbell Boulevard, in the city's industrial park. The unit was a maintenance outfit, so there wouldn't be any real military vehicles there, to amount to anything. At least no major combat vehicles.

There were a few Humvee's of course, and trucks, but George wasn't especially interested in them, although a Hummer would be nice, if time allowed. What he was really interested in was the armory, and the supply section.

He had approached the armory cautiously, aware that someone might be there. He also worried that the idiots they had taken out at the Wal-Mart would have been there.

He needn't have worried. They had apparently decided that they had all they needed under one roof. As near as George could see, no one had disturbed the armory at all.

He had thought sure that at least some of the Guardsmen would have reported for duty, but it appeared that no one had. He shook his head sadly. As fast as the virus had moved, it was entirely possible that most of them had succumbed to it before they could get here.

And if they hadn't, who could blame them for staying with their families? It wasn't like there was anything they could have done. There was no way for them to fight something they couldn't see. They couldn't win against such an enemy. Activating them would have been nothing more than a feel-good gesture, made for the public.

George examined his handiwork. He had finally managed to open the armory. The weapons had been undisturbed, as had the ammunition supplies, and various and sundry parts and equipment.

He had managed to find a large U-Haul trailer, and had spent the day loading everything he could find onto it. Rifles, handguns, heavier weapons, though there weren't many, even some grenades. Every part and piece, cleaning equipment, tools, whatever he found. He had found several cases of MRE's, which he had also loaded.

BDU uniforms, boots, radio equipment, a small generator meant for field deployment. Finally, he'd selected an armored HumVee from the motor pool and attached it to the trailer, then loaded it to the brim as well.

He had left behind some things that might be useful, but weren't needful. That was the way of things, he knew.

He also knew that they would never need such a great amount of weaponry, but it made sense not to leave it for others to use against them. Satisfied that the truck and trailer were ready, George climbed aboard, and headed out of town.

He would store the truck and its trailer behind what was left of Regina Townsend's home, and probably sleep in the cab.

He could always hitch a ride back with the returning trucks.

Billy surveyed the line of trailers at the Clifton Farm, and felt some relief. They had elected to store them here, since it was out of the way, and far enough past the other houses to be out of sight. Billy figured if someone made it this far, there was no way to save anything, anyway.

He had also started thinking about a back-up plan. Among other things.

"What we need is a school bus," he murmured, unaware he'd spoken out loud.

"What?" Terry Blaine asked, standing nearby.

"What?" Billy looked at him.

"You said school bus?" Terry looked at him.

"I did?" Billy frowned. "Well, I was thinkin' it, anyway," he shrugged. "We need a good school bus. We got a lot o' people, now. Say we all wanted to up and go somewhere. Or had to run for it. Ain't no way we could make it, with ever body pilin' in the few trucks we got. We need somethin' that'll carry most everyone, and use the trucks to protect it. Ought to have one o' these rigs packed with enough gear to start over somewhere, too, was we to have to."

"Huh," Terry grunted. He hadn't thought that far ahead. He shook his head.

"You don't think so?" Billy asked.

"No, I think you're right," Terry laughed, though without any humor. "I just hadn't thought about it. And I should have," he added with a grimace.

"Why?" Billy asked.

"Because this is what I do," Terry told him. "I've always been prepared for anything, Billy. If I could imagine it, I was ready for it. Done it my whole career. My whole life. I shouldn't be over looking these things. And you always seem to think of them. Boggles the mind," he sighed.

"Because I can think of them?" Billy asked, frowning. He didn't like the way that sounded.

"Because I *don't*," Terry corrected him. "Hell, Billy, I was trained to think about these things."

"So was I," Billy shrugged. "All my life."

"You were?" Terry asked in surprise.

"Yep," Billy nodded. "My folks was always prepared for any emergency. All the time. Never did have anything catch'em by surprise that I knew of."

"Well, that's good," Terry nodded. "Most folks don't bother. They just assume the government will take care of it." Billy snorted at that.

"My momma and daddy didn't have a real high opinion of the gover'ment's ability to take care o' nothin'," he said.

"Wise thinking," Terry nodded. Having served his twenty and a little more, he knew all too well how inept the government could be. Anyone left alive after the plague should be able to see it now.

"Anyway, once we've rested up, I think I'll work on it," Billy told him. "Make a plan for in case we have to head out, unexpected like. We got a plan, we can avoid makin' a mistake."

"You're a big believer in plans, aren't you?" Terry asked.

"Got to have'em," Billy said firmly. "You ain't got a plan, and don't stick to it, you're askin' for trouble. Be runnin' around like a chicken with it's head cut off."

"One last run," Billy said, as he and Rhonda crawled into the cab.

"Yep," she replied, tiredly. She had wanted to come, but she realized now that Billy and the others had to be near exhaustion. All she had done was ride, for the most part. And she was give out.

The trip was uneventful, and quiet. The entire group was tired. The radio startled them.

"*Anyone awake out there?*" George's voice cut across the air.

"We're here," Rhonda replied.

"*Need you to stop at our new friend's place, and pick me up, you don't mind,*" George told her. "*Didn't feel like walking back, last night.*"

"*We'll get him,*" Toby's voice came through. Billy wondered why George was out there, but figured he had a good reason. They'd know soon enough.

Peter and Toby caught up quickly after stopping to get George. The three rigs were backed in to the trailers and hooked up shortly. They were all getting good at that, by now.

"What were you doin' all the way out there?" Billy asked, as George got out of the Ford.

"Took a Hummer and trailer from the Guard. Loaded it up from the Armory," George smiled.

"Huh," Billy grunted. "Never even thought o' that," he admitted.

"I have to get one on you every now and then," George winked. Billy just chuckled.

"All right, are we sure this is it?" Jon asked. "Something about this morning is giving me the willies."

"This is it," George nodded. "Have to stop on the way out and get the truck I left, but that's all. Won't take five minutes."

"Well, that's good. We can be home. . . ." Jon trailed off as Billy held up a hand.

"What is it?" Terry asked, hoisting his rifle and looking around.

"You don't hear that?" Billy asked softly, frowning.

"I don't hear. . . ." Terry trailed off, looking alarmed.

"The train."

-

The drivers hurried to their trucks, and soon the rigs were on the road. The Ford brought up the rear, since that's where the threat would be.

"Maybe we should leave the U-Haul, George," Pete suggested.

"No," George said at once. "Too much on it. And if this group ever comes after us, we'll need it."

"Point," Pete nodded. "We really need a couple more guys," he added.

"Have to make do. Do what we can with what we got," George shrugged. Pete pulled up to the Hummer, and George jumped out.

"You guys get going," he ordered.

"Soon as you do," Peter nodded.

"I mean now!" George snapped back.

"Whatever," Peter muttered, backing the truck out onto the road. He jumped out, rifle in hand.

"What do you say, Toby?" he asked, as the boy slid over behind the wheel.

"We run, or we wait?" Pete was testing his young friend.

"We wait," Toby said at once, gathering up his own rifle. "He won't never be able to drive that rig and shoot back."

"Good man. Be ready to tear outta here as soon as he's out of sight."

Toby nodded, watching George. They couldn't use the radios, for fear the signal might be picked up. All they could do was stick to the plan.

"Hate to leave the others with no rider," Toby said quietly.

"Me too," Pete admitted. "We'll catch up soon enough," he nodded as George came tearing out of the Townsend driveway.

"You idiots get moving!" he yelled angrily. Toby smiled, and waved, and sat still.

"Right behind you!" Pete yelled. George looked mad as he pulled onto the road, and floored the big truck.

"He looks madder'n a wet hen," Toby laughed. Pete nodded.

"We'll hear about this later, you can bet," he told the teen. "But I don't mind getting chewed on for doing the right thing."

"Me neither," Toby surprised himself by admitting.

"Hear that?" Pete asked. Toby could hear it. Motorcycles. He looked to see where George was. Out of sight.

"George is up the road," he reported.

"Just in time, too," Pete said, raising his rifle. "Here come the neighbors."

Two motorcycles, much like the two that Billy had destroyed in Cottonwood, came into view. Both slowed at the sight before them, and one raised his hand to his head. Assuming it was a radio, Pete opened fire, spraying both bikes, and both riders, with a hail of jacketed bullets. Both fell to the pavement, and one of the bikes caught fire.

"Time for us to move on, kid," Pete ordered, sliding into the back seat, and opening the rear window. "Get us moving!"

Toby needed no encouragement. He floored the big Ford, and it took off, heading down the highway, with Pete watching their rear the whole way.

-

"I'd like to know what the two of you thought you were doing?" George almost yelled, as Pete and Toby stood before him.

"Our job," Pete shrugged. "We were the escort. Our job to make sure the rest of you made it out of town."

"And we did, too," Toby added. George's glower cut his smile off at the knees.

"I told you two to get down the road!"

"And we did, right after you," Pete nodded.

"I meant right then!"

"You should have explained yourself better," Pete shrugged. "Not our fault."

George looked apoplectic.

"We did what we was 'sposed to do, Mister Purdy," Toby said firmly. "I don't see what the big deal is." George looked at him, but said nothing. Finally, he sighed.

"So, you did, Toby," he said at last. "Good work. Both of you."

"That's more like it," Pete nodded.

"Don't push it, Injun."

-

The news traveled fast that everyone was home, and that they had encountered the train. Ralph and Amy decided to go up and see what had been found, and asked Debbie to come along.

"I don't think so," Debbie shook her head. "I don't feel too well, at the moment," she admitted. "Would you mind letting Georgie go with you? To see his father?"

"Of course not," Ralph said at once. Amy looked at Debbie in concern.

"Deb, are you okay?"

"Oh, I think so," Deb nodded. "Just a little off, that's all. I've been having trouble for a little while. I think it's the different foods we're using now. I've tried to make more things from scratch than I used to. I think once we're adjusted to the diet, I'll be much better."

"None of us have had any trouble," Amy pointed out.

"And be glad for that," Debbie told her, grimacing. "It's not all that bad, just irritating. And tiring. Seems like I'm always tired, lately," she admitted.

"Well, why don't you try and rest while we're gone," Amy told her. "The house will be good and quiet."

"I think I will," Debbie nodded after a minute of thought. "I really am tired."

"If you need me for anything, give me a call, okay?" Amy pressed.

"I will," Debbie smiled tiredly. "Tell George I'm glad he's back okay," she added hesitantly.

"I sure will," Amy smiled. She really did like Debbie, when she wasn't trying to stir up trouble. Amy still had no idea why she was so prone to be that way. There didn't seem to be any reason for it.

But, it wasn't her business, either, she decided. Debbie was grown.

Georgie in tow, the couple started up the road.

Behind them Debbie rose tiredly to her feet, and started for her bedroom. She had taken three steps when a wave of dizziness and nausea struck her. Before she could react, she fell to the floor, unconscious.

-

"Well, that's a load you boys got," Jerry said approvingly. Ben Kelvey nodded in agreement.

"Enough materials to build a house, pretty much," he added, looking into the two trailers that carried the building supplies.

"Got a decent haul from a pharmacy, too," George told them, nodding to Amy. "Might want to look through it."

"I will," Amy nodded.

"What's in the Army rig?" Ralph asked. George grinned at him.

"I raided the Guard armory at Columbia," he told them. "Got a whole bunch o' goodies, too," he added with a snicker.

"I bet," Ralph grinned back. "Anything interesting?"

"Well, I think there's enough tack vests for all of us to have one," George nodded. "Plus BDU's, boots, everything we need. Even radios."

"Nice," Ralph nodded. "Debbie said tell you she was glad you were back safe," he added, more quietly. George nodded, hoisting Georgie up in his arms.

"I'll. . .I'll try to visit," he said quietly. "Good to see you, little man," he told his son,

"Where you been, Daddy?" the youngster asked. "Missed you."

"Aw, I missed you, too, little buddy," George replied with a tight hug, trying to keep his emotions under control.

"Big truck," he said excitedly, pointing to the rigs.

"Very big truck," George nodded. "Wanna see'em closer?" he asked.

"Sure!"

Terry walked his son over to the rigs, wondering what a conversation with his wife would bring. He decided he would go and see, after he spent some quality time with his son.

Maybe Debbie would be in a mood to talk sensible.

-

"Well, that was fun," said Rhonda as she and Billy unloaded his gear from the rig and placed it in the Ford.

"Sure was," Billy said tiredly. He really wasn't paying attention. He was beat.

"Billy, I think you need a day or two of rest," Rhonda told him. "You're about done in."

"I'll be fine," Billy waved her off. "Will be good to sleep in my own bed again, though," he added. "I am tired," he admitted. "Still, we got a lot o' stuff done. We're in a lot better shape now than we been a bein'."

"I'm sure we are, but it's time you got some rest," Rhonda told him flatly. "And there's plenty to do at the farm for a week or two, so you don't have to worry 'bout having something to do."

"Yeah, I'll need to get caught up," Billy nodded. "About time to start plantin' our cache tubes, too," he added.

"Okay," Rhonda nodded. "Let's go home and get cleaned up first, and get some rest. I'm tired."

-

George walked back with Ralph and Amy, Georgie riding on his shoulders.

"You gonna live with us again, daddy?" the boy asked, and George felt a lump in his throat.

"I've always lived with you Georgie," he said honestly. "Why would I stay away?"

"Don't know," the boy admitted. "Just missed you. Afraid you was gonna stay gone."

"No, buddy, I'm not staying gone," George promised. Right then he made his decision to do whatever it took to work things out with Debbie. He could live in misery if it meant his son didn't. That was a sacrifice he was willing to make.

At the house, Amy opened the door, and Ralph stepped in behind her, followed by George and Georgie. By the time George was inside, Amy had already ran to where Debbie lay on the floor.

"Ralph, get my bag. Hurry!"

CHAPTER FORTY-EIGHT

"What's wrong with momma, daddy?" Georgie asked quietly.

Debbie had been moved to their bedroom, and Amy was examining her as George and his son sat in the living room. Ralph was in the hallway, in case Amy needed any assistance.

"I don't know, buddy," George told him. "But Miss Amy is with her, so I'm sure she'll be okay."

"I like Miss Amy," Georgie nodded. "She's nice."

"She sure is, isn't she," George nodded. He was trying to maintain his calm, but it wasn't easy. He needed to be strong for his little boy, though. He heard Amy speak, though he couldn't make out the words. Ralph nodded, and walked into the living room.

"Amy can't figure out exactly what's wrong," he admitted. "Blood pressure is up and then down, and she's real pale. No idea why, exactly. Amy says there's two or three things might cause it. One of 'em is some kinda poxy something, but that only happens to pregnant women."

"It can't be that, then," George shook his head. "Debbie can't have any more children, remember? Doctor told us that back when."

"She can't, or ain't supposed to?" Ralph asked, eyeing Georgie carefully.

George Senior blinked.

"Ah, he said couldn't. And we, uh, you know, never used any sort of, ah, preventive measures."

"Maybe you should go talk to Amy," Ralph said, weighing his words with care. "Me and Georgie can wait here. Can't we buddy?"

"Well, I guess," George Junior said, nodding.

George walked to the bedroom door, and looked in. Amy looked up at him, motioning him into the room.

"George, are you sure, I mean absolutely sure, that she can't get pregnant?" Amy asked.

"Well, the doctor told us after Georgie was born that Debbie had suffered some damage that would make it impossible for her to conceive again," he answered. "That sounded pretty definite."

"What was her problem, exactly?" Amy pressed. "Was it a breached delivery?"

"Well, yeah, I think that's the term. I know that Georgie was turned wrong, and making sure he was right caused a lot of damage. Deb almost bled out, in fact, it was so bad. We were lucky to save her. Or little man, either, for that matter." Amy chewed on her lip, thinking.

"I can't run the tests I need to see what's wrong," she admitted to him, finally. "I don't know what to do, exactly, without that. If she's not hypoxic, then it might be internal bleeding. That could be an ulcer that let go, or it could be something else. Her spleen maybe."

"She doesn't have one," George suddenly remembered. "She had an accident when she was a teenager. Had to be removed." Amy nodded.

"Okay, that helps." Amy chewed on her lip again. Suddenly she started.

"I know you and her are having problems, George," she said. "But are they normal? Has her behavior been off? I mean really off. We've all been off lately," she added.

"Yeah," he sighed. "You saw how she was about that girl, Mary. She's been on about that, and then about the Tatum boy. Always downing Billy and Rhonda about the two kids." He shook his head sadly. "It's been like she's trying to start something, you know?"

"Yes," Amy nodded. "And you're saying that's not normal behavior? I'm not trying to pry, George, but anything that might help me get a clue here is important. Has she ever been treated for depression?"

"Yes," George nodded. "After Georgie was born."

"Any other time?" Amy pressed again.

"Not that I. . .well, wait," he paused. "There was one time. A student of hers, really bright girl, was killed by her stepfather. He'd been abusing her for a long time, and she finally stood up to him. Deb was devastated. She cried for a week, off an on, sometimes just breaking down all out of the blue. We finally had to go to the doctor, and get her treatment for it."

"What was the treatment?" Amy asked. "A drug?"

"Yeah, something with a P, I remember," he nodded, thinking. "I can't. . .you know, I remember kidding her it rhymed with axle, but I can't. . . ."

"Paxil?" Amy asked.

"Yeah, that was it."

"How long did she take it?"

"Well, she was still taking it," George mused. "Or at least I guess she was," he added. "We never talked about. I hated to say anything, since it always made her cry." Amy sighed, leaning down to the point that her head could touch the bed.

"So, she hasn't had Paxil since at least the plague, is that it?"

"I can't rightly say," George admitted. "I'm sorry."

"Where did she keep her medicines?" Amy demanded. "Anything that she might take for illness?"

George led her to a small bag in their bathroom, which Amy upended on the counter. She scrambled through the bottles, finally finding what she was looking for.

"This is 20mg Paxil," she breathed. "Strong. And there's three pills left. Out of ninety, dated right at the start of the Plague. She was trying to stretch them. And I bet wean herself off them," she added. "Smart girl."

"What?" George asked.

"This drug is addictive," Amy told him. "Almost impossible to stop taking, without a doctor's help. And she didn't have a doctor. She knew she wouldn't be able to get more, so she's been stretching what she had, and making do." Amy sighed.

"We can fix this," she said confidently. "It will take some time, but we can fix it." She looked up at George.

"This may explain her recent behavior," she told him. "I'd bet on it, in fact."

"Really?" George asked. He so wanted things to be right. "I had no idea she was still taking it. She never discussed that kind of thing with me. And I didn't pry. Maybe I should have."

"Takes two to communicate," Amy said kindly. "You may shoulder some blame, but so does she. The important thing is, we can help her now. Probably. She should come around after she sleeps. I'm almost positive that she's suffering from fatigue as much as anything else. She's hasn't been eating good, she's been scrimping on her meds, though out of necessity. She's stressed, and she's depressed. Not a good combination." She laid her hand on George's arm.

"Don't worry, George," she told him confidently. "We'll make it right."

-

Debbie came around slowly, her eyes adjusting in the dim light. She looked around, her gaze coming to rest on George, asleep in a chair near the bed. His head was over on his shoulder, one hand bracing it, elbow resting on the chair arm. She tried to rise, but her head spun, and she lay back with a groan.

George was awake in an instant. Two seconds later he was kneeling by her side, holding her hand in both of his.

"How are you?" he asked softly. One hand came up to smooth her hair back from her face.

"Whmmphh," she tried, but her mouth and throat were bone dry.

"Wait a minute," George reached out to her night stand and took a small glass with water, holding it up for her to drink. She did so greedily, and drained the glass.

"Want more?"

"No," she gasped. "What happened?" she asked, lying back again.

"You fainted, I guess, for lack of a better word," George told her, replacing the glass on the night stand and reclaiming her hand. "Amy says you're suffering from fatigue, among other things. And that you're suffering from withdrawal from the Paxil."

"I thought I had that under control," Debbie replied, her eyes closed. "I really did."

"Baby, you should have told me," George scolded lightly. "Why didn't you?"

"George, you had so much on you," she said softly, a single tear trailing down her cheek. "I. . .I just couldn't add to that. And it was my problem to deal with."

"That's bullshit," George told her firmly, though his voice was kind. "We're married, Debbie. Any problem one of us has, both of us have."

"Things were so. . .so messed up," she sobbed suddenly. "I could hear myself saying things I shouldn't, and for the life of me I couldn't stop. I know, I *knew*, I was hurting you, and making everyone else mad, and I still couldn't stop myself. I was afraid that anything I said would just sound like an excuse."

"Debbie, you can't keep stuff like that from me," George told her. "Now, more than ever, we have to be there for one another, and support one another. And it's not just for us, either. We have to be strong for one another so we can both be strong for Georgie. He's gonna grow up in a much harder world than we did. We've got to work together, for our own happiness and for his."

"I know," Debbie cried softly. "I'm so sorry I've added to your burden, my dear husband. I never meant to. I tried so hard, but I couldn't. . . ."

"No more of that," George placed a finger to her lips. "None. From now on, we talk about things like this. Amy says we can beat this. You just need help, that's all."

"And I'll be here for you, no matter what."

Word passed slowly but surely throughout the small community about Debbie's condition. No one bothered to inform the new arrivals, figuring it wasn't any of their business. They hadn't been here, anyway, so there was no reason for them to know anything.

Amy looked through the meds that Billy and the others had brought back from Columbia and found a couple that would help Debbie.

"I think she'll be fine in a few weeks," Amy informed George. "She'll have some rough spots as the drug flushes out, and then she'll have some more as she relearns how to cope without the meds. Just be patient. She'll need it."

"I will," he promised.

Billy had ridden over to talk to George that afternoon, wondering if he was intending to go out anymore, with Debbie in such a condition.

"No," George said firmly. "She needs me to be here, and so does my son. I'm staying put."

"Think that's a wise decision," Billy nodded in approval. "Meantime, I got a project or two I can work on. Imagine ever body else does too. We made a goodly haul, back there. I think we can afford to sit home a spell."

"You did really good back there Billy," George said. "Really good." Billy nodded, but said nothing. He didn't know what to say, or what to think about it, anyway.

"I'm glad you went with me," George added, smiling.

"Enjoyed it myself," Billy grinned. "Reckon I'll be gettin' home. Gonna ride up and check on the new folks first, I guess. You need anything, you let us know, hear?"

"I will Billy, and thanks." Billy nodded again and pulled Samson around toward the Clifton farm, Rommel already out in front.

As he rode, Billy thought about the last few weeks. He'd been busy, and hadn't really figured things together like he normally would. He didn't like that. Too easy to forget, to make mistakes.

Their food situation was pretty good at the moment, and being able to clean out two trucks of canned goods, along with a good bit of flour, meal, and oil, hadn't hurt. True, they had more mouths to feed now, but a lot more food, too. And three more adults and two teens to help share the work load that new mouths entailed.

The train arriving in Columbia had bothered Billy. He had wondered where they were, and if they had gone on to greener pastures. Now, he knew they were still around. Still moving from place to place. They wouldn't find much to their liking in Columbia, Billy knew. But they'd find plenty of fuel, and likely some other goodies still lying around.

If they took the time and effort to look through the houses, they'd likely find some usable goods, as well as guns and ammunition, but they wouldn't find any in the stores. And thanks to George, they wouldn't find anything at the Armory either. Billy paused, thinking about the weapons from the armory.

Those would be real military weapons. Automatic rifles, machine guns, maybe some heavier stuff, he didn't know for sure. A lot of firepower in the wrong hands.

And right now it was sitting inside a truck and trailer in a pasture. Along with every round of ammo the armory had contained.

That just wasn't safe, he figured. That stuff needed to be broke apart into smaller groups of equipment, and hid. Stashed where it could be got to in a hurry.

Thinking of that reminded Billy that his own cache's still weren't in the ground, either. He shook his head in disgust at that realization. What was he thinking? Was he getting lazy?

No, no chance of that with Rhonda around. She kept him jumping like a frog in a fireplace. He wasn't lazy, but he had forgotten. There were plenty of excuses he could make, he figured, but he tried not to use excuses. If he got into a habit of it, then he'd start using them all the time.

And that just wouldn't do at all. He had to keep focused. Had to keep things going. He wasn't just responsible for himself, anymore, or even just him and Rhonda. Now there was Mary to think on, and Danny as well. He had to figure them into everything, and make sure they were safe, cared for, and well provided for.

That was his responsibility.

Which reminded him that he hadn't taught Danny to shoot, yet. Well, he already knew how to shoot, but Billy hadn't gotten him a better rifle, and made sure he knew how to use it.

Mary needed the same thing. She had that Ruger, but it was awful heavy. She needed something light. Easy to shoot. He wondered what was in that stuff from the armory. There might be a light carbine in there. He might need to look through it, unless Rhonda had something for her. They could ride over to the gravel pit range and get the two youngsters used to their new weapons.

Which reminded him that Danny couldn't ride a horse. Something else he needed to take care of. These days, people had to know how to ride. They didn't have a finite supply of fuel, and they couldn't waste what they had running around here on the farms.

He'd have to teach Danny to ride. Fortunately, there were some new saddles and tack they had picked up at the Tractor Supply in Columbia. They'd be able to outfit the boy. Even had some boots. There'd be a pair in there somewhere he could wear. He'd have to add clothes and weapons for the two kids to their caches, he realized with a start. And up the amount of food in them.

And that reminded him that his own caches weren't out, yet. Which in turn reminded him again that the equipment from the armory was still sitting in a barn lot. . . .

He reined Samson around with a sigh, shaking his head at himself as he headed home.

He had way too much to do to be out visiting.

-

"Whatcha doin'?" Danny asked, finding Billy in the barn. Billy had only just closed the floor door and recovered it when the boy popped in.

"Just workin' some," Billy told him. "What you up to?"

"Nothin' at the moment," Danny shrugged. "Miss Rhonda sorta ran outta things for me to do, so I got while the gettin' was good."

"Smart boy," Billy nodded in approval.

"You need any help?" Danny asked.

"As it happens, reckon I do," Billy told him. "We need to get you outfitted."

"What's that mean, 'xactly?" Danny asked.

"C'mon and I'll show ya."

"Well, look at you!" Rhonda exclaimed as Danny came into the yard. He was wearing a pair of Carhart overalls, a wide brimmed Stetson, and Durango boots. He was also carrying a saddle, complete with rope, saddle bags, and rifle scabbard. Beneath the overalls was a deep blue denim Carhart shirt. Billy was carrying bags which apparently held other clothes for the boy.

Danny blushed under the scrutiny.

"Danny, you look mighty handsome, all dressed up like that!" Rhonda praised the boy. Danny's face got even redder, and he looked at the ground, scuffing his right boot along the ground.

"Aw, cut that out," he protested.

"You go and put your things away, Danny," Billy told him. "Tomorrow, we start teachin' you to ride."

"Oh boy!" Danny enthused. He almost ran to the barn to store his saddle. He was back in a flash, gathering his new clothes and streaking toward the house.

"Ain't gonna make tomorrow get here no quicker, runnin'. And you trip and hurt yaself, you ain't gonna be able to ride!" Billy yelled, laughing.

"I'll be careful!" Danny promised, never slowing, or turning. Rhonda laughed as the boy ran out of sight. She turned to look at Billy.

"I thought you had stuff to do today?" she remarked.

"I do, and I did," Billy nodded. "I got stuff to do right here. That boy needed outfittin', and he needs to learn to handle and care for a horse. And he needs a new gun, and learn to use it. Mary does too, for that matter."

"Plus, we gonna have to redo them caches, makin' allowance for the to o' them, and then get'em hid. And there's work to be done here, that I ain't been gettin' done."

"So that's changin' as o' now. I'll be spending a while at home, for a change."

"I'm glad to hear that," Rhonda smiled beautifully at him.

CHAPTER FORTY-NINE

Danny Tatum did not enjoy flying. Rather, he didn't enjoy landing, once he had been sent flying by the mule headed gelding he had picked for himself from the herd of horses gathered from the surrounding area.

"Oooofff!"

"Git up, and try it again," Billy ordered.

"That's five times already!" Danny protested, getting slowly to his feet and brushing himself off.

"Be six, you don't stay on'im this time," Billy said flatly. "Ain't his fault, it's yours. Horse is saddle broke, and has been near on two years. He ain't been rid in a while, so he's starchy, but you can't just heave up on a horse, and 'spect him to allow you to be givin'im orders. You got to take charge, and be confident. Horse can smell fear, same as a dog can. You're showin'im fear, and he's dumpin' ya cause of it. Now git back on."

Danny muttered under his breath as walked to where the horse was standing. How could he show confidence? An idea came to him, suddenly. He reached the rein, and pulled it in, taking the halter in his left hand and pulling the horse's head toward him. He looked right into the gelding's eyes as he spoke.

"Now you listen here, you glue factory reject," he said, voice soft but stern. "I'm tired o' this. Me and you, we gonna be friends whether you like it or don't. So, the best thing you can do is stop all this flighty nonsense, and learn who's the boss. And that's me, case you ain't got it yet, hear?" The horse snorted, but Danny held its gaze. The horse was the first to look away, stamping the ground as it did so.

"Billy, is this safe?" Rhonda asked quietly, concern plain in her voice.

"'Bout as safe as wrasslin' a wildcat," Billy nodded, never taking his eyes off Danny. "But he picked the horse. And that paint is a good horse, too. Danny needs to get'im under control. Once he does, that horse'll be a fine mount for him for years to come."

"What if he get's hurt?"

"He get's hurt," Billy shrugged. "Life's like that. What if somethin' happened to you and me tomorrow? Sure, the rest will help'em, but these two gonna be on their own for the most part. They got to learn." Rhonda could see the sense in that, but she was still worried as Danny stepped into the saddle again.

Once seated, Danny took the reins, and nudged the big gelding's flanks with his heels. The horse tried to buck, but Danny was ready this time, and grabbed the saddle horn with one hand while yanking the horse's head up with the other. The gelding fought him, and tried to turn, but Danny had seen that move too, and instantly pulled the reins in the other direction.

The gelding surprised him then, going with the reins, only faster. Danny almost went flying again, but managed to dig his feet into the stirrups, which coupled with his death grip on the saddle horn helped him stay on. As the gelding floundered for a second, Danny quickly wrapped the reins around the saddle horn, and used his now free hand to smack the horse soundly between the ears.

The gelding's ears went flat, and he bucked. Or at least he tried to. With the reins around the saddle horn, the horse was unable to get his head down enough to buck sufficiently hard enough to dislodge the teenager.

Billy watched with approval as Danny met the horse halfway every time the gelding tried to move. After what seemed like an hour to Danny, but was actually less than five minutes, the gelding suddenly stopped, whinnying slightly in defeat. Danny held him a bit longer for good measure, then reached down to pat the horse's shoulder. Reaching into his coat pocket, the boy produced a quarter of an apple, which he leaned forward and offered to the horse. The gelding sniffed at it, the carefully took the offered fruit, munching it loudly.

"Good boy," Danny patted the shoulder again, stroking the horse lightly. The horse's tail flickered, and he whinnied again, this time more friendly. Danny rewarded him with another piece of apple, then nudged the big gelding slightly, guiding him to where Billy and Rhonda sat watching.

"How 'bout that?" he grinned, and Billy nodded in satisfaction.

"I think you've convinced him," he said, leaving his perch. "Now, let's see can you ride him around the farm 'thout him givin' ya the heave."

-

Once he had mastered the gelding, Danny wanted nothing more than to ride every minute of the day. He paid careful attention as Billy showed him how to care for the horse, and made sure he repeated Billy's motions. He rubbed the horse down faithfully when he rode him, made sure he was clean and healthy. And every now and then slipped him a slice of apple.

"What are you gonna call'im?" Billy asked, as Danny was saddling the gelding for a ride over to the gravel pit.

"Call him?" Danny asked. "I hadn't give that no thought at all."

"Reckon you ain't got to name'im," Billy shrugged. "Most do though."

"Hmm," Danny hummed thoughtfully.

Billy left the teen to ponder the question while he finished loading their gear. He and Rhonda were taking the two kids to the gravel pit today. Rhonda had produced one more CAR-15, which would be going to Mary. Billy had selected an M-4 for Danny, albeit one of the civilian models. Both had holographic sights on them now, as well as slings. The M-4 also had iron sights, and Billy saw no reason to remove them. The CAR didn't have iron sights, being a ready for optics model.

They had looked long and hard at handguns for the two. Mary's small hands had presented a problem, at least for now. She would eventually, probably anyway, grow into a larger pistol, but for now her choices were limited. Rhonda had one 3906 S&S, a single stack nine-millimeter, which Mary had been able to hold comfortably. It was on the large size for her, but the single column mag meant that the grip was much smaller than say a model 59 variant. They had also chosen a pair of revolvers for her.

The first was a 2 ½ inch barrel Model 66 Smith. It was heavy, but the grip was good in her hand. It was chambered for .357, but would also take the less powerful .38 and .38+p rounds. The other was an even smaller Tarus model 85, a 2inch barrel five shot revolver. Both would be well within her ability to use now, and would still be fine when she was older and stronger.

Danny would get a pair of SIG pistols, model 229's, that they had found in the shop at Cottonwood. Both were nine-millimeter, and his hand was already large enough to hold them. He also received a SIG .380, gotten from the same source, to use as a back up or hide out weapon.

The selection process was rounded out with a shotgun apiece, an 870 12ga for Danny, and a Mossy .410 pump for Mary. Billy had chosen a nice Remington 700 chambered for .270 for Danny as well, as a hunting rifle.

All in all, it was quite a load. Billy had decided to take a pack horse this time, since they would need a good bit of ammo, and would be gone much of the day. Finally packed, he waited as Rhonda and Mary 'got ready' and made their way out.

"Thor!" Danny exclaimed suddenly, and Billy turned to look at him.

"What?"

"I'ma call'im Thor!" Danny said proudly. "My horse, I'm gonna call'im Thor," he added, at Billy's look of confusion. Billy thought about that for a moment, then nodded.

"Good strong name," he approved.

"Here we are!" he heard Rhonda announce.

"And 'bout time, too," Billy muttered under his breath, where Rhonda couldn't. . . .

"I heard that!" Rhonda shot back, sticking her tongue out at him. Shaking his head, Billy mounted up.

"Rommel, Dottie, lead off," he ordered, pointing in the direction he wanted to go. The two Rottie's obediently took off, Rommel as usual in the lead, while Dottie stayed closer to the horses.

—

"Well, that should do it," Billy nodded. The sun was much further along in the sky now. Both teenagers were busy collecting their empties. The lessons had gone well, and both had shown very good proficiency with the new weapons.

"I'm proud of them," Rhonda nodded from beside him. "Especially Mary. She took to it very well."

"She did," Billy agreed. "Danny wasn't kiddin' when he said he was a fair shot. Once he got the sights right, he was all x's. Boy's a fine shot."

"Yeah, he is," Rhonda said, almost wistfully.

"What is it?" Billy asked, turning to look at her.

"I hate this," she admitted, looking up at him. "I hate that these kids have to learn this."

"Good for'em," Billy shrugged. "I don't hate for'em learnin' to shoot. Ever body ought to know how. But I know what you mean," he added. "I hate to think they'll have to use'em for anything 'cept huntin' and sport."

"I'm afraid they will, though," Rhonda said softly. "I don't know why, but I'm afraid. Things have gone entirely too well, for us, Billy. And you know that."

"Well, I think things has gone well, considerin'," he nodded. "That don't mean it'll change, though. We been mightly careful. I mean, sooner or later somebody's gonna find us, or we're gonna tell'em where we are. Reckon we can't stay hid out forever."

"That don't mean it'll be bad, though," he went on. "Just means we'll need to have a good plan for it. Like ever body here knowin' how to defend themselves, and the place."

"I hope you're right," Rhonda sighed. "I really, really do."

They rode home in silence. The two kids cleaned their weapons under adult supervision, while hearing lectures on safety and security. Both teens soaked up the instructions like a sponge. They had been through rough times already. They had no need to be taught how bad things were, or how bad they could get. They knew all too well from first hand experience.

"Reckon we'll get supper on," Rhonda announced as she and Mary finished up.

"We'll see to the horses, and make a round, make sure ever thing's okay," Billy agreed.

Supper was a quiet meal, with the teens chattering away about their exciting day, while the adults thought about their discussion.

It was almost normal.

-

Billy spent the next week working all over the farm, with Danny right alongside, learning as he went. Billy showed Danny how to care for the stock, how to see when something was wrong with the cattle. He told him about warning signs for sickness, the dangers of ticks and other parasites, whether to horse, cow, dog, or human.

Billy taught him everything he could think of, in fact. He took his own notes and read them off to him, going over the things that needed to be checked every day, or every week. He showed the teen the battery bank for the solar system, teaching him how to check the meters, and the batteries. He showed him the generator, how to service it and check to see if it was ready to run, then how to start it, and how to turn the power into the house when needed.

He taught Danny how to use a chainsaw, and the wood-splitter, as well as split wood by hand. He started showing Danny how to track, teaching him the signs that each animal made. He also brought out one of his father's books on tracking, and another on edible plants. Danny gobbled them up, eager to learn.

Billy presented Danny with an excellent knife, an RTA III, along with a smaller RTA belt knife, and two good multi-tools.

"Why two?" Danny asked.

"Two is one, and one is none," Billy quoted.

"What's that mean?"

"I don't really know," Billy admitted. "I just always heard my daddy say it, and I kept it to mind. I think it means that having one of anything is just like havin' none. When it breaks, when you use it up, when you lose it, then it's gone, and you ain't got nothin' else."

"Make's sense," Danny decided after a minute. "Two is one, and one is none." He suddenly whipped out a small notebook, and scribbled a note to himself.

"What's that?" Billy asked, not quite frowning.

"My notebook," Danny said, putting it away. "I write down important stuff, so's I don't forget. It helps me, cause I can always go back over it again, and read what I wrote down. Helps remind me."

"Good thinkin'," Billy grunted.

"Just good plannin'," Danny shrugged.

"So, it is," Billy grinned. "Let's go up to the house, and I'll show you how to sharpen them knives."

"Neat!"

"Howdy neighbor!" Ralph called as Billy rode into the yard. "Haven't seen you in a while."

"Been keepin' busy," Billy admitted, stepping down. "Had a lot to catch up on."

"I imagine," Ralph nodded. "Don't think anyone's strayed too far from home last week or two."

"How's George?" Billy asked.

"Fine. Needs to sleep more, but I don't blame him none for that. Deb's doing better, but going through a rough patch at the moment. Amy says it'll pass, but just takes time."

"Glad she's doin' better," Billy nodded. "Got a favor I need," he went on. He held out two bundles.

"Whatcha got there," Ralph said, taking the two parcels and placing them on the table in his shop.

"One's a calf hide I tanned," Billy told him, as Ralph was pulling the hide out.

"Nice," Ralph complimented. "Very nice work. What you want done with it?"

"This is a coat of Rhonda's," Billy told him, holding out the other parcel. A waist length denim coat. "Think you can make her a coat from the hide, usin' this as a pattern?"

"Don't see why not," Ralph nodded. "Denim jacket won't survive the process, though," he warned.

"She's got three of'em, I think," Billy shrugged. "Two for sure. And this calf hide oughta last a long time."

"It sure will," Ralph nodded. "Billy, this is a really great job. You'll need to show the rest of us how to do this."

"Get time, I will," Billy agreed. "Meanwhile, reckon you can have that done for Christmas?"

"Two weeks?" Ralph figured. "I think so. I don't have a lot going on at the moment."

"How much?" Billy asked.

"For you?" Ralph snorted. "Nothing. I'd consider it a way for me to give back after all you've done for us."

"I reckon I can pay," Billy said stubbornly.

"I'm sure you can," Ralph nodded. "But I reckon I can decide what my services is worth. And for you, they're priceless. Your money's no good on this one, Billy. My treat."

"Ralph, I don't want. . . ."

"Stow it, Billy," Ralph said pleasantly. "I've wanted to find a way, any kind of way, to show my appreciation. You just don't ever seem to need anything. Now, you've give me a way to do it. I'll have it ready by Christmas Eve, Lord willing. Don't you fret."

"Thanks, Ralph," Billy nodded. "'Preciate it."

"No problem. What are neighbors for?"

Billy rode back home to find Rhonda saddling her own horse.

"What'cha doin'?" he asked.

"Goin' up to see them new folks," Rhonda smiled. "Thought I'd check in on them before we ride over to the Silvers' for dinner."

"Mind if I ride along with you?"

"Course not!" Rhonda beamed. "I might need you to protect me from lions, or bears, or. . . ."

"Plain old yes or no would be fine," Billy held up his hand. "I ain't even been up there since we got back. Reckon I should at least drop by."

"Reckon we ought to start puttin' the cache's out soon," Billy noted as the two started up the trail.

"They're done, then?" Rhonda asked.

"Yeah. Decided to just place two tubes each time, instead o' tryin' to make bigger one's. Just put their stuff in the new one."

"Good idea," Rhonda nodded.

"I used some of daddy's old guns for them," he added. "SKS for Mary, and an AK for Danny. Gave'em a couple o' CZ handguns that daddy found somewhere years ago. Pretty good guns."

"My daddy always said so, too," Rhonda nodded. "I wonder what he would say, if he could see me now," she sighed.

"He'd say he taught you right well, I'd imagine," Billy replied without hesitation. "He'd be proud, too."

"I hope so," Rhonda sighed again. "I miss him every day, but some days are worse than others. Like when I really need his advice on something or other."

"I know how you feel," Billy said quietly. "There's many a time just since all this started I wished I could talk to my folks for just five minutes. Course, I'd just want five more after that."

"Yeah," Rhonda nodded sadly. She forgot, sometimes, that Billy had been on his own for over three years before all this had happened. He'd had to learn to get by on his own. And he had. The two of them had made errors, but they hadn't done too badly considering.

The ride didn't take as long as it seemed to when they had first rode up. Now days, the trip was a regular thing, and everyone was used to riding horseback by now. Rhonda noticed that a buggy was parked in front of the house.

"Looks like Emma's here too," she noted. Emma could ride, but much preferred the buggy that Jerry had refinished for her when things had gotten so bad.

"Looks like," Billy said, dismounting. "Reckon me and Rommel will take a look around," he told her. "Make sure everything's looking okay."

"Okay," Rhonda smiled. "I'll be inside if you need me."

Billy nodded, and he and Rommel started over to the trailers first. After that he figured they'd look around the tree line behind the house, and then circle it good.

Paid to be cautious these days.

Rhonda went inside, where she found Emma and Michelle visiting with Regina and the others. Michelle was holding the one year old in her arms, cooing softly to him.

"Hello neighbors," she smiled. "I bring gifts," she announced, handing over a basket with some fresh bread, jelly, and cookies. "I thought the young one's might enjoy the sweets."

"I'm sure they will," Regina smiled, handing the basket off to one of the twins to secure. "How are you Rhonda?"

"Why I'm fit as fiddle, I reckon," Rhonda twanged back, and all the women laughed. "Billy's making a check around outside. He'll be along after while."

"Ralph was up here this morning to check on us, too," Regina nodded. "I don't know what we'd do, where we'd be, if not for all of you."

"Well, you're here, now, dear, and that's all that matters," Emma smiled. "Rhonda, dear, how are you?"

"I'm good, Miss Em. Shelly."

"Hi," Michelle looked up from the baby. "Isn't he gorgeous?"

"Yeah, he's a cute little tyke."

-

Billy had a bad feeling. Like the hair was wanting to stand up on his neck. He looked to Rommel, and noticed the large dog sniffing the air.

"Easy, boy," he warned gently. "Let's just ease along, and see what's what, okay?" Rommel ratcheted down a notch at Billy's words, but he was uneasy.

Billy didn't like that. If both of them were uneasy, then there was probably a reason. That gave Billy a dilemma. Should he risk going to check on his own? Or should he get someone else up here to back him up? He weighed the two ideas for a minute, then decided to check things out a little more first. No sense in alarming everyone for no reason.

Nodding to Rommel, Billy let his sling catch his rifle and started ambling along, with no clear direction in mind, or apparent to someone who might be watching. In fact, though, he had a very clear destination in mind. There was a small trail inside the tree line, and Billy was heading indirectly for it. For some reason that he couldn't place, he had an idea someone was in those woods, watching. Or had been. And he didn't like that one bit.

Easing along, he acted like he was just out looking things over, with no real reason to be here other than that. Rommel stayed close, helping that idea along without knowing it. *Probably* without knowing it, Billy decided. Rommel was an uncommonly smart dog.

When he was within thirty yards of the woods, three white tail deer suddenly lunged into the field, running. Billy instantly threw his rifle up, but held his fire. His M4 wasn't the best rifle to try and take game with, and he didn't really need the meat at the moment. No one did. Allowing his rifle to fall back into rest, he acted like he was watching the deer. What he was really doing was eyeing the area they had run out of.

"Easy, Rommel," he ordered softly, as the dog quivered, wanting to give chase. Rommel calmed, but kept his eyes on the fleeing deer.

"C'mon, boy," Billy ordered loudly. "Ain't no need o' tryin' to get'em. They's too far gone, anyway. We can see if there's more, though." He spoke loudly for the benefit of anyone who was watching, if there was someone watching.

Angling for the spot where the deer had come from, Billy walked slowly but steadily in that direction. No hurry, here, friends. Just walking about.

He was inside the trees before he realized it. As soon as they were in the tree line, Billy started moving more carefully. If there was someone in here, Billy wanted them to have to work at seeing him.

"Let's go, boy," he whispered to Rommel. Billy led him back toward the area that had made him uneasy, working slowly through the wood, quiet as he knew how. He did this for almost ten minutes, during which he traveled less than thirty yards.

Kneeling beside a large oak, he found what he'd feared. Pressed grass, cigarette butts, and a candy wrapper. From the look of it, at least two had been watching. Billy looked around carefully, but saw no other signs. He traveled another twenty to thirty yards, but found no other sign.

Steadily making his way through the woods, he emerged behind the house again, this time on the opposite side where he'd entered. He'd found no other place where anyone had hidden and watched the Clifton house.

But one was enough. More than enough.

CHAPTER FIFTY

Billy was antsy the rest of the time they spent at the Home. Everyone had taken to calling it that, since it's purpose had been to house orphans. It was now housing orphans.

Rhonda recognized his fidgeting, and made an earlier exit that she'd intended to. As they mounted up to leave, she asked him what was wrong.

"Who said anything 'bout somethin' bein' wrong?" he asked evasively.

"Billy, you really are a horrible liar," she told him, grinning. "I can tell when something's bothering you, and you've been worrying over something ever since you took that walk."

"Someone's watchin'," he said softly. Rhonda looked at him, dumbfounded.

"What?"

"Some body's watchin' this place," he repeated. "Like as not been at it a while, though I can't be sure o' that. Found where they been layin' out in the woods, keeping an eye out."

"Who could it be?" Rhonda asked. "Oh, duh," she added a second later.

"Yeah," Billy nodded. "Ain't no way o' knowin'. Not really. Not until we catch'em. I'm gonna ride down and see Pete. Reckon he'll help me stand a watch tonight. We'll have to figure out who it is. Maybe we can follow'em back to where ever they're camped."

"Meanwhile, we need to let every body know what's happening, so they can be watchful. I'll leave it to you to stop by the Kelvey's, Ralph and George's, and tell Jerry and Miss Em. I'll head on down to see Pete."

"Aren't you gonna tell Regina and them?" she nodded back to the Clifton place.

"Tell'em what?" he asked. "They're nice folks, but border line useless at the moment. Which is somethin' else we got to change," he decided. "I'll talk to Terry about that. We need to get them women checked out on rifles. They need to be able to defend themselves and them kids. I never imagined we'd have someone behind us like this. I mean, it's like five *miles* back there to the nearest road!"

"Even fire trails and the like?" Rhonda asked. Billy actually stopped his horse at that.

"I didn't think o' that," he admitted. "Even so, it's still got to be somebody that's familiar with the area. Either that, or somebody flew over us with a plane, and saw all them trailers. Or at least the cattle."

"What can we do?" Rhonda asked.

"All I know to do is find'em, and kill'em."

-

"Watching the Home?" Terry asked, concern on his face.

"Ain't nothin' else up there to watch as I know of," Billy replied. "Reckon they saw the trailers, or something else they wanted."

"Like the women, maybe?" Pete asked. Billy shrugged.

"Well, we got to do something about that," Terry said casually.

"I figured to ask Pete to help me stand a watch up there," Billy said. Pete nodded.

"No problem," he said at once.

"Won't be just that simple, though," Terry mused. "They've got to have a camp somewhere back in there."

"That's what I figure," Billy admitted. "What I thought was if we can catch the one who's watchin', we can convince him to tell us all about it. Then do what need's doin' from there."

"Simple and direct. I like it," Terry approved. "We'll stake'em out tonight. In fact, let's just head on up there now, and get situated. We can plan on two or three days, so we need a good hide."

"Was hopin' you'd do somethin' else," Billy said. Terry frowned.

"Really? What?"

"Them women need to be armed, and taught to shoot. I was hopin' you'd help Rhonda with that. Maybe Shelly can help too. Or Toby. Thing is, we can't leave any one place empty for more'n a minute or two. I got to thinkin' on the way down, we ain't got no idea if they're only watchin' the home. Hell, somebody could be watchin' us right now!"

Terry hadn't thought about that, but he agreed it was possible.

"Well, I can do that," he nodded. "And you're right. We should have already seen to that. Damn it all. We were counting on isolation keeping the Home hidden, and now it's the one we know for sure is being looked at. Ain't that just the way of it?"

"So, it is," Pete nodded. "I think it's about time we opened that truck and trailer George brought back."

"And moved it," Terry added. "Like today."

"Rhonda's warnin' all the other houses. I ain't said nothin' at the Home as yet, since ain't none o' them could lend a hand no ways."

"They'll be able to in a couple days, I promise," Terry assured him.

"Meanwhile, we should go get that truck, and start loading some mags," Pete pointed out. "For all we know, there's a whole platoon of them, just waiting to see what all's here, and how many of us there are."

"Be nice to have a few more fellas right now," Billy said. "But I reckon we'll have to make do."

-

The HumVee and it's attached trailer were moved to Billy's place an hour later. Ralph had decided that there was some work he and Ben Kelvey just had to do up at the Home, and had taken off as soon as Rhonda had mentioned things.

"If nothing else," Ralph had grinned, "Ben can show me how to be a fireman."

There was at least one able bodied man at each house, except Terry's, and his wife had the house locked down, with a radio in hand.

"Let's pull about two dozen rifles," Terry ordered. "And say seven mags per. We need to have at least one auto at each place. Even if no one can really hit with it, the sound of rock and roll will make the bastards more timid, anyway."

"I like it," Pete nodded.

The three worked quickly, and Danny and Rhonda pitched in to help. Toby arrived not long after they started, and pitched in as well. It took less than an hour, with all hands on, to get the work done.

"Well, let's get these spread out, I guess," Terry ordered.

"We'll do that," Billy told him. "You get on home. Your house is more exposed. Let's not take too many chances."

"Thanks, Billy," Terry nodded, his relief palpable. "I appreciate it." Terry took two rifles, and their magazines, and went home.

"Toby, you help Rhonda get a pair o' these to the Kelvey's and The Purdy's, then come back and take two more home. Me and Pete gotta get ready."

"Sure thing, Billy," Toby nodded. Pete looked at Billy.

"Meet you there about an hour before dusk."

"Works for me," Billy nodded. When Pete had gone, Billy looked at Danny Tatum.

"Danny, this could get bad 'fore it get's any better. I want you to stay near the house. Rhonda tells you to do somethin', you do it, and don't argue. This ain't no game, boy."

"I won't let you down," Danny promised.

"I know you won't. You keep a sharp eye out. You see somethin' ain't right, you call out on the radio. Got that?"

"Got it," the boy said firmly.

"Good deal. Now I got to get ready to go."

-

Billy and Pete met in the tree line just down the road from the Home. Both were prepared for an overnight stay, and carrying night vision goggles. Billy had changed his optics for a night vision scope as well, and noticed that Pete had done the same.

"I skulked around here a bit when we got here," Pete said softly, "but I don't know the area half as well as you do. I was thinking the first thing we need to do is for you to show me about where you found the OP."

"I can do that," Billy nodded. He led Pete the short way up the road, and pointed to where he'd found the spot used to observe the house.

"Why don't you slip into the barn and take the loft," Billy suggested. "I know a place or two where I can hide just fine. I'll probably move around to the other side o' the house, and take up a spot there, just in case they change up on us. Ain't no tellin' how smart, or dumb, these guys may be."

"True that," Pete replied. "Works for me. Be careful," he added. Billy nodded, and started back, working his way around the house where he wouldn't be seen. Pete eyed the spot through his binoculars for a minute, then worked his way carefully into the barn. Two minutes later, he was set. The rear loft doors gave him an excellent view, and he settled in for what might turn out to be a long night.

Billy carefully worked his way to the other side of the main house, slipping from cover to cover. His destination was a large cedar tree, about thirty yards from the house. Keeping the tree between him and the woodline as much as possible, he secured a good place, about five feet up into the tree. With a few judicious snips of his short-handled loppers, he had created a good field of view, yet remained confident he was hidden.

A short piece of two by eight board provided him a seat, with a little padding for comfort. He slid into his makeshift tree stand, and made himself comfortable.

Now, they waited.

Peter Two Bears had learned to be still and quiet as a child. To wait quietly for long periods of time, with little or no movement. His people had always been warriors, and hunters, and still taught those skills even in the modern world.

As he sat in the loft scanning the tree line, he allowed his mind to wander. He wondered how his people were faring. How his family were doing. His mother and brother lived with his maternal uncle on the Rez. If they had survived the plague, they would be safe there, he knew.

His uncle was a veteran, and was also one of those people who believed in being prepared. He would be ready for this new world if anyone was. While not rich, his people were wealthy by reservation standards, with sheep, horses, and not a few cattle. Fresh water was available, and his uncle knew how to live off the land.

There was no way to contact them that he was aware of, and certainly no way to go and look for them. He knew they would wonder about him, as well, but would also realize the same thing he did. They would likely never see each other again.

Peter wasn't one to get emotional about such things, and had learned to accept things that were beyond his power to control long before he'd joined the Army. His family was no different. If he got to see them again, he would be glad. If he didn't, he would survive.

He was glad to be where he was, anyway. Terry Blaine was the best friend he'd ever had, and George Purdy was a close second. The three of them had shared some wild times together, some good, and some not as good. They were his family, now. Had been for a long time.

Billy Todd was becoming that way as well. He hadn't really intended for that to happen, but he saw a kindred spirit in Billy. Terry and George had once shared that spirit, but it had been tempered over the years by family and responsibility. That wasn't a bad thing, he figured.

Now, he was looking at Michelle Silvers in much the same way he imagined Terry and George had looked at their wives when they had first met them. Sure, it was far too early to think on that, but it was still there in the back of his mind. He knew from listening, especially from Michelle herself, that had he met her before the world had died, he probably wouldn't have liked her nearly so much. That was how the world worked, he figured. Sometimes crisis brought out the worst in people, and sometimes it was the best. In Michelle's case, it seemed to have been the best.

In his mind's eye, he could see himself with her, married and with a home. Maybe with little half-wild, half-Apache kids running around. It could happen, he decided. Unlikely, to be sure, especially so early in their talking. Still, a man could hope for a brighter future. And that hope didn't cost anything.

Of course, Jerry didn't really seem to be high on the idea. Not that Pete blamed him. Who would want a half-wild savage like him easing around to speak to his daughter? If he had daughters, he would be sure and keep them far, far away from someone like. . . .

His drifting stopped suddenly as he caught movement in the tree line. Right where Billy had said. He watched closely, using a spotting scope to get better detail. Right. . .there. Two men, on the ground, one with a pair of binoculars.

Pete eased himself onto the loft floor, using a pair of square hay bales to hide himself. The two men in the woods were sloppy, coming back to the same place over and over, and leaving trash to betray their presence, but that didn't mean they were entirely stupid. And they might have just as good a scope as he did.

He reached slowly for his radio, bringing it to his lips. Just as he was about to key the mike, someone else beat him to it.

-

Billy had sat completely still in his hidey hole, completely hidden by the branches of the cedar. He had brought a rifle scope with him, and was using it to periodically scan the wood line. As he sat there, watching, he had been thinking on things.

He had hoped, once Columbia was behind them, that he could relax a little, and take care of some things around the farm. And he had, he reminded himself. Danny could ride, now, and had a horse of his own. Both he and Mary had learned to shoot pretty well, and had their own weapons. The caches were hidden, complete with additions for Danny and Mary.

That wasn't nothing, he reasoned. But there was still a great deal to do. It would soon be real winter. Sure, they'd endured one storm already, and had a little more snow while in Columbia, but it was still two weeks till Christmas. They hadn't seen any real winter yet. When they did, Billy feared, it would be bad.

He was fairly confident that their little community was set for the winter. There was plenty of cut wood, although they would need to cut some more now that so many were staying at the Clifton house. Thinking of the Clifton house reminded Billy of why he was sitting cold and miserable in a cedar tree, and he lifted the scope to his eye, scanning the entire wood line carefully.

Nothing.

Lowering the scope, Billy continued working out in his mind things that still needed to be done. They needed a propane tanker. He mentally kicked himself for not thinking of that in Columbia. He was sure there was propane there, but it was probably far too dangerous to go back for it. There was propane in Cedar Bend, too, of course. They could get plenty there. But when it was gone, then what?

And what about their heaters? When they broke down, did they have the parts to fix them? He knew they'd managed to get a few propane heaters in Columbia, but they were seasonal items, and it had been summer when the plague hit. Not too many heaters sold in summer, he figured. Still, he knew there were some.

All the houses had either wood stoves, or fireplaces, and some, like his place, had outdoor furnaces that heated the house and provided hot water. The Clifton place had one, too, he remembered. Which reminded him why he was sitting cold and miserable in a cedar tree, and he lifted his scope once more.

He had gotten used to seeing nothing, and so passed over the two men at first, their presence not registering on him. Realizing a second later what he'd seen, he whipped the scope back on target, and dialed in.

Two men. Right in the same old spot.

How dumb can you be? he thought, then decided not to question such a gift. He carefully scoped the rest of the wood line, but could find no sign of any other watchers. Apparently these two were the only ones.

After five minutes of careful observation, he slowly lifted his radio to his mouth, and called Pete.

"*I got'em,*" Billy's voice came through the ear plug loud and clear.

Jeez Billy, you just scared the crap outta me! Pete thought, shaking his head.

"I see'em too," he replied. "Two men, right in the same spot."

"That's them, all right," Billy's voice came back. *"Want to sit on'em and then follow'em, or just ease on up and have a talk with'em right now?"* Pete pondered that for a minute.

"Let's wait," he decided. "They may not be alone. If they aren't, they just might lead us back to the rest. What do you think?"

"*Sounds good to me,*" Billy replied. "*I'd as soon get'em all and be done with'em. We got other things need doin'.*" Pete shook his head, grinning at Billy's plain-spoken statement.

"Okay. I'll take first watch, if you want to catch some sleep."

"*Thanks.*"

Pete settled in to watch the two stalkers, who were blissfully unaware that they were now the prey.

CHAPTER FIFTY-ONE

"*Billy, wake up. They're moving.*"

Billy was awake in an instant. It took him a minute to realize where he was. Finding himself in a tree, cold and miserable, made him panic for a few seconds, until he remembered why he was there.

"*Billy, you copy?*" Pete's voice spoke into his ear. "*We need to move.*"

"I hear ya," he said softly into the earbud's microphone. "I'm awake. What's the plan?"

"*Meet me where they were laid up,*" Pete ordered. "*I'm moving now.*"

"Got it," Billy replied. He moved to get down, and stifled a groan as his muscles protested movement after so long still and idle. He managed to get to the ground without making any noise, and took a few seconds to stretch the soreness out. Then he was moving.

It was almost dawn, he realized. Billy was puzzled by the watcher's movements. Had they always been watching at night? And if so, why? There wasn't much to see after dark, especially in winter time. So what would be the point? Something about that nagged at him, but he couldn't put his finger on it just yet.

He met Pete at the observation post, where his friend was already studying the ground. Billy joined him. He could see tracks and sign for two men. They had left a trail that a kid could follow.

"Awful sloppy work," Pete murmured. "They're either amateurs who think they've learned something from videos, or they don't think we're a threat. I wouldn't bet a nickel on the difference, either."

"I don't see why they bother watchin' in the night," Billy voiced his concern to Pete. "Ain't nothin' to see in the dark. Ain't no way they can gather no information in the dark, are they?" Pete pondered that.

"I had thought that too," he admitted. "Like I said, they may be amateurs. And, we don't know they're always watching at night. They may be watching at all different times of the day, getting an idea how many people are around, how the comings and goings work, that kinda thing."

"Yeah, I'd just wondered," Billy agreed. "Anyway, let's get after'em."

"Slow and easy, Billy," Pete warned. "If they're any good at all, then they may leave booby traps along their trail, or have warning lines spread to alert them to followers. We can't assume they're stupid." Billy nodded his understanding, and the two began to move.

The tree line started about twenty yard from a hill behind the Clifton house. The trail went straight up the hill. Pete started to follow when Billy stopped him.

"Easier way," he mouthed, and motioned for Pete to follow. Billy led them north about fifty yards where a small game trail was carved into the hill. Over the years, use of the trail by both man and beast had left almost step like depressions in the ground, some supported by tree roots. The two men scrambled up the trail quietly, and moved back to pick up the enemy trail.

Billy knew these woods as well as any man could, having used them all his life. Pete took advantage of that as the two moved, allowing Billy to point out easier going that often let them travel faster than simply following. Suddenly, Billy stopped short.

"I think I know where they're goin'," he said softly. "If I'm right, I know a better way to get there."

"If you're wrong, then we'll have to come back," Pete warned.

"Don't think I am," Billy shook his head. "There ain't but one good place to camp out here. If they ain't got a house somewhere, this is where they'll be." Billy's confidence won Pete over, and he nodded for Billy to lead the way.

Billy moved swiftly over the ground with the assurance that came only with long use and familiarity. The two of them moved quietly for all that they moved fast, and Pete had to admit that Billy's way was far easier than the trail the two watchers were taking.

That probably meant that they weren't dealing with anyone local. But only probably, he cautioned himself. There was no room here for assumptions. Or mistakes.

Suddenly Billy stopped short, raising his hand. Pete watched as Billy cocked his head slightly, then grinned. He turned to Pete, making a shush motion with his finger to his lips, and then motioning again for Pete to follow.

The two of them moved at a much slower pace now, almost creeping. Suddenly they were on the lip of a small hollow, looking down at a clearing near a spring fed stream. Even as Pete watched, two men came into camp, and sat by the fire, both helping themselves from the pot still hanging over the fire.

Others were stirring now, and Pete counted them without thinking. He stopped at nine. Seven men and two women. The women weren't captives, this time, judging by their actions, and the fact that they were both armed. Pete was determined not to make that mistake again.

A large man with a shaved head emerged from one of the tents and walked to the fire.

"Well?" he demanded of the two that had just returned.

"Still nothing," one of them replied between mouth fulls of what appeared to be stew. "One of the trucks was moved today, the little one. The U-Haul. All the others are still there. Every now and then, someone comes and takes stuff out."

"Probably enough food and supplies to last us the rest of the winter, at least," another man remarked. The apparent leader nodded absently.

"How many people?" he demanded. The man who had replied to the first question consulted a small notebook.

"We've counted seven different men, and four different women in the last week," he replied. "At least two of the women are living in the house, but rarely venture outside. The rest are living in other houses, but we haven't been able to determine which ones. We do know that two houses down the road are occupied, and at least two men and one of the women live there."

"So they're spread out," the leader mused out loud. The speaker nodded.

"I say we hit'em, take what we want, and move on," the man across the fire spoke again.

"And I say it's a nice place to spend the winter," the man with the notebook shot back. "Food, water, power, plenty of firewood. Women. Even moving vehicles with gas enough to run around on. And horses aplenty, too."

"Could be if we asked, they'd just help us," one of the women spoke up.

"Why ask, when we can just take?" the surly one snorted. "I say we take it all."

"And I say I make the decisions around here," the leader told him flatly. "Anytime you don't like that, you're free to leave."

"I figure I done seen enough," Billy whispered, moving his rifle into firing position. Pete's hand stopped him.

"Patience, amigo," he whispered back. "They aren't a threat at the moment. And now we know where they live. We can get information just listening to them." Billy frowned.

He clearly didn't like the idea, but with a deep sigh he relaxed. Pete stifled a sigh of his own as Billy stood down. Then he went back to watching.

"We already lost two people when the blizzard hit," the surly man who wanted to 'take' noted. "There's no sense in waitin' around until we lose more. They've got what we need, at least to get through the winter. I say we take'em now, and then we're set for the winter."

"So long as we stay, I agree," 'notebook' nodded. "I'm tired o' livin' in the woods, or abandoned houses, and scrapin' by. This is a good set-up. We get rid of them, and we take over ourselves. Live comfortable."

"We have to keep moving," Leader said firmly. "We can lay up a little while, but we got work to do. You all know that."

"We can't get work done in bitter weather," Notebook objected. "They got to understand that. All of us ain't sittin' comfortable somewhere for the winter. We need a place to rest up."

The leader watched his men, and women, debate their ideas for a few minutes. Finally, he held up a hand.

"That's enough!" he said forcefully, and all talk came to a halt.

"We take'em," he announced. "We do it now. Today. Everyone get their gear and. . . ."

"Time to make this go away," Pete whispered raising his rifle. "I'll take the leader, and Surly. You take the two watchers. After that, targets of opportunity. On three?" Billy nodded, sighting his rifle.

"One. . .two. . .three!"

The two rifles cracked as one, and Leader and Notebook fell. Before anyone could react, both fired again, Surly and the other watcher hitting the ground. After that, things got interesting.

One man jumped to his feet, sending rifle rounds wildly into the woods. A single round from Pete's rifle stopped him.

The two women were shrieking loudly, and one drew her pistol, looking around wildly as she screamed in rage. The other one tried to grab a shotgun leaning against a log nearby. Billy didn't hesitate, cutting her down. Pete hesitated no more than a second before shooting the woman with the handgun. She had been the one arguing for the group to just ask for help.

Tough.

The two remaining men managed to get behind a pair of downed trees. These two had figured out which direction the shots were coming from, and started to fire back. Their shots weren't near Billy or Pete, but they were working their way down.

Billy took the left one, watching carefully until he had the shot he wanted. The man raised his head every time he took a shot, then ducked back quickly. But he got into a rhythm, and he didn't change his position. Billy waited patiently, and on the fifth shot, fired once. The round took the man in the forehead.

Pete's target was more careful, but Pete was just as patient as Billy was. This man was changing his position after every two shots. His mistake was doing that after *every* two shots. The shooter still wasn't certain where his attackers were, and should have remained hidden and silent, waiting for a shot. Instead, he was sending rounds into the woods at random, and hoping for luck.

His luck ran out.

Pete had let the man shoot and scoot three times. Satisfied that his target was locked into his two shots and move pattern, Pete waited for the first shot from his new position. When it came, Pete simply sighted in on the spot, and waited.

Sure enough, the man exposed himself again to take the second shot before moving. Pete was already squeezing the trigger when his target appeared, and a single rifle shot put him down forever.

The two men waited for ten minutes, perfectly still, watching the campsite. After ten minutes of no movement, they began to cautiously make their way down the hill, and into the camp.

It had been a clean sweep. Those not killed immediately, had died in the interim. Neither Billy nor Pete wasted any emotion on the pack of killers.

Pete began rummaging through their belongings, looking for information on where the group had come from. Billy began methodically stripping the bodies of weapons, ammunition, anything that might someday be of use to them. All of the group had been well armed. In fact, looking through their gear, Billy realized that all of the group's gear was good stuff. But there wasn't much food. Just some MREs and a few bags of beans and rice that looked like it had been rescued from the rat population.

"This bunch was pretty well heeled," he noted to Pete, who nodded.

"They were at that. And they've traveled a long way, according to this map." Pete held up a well marked map that he'd taken from Leader's tent. "They started out in Nashville, and apparently walked most of the way here. Took a wandering path. Looks like they've drifted from one area to another, stripping each place as they went. I'm curious how they haven't managed to find enough gas to keep vehicles running."

"Maybe they just ran out," Billy suggested. "This is a buncha stuff, Pete. And even with them game carts," he pointed to where the carts sat abandoned behind the tents, "there ain't much way they humped all this stuff this whole way." This time he pointed to the route traced on the map.

"True enough," Pete conceded. "Take a look at this map, though. Look at all these notations. I think I need to look for a notebook or something." Pete went back to looking, while Billy went and collected two of the game carts. He didn't want the MRE's or other food, but the guns and ammunition were all good quality. So were most of the other gear, including spotting scopes, binoculars, compasses, packs, knives, and everything else. This bunch had made out pretty well scavenging.

Odd Billy Todd

One thing that Billy took for himself was a Kimber forty-five like his own. The pistol looked practically brand new, with several mags and an excellent Bianchi holster. He decided he would take the whole outfit. He doubted he'd have the opportunity to secure another Kimber any time soon. Or ever.

The rest he piled into the game carts, using blankets to pad and protect the gear. And conceal it, he admitted.

"Look here, Billy," Pete called. He was holding a small leather notebook, and a large one as well.

"These guys have been spotting large amounts of supplies. Inventorying them. Why in the hell would they be watching us, and planning to take our stuff, when they've got all this already spotted?"

Billy looked at the notations on the map, and had no trouble matching them to notations in the book. As he looked at the places on the map, most of which he knew of, even if he hadn't been there. There was something nagging at him about these places.

"This book looks like radio codes," Pete held up the other radio. "Later on, there's a logbook. I've only read the first three pages or so of the log, but it seems these guys were in regular contact with someone."

"None of'em got a railroad!" Billy exclaimed. Pete looked up at the non-sequitur. "What?"

"Ain't none o' these towns got a railroad," Billy repeated, pointing to the map. "Not a one. You say these guys are reportin' to somebody else. How 'bout that damn train? Are they gatherin' intel on what's available off the tracks, so that bunch on the train can form a convoy, and strip even more stuff from the towns around us?" Pete looked stunned at the idea.

"I. . .I don't know, Billy," he said after a minute. "It's possible, I guess."

"I'd bet it's likely," Billy declared. "Did you find their radio?"

"Not yet," Pete went back to looking through Leader's tent. "I'm assuming it would be in here, somewhere. But maybe someone else was the RTO. Radio operator," he clarified. Billy nodded, not bothering to add the he'd know what Pete had meant.

"Check the other tents," Pete ordered. "I'll help. Let's see can we find a radio here. Wait!" Pete stopped him. "Have you ever seen a sat phone?"

"Not as I know of," Billy shook his head.

"If you find a weird looking phone with a antenna looks like it's bent, bring it to me. They might be using a satellite phone instead of a radio."

The two went to work, scouring the campsite for communications equipment.

"Got it!" Pete called out five minutes later. He lugged what appeared to be a sturdy looking brief case out of one of the tents, setting it on the ground. He opened it up revealing a small folding satellite receiver, a metal box with numerous gauges, dials and readout panels attached, and a telephone headset.

"This is a pretty good setup," Pete noted. "It's old, compared to modern military hardware, but still a good rig for what they're using it for. You can hit a satellite with this, and talk to your base from damn near anywhere in the world."

"Or to a train that's got one just like it?" Billy asked. Pete looked up at him.

"Yep."

The two of them spent the next three hours scouring the campsite. Every scrap of paper they found went into a duffle they had appropriated for the purpose. They would go through it all later.

Billy had pulled the bodies away from the camp site, and the creek, stacking them like cord-wood. He rummaged around the camp until he found two gallons of kerosene, which he proceeded to pour onto the bodies. Pete looked at him.

"What you aim to do?"

"Burn 'em," Billy shrugged. "Don't want them rottin' out here, and poisonin' the water. Or ruinin' this campsite. Like I said, only decent one around this little area. Might need it sometime." Pete nodded, understanding.

"I'll come back 'fore summer, and get rid o' what don't burn up," Billy went on. "Ain't no sense in the women folk or none o' them kid's gettin' a look at such as this."

"Good idea," Pete nodded. He watched as Billy tossed a burning branch for the campfire onto the pile of bodies. Billy had gathered up a good amount of dead fall and brush, which he had placed under, on, and around the stack. It caught up quickly, and began to burn. Both men sat down up wind of the fire.

"The more I think on it, the more I think you're right, Billy," Pete said after a few minutes. "It could be something else, I guess. Maybe a patrol from some MAG outfit, looking for salvage. But the way they spoke so casually about killing us and taking our place makes me wonder."

"I don't care who it is," Billy said flatly. "Anybody aims to *take* from me and mine better have friends. And a sack lunch."

"Sack lunch?" Pete looked at him, grinning.

"Gonna be an all-day job," Billy nodded without humor. "Might get hungry 'fore it's over."

Pete was still laughing when the sat phone began to beep.

CHAPTER FIFTY-TWO

The two men jumped slightly at the sound. They both turned to look as the case beeped again. They exchanged looks of surprise and confusion, and then shrugged, almost in unison.

"Might as well answer it, I guess," Pete said, looking back at the phone's case.

"Might's well," Billy nodded. Pete went to the case and hurriedly hooked up the receiver, then picked up the phone.

"Go ahead," he said gruffly, hoping that his voice wouldn't sound different enough to cause a reaction.

"*Status.*" The one-word demand was short and sharp.

"Unchanged," Pete said, replying with the same tone.

"*Understood. Out.*" Pete waited, but there was nothing more. He replaced the handset, and broke down the antenna.

"Well, that gives us a little more time, maybe," Pete said thoughtfully.

"Works for me," Billy nodded. "Only thing worries me is whether or not these idiots told whoever that was where they were campin'."

"That's an issue," Pete acknowledged. "Or what was here, for that matter," he added after a minute's thought. He stood.

"I reckon we best be heading back, Billy," Pete told him. "I think we're gonna need to share this with the group. At least with George and Terry, and Mister Silvers."

"*Mister Silvers* is it?" Billy grinned, and Pete almost blushed.

"Trying to stay on his good side," Pete admitted. "That don't come easy to me, either."

"You treat Michelle right, and be a man, Jerry won't have no problem with you," Billy assured his friend. "His bite is as bad as his bark, mind you. But he's a good fella. And a fair-minded man."

"He seems like a good guy," Pete nodded.

"He is, or him and daddy wouldn'a been friends," Billy confirmed. "Trust me on that." He looked to where the bonfire had finally burned down. Charred bones were clearly visible in the pile, but Billy wasn't bothered by that. They had gotten off easier than was deserved, to his way of thinking.

"Reckon we can head on back," he commented. "Don't think that fire's goin' nowhere." Pete nodded in agreement, and the two men grabbed the carts they'd filled and started for home.

-

"What are we gonna tell the rest?" Billy asked, as he and Pete neared Billy's house.

"Huh?" Pete looked at Billy, puzzlement on his face.

"What you aim to tell the rest?" Billy repeated. "About what we found."

"Uh...just figured I'd tell 'em the truth," Pete shrugged, confused.

"Reckon me and you can do somethin' 'bout this train, we was to set our minds to it," Billy told him evenly. "If'n you want, that is."

"All two of us?" Pete asked with a snort. "That's good attitude, Billy, but I can't see how the two of us can stand up to that train."

"I might know a way," Billy shrugged. "I wanna take a look at that map again, and that radio book, 'fore you let it get away from ya. Mind?"

"Hell no," Pete shook his head. "Wasn't for you, we wouldn't have it. Which reminds me, we need to get a patrol started. Horseback'll do, I think, but we need to make at least two circuits a day around the entire area, and have some on listening post duty through the night. Maybe even making some checks."

"Sounds like a good idea," Billy nodded. "Need an alarm o' some kind, too. Maybe where anybody in any house can trip it off. Add in some lights at each house that'd come on when the alarm went off. I don't know. Some kinda way for an alert to sound."

"Good idea," Pete agreed. "Let me think on that. We might could set up a switchboard type deal, where the alarm triggers a light at the post. Hmmm." Pete went quiet, lost in thought. Finally, he snapped his fingers.

"We need to talk to Howie. And we need to go to Cedar Bend, maybe. I got an idea."

-

"Yeah, I can do that," Howie nodded. "We can use wireless stuff to send the alarm, and it'll sound off in the alert shack. No problem."

"Without phones, we need a way to make sure we can round everyone up," Pete reminded him. "Radio is okay, but it might not wake a man up from a sound sleep. And we might need everyone awake, even if they aren't needed. Especially if we were being attacked."

"Hmm," Howie mused, rubbing his chin. "Let me think on that. Meanwhile, let's look at what we'd need for the alarms. If we can find the parts and pieces, we can actually wire the windows and doors to alarm when someone breaks in, you know. Let's start looking at how many places we're talking about, and how many windows."

-

"Okay, I think we've got a good count," Howie said finally. "A local alarm is no problem, provided we can scrounge the components. And even if we can't, I can probably make something that will work."

"Rigging a system that will alarm remotely presents other challenges, but they're not insurmountable. Just. . .difficult. The main problems are power, and transmission. Well, supply is a problem, if we can't find what we're looking for."

"We got a lot of stuff like that at the Lowe's in Columbia," Pete mentioned. "Alarms, cameras, stuff like that. Maybe that will help."

"Great!" Howie enthused. "We really need a Radio Shack, or some other radio supply, too. We'll need wire, for one thing. And we'll need something to relay transmissions from the cameras and motion detectors to the alert shack."

"Well, there was a Radio Shack, I think," Pete sighed. "But we didn't go there."

"Any chance the Train people didn't hit it?" Howie asked.

"Ain't no way o' knowin', 'cept to go look," Billy replied. "I'm game."

"Me too," Pete agreed. "You want to go?" he asked Howie.

"I sure do!" Howie smiled. "I'd love to get out, even for a day!"

"Well, I guess we'll take a road trip," Billy nodded.

Odd Billy Todd

Rhonda was not amused.

"You said you was gonna stay around here!" she protested, when Billy informed her of the trip.

"Come with me," Billy said quietly, though firmly. Taking her by the arm, he led her out the back door, and over to his small 'shack'. Inside were the weapons and other equipment he and Pete had taken from the group that had been scouting the farms.

"See all this?" he demanded. "This here is what we took from nine people this mornin'. People who were gettin' ready to come over that ridge behind the Clifton place, kill us all, and take ever thing we own." Rhonda's face lost the rigidity of anger.

"What. . .I mean, where are they, now?" she asked.

"Dead," Billy told her flatly. "And the bodies burnt plumb up," he added. "This here ain't no game, Rhonda. Them people meant to do us harm. And they was workin' for somebody else. Somebody that might just know right where we are, right here this very minute."

"I can't help what other people do, you know," he went on. "This here wasn't somethin' I knowed about when I said all that. And it can't wait. We got to have some better security around here, or we gonna wake up dead one mornin'."

"Howie says he can do that, but he needs stuff. 'Lectric stuff. Don't get me started on what all, on account o' I don't rightly know. All I know is, he says we need it. So, we got to go get it. And that means we have to *go* and get it. It ain't gonna come to us."

Rhonda held her peace as she digested what Billy had told her.

"I. . .I didn't think. . .I mean, I thought we were safe," she managed after a minute.

"Might be we are," Billy nodded. "But I ain't willin' to take a chance on it. We been runnin' ass over tea kettle for over a month. Longer, really. We got to stop, and take stock. We're vulnerable, and not a little bit weak. We need ever edge we can get, and having motion detectors and cameras and what nots is a pretty good edge. We need alarms for the houses, too."

"And while Howie is a sure 'nough redneck genius, reckon he can't just make somethin' outta nothin'. He needs stuff to work with. We got to get it for 'im. Simple as that."

Rhonda nodded, realizing at last why Billy was so set on doing this.

"Be careful," she said, her voice almost hollow. "I can't do this without you."

"Yeah, you can," Billy assured her. "Just keep your rifle to hand, and stick close to the house whilst we're gone. Should be back this evening, although we might not make it until tomorrow. We got to see what we can find for Howie to use."

"Now I need you backin' me. I can't be doin' what all needs doin' with you gettin' all mad at me ever time somethin' ain't to your likin'. Won't work. We all got to do what we can do. This here, I can do." He fell silent, breathing a bit hard. Rhonda realized that Billy was really worked up over this, and tried to soothe him.

"I didn't mean to come off like that," she admitted. "I just. . . ."

"You just wanted me not to be goin' no where," Billy cut in. "Won't cut it. We need this stuff. All of it we can find. That means we need to get out and lookin' for it. We been uncommonly lucky with weather so far, considerin'. But it won't last. We got to gather the harvest 'fore it gets too cold."

Billy, Pete, Toby and Howie crammed into the Ford early the next morning. Toby had readily agreed to making the trip again, although Jerry wasn't eager to see that. He also wasn't willing to stop him. Toby had grown up all of a sudden. Jerry hated that it had taken the end of the world to make that happen. Still, he was glad that Toby was doing his part.

"So, what is it we're after?" Toby asked, getting settled.

"Electronic goodies," Howie grinned. "Cameras, microphones, wire, alarms, motion detectors, wireless transmitters, receivers, monitors. . . ."

"The whole shebang, then," Toby nodded. "You're aimin' to wire the whole place."

"You got it," Howie nodded.

"Have you thought about how you're gonna get power to'em?" Toby asked.

"Uh, still working on that," Howie admitted. "Gonna be a problem."

"Some of that stuff works on batteries," Toby mused. "Gonna need to find rechargeable batteries for that. Lot of'em."

"True, true, but we'll work something out. Just have to put some thought into it, that's all," Howie waved the problem away.

"Just use solar," Toby shrugged. "Be done with it."

"Finding that many solar chargers will probably be an issue," Howie replied, speaking as teacher to student.

"Nah. Just take'em from solar power lights. That'll work fine."

Howie turned to look at Toby, giving the teenager his undivided attention.

"Say what?"

"Solar cells from solar powered lights," Toby said again. "You know, like you put along garden paths, driveways, and such like. You can solder them into the power system, and they'll keep the rechargeable batteries charged on the spot."

Howie stared at Toby for a long minute. Toby simply stared back. Finally, Howie smiled.

"We need to talk, kid."

Behind the wheel, Billy managed not to chuckle. Toby was showing his worth more and more everyday.

-

"Okay," Billy said as they approached Columbia. "I can't see how anybody'll still be around here no more. Not after the train came through. But we ain't takin' that for granted, understand? So be on your P's and Q's."

"Keep track of what you see, too," Pete added. "There's several places we didn't quite get to. You see something useful, grab it. If it's too much for us to carry today, we can always come back for it."

"Might be we can check for gas, too," Toby opined. "Might be the train people didn't take it all."

"Good idea," Billy nodded. "Okay, that CB place is just up here, so we'll start there."

The foursome spent the rest of the day moving cautiously through what was

Odd Billy Todd

left of town. Pete had noted on the way in that the two motorcycle riders he had taken out were still there. No one spoke as Billy guided the truck around the bikes and bodies. There wasn't really anything to say, anyway.

They quickly took everything they could find that might be useful in securing the Farms. Billy, by far the least able to identify useful electronic items, stood guard while the others searched for and retrieved the things they wanted.

The Train had not, for whatever reason, hit the Radio Shack, or any of the other places that dealt in electronics. Howie cackled like a mad man at times, finding stashes of equipment that would help him wire their homes.

As the sun began to wane, it was time to make a decision.

"If we're gonna stay, we can keep lookin'," Billy told them. "If we're goin' back, then we need to be thinkin' on headin' that way. What's the verdict?"

"We're not finished," Howie said at once. "There's still other places to look. And we need this stuff."

"Like as not be snowin' by mornin'," Toby put in, looking at the sky. "Colder now that it was just an hour ago. And it ain't just cause the sun's gettin' on over. Air smells wet."

"You right about that," Billy nodded in agreement.

"I say we bivie here and keep working," Pete said finally. "I'd really like to get done, and get home. I don't like so many of us being gone like this."

"Then let's stay at it," Billy ordered. The group continued to work on through the night. Howie and Toby had even started removing surveillance cameras from stores, along with their routing equipment.

"Won't do much for remote's, but where we can get power to them, these cameras are great," Howie pointed out.

"And we can use'em on barns, along the pasture areas, anywhere there's a nearby source of power," Toby added, handing down another camera.

"Where'd you learn all this stuff, kid?" Howie asked. Toby grinned.

"Hey, man. It ain't all about the Xbox, ya know?"

It was late when they finally stopped. They decided to make camp in the convenience store they had just stripped. A watch was set, and they settled in.

Billy was the last on watch, and Pete shook him awake at four in the morning.

"Snowing, Billy," he said, as Billy came awake.

"Figured," Billy said gruffly. "How bad?"

"It's pretty heavy right now," Pete admitted. "Been that way last hour or so. And it's cold. Colder than it's been being since the blizzard."

"That might be bad," Billy mused. "You better get some sleep," he told Pete. "Liable to be a long day." Pete nodded and settled into his bed roll. Billy got to his feet, went out the back to relieve himself, and then settled in at the counter to watch.

He was convinced this was a good idea. But he agreed with Pete. He didn't like it that so many of them were away at one time. They just didn't have enough manpower to do all the things that needed doing.

But what choice was there? What they had was what they had. It wasn't like they could just advertise for new neighbors.

Well, they could, of course. There were plenty of people out there right now that would give their eye teeth to be living on the Farms. He thought then about the people left in Franklin. How many of them were cold and hungry tonight? How

313

many had died in the blizzard that had hit just a few weeks ago? They were short on food, and probably fuel. What else would they need?

There was no way to help the town, either. Billy hated to say it, or think it, but that's just the way it was. The resources at the Farms would do fine for their number, and maybe a few more, and for some time to come. But with so many others, their supplies wouldn't last more than three weeks, Billy guessed. Maybe a month, at the outside.

There was no point in trying to help others, only to wind up needing help themselves. Didn't make sense. There was only so much they could do, and right now, the way Billy saw it, they were doing it all.

He had wondered about maybe taking three of four steers to Franklin. Riggs could distribute the beef once it was slaughtered. People could live for a while on beef, especially with some rice and beans. The Farms didn't have enough rice and beans to go around, but they could part with a few head of cattle.

And, he admitted, it wouldn't be a bad way to take a look at the people still in and around Franklin. Maybe there were two or three others who might be interested, and that could be useful.

But all that would have to wait, at least for a while, he decided. He realized with a start that it was daylight. The snow hadn't let up, but they had work to do.

He decided when they got back, and everything was done, then maybe they could have a meeting, and decide what to do. For now, though, they had to get to work.

He rose from his seat and started waking the rest of the crew up.

CHAPTER FIFTY-THREE

The trip home was long and tedious. Roads were slippery, and the salt and plow trucks weren't running anymore. No one was left to drive them.

"Salt," Billy muttered as he drove.

"What?" Pete asked.

"What?" Billy looked over at him, then straight back at the road.

"You said 'salt'," Pete told him. Behind them, Howie and Toby were already working out how best to cover the Farms.

"I did?" Billy frowned. "Well, I was thinkin' it, anyway. We got that truck, and then a plow, and didn't get no salt. We shoulda got some salt."

"Oh. For the roads, you mean."

"Yeah. Helps melt the snow and ice. Won't matter none, can we get home, anyway," Billy added. "Long as we get back, we're good."

"Will we?" Pete asked, looking at the still falling snow. Already several inches of powder covered the landscape.

"We will," Billy nodded firmly.

"We still need to do something about that sat phone," Pete pointed out.

"Such as?"

"I don't know, just yet. We may have missed a call these last two days," said Pete, as the thought occurred to him. "That might be bad."

"They'll figure it out sooner or later, anyway," Billy shrugged. "Thing is, we need to be ready. They ain't no tracks near us. Long as them coyotes didn't mention us to their friends, there's no reason for 'em to come lookin'. And I don't think they did."

"I don't either," Pete mused, looking off into the distance. "According to what we've seen so far, they were marking supplies for later pickup, and then moving on. They probably saw us as a chance to get some for themselves. If they had reported in about us, then they'd have to just mark it, and move on."

"What I was thinkin'," Billy nodded.

"So, we got some time," Pete sighed. "We better make good use of it."

"Yep."

-

It was after dark when Billy finally rolled into his own yard. The electronic equipment was now in the same barn with the bio-diesel set-up, safe and dry. Everyone was at home, dropped off as Billy went.

He parked the truck close to the house, and grabbed his gear, hurrying as much as he dared to get out of the weather. It had turned colder, and the snow was still falling. Rhonda met him at the door.

"Are you okay?" she asked, hanging his coat to dry, then helping with his gear.

"Just tired," he smiled, working his boots off. "And hungry," he added, sniffing the air.

"Chili," Rhonda smiled. "Just about ready, too."

"Leaves me time to clean up some, then," Billy told her.

"Sure. It'll be on the table when you come down."

Billy and Danny cleared the snow away the next morning. The snowfall had stopped sometime during the night, after Billy had gone to bed. It was still cold, but work had to be done. Danny, as always, was ready to go. As they worked, Billy talked to him, teaching him things, preparing him for what might come.

"But how 'bout them people in the woods?" Danny asked, as he and Billy finished putting the Ranger away.

"What about'em?" Billy asked.

"What happened to them?" Billy looked at the teen for a long moment, then sighed.

"You gotta understand, Danny, them people meant to do us in. Kill us all, and take what we had. Only maybe not kill the women, if you take my meanin'," he added. Danny's eyes narrowed at that.

"I get it," he nodded seriously. "Kinda like coyotes."

"Exactly like'em," Billy nodded. "And what do you do with coyotes?"

"You kill'em," Danny replied flatly. "So, you and Pete got rid of'em, yeah?"

"We did."

"Good," Danny nodded firmly. "Wish I coulda helped."

"No, you don't," Billy told him softly. "Ain't no glory in killin' a man Danny, or a woman, neither. Even when they got it comin', it ain't somethin' to take light of. Understand?"

"Not really," Danny looked puzzled. "They meant to hurt us."

"And we made sure they can't," Billy replied. "But killin' folk ain't really nothin' to be proud of. It's just somethin' that needed doin'. Like when you kill a coyote. You bother braggin' on it?"

"Well, if it's a great big'un, yeah," Danny shrugged. "But ever body kills coyotes. Ain't no real big deal."

"And this ain't neither. It ain't nothin' to be prideful of, or to go braggin' about. You do what has to be done, and you make sure it gets done. But killin' folk ain't a thing to be proud of. And these days, it ain't nothin' short of a sinful waste. Ain't many people left in the world no more. Losin' even one is a bad thing."

"Only sometimes, some o' the people what's left, they ain't good people, Danny," Billy went on. "And that's a shame. We all need to be workin' together to make sure we survive. Make sure we rebuild. But some, they don't care 'bout that."

"They don't think on the future none. All they care 'bout is right now. What they can get right now. They don't think past the nose on their face. And they'll take whatever they can from whoever they can, and hurt anyone tries to stop'em. If they can," he added.

"But we don't aim to let'em," Danny was starting to see Billy's point. "Do we?"

"No, boy, we don't," Billy said flatly. "Anyone comes here needful, we'll try and help, if we can. Anyone comes here willin' to work, if they can, is welcome, long as they remember this is ours, and it ain't here for them, but for us."

"And if somebody comes aimin' to make it their's?" Danny asked.

"We convince'em it ain't healthy, boy."

-

"So, from now on, you don't go wandering off alone, Missy. Understand?"

"I don't see why," Mary sighed, as Rhonda finished. "I can take care o' myself, you know."

"I know you did," Rhonda nodded. "But this ain't the same. These people were about to attack us, Mary. Kill most of us, and keep a few women alive for. . .well, for." Rhonda looked at her. Mary stared back a minute, and then suddenly her eyes widened as the point sunk home.

"Oh," she said quietly. "I didn't think about - "

"And we didn't want you to have to," Rhonda told her sadly. "Unfortunately, there's not a way to keep from that. We all have to be more careful. We should have been doing it all along, mind you, but we got complacent. Everything was going pretty well, and we started to get. . .not careless, really, but just complacent. Like things were always going to be okay, as long as we stayed here on the farms. The valley would be safe, no matter what."

"So, it ain't safe?" Mary asked.

"It is," Rhonda nodded firmly. "And when Toby and Howie get done, it'll be safer still. But that doesn't mean there's no danger about. We have to start being more careful. And we're going to. Including you."

"Okay," Mary sighed. She had become accustomed to having free reign anywhere in the valley where the Farms lay. By now she knew the surrounding area almost as well as anyone, except Billy and Toby. And Jerry, of course.

Now, she'd have to stop that. She could still feel free to be about her business on the Todd farm. There was always someone nearby, if she needed help. And Dottie usually followed her wherever she went.

But her rambling from house to house was over. At least for now.

"So, what are we gonna do, then?" Mary asked.

"What do you mean?" Rhonda asked as she placed the dough she'd been working on into the oven.

"Well, if we might not be safe, we have to make it where we are safe, right?" Mary reasoned. "How we gonna do that?"

"You leave that to the grown-ups," Rhonda chided humorously.

"Toby ain't no grown-up!" Mary shot back.

"Oh, he most certainly is," Rhonda replied. "And don't you ever think or say otherwise," she added, emphasizing her point with a shaken finger.

"He ain't to me," Mary almost sulked.

"Then you keep it to yourself, young Lady."

"Fine."

-

Pete visited on the third day after the snow fall. The snow was mostly gone now, as the temperature had climbed slowly back into the fifties.

"Nothing on that sat phone at all," he told Billy. "I'd say they know we ain't them."

"Prob'ly," Billy nodded. They were in his 'shop'.

"I don't know what we can do, now," Pete sighed. "I'd like to have some way of tracking that bunch, but I just don't see a way to do it."

"We need to get the word out," Billy said after a few minutes. "We need to start broadcasting on the radio. Make sure people know about that train."

"We do that," Pete shook his head, "and they might be able to DF us."

"Dee Eff?" Billy asked.

"Directional Find," Pete clarified. "They can use the transmissions to locate us."

"So, we make the transmissions from somewhere else," Billy considered. "Maybe even somewhere they already been. Somewhere away from here."

"Like where?"

"Well, there's always Columbia," Billy shrugged. "I'd like to go back there again, to be honest. There's things we need to check on. See what else is left."

"Like what?" Pete frowned.

"Well, did they take all the fuel, for one," Billy replied. "And what about propane? Be nice if there's some left. And we could get a truck or three runnin' to bring it back in. Maybe enough to keep us warm and toasty for some time. And did they get all the batteries that we couldn't get to? We'll need'em for the solar arrays sooner or later."

"Huh," Pete grunted. "You think a long ways ahead, don't you."

"I try to," Billy shrugged. "Trouble is, I'm forgetful. I think o' something, then don't write it down, and it gets lost. I had thought about propane before. Even thought of it when we was in Columbia gettin' them electric parts. But did I remember for us to check? No. Started snowin', and I lost it. The thought, I mean."

"Well, I got nothing against going back," Pete grinned.

"Good," Billy nodded. "We'll see first if the weather don't clear a bit. Few days. Maybe a week. Meantime, we need to all be helpin' Howie get things set up. Well, not all of us," he corrected himself. "We need us some place for a monitor station, I guess. A security shack, or somethin'. Where we can have people on duty watchin' them cameras, and listenin' in on the radio, and such like."

"That'd be good," Pete agreed. "Tomorrow?"

"What's wrong with today?" Billy asked. "And why are you so dressed up, anyhow?" Pete was dressed very nicely, and wasn't wearing the gear he normally wore when out and about.

"Ah, well," his face reddened slightly. "I'm, uh, kinda going over to, uh, the Silvers' for, ah, supper, see."

Billy sat completely quiet for five seconds and then busted out laughing.

"I don't see how that's funny!" Pete retorted.

"Have you seen yourself?" Billy asked. "I mean, when you explain where you're goin', not how you're dressed. You look like a kid done got caught stealin' candy!"

Pete stayed red faced a bit longer, but then started laughing himself. The two of them laughed like that for a good few minutes.

"I suppose I do, at that," Pete was finally able to reply. "Course, I doubt Shelly would like being referred to as candy."

"More like castor oil," Billy nodded. Pete frowned.

"Don't pay me no mind," Billy waved his comment off. "I knew her 'fore she was nice people, that's all. She's a lot better now."

"Well, anyway," Pete stood. "That's what's wrong with today."

"Tomorrow's fine," Billy nodded. "And Em's a good cook."

"Shelly's cooking."

"Oh. Well, I'm sure Em's supervising." Billy looked up slyly. "We gonna need to find you a house soon?" he teased.

"Probably not soon," Pete shrugged. "But one day. . .maybe."

"We'll start lookin', then," Billy turned serious. "There's a few nice places about. We'll get one staked out, in case. Make sure we don't let nobody else have it."

"Thanks, Billy," Pete said, his voice sincere.

"Ah, what're friends for. I mean, other than to laugh at ya?"

CHAPTER FIFTY-FOUR

The next day was blustery, but still warmer, for which everyone was thankful. It was ten days until Christmas. Billy shook his head as he realized that. Seemed like time had drug along at times, and then raced by at others. He didn't know which he liked better.

He, Pete, Ben and Jon Kelvey, Jerry and Toby, George, Ralph and Terry labored through the day erecting the security building. Howie was along as well, and after about thirty minutes of studying a map Billy provided, had decided that the spot Pete had selected was 'do-able'.

After a brief discussion, it was decided they would use the last single car carport for the security shack. It was easy to erect, and with a few hours work could be enclosed, insulated, and made ready to occupy.

As they worked, they discussed how the station would be manned. There was a lot to do, and a great deal to be decided. Howie explained what he could accomplish using what they had, and the crowd was suitably impressed.

It took most of the day, since the days were getting shorter all the time, but by the time they stopped for the day, the 'shack' was ready. PV cells were in place, battery bank charging, and a small emergency generator was in place as well. Using it would be only in a true emergency, since it would make noise, possibly leading someone to the building. It was decided that an alternative to having the generator on site would be looked for. But for now, it was workable.

"This ain't a bad deal," Billy nodded, looking at the finished structure. "Ought to do just fine."

"Yep," Howie nodded. "Almost certainly. Once we're finished installing everything, we should be able to literally sit here and see everything."

"Might want to add an observation deck," Pete suggested. "At some point, anyway. Maybe with some high-powered binoculars. Even a small telescope, we can find one. Sometimes you need to get eyes on something, to really see it."

"That ain't no bad idea," Billy mused quietly. "We need to think on that."

"We'll work on the cameras and stuff tomorrow," Jerry announced. "I'm done in, myself. See you boys tomorrow."

—

The women had not been idle whilst the men were working. Emma and Rhonda had gone up to the Clifton farm and helped fit clothes for the children there. Rhonda, because of her and Billy's thorough salvaging, was able to provide the women with shirts, jeans, coats, and shoes from her stores. All were most appreciative.

Rhonda and Emma had also tried to think of little things for the women, who had lost everything. They had given each one a bound notebook to use as a diary, along with pens and pencils. They had brought toys, as well. The older children were thrilled to see that, and were soon enjoying the bounty that Rhonda and Em had provided.

"I don't know how we'll ever be able to thank you," Regina told them, her eyes a bit damp.

"Well, happens we have any more children, with no one to care for them, you'll probably be called on for that," Rhonda shrugged. "The four of you can do a great deal that way. And once spring rolls around, we'll be planting gardens. We'll have one here, for you and the others. We'll help all we can, but you four, and the older children, will likely have to do most of the harvesting."

"I love to garden," Regina told them. "Always have. There's nothing much better than sitting down to a good meal with food you grew for yourself."

"Amen to that!" Emma nodded. "I'd always rather have mine."

"Did Terry get you all set up at the range?" Rhonda asked.

"Yes, he did, thanks," Regina nodded. "We all managed to do well enough that he said it was 'not a waste of resources' for us to be armed," she added, laughing. "We have pistols and rifles here now, and two shotguns. And we all know how to use them."

"Good," Emma nodded. "Keep them handy. Don't go out without them, not even to just have a look around. These are dangerous times. But then, I don't have to tell you that, do I?"

"No ma'am, you don't," Regina smiled slightly. "I'm afraid we're more than aware of that."

"It's a shame it has to be that way," Emma commented sadly. "With so many gone, it's just a waste to lose anyone now."

"Shameful," Rhonda agreed. "But, can't let the coyotes in with the chickens."

"And that's the truth if ever if was told," Emma nodded.

"Well, let's start sorting through stuff, and see what we can come up with," Rhonda said brightly.

-

For three days afterward, almost everyone who could help with the security project did so. Hundreds of yards of commo wire, courtesy of Radio Shack, Ricky's Radio's, and the National Guard among others, were woven into the landscape around the valley, surrounding the area known as The Farms. All of those wires, regardless of where they originated, terminated at the new security building, itself hidden and camouflaged. Some cameras were hard wired straight to the shack, while others were wired to wireless transmitters, which in turn sent them to the shack.

Cameras, motion detectors, microphones, heat sensors and loud speakers were placed everywhere it was feasible to do so. Once all the critical areas were covered, then everyone began looking for random areas that might benefit from extra coverage.

Every piece of equipment was numbered, and wired into a console. The Farms were divided into four areas, each a square that combined with the others to make a larger square. It looked terribly complicated, but Howie assured them that once it was online and working, it would be much easier to use than it looked.

"Heck, a caveman could do it!" he laughed, emulating a famous commercial. Most everyone laughed, albeit tiredly.

At long last, as the third day drew to a close, the job was finished. Howie turned everything on, and started flicking switches. Soon, the monitors in the room began showing the areas around them, the screens flickering from one view to the next.

"I'm going to stand the watch tonight, at least most of it," Howie announced. "There's a lot of fine tuning I need to do, and I can sit here and get that done while I make a manual of sorts for all of this. Liz will help me," he grinned at Elizabeth, who smiled at everyone shyly. She had improved, but still rarely came out of her shell.

"Starting tomorrow, we'll need someone in here all the time, I'd say," Howie went on. "One person or two person shifts. I'd recommend two, since there's so much to cover. I'll leave that to you guys, though. I got work to do here."

"We'll see you in the morning," Jerry nodded.

As the crowd broke apart, Billy wound up beside George.

"How's the misses doin'?" he asked. George shrugged.

"It's hard," he admitted. "If this wasn't so important, I wouldn't be here. She's okay, with Amy there with her, but every time I leave her, I feel like I'm letting her down, somehow."

"I can see that," Billy nodded. Hearing that made him think about himself and Rhonda. He hated leaving her so much, as well. While he was out working, Rhonda kept their place going, with only Danny and Mary to help. He felt guilty about the time he had to spend away, but couldn't see a way around it for now. Things had to get done.

And, he wasn't the only one leaving family behind him to get things done for the group as a whole, he reminded himself.

"I hope she get's better," he said to George. "I pray for her," he added quietly. George looked at him.

"Never took you for the praying kind, Billy," he said kindly. "I appreciate that."

"Reckon I don't make a big deal of it, but I pray all the time," Billy shrugged. "When I can't see a way to make somethin' happen, when I can't do no more 'bout somethin', then I tend to hand it to God, and pray for things to be like he wants. All I can do," he added.

"That's always a good plan," George agreed. "Reckon some don't believe, but. . .I seen a lot of bad things, Billy. And I've seen stuff come out of it I can't describe as nothing more than a miracle. Seen a house blowed to little bits once, and then found a baby inside, not a scratch on it. See something like that, there's no way you can't credit it to a higher power."

"Imagine so," Billy nodded. "Heck, the fact someone like me can make it on his own ain't much short of a miracle." George snorted.

"You sell yourself too short, Billy," he told the younger man. "It's not a miracle. It's just plain hard work and determination. You're a rare kina man, buddy. I don't think you know how to quit." Billy flushed slightly, and said nothing.

"Anyway, I appreciate it," George went on, not wanting to make his friend uncomfortable. "I'll see you tomorrow."

"Take care, George."

-

The Silvers' came to the Todd's for dinner that evening. Rhonda, Shelly and Emma had all been cooking while the others were working to help finish the security arrangements. There was a good feast waiting when Billy, Jerry, Toby and Danny arrived at the Todd house.

After grace had been said, and everyone had filled a plate, conversation began to drift around the table.

"Be Christmas in a few days," Toby pointed out.

"Yeah!" Mary and Danny exclaimed at the same time.

"Reckon we ought to have a party," Jerry nodded.

"We're ahead of you on that one," Emma smiled. "We're all going to gather at the Clifton place this time. That should be the easiest, and that way the younger children won't have to be out in the cold. Regina and the others can enjoy the party without worrying about leaving when the children get tired."

"Good idea," Billy nodded, speaking around a mouthful of cornbread.

"Don't talk with your mouth full," Rhonda said automatically, elbowing him. Billy nodded, but kept eating. He was used to that by now.

"We need to take a day and think over some gifts, especially for them kids," Jerry mentioned. "Tiny young'uns need toys at Christmas."

"Could always go and find toys for'em," Billy shrugged, dodging another elbow from Rhonda.

"Not a bad idea," Shelly smiled. "There's probably toys still on the shelves even in Cedar Bend. We could have a shopping trip."

"We should make a list of all the kids, and then make sure that each one has something nice for Christmas," Rhonda opined. "Next year, it might be home made toys and gifts of necessity. This might be the last time they get anything like conventional toys."

"We could go tomorrow," Billy shrugged. "Get into town and get it done. Have plenty of time to get'em wrapped and what not." Everyone nodded at that suggestion.

"Tomorrow it is, then," Jerry affirmed. "Now, is that a pie I see over there?"

-

The Great Christmas Shopping Trip would be remembered by all who went for a very long time. Rhonda and Billy insisted that Mary and Danny stay home, which resulted in much sulking. Shelly insisted that Pete go, which resulted in only slightly less sulking. Jerry and Emma asked Regina to come along, in order to help with finding gifts for the other children, which resulted in still more sulking as the other three women were left to tend to the children.

At the last moment George and Debby asked to go, much to the surprise of all. Debby hadn't been about since her spell, and no one had even suspected that she might want to go. No one objected, however, relieved that she was willing to get out for a change.

The Kelvey's weren't interested, and offered to stand the watch while the others went, Howie agreeing that it would give him time to 'tweak' the systems they had put into place. Amy asked Emma to look for a few items for Amanda, and offered to sit for Georgie, and for the Blaine children.

Terry was reluctant to leave with so many already going, but had no problem with Maria making the trip. He would remain behind to assist the Kelvey's. Toby, to the surprise of all, declined the invitation, and agreed to stand watch at the Silver and Todd Farms, and be ready to help if anything happened.

Odd Billy Todd

So it was that a small convoy of three trucks went into the ghost town of Cedar Bend to look for toys and trinkets for the children.

Despite the gloom of the dead town, the shoppers were excited. This was almost normal. Shopping for last minute Christmas gifts. The cold had driven the rats into hiding, and the town was mercifully clear of them, at least for the day. No one complained about that.

Billy stood watch as the rest combed the stores. He had spoken to Rhonda about it, and the two had decided that George needed to be with Debby, and that it wouldn't be right to pull Pete away from Shelly during their first Christmas, such as it was.

So, Billy was alone when it happened.

-

When it had become apparent that the virus was going to kill most of the population, a number of safeguards were put into place at the last minute.

All nuclear plants were idled. No one wanted to imagine what any survivors would go through if a runaway nuclear reactor cooked off with no one capable of stopping it left.

For similar reasons, America's nuclear arsenal was buried in secret, and vital components removed. Someone might, one day, retrieve some of the weapons, but it was unlikely that the sophisticated components of modern nuclear devices would still be serviceable. Missile components were like wise stripped away, and the rockets hastily buried in rock and concrete.

Hazardous materials at various places around the country were locked away in vaults that would take weeks to try and open. In prisons around the country, violent prisoners were euthanized, while non-violent offenders were set free, and left to their own devices.

And radical animal rights activists in almost every major city raided zoos, releasing thousands of non-indigenous species into the wild. Many were mauled by the animals they were trying to 'save'. No one was left to try and contain the animals, who found themselves on their own, in a land not their own.

Many died quickly, unable to transition from being kept in a cage and fed everyday to self reliant hunters or foragers. Some were unable to cope with native predators, and were all but eliminated.

But many, far too many, of the more violent predatory species survived. And one had found his way south from Nashville to Cedar Bend.

Just in time for shopping day.

-

At first Billy refused to believe what he was seeing. It simply wasn't possible, so that meant he was hallucinating, or he was just wrong about what he was seeing. But as he continued to watch, it began to dawn on him that he wasn't imagining things.

There really was an African lion trotting down Main Street, Cedar Bend, Tennessee.

At about the same time Billy decided that Leo was real, Leo noticed Billy. The great cat stopped short, lifting his nose to sniff at the air. Billy remained stock still, for once unsure what to do. His M-4 was equal to most tasks, but Billy had a terrible feeling that this beast wouldn't like being shot by a tiny .223 round at all.

At all.

The others, unaware of what was happening, were talking and laughing inside the store. The lion could hear them, and started pawing and snorting, as if answering a challenge. Billy moved so slow that it felt like years passed before his hand found his radio.

"Everyone be quiet, and stay still," he whispered into the mike. "Don't answer me, and don't open the door. Just stay where you are and be quiet." He released the button.

"*Billy what's wrong?*" Rhonda asked at once. Billy closed his eyes and shook his head.

The lion charged.

CHAPTER FIFTY-FIVE

Rommel's head came up sharply. He sniffed the air, tasting an unfamiliar scent on the wind. If he could have frowned, he would have. He had never encountered that particular scent before.

Rommel had slipped away from the others in Cedar Bend, allowed to roam as Billy and the others took stock of what was left. He was rarely far from Billy's side, but the distant familiarity of Cedar Bend had gotten the better of him, and the huge canine had wandered the area around the shops.

Now he stopped, testing the air once again. That scent was strange, but every instinct told Rommel that it was predatory. And that, he decided, made it his business.

He had already taken several steps toward investigating when he heard shots.

Billy threw his rifle to his shoulder and tried to get the charging lion in his sights. Every instinct he owned told him to run, yet those same instincts said if he did, Leo would kill him.

His first shots were off. His target was bounding towards him in giant leaps, which made targeting difficult. It didn't help that his heart beat was pounding in his ears, and his hands were shaking. If he had ever been more scared in his life, Billy couldn't remember it.

Concentrate.

Billy took a breath, wasting a second he really couldn't spare, trying to get his heartbeat under control as well as his breathing. He fired again.

The lion jerked slightly as the bullet ran along his shoulder. All that did was make him mad. Billy kept firing.

Another bullet nicked the lion, and he roared a challenge as he covered the last twenty yards to his next meal. Billy had emptied his rifle by now, managing to score three more hits, one he was sure in the lion's chest.

But the lion didn't seem to notice.

Billy didn't have time to reload, so he dropped the rifle, allowing his sling to catch it, and drew his pistol. The Kimber barked once. Twice. A third time. The first and third rounds hit, and the big forty-five slugs did get the lion's attention.

Just not in a good way.

Billy was aiming for one last shot when a large, black blur hit the lion from the side, knocking the big cat off his feet, and sliding him several feet along the roadway.

Rommel had followed the noise, knowing that his person often made such noises. Along the way he encountered the predator's scent again, stronger now. And different. Rommel broke into a run, a ground eating lope that carried him quickly back to where he'd left his person.

Rounding the corner one block up from where his person was, Rommel finally put a picture with the scent. He had no idea what he was looking at, but knew that it was a danger. That was really all he needed to know. In less than a second the

326

large hound realized that this new predator was attacking his person.

And Rommel just couldn't have that.

He broke into a run, paralleling the giant cat. He gained ground on the beast, and just short of where his person was standing, attacked, hitting the beast in the flank. Catching the large cat off guard, Rommel managed to knock him off his feet.

Rommel hesitated for less than a second before pouncing on the predator.

"Rommel! *NO!*"

The big dog ignored him, and hit the cat with a fury. Billy could only watch as Rommel tore into the off balance and wounded cat with jaws that Billy had seen crush another dog's spine in one bite.

But this wasn't another dog.

Rommel found that out the hard way.

The lion rolled onto his back as the yapping beast launched itself on him. Large teeth tore at him, inflicting still more damage on his body, but the cat managed to get his back legs up and under the dog.

With a strength grown from desperation, the lion kicked out, and was rewarded with a yelp of pain as the dog went flying.

Billy, seeing Rommel be sent into flight, took aim again. He had reloaded his rifle, and now began emptying it into the lion from close range.

The lion tried to get to his feet, but the damage was taking it's toll. Billy continued to fire, more of his shots hitting home than before. The lion staggered, then collapsed into the street.

Billy walked to where the lion lay, still gasping, and placed one more forty-five into the beast's head, then ran to where Rommel was struggling to get to his feet.

"Easy, boy," Billy soothed, trying to quiet the dog. "I got you buddy. I got you."

Rommel was in bad shape. How bad Billy couldn't say just yet, but there was a lot of blood. At least the cat hadn't managed to get a good purchase with his hind claws, or he knew Rommel would be dead.

"Easy, boy," he repeated, as the others boiled out of the store.

"What happened?" Pete asked, then stopped short, seeing the dead lion.

"Holy shit," he blurted. Then he turned to look up and down the street. Just in case. He saw nothing, but his guard stayed up. Lions lived in prides in the wild. If there was one, there was no reason there couldn't be more.

Rhonda ran to where Billy was desperately working to halt the flow of blood from Rommel's torn stomach and sides.

"Billy, what happened?" she cried, sliding in beside him.

"What part," Billy snapped as he tried to use a bandage from his first aid kit to staunch the blood flow, "of *don't answer me* didn't you get?"

"What?" Rhonda looked at him.

"I *told* you, *don't answer me!*" he snarled. "Just be quiet. And the *first thing you did is to ask me somethin'!*" Rhonda looked stricken, but Billy didn't care.

"If you had just been quiet," Billy went on, his voice dangerously low, "*like I told you*, I might could have shot the damn thing in the head, and been done with'im. But no, you can't *ever* do anything you're told to, can ya? Always, *always*, got to argue." Billy managed to tie off the wound, finally, and gathered the still struggling Rommel into his arms.

"I got to try'n git'im back," he told everyone and no one in particular. "Reckon you'll have to finish shoppin' 'thout me."

"I'll go with you," Rhonda told him, but Billy shook his head.

"Think you done did enough for one day, thanks," he didn't quite snarl. Rhonda jerked as if he'd hit her.

"I'll drive you," Pete offered. Again, Billy shook his head.

"You need to stay with 'em. I got it." With that Billy put Rommel into the front seat of the Ford, and took off home. Rhonda watched him go with tears in her eyes.

"He's just worried, dear," Emma soothed, seeing the young woman's distress.

"He's right," Rhonda shook her head. "I never just do as he asks. I always have to argue. And this time I might have killed him. May *have* killed Rommel."

Emma couldn't argue the point, so she said nothing else.

There really wasn't anything else to say, anyway.

-

"Just hold on, boy, we'll be home right quick. Get you all fixed up good." Rommel licked the hand Billy was rubbing him with, whining in pain at the effort.

"Just take it easy old boy," Billy told him, driving far faster than he was comfortable with. Or used to.

Some luck remained, however, as he managed to slide into the driveway where Amy lived. She ran to the door, looking out.

"I need your help!" Billy called, racing around the truck to get Rommel out. The dog's breathing was ragged now, and he was still. Billy looked at Amy, his eyes desperate.

"He got hurt by a lion," he told her. "Saved my life. He's hurt bad. Please tell me you might may can help."

"Bring him to the shop!" she shouted, and ran back inside. She ran to the closet where she kept her medical supplies and started filling a plastic bag.

"Amanda, watch the kids!" she called over her shoulder, running out the back door.

Billy had placed Rommel on Ralph's work bench, and was working on stopping the flow of blood again.

"Move!" Amy shouted, and Billy moved. Amy stripped away the field dressing quickly and expertly, looking at the wound for less than ten seconds before grabbing for what she needed.

"Did you say lion?" she asked, working quickly.

"Yes'm," Billy nodded. "Big ole lion right outta the movies," he told her.

"Where in the world did you find a lion?" she asked, her hands still moving. Rommel had lost some blood, but to her eye, it was less than it appeared, at least at first. And dogs were tough. This one more than most.

"He found me," Billy admitted. "In town. Must 'o got out from some zoo some wheres."

Amy used peroxide to clean the wound quickly.

"Hold him," she ordered. "He won't like this." Billy took Rommel's head as she doused the wound, using clean gauze to clear away blood.

"Boy, he got you good, didn't he Rommel," she asked, never taking her eyes from her work. Rommel whined a little at his name, but offered no resistance. Amy found two separate sets of claw marks, one on the right side of Rommel's belly, the other well up on his opposite flank. Two tracks looked deeper than the others, but all of them were bleeding.

"You got lucky, Rommel," she told the dog. "Another inch or two, and he'd have gutted you." Amy grabbed a pre-made suture, and started stitching.

"Hold him tight, Billy," she warned. "This will hurt."

Rommel tried to struggle as the needle bit into him, but Billy held him tight, and the dog was simply too weak to put up much of a fight. Amy's hand's seemed to be everywhere at once as Billy watched, fascinated by her ability.

It took almost an hour for Amy to get the wounds cleaned, and then closed, during which time Rommel had lost consciousness. Billy had almost panicked at that, but Amy assured him it was probably okay.

"His system knows it needs rest," she told him, hoping she was correct. She wasn't an animal nurse, after all. She stood back, exhausted all of a sudden.

"That's it, we're done."

"Reckon he'll be okay?" Billy asked hesitantly. He stroked Rommel's massive head without realizing it.

"I think he might," she hedged. "I'm not...thing is, Billy, I can fix the damage, but I don't know squat about canine physiology. How his body works," she explained, when Billy looked puzzled. "I think he'll be okay, but I don't have any way to be sure. So long as he hasn't lost too much blood, the main threat, now, should be infection."

"I got animal meds," Billy told her. "Got'em from the vet's office. Even some anti-biotics."

"That's good," Amy nodded. "Best to use them rather than ours. I think they're the same, but I don't know it for sure. Better to use something from a vet's. You have any books about dog health?" Billy nodded.

"As soon as you make him comfortable, start looking for information. There should be a section in there about what to watch for in the way of signs, whether it's infection or any other kind of distress. I'm afraid I've done all I know how to do," she admitted.

"It's more'n I could'a," Billy told her somberly. "Reckon I'll pay you back however you want," he added.

"Billy, I'm glad to do it," Amy smiled faintly. "It's not like you've never done anything for us, now is it?"

"I'm obliged, ma'am," Billy told her, and Amy was struck by Billy's humility. He clearly credited her for saving his beloved Rommel.

"Billy, you kept him alive," she told him. "If you had panicked, and not bandaged him like you did, he would have lost so much blood there would have been nothing I could do by the time you got him here."

"Be okay to take'im on home, you reckon?" Billy asked.

"Just be careful," she nodded. "Make him comfortable. He probably won't be able to go out for his business, which means you'll have to clean up his mess. And that's important. Make sure he doesn't lay in his waste. That'll make his wounds go septic, and then we'll loose him for sure."

"I'll mind it," Billy promise. "Wait on him hand and foot. He hadn't helped me, that old lion would o' got me sure 'nough. I was shakin' so bad I couldn't hit him to save my own life."

"I can't even imagine," Amy nodded, understanding. She walked to the truck and opened the door for him.

"Ma'am, I can't rightly thank you enough," he told her.

"I'm thanking you, Billy," she assured him. "Now, go and take care of things. If you need anything, give me a call."

When Rhonda came in from the shopping trip, having ridden in with Jerry and Emma, she found Rommel in the study, on a large sturdy pillow, water and canned food next to him. The dog was asleep, his breathing labored, but strong. Billy was sitting next to him, reading. Dottie, who had remained with the house, was lying next to her friend. The female looked up at her, but didn't offer to leave Rommel's side.

"Hey," Mary said, walking into the entrance way. "Had some excitement, huh?" Mary didn't smile.

"Some," Rhonda nodded. "How is he?"

"You mean Rommel, or Billy?" Mary asked.

"Either. Both."

"Billy's right quiet," Mary replied. "Ain't said prob'ly ten words since he got back. Been readin' that book since he got Rommel situated. Readin' 'bout dog injuries and such. Rommel's pretty beat up, but might be okay, maybe, according to what Amy said. She stitched him up, Billy said," the girl added.

"Thank goodness," Rhonda sighed. Her greatest fear had been to get home and find Rommel had died.

"Reckon Billy's a might touchy at the moment," Mary added. "He ain't. . .he ain't been ugly, mind, but he ain't what you'd call over eager to speak to nobody, neither."

"Especially me, I'd imagine," Rhonda nodded. "Get Danny and put these things away. And don't peek. Please."

"We won't," the girl promised. She went to find her fellow orphan. Rhonda stood in the study door, peering in at Billy, deep in concentration over the book in his lap. Every few seconds, he'd look up at Rommel, and then back to the book.

"How is he?" Rhonda ventured to ask.

"He's alive," Billy told her curtly. "Hopefully he'll stay thatta way. Ain't no way to know save to wait on it." He never looked up.

"Billy, I am so sorry," Rhonda offered. Billy didn't respond. Didn't move.

"Billy, honestly, I didn't mean. . . ." Billy snapped the book shut suddenly, with a force that made her jump.

"Reckon you didn't," he said quietly. "Happened anyways." He didn't look up at her.

"I should have done what you said," Rhonda tried again. "I didn't think. All I knew was something was wrong. If you had told me - "

"I shouldn't have to tell you," Billy interrupted. "I shouldn't have to explain ever little thing like that. I should be able to ask you to do somethin', or tell you, and you just trust me, and do it." He looked up at her finally, and Rhonda winced inwardly at the look in his eyes.

"That lion could o' killed me." Billy's voice was very low. "When he heard you on the radio, he charged right at me, when he had been sittin' still. Had you just done what I asked you to, he might o' stayed still long enough for me to put a bullet right 'tween his eyes, and dropped'im right where he stood." He got to his feet, book still in his hands.

"'Stead, he come a runnin' at me, a leapin' and a jumpin' all over creation, and I couldn't hit him hard 'nough to put'im down. I was so scared, my hands shakin' so bad, I couldn't hold steady 'nough to git a good shot. Not for Rommel, he'd o' got me. And he did git Rommel." Saying the dog's name made Billy look at Rommel again, to make sure he was still breathing.

"Billy, I didn't know," Rhonda said quietly. "All you said was to be quiet, and I was afraid something was wrong, and I wanted to know. . . ."

"You always want to know," Billy nodded. "You always got to know, got to say, got to be, got to argue. Even when you know things is how they got to be, you still argue." He sighed, then. A long, sad sound.

"You always got to say," he said again. "This time, you had your say, just like always. Was it worth it?" There was no sting in the words. Just resignation. Sadness.

"No," Rhonda admitted quietly.

"Well, that's somethin', anyway," Billy sighed again, this time tiredly. "I'm gonna try and rest a while. I'll be in here if you need me."

"In here?" Rhonda asked, stunned. Was he shutting her out?

"Can't leave'im," Billy pointed at Rommel. "He can't even get up enough to go tend his business. I got to clean him up ever time. I don't, he'll get a infection. Can't have that. Might kill'im, even if the blood loss don't. So, I'm sleepin' here." He pointed to where he'd rolled out his sleeping bag.

"I'll stay with you," she offered.

"No," he shook his head. "Ain't no need o' both of us sleepin' on the floor. Just. . .just go to bed, when you get ready. Like I said, I'll be here, you need me."

With that he shut off the light, and got into his bed.

"You don't care, pull 'at door to when you go."

Rhonda gently shut the door, and made her way upstairs. She had been hungry, but now had no appetite. She looked at the bundles in their room, the results of their efforts before the lion attack.

"All this for some Christmas presents," she said to herself.

And then the tears came.

CHAPTER FIFTY-SIX

Christmas dinner was a hit for most of the small community. For once, things just sort of fell into place. Pete had offered to stand watch, and Shelly had offered to help, so the two of them made up a basket from the assorted foods and left quietly, Jerry's frown following them. He didn't mean to frown, he told himself. He liked Pete. But that was his daughter, and he felt like he was duty bound to frown. So he did.

Billy made only a brief appearance, wishing everyone a merry Christmas. Then he too made up a basket and headed home. Rommel was better, but not enough. Rhonda watched him go, not bothering to tell her good-bye. Billy was distant, if not outright cold, and it hurt. Knowing that he was right to be that way made it hurt more.

"What's wrong, dear?" Emma asked, having seen Rhonda's expression.

"Nothing," Rhonda told her quietly, smiling. "Just watching the doings."

"You can lie to yourself, honey, but I know better," Emma patted her hand. "You're tore up pretty bad. Is he still angry?"

"He's not. . .angry," Rhonda struggled to find the right word. "If he was, I'd actually feel better. If he'd yell, or scream, or break something, then I'd think we were making progress. But he doesn't. He just sits there. When he speaks, he's proper and polite, his tone is gentle. I. . .I just don't understand," she admitted, tears beginning to flow.

"That's just his way of coping, dear," Emma told her softly. "Billy has always had to ride hard on his anger. One of his main failings is that when he allows himself to get mad, he's 'mad all over', as my grandmother used to say. He's mad, and he can't control himself. He knows that. So he keeps himself bottled up. I'm afraid one day that will do him more harm than good."

"What do you mean?" Rhonda asked.

"Oh, I don't mean he'll hurt anyone," Emma assured her at once. "But bottling all that anger up inside isn't healthy. It's hard on the system. Something else my grandma used to say," she grinned. "Hard on the system. He's penning all that rage and frustration up inside, and it can hurt him, over a long period of time."

"How?"

"Well, it can cause health problems. Stress causes all kinds of problems, honey. Heart disease, stroke, that kind of thing. Billy's young, and healthy as a horse, so I doubt it's hurting him right now. But as he gets older, it will, I'm afraid. He has to learn to find an outlet for all that."

"Maybe I can help," Rhonda mused. "Once he's talking to me normal again, anyway."

"Maybe you can."

-

Rhonda left the party and walked home. It was a long way, but she enjoyed it. She was armed, of course, and Dottie was with her. Mary and Danny had asked to stay the night, with the other children, as had Georgie and Amanda. Mary had pleaded for Toby to stay as well, but he was having none of it.

"I ain't no kid," he muttered, shaking his head. Mary pouted a bit, but Toby was immune to that, and went home with his family.

As Rhonda walked, she mulled the problem over in her head. She and Billy had enjoyed a wonderful relationship up to now, and she missed that. She knew that she was prone to insist on things, but she was usually right. At least that's what she told herself.

But she admitted that sometimes her insistence made things hard on Billy. Like when she complained that he would leave, to go and take care of something. Deep down, she knew those things had to be done. But she was tired of Billy always being the one to do them.

The others had problems of their own, of course. George with helping Debby, Terry with two children, living in a house farther away from the others. Jerry and Emma were older, and not really able to get out and about like the others. The Kelvey's were still in stages of recuperation from wounds suffered during the Franklin raid, with Ben taking up the 'slack' of Jon and Howie not being quite back to battery as yet.

Regina and the others had their hands full with the children. Ralph was busy with the bio diesel experiment, and with George staying close to home, Ralph was also doing the lion's share of the work with the community herd.

That meant that it usually fell to Billy, Toby, and Pete to do the leg work. The others all participated in some things, but the three of them bore the greatest part of the burden. All were young, strong and capable. And had the least responsibility. True, she and Billy had Mary and Danny now, but both were teens that had managed to survive on their own for months, and were quite able, and more than willing, to work hard around the Todd farm. Now days Danny took care of the Todd herd, and the horses, performing most of the farm chores himself, including helping Jerry with the pigs.

Mary worked around the house, and helped Danny with chores, and took almost exclusive care of the chickens. When it came time to garden, and then to can, Danny and Mary would be there to help then, as well.

She had said herself that it was hard work, maintaining a farm, Rhonda remembered. And it was. It was also an everyday thing. Animals had to be fed, even when it was Christmas. When it was cold, hot, raining, snowing, the weather didn't matter, chores had to be done.

And, she admitted to herself with a sigh, salvaging the things they needed to be safe in their own community had to be done as well. She didn't have to like that Billy was gone so much, but she did have to accept that it was necessary. Period.

"Time to grow up a little, Rhonda," she murmured to herself, as she approached the house. "You've had things pretty much your own way since you got here. Time you learned to give a little."

She knew that it was. The problem was how to do it. And to convince Billy that she was going to.

-

She was surprised when she got home. Billy was outside, with Rommel getting about, albeit gingerly, in the backyard.

"Hi, Rommel!" Rhonda greeted, as Dottie ran to where Rommel watched them coming. The two dogs pawed and sniffed slightly, though Dottie was obviously

Odd Billy Todd

conscious that her buddy was still injured. Rhonda paused to ruff Rommel's great head, which he accepted with a whine, licking his face. Rhonda laughed, realizing that Rommel was getting back to his old self.

"Hi, baby," she said to Billy.

"Hi!" Billy smiled, and her heart warmed.

"I see the Beast is better," Rhonda smiled back, sitting down beside him.

"Seems to be," Billy nodded, kissing her lightly. "He was up'n about when I got back. I opened the door, and out he came."

"He looks good," Rhonda agreed, taking Billy's hand in her's. "I'm glad."

"Me, too," Billy agreed, and squeezed her hand lightly. "Had me worried for a bit."

"I know, baby," she said softly, hugging him. "I'm so sorry," she added.

"Ah, it's under the bridge now, I reckon," Billy shook his head.

"No, it's not," Rhonda shook her head, and Billy looked at her.

"I ain't been right by you, Billy," Rhonda said, looking him right in the eye. "I complained about you havin' to go and do, even when I knowed it had to be done. And, I do almost always object, or argue, or complain, wantin' to know what's what."

"It scares me that I almost got Rommel killed," she admitted. "And it terrifies me that you might have been hurt, or killed, because I didn't do what you said. I'm sorry for that."

"I can't change what I did, or what happened cause of it. But I can change how I do things in the future. I know there's things you have to do. You, Pete, and Toby are about the only one's that can do some of this stuff. Everyone else has so much else on'em. So from now on, I'll do my best to be supportive of times when you have to go and do and take care of things. I promise."

"Well, I don't care that you ask, or even that you argue," Billy shrugged. "But what happened in town, that wasn't. . .that was the time not to, is all. I. . .I needed it to be quiet. I couldn't even believe what I was seein' at first."

"He could hear ya'll in the store, and he started pawin' and snortin' like a old bull or such. He was gettin' ready to 'tack, I thought. That's why I called to ya'll to be right still. Thought it would make him pause."

"And then I had to ask what's wrong," Rhonda sighed.

"He lit right out after me," Billy nodded in agreement. "I was so scared I couldn't even get a good shot on'im. And it didn't help none that a .223 ain't really the ideal big game bullet, neither," he grinned. "I couldn't hit nothin' vital, and I reckon it wasn't much more'n a bee sting to'im. He just kept a comin'."

"I figured I was pretty much a goner when Rommel hit'im from the side," Billy continued after a minute. "Hadn't been for him, that lion woulda killed me most like. Hurt me bad for sure." He looked at her then.

"I know I said mean things to you. I can't rightly recall what, to be honest, but I'm sure I did. I didn't mean to. I was scared, and I was mad. But still, I hadn't ought o' done it. And I'm sorry."

"I had it coming," Rhonda patted his arm.

"No, you didn't," Billy shook his head. "That kinda thinkin' don't work for me, Rhonda. You start thinkin' like that, you can justify all sorts o' things. I can't be that way. I gotta hold the line, and do right. I don't, I do wrong. Bad wrong, sometimes," he almost whispered.

"Billy, you ain't gotta 'bad wrong' bone in your body," Rhonda smiled. "You just react to things, that's all. And I put you in a bad place. I promise to do my best not to do it anymore. Ever."

They sat together for a good while after that, enjoying each other's company, and watching the two dogs go around the yard. Finally Rhonda turned, and whispered into his ear.

"Ya know, the kids stayed at the Clifton Home tonight. Ain't nobody but us in this big ol' house tonight. All alone." Billy grinned.

"What will we do?" she asked, batting her eyes at him.

"Reckon we'll just have to do the best we can," he grinned even broader, and leaned in for a kiss.

-

The Christmas party had gone so well that another was planned for New Year's. The Clifton House was again the location, having so much more room than anywhere else. The weather was cold now, so any outdoor activity was accompanied by bundled clothes and then followed by runny nose's and sore throat's.

With Rommel recovering nicely, Billy was happy to go to the party. He and Rhonda had talked a good deal over the last few days, and he felt much better about their relationship. In fact, they both did.

They elected to drive, because of the cold, and arrived early so Rhonda and Mary could help with the party preparations. Billy and Danny looked around the farm for chores that needed doing, and took care of them, including filling the outdoor furnace, checking the fuel and oil on the small generator, and the fuel line from the propane tank to the furnace. A last chore was to fill the wood box on the back porch for the fireplace.

By the time they had finished, the others were either there already, or arriving. The two slipped inside, took off their coats and went to warm by the fireplace.

Soon the house began to fill up. There was no actual meal this time, just plate after plate of finger foods, deserts, and corner sandwiches. Everyone simply grabbed a paper plate and fixed something, then mingled.

After an hour of general talk, music started, and people began to dance, and laugh. There was no televised ball dropping in New York, so Regina and the others had rigged their own. There was alcohol, of course, and wine, and soon the house was getting louder and louder.

Billy and Rhonda had danced for a while, then sat out as Rhonda helped watch the smaller children, who were having their own party upstairs, giving the women from the day care a chance to enjoy the fun.

Billy sat by himself for a while, then allowed Mary to pull him onto the dance floor once, to dance with her. The music seemed louder to him, now. Someone had rigged a few lights, probably Howie, and they were flashing on and off at times with the music.

Billy struggled as the music, lights, talking and laughing all seemed to run together into one big noise. He'd never been to a party. Ever. The noise was intruding on his calmness. He began to fidget, and then to sweat.

Soon, without even realizing it, Billy was becoming irritable. He turned from side to side in his seat, frowning at every new sound, every flash of light. Then, someone found the light switch and began turning the overhead lights on and off. On and off. On and off.

Suddenly Billy jumped to his feet. It was too much. Too much noise, too much light, too much. . .people. He ran out the front door, and into the yard. A few noticed him go, but didn't think anything of it, assuming he wanted fresh air. Which was the case, to a point.

Pete had been sitting with Shelly, watching the goings on when he saw Billy hit the door. He frowned to himself. Something was wrong. He excused himself, and followed his new friend outside.

He found Billy nearly to the tree line, wandering aimlessly, shaking his hands as if trying to air dry them. He was also talking to himself. Pete frowned again. That wasn't good. He walked slowly toward Billy, stopping a few yards away.

"Calm, calm, calm," he heard Billy say over and over.

"Billy, you okay?" he called out. Billy stopped short, his head swiveling toward the call.

"Are you okay, buddy?" Pete called again, as Billy just looked at him.

"Too much," Billy said. "Too. . .too much."

"Too much noise?" Pete asked, understanding at least in part.

"Too much everything," Billy shook his head. "Too loud, too bright. Too much people."

"Bothering you, is it?" Pete asked quietly.

"Too much," Billy repeated.

"Want me to get Rhonda?" Pete asked.

"NO!" Billy shouted, and Pete drew back a step. "No," Billy repeated, calmer. "Don't want her to see. Want anybody to see. Not like this. Gotta keep calm, that's all. Gotta. . .calm. Calm. Calm."

Pete stayed quiet, contemplating the problem. He'd never seen Billy like this. He knew Billy had some issues, but didn't know exactly what they were. Pete was at a loss as to what to do. He watched Billy walking for another minute before speaking.

"Billy, why not talk to me?" he asked. "I can listen. And I won't tell anybody what you say. We're friends, you know? What was bothering you?"

"Too many people," Billy told him, still walking in a small circle. "Too crowded, too much noise. I can't. . .I need to focus, that's all. I need to keep calm. Calm, calm, calm. That's all. I just need to be calm. That's all."

Pete felt frustrated. He wanted to help, but had no idea how to get through to him.

"What helps calm you down, Billy?" Pete asked, keeping his voice conversational. "What makes you feel calm?" Suddenly, Billy stopped. He looked at Pete as if he had three heads.

"What?" he asked.

"What helps you calm down?" Pete repeated patiently. This seemed to be working.

"I don't. . .I don't know, really," Billy replied slowly. "Usually just reminding myself that I need to be calm does it. It's just. . .too. . . ."

"I know, Billy, it's too much," Pete nodded, not wanting to let Billy get back on that train of thought. "I even understand, a little."

"You do?" Billy peered at him in the darkness. "How?"

"I was raised on a reservation, Billy," Pete told him. "Wide open spaces, lot's of solitude and empty space. Lot of it was desert, of course, but there were also some grass lands. I've watched over my uncle's sheep, my grandfather's cattle and horses, sometimes weeks at a time in camp. When I came back, all the noise and people talking put me on edge for a while."

"I was so used to being alone, to the quiet, to concentrating on my work, that I couldn't always drop back into being around my family. Sometimes it took several days for me to get used to being around them again."

"You're not used to being around so many people. At least not in a confined space like a house. And let's face it, there's a lotta people in there, and it's loud."

"Too loud," Billy agreed, but seemed calmer. "And too close together."

"Yeah, I know," Pete sighed. "Like I said, it bothers me sometimes. I don't much care for loud noise like that, because I can't hear what's happening around me. I like to know what's going on around me."

"So do I," Billy nodded. "Awareness. You got to be aware. You gotta be able to see under the hood, gotta see what's going on." Pete nodded, rightly suspecting that this was a reference to Billy's days as a shop owner.

"Yeah," Pete said. "When you don't know what's happening, you don't feel like you got any control. That's important to me. I bet it is to you, too. Ain't it?"

"Got to be in control," Billy nodded jerkily. "Gotta be aware and calm. All the time. When ya ain't, ya make mistakes. Mistakes ain't no good. When you're calm, you don't make no mistakes."

"Well, I do," Pete admitted. "Sometimes I just do the wrong thing. But when I realize it, I just try to go back and fix it. About all I can do, most times."

"Fix it?" Billy was still struggling, but Pete was relieved to see that he was listening. And thinking.

"Yeah. You know, go back and correct whatever mistake you made," Pete nodded. "Make it right."

"Go back and fix it," Billy repeated, as if memorizing it. "Never. . .I ain't ever thought about that. Always just tried not to make'em in the first place."

"Well, that's the best policy," Pete agreed. "Just don't always work."

"Sometimes you can't," Billy said quietly. He looked calmer now, Pete was glad to see. "Sometimes, you git it wrong, and that's it. Done."

"All too true I'm afraid," Pete nodded, sighing. "Billy. Everyone makes mistakes. You ain't alone in that, you know. Ain't none of us perfect in no sense of the word."

"Guess that's true," Billy nodded in agreement. "It's just. . .I make. . .I have to concentrate. If I don't, I lose my way, sometimes. I get caught up in a circle, and I can't git out of it."

"Start thinking about one thing, and it leads to another," Pete nodded. Billy looked at him again.

"You do know what I mean, don't you?" he asked. Pete nodded.

"Yeah, 'fraid so," he sighed again. "I spent a lotta time as a scout. Observer, tracker, that kinda thing. Lot's o' time alone, having to be real quiet like. Leaves you with not much but your mind, roamin' all over the place. You think about

Odd Billy Todd

something, and after a while, that makes you think o' something else. Pretty soon you're thinking on a thing, and you can't even remember how you got there. I have to back track to see how I wound up where I'm at."

Billy's eyes widened a bit at that.

"Same thing happens to you, I guess," Pete took a chance. "Don't make you weak, or stupid, Billy. Just makes you like others. Human, I guess. We all do it, one way or another."

"I always. . .I guess I just always figured it was cause I ain't. . .cause I got problems," Billy managed. "That it was just part o' my. . .part o' what made me like I am."

"How are you, Billy?" Pete asked.

"I'm. . .I'm slow, I guess," Billy seemed hesitant. "I ain't. . .I can't think on things like most seem to. Have to write stuff down. I need a plan, and when I get one, I stick to it. If I ain't got a plan, then I make mistakes. Dumb'uns, that cost me time, and sometimes more. I can't. . .I can't always focus just right. Havin' a plan helps me to focus. Stay calm. Not. . .not get rattled, I guess. Good as any way to describe it I reckon."

"We all get rattled sometimes," Pete shrugged. "Overwhelmed. Sounds like you got a good way to deal with it, though. Your folk's teach you?"

"Yeah," Billy nodded, looking at the ground around him, as if looking back in time. "They helped me learn."

"My grandfather did that for me," Pete told him. "Taught me the 'old ways' as he called'em. Said it was things our people had learned the hard way. Things that would work when the white man's magic had died. Looks like he was more right than he knew," he chuckled.

"Reckon so," Billy nodded.

"You okay, now?" Pete asked. Billy nodded.

"Reckon I am," he replied. He looked at Pete. "Thanks, Pete. I. . .I usually ain't so bad, these days."

"Just a shock to the system, that's all," Pete shrugged.

"Guess so," Billy nodded.

"Ready to go back inside?"

"I am," Billy nodded again.

CHAPTER FIFTY-SEVEN

The new year entered with a both a bang and a whimper. Most of the adults who had attended the party were slow to wake, and woke to painful reminders of having imbibed a bit too much, or delayed going to bed too long.

Billy hadn't had anything to drink, but his 'episode' had left him restless, and he hadn't slept well. Nonetheless, he was up early. Chores had to be done. He found Danny waiting, as usual, and the two had spent most of the morning completing their chores, and doing a few odd jobs that had been put off too long.

About ten that morning, Billy had stopped for a moment, and was looking into the distance. Danny followed his gaze, squinting a bit. Finally, he asked.

"What is it?"

"I think we're gonna to get some snow," Billy told him, sniffing the air.

"How do you...what do you smell?" Danny asked.

"Air smells wet," Billy told him. Danny sniffed hesitantly at the wind, his eyes widening.

"Wow. I never noticed that."

"That's cause it ain't been there long," Billy nodded. "Check 'at thermometer over there. I'd say the temperature done dropped five degrees in the last hour or so." Danny dutifully obeyed, and nodded as he read the mercury.

"You're right, at least 'bout the temperature," he reported. "Was about forty when we came out. Now it's thirty-five."

"Okay," Billy replied, blowing his breath out in a long, thoughtful moment. "We got work to do. Saddle your horse, and start makin' the rounds. Let ever' one know we probably got weather incomin'."

"What else?" Danny asked.

"Check the fences on your way out," Billy told him. "It'll save time."

"I'm on it."

Billy started finishing their work, already thinking about what he'd need to do to ready the farm for what he was sure would be a rough storm.

It started about four. The wind had been steadily increasing for the last hour. The home weather station that Billy watched indicated that the wind was up to twenty-eight miles an hour, with gusts to near forty. The temperature had already dropped to twenty-six degrees.

Danny had made the rounds as quickly as he could, and then returned to help secure the farm. They were as ready as possible.

Billy watched as the snow began to fall.

The storm raged for four days. Snow, ice, even thunder at one point, which had been nerve wracking. Billy had heard tell of such things, but never encountered them.

The temperature had dropped to near zero at times, and the wind had held steady at forty-five miles per hour for a long time. Gusts had been even higher, with one hitting sixty-one mph for nearly a full minute. Billy heard more than one tree hit the ground in the woods surrounding the farm. He hoped there was no damage around the area.

The Todd's spent the time indoors in various ways. Video games, card and board games, movies with popcorn, reading. There were plenty of diversions.

But everyone would eventually turn back to the windows. Looking outside. Trees bent, snow flew, ice coated. This was a real blizzard. The storm in November was starting to look like a flurry.

Billy and Danny had used their time wisely, making sure that sufficient food and water were available to all the animals. Billy hadn't wanted to venture out into the weather more than necessary. They had run ropes to the barn, the pig lot, and the feed shed in the pasture just in case. With the wind blowing so hard, it would be easy to get lost in the snow.

On the third day, the two of them had made use of the ropes to check everything during a small respite. All the animals were okay, though the horses were restless. They spent a little time calming the horses down, rubbing them down, and giving them treats before heading back to the house. By the time they returned to the house, the wind was picking up again and the snow was falling heavier.

At night the wind literally howled. With the night so dark the howling wind added to the feeling of isolation that people all over the valley felt. Blankets were pulled tighter to ward off chills that weren't entirely caused by falling temperatures. Startled eyes would turn to the windows whenever an especially strong gust of wind would hit, rattling the windows, and sometimes even the doors. The crash of trees overburdened by the weight of snow and ice falling in the dark hours likewise drew wary glances, and caused more than one person to flinch, or look at their roof.

Even Jerry couldn't remember a worse storm. He watched from his bedroom window, then from his den as the snow piled higher and higher. He and Toby had taken the same precautions as Billy had, but he worried none the less.

When the storm finally blew itself out, there was none of the usual after effects, such as clear skies and calm winds. The sky remained dark and grey, clouds hanging low, and seeming to threaten still more falling weather at any time. The wind, while no longer a gale, was still strong, and gusty.

Billy and Danny ventured out at once on the first morning, ignoring the wind and cold as much as they could, to do their chores. Water that had turned to ice was broken, and fresh water pumped into troughs. The horses were released into the corral to work off excess energy. The two of them used the Ranger's fixed blade to plow walkways to the barn, pasture an pig lot, then on through the woods to the Silvers' homestead. They met Toby, plowing in their direction with his four-wheeler.

"Cold out!" Toby shouted.

"Sure is," Billy nodded. "Ya'll okay?"

"Reckon so," Toby nodded. "Tree's are down all over, but ain't none hit nothin' here. You been out?"

"Just here," Billy shook his head. "Ya'll heard from ever body?"

"Pa talked to ever one on the radio. No damage to any houses. Ralph says we lost two calves, but that's all. Reckon that's not bad, considerin'."

"Him and the others manage okay with the big herd?" Billy asked.

"Yeah. Pa told'em they needed any help, to call." Billy nodded at that. "Pa reckon's we'll get more o' the same, soon," the teen added, looking at the sky.

"I figure that too," Billy agreed. "Reckon we better get back at it."

"See ya!" Toby waved as he turned for home.

"Reckon we better see to gettin' some wood up, and then collect the horses," Billy said, as Danny turned the Ranger around. "I don't think this is over."

-

It wasn't.

Snow began falling again just at dark that evening. No one had been idle. Rhonda and Mary had seen to the chickens, and collected the few eggs. They also swept away the snow that had accumulated on the front porch, and shoveled away the snow that had blown under the awning at the rear of the house.

Danny and Billy had set two heaters up in the attic to help remove the snow from the roof, and the resulting runoff had formed large icicles all along the roof edge. Breaking them off had proved challenging, but no one wanted the razor sharp or needle point ice spears falling on them.

Rhonda had made a hearty beef stew with fresh bread, and they were about to sit down to dinner when the snow started again. Large, heavy, wet flakes were soon falling so thick and so fast that visibility fell quickly to almost nothing. Billy looked out the kitchen window as he enjoyed the hot chocolate Rhonda had made.

"How much more, do you think?" Rhonda asked softly, coming to his side.

"No way o' knowin'," Billy admitted. "Ain't no weather reports no more, so all we got is what we can see."

"Will we be okay, Billy?" she asked.

"Yeah," Billy nodded firmly. "We're in good shape. All of us is. Be rough gettin' through, was somethin' to happen, but we're good. Just have to wait it out."

"Why is it so bad?" she asked.

"Ain't many people left," he shrugged. "No more cars runnin', no more heat from exhaust, from factories, from. . .nothin'. Ain't too much to keep the cold at bay. Things is back like they used to be. I imagine this here is what we can expect for winter from here on, most like."

She took his hand, and they watched together for time, until supper time.

Meanwhile, it snowed.

CHAPTER FIFTY-EIGHT

For three long months, the snow would come and go. Winter was one long blizzard it seemed, with short periods where the temperature would be milder, sometimes even into the fifties.

But those short periods never lasted. Three days, five, once an entire week. But always the milder, drier weather gave way to more freezing temperatures, and more snow. Much more.

The short periods of thaw were used to work around the farms. There was no visiting, no socializing. Time was too precious to waste. The group had lost cattle, pigs, and even three older horses to the cold, wet weather. The losses were bearable, but they were losses.

Hay was used much faster than anticipated. There was no grass, anywhere, that remained viable. Most of the times it was simply unreachable. The decision was made in early February to cut back on haying, to ensure that there was enough to get the herd through. The cattle would lose weight, but they would regain it once spring and the grass returned. It wasn't a perfect solution, but it would work.

During the days, and sometimes weeks of snow and bitter cold, plans were made. Each house was determined to be better prepared for the next winter. A year ago, this would have made everyone laugh, to be worrying over next winter while in the middle of a blizzard. Not anymore.

Everyone was realizing that the non-winter months would now become a race to prepare for the coming winter. Nothing else would matter. Crops would have to be put in, and harvested. They would need much more hay for the cattle. And at least one new hay barn.

Roof structures would have to be checked, and any with signs of weakness repaired or strengthened. The weight of two or three feet of snow could collapse a roof. The homes were all sturdily built, but neither their designers nor their builders had ever anticipated this kind of weather. Adjustments were planned for spring time.

Horses in their barns stomped and kicked, built up energy making them restless. They were allowed to run during the brief thaws, possibly all that kept them sane and manageable. Barely.

Every single thing they could squeeze into the thaws was done. If there was thirty minutes left, they were used for something. For some, the need to simply get out of the house was often overwhelming. For others, the need to get work done was the main factor. For all, the winter was wearing.

Day after day of heavy gray clouds. Driving snow and sleet. Drizzling freezing rain. The sound of trees falling around them became common place, as those over whelmed by ice finally gave in to gravity.

There would be plenty of downed trees to cut for firewood come spring time.

Billy figured there would also be a lack of wild game. In these conditions, game animals would be hard pressed to survive. Many would leave, he figured, moving further south in hopes of finding better ground. Perhaps they would return with the spring.

Perhaps not. He didn't know. No one else did either, he guessed.

He had never seen a winter this savage. Knowing it was possible, even expecting it, had not prepared him to see it. There were days when he looked outside that he wondered about his sanity. Everywhere you looked, there was nothing but white.

The others weren't dealing with it any better. Many refused to look outside anymore. They ignored the white. They read, they wrote, they slept. They worked on indoor projects. They dressed in sweats, and covered themselves with blankets to accommodate the colder temperatures. Fires and furnaces were kept low, to preserve fuel.

Mealtimes were boring. There were only so many ways to prepare the same foods. There was no where to 'eat-out' anymore. There were no social gatherings. No cook-outs, no 'visiting'. Movement was difficult when the snow was upon them. When it wasn't, no time could be wasted 'socializing'.

The radio told a sad tale of it's own, as signal after signal stopped transmitting. People they had heard on the HAM frequencies since civilization had died went silent. More and more isolated, everyone began to draw more into themselves.

It was a harsh and rugged world they now lived in. One where a simple mistake could lead to death. No more hospitals. No more doctor's clinics. No EMS ambulances. Nothing.

For the first time, the residents of the farm community realized they were well and truly on their own. There was no one else. No one to come riding to the rescue if something happened. No one to lean on, depend upon, but themselves.

Not one of them had ever considered the mental issues that this realization could cause. It hadn't seemed important. They had survived, and would continue to do so. That should be all there was to it.

But it wasn't. Week after week of continued confinement, worry, and fear increased stress levels to the breaking point. Nerves were in tatters from the forced isolation. Tempers flared and snapped. Even couples tended to drift apart, looking to isolate themselves from one another. Books were read, read again, then traded to others for still more books that had already been read.

Video games that had initially occupied the attention of children became boring, and then disgusting. Movies that had been seen five times over and were once favorites became hated. Music that once had soothed the soul now jarred already fractured nerves.

It seemed there was no end in sight. Many bundled up and ventured outside just to relieve the boredom, only to be driven inside within minutes by biting winds and wet clothing.

By March, it would have been difficult to find anyone who wasn't near the end of their rope.

But some had used the time to prepare for things other than the next crop. The next need.

And they were just as ready for the thaw as anyone else.

CHAPTER FIFTY-NINE

It was late into March when the first long break of good weather seemed to stick around. Good was relative, of course, with temperatures in the fifties and strong winds. Still, it beat being buried in snow.

As the small community began to dig out, they surveyed the damage. Thankfully none of their own homes or buildings were damaged. Their perimeter system had suffered, and Howie took this long period of good weather to start working on that. It took him almost a week, but the alarms and cameras were finally all running again.

Billy and Danny spent three days working on the Todd farm to get everything back to battery. Once that was done, Billy told Danny he trusted him to look after the animals from now on, but to call if he needed any help at all. Danny took this trusted post with a swelled chest, proud that Billy would trust him so.

Billy then disappeared into his 'shop'.

He had work to do.

-

Billy was sitting outside studying a map when Pete rode into the yard.

"Hey, Pete!" Billy grinned. "How ya doin'?"

"Passin' fair," Pete nodded, grinning in return as he stepped down off his horse. "You guys about caught up?"

"Have been a couple days," Billy assured him. "Got lucky this go 'round."

"I think we all did," Pete nodded. "Was headed over to see Michelle, thought I'd stop in and say hello."

"Guess it was a long winter for ya, huh?" Billy grinned.

"Made some snowshoes," Pete chuckled. "Spent a lot o' time at the Silvers' place."

"That's the way to plan," Billy laughed.

"What you doin', anyway," Pete asked, his head nodding at the map.

"Ah, just lookin' at stuff," Billy replied vaguely.

"What kind of 'stuff'?"

"Railroad trestles and such," Billy told him, his voice low.

"So that's your idea," Pete said, comprehension dawning. "How you plan on going about it?" he asked, interested.

"Ain't made up my mind just yet," Billy admitted. "Still studyin' the layout so to speak. And a lot depends on what they do."

"Well, I'm in, whatever it is," Pete grinned suddenly. Billy looked at him for a long minute, then nodded firmly.

"Works for me."

-

"Jerry, reckon you're the one knows what's best, here," Billy mentioned. "Reckon you oughta start us off." Everyone who would be part of the communal work on the farms was gathered for a meeting. They all realized that there was no time to waste. They needed to get crops in the ground, and other work started. Sooner would be much better than later.

"Well, we got to get as much land broke up and fit to plant as we can manage, o' course," Jerry told them. "And some o' that's gonna depend on fuel and manpower. But we got to decide what we aim to plant, and make sure we got seed enough to do it."

"We need plenty of rapeseed, for the bio fuel," Ralph spoke up. George nodded his agreement.

"And we need a lot o' corn for the hogs," Billy added, brow furrowed.

"And we got to have more hay," Jon Kelvey spoke up. "Ran way too low, this time."

"Now you're startin' to see the problem," Jerry sighed. "Can't just throw some seed at the ground, and that's it. Takes plannin', and good management. Gotta plant so that everything don't come ready at once, or you loose some of it. Not to mention, we need a place to store the grains. Ain't got near enough o' that, right now."

"So we get the crops in, and then start working on the storage?" Terry Blaine asked. "I can see that working. And it's a good management of our time, seems like. We don't have to be ready at planting time. Just at harvest."

"That's simplified, but mostly right," Jerry agreed. "Thing is, if we make a mistake, we may not have enough time to fix it. And we don't want everything in one place, neither. We need to spread everything around some."

"Okay, so all we're gonna plant is corn, rapeseed, and hay?" George asked. "And none o' that is for us, right?"

"Right," Jerry nodded. "Everybody will need to get gardens in, and grow their own. We'll plant some wheat, though, and make sure everybody gets flour. And we'll set aside some corn for meal, too."

"Sounds like a long summer to me," Toby sighed. He wasn't really surprised. This wasn't anything different from the way the Silvers' had lived all his life.

"Well, we can get the breaking done right off, I should think, we got plenty o' tools, and drivers."

"Well, then, let's get down to the bones o' this plannin', and we'll start plowin' tomorrow, right?"

-

The work was hard, but not especially difficult. After a few trial runs, the consensus was that Jon Kelvey and Jerry Silvers would be the drivers. Both men were much better than the others handling the tractors and equipment needed to get ready for planting.

There were issues. The noise of the equipment would attract anyone in the area to come take a look. It was agreed that the security shack would be manned around the clock starting immediately. Everyone was given a weapons refresher, and those who didn't have sidearms were issued them, and told to wear them at all times, or keep them near when sleeping, bathing, and so forth.

Spotters would also accompany Jon and Jerry as they worked to prepare various fields for planting. Their attention would of necessity be focused on operating the tractors. Someone would need to watch their backs.

After three weeks of pleasant weather, it was decided to go ahead and start the gardens. There were several plants that could be planted early, that a frost wouldn't hamper. In three days time a decent greenhouse was started on the Todd farm, and several of the women gathered to get starter plants going inside. When the weather permitted additional planting, they'd be prepared.

By mid April, the gardens were planted, as were the fields. It had been hard work, and almost everyone was tired. After months of enforced inactivity, the sudden spurt of hard work had everyone tired and sore. It was decided by the women that a social gathering was indicated.

The outing would take place at the Todd household this time. Billy, Danny, Toby and Pete left early one morning in two trucks, returning in the afternoon with various playground equipment. They worked the rest of the day setting everything up temporarily the Todd farm, with plans to relocate most of it to the Clifton Home once the gathering was passed. Kids needed playtime, Billy had decreed.

One of the fatter calves, and two shoats were slaughtered and cooked over open fires for most of a night, to be ready for serving on the next day. As usual the men folk gathered around these fires and performed manly bonding rituals.

Pete volunteered to man the security systems, and Michelle Silvers, unsurprisingly, offered to help. Billy joined the 'circle', but he and Toby remained completely sober, just in case. There was no getting around the fact that these were dangerous times.

The day of the 'social' as it was being called was a full day of food, games, talking and playing. Everyone had a good time, with the men taking turns on watch. Every two hours, two of them would saddle horses and ride the perimeter of the farms, as the two currently on watch would return to the gathering. The same schedule was used for the security shack, making sure that everything was safe while everyone got a chance to let their hair down and recover from the long winter.

Debby Purdy joined the party too. It was the first time she'd been away from the house since her problems had come to a head. She was shy at first, uneasy as to how people would take her being there. But Amy had explained to everyone what had happened, and the fact that Debby wasn't truly to blame for what had happened to her, and the others were willing to let it go.

As the day wore on, and Debby realized that everyone was glad to see her back on her feet, she relaxed, and began to enjoy herself.

All in all, it was a very good day for the little community, and one that was long over due. Tomorrow would bring a new round of chores for everyone, and the work would start early. But today, everyone just enjoyed the company.

CHAPTER SIXTY

It was the first of May. Billy and Danny were looking over their own herd, which had grown considerably. There was talk of taking some cattle to Franklin for trade, and the two of them were discussing what members of their herd might be suitable for that.

"I don't think we should take the bull," Danny said. "He's young, but he'll be a good new bloodline."

"Be hard for us to use 'im," Billy shook his head.

"But there's other cattle," Danny pointed out. "We can use 'im in the big herd. Trade 'im out for one over there." Billy considered that.

"Good point. New blood for us, and for the big herd," he finally nodded. "Good idea. We'll do that." He looked at his adopted son.

"You know, we're gonna have to keep good strict records on the breeding," he noted. "Reckon you can handle that?" Danny looked up at Billy.

"You'd trust me to take care o' somethin' like that?" he asked.

"Why shouldn't I?" Billy countered. "You're plenty smart."

"I. . .sure, I can do it!" Danny grinned.

"Might want to get a good notebook from Rhonda, and get started then," Billy told him. "You need to keep good notes, and make sure they're accurate. Might not matter right now, but down the road, it'll be important. We need to keep the herd healthy, and strong."

"I'll start today," Danny promised.

"We got records already for the original herd of ours," Billy told him. "I'll get 'em for you when we get back. I want you to get Mary to help you. We need everybody able to take care o' things."

"Okay."

"Let's head over to check. . . ." he stopped as he saw Mary running toward them.

"Pete needs to talk to you!" she shouted before she reached them. "He called on the radio, said he's on his way over, and it's important!"

-

"We maybe got a problem," Pete said, as he took the offered glass of water. Danny was walking Pete's horse, which had been winded by the ride.

"What kind o' problem?"

"There was a small settlement west of Nashville. A town called Weber. More of a community than an actual town, but it was doing pretty well. Kinda like us, with people moving in there to work together."

"Okay," Billy nodded. "What about 'em."

"Well, they were on the radio about once a week," Pete told him. "Just average stuff. Sharing weather info, looking for trades, that kinda thing. Terry or Jerry one have talked to them off and on all winter." He paused, looking off for a minute, then taking a deep breath.

"We ain't heard from them in almost three weeks. Not a peep." Billy frowned.

"Maybe they lost their generator?" he asked. Pete shook his head.

"They're using a combination of solar and pedal power for their radio," he told Billy. "They got more than one radio, too," he added, pensive.

"So, you think something happened to'em," Billy said.

"I think it's likely," Pete nodded.

"So, what you wanna do?" Billy asked. "You wantin' to take a ride up there, and see for yourself?"

"I. . .well, I don't know," Pete shrugged. "On the one hand, it would be nice to see what's wrong. To know, you know? If it is radio trouble, we could take them one of the spares we have, maybe get'em back running."

"On the other hand," Pete went on, "there's the possibility that we'd run into trouble ourselves. I don't know what to do, Billy. I guess I was hoping you'd have an idea." Billy frowned.

"I don't know," he mused. "How far is it?"

"About seventy miles," Pete admitted. "Maybe a bit more or less. And we don't know anything about the road conditions between here and there. At least not once we're out of our area." Billy pondered that. Finally, he sighed.

"I don't see how we can help," he admitted finally. "I mean, that's a long way, into an unknown area. And we don't actually know anybody up there. We might wind up walkin' into somethin' tryin' to help."

"And we can't really spare anybody from here for a long time," he added, rising from his seat and beginning to pace slowly. "We can barely cover what we got as it is. Send two or three people that far away, we might be askin' for trouble here at home." He looked back at Pete.

"I hate to say it, buddy, but I think it's too much to risk," he said finally. Pete nodded slowly.

"That was the decision I came to," he said sadly. "I guess I just wanted someone to tell me I was right. I feel bad not going, but I'd feel worse if something happened here while I was gone."

"I know how ya feel," Billy agreed. "But we got to look out for ourselves first. I'm all for helpin' anybody we can, so long as it don't hurt us. Know what I mean?"

"I agree," Pete nodded firmly. "There's to much to risk here. Thanks, Billy."

"Anytime."

-

"You're awfully quiet," Rhonda said, as she and Billy cleaned up after supper.

"Just thinkin'," he told her.

"What about?"

Billy told her about his conversation with Pete earlier in the day. She listened without comment, but was visibly relieved when she realized that Billy had been against going to Weber.

"I ain't gonna put us a risk," Billy told her flatly. "I'd like to be able to help, but it's just too far. And too risky."

"I know you want to help, honey," Rhonda told him. "But I'm glad you won't be going. I. . .I don't want you getting hurt."

"I know. And it ain't fair to you and the kids to keep runnin' off. Can't say we won't have to some times, but when it's too much to risk, I just can't see that it's worth it."

"Good," she hugged him.

Odd Billy Todd

Billy woke up abruptly around three in the morning. Something was nagging at him, and he couldn't figure out what it was. There was something he had missed, somewhere. Taking care not to wake Rhonda, he eased out of their bedroom and started downstairs. Rommel was at the foot of the stairs, keeping guard. He raised his head, looking at his person, and Billy stopped to ruff the great dog's head, then went into the study.

A map of the area was pinned to the wall, and he walked to it, studying. He soon found Weber on the map. A tiny dot along a state highway. He looked at the area around the small farm community, finally seeing what had bothered him.

A railway. Less than five miles from Weber. Crossing the same highway that bisected the small community.

Perfect for a train borne convoy.

-

Billy shared his revelation with Pete the next day, but both agreed there was still too much risk for them to go and see for themselves. Both hated that fact, but realized there was nothing they could do to change that. The two of them decided they would make a circuit of the Farms, making sure of their own security. It was early, and they packed food and water for the whole day.

It was a chance for Billy to show Pete more of the back country, too. The Native American ex-soldier had an uncanny ability to remember terrain, and once Billy showed him something, it remained Pete's knowledge from then on. So he spent the bulk of the day showing his friend various fire and game trails all over the valley, as well as 'shortcuts' that allowed much faster travel from point to point.

"This is great country, Billy," Pete noted, as they sat on the rim of the valley, looking out over the Farms.

"Yeah," Billy nodded. "I ain't never lived no where but here. Ain't never really *been* nowhere but here, and a few places around. It's always been home."

The two of them rode back by a different route, taking their time, watching for anything out of place or suspicious. They checked on a number of places that seemed to offer natural lookout posts, but found nothing anywhere to indicate they were being watched.

"Well, reckon it's gettin' on for five or so," Billy looked at the sky as they approached the house where Pete lived with the Blaine's. "Reckon I better be gettin' on back." Pete looked at his watch, shaking his head. It was ten till.

"You're gonna have to tell me how you do that, sometime."

"Do what?" Billy asked, puzzled.

"Never mind," Pete sighed. "I'll see ya tomorrow, Billy."

"Take it easy," Billy waved, and headed home.

-

Two days later, Billy was working in his shop when his his radio crackled. They didn't use the little GRMS radio's except in an emergency, to avoid anyone monitoring frequencies to overhear them, and come looking for the Farms.

"*Billy, Pete, Terry, we got visitors,*" Howie's voice came through clear. He was obviously excited, but he kept his voice as calm as he could. "*There's a group on foot, looks like ten adults and maybe that many kids, on Cedar Bend Road. They're east of the crossroads. Less than half a mile from it.*" Cedar Bend Road was the road into town from the Farms. The intersection he spoke of was where the road to the Clifton Home, and to Terry Blaine's house, crossed the main road.

"*Are they armed?*" Blaine's voice came back almost at once. The group had decided that when there was a 'tactical' matter, Terry or Pete one would be in charge if they were available.

"It's hard to tell from this distance," Howie admitted. "*But at least three of the men are carrying long guns. Two of the males are out front by fifty yards or so. They're already at the intersection. Waiting for the rest, looks like.*"

"*Billy, I want you and Toby to take the blind east of the intersection. You should be able to get into it unseen. Pete and I will make contact. You back us up.*"

"Got it," Billy agreed at once, already heading for the house.

When he exited the house, rifle in hand, Toby was standing in front of the porch, trying to get his breath back.

"F. . .further than I re. . .remembered it b. . .bein'. . .on foot," he gasped.

"We done got lazy," Billy grinned. Rhonda came out behind him.

"Please be careful," she said softly. "Both of you," she shot a look at the gasping Toby.

"We will," Billy promised, giving her a quick peck. "Let's go, Toby."

The two of them set out at a run for the blind, a small hunting blind built twenty-five yards from the intersection. The two of them made good time, slowing slightly to avoid making noise as they entered the blind.

Billy could clearly see the two armed men at the intersection. One was holding a police style shotgun, while the other was carrying an AR-15. Both were ragged looking, and appeared malnourished.

"We're in position, both men in sight," he whispered into his radio. He had taken time to insert his ear mike, and Terry's voice came back clearly.

"*We're on our way. Approaching from our place, on horseback. You should see us in less than a minute.*"

"Toby, you take the one with the shotgun," Billy ordered. "I'll get the one with the rifle."

"Are we gonna have to shoot'em?" Toby whispered back.

"Hope not," Billy replied. "They look about done in. I'd say they're on the run from somethin'. Maybe they'll be friendly if they need help, and we can help'em."

"*This is George,*" another voice came over the radio. "*I'm in position about thirty yards up the Clifton Road. I have them in sight as well.*"

"Okay, we see them," Terry called. "*And they see us. I'm switching to Vox so you can hear what's said. Here we go.*"

Terry and Pete rode abreast, but were separated so that no one move on their visitor's part could get both of them at once. Both were wearing body armor.

"*Terry, the rest of the party has halted, they're still about fifty yards or so back. They've huddled around the children, looks like, with one man to their front, another to the rear. Both are armed.*"

"Roger that," Terry answered quickly, grateful for the information. Howie was doing a good job. He surveyed the scene to their front. He saw one of the men look their way, stiffen, and grab his companion's arm.

"Hold up, there," Terry shouted, raising an empty hand. "We aren't unfriendly unless you are. And there are three rifles pointed at you right now!" The two men looked around them in panic, but could not see the threatening rifles.

"Don't raise your guns!" Pete called. "We want to talk, and see why you're in our area. If you raise your weapons, you'll be fired on. Let's all just be peaceable, and maybe we can settle all this without anyone being hurt."

The two men hesitated, looking at one another. Finally, one shrugged, and lowered his gun. The other followed suit after another few seconds.

"We're just passin' through," the first called. "You got no call to be comin' on us like this."

"We've got plenty of 'call'," Terry informed him. "Our families live here. We're responsible for their safety and well being. Seeing armed men in the neighborhood is 'call' enough for us to see what's what." He dismounted.

"I'm Terry Blaine. This is my friend Pete. This is our home," he waved his arm around the valley. "And it's not exactly on the beaten path. What brings you this way?"

"Like I said, just passin' through," the first man replied, not offering his name.

"Where you headed?" Terry asked. "We're not really on the way to anywhere. Seems odd that you'd pick to come through here."

"We were hopin' to find food," the second man offered. The first man glared at him, anger on his face.

"Shut up Fred!" he hissed.

"Kiss my ass!" 'Fred' shot back. "We been doin' things your way for long enough. We need food for the young'un!"

The man with the AR lifted his rifle in one smooth move and slammed the butt into 'Fred's head. Fred hit the ground like a sack of potatoes. His assailant raised the rifle for a finishing blow, but before he could finish it, his own head exploded in a fine mist, his body flipping backwards to rest on the pavement ten feet away.

From start to finish, the entire scene had lasted less than five seconds.

"*You guys okay?*" Toby's calm voice came across the radio. A still stunned Terry Blaine raised his hand to his radio without conscious thought.

"We're good. Was that Billy?"

"*Yeah. He didn't know if the guy was gonna kill his partner or turn on you guys.*"

"No problem," Terry acknowledged. "Tell him nice shot."

Fred was struggling to sit up, blood running down his face from a gash on his temple. He saw his attacker lying across the road from him, and looked at the body for a moment, then buried his face in his hands, scrubbing his face harshly.

"Sorry about that, buddy," Terry said, still standing where he had been. Fred looked up at him, eyes widening.

"His friend!" he shouted suddenly. "He's got a friend with the women and children! If they see what's happened, I don't know what the guy will do!"

"What's he look like?" Pete asked at once, moving to Fred's side. "I need to know what he's wearing, and how he's armed."

"Uh, he's tall, tallest one in the bunch. Got a rifle like Todd," he pointed to the dead man. "He's wearin' an old army jacket. Got patches all over it." Pete keyed his radio mike.

"Billy can you see the main group from where you are?"

"*We can see 'em,*" Toby answered. "*One of 'em's yellin' at the others. Billy don't think he's too stable.*"

"He's not! Tell Billy to take him if he. . . ." Pete's voice was drowned out by the sound of a high-powered rifle shot.

"*Billy says he's down. No movement.*" Toby said calmly. "*Rest are just sitting there.*"

"We're gonna head up there," Terry announced as Pete pulled 'Fred' to his feet. "Keep us covered."

"*Will do.*"

"So, Fred, what brings you guys our way?" Terry asked, as the three of them walked toward the rest of the group.

"We been on the move since winter let up," Fred shrugged. "We cut through here hoping there was something to eat. We been on tight rations for a while. Harder on the kids, than on us."

"Ya'll a family?" Pete asked.

"Not really. My wife is along, and there's another couple. The rest were just friends and neighbors. Todd and his buddy Wilkins showed up a month or so after the virus, offerin' to help. Pretty soon, they was runnin' things." He looked at the two men, shame faced.

"They was soldiers, at one time, I reckon. Wasn't no way for us to stand up to'em. They always kept on guard, one of'em always awake and watchin'. Long as things went their way, things were fine. If anybody bucked'em, things got ugly."

"If. . .they threatened to hurt the women and the kids if we tried anything," he admitted. "I don't think we could have took the two of them. We couldn't win, no matter what. If we failed, then they were alone with the others. If we took'em, but they got all of us, then the rest were alone." He sighed.

"Ever been in a no-win situation?" he asked sadly.

"Yeah, we have," Pete nodded. "You did what you could. And now, you're free of them."

"Yeah, and starvin'," Fred nodded. "We don't get the kids somethin' more substantial than dandelion soup soon. . . ."

"Let us see about that," Blaine told him as they arrived at the small group of huddled, ragged, hungry people. "Why don't you introduce us?"

CHAPTER SIXTY-ONE

Fred looked at his people.

"It's okay," he told them. "Todd's gone too. They aren't going to hurt us. If they were, they could've done it already." The two men, four women, and nine children looked at him wide-eyed, clearly in shock. Their belongings were in several carts and small wagons being pushed and or pulled along the road.

"I think we should move this somewhere else," Pete murmured to Terry, nodding at the corpse in the road. Terry nodded.

"Look, folks," he said to the group. "I know you're scared, but you look like you could use a good meal, too. And maybe a chance to clean up, and get some better clothes. We can help with that. Let's get all of you somewhere a bit more secure, and these kids away from. . .well," he nodded to the body himself. "Sound okay?"

A few nods and muttered agreements met his statement.

"Any suggestions?" Terry asked.

"Bring'em to the house, for now," Billy's voice made both men jump. They turned to see him and Toby looking at them blandly. No one had noticed them coming up.

"We moved the other. . .fella," Billy nodded back toward the intersection. "I called Rhonda, too. She's got Shelly and Miss Em workin' on a meal for'em, and Jerry and Danny are riggin' an outdoor shower. Rhonda sent Mary over to get Amy, too," he added.

"Well, that sounds like a good a plan as any," Terry agreed.

"You two take'em on down," Billy ordered. "Me and Toby'll clean up here."

"All right," Terry nodded. "Once we've got them to the house, Pete and I will make a round, just to make sure there's no one else coming. Or anyone following this bunch."

"Sounds like a plan," Billy agreed. "Rhonda and them will be waitin'. Toby, run on ahead, and bring back the little track hoe. We'll get rid o' them two, and head back."

-

"My name's Fred Williams," Fred filled the other two in as they walked. "This is my wife, Cora," he indicated the woman walking next to him. "That's Harry March, and his wife Bethany, with their sons, Henry and Jacob. These two are Jennifer and Janice Beal, sisters. Their parents were our neighbors," he added.

"The rest of the children were kids in our neighborhood, or that we found trying to make it on their own." He rattled off the names of the three boys and four girls, aged anywhere from six to sixteen. Terry lost the fight to remember them all.

"Well, I'm sure we'll get to know each other better, over the next few days," he said kindly. "Right now, let's concentrate on getting you folks in better shape than you're in now, okay?" Nods from all around met this declaration.

"How many of you are there?" Fred asked. Terry looked at him, grinning slightly.

"A fair few," he answered, and Fred flushed slightly.

"Sorry, that wasn't how I meant it," he said.

"I figured not," Terry nodded. "We're just a cautious bunch. Had more than our share of trouble."

"Well, you're being mighty helpful to us, so I can't question you," Fred shrugged. "And we're beholden to you."

"Nah," Pete waved him off. "It's just the right thing to do. Ain't many people left these days. Those of us left have to take care of each other, if we can."

"That's a mighty Christian attitude, young man," Cora Williams offered.

"Well. . . ." Pete shrugged, but said nothing else.

It was a slow walk to the Todd farm, with the new arrivals in such poor shape. By the time they had arrived, they had already met Toby returning to the scene with the small trackhoe they had 'liberated' last fall, and a table of quick food was already set out on the benches behind the Todd farm. A temporary wash station was also available for the newcomers to wash at before eating. Behind Billy's shop, Jerry and Danny were almost finished with the temporary showers, wooden frames covered with tarpaulins, and water nozzles hanging from three garden hoses.

The small group stopped short, seeing all of this, looking on with wide eyes.

"We haven't seen so much in. . .a long time," Fred murmured. The adult men made no move toward the food, insisting that the women and children eat first.

"There's plenty for everyone," Emma Silvers promised. "And more cooking. This was what we could get ready before you got here." Everyone looked goggle eyed at the pronouncement.

"It's plain fare," Emma went on, "but there's plenty of it."

The men reluctantly headed for the table, clearly glad to be able to eat, but still hesitant to take even one bit away from the others.

"They've had a hard way of it," Em whispered to Rhonda. She nodded.

"It looks like it. Those poor kids," she whispered. "I wonder when their last good meal was, poor babies."

"Looking at them, I'd say it was a while," Em commented. "We need to call Regina over here," she added. "Some of these kids will almost certainly wind up over there. And she may find some help with those two," she nodded to the Beal sisters, who were ignoring their own hunger to ensure that each child was clean, and eating properly.

"I'll send Mary over there."

-

"What are we gonna do with that bunch?" Toby asked, as he and Billy finished burying the two bodies. They hadn't bothered with a marker. Just buried them deep enough that no scavengers could get at them.

"No idea," Billy shrugged, wiping his brow. It was turning out to be a warm day. But after their winter, he wasn't complaining. "Ain't up to me."

"May not be up to you, but damn sure they're all gonna wanna know what you think, Billy," Toby pointed out. "Most everybody here looks to you before doin' anything. Hell, my daddy always wants to know your opinion before he does much outside our own place." Billy looked at him quizzically.

"Why? He knows a heap more'n I do."

"Because you see things differently, I guess," Toby shrugged. "Every body else is trying to make decisions based on how things used to be. You don't."

Odd Billy Todd

"Well, ain't no point," Billy shrugged. "Things *ain't* like they used to be. Gotta be adaptable, ya know. We got to find new ways to do things."

"And you been better at that than the rest of'em, Billy," Toby declared. "Plain and simple. When ever you've come up with somethin', it's worked. None o' the rest of'em can say that. Sometimes they're so busy arguin' over the old ways, they forget none of'em 'll work!"

"Well, that may be true," Billy shook his head doggedly. "But that ain't got nothin' to do with a buncha new folks. I ain't got no dog in that hunt." There was a note of finality in his voice.

-

"So, Billy, what's the best way to go where these new folks are concerned?"

Billy ignored Toby's smirk as he looked at the assembled faces before him. Jerry was waiting expectantly for an answer to his question, and Terry, George, Ralph, and the Kelvey's were leaning in to hear what he had to say.

"Why you askin' me?" Billy replied. "I ain't even met none of'em, yet."

"Well, we wanted your input," Ralph explained. He looked a little sheepish.

"Don't rightly know what to tell ya," Billy shrugged. "Reckon if they ain't trouble makers, we can put'em up around here somewhere. Any of'em know how to do anything useful?"

"You mean you'd kick'em out?" This from Emma, as she and Rhonda joined the fray.

"I didn't let'em in," Billy sounded exasperated. "And I done said, I don't know none of'em. Was just askin' is all."

"We can't just kick those kids out," Rhonda said firmly, eyeing Billy a bit hard. "It's not right."

"Look, I ain't said nothin' about kickin'. . . ."

"If Billy thinks they need to go, reckon I'll back him," Ralph shrugged.

"I ain't said they. . . ."

"We are *not* kicking those children out of here, Billy Todd!" Emma said sternly.

"Miss Em, I didn't say a thing. . . ."

"If Billy thinks that's the way to go, then we'll have to think on it," Jerry put his oar in. "Though I am surprised," he added.

"Well, there are a lot of'em," George shrugged. "Finding a place for that may prove difficult. Where did you have in mind to put them, Billy?"

"I hadn't thought about that because. . . ."

"Because you were plannin' on kickin'em out?" Rhonda challenged.

"*HEY*!!!"

Everyone fell silent and looked at Billy.

"First off, I ain't said nothin' 'bout *nothin*'!" he declared. "I don't know them people, don't know where they come from, how they got here, not even their names. I ain't said nothin' 'bout them being kicked out, where they'd stay, nor nothin' else, on account o' I ain't managed to get a word in sideways since I walked into the yard. My *own* damn yard at that!"

"Now, I killed two men this mornin', and I just got done helpin' Toby bury'em. We're both tired, hungry, and not a little put by. I told you, I ain't got nothin' to say about all that. Ya'll need to get together and come up with somethin'. Toby, I'm gettin' somethin' to eat. You comin'?"

"You got it, Boss," Toby grinned, then ducked hurriedly as Billy sent a backhand his way. He then followed Billy to the table, and dug in.

"Well, I don't see why he's so upset!" Emma stated, and Rhonda nodded in agreement.

"Reckon I do," Jerry admitted, a bit flushed. "Here we are, ever one of us older'n him, and got more experience. Yet we're so used to turnin' to him, because he always seems to have the answer, that we did it again. We're more than capable of dealing with this without bothering him about it." Just then Toby ran up.

"Billy says not to put'em in the George place, he's got it put by for somethin'. Other than that, he figures the young'uns that ain't got no parents should go to the Clifton House, along with them two sisters who seem to be keepin' an eye on'em."

"He says too that the Halsey place is in good shape for a family, and that the Crowder place is a fair starter place for someone with no kids." With that Toby ran back to the table, leaving the others to stare at each other.

"Okay, then," Jerry nodded firmly. "Reckon you heard that. Now we need to start in talkin' to these folk. Reckon we can at least handle that on our own?" he asked, chuckling.

The others laughed at that, then started circulating among the new comers.

CHAPTER SIXTY-TWO

"Your name is Todd?" Cora Williams asked, frowning.

"Yes ma'am," Billy nodded. "Nice to meet you."

"The man who was terrorizing us was named Todd," Harry March noted. "How do we know you aren't kin to him?" he all but demanded. Billy looked at him, but said nothing.

"Hey now," Toby spoke up. "Ain't no call for that. You need to remember who helped you, buddy." Toby's tone was almost truculent. He didn't like where this was headed.

"We have a right to know!" Bethany March didn't quite screech. "We won't go through that again!"

"Hey, you need to calm down," Toby ordered, coming to his feet.

"What's going on here?" Emma asked, seeing her son red faced and angry with the others. "Toby, where are your manners?"

"Where are *their* manners?" Toby shot back. "They're all but accusing Billy o' bein' in some kinda cahoots with that guy they was followin'." Emma frowned, turning her gaze on the newcomers.

"Is that true?" she asked icily.

"He's got the same last name," Cora stated firmly. "We demand to know what relation he may be."

"I ain't related to nobody," Billy said quietly. His already bad mood wasn't improving. "I got no family, nowhere, anymore, except Rhonda and the kids. And the folks around here," he added, placing a hand on Toby's shoulder to guide him back to his seat.

"Whoever that fella is, *was*, he ain't no kin o' mine."

"And we're just supposed to believe that?" Harry asked scornfully.

"I don't care what you believe," Billy shrugged. "Ain't no never mind to me."

"You can't possibly expect us to stay here with him," Cora informed Emma. "There's no way we can trust him, not knowing for sure."

"I know for sure," Emma told her firmly. "I've known him all his life. I knew his parents, and their parents. There's no possible way for Billy to be related to the man who caused your problems."

"We don't know that," Bethany refused to budge.

"Well, I guess that takes care of the problem o' where to put'em," Toby declared. "Reckon they can just move on."

"Toby," Emma chided.

"Why should we move on?" Harry demanded. "There's plenty of room here for us! And food as well."

"Mister March," Jerry spoke up, having moved up and listened to the exchange, "we aren't a charity. Everything you've eaten today is the fruit of our labor. We are charitable people, but we can't support so many mouths by ourselves. Everyone here works to support themselves."

"We're willing to work," March said. "I just don't think we can trust him," he pointed at Billy.

"You trusted him this morning," George decided to weigh in. He didn't like the tone or attitude their visitors were taking.

"What's that mean?" Harry March demanded.

"Who do you think shot the man who was about to kill you?" George asked Fred Williams. "Or the man threatening the rest of you?" he asked March. "Who offered his home as a place for you to clean up, be fed, and let us see to your needs?"

"Billy Todd, that's who," he told them. "This man saved your life this morning, Fred," he added. "No way we could have stopped him before he killed you. Not for Billy, you're not here right now."

The group grew silent over that, thinking it over.

"Bottom line is this," George went on, noting that Billy was still eating quietly. "We were considering offering you a place here. If there's a problem between you and one of us, especially Billy, then there's no place for you here. Period. We're willing to take the children who don't have anyone to care for them, because we have a home for them already with children who's parents perished in the plague or it's aftermath. That's up to you as their present caretakers."

"Think it over," he shrugged. "It doesn't matter to us, one way or the other." With that he walked away, leaving the small group to talk things over. Billy stood, and looked over at them.

"You need to think fast. I don't aim to extend much hospitality to folks that ain't got even basic good manners. I want you off my farm 'fore the day's out. You can work where you go out with the others." With that he stalked away, angry.

Toby stood, collecting his own plate, and followed. Though not without one last glare at the people he'd help save just hours ago.

"Well, congratulations," Jerry told them sarcastically. "You've just offended the one person in this group who is almost impossible to offend. Not to mention the man who was first in line to help you folks." With that he and Emma walked away as well.

"Better have a word with the lil'un," Jerry told her. "Billy ain't like to be in a good mood for a while."

"I'll just do that," Emma nodded, wondering if Rhonda would be any less inclined to be angry at the insult levied at Billy.

-

She wasn't.

"I want them off this farm, *now*!" she growled, eyes sparking with anger. "I don't care where they go, but they aren't staying here!"

"Billy already told them they had to go by the end of the day, dear," Emma soothed.

"That ain't good enough," Rhonda didn't quite yell. "I mean *now*! I will not have them on this property, eating our food, and then dare to accuse him of something so. . .so. . .*aaahhhhh*!" She did scream then, a primal sound that was scary enough to bring several of the men to investigate.

"We're fine, nothing to see here," Emma assured them. "Move on, now. I'm sure you all have work to do." Just then, Billy came out of the house, having cleaned up.

"What's with all that caterwaulin'?" he asked.

"Rhonda was just. . .expressing her displeasure with our visitor's opinion of you."

"Well, that's okay," Billy shrugged. "I ain't all that happy, myself."

"I want them *off. This. Farm!*" Rhonda repeated, biting her words off angrily. "I will not have them sitting here, on our farm, putting you down!"

"Easy, tiger," Billy grinned. "I told'em to get gone by dark. Let'em get fed. Especially them kids. They ain't said nothin' 'bout me," he chuckled.

"How can you be so *calm* about this?" Rhonda demanded.

"I ain't calm," Billy assured her. "I'm mad as hell, you wanna know the truth. But I ain't gonna punish them kids because they happened to fall in with a buncha ungrateful as. . . ."

"Billy Todd!" Emma scolded laughingly. "That's quite enough!"

"Yes'm," Billy nodded, grinning unrepentantly. "Anyway, give'em time to get cleaned up, and get fed. They might feel better after that."

"I don't care how they feel, they are *not* staying here!" Rhonda fumed.

"Wasn't you givin' me the evil eye earlier on account o' you had decided I *wasn't* gonna let'em stay here?"

"That was different!" Rhonda shot back. "That was before they. . . ."

"Bad mouthed me?" Billy asked.

"Yes," Rhonda hissed.

"It's okay, Rhonda," Billy put an arm around her and drew her to him. "Let'em eat, and then they can get gone."

"Fine."

It was perhaps and hour later that a shame faced Harry March approached, his wife Bethany, and Cora Williams following. Fred Williams stood back, arms crossed, a very determined look on his face.

"Uh, Mister Todd?" Harry said haltingly. "I think we owe you an apology for earlier. We were just. . .well, that man has terrorized us for months. I can't say that's excuse for us to take it out on you, especially considering how good you've been to us today. We're heartily sorry."

"We really are," Cora added, and Bethany nodded her agreement. "I hope you can forgive us."

"Reckon I can," Billy shrugged.

"*Not likely,*" Rhonda hissed at the same time. They looked at each other.

"Rhonda, they been through a rough patch. Reckon it ain't right to hold a grudge," Billy said easily.

"There's no excuse for what they did," Rhonda insisted. "I want them off this farm, and I mean *right now!*" Billy studied her for a moment, then nodded.

"Okay," he agreed. He looked back to the three newcomers.

"Reckon you folks better go," he ordered. "I'm sure the others have made arrangements for ya. Better see what they are." The three of them scuttled away, passing Fred Williams on the way. Billy looked at the other man, and Williams caught his eye, nodded in thanks, and then moved to follow his wife and the others.

"Well, guess they're goin'," Billy said to Rhonda.

"And not a moment too soon, neither!" Rhonda was still angry, and she didn't plan on getting over it any time soon.

"Rhonda, they're leavin'," Billy told her. "Let it go."

"When they're gone, I'll think about it," she groused. "Let's go see what they're gonna do."

George was explaining their options when Billy and Rhonda walked up.

"Like I said, the decisions are yours to make," George was saying to the twins. "If you two want to take the children, and take up residence in the Clifton Home, Regina is in charge of the Home, and you'll work for her."

The two sisters looked at each other, apparently communicating silently. Each nodded to the other as the same time, and both turned to George as if on command. It was a little creepy, Billy thought. *Must be a twin thing*, he decided.

"We will go to the Clifton Home," they announced as one.

"Another set of twins," Regina shook her head. "Welcome to Clifton House, then," she smiled. "I think you'll like it just fine. Let's gather the children up, and get started. We'll need to get them squared away and let them rest. It's a good walk."

"I'll carry you up there in the truck, Regina," Rhonda volunteered. "Mary and I can see about clothes and such."

"We'll help, too," Emma said, looking at Shelly. Her daughter nodded at once.

"Why don't we go ahead and try to find them some clothes, and some personal items, and then we'll head on up," Rhonda decided. "I've got some stuff that might work in that trailer," she pointed to one of the U-Haul trailers. "Let's see what's there."

Rhonda had gotten Mary and Danny to help her rework the things she and Billy had collected over the first months after the plague. She had wisely moved an assortment of clothes and personal items to this one trailer, to avoid allowing anyone to know just how much she and Billy had. At her wave, the women herded the newly arrived children in that direction. George watched them go, then turned back to the others.

"Well, that leaves the rest of you. What do you want to do?"

"We'd like to stay, if there's a farm we can work," Fred stated. "I don't have any tools or. . .well, I don't have anything but the clothes on my back," he admitted. "But if you can loan me a few things, I can at least make a start."

"We can do that," George assured him. "And there should be some tools left at the Crowder's. You can take their place. It's cleaned out, if you know what I mean, but you'll have to clean it up good. What about you folks?" he turned to the March's.

"I. . .we don't know," Harry admitted. "We need another few minutes to talk it over." George nodded, and the two withdrew. He looked at the last member of the party, a tall rangy looking man whose features were pinched, and not a little suspicious looking. His name was Murphy.

"Well, Murphy, what do you think?" George asked. He tried to be nice, but this man gave off a bad vibe to George. He didn't like that.

"Well, I ain't no farmer," Murphy admitted. "I don't mind workin', just don't know how. I'll try, but somebody'll have to show me what I need to know."

The others thought about that. The truth was, no one wanted the man around, but he hadn't done anything that rated being kicked out.

"I could stay up at that orphanage you got," Murphy smiled. "Help them out with stuff that's heavy and what not. Long as they can show me what to do."

Billy's hair tingled at that. Suddenly he knew what Murphy was. He realized why he didn't like the look of the man. Murphy was a predator. With the other two gone, he thought he was free to roam, now.

This presented a problem for Billy. He didn't want Murphy anywhere near anyone in the valley. Period. But he also didn't want to let Murphy go his way. No telling what the man might do to others he might come across.

"The Clifton Farm is well looked after," Jerry Silvers announced in a voice that said, he, too, recognized the man for what he was.

"Just offering," Murphy shrugged. "What else can I do?"

"You sure you wanna stay on here?" Billy asked blandly. "Ain't no law says you got to, I mean. You're a free man. Go where ya like."

"Sure, I do. Ya'll got a good place here. I'd love to stay here with you." Murphy grinned, and just then his eyes darted toward the collection of children and women at the trailer. Billy's hand drifted toward his side of it's own volition.

"Well, reckon I know a place that'd suit ya," he said easily. "Hafta drive ya up there. It's not too far, and we can get ya a horse, tomorrow or so. It's a small house, got two bedrooms, and a good well. Interested?"

"Hate to be so far away, but other than that it sounds good," Murphy nodded reluctantly, casting another furtive glance at the women and children.

"Well, how 'bout I carry ya up there, and let them settle the others. That sound okay?"

"Sure, friend," Murphy nodded, licking his lips in a nervous manner. "I sure appreciate it."

"No problem," Billy smiled.

"I'll ride up there too," Pete offered suddenly. Billy looked at his friend sharply, but Pete's face was a mask of innocence.

"Well, let me get you a bed roll, and you fix you up a couple meals, then, and we'll head out," Billy nodded. He started off toward the barn, while Murphy went eagerly to the table.

"Wait a minute, Billy, I'll help ya!" Pete called, and set off after his friend. Billy waited, reluctantly, until Pete had caught up.

"What are you thinking, Billy?" Pete asked at once.

"I'm thinkin' I can carry him up there all by my lonesome," Billy tried not to growl. Pete snorted.

"That's not what I meant. I meant what are you thinking about *him*," he nodded back at Murphy. Billy gave Pete a long look, as if weighing what he should say. He seemed to come to a decision suddenly.

"I'm thinkin' we don't need the likes o' him around here," Billy replied. "He smells. Makes me feel like I need a shower just talkin' to him."

"Yeah, I thought that too," Pete nodded. "If he ain't a predator of some kind, I'll eat my shoes."

"I don't aim to let him stay here," Billy declared openly. Pete looked at him.

"Be a risk to just run him off," he said evenly.

"It would," Billy nodded.

"Folks might wonder where he got to," Pete mused.

"Might."

"Billy, I don't know if I'm comfortable with this," Pete admitted.

"Didn't ask you to come along," Billy replied flatly. Pete was taken aback by that. And by the tone of Billy's voice.

"You're sure this is what you want to do?" Pete asked, uneasy.

"I don't want to, no," Billy admitted. "But he's a risk I don't aim to take. Period. You ain't got to go. Just act like you changed your mind. No problem. And keep your mouth shut." Pete looked at his friend as if seeing him for the first time.

"Billy. . . ."

"It's your choice," Billy cut Pete off. "You want to go, you can. You want to stay, that's fine. But he's not gonna stay here. Come tomorrow he won't be anywhere he can hurt anybody."

"We don't know for sure he will hurt anybody," Pete pointed out.

"I know what he is," Billy said stubbornly, "and so do you."

"Let's ask Fred about him, before we make a decision," Pete temporized.

"I already made my decision," Billy shook his head. "You want to go talk to Fred, you go right ahead. I got stuff to do." With that Billy turned and headed toward the barn. Pete watched him go, dumbfounded.

This is not good, he thought to himself. *I better talk to Fred pretty quick.*

-

"Well, there was always talk, you know," Fred said quietly, looking at Murphy. "But as far as I know, that's all it was. Talk."

"But you don't like him," Pete pressed.

"I never have," Fred admitted. "He pays too much attention to things he shouldn't, if you know what I mean."

"Why did you bring him with you?" Pete asked.

"Wasn't my decision," Fred shrugged. "Todd took a liking to him, and brought him along. No one could stop him."

"What was he like while you were on the road?"

"He was always looking at the Beal sisters like he was hungry, and they was lunch."

"He never tried anything with them?"

"No, Todd wouldn't allow anything like that," Fred admitted grudgingly. "He was a son-of-a-bitch, but he wasn't like that at all. He would probably have killed Murphy if he'd tried anything."

"Did he pay any attention to your wife, or Mrs March?" Pete asked. He had an uneasy feeling in his stomach. The Beal sisters couldn't have been much older than sixteen, and Murphy was well into his forties.

"No, but he did pay far more attention than was called for to two of the older girls," he nodded to a pair of girls in the group by the trailer. "Look, I don't want to do or say anything that would get us kicked out of here, but I wouldn't trust him as far as I could throw him. Period."

"Just keep this between us," Pete nodded. "I think we'll just encourage Mister Murphy to find his way somewhere else."

"Just be careful," Fred warned. "He's a snake."

"No problem."

-

"Feel better now that you're all cleaned up and fed?" Billy asked, as Murphy

Odd Billy Todd

walked toward his truck.

"I admit I do," the other man nodded. "Where's your friend?" he asked, looking around.

"May have changed his mind," Billy shrugged, hoping that Pete had done just that. "I don't aim to wait for him, either, you don't mind. We'll get you set up, and then it's been a long day. I'd like to get back, and cleaned up." He waved at Rhonda as she went to the Ford to get ready to carry everyone to the Clifton Home. Murphy turned to look, and Billy noticed how the man's eyes devoured Rhonda's petite form as she walked. He was smiling when he turned around, and Billy's face was bland as ever.

"Right nice little gal you got there," Murphy smiled, but the look didn't reach his eyes.

"Yeah, she is," Billy smiled. "Thanks."

"We ready to go?" Pete walked up. Billy didn't curse, but he wanted to.

"Reckon so," he said instead. "Climb in Mister Murphy. Let's get you put in the right spot. You got to be tired."

"I sure am," Murphy nodded, looking nervously from one man to the other. He seemed reluctant to climb into the truck, but could see no way to avoid it. He eased into the cab, and found the other two men on either side of him.

"Here we go."

-

The man called Murphy rode uncomfortably between the Idiot and the Indian, as he'd taken to calling them. They couldn't have three brain cells to rub together between the two of them. As he rode, he thought about his good fortune.

He'd been careful to keep his distance from Todd and his cohort, just in case something like this happened. He didn't want to be seen as too friendly to them, so that if something like what happened today came along, he'd be able to ride into a new place, just like this.

And what a place! Food, water, women, everything a man could want, right here. He cursed his luck again at the Idiot having stuck him so far away from the others, especially those Beal twins, and the little blond they were so fond of. But, if he worked it just right, this might be better. They'd be hard pressed to prove he'd done anything, and him so far away.

And that little redhead! True, she was a little older than he liked'em, but man, what a morsel. He'd definitely enjoy time spent with her. Served the Idiot right, too. Sticking him way over in the woods like this.

"How much further?" he asked, trying to keep his voice interested and hopeful.

"We're here," Billy told him, turning into a dark drive. It was past dusk, by now. The head lights showed a small, rundown house with a wildly overgrown yard.

"I know it don't look like much in the dark, but it's a pretty nice place," Billy promised. "And she's in real good shape, too." The three men got out of the truck, and Billy picked up a battery lantern, switching it on. He handed it to Pete, and took out the roll of blankets.

"Long way from everybody else," Murphy lamented. "But it's sure nice. Reckon I'll need that horse if I aim to visit any." He was about to say something else when he felt an arm snake around his neck. Before he could react, a sharp pain hit him beneath his shoulder blades. He felt weak, suddenly.

"You didn't really think we'd turn you loose around our women and children, did you?" he heard Billy Todd's soft voice in his ear. Murphy tried to speak, but no words would come. His last thought was ironic.

But he's just an idiot.

"Well, that's that," Billy said evenly as he put the last shovel of dirt over the late Mister Murphy. "And good riddance to bad rubbish, as my Pa used to say."

"You were right," Pete nodded. "Fred had nothing but bad things to say about him."

"Well, let's get the hell outta here," Billy stated. They had put Murphy across the old road from the house.

No sense messin' up a good house place with a good well, Billy had shrugged, when Pete had asked him why. Pete had seen a new side of Billy tonight. He wasn't sure what to make of it yet.

"How do you feel, Billy?" he asked cautiously.

"Better," Billy said firmly. "He looked at Rhonda like a wolf looks at sheep. That was enough for me to kill 'im right there. But the way he looked at those girls. . . ." Billy shook his head, as if to clear his anger away. "He had to go."

"That doesn't make it any easier to do," Pete said softly.

"I told you ya didn't have to come," Billy reminded him.

"That's not what I meant," Pete shot back. "I've killed many a man, Billy, but in combat. Self-defense. This was. . .different."

"You're right," Billy nodded. "He wasn't no soldier. He was vermin. You don't give a wolf that's chasin' your stock a chance to bite you. You kill it, and be done with it. I ain't by nature a violent man, but I reckon I know what's got to be done, and do it. This here? This had to be done."

"I couldn't live with myself if he stayed here, and hurt somebody. And I couldn't live with turnin' im loose, neither. He mighta brought somebody else down on us, or hurt someone else down the road. This here was for the best, no matter how bad it seems tonight."

"You're right," Pete nodded firmly. "Just seems. . .wrong, somehow, killin' a man without even a trial. I don't know if I'll sleep tonight."

"I will," was all Billy said. The rest of the trip was made in silence.

CHAPTER SIXTY-THREE

It was three days before anyone asked after Murphy. Billy kept it simple.

"He didn't like it," he shrugged. "Said he'd take his chances somewhere else. We got him up an outfit, and he was gonna head out the next day."

"Funny. He seemed like he liked it here," Jerry observed, rubbing his chin. "Well, no accountin' for folks, I guess." Terry Blaine said nothing until they were alone, then eased up to Billy.

"We need to talk," he said quietly. Billy nodded, and the two of them walked out to Billy's barn.

"Where's Murphy?" Blaine asked, his voice edgy.

"Don't rightly know," Billy shrugged. "Ain't seen him since he settled in over yonder. Thought he'd stay. Seemed to like the place, 'cept for it bein' so far from the rest of us."

"And you don't have any idea where he went?" Blaine's face was red. Angry.

"Ain't none o' my business, I reckon."

"Dammit, Billy, if he lit out, he might lead a bunch right back down on us!" Terry exclaimed. "We'll have to set extra posts now, and be on the lookout!"

Billy looked at the older man, and weighed his options. He couldn't allow extra people to be out all the time. Everyone would be tired, and work would stretch them thin. Plus, he didn't want Terry to be worried about Murphy coming to call with bandits.

"He won't be doin' that, Terry," Billy said softly, cutting into Blaine's worried mutters.

"What?"

"I said Murphy won't be bringin' nobody back. He won't be comin' back neither."

"What the hell does that mean?" Blaine demanded. "If he decides to. . . ." he trailed off. "Oh," he said finally. He looked at Billy for a minute, then sat down on the bench outside Billy's barn.

"Care to tell me what happened?" he asked.

"He didn't belong here," Billy shrugged. "He was a bad man. He was lookin' at them girls all wrong. He had to go." Billy's statement was simple. Factual.

"And you just decided all on your own to get rid of him?" Terry asked.

"Yep," Billy nodded. "Like I said, he was a dangerous and low-down feller. He ain't got no business 'round these women and kids. Period."

"Billy, don't you think that's something we should all have a say in?"

"Say anything you like," Billy shrugged. "You want to be around somebody like that, have them around your wife and young'uns, go right ahead. Only it won't be here, on account o' ain't nobody like that ever gonna live in this valley. *Ever*."

"You know Billy, the rest of us deserve a say in things like that."

"So, have your say," Billy shrugged again. "I ain't stoppin' ya. Wouldn't if I could. But rest of ya or not, ain't no animal like that gonna be 'round Rhonda and the girl. And I don't care who says otherwise."

"Billy, you just can't do things like that," Terry's voice was an urgent hiss.

"What if people find out?"

"They won't less you or Pete tell'em, so that's up to you." Billy looked the older man in the eye. "But I'm tellin' you, one more time. Any predator like that comes into this valley won't be leavin'. You can all take a vote, draw numbers, throw chicken bones for all I care. But in the end, I'll still make sure that nobody like that ever gets near the women and kids in this valley. No matter what."

Terry studied Billy for a long time, during which he didn't see Billy blink even once. Or ever even offer to look away. He simply looked back. Waiting.

Where does he get that patience? Terry wondered. *Anyone else would have looked away by now, but not him.* He studied the young man in front of him again. Cold, calm, reasoning.

"Billy, I don't know what to say," Blaine finally admitted.

"Then don't say nothin'," Billy told him flatly. "'Cept just what I said. Murphy decided to move on. And he ain't comin' back."

"Others might ask questions."

"Might," Billy nodded. "Don't mean we'll have answers. Can't be making excuses for someone we don't know that well. He decided to see what was over the next hill. Leave it at that."

Finally, Terry nodded. There really wasn't much else to do. Or say.

"So where you headed?" Terry asked, nodding to where Rommel waited by the Ford. The truck door was open, and he could see Billy's rifle inside.

"Takin' a ride," Billy shrugged. "We got to do somethin' 'bout how easy it is to find us. I ain't sure what, just yet. Gotta get out'n take a look. See under the hood."

"What do you mean?" Terry asked.

"We got to *hide*," Billy stressed. "We hadn't been watchin', Howie hadn't warned us, that whole bunch would o' been in our lap 'fore we knowed what was happenin'. We can't take that chance, not no more. We got ta hide. Anybody left from 'round these parts might know this place is here, but not many more do. We got to keep it that way."

"What do you figure to do about it?"

"Don't rightly know, yet," Billy admitted. "Why I'm goin' to look." Terry studied Billy a minute longer, then nodded.

"Mind if I ride with you?"

-

"Where are you going?" Rhonda asked, seeing Billy fixing a lunch.

"Think to Cedar Bend today," he answered. "We got to find a way to hide our road. Something that'll keep people from just walkin' right up on us. I can't figure that out until I go and look."

"You've seen it a million times," Rhonda told him.

"I ain't never looked at it like I was aimin' to hide it," he shook his head. "I'm gonna have to study on this. Don't do it right, it'll look wrong. Won't fool nobody."

"Can I come?" Rhonda asked.

"Terry's goin'," Billy told her.

"So?"

"Just wanted you to know. You wanna come with, you're welcome to. You know that." He punctuated that with a kiss. Rhonda smiled at him when they broke apart.

"I'll just get ready then."

"Okay."

They sat at the intersection where the road to the Farms hit the street into town. Billy was squatting on the ground, as he had been the last fifteen minutes, looking back up the road the way they had come, his face a mask of concentration. He had picked up two rocks, and was tumbling them together in his hand as he studied the road in front of them. Occasionally he would move a short distance, look around, then squat again, tumbling the rocks once more.

Terry and Rhonda stood a short distance away, keeping lookout. Rhonda sighed heavily for at least the fifth time in the last five minutes, but she said nothing. She knew that look. Billy would be done when he was done, and not until.

"You think highly of him don't you," Terry broke their silence.

"I love him," Rhonda said simply, shrugging.

"It shows," Terry smiled. "He's an unusual sort of man."

"One of a kind," Rhonda nodded firmly.

"He has a very direct way of looking at things," he added. Rhonda looked at him, then.

"Yes, he does."

"Is that always a good thing?" he asked. "For the two of you, I mean?"

"What are you really asking, Mister Blaine?" Rhonda demanded, her voice a bit sharper than she'd actually intended.

"Just making conversation," he held up his hands. "I know what it's like, being with someone who's so different from you. Maria and I grew up in totally different cultures. When we first got together, we struggled a lot, trying to be considerate of the others feelings. You two seem to be doing just fine, to me."

"We aren't as different as you think," Rhonda told him. "True, Billy has some learning issues, but his mind is sharper than most. Nothing gets by him, and I mean *nothing*. It's almost scary, sometimes, how much he *sees*. How often he's just instinctively right about something, or someone."

"I think part of that is the work his parent's put in raising him. He was never allowed to think of himself as helpless or disabled. They would explain to him how he could solve a problem, but they would never solve it for him. He had to do that on his own."

"He's a first-rate problem solver, that's for sure," Terry agreed, scanning the area around them again with binoculars.

The pair grew silent again, though Rhonda couldn't help but wonder what it was that Blaine was getting at. Her almost automatic defensiveness of Billy threatened to make her demand an answer, but after a moment, she decided that Blaine was just making conversation. Still, she decided to watch him a little closer for a while. Some instincts couldn't be repressed.

Suddenly Billy stood up, tossing the rocks back to the roadway.

"I've got it," he announced. "We can do this pretty easy," he added, walking toward them.

"What you got in mind?" Terry asked, eager to hear what Billy had come up with. All Terry had been able to think of was tearing out the road. And that wouldn't hide the fact that a road had once been there.

"We're gonna cover the road, from here to that hill," he pointed. "Then, we'll plant grass, and lay down just a little gravel, here and there. Then, we add a gate, a cattle gate, 'bout halfway up. Once we take down all the road signs, it oughta look like it's just another pasture road. One we can still use," he added.

"If that don't look real enough, we'll get a house trailer, and pull in here. Make it look like it was a house place, sitting near the gate. That should do the trick."

Both Rhonda and Terry studied the layout trying to put Billy's idea into their thoughts. They looked each others way the same time, then back at Billy.

"That's a great idea," Terry nodded. "All I could think of was to tear out the road."

"Don't wanna do that," Billy shook his head. "Might need it."

Terry shook his head at Billy's long-sighted solution. He hadn't considered that at all.

"Sometimes you amaze me, Billy," was all he said. Billy blushed a little, but just shrugged.

"Well, now we got a plan, we can see about gettin' it done," he announced. "Ya'll ready to head back?"

-

"So there it is," Billy told the men who had assembled at his place to hear the plan. "We can do the same thing at the other end, 'cept that'll be easier. Road down toward the highway's got a field either side of it, so we just bury the road, and make it look like one big ole field."

"That sounds like quite a job," George noted. "Reckon how long it'll take?"

"Three, maybe four days on the road in town," Billy shrugged. "'Bout the same on the other end, although that'll be easier done."

"Any idea where we'll get the mobile home?" Ben asked.

"Used to be a dealer in Columbia. Reckon might be some still there," Jerry noted.

"You think?" This from Howie.

"Should be," Jerry nodded. "Ain't no idea what shape they'll be in nowdays."

"Well, so long as they're still sound, that's all we need," he shrugged.

"What you got in mind, Howie?" Pete asked.

"Well, for one thing, we could find a small one to use as our security shack. The one we're usin' now was just knocked together. And in the winter, it's cold. Plus, it would be nice to have a bedroom to sleep in, stead o' that cot."

"Makes sense," Jon agreed. "And I can get one in there, if we find one small enough."

"You know, what if we could find more than one?" Jerry mused. They all looked at him.

"Look, we can't keep spreadin' out like we have been," he pointed out. "If we grow much more, we're gonna need houses. We got couples already formin', and we got teenagers that ain't gonna stay teenagers for much longer. We're gonna have to have a place to put'em."

The others nodded at that. No one had really thought that far ahead, but it was an excellent point.

"If we're gonna set up places to live, we're gonna need to find septic tanks

Odd Billy Todd

for 'em," Billy pointed out. "Speakin' o' that, we need to find one o' them pump trucks that empty septic tanks when they git full."

Several men groaned at that.

"Every time we turn around, there's something else we need, or need to take care of," Terry shook his head in grim amusement. "I didn't work this hard in the Army. *Including* when I was in combat!"

"Ain't but another day on the farm to us," Toby grinned. "Always somethin' to be done round here!"

"Well, let's get to plannin' then," Terry grinned. "This is gonna take a good two to three weeks. Let's make sure we got everything nailed down. Less time we're exposed, the better."

—

They decided to make the trip into Columbia first. George drafted Williams and March to help, enlisting some of the ladies to assist their wives with tending to their gardens.

George, Ralph, Ben Kelvey, and Howie would stay behind along with Jerry to watch over the valley. The rest would make the trip into Columbia, hoping to be able to get everything they needed in one trip. One problem did emerge, though, as work assignments were set out.

"I ain't drivin' no big rig."

Billy's voice was calm, clear, and left no room for argument. The others looked at him.

"Billy, we ain't got that many people who can drive one," Terry pointed out. "If we're gonna make this in one trip, we'll need you to pull a trailer."

"No sir," Billy shook his head. "I ain't doin' it. Not again."

"C'mon, Billy," Pete urged. "This is all hands on deck. One trip and haul ass."

"I can drive a rig," Harry March spoke up. "Haven't in a few years, but I used to OTR back when I first got married. Me and Bethany worked together until she got in the family way. Decided to take regular jobs close to home after that."

"There ya go, then," Billy nodded. Terry sighed, but nodded.

"Okay, Harry. You're elected. I don't suppose Bethany still drives?"

"Oh, she didn't drive," Harry chuckled. "She just kept me company, and kept the books up. Sorry."

"No problem. Didn't hurt to ask. We'll take all three trucks, then. We're after mobile homes, and septic tanks. Billy, you may have to drive one of the flatbeds with the septic tanks. Okay?"

"Yeah," Billy nodded, unhappy but willing to compromise. "I reckon I can do that."

"Well, if you do that, then we should be able to pull three mobile homes. What else are we going to try and get?"

"Propane trucks, if there's any gas left," Billy spoke up. "Even one would go a long way. Doubt there'll be much gas left, but it's worth a look."

"Good idea," Jon nodded. "And we can always treat the gas, or diesel. For that matter, we can add the diesel to the bio fuel. Once it's mixed, should run just fine, no more than we'll need it."

"Well, that's our plan, then." Terry took charge. "Billy, you lead off, with Pete and Toby. Me, Jon, and Harry will follow in the trucks. Fred, you run shotgun with

Harry until we hit town. As it is, we can drive two more trucks back, whether it's fuel, or something else. I want to be on the road, and already through Cedar Bend by sun-up, so everybody get some rest. We'll meet at the crossroads in the morning around four. Any questions?" There were none.

"Then I suggest we head out, and get our chores done tonight." The meeting broke up, people heading back to their own places.

Billy started walking toward home from the Blaine house, thinking as he walked, Rommel pacing him. There was a lot to do. He already knew where he could get all the dirt they would need. They only had one dump truck, but he figured they could scare up another one, maybe two more, in town. There was a state garage just on the other side of town, and they hadn't even looked there. Might be a lot of other things they needed there too. Even a gas tank. He took out his notebook and made a note of that.

He made another note to take a look around Columbia again when they were in town. He had a phone book from there, so he could search the yellow pages and see if there were any places they hadn't already looked. Might not find anything, in fact he figured they wouldn't. But they wouldn't know until they looked. If they happened on a sewing store, they could take fabric, sewing machines, and what nots from there to bring back. He figured some of the women might like that. Rhonda was using Billy's mother's machine, and he knew Emma had one. He didn't know about the rest.

He added another note to check for rechargeable batteries, including car batteries, and especially deep cycle marine batteries. They were the best for the solar grids many of the homes were using. He paused for a minute, thinking about that. Rommel went on a few steps, then stopped, looking back.

Sooner or later, Billy knew, their power would give out. It would be a while, but there wasn't any real way to stop it. Batteries didn't last forever, and solar panels got broke sometimes. So, what if they used a big mobile home, one of those double wides, to make a sort of community work center? Sewing, canning, laundry, whatever would need power? There was no way to provide power to the homes the new people were using. None of them had solar cells, and there just weren't enough left to power even one home, let alone both. And there was nothing left for the newer homes, either.

He scribbled furiously in his notebook, writing down everything as fast as he could before he forgot it. Even as he wrote, there was something niggling at the back of his mind, but he couldn't quite get at it.

He scribbled another note to be on the lookout for a large diesel generator. If they could erect a building around it to muffle the noise, something like that could power his community work house with no trouble, and their bio diesel would power it just fine.

That made him think about all the chemicals Howie and Ralph and George needed for their bio-diesel, and where they might be found in Columbia. Which led him to the fact that they needed larger containers for their bio-diesel operation, or at least more like the one's they already had. More scribbling.

Still, there was something tickling his brain. Something he'd thought of for a brief instant, then forgotten. Of all the problems he had, that one caused him the most grief, usually. Having just a hint of a good idea, and then losing it before he could get it down on paper. It was frustrating no end to him. And there was nothing he could do about it, except concentrate and hope it came back to him.

He resumed walking, notebook still in hand.

Power, power, power. It had something to do with power. It was right there on the edge of his brain, but he still couldn't reach it. Power, power, power. Sure would be nice if they had a dam somewhere, generating. . . .

"That's it!" he said aloud, stopping short again, and writing furiously. Then he started walking again, a lot faster.

He needed to talk to Howie.

-

"You mean a waterbug?" Howie asked, trying to follow Billy's excited rambling.

"That's it!" Billy snapped, pointing a finger at Howie. "That's what I been tryin' to think of! Can you build one?"

"Well, sure," Howie nodded sitting back. "All you need is a. . .well, I'll be damned," he snorted. "Why in the hell didn't I think of that?"

"I dunno," Billy answered him without thinking. "But look, there's five good creeks crosses this valley, and there's at least four springs. Can't we make these bug whatsits, and use'em?"

"Water bugs," Howie grinned. "And yeah, we can. All we need is a barrel with some kind of coating that will make the water turn it, and a car alternator or generator for the wheel to turn. But there's something even better than that, Billy, if we can find a place for one."

"What? And what kinda place?" Billy wanted to know.

"A small hydro-electric generator. Water turns the blades just like on a big dam. The water has to be running down hill, though, and fairly fast. We divert the water through a tube, run it down the creek a piece, and then dump it right back into the same creek, only through that generator. It'll turn some power, and all we have to do when we're not using it is. . .well, shut it off."

"Can you build one o' them?" Billy asked.

"Well, I think so," Howie mused. "I know in principal how they work. It should just be a matter of finding the parts I'd need, and putting them together. I. . .I think maybe I should go along with you tomorrow."

"I think so, too," Billy nodded firmly. "You start makin' a list of what you think you need. Oh, and make a list o' them chemicals ya'll need for the bio diesel, too. And I got to go round up some more help." He started for the door, then stopped.

"And pack a sleepin' bag. Just in case."

-

"Well sure, I'll go," Rhonda nodded. "I'd love a chance to look for fabric and sewing machines, and what not."

"Just remember, this ain't like what we used to do, okay? This is for ever body."

"I know that," Rhonda agreed. "But I'm part of every body, too. And I might need something. It's a great idea, Billy. A place like that will be great!"

"Well, we ain't got it yet, but I'm hopin'," Billy told her. "Even if I have to drive one o' them durn big rigs. Be worth it for this."

"Who else can we get to go, you reckon?"

"You bet!" Shelly said at once. "I'm game for it. I'd settle for seeing a ghost town after this winter."

"Might be just that, just so's ya know," Billy warned. "It'll be hard work, but worth it, I hope."

"Sounds like it," she nodded. "We can look for any kind of canning supplies that are left, too," she added. "Especially lids and rings."

"Good idea," Rhonda nodded.

"We're gonna need more help," Billy said, shaking his head.

"Leave that to us."

CHAPTER SIXTY-FOUR

-

"What are they doing here?" Terry asked, seeing Rhonda, Shelly, Howie, Amy, and Ruth Townsend. They were all piled into the Ford, while Billy was driving his own truck.

"They got things to see to in town," Billy replied, and briefly explained. "Plus, Rhonda can drive a truck as good as any of us, happens we have more stuff than we hope."

"Billy, we already had this worked out," Terry sighed in exasperation. "Now that's all got to be - "

"No, it ain't," Billy shook his head. "Only thing that's changin' is Pete is goin' with them," he pointed to the Ford, where the women sat waiting. "Me and Toby'll take my truck and scout ahead." Terry was about to object when Billy added, "And I'll drive one o' the rigs."

"Deal," Terry said at once. Getting Billy to drive a truck was worth the extra work. "Well, have they got a plan made up?"

"We do," Rhonda called from the truck. "And time's a wastin'!"

"Fair enough," Terry called back, chuckling. "Let's head out!" Everyone piled into their respective vehicles. As Pete headed for the Ford, Billy grabbed his arm.

"Figured you'd feel better lookin' after her," he nodded toward Shelly.

"Thanks, Billy," Pete grinned. "And I won't have to work so hard as you will, neither."

"Just make sure nothin' happens to any of 'em," Billy told him.

"No doubt."

Five minutes later, they were on the road.

-

Once in Columbia, they separated. The trucks went to the mobile home yard first, since that was high on the list. Billy and Toby went in search of septic tanks. Rhonda and the others started looking for the stores they had picked out in the phone book.

"Why do we have to get the septic tanks," Toby made a face. He was driving, while Billy looked at the map he'd brought.

"They ain't used, Toby," Billy said dryly. "They're new. And we need 'em for the trailers."

"And a septic tank pumper," Toby's face screwed up even tighter. "That's got to be the nastiest job in the entire world."

"Well, I expect that's true," Billy nodded. "That reminds me," he said suddenly, taking out his notebook and writing something down.

"What's that?" Toby asked.

"We need to look for some activated charcoal," Billy told him. "Well, I guess regular charcoal would work in a pinch, but we need the other, if we can git it."

"What's it for?" Toby asked. "And what's the difference?"

"We can start re-pipin' the houses, and turn the washers, showers and sinks into a sump filled with sand, gravel, and charcoal. It'll filter the soap and what have you out, and let the water go back into the ground, 'stead o' in the septic. Make the tanks last longer. Speakin' o' tanks, be watchin' for old appliance places. We need some more o' them water heaters for the bio diesel outfit." He made another note. "And I ain't rightly sure what the difference is."

"Billy, how can you keep up with all that?"

"I write it down, that's how," Billy told him. "If I don't, I won't remember it passed the end o' my nose. If it gets that far." Toby laughed.

"You need to start payin' attention," Billy warned. "We don't know for sure ain't nobody else around." Toby sobered at once.

"I'm on it."

-

Billy kicked, cursed, spat and hissed as he worked on the loader. He had to get it running if they were going to load the three septic tanks he'd picked out. Without it, he didn't think they'd get them loaded. Right now, all he had to show for at least two hours of work was three busted knuckles and a bad temper.

"Billy, how we gonna haul these?" Toby asked suddenly. "And get'em unloaded."

"What's that?" Billy's head shot up. *Unloaded*?

For just a second, Billy stared at Toby as if he had two heads. Then he flew into another round of kicking and cussing.

"Dammit *all*! I never thought o' that! You see what I mean, Toby? I don't write things down, I don't think things through, I wind up screwin' up! How in the hell *are* we gonna get these cursed things off this truck? *Any* truck!"

"Uh, I don't know," Toby replied. "How?"

"I don't *know* how!" Billy almost yelled. "All this work, and I ain't got a damn *clue* how we gonna get this done!"

Silence reigned for a minute, as the two of them looked at each other. Billy looked at the sky, and shook his head.

"Already after noon, too," he muttered. Purely from reflex, Toby looked at his watch. Twenty-six minutes after high noon.

I really want to know how he does that.

"Reckon we'll just have to take this thing with us, someway," Toby announced at last.

"Right now, this thing ain't workin'!" Billy reminded him.

"It will be," Toby stated with absolute confidence. "You'll fix it."

-

And he did. He wasn't sure which 'fix' had made the difference, and honestly wasn't caring at that point. What he did know was that the thing ran.

"Now, we need a truck," Billy sighed. "I guess we need a good flatbed trailer. And some tie down straps, for sure. At least we don't have to carry this thing," he pointed.

"Why not?" Toby asked.

"I figured we could use the backhoe to unload it. Just need some chains and straps, and this place has got'em aplenty. We'll do that. Still need a truck though."

"Well, let's us eat, first," Toby suggested, breaking out the food they'd packed along. The two dug in, Billy especially hungry.

"Wha' we 'onna 'o now?" Toby asked over his sandwich.

"I ain't sure yet," Billy admitted, then took a long drink of cold water. "Reckon we'll have to get a truck runnin'. I hadn't thought about that. If we can, and get a trailer for it, that means the other three can haul back three o' them mobile homes."

"Sounds like a plan," Toby nodded. He finished, and stowed their gear as Billy cleaned up a bit.

Then they were off.

-

"Well, I'd say you found some things worth hauling, ladies," Pete grinned, as the four women stood inside a store called *Pat's Sewing World.*

"I'll say," Amy nodded. "It's like the owner just walked away, and no one came in after she left."

"Well, we can admire it later," Rhonda sighed, thinking of all the work. "Meanwhile, Pete why don't you get the trailer backed in for us. I know you two have things to do. We can load this."

"Okay," Pete nodded, and went to do as he was told.

"I used to come here all the time with my mom," Ruth Townsend sighed. "I always liked looking through the fabrics, and seeing the new machines."

"Well, you can pick yourself out a machine, now," Shelly told her. "In fact, let's all get to work. I don't know about you girls, but I don't want to be here any longer than I have to."

"I heard that."

Pete came back in, having arranged the trailer for them.

"I want one of you watching all the time," he ordered. "I know it's a hassle, but we can't be too careful. Make sure you all get your gear, so you'll have it with you. Just in case." The women trooped outside dutifully and collected their 'kit', as Pete often called it. Ruth had a pistol, but hadn't brought a rifle. Instead she's opted for a shotgun. She hadn't mastered rifle shooting yet, but with a shotgun she did just fine.

"All right, Howie, let's see if we can find what you need."

"Ready to go," Howie smiled. The two piled into the Ford, and took off, searching for the parts and pieces he needed to build his projects.

Shelly watched Pete drive off, and sighed.

"Pretty serious, huh?" Rhonda asked softly.

"Yeah," Shelly admitted. "It just. . .sometimes I wonder if there's a point."

"What d'you mean?" Rhonda asked, packing a plastic tub with thread.

"Well, he's always goin' off on one of these 'trips' for one thing," Shelly noted. There was no complaint in her voice, just worry. "I. . .I try not to worry, but it's hard, y'know?"

"Sister do I," Rhonda chuckled, though without much humor. "Billy's always got somewhere he 'needs' to go, or something he 'needs' to get. I'd like to say it gets easier to watch him drive or ride off, but honey that'd be a lie."

"Pretty much what I figured," Shelly nodded. "We both want a family you know, but. . .I swear, Rhonda, with the world like it is, how responsible is it to bring a child into the world?"

"Good point," Rhonda conceded.

"What about you and Billy?" Shelly asked. "You two ever talk about havin' kids?"

"Not so far," Rhonda shook her head. "Really ain't been a time for it. And we've got Danny and Mary to look after."

"Hey, built in baby sitters," Ruth mentioned from across the room.

"Don't knock that, either," Amy chimed in. "It's nice to have someone who can watch after a little one for you."

"Well, I don't think they'd appreciate that too much," Rhonda laughed. "But it's something to keep in mind. I wouldn't mind a baby or two, in all honesty. But we're both young. And there's either gonna be time, or there ain't. Can't see any need to rush things. Once things are more settled, we'll see, I guess."

"Yeah," Shelly nodded. "I think if we could establish a more stable way of life, once we do, I mean, having kids might be more comforting than worrisome. Have to see what happens I guess." She was looking out the window, taking her turn at guard duty.

"I think if Billy get's his community service center going, and it works out, then we can see about building a real community center," Rhonda noted. "Somewhere we can all gather to eat, play, and what have you. I'm gonna press him for something like that, anyway. We all need a place other than someone's home. A place where there's more room, and its neutral ground, you know?"

"I'd like that," Amy nodded. "We'd love to have a place to throw a dinner, or a party. We just don't have the room!"

"Not many do," Shelly agreed. "Having a good-sized place to gather would help us all."

"I can get behind that," Ruth spoke up. "With so many kids around, it's not possible, really, to have any kind of grown up fun. Maybe have a night off, play cards, something like that." The other women looked at her, then, and she grew a little uneasy.

"What?" she asked.

"I hadn't thought about you guys up there with the kids all the time in that way," Shelly answered for the rest. "I mean, no matter what the weather is, or anything else, you've got a whole house full of kids to see after. And that's a job that never goes away, and can't be put off."

"Tell me about it," Ruth laughed.

"No, I don't think that's what she's getting at," Amy was catching on. "It's not right for you guys not to get a day off, now and again. We need to do something about that."

"Like what?" Ruth raised her hands. "Like she said, it's got to be done."

"But not by the same people, day in and day out," Amy shook her head. "All of us manage a day here and there. I mean, sure, there's always housework and cooking and cleaning, no matter what. But we'd have to do that anyway, even if the world wasn't upside down."

"Yeah," Rhonda nodded. "Maybe we can form a posse of sorts," she smiled. "Two of us come up there once a week, and let two of you have a day off. Wouldn't do to take all of you away from the kids every day, but we could spare two of you for a day, and let the others show us what to do."

"Exactly," Amy nodded firmly. "Those with kids can bring'em along! Heck, Amanda stays up there about half the time anyway."

"Well, yeah," Ruth nodded. "And she's a big help, too, by the way."

"I'm glad," Amy smiled. "Anyway, when we get back, we need to sit down and make up a schedule. We can work this out."

Heads nodded all over, as they got back to work.

-

"Well, this is a great start," Howie nodded. "But we're almost out of room."

"We can pile it a little higher," Pete shrugged. "Just have to be careful."

"We can make another trip, too," Howie suggested. "There's a lot of good stuff still laying around. Things I can use to make other things we need. Heck, we can build a windmill, even!"

"We'll have to see about that," Pete cautioned. "We can't just up and come up here anytime. And we can't come up here alone, either. Too much can happen."

"Yeah, I know. But another good trip and we can collect enough stuff to really make a difference. Heck, we can make stuff to trade and sell, too!" Howie's enthusiasm was growing.

"Like I said, we'll have to talk it over as a group," Pete replied. "But I think it's a good idea. Still, for today, let's just concentrate on what we need to get by."

"Okay," Howie agreed. "We still need to check the chemical place," he said, looking at his list. "We need some ingredients for the bio diesel set-up."

"Well, let's get on that."

-

Terry Blaine resisted the urge to scream curses at the sky. It wouldn't help, and might attract attention.

Not that we need any help attracting attention, he sighed. *We're making enough noise to raise the dead.*

"I think we've about got it," Jon announced.

"This time?" Terry asked.

"Hey, none of us have ever done this," Jon shot back. "And I ain't seen you helpin' any. You ain't got nothin' constructive to add, then I'd just as soon you stayed quiet." Terry bristled at that, but then cooled. Jon was right.

"Sorry," he murmured. "I'd just like *something* to go right."

"You and me both," Jon agreed, mollified. "And it may have. I think we've got the fifth wheels fixed. We're gonna try to pull one, and see what happens. If it holds, then we can rig the others the same way. And then get the hell outta here."

"Suits me," Terry nodded. Jon turned and gave the wind-up signal to March, who was already in his truck, engine idling. He waved back, and eased the truck into motion. There was a lot of creaking and groaning, but the truck gradually eased the trailer out of the lot, and started down the drive. After one hundred yards, he pulled to a stop.

"Well, I think that's got it," Jon sighed gratefully. "Now we can get the other two hooked up." With that, he went back to work.

-

"I don't think this will hold all three, Billy," Toby shook his head.

"Probably not," Billy agreed. "But I've got it runnin', and it'll hold at least two. And that's all we need, for now. Let's head back. We still got to get loaded."

Toby trailed Billy back to the site, and they set to work. Sooner than Toby would have imagined possible, Billy had two of the large septic tanks loaded. It took far longer to properly strap the tanks down than it had to load them. By the time they had finished, an hour had passed, and both were wringing wet with sweat.

"I can't believe we finally got everything loaded," Amy was almost breathless as she spoke. She took a long drink of water. "And the trailer's only maybe two thirds full!"

"Proper packing," Rhonda said, drinking from her own water bottle. "Now, as soon as the boys get back, maybe we can go find some canning lids and rings."

"There's a possibility that Mister Hanson's store has some. He always kept those things on the shelf, year round," Ruth Townsend added. "It's only a few blocks that way," she pointed east.

"We could walk over," Amy suggested.

"No way," Shelly and Rhonda spoke at the same time. "We have to stay together," Rhonda went on. "And where we're supposed to be. That's the most important thing when we're out like this. No one goes off on a tangent. We stick to the plan, period."

"Okay," Amy raised her hands. "Just an idea."

"And normally a good one," Rhonda nodded. "But this ain't normal times. So, we sit tight."

Since Billy didn't know where the women were, he drove to the mobile home place. He was pleasantly surprised to see all three trucks ready to go, two pulling the sides of a double wide trailer, another pulling a small two-bedroom single wide.

"I see you found some septic tanks," Terry grinned.

"Yeah, several of 'em. Can't find a bigger trailer though, so this'll have to do, today," he nodded at the small flatbed.

"We'll take it," Terry nodded. "Nothin' has gone right for us, much either. Jon did make it work, though."

"We ready to roll?" Billy asked.

"Soon as the others get here."

"Do we know where they are?" Toby asked. He was driving Billy's truck.

"Nope," Terry shook his head. "And I don't like that, either."

Well," Billy looked skyward, "they still got about a hour and a half 'fore they're s'posed to meet us here. We'll wait for 'em. After that, we'll have to go lookin'." Terry looked at his watch.

"Don't bother," Toby told him. "He's within fifteen minutes, or the next one's free," he snorted. Sure enough, the others still had just over ninety minutes.

"How the hell do you do that?" Terry asked, not for the first time.

"I don't know, I just do," Billy shrugged. He had grown passed being irritated when someone demanded how he could always tell what time it was. And he *didn't* know.

"Well, I guess we'll wait, then," Jon sat back against one of the trailer wheels. "So, what all trouble did you two have?"

"Okay, that's it," Pete said. "This truck is over full. Time to get back to the women folk."

"Okay by me," Howie nodded. "I think I got more'n enough to get started on, anyway." The two men hopped in the Ford, and ten minutes later were back to the

Odd Billy Todd

fabric store.

"One more stop to make," Rhonda said as Pete hooked up the trailer.

"Where?" he asked.

"There's a small store a few blocks that way that Ruth thinks might have some canning rings, and lids. If they do, we need 'em."

"Do we *need them*, need them, or just *want them* need them?" Pete asked.

"You wanna eat this winter?" Shelly demanded.

"Of course, I do!" he replied.

"Then we *need 'em*, need 'em," she teased. "Got it?"

"I got it," Pete sighed. "Well, get in. We ain't got all day!"

It was indeed only a few blocks to the store. It was a small operation, and according to the sign it had been in continuous family owned operation 'since 1952'.

"I guess it's out of operation now," Pete said softly. "Wait here," he ordered, and went inside to check the place out. He was gone less than five minutes.

"Looks okay. Rhonda, you're on guard inside. I'll watch here. Howie, you help them, will ya? Let's try and get done soon as we can. We're runnin' out of time," he added, looking at his watch.

The others trooped inside, and were some exiting with boxes. Shelly took a long look at the trailer.

"What is it?" Pete asked.

"We found a lot o' jars, too," she told him. "We're gonna try to get all of 'em. Just lookin' at what room is available." The work went fairly quickly, considering how tired everyone was starting to get. The jars took the longest, since they had be secured against breaking on the trip back. Shelly and Amy re-worked the load twice, but finally gave up. There was simply no way to get them all in the trailer.

"We're going to have to leave some of them," Shelly told Rhonda. "I just can't see a way to get them all in the trailer."

"No problem," Rhonda nodded. "We'll put them in the truck. We can ride on the sideboards, or on top of that crap those two brought back. We ain't goin' far till we meet up with the others. We can split up, ride in the trucks. Fill the back seat to the top." Shelly nodded, and went to tell the others.

Finally, fifteen minutes after they should have been back, they were loaded.

Pete rolled the windows down, and everyone who had sat in the back stepped onto the sideboards. Finally, he and Shelly were in the front seat.

"Take it slow, cowboy," Rhonda teased. "Don't buck us off."

"Well, I'll try not," he grinned back. He eased the big truck around and started for the meet up.

-

"Okay, they're officially a half hour late," Terry complained. "We're gonna have to go and look for 'em, or risk calling on the radio."

"Wait," Billy shook his head.

"Billy, we're on a tight schedule here, and. . . ."

"Hush, and listen," Billy held up a hand. The others fell quiet, and Billy moved away from the now idling rigs. Suddenly, he smiled.

"I hear the Ford," he told them.

"How can you be sure it's not someone else?" Terry demanded, hefting his rifle.

"I know the sound of ever car and truck I've ever worked on," Billy told him. "That's our Ford." Terry was about to argue the point when the slow-moving Ford pulled into view, three women and one man hanging on the side.

"I'll be damned," Terry muttered.

"Nah, you're a pretty good guy," Toby slapped him on the back. "Just learn to trust the Boss. He won't say nothin', less he knows he's right." Terry shot the boy a stern look, but his eyes betrayed him. Toby snickered and went to meet the truck.

"We found a bunch of cannin' stuff," Rhonda announced. "Had to get as much as we could. Sorry we're late."

"No problem," Terry lied. "I guess some of you will be riding back in the rigs?"

"Looks like," she grinned.

"Works for me," he shrugged, then turned to Toby. "Looks like you and me on point, kid."

"Cool," Toby nodded, and went to Billy's truck.

"Everybody find a ride, and let's get going!" Terry ordered.

"Give you a lift, lady?" Billy asked Rhonda, grinning.

"If you want to eat tonight, you'd better," she shot back, smiling.

"Sounds like a good trade."

Everyone found a ride, and five minutes later, they were on their way home.

"You know, even though things haven't gone that well, it's still been a good trip, overall," Billy mused.

"Don't jinx it," Rhonda said sternly. "We ain't home yet."

CHAPTER SIXTY-FIVE

Things hadn't been idle on the Farms while the others were in Columbia. There was always work to be done, and with so many away, there was plenty to do.

Regina had decided to take the day away from Clifton House and help with the new arrivals gardening. She couldn't have done it with Ruth away, but the Beal girls were very capable. Leaving the house was a luxury she was rarely afforded, but she needed a break. No one could stand the strain of so many children day in and day out, around the clock, forever. She had allowed everyone else a day off here and there, but never herself. Today she decided she would get away for a while.

So she, Emma Silvers, with George and Debbie Purdy, went to the Williams house first, where Bethany March was already helping her friend get ready to plant. George had a tiller, and unloaded it while the women got acquainted, and decided what to plant first.

Elizabeth Kelvey, (she and Howie still weren't married in the eyes of man, but they were in God's eyes, she figured, and had adopted his name) manned the security station alone, which wasn't a problem. By now she knew everything as well as Howie did. She kept a close watch on everything.

Jerry, meanwhile, had taken a four-wheeler and some lunch, and his water jug, and was out surveying the fields. He would be gone a large part of the day, but had taken his rifle and pistol, and had a radio in case Elizabeth needed him for anything.

Ben Kelvey was staking out the sight of a new hay barn behind his place. They had decided after the rough winter they would need to bale and store much more hay. This layout was for the first of three new barns they hoped to get put up before winter. The only problem they could see would be finding sufficient tin for the roofs. That was one of the trades they hoped to make with the people in and around Franklin for beef on the hoof. They had plenty of housing in the area, and shouldn't need the tin, or many of the building supplies that might still be in Franklin. The Farms did.

Work was steady for everyone through the day. Once Jerry finished checking the fields, he rode over to see if he could help Ben. The gardening party finished at the Williams home, and made its way to the March place to start over. With so many working, it didn't take long to get both new places a good garden growing. Both women were assured that there would be plenty of food to keep them going until their garden began producing.

As they chatted, the women in particular worked out plans for future projects, one of which would be the grinding of the wheat crop that had been planted. Without the wheat, there wouldn't be much bread, so it was important. There was also one small corn field whose production was set aside for cornmeal. It wasn't large, just about ten acres, but it should provide enough ground corn for sufficient meal to get through the winter.

Beef, beans, and cornbread might well be a staple for some time to come, supplemented with corn and other veggies grown in their gardens. Anything that added variety to their winter fare would be welcome.

Ben and Jerry managed to stake out a second hay barn sight before calling it quits. They decided against worrying with another one as yet, since they still needed to build the first two. As always, you did what you could, while you could, and then came back later to do more.

All in all, it was very good day, and a great deal had been accomplished, with more plans made, when the convoy from Columbia pulled into the community, with perhaps an hour to go before dark.

Willing hands helped guide the trucks into a spot at the Clifton House near the barn, while the trailer was taken to Billy's for the time being. The women agreed to come and sift through it's content the next day, to divi up the spoils.

It was tired but pleased group of people who bedded down that night.

-

It took most of the next day to site the small trailer for the new security building. Elizabeth liked it, announcing that she and Howie could make do nicely with the small house. Putting down the septic tank would take a little longer, but by the end of the week, the two had all but moved into the small trailer, using one bedroom for the monitors, the other for themselves.

Howie decided to use the old 'shack' as his new shop, and was soon working on his projects. Billy often helped him, over the next two weeks, and the two made a good team. Soon, they were ready to start testing the water bugs, and Howie had sketched out a full fledged wind mill, with Billy's help.

Meanwhile, the double wide was stripped down, and turned into a community wide service center. One room was fixed as a laundry room, with three washing machines, and three dryers, although the dryers were only to be used in bad weather. A large, beefy clothes line was put up behind the place, for drying clothes in better weather. The kitchen was re-worked, three ranges, along with several sturdy home-made tables, for canning and preserving work. Billy's propane generator, the one he'd taken from in town, was hooked to the house. It would only be run when necessary. If more PV panels and equipment could be found or traded for, then they would be added to the center as well.

The trailer had been parked across the road from Billy and Rhonda's house, in an area carved out of some woods. A fire trail led to the open area, and grass was planted around the center, with the playground equipment left at Billy's moved there as well. All in all, after nearly a full week's work, if wasn't half bad, everyone agreed.

Soon it became a social spot, as the women began to make preparations for canning. The time was really flying, it seemed, with June in swing, and July on it's way.

That was when the men decided it was time to travel to Franklin.

-

"I just don't know," Jerry shook his head. "We haven't been in contact with anyone over there. We don't even know what shape the roads are in. For all we know, there's roadblocks all the way there and back."

"I'm afraid that's true," Ralph nodded. "But the only way to know is to go see."

"Why are we so hot to set up trade anyway, right now?" George asked. "We've been able to get a good bit of the stuff we want and need from Columbia, and from

Odd Billy Todd

Cedar Bend itself. Why take the risk of heading over that way? Things were bad when we left. How much worse could they have gotten by now?"

"Again, that's all true," Ben nodded. "And we can't know until we go see."

"My point is, why go see at all?" Jerry asked. "There's too little gain, and far too much to lose, if things are rough."

"Gotta agree with that," Terry nodded. "I'd like to know what's happening, just so we'd *know*. But I don't want to know so bad that we risk losing someone, whether it's on the way, or there in town."

"So we just sit here, and not try to open trade at all?" Howie asked. He had been working on things to make and trade with others. Things that others might need, and be willing to trade stuff he wanted. Ralph was the same way.

"Well, I don't want to isolate ourselves like that," Jerry sighed. "Sooner or later, we'll have to come out of hidin'. Or someone will bring us out, either way. But I do question whether this is the time, that's all. We're doing good, right now. Is it worth the risk? I think that's the bottom line, right there. Is the reward worth the risk?"

The others mulled that over in silence. Jerry had a point. They had to weigh the risk against anything else. It was Billy that spoke up first.

"We need a recon," he said simply. Everyone in the room looked at him.

"We do," he shrugged. "Instead o' worryin' about headin' over there with a trailer load o' cattle, or anything else, we need to just do a look see, and find out what the situation is. Maybe they need food, and maybe they don't. Them that's survived the winter is likely one of two things. Plantin' their asses off, or been livin' on others."

"We know that several small places has been either took over or maybe wiped out. We been willin' to blame the train for that, but fact is, we don't *know*. For all we know, Franklin is the home of whoever is doin' all that. See what I mean? We need to go and see under the hood, 'fore we go decidin' whether we even *want* to trade with'em."

"I think Billy's right," Terry sighed. He seemed to be saying that a lot these days. "We need to just go and have a look. That'll end all the speculation. We see what we can see, and then make our decision based on that."

"Who goes, and how do they get there?" George asked. "I'd say drivin' into town is out. That's gonna attract a lot of attention. By now, their fuel is probably low, or gone completely."

"We can take the Hummer you brought back," Terry shrugged. "It's armored. Even got a gun tub. We take three, maybe four at most. Hide the truck nearby, and recon on foot. Take three days or so, look the place over, maybe even go into town. Then we head back. The others can hear what's been found, and then we can make an informed decision. We can take a camera, even a video camera, just in case."

"I take it you're going?" George asked. Blaine nodded.

"I am. I want to see."

"Who would go with you?" Jerry asked.

"Anyone who wants to," George shrugged. "Pete, you wanna go?" he asked. Pete grinned.

"Sure, Kemosabe," he joked. "I ride with you to white-eye town." Everyone chuckled at that.

383

"Anyone else?" Terry asked. Billy looked at him, but stayed silent.

"I'll go," Toby raised his hand. "I mean, if you'll have me," he added.

"Toby," Jerry started, then stopped. His son was a grown man. He had to start letting him make his own choices. Even choices he didn't like.

"You do what I say, when I say, and no questions?" Terry asked.

"Yes sir," Toby nodded, solemn. He was scared, but not allowing that to make him stupid. Terry liked that. A man that wasn't scared doing something like this was a liability.

"Well, I guess that's that, then," Terry decided. "Let's go take a look at that Hummer. Maybe break out a fifty to go on it. George, I know you found a few."

"I did," his friend nodded, grinning. "C'mon, and let's get you fixed up." Pete looked at Billy.

"You wanna come, Billy?" he asked. Billy slowly shook his head.

"I don't think so," he replied. "I. . .I been goin' too much, here lately," he added. "Time I stayed home a while, and took care o' my farm." *And my family*, he didn't add. But he didn't have to.

"Appreciate it, you help George look after my Misses and the young ones while we're gone," Terry said quietly. Billy nodded.

"You can count on it, Terry."

-

Two days later, the three men piled into the Hummer, ready to make their reconnaissance. Pete took the back seat, where he could man the heavy machine gun if necessary. Toby pulled shotgun, with Terry driving. They had food and water for a week, and plenty of ammunition.

"I figure we'll take a day getting there, moving slow, and finding a place to hide the truck," Terry said. "Then, we'll spend three, maybe four days looking things over. After that, we'll head home by a different route, just in case."

"We'll use the radio sparingly, but we'll call once we're set up. You'll hear us say "Eyes to Base" and then we'll give you a report. No names, and no locations. Good enough?"

"Sounds like a plan," George nodded. Jerry looked at his son.

"Toby, you be careful, and do what Terry says, son."

"You know it, Pa," Toby smiled.

Pete and George took a few minutes to say good bye in private, and then the three of them were off. Jerry, George and Billy stood watching them out of sight, while Rhonda stood with a teary-eyed Shelly, and a very stoic Maria.

"They'll be back," Billy broke the silence, his voice confident.

"Sure," George agreed.

No one argued. No one wanted to.

-

Despite their worry, there was work to be done. Everyone drifted back home to get to it. Maria would be alone, but she'd been there before. And George and Billy would be looking in on her regularly.

The March's and Williams' had been informed of the trip as well, and they would be on the other side of Maria. Thinking about that, Billy had decided that it was time to take the new folks out to the range. Rather than use horses, he decided to just drive the Ford, Rhonda came with him. Before going, the two had ventured into the barn, and selected a few choices for the new folks.

Since all of them were either middle aged, or approaching it, Rhonda made sure to lay in a few revolvers, as well as two twenty-gauge shotguns for the women. Ruth Townsend carried one, and wouldn't have traded it for the finest rifle in the world.

The foursome readily agreed to the training day, and Billy stopped to drop the March kids off at home, admonishing Mary and Danny to keep an eye on the two boys.

The women were a bit squeamish at first, so Rhonda took them to the side to work with them. Billy took the two AR's the two men had taken from their dead 'friends' and looked at them.

"These things are about done in," he announced. "And they ain't user friendly, neither. Man usin' one o' these has got to know how to take care of it, and make sure the ammo is right, and so forth. I take it neither one o' you has ever used one?" Both men shook their heads.

"All right, then," Billy nodded. "Tell me what ya have used, and let's go from there."

-

It took a while, but by the time they left the gravel pit, all four were armed, and knew how to use their weapons. The women both elected to use the smaller shotguns, opting for small revolvers as a side arm. Rhonda agreed it was a good choice, as both would use them only in self defense.

The men had selected a pair of twelve-gauge weapons, Mossberg pump actions, and had likewise decided to go with revolvers as sidearms, albeit larger ones than their wives. They had each selected a simple hunting rifle as a long arm. Neither was proficient enough to handle anything more, and they were both good shots with the auto loading 30-.06 rifles they'd selected.

By the time they had returned everyone home, it was getting late, so the two of them rode over to the 'shack'. Howie was in his shop, and came out to meet them.

"Any word?" Billy asked. Howie shook his head.

"And I don't like that," he added. "I'd have thought they would have made it by now."

"Well, remember, Terry did say they wouldn't call until they were set-up. For all we know, they're there, and just haven't found a hidey hole just yet."

"True," Howie mused. "If it wasn't so far, I'd expect him to use his own place, really," he added. "It's got an underground garage. Well, the whole house is mostly underground, to be exact. Things built like a bomb shelter."

"Wonder he came here, then," Billy mused. "Sounds like he had a good set-up where he was."

"Oh, he did," Howie assured him. "I think he and Maria decided this was a better place for their kids than keeping them under ground."

"I can see that," Rhonda nodded. "And they're adorable." Just then Elizabeth came to the door.

"We just heard," she announced. "They're set up."

"He add anything else?" Billy asked.

"No. But he wouldn't have, unless it was important. He gave me a sheet of code words he would use, if he needed to relay anything important enough to risk the radio again."

"Well, sounds like they made it, and are okay, then," Howie let out a long breath. "Now, we just have to wait and see what they come up with."

"Well, I think we'll wait at home," Rhonda replied. "It's been a long day, and I need a shower. And I'm hungry."

—

The next day passed without event. Billy and Howie managed to get a working waterbug installed in a creek behind the shack. It was tedious going, but after three hours of work, Howie was satisfied it was going to work.

"How much power can this thing make?" Billy wanted to know, as the two of them rested, eating their lunch.

"Well, it depends," Howie replied. "On several things. First, how fast is the water moving. Second, how big the generator or, in this case, alternator, the bug can push. Another is how many batteries you can co-ax together, how many the generator or alternator can handle. And finally, how far you have to run the power. For every hundred feet or so of line, you lose some power."

"How much?" Billy asked.

"Depends on the line, the power source, there's a lotta variables," Howie told him. "But, so long as we can make them, and this proves we can, we're okay. There are a couple things we should try and come up with, though."

"Like what," Billy took out his notebook.

"Well, if we could find a place that used battery powered forklifts, or even better, that built them, we could take those batteries. They're pretty strong. Lot better than tying car batteries together. We could run two or three bugs like that one," he pointed to the creek, "to one of those, and probably keep it charged pretty good. I mean, it still won't be enough to run a whole house or anything, but it's a lot better than this little rig."

"But this is just a test, right?" Billy asked, clearly thinking ahead.

"Sure," Howie nodded. "I wanted to make sure I had my plan workin'. Now that I know, I can build as many of them as I can find parts for."

"Well, there's a ton o' cars settin' out there right now, all with batteries and alternators on'em," Billy pointed out. Howie grinned.

"Hadn't thought of that. Some of those batteries will be beyond saving, of course. But some will work, at least for a while. Even those that won't hold a charge will serve to pass the current from the alternator along the line. Not the ideal set-up, but it's doable."

"What will we do when the batteries run out?" Billy asked. Howie shook his head.

"I don't know, yet," he admitted. "I got a few ideas, but I haven't come up with anything that'll work so far. I'll keep at it, though," he added.

"You do that," Billy nodded. "We need to find a big ol' library, that's what we need to do."

"Huh?"

"A library," Billy repeated. "There's all kind's o' stuff in a library, Howie. Lotta information in them books. Seems like one of 'em would be able to show us how to build a battery. Even a big'un."

"Well, yeah!" Howie started getting excited. "It would. Even better might be a college library!"

"Just so happens there's a community college in Columbia," Billy mused.

"And they probably had a public library, being a pretty good sized town," Howie added.

"We, Rhonda and me, took a lot of books from the little library in Cedar Bend, but it was mostly stock books and the like. Might be we could find somethin' there, was we to look."

"Sounds like a good place to start," Howie nodded in agreement.

"We'll head in, once Terry and them git back," Billy promised. "Meanwhile, we can keep workin' on these," he pointed to the creek. "If nothin' else, we can use'em to power cameras and motion sensors near creeks and the like."

"Good idea. Let's get back to the shop. I need to sketch up my idea for the lift batteries anyway. Before I forget it," he added sheepishly.

"Good plan," Billy agreed.

They worked for another four hours, stopping once in a while to discuss things. Howie knew that Billy had some disabilities, but for the life of him, he couldn't see them. Billy's mind was sharp. He knew what he knew, but more important, he knew what he *didn't* know, and that wasn't always the case.

He figured he and Billy could keep the Farms going for a good long while, together.

-

"*Billy, George, there's a vehicle coming in the back way.*"

Billy sat up straight from where he'd been lounging in his living room. He picked up his radio.

"Just one?"

"*All we can see,*" Howie replied. "*Light's on, no attempt at being subtle.*" It wasn't quite dark yet, but it was dusky. Billy gathered his gear, and headed outside, motioning for Rommel to follow. With a bound the large canine was out the door, and starting for the truck.

"You tell what kinda vehicle it is?" he asked, walking to his truck. Terry and the others had been gone five days.

"*Not yet. Headlights are making it hard to see.*"

"*Billy, where are you?*" George called.

"I'm headin' down that way in my truck," he replied. "Reckon they don't need to get in here."

"*I'll be right there,*" George promised.

Billy drove a slight ways past the Silvers' driveway, then parked his truck sideways of the road, sitting on the small bridge that covered one of the main creeks in the valley.

"Reckon we'll just wait for'em right here," he told Rommel, who wagged his tail stump. Billy rubbed his head, then opened his door and got out, allowing Rommel to do the same. The dog ran around the truck, sniffing the air, then settled down by Billy's side.

It wasn't long before Billy could see the headlights, bouncing up and down along the road.

We got to git that road hid, he thought to himself. *And the sooner the better.*

"*Billy, it looks like the Hummer,*" Howie came over the radio again.

"Okay," Billy answered, never taking his eyes off the headlight. If it was a Hummer, then maybe it was them. Only way to know was to wait see, he decided. As he waited, he heard George drive up behind him.

"Made good time," Billy mentioned, his eyes never leaving the potential target.

"Traffic was light," George chuckled, and Billy shook his head, grinning.

"You heard Howie?"

"You mean about how it looks like a Hummer?" George asked. "Yeah. Don't mean it's our's, though. There were a mess of'em made, you know."

"Was thinking that myself," Billy nodded. The two stood there in silence until the Hummer eased to a stop. Terry Blaine slowly climbed out of the driver's door.

"We didn't expect a welcoming committee."

"Last minute thing," George chuckled. "Good to see you, man."

"Good to see you too, brother. All right if we pass through?" Terry looked dead on his feet.

"Sure, just didn't know it was you," Billy nodded.

"We all need to get somewhere and talk. But we need to cleanup first." All three were ragged and filthy. George nodded.

"Why don't all of you take an hour, get cleaned up and fed, and we can meet. . . ." he trailed off. Where could they meet?

"Let's just let it be my place," Billy offered. "Sort of between their places. Make it easier."

"Sounds good," Terry nodded, already walking back to the Hummer.

"Terry?" George asked. "What was it like?" Blaine turned back.

"Well, it was bad."

CHAPTER SIXTY-SIX

The hour passed very slowly for Billy and the others, gathered around his table waiting for the report from Terry, Pete, and Toby. George and Ralph were there, along with the Kelvey brothers. Jerry would be along with Toby in a few minutes.

"What do you think they found?" Ralph asked, more to fill the void than in any real expectation of an answer.

"I don't know," George replied. He looked worried. "I've know Terry a long time. Been through a lot of bad times with him. If he said it was bad, I honestly can't imagine what he saw. What they saw."

"He don't say 'bad' very often, I take it?" Rhonda asked.

"Not very," George admitted. "Some of the things. . .well, there's no sense in going there," he cut himself off. "We'll know soon enough." Just then they heard a vehicle pull up out front.

Terry and Pete entered the front door at almost the same time that Jerry, Toby and Shelly entered the back. Shelly went immediately to Pete, and the two of them took a moment to re-unite in private before joining the rest. No one spoke at first, as Terry and the others sat quietly, collecting their thoughts. Toby reached into the backpack he had brought, and produced a video camera and a still camera.

"Not. . .not yet, Tobe," Terry shook his head, the first words he had spoken. The pale faced teen nodded jerkily, and left the two devices on the table. He removed a I-Pad from his bag, and the cords needed to transfer the data, but made no move to attach them.

"Terry, are you guys okay?" George asked, concerned.

"I. . .I don't know," Terry admitted at last. "First off, I want to say something. We. . .what we saw was. . .bad. I can't really emphasize how bad. You'll see soon enough," he pointed to the cameras. "Toby, I want to tell you this in front of everyone. First, I'm proud of you. You'll always be welcome to come with me, anywhere. There's no question in my mind that you're through being a 'boy'. You're a man grown, and a damned good one at that."

"Second, I'm sorry I let you come along. Not because of anything you did, but because you shouldn't. . .you shouldn't have had to see any of that."

"It's okay, Mister Blaine," Toby said shakily. "I'm. . .I was just glad to do my part, that's all."

"You did that and more," Terry nodded. "Well, I guess it's time. When I say it's bad, I mean. . .horrible. I never imagined. . . ." He broke off for a moment, clearly gathering himself. Pete was silent, but Shelly could feel a simmering rage underneath his normally calm exterior. It frightened her more than she would be willing to admit, even to Pete. She didn't know what had happened, but she was sure that Terry was understating it.

"We got there okay, managed to hide the truck about a mile from town. We thought about leaving someone with the Hummer, but decided we were better off together."

"We walked to town, easing into a good position over the town. . . ."

"This is a good spot," Terry whispered harshly. "We'll set up here, make a cold camp. We can see the town, and I've seen a few people. We can see the old market place, too. We'll watch tomorrow, see what happens."

"And that's what we did," Pete spoke for the first time. "We watched the comings and goings. With the spotter scope, we could see pretty far. We weren't on a real hill, but it was a small rise, and that helped."

"Everything was fine at first, it seemed. . . ."

"Lot of people coming and going," Terry observed. "You know, I admit it, I didn't expect so many folks. They came through the winter better than I expected."

"Good for them," Pete smiled. "I didn't figure they did so well, after the attack."

"Me either, to be honest. I'm surpr. . . ."

"Truck comin'," Toby whispered. "Make that trucks," he amended. "Look."

Sure enough, there was a small convoy coming to the community center building. Terry counted seven trucks in all, two of them pickups riding fore and aft, like guards. He nodded, knowing from experience that security was important if you were moving anything of val. . . .

"Terry, I don't like this," Pete whispered. "Those are people in those trucks, I think."

"All of 'em?" Terry asked. What the hell?

"I can't be sure of that," Pete admitted. "But there were people in that lead truck, for certain."

"Toby are you taping this?"

"Yes, sir," Toby whispered back. "Want me to stop?"

"No, no. You're doing fine," Terry patted the teen's shoulder, smiling. He was a good kid.

As the three of them watched, the trucks came to a halt, and two men exited each truck, yelling and pounding on the back of the trucks. Sure enough, people began to pile out of all five of the larger trucks. Military trucks, the old 'deuce-and-a-half', still found in many National Guard armories.

Terry was starting to get a bad feeling about this. He looked at Pete, and noticed a similar look on his friend's face. As they continued to watch, the people were separated into two groups. One was comprised primarily of attractive young women, teen age girls, and children. Another was able bodied men, and women who didn't seem to 'qualify' for the first group. The last was older or infirm people, those who had trouble getting around, or didn't seem to be able to cope on their own.

"I really don't like this," Pete said softly.

"Neither do I," Terry agreed.

As they watched, four of the men standing guard stepped forward and ordered the able-bodied men, all cuffed and shackled, to start moving. They marched slowly out of sight, to where Terry wasn't sure. As he thought about what he knew of the area, he decided they were possibly headed to the jail. Maybe they were criminals?

He shook that thought off. Those kids weren't criminals. This was something else. They continued to watch, Toby taping it all, to see what would happen next.

"We didn't have to wait too long," Toby added his voice to the tale. "I was still tapin' everything, but I could hear another truck comin'. Least I thought it was a truck."

"Hey, there's a school bus," Pete pointed. Toby swung the camera around, catching the yellow vehicle as it pulled into the lot. Two men, and five large, rather angry looking women exited the bus. They headed as a unit to the first group. The one with the women and children.

Each person in the group was given the once over, usually twice over if the woman or girl was particularly attractive or well built. They were ragged, hungry, and scared to death. All three of them could tell that, even at a distance.

Each adult and able-bodied teen was secured with plastic cuffs. One boy, about twelve or thirteen, tried to fight. With no more thought than if swatting a fly, one of the men hit the boy in the head with a large club. From the sound, it was likely metal, Terry decided.

The boy hit the ground, and didn't move. One of the girls, probably a sister, cried out, and tried to go to him, but one of the women guards grabbed her by the hair, and started yelling. This was the first time they had been able to hear what was said.

"'You better get that idea outta yer head, girl. You belong to us, now, and you do what we tell you, when we tell you, or you'll get the same thing he got. Hear?'"

Pete and Terry looked at each other, their faces slack. They looked back to the scene before them.

"'They'll bring a good price'" the largest woman nodded in approval. "Good job.'"

"'What about them?'" the man they assumed was the leader asked, nodding to the last group.

"'Take 'em inside. Butcher's are waitin' on 'em. We got hungry people to feed.'" The man nodded, and shouted orders to his men. They began herding this last group toward the civic center.

"Did she just say what I think she said?" Pete asked, looking at Terry with something like terror in his eyes.

"I'm pretty sure she just said they was gonna eat them people," Toby observed, his voice cracking.

"*Eat* them?"

Every voice at the table spoke as one. Terry and Pete nodded.

"Yeah," Toby answered. "That's what she said."

"We need to get the hell outta here," Pete said firmly. "This is. . .Jesus..." he trailed off, looking on in horror. How in the hell had this come about?

"We need to know what's going on," Terry shook his head.

"I'd say we see what's going on!" Pete hissed sharply, but quietly. "They're. . .they're cannibals!"

"We think so, but we don't know," Terry motioned for Pete to calm down. "We do know, now, that things aren't right. We came here to recon. We're going to *finish."* He looked at Pete.

"These sonsabitches may well come our way, one day," he pointed out. "I want to know what we'd be up against, Pete. Don't you?"

The hot-blooded native began to calm down, and nodded. His first inclination was to start shooting, and his second had been to return home and start preparing for the day these...people...came calling on them. But Terry was right. They were already here, in place. They should finish.

"So, what are we gonna do?" Toby asked. He was still taping.

"We aren't doing anything," Terry told the teenager. "You're going to sit right here. Pete and I will try to get down there and see what's really happening."

"Oh, hell no!" Toby hissed. "There's no way in hell you're leavin' me up here by myself! These people are nuts!"

"Toby, this is the safest place for you," Terry shook his head. "You stay."

"Not a chance," Toby insisted. "I am not gonna be their next lunch. And if somethin' happens to you two, what the hell am I supposed to do, huh? No, sir. I'm goin'."

Terry frowned in frustration.

"You promised to do what I said!" he hissed.

"That was before I knew I could be on the damn menu!" Toby shot back, unimpressed with the look Terry was giving him. "I'm not lettin' you two outta my sight. Side's, if I go back without Pete, my sister will *kill me!*"

In spite of himself, Terry snorted, trying to contain his laughter. Pete grew a bit red faced, but grinned. Toby, however, didn't. He was serious.

-

"I have to admit, Toby's courage was never in doubt," Terry complimented, and the teenager blushed. "His obedience qualities leave something to be desired, of course," he frowned mightily, but cut it with a grin. "His loyalty, however, is beyond question."

"I can't believe you went down there," Shelly almost whispered. "You could all have been killed."

"And eaten," Ralph was aghast at what he'd heard so far.

"It was a risk I decided we had to take," Terry shrugged. "We needed to know."

-

The three of them worked their way down to the civic/community center building carefully. They moved slowly and carefully, dropping out of sight at the slightest noise. Discovery would mean death. They had no illusions about that. Even Toby, young though he was, knew that. And he was scared. Which was fine, since Terry and Pete were scared, too, and had let him know it.

They came to the parking lot of the civic center. There were very few places to provide cover. They would be forced to cross open ground if they wanted to get any closer.

Terry motioned to Pete with a series of hand signals. The younger man nodded, and began working his way across the open ground, using everything from the few abandoned vehicles to light poles. It took him only two minutes to reach the plants and bushes that remained of the landscaping around the building. He studied his surroundings for a few seconds, then motioned for Terry and Toby to follow.

Terry grabbed Toby's harness, pulling him to his feet.

Odd Billy Todd

"Let's go, kid."

The two followed the same path Pete had used, albeit faster, with Pete watching over them. When they arrived, Toby watched as both men pulled their hand guns, and began to screw long tubes on the end of the threaded barrels.

"Are those. . . ." he started, but was cut off by a glare from Terry, and a 'shush' motion from Pete. Toby nodded, blushing at his mistake.

More hand signals from Terry, and Pete started toward the door. Terry leaned down, pressing his lips to Toby's ear.

"Stay quiet. If we enter the building, I want you to stay there, and keep watch. Don't shoot unless you absolutely have to. Got it?" Toby nodded his understanding.

The two then followed Pete, who had found the door unlocked. There was no sign of a guard, or even that one had been there. Pete shook his head, as if to say 'amateurs'. Terry glared at him, and Pete rolled his eyes, but returned to the job at hand. Toby, meanwhile, had found a small alcove well back from the door, and pointed to it, then to himself. Terry nodded, then winked, pushing the teen gently in that direction. Toby handed over the video camera, and moved on.

Pete motioned for Terry to follow, and stepped through a nearby door. As the door opened, the overwhelming smell of copper hit Terry full force. There was only one thing that produced that smell.

Blood. And lots of it.

He moved quickly, catching up to Pete as the younger man waited outside the doorway to the auditorium. They looked at each other, eyes speaking where words were dangerous. Terry nodded, and hefted the camera.

-

"Is that what you didn't want to show us, yet?" Jerry asked. His face was drawn, and hard. He had put a hand on his son's shoulder, squeezing firmly. That grip conveyed more than any words he might speak to the younger man.

Though no one in the valley knew it, Jerry had fought in Vietnam. One of the last groups of young men to be sent over before America decided it was time for the South to stand on its own. He had stayed almost two years, and had seen a good deal of action that would never be recorded into any history book, not all of it in Vietnam, either. Terrified, alone save for his comrades, and far from home, Jerry had never again experienced such heart stopping fear.

He had hoped his son would never be in such a position. That hope appeared to be gone forever. His son looked. . .haunted. He was still strong, but his illusions were gone now. His innocence, what had been left after this last year, was a thing of the past.

Though proud of his son, Jerry was sad that he had to see something so horrible, so young.

-

Terry put the camera against the small window in the door. He looked at the small screen as he panned the camera around. What he saw threatened to turn his stomach inside out.

Terry Blaine was a hardened warrior. Had seen combat not only in Iraq and Afghanistan, but the Philippines, South America, and Africa. After twenty-two years and five continents, he thought he had seen the worst mankind had to offer.

He was wrong.

The people that had been herded inside the building earlier had all been slaughtered. And that was an apt description. Their bodies, stripped of clothing, were hanging from a series of meat hooks suspended from the ceiling. Seven people, four men and three women, were 'working' on various jobs, literally processing the bodies into....

"shitaa' ch'įgonÁ'ÁÍ," Pete breathed. In his shock, he had reverted to his native language, the language of his True People. Terry had heard him speak Apache only a few times. Most of those times right before Pete exploded in violence.

Before he could finish that thought, Pete was through the door, pistol in one hand, knife in the other. Not the combat knife he carried everywhere, but the huge khukri blade he carried on jobs like this. The same one he had carried on three tours in Afghanistan.

"Pete!" Terry hissed, but it was already too late. The largest of the men turned to see who had entered, and then roared a challenge. Terry shot him in the head without pausing, the pistol much quieter than it normally would have been.

But not silent.

The knife claimed the next two, slashing one way, then another, decapitating a woman, and slicing a man's throat almost to the spine. Another shot sent a third man to the floor, dead before he finished falling.

Terry was in action by then, forced by Pete's actions to forgo any chance of subtlety. His pistol coughed twice, the sounds making him wince as he double tapped the last man in the room. His next two shots went into a woman charging him with a cleaver. She took a third shot before hitting the floor.

Pete had already dispatched the last woman. The two stood eyeing the destruction they had caused, breathing heavily. The entire action had taken less than ten seconds.

"What the hell are you thinking?" Terry hissed, grabbing Pete's arm. "We were supposed to be looking!"

"They couldn't be allowed to live," Pete shook his head. "This...this is an abomination. We can't allow it."

"How the hell do you suggest we stop it?" Terry demanded, fear and anger making his words harsh. "We're just a little outnumbered, you know."

"We have to destroy this place," Pete remained unmoved. "Take the boy and go. I'll catch up."

"That's not going to happen," Terry told him flatly. "We're all leaving, together. Right now!"

Pete looked around, eyeing the small generator still running in the far corner of the auditorium. Not far away was a small gas can. He walked to it, picking up the can and sloshing it around. At least half of the five gallons it would hold. Enough, he decided.

"Pete, I said let's go," Terry ordered.

"Not until I erase this stain," Pete shook his head. "We cannot allow this to remain. I told you, take the boy and go." With that he began to slosh the gas around the large room.

Terry sighed, shaking his head in defeat.

"We'll wait at the door." Pete nodded, never stopping.

"Make it fast, okay," Terry said finally, and turned to leave.

Odd Billy Todd

To see Toby Silvers standing in the doorway, his face a mask of revulsion.

"Toby, I told you to stay at the door," Terry said carefully. "Toby!" That shook the boy from his trance.

"Sorry," he stammered. "I was afraid you needed help." With that he turned away, hurrying back to his post. Terry shook his head again. This was his fault. A total breakdown in command.

And the boy had seen the room.

"God help us," he murmured softly, then followed Toby out. The two of them waited near the entrance, not speaking, careful to keep an eye out. Two minutes later, Pete appeared still sloshing gas. Finally, he set the can down, then tipped it over. He had a rag in his hand, and now took his lighter from a pocket, and lit it. He made sure the rag was burning, then turned to Terry.

"Go!" he ordered, and then tossed the rag.

Flames erupted all through the building as the fire followed the trail of accelerate. They had cleared the door before the fire reached inside the can, igniting the remainder of the fuel, and the vapors around it with a 'whoosh'.

"Get back to the hill!" Terry urged. They were running flat out, hoping to get out of sight before anyone appeared to investigate.

They had only barely settled into their hide when the first people began to show up.

-

"Oh my God," Rhonda said softly, his hand coming to her mouth. Shelly lost the battle she was having with her stomach and bolted for the hall bathroom. Ralph headed out the back door for the same reason. Rhonda lasted a minute longer, and then hit the stairs for her own bathroom.

The others sat very still. Billy hadn't moved, nor had Jerry. The Kelvey brothers looked ashen, no doubt wondering what might have happened to people they might have know in Franklin.

"Did it burn?" Billy asked softly. "The building? Did it burn down like you wanted?" he asked Pete. His friend nodded slowly.

"Yes, their spirits are free," he almost whispered back. "Among. . .among my people, cannibalism is the vilest of crimes. One. . .one small tribe once practiced it, many generations ago. They were ostracized, and finally hunted down. Only a few lived. We. . .we are taught from childhood to fear them. Despise them. They are unclean."

"Sounds like a good policy," Billy agreed. "Good job."

"No, it wasn't," Terry shot back. "It alerted those. . .*people*. . .that someone's around. That is not a good thing."

"They'd have found us sooner or later, I imagine," Billy shrugged philosophically.

"That is not the point," Terry grated.

"I know that," Billy nodded. "Still, I agree with Pete. That had to be done. And it just might tell them. . .*people*. . .they might not be the only dog on the block. Might just make 'em hesitate. And that'll give us some time to get ready."

The others began to return then, Ralph first. He settled into his chair, looking a bit green.

"Sorry about that," he grinned weakly.

"Ain't nothin' the rest of us ain't done," Toby assured him.

Shelly and Rhonda returned just then, neither looking all that well. Rhonda poured herself, Shelly and Ralph something to drink before sitting back down.

"Is that all?" Jerry asked.

As the three of them watched, men and women arrived in groups of two or three, along with a fire truck. They worked hard, but were disorganized and without training. After an hour, they gave up. The truck had long since ran out of water, and the water mains that supplied the hydrants hadn't worked in nearly a year.

As they watched, two men and one woman met in the parking lot. From their shouted orders, it was obvious they were in charge. The woman was the same one who had taken the women and children away. The men were new to them.

There was no way to hear their animated conversation, but it was obvious they were pissed, and looked to be trying to blame one another for what had happened. Others around the building actively avoided them.

"I think it's time we thought about leaving," Pete whispered. Terry nodded.

"I was just thinking that myself. I'd say we've overstayed our welcome. Toby have you been getting all of this?"

"Yes, sir," the teen nodded. "All of it."

"Well, this will at least give us an idea of how many there are," Terry sighed. "Okay, Pete, take point, and get us back to the Hummer."

"It took us about three hours to get back, taking it slow and working our way out. We took a round about way, just in case. And we sat on the truck for a while, to see if there was any action around it."

"Once we realized it hadn't been disturbed, we saddled up and hit the road. We stopped several times on our way out, making sure we weren't being followed. And, here we are."

The others sat quietly for a time, no words coming to them. Finally, George asked the question that was on everyone's mind.

"What do we do?"

"What *can* we do?" Jerry asked, leaning forward, his elbows resting on the table.

"We should try and help those people," George shrugged. "If we can."

"I don't see any way to do that," Jerry replied. "I admit, it's a bad thing, all around. But what can we do?" he repeated.

"There's a lot of 'em," Toby put in.

"Sounds like a rough outfit, any way you slice it," Ben Kelvey put in. "I wonder if anyone's left that we know?"

"You can watch the video, I guess," Toby shrugged. "See if you can recognize anyone. I'd fast forward through the stuff inside, was I you," he added.

"How many people came to the fire?" Jon asked.

"I didn't count, since we had the film," Terry admitted. "I'd guess it was forty, at least. But that *is* just a guess."

"Well, that pretty much settles it, then," Jerry leaned back again. "I don't see what we few can do about all that."

"There's got to be something we can do," George shook his head. "And we need those people they're keeping captive. If we can release them, they would probably help us. The men, anyway. Can't expect those kids to. Some of the women might be able and willing though."

"We don't even know that the men are," Terry argued. "What happens when we release'em, and they just go running for the hills?"

"They'd be a distraction, at least," George offered. He looked around the table.

"Look, I know it's a long shot. But we gotta face some facts, here. These. . .*people*. . .are systematically stripping everything around them. Sooner or later, they'll come here. It's better to fight them where they are, than wait until they're here, where we live."

No one disputed that assessment. In fact, most agreed. That still didn't mean there was anything they could do about it. Or was there?

"I think we need to go about this a little different," Billy offered finally. He hadn't said much as the discussion traveled back and forth, other than his observations about what Pete had done.

"Such as what?" Terry asked.

"Well, it ain't like we can rush'em, is it?" Billy asked. "There's a bunch o' them, and just a few o' us. We got to go about this a little smarter." He looked at Pete.

"You interested in goin' back?"

CHAPTER SIXTY-SEVEN

"This is a bad idea."

Pete looked around at Terry from packing his warbag.

"You've said that before," was all he said.

"And I'll keep saying it, until you listen," Terry shot back. "This is a crazy, no, it's a *stupid* idea. I know you and Billy are friends, but this is one time you need to call him, and stop this idiocy."

"My being his friend has got nothing to do with it," Pete said easily. "George is right. This needs to be done. Sooner or later, we'll have to face them. It's better to do it there, than here."

"It's better to make sure they don't find us at all!" Terry exclaimed. "We need to be working on that, not running off trying to wage war against a group that size."

"So work on it," Pete shrugged. "You don't need us for that. Meanwhile, we'll be keeping them so busy, they won't have time to bother you."

Disgusted, Terry shook his head and walked out. Pete watched him go, then continued packing.

-

"I'm begging you, Billy. Don't do this."

Rhonda was in tears. Holding them back through force of will alone, a few were leaking out anyway.

"Rhonda, I ain't gonna just sit here, waitin' for them people to come and take you away like that. Nor Mary and Danny, neither. I ain't."

"You don't even know that they'll find us!" she almost wailed. "You're just doing this because you think you *have* to!"

"I *do* have to,' Billy replied gently. "Ain't nobody else. And I don't *want* to, ya know. If I had my way, I'd never get within ten miles o' them people. But I don't see another way. We can't let them get close to us. Let alone find us. There's too much to risk. We got all these kids here, too. That bunch is preyin' on kids."

"Then you should stay here and protect'em!" Rhonda shot back.

"I can't," Billy sighed, and sat down. "Don't you think I ain't done thought about that? You think I tried ever way in the world not to have to do this?"

"No, I don't," Rhonda snorted. "I think you see a chance to run off an do somethin' stupid, and you're takin' it!" Billy's face went slack at that.

He stood abruptly, and Rhonda took a step back instinctively.

"Is that what you think o' me?" he asked, his voice soft.

"Billy, I. . . ." Rhonda choked off her reply.

"You listen here," Billy kept his voice calm, and Rhonda could see that he was struggling to keep his temper in check. "I've done thought about this ever way I can see. There's a simple fact, here. I can't keep you safe here, against a mob like that. We ain't got the people. Period."

"A buncha no goods like'at 'll go through this valley like a dose o' salts, Rhonda. Sure, we'll kill a bunch of'em. But it won't be near enough. We lose one o' us for ever five o' them we kill, still won't be enough. All it'll do is make it easier on 'em to stay fed. And with what we got here, they'll be fat and happy for a long time. What happens when they look in the barn? Huh? What happens when they find all that stuff we been hidin'?"

"It ain't just about us, no more," he said firmly. "Don't you see that we can't have no kinda life, them kids can't have no kinda life, with this hangin' over us? We'll be fearful all the time, day and night. And sooner or later, we'll let our guard down, just a little, and sure as God made little green apples, that'll be the time they hit us."

"How many actual fighters we got Rhonda? We got a lot o' people here, nowadays, but how many can we depend on? House full o' young'uns, old folks, cowards like March and Williams that already failed once, ag'in just *two men?* When you start addin' up real numbers, we ain't got'em."

Rhonda listened to him as he rattled off the facts, and despaired. He was right, damn him. They had only a handful of people who could actually fight against anyone who attacked their hideaway. They could stay hidden for a while, but he was right. Fear would be their constant companion. She dropped her head, and gave up the fight to keep her tears at bay. She literally shook with sobs.

Billy frowned, feeling responsible. But he couldn't help what he couldn't help. Facts was facts, and he couldn't change them. He stepped to her, and wrapped her in his arms. She leaned against him, burying her face in his chest, and cried.

He rubbed her back gently while she did, talking softly to her about anything and nothing at the same time. He'd grown a lot in the months since the world had gone to hell. A year ago, he wouldn't have done anything. He wouldn't have known how.

Finally, her sobs subsided. She looked up at him, and he felt pain at the look in her eyes.

"I'm sorry," he said softly. "I hadn't shoulda said all that. It's. . .I live with that fear ever day. Ever day I worry 'bout somethin' just like this. Somethin' I can't protect you from. Protect the kids from."

"I ain't but one man. I ain't a soldier, ain't too smart, either. I know what my limits are. Been livin' my whole life knowin'em. Ain't no gettin' round the facts. But this here is somethin' I can do. If nothin' else, we'll buy some time for the fellas to get the work on the road done. They do a good enough job, even somebody knows it's there have a hard time findin' it."

"Please, *please*, promise me you'll be careful," she pleaded softly. "Please don't go there and get killed, an' leave me here all alone."

"I promise I'll do my best," he replied. "And ole Pete, he'll be lookin' out for me. He's right smart, and *was* a soldier. He won't let nothin' happen to me." He smiled to show her he was confident, but the truth was, he wasn't.

Billy didn't have any real expectations of what was to come. He knew that he and Pete had a good chance. But that's all it was. A good chance.

"Do you think you can stop all this for a while?" Rhonda asked him, her eyes pleading with him.

"I imagine so," he nodded, his voice as soft as hers.

Without another word, she took his hand and led him toward the stairs.

A similar discussion was taking place not far away.

"Why are you doing this?" Shelly Silvers asked, as she and Pete sat on the porch swing at her parent's home.

"It has to be done," Pete told her simply. "Billy's right. We can't wait for them to come to us. We just don't have the manpower to stop them. They'll ride through this valley and kill us all eventually, no matter how hard we fight."

"They might not," Shelly replied. "They might not even know we're here."

"But they will," Pete assured her. "They're being very methodical. I think if it wasn't for your father, making sure no one was on the radio, they might have found us already. I think the people they had the other day were people who had been using their radios. Easy to track that kind of thing, if you know how."

"You don't know if they can do it or not," Shelly pointed out.

"That's true," he nodded. "But we can't take the chance. Or *any* chance, for that matter. We have to do what we can, now. Summer is campaign weather. They're using the good weather to move, and do their damage. If we let them have free reign to do as they please, Shelly, they'll find us. They can't miss us."

"Why does it have to be you?" She was trying not to whine, but she really didn't want him to go.

"Who else is there?" he asked. "George and Terry both have kids. The Kelvey's are needed here, and they don't have the know how for something like this, anyway. Your father might, but he's too old. Ralph's a great guy, but this isn't his thing, and he'd be the first to admit it." He shrugged.

"Leaves me and Billy."

"It's not like you two don't have anyone here, you know!" she struck back. "And Billy and Rhonda have Danny. And Mary."

"And they're both near grown for the times we live in now," Pete replied calmly. "It's not that we want to go, you know," he pointed out. "It's just that we're the two best qualified to do it. There's no way to get around that, honey."

"Billy ain't a soldier!" she said suddenly. "He's not even. . . ." she broke off sharply, her face reddening. Pete frowned.

"I *hope* you weren't about to say what I think you were," he said, his voice firm and unyielding. "Billy may not be smart the way you see it, but I'll tell you straight out. I'd have traded three or four of the guys I fought with in Iraq and Afghanistan for one like Billy Todd. I don't know how he knows as much as he does, but I can promise you he's smart. And he's a better shot than I am, especially at long distance."

"I'm lucky to be going with him instead of some of the people I've served in combat with," he finished, giving his friend the greatest compliment he knew.

"I. . .I didn't mean it like that," Shelly said softly. "I. . .I used to make fun of Billy, but I haven't in a long time. It's. . .it's just that, this time, I'm depending on him to make sure you come back to me." Pete laughed softly.

"I'd imagine Rhonda is thinking the same thing about me," he assured her. "And we will come back. I don't know how long we'll be, but we've already discussed precautions to make sure that no matter what happens, we'll get home. Might take us a while, but we will."

"You know I'll be sick with worry every minute you're gone," she finally said, giving up.

"No more than I'll be missing you, honey," Pete promised her. He leaned forward then, and kissed her.

There was no more talk about his trip after that.

Billy was up early the next morning. He had a lot to do today. He and Pete would be leaving in the morning, and there was no real way to know when, let alone if, they would be back.

"I'm dependin' on you to keep things goin', Danny," Billy told the teenager. "You know what's got to be done, so don't let things get away from you. You need help, you ask for it."

"I'll get it done," Danny promised. "I wish you wasn't havin' to go, though," the boy admitted. "Scares me a little."

"Me too, bud," Billy nodded. "You won't have to worry too long, I reckon. We'll be back 'fore ya know it."

"Ever thing'll be here like ya left it," Danny promised solemnly.

"I want you to take Rommel with you when you're out and workin'," Billy told him. "He's a good dog, and he'll give you fair warnin' when somebody's about. Don't let him in the pasture, though," he added, remembering when he'd taken the big dog in with him. "Him and the cows, they don't get along too well."

"I'll remember."

"Carry your rifle with ya when you're out. Make sure you got your pistol on you when you walk out the door. And pay a mind to what's around you." The boy nodded again, his face as serious as could be.

"All right, then," Billy slapped him on the shoulder. "Reckon that's it. You best get to work. I gotta lot to do, today." Danny nodded once more and headed away to do his chores.

Billy watched him go, and then headed to the barn. He had things to gather up. Just as he reached the barn, Pete rode into the yard.

"Hey Billy," he grinned, stepping out of the saddle.

"Pete," Billy nodded.

"Whatcha doin'?" Pete asked.

"Makin' sure ever thing is ready for me to leave," Billy replied. "You?"

"About the same, I guess. I wanted to see what you were carrying. No sense in us taking too many different calibers. Make it hard for ammo."

"Good idea," Billy nodded.

"We need to work on the cache tubes, too," Pete reminded him. "We can bury them along the way. Might be good to have a few small one's we can spread out in town, too."

"'Nother good idea," Billy allowed. "Reckon I'll take my rifle," he added.

"Well, yeah," Pete snorted. "Considering what we have in mind, that'd be a good idea." Billy reddened at that, but said nothing. He looked into the barn, then back at Pete.

"What is it, Billy?" Pete asked. "You okay?"

Billy considered his options. Should he show Pete the Room? Let him in on the big secret? No, he decided. That wouldn't do. He liked Pete, and he trusted him. But some things were for him and Rhonda only. And the kids. The Room was one of them.

"I'm just tryin' to get things straight," Billy pointed to his head. "Lots to get done 'for we go. I don't wanna leave nothin' undone, and I don't wanna get there an' realize I done left somethin' I need."

Odd Billy Todd

"Yeah, I know that score," Pete chuckled. "Left my radio behind once. Thought ole Terry was gonna tear my head off."

"What say we meet up in a couple hours?" Billy asked. "I'll have Danny bring the truck over, and you can load your gear, then we'll look over ever'thing good and proper. All we'll have to do then is load stuff in that Hummer, and take out."

"Sounds like a plan," Pete nodded. He could tell Billy was wanting to end the conversation, so he mounted his horse. "See you in say, three hours?"

"Works for me," Billy nodded.

-

Billy looked at the equipment he had assembled. His face was as grim as his mind. This would be an ugly thing. He took no pleasure in what was coming, but try as he might he still couldn't see any way other than the one he and Pete had come up with me.

He shook his head, trying to throw the thoughts out. They served no purpose. The Ford rolled into the yard just then, with Danny bringing Pete along. Pete got out, his jaw dropping at what he saw displayed on the table.

"Billy, is that. . . .?"

"Yep," Billy nodded grimly. Lying on the table in front of him was a Barrett Rifles M82. Several box magazines were spread out alongside the big rifle.

"Where did you get that?" Pete asked, his voice almost a whisper.

"My daddy left it to me," Billy told him. "Never thought I'd have no use for it, but. . . ." He shrugged, as if to say *I was wrong.*

"So this is what you meant when you said you were taking your rifle?" Pete asked.

"Well, no," Billy shook his head. "Truth is, I ain't. . .see, I can't see how we're gonna be able to carry ever thing we need," he admitted. "I want to carry my 700 too, and I reckon we'd better carry our M-4's, 'count o' we may need'em, we get into a sure 'nough fight. But that's a lotta stuff to carry. Hard to move with all that."

"It is," Pete nodded. "It's an age-old problem, Billy. You just have to look for the best compromise you can come up with."

"I ain't come up with one as yet," Billy admitted.

"Well, let me see if I can help you."

-

"So that's what we'll do," Pete finished.

"I like it," Billy admitted.

"That will be our first priority, then, when we get there. We'll stash supplies in several of the outlying houses. None of them looked to be used when we were there. We'll waterproof the stashes, so we can hide them outdoors, too. That way, we don't have to hump so much stuff all the time. When we get low on food, water, or ammo, we'll just head to one of those stashes, and resupply."

"Kinda like cache tubes, but purpose built, like," Billy nodded.

"Yeah, just like that," Pete replied.

"Well, reckon we'd better get to work on that, then."

-

They were ready. At least as ready as they could be. Terry, George and Jerry were standing with them, going over last minute things.

"We'll start workin' on the road tomorrow," Jerry told them. "Hope you boys can find your way home," he chuckled.

"We'll be back," Billy nodded.

"Look, I still say this is a stupid idea," Terry cut in. He wasn't in the mood for any jokes.

"And I still say it's all we got," Billy shrugged. "I don't like it neither. I ain't never. But we can't let them people find us, Terry. We can't beat'em. Not here. And you know that, better'n I ever will."

Terry sighed, refusing to acknowledge that Billy was right. He'd studied the terrain, figured on everything they had available, the people who were able to fight. There was no way to defend the valley against them. None.

"You guys watch yourselves," George told them.

"We will," Pete nodded.

"So, you're leavin' out first thing?" Jerry asked.

"Fore day light," Billy nodded. "We wanna be well on our way 'fore the sun's up."

"Good idea," Jerry agreed. "I wish I was twenty years younger. I. . . ." he stopped. He wasn't, and nothing would change that. He looked at Pete.

"You had better come back," he warned. Pete smiled.

"Do my best, sir."

"And you too, Billy," Jerry turned to his young neighbor. "I think we've proved this place can't hardly manage without you." Billy flushed at that, but merely nodded.

"Good luck," was all Terry could manage. He wanted to go. He wanted them not to. He wanted things to be normal. He wanted to keep bad things from happening.

And he had never felt so powerless as he did right now.

-

Morning was still dark when Billy walked out his front door. Rhonda followed him, tears falling silently down her cheeks.

"I will worry myself sick until you come back," she told him.

"I know," he nodded. She would.

"Please, Billy, don't take so many chances," she pleaded. "Come home."

"I plan to," he promised. "I really do." She stood on her toes and kissed him, then suddenly fled into the house. The Hummer was waiting, Pete behind the wheel. He had experienced a similar morning.

"Ready for this, Billy?" he asked.

"No, but I reckon it's got to be," Billy admitted. Pete nodded, and put the truck in gear.

"Here we go, then."

CHAPTER SIXTY-EIGHT

"Looks like three," Pete whispered. Billy nodded, looking through his rifle scope.

"Which one you think looks like the leader?" he whispered back.

"I'm going with the one on our right," Pete replied after some consideration. "He looks like he's giving orders."

"Works for me," Billy answered.

They had been in position for almost three days. Arriving without any problems, the two of them had first looked for, and found, a secure place for the Hummer. A garage on the south west corner of town in a neighborhood that looked like it hadn't seen any visitors since the virus proved to be just fine. There was a small loft above it, and they decided to make a stash there as well.

The next two days had seen the two running scout all over their side of town, and eventually making an entire circuit, leaving small caches of supplies in the least likely places they could think of. GPS was still working, at least for now, so in addition to written notes and map notations, they entered the coordinates of each one as well.

They weren't really anything special. Ammunition, MRE's, a knife, a multitool. Water. First aid kit. Socks. Things that someone might really need in order to get out of a bad scrape. Even if they didn't use them, the cache's would be here the next time.

Finally, they had spent an entire day looking over the center of town, where the activity was concentrated. The two men had selected five houses that had upper levels, giving them a good view of their surroundings. In addition, there were a few multistory buildings that would give them good vantage points.

The trick, the key, was to stay hidden.

-

"Reckon we start with him?" Billy asked.

"I don't see why not," Pete shrugged. Before he could add anything, the huge rifle split the atmosphere in half.

Below them, two men stood stunned, and speechless, as the man they took their orders from disintegrated in front of their eyes. One minute, he was there, and everything was normal. The next, he was in several pieces, with blood and bone and body parts everywhere on the sidewalk.

Before they could recover, another one met the same fate. The third, realizing he would be next, took off running back in the direction from which they had come.

Billy let him go.

They needed someone to tell the story, after all.

"Time to move," Pete noted, gathering their things.

-

Rather than strike again that first day, Pete and Billy elected to watch the reaction to their attack. The 'mess' was cleaned up by very hesitant people, each looking around them frantically, as if they could somehow ward off the destruction if only they could see it coming.

Everyone who came to the scene left terrified. Which was just what Billy and Pete intended.

The next day, almost a mile from where they had first struck, the big rifle boomed again. One moment a young girl was being forced down the street by the woman Pete remembered from the bus, the next moment the girl was alone, her captor spread all over the sidewalk.

The girl screamed. Men and women came running from every direction to the noise of the shot, and the scream. One man, who might or might not have been in charge, they didn't know, hit the girl in the face, knocking her down. He screamed at her to tell him what had happened or he would kill her, and drew his gun to emphasize the point.

Three seconds later, his head exploded, along with most of his shoulders, covering his 'friends' in a mist of bone fragments, blood, and parts of their former leader. Everyone ran for cover, leaving the girl unattended.

Pete and Billy were on the move again before everyone found a hiding place.

-

They didn't limit their damage to the people, either. Billy's rifle put six vehicles out of commission over the next three days. Broken engine blocks were hard to replace, and the big fifty caliber rounds went through even the toughest blocks. They only targeted the moving vehicles, a fact not lost on the people in charge of the town.

Also not lost on them was the two deaths and three injuries caused by the exploding engine blocks and over penetration of the heavy rifle rounds. By the seventh day, no one was driving anywhere.

Search parties were sent out looking for the shooters. Billy and Pete moved each time they shot, and often moved yet again before taking another shot. When whoever was in charge wised up and sent almost every man and woman out to search, they withdrew, watching until the search parties returned, carefully counting each one to make sure no one had stayed behind to ambush them.

"I would have left at least two men out here, lying low, to watch for us," Pete told Billy. "Either no one down there knows anything about tactics, or we killed the one who did."

"Makes it easier for us," was all Billy said.

-

They took the next three days 'off', setting up in a good location, and taking no shots. The idea, Pete told Billy, was to let them relax, think it was over. Gradually, they would relax their guard, and try to get back to whatever was normal for them.

"Once they get back to their beat, we'll start again."

So, they watched, and they waited for three days. The time wasn't wasted, as they observed the comings and goings in the town. Slowly but surely, they started to get an idea of what they were up against.

There was no set group of people. That was something that stood out. The thugs running what was left of the town were from all walks of life, if their dress was anything to go by. A few wore leathers that reminded Billy of biker gangs. Pete had recognized two different army patches among those wearing military style clothing. A few were dressed as farmers, or ranchers.

Odd Billy Todd

"We can't really be sure, though," Pete mused. "They could have taken those clothes from anywhere. The two guys I saw with the army patches, though, they sort of look the part. Still, if they had any experience at all, they'd be laying in wait for us, not walking around town."

They had narrowed down where the prisoners were being kept as well. The men were being held in the old jail, they were sure. A few had been brought in and out to perform one menial task or another, always under heavy guard.

They were also fairly certain that the women and children were being held in what had been a hotel. There were always men on guard there, as well as some tough looking women. Neither wanted to think what went on inside the hotel.

"Reckon there ain't much we can do for them," Billy lamented.

"I know," Pete agreed. "But we'll keep a look out. If we get the chance, we'll try and spring them. I'd say try to get the men, first. If we can arm them, they might be of some help."

-

While Billy and Pete were working to keep the gang in Franklin off balance, the others were working hard at home. The morning the two had left, Every able bodied man and woman reported to the community building. Soon, they were headed into town. It took a few hours, but they managed to get three additional dump trucks running. They took the trucks back to a small hillside near the gravel pit, and started loading them with dirt, using a front end loader.

Soon, the trucks were moving back and forth to the highway, what was considered the 'back' way into the valley. Starting at the edge of the right-of-way, the trucks started dumping load after load of dirt. As the small dozer they were using spread the dirt out, others walked behind, sewing hay seed. With any luck, the roadbed would soon match the fields around it, flowing with hay.

They worked for three days, almost non-stop. Most ate on the road, or when they were waiting for new dirt. It was hard work, and grimy in the hot sun, but no one complained. Everyone knew what was at risk. If they wanted to live, to survive, they had to hide.

By noon of the fourth day, they had covered the mile-and-three-quarters of road that ran to the tree line. Five people spent over an hour trying to see the road from the highway, from every angle they could find. Terry finally lowered his binoculars, and pronounced the job done.

"Take about three weeks, or so, for that alfalfa to start risin'," Jerry remarked. "After that, I reckon no one that don't know that road's there will be able to find it."

The next day, they started the process over in Cedar Bend. The job there was both easier, and more difficult. Easier because of the small rise that would hide the rest of the road, once they had covered what was visible, and harder because more work was required to camouflage the street. The road sign was pulled from the ground, as was the highway sign that indicated an intersection ahead.

In the end, a small shed was moved from elsewhere in town, and filled with and odds and ends assortment of hand tools and wire. The things that a small shack like that would have on a farm or ranch. It took two days to complete on this end, and the result was just as good.

This time bluegrass was used, instead of hay. It would look good, and grow fairly quickly. Once it was growing, nothing would remain to suggest that a road had ever been there. The last touch was a cattle gate, secured with a rusty looking lock. It wasn't actually rusty, but only a close inspection would reveal that.

"I think this is actually better than the other side," Jerry approved. "Heck, I been livin' here all my life, and if I didn't know there was a road there, I'd never suspect."

"Good," George nodded, wiping his brow with a gloved hand. "That's the point, right? So, what's next?" he asked Terry Blaine.

"Tomorrow we start working on defensive structures."

-

Terry had found a geographical map of the small valley, and used a copy machine to enlarge it and make extra copies. They used the machine sparingly, since they didn't have much of the toner the machine needed, but this was something they needed.

"We're going to build some defenses along a rough ring around the houses," he told the assembled valley folk. "We have a few heavy weapons, and we'll sight places for them where they'll do the most good. In addition, we'll construct some dead-fall roadblocks that we can move into place given a few minutes warning. We'll also look at booby trapping certain areas where we don't go, and others might use to sneak up on us. It's important to keep the children away from these areas," he reminded everyone. "Right now, we'll concentrate on fighting positions. They need to be strong, well concealed, and offer good fields of fire." He paused, looking them over.

"The only way we'll beat off a determined attack is fighting from cover, and inflicting as many casualties on our attackers as possible. We don't have the manpower, or the equipment, to face a large group in the open. So, we learn the terrain, we stash weapons and ammunition in places around the valley that can be accessed in an emergency, and we train to use them."

"Once our defenses are in place, we'll run some drills. See how fast we can respond, and what works and doesn't. We'll likely have to make adjustments after the drills, but that's what they're for, so don't worry about that."

"We'll start here, here, and here," he told them, pointing to where he'd made red dots on the map. "We should be able to get those done tomorrow. These will be the places we'll set up our heavier weapons. Once that's finished, we'll start creating supporting positions."

"So, everyone get a good night's sleep. We'll start bright and early in the morning." He ignored the groans of protest. He agreed with them.

But it had to be done.

-

John Easel, known as 'Big John' to everyone in what was left of Franklin, was a thinking man. Not many would have guessed that, since he was a huge, hulking brute, and cultivated the reputation of an ignorant bully. No one challenged his leadership of the group because of that, and the three men who made sure he stayed in charge.

But he wasn't dumb. Not by a long shot.

He'd lost seven people so far to the Shooter. That's what his people had taken to calling the sniper that had plagued them for the last week. Seven killed, and three that were left useless, arms or legs lost to the heavy rounds. Those three wouldn't make it much longer. There was no place here for people who couldn't do their share. They'd be dealt with, and soon.

Meanwhile, he was experiencing a reluctance among his followers to get out and work. The Shooter hadn't struck in three days, though, and Big John's patience was wearing thin. So he'd ordered everyone back to work. He had to replace the ruined vehicles, for one thing. There were plenty around, but getting them running wasn't always easy. None of his men were real mechanics, and John wasn't either.

Times had been hard over the winter. So hard that he and his followers had crossed a line that few men crossed. There had been revulsion at first, not merely reluctance but outright refusal. He hadn't worried about that. Sooner or later, everyone gave in to a hungry belly.

In hindsight, once they had crossed that line, no one seemed to care anymore. It was as if their last vestige of humanity had left them. No longer concerned with civilized behavior, the people he led had given themselves over to the depravity that often accompanied such acts.

By spring, they had lost any sense of humanity. No regret, no morals, no restraints left. It was almost as if they suddenly realized there was no more real authority left, and they could do all those nasty things that they'd always wanted to, but were afraid of the consequences. And there were no more consequences.

Well, other than Big John. He had to put his foot down once in a while. Had to be some discipline, after all. Couldn't just have people running around willy-nilly doing as they pleased.

No, someone had to be in charge, and Big John had decided that was him. Things had been fine until a few weeks ago, when the slaughterhouse had been burned. That had left them short on food, and he'd reluctantly taken from the 'stores' he had meant to sell or trade to the train people. He hated to lose out, but people had to eat.

If only the train got here soon enough, they could trade the rest of their prisoners, minus a few of the prettier women and a handful of promising kids, for supplies they needed. He didn't know what that bunch wanted all these people for, and didn't really care, so long as they payed him.

Now that the Shooter seemed to have been scared off by the search parties, it was time to. . . .

His thoughts were interrupted by a loud boom echoing across town, and a gurgled scream just outside his building.

—

"He was guarding something," Pete whispered. "Wonder what?"

"Guess we'll see," Billy shrugged. "Want to move?" Pete considered that, and shook his head.

"Not yet. This is a good spot, and you're well back into the room. Let's stay here, and see who comes to have a look see."

"Okay."

They waited for almost ten minutes. Finally, a crowd started to gather, looking at the latest mischief of The Shooter.

"Take that big one," Pete suggested. "The one that looks like he's giving orders. Or arguing. I can't tell. He's wearing overalls, and a web belt."

"I got'im," Billy replied. Slowly he squeezed the slack from the trigger, let his breath out about half way, and finished his squeeze.

"Big John, somethin' got to be done!" the man across from him complained. "We can't keep goin' like this!"

"I know that, Abel," John replied calmly. "I'm workin' on it, but these things take time. I got two men out there right now, tryin' to track him down."

"Two! That ain't nowhere's near enough, John! Oughta be at least ten. Or twenty even!"

Big John never got the chance to answer as Able's large body was suddenly de-constructed right in front of him. Parts of Able went everywhere, including on to Big John. The big man stood stock still for a full five seconds, blood and gore drenching him. Finally, he took a breath.

"I want him *FOUND*!" he screamed at the top of his lungs. Underlings spread out like ducklings, racing to find somewhere else to be.

"Find'im! And *kill'im*!" he ordered his lieutenants. They nodded and hurried to organize search parties from among the extremely reluctant participants.

"DAMN YOU!" John roared, still rooted to his spot on the sidewalk. Abruptly he turned and stomped back into his building to wash Abel off of him.

-

"Reckon we know who's in charge now," Pete observed.

"Yep," Billy nodded. "Reckon I'll take him, he comes out again."

"We got to move, for now," Pete shook his head. "Don't worry, you'll have your chance. But for now, let's make tracks."

-

The two men Big John had dedicated to finding the Shooter had heard the first shot, and gone still. They were near the Shooter, it sounded like, so they held up.

The second shot confirmed their belief, and the two men started to move in what they believed was the right direction. Neither man was military trained, but both were hunters. They had hunted all their lives and were good at it.

Unlike the others in town, they hadn't crossed the line into cannibalism. They had managed to live off the scarce game left around the edges of town, a few cans of vegetables still hiding in houses outside of town, and their knowledge of edible roots and plants. They needed things from town, sometimes, though, and had let themselves be employed by John in exchange for things like ammo, and the occasional access to the town's 'entertainment'.

The two men were cousin's, Rob and Kent McMahan. Raised miles from town, the two had always been a rough pair. In trouble with the law from their early teen years, the two had never had much respect for others, and the fall had simply completed their descent into lawless depravity.

They were perfect for this kind of job. And the promised payment was enticing. Their pick of the women awaiting sale to the Train. Neither was intending to miss out on that.

With that in mind, the two cousins began their tracking.

CHAPTER SIXTY-NINE

Pete took a careful look at their surroundings before heading out of the building. They hadn't encountered any trouble up until now, but neither had allowed their caution to wane. This was a deadly dangerous place for them to be, and they never forgot it for even a second.

Pete motioned to Billy, and the two of them moved across the alleyway behind the building they had just vacated. Heading down the small alleyway, they entered another building, going straight through, and up to the second floor, where they set up to watch.

"We'll watch our back trail a bit, and see what happens," Pete whispered. Billy nodded, and set to cleaning his rifle. He was still working when he saw Pete stiffen slightly.

"What is it?" Billy asked. He silently closed the action on the rifle, and set it aside.

"I think there's a couple guys following us," Pete told him, amusement in his voice. "They're either bait, or stupid."

"Could be both," Billy suggested with a shrug.

"Suppose so. They're working through the building we were using. Probably looking for sign."

"We didn't leave anything," Billy shrugged.

"No, but a good tracker will be able to tell we've been there," Pete pointed out. "I'm tempted to move while they're in there. On the other hand, I want to wait and see what they do. Where they go."

"We could always follow them," Billy suggested. Pete considered that for a moment.

"We'll see. Depends on what they do."

-

"Look here, Rob," Kent whispered harshly. He pointed out the window, and Rob realized is lined up with where others were still cleaning up pieces of Abel.

"See here, too," Kent added, pointing to the dust. "I think. . .I think they's two of'em," he decided. "They's two outlines in the dust, here. One a layin', one a sittin', best I can tell. They're pretty good, too. Wasn't for this dust, we'd likely not seen no sign of'em a'tall."

"Reckon you can suss out whichaway's they went?" Rob asked. Kent studied the scuffs in the dust for a moment.

"I kin try. Them's army boots, right there," he pointed. "Pretty sure both of'em are. We kin try tailin'em from here. Long as the dust lasts, or if'n they make a mistake, we'll find'em."

"I'd sooner find'em now, and be done, as have to go back and tell Big John we ain't yet got'em."

"Well, alrighty then. Looks like we go huntin'." The two men left the room, Kent trying to maintain a trail of some kind in the thin dust along the building's floors.

"Reckon they went out the back," Kent announced, after a few minutes of studying. "Right in'ta the alley, there."

"Can ya get a track on'em out there?" Rob asked.

"No idee," Kent shrugged. "Hafta go and have a look-see." The two made their way outside, cautiously. They weren't taking any chances with someone like the Shooter.

-

Little did the cousins know that the 'Shooter' and his assistant were watching their every move.

"You know, I take back what I said," Pete mused. "They found enough sign in there to follow us out that particular door. That means they know a little bit, anyway."

"Look like hunters," Billy observed. Pete considered that, and nodded.

"Yeah, that makes sense."

The two fell silent, watching to see what the two men tracking them did. Pete's worst fear was that the two would call for more help, and search all the buildings. If that happened, he and Billy would have to get out of the area fast and unseen, or they'd be in a fight. One they would probably lose at this juncture.

-

"Reckon we oughta call for help?" Kent asked.

"Help? For what?" Rob demanded. "We call for help, you can forget about that little redhead gal. Somebody else'll be taking care o' her come winter."

"Was thinkin' that we could get some help to search out these here buildings," Kent explained. "Reckon if we find'em, John ain't got no call not to give us our due hire."

"You really think he'll go for that?" Rob demanded.

"I bl'eve he'll be so happy to have that Shooter, he'll give us pretty much whatever we ask for," Kent said simply. Rob considered that.

"Might be you got a point, cousin," he said at last. "But let's see if we can't narrow it down a bit more, 'fore we go callin' the calvary."

-

". . .fore we go callin' the calvary."

Pete sighed in relief, and lowered his rifle. The two would likely never know how close they had been to dying right then. The noise suppressor on Pete's M-4 wouldn't make the rifle completely quiet, but among these buildings, it would prevent the noise from traveling very far.

"I think we need to take them two out," Billy whispered. "They liable to be a problem 'fore this is over."

"I agree, but I'm not sure we should do it here," Pete replied. "We're still way too close to where we were. There's almost bound to be people just on the other side of that building," he nodded to where they had been earlier. "No way they don't hear."

Billy considered that, grudgingly agreeing. Letting these two go was unsafe. They were clearly hunting for Pete and Billy. Might show up anywhere, at anytime. Eliminating them was the better option. He sat back.

"So, what'da we do?"

"We wait. They just might come to us."

-

Odd Billy Todd

The cousins looked the alley over carefully, Rob depending on Kent more than himself. Kent was by far the better tracker of the two, and Rob let him take the lead. Kent, for his part, examined everything carefully, but came up short.

"There ain't a lick o' nothin' here I kin foller," he told Rob. "Don't mean they's all that careful, but this pavement ain't much for leavin' no traces. And I ain't seen nothin' outta place, neither."

"Reckon they ducked inta one o' these here buildin's?" Rob asked, nodding to the building they were in rear of.

"Could be," Kent mused. "Don't rightly know. Ain't no sign of it, but then, they wouldn't be, less they dropped sump'n."

"Let's check it out, then," Rob ordered. "Real quiet like." Kent nodded, and led the way into the building.

-

"Well, here they come," Pete sighed.

"Should be more careful what ya wish for," Billy grinned. Pete just shook his head. He nodded to Billy's M-4.

"Got a can for that?" he asked.

"Can?" Billy frowned, then brightened. "Silencer, ya mean?" Pete nodded.

"Yeah, I got one," Billy surprised him. He quickly detached the flash suppressor, and removed a gray piece of tubing from his pack.

"Where'd you get that?" Pete asked.

"Made it," Billy replied, carefully screwing the silencer onto the rifle.

"You *made* it?" Pete goggled.

"Yeah," Billy looked up. "What?"

"Billy, that thing's got to be right on, or it could blow up in your face!" Pete hissed. "And it's got to be quiet."

"It works," Billy assured him. "And it's quiet enough."

"I hope so, because they're coming." Pete moved to the hallway. The stairs were centrally located in the building, opening up into a main hallway that led to now long empty offices.

"I'm going to cross over, and set up in one of those doorways. You set up here. Let them both get on the landing, then we take them together. I'll take the first one up, you take the second." Billy nodded, and settled in as Pete hot-footed across the landing as quickly and quietly as he could.

-

Kent eased up the stairway, carefully testing each step. Rob was close behind, covering his cousin, depending on him to make sure they didn't make noise.

"I think they's up here," Kent whispered. "Tracks in the dust. Army boots."

"Shh," Rob hissed, motioning for Kent to keep going. The other man nodded, and continued his climb, lifting his rifle as he did so. As he neared the top of the stairs, the hairs on his neck rose. He stopped at once, dead still.

"What?" Rob asked, almost in Kent's ear. Kent sniffed the air, and then looked back at Rob.

"I can smell'em," he whispered back. "I think it's time to call in that calv'ry you was talkin' 'bout. Reckon we're walkin' right into an ambush." Rob looked at him for a moment, then sighed. Nodding in agreement, he took out his radio, and turned it on.

"...answer me right now, or you can forget any reward for takin' out that shooter!" Big John's voice boomed through the building.

"Turn that down!" Kent hissed though his teeth, just as they heard a voice at the top of the stairs.

"Now Billy!"

Pete had watched, holding his breath, as the two edged closer to the landing. He wanted them both out in the open, and clear. They had to take them quickly, and then get moving, in case there was someone nearby.

Even as he watched, the front man stopped, and sniffed the air.

Damn he's good, Pete thought, dejectedly. They would have to take their. . . .

"...answer me right now, or you can forget any reward for takin' out that shooter!"

"Turn that down!" he heard the man in front hiss. It was now or never Pete decided. He leaped to his feet, bringing his rifle to bear.

"Now, Billy!" he shouted.

The two men on the stairs froze for a split second. Kent's eyes had just enough time to recognize the threat before Pete's rifle *burped* a three-round burst into his chest. Rob, caught by surprise at the sight of his cousin being shot, raised his own rifle too slowly. Even as he brought the rifle to bear on Pete, he felt something smash through him.

Kent was right, his last thought came in a rush. *There are two of. . . .*

"Let's go!" Pete ordered. The two men returned to their 'room' and grabbed their gear. As they ran down the stairs, Pete eyed the radio, and grabbed it in one hand, never slowing. He quickly shut it off, and jammed it into his pocket. The two of them hit the street outside at a run.

Right in the middle of a work detail. The two guards were already alerted, and their rifles raised.

Pete didn't hesitate. He snapped a three-round burst into the man to the left, hoping that Billy would be able to take the man on the right.

He didn't have to. One of the four prisoners grabbed the man's rifle, wrenching it from his grasp. Without a pause, the prisoner struck the suddenly disarmed guard, still reeling in shock, in the throat with the butt of his own rifle. The guard collapsed choking and gagging, his larynx crushed.

Pete had his rifle on the other three, while Billy covered the now armed prisoner.

"Reckon you better lower that rifle, friend," Billy said calmly.

"Jesus, it's him!" one of the other prisoners exclaimed. "It's the Shooter!"

"Are all of you prisoners?" Pete asked, his rifle still on them.

"Hell yes! But not no more!" Two of them took off, and nothing Pete did or said could stop them. He looked at the man who had disarmed the guard.

"Look we can't stay here," Pete told him. "You need to make up your mind what you're gonna do."

"I'm coming with you, if you're still aimin' to kill these bastards," the man snarled. "If not, then I guess I'm staying. At least until I can get my sister."

"What about you?" Pete asked the other man.

"Better'n the alternative," he shrugged. "I'm game."

Odd Billy Todd

"Then let's beat feet!" Pete urged. "Billy, site Three! Take the lead, I'll take drag. Let's move!" Pete's command was all they needed. Billy moved out quick, making tracks in a round about way to one of their stash points. Site Three was a larger stash, with ammunition, food, water, and a first aid kit. By Billy's reckoning it was about nine blocks away.

Moving carefully but quickly, they negotiated the distance in twenty minutes or so, by Billy's reckoning. During that time, they saw no one, but that didn't mean no one saw them, and Billy knew it.

"We can't stay here," Pete warned. "Someone may have seen us. We need to grab this gear, and get moving again. You two bear a hand. Once we get where we're going, we'll get you some food and water."

The two freed prisoners grabbed the supplies, and then the four of them were on their way again.

"Billy, find us a hole!" Pete urged.

"Workin' on it," Billy replied. He led them further afield into the edge of town. After thirty minutes of non-stop movement, they halted in front of an old Brownstone.

"Look's good to me," Billy suggested. Pete nodded his agreement.

"Sweep and clear," he ordered. Billy nodded, and stepped inside, the others following. Billy was already deep into the house, his tactical light leading the way. The windows still had heavy drapes, and the natural light of day couldn't penetrate them.

Billy moved upstairs, with Pete covering the ground floor. The two former prisoners remained with him. Soon, Billy was at the head of the stairs again.

"Clear," he called. "C'mon up." The others joined him on the second floor. Billy was already in one of the front bedrooms, looking out over the street.

"Look's clear, for now," he reported. There was a shot in the distance, then another, followed quickly by two more.

"That'll be your friends, most like," Billy drawled.

"They wasn't our friends," the armed prisoner retorted. "Ass kissing suck-ups, the both of them. Always trying to get in good with anyone who'd listen. Couple o' guys had worked out a plan to jump the guards, free ourselves, and them two ratted 'em out. Good riddance to bad rubbish."

"Ya'll sit down," Billy ordered, motioning to the bed. He reached over and took the rifle from the prisoner before he could stop him.

"I'll just hang on ta this for ya, next little bit," he smiled. The man started to object, then shrugged, and sat down.

"Who are you guys, and where are you from?" Pete asked. "More to the point, how'd you wind up here?"

-

It was hot in the valley. Details had been working for two straight days on the fortifications. Even Terry was pleased with what they had accomplished in such a short amount of time.

Three permanent posts had been put in place. Jerry, Ben, and March had gone into town, and managed to scrounge enough cement to pour thick concrete walls and a roof over the three machine gun positions. The top and outside were then hidden behind a log wall, which was then camouflaged with shrubbery and debris.

From a distance of fifty feet, even knowing where they were, spotting them was difficult.

They were divided into two teams, one led by Terry, the other by George. They knew the most about this sort of thing, save for Jerry, who had conceded their greater knowledge at once.

"Forty years ago, boys, or near enough it makes no difference," the old farmer shook his head.

With the three main positions dug along the only three ways into the valley, the teams took to erecting fighting positions along the roads, and constructing the dead fall roadblocks that Terry had wanted.

The fighting positions were layered dirt and log structures, some covered and some not. Meant to provide cover and concealment, they were scratched out anywhere that the terrain favored such a thing, and well hidden.

The roadblocks were simple, and efficient. Heavy logs were banded together with odd bits of chain and cable, whatever could be scraped together, and placed just off the roadways. Longer lines were then run through the woods to the nearer houses, where they could be hooked to a truck or tractor, and then pulled across the road. They wouldn't stop a determined attacker, but they would slow them down. Which would give the defenders time to prepare.

By the end of the third day, both men were satisfied that the work was pretty much done.

"We'll need some extra work, along, and we'll be adding to these, and improving some of them, as we go, but this is a good base to start from. I know we're all give out, so I'm calling a day off. We all got chores to see to, and we need some rest."

"We'll wait a couple days, get caught up, and then we'll start some real training. Nothing fancy, just familiarize you with the weapons we'll be using, and some basic tactics that might help us if we're attacked."

"Okay, everybody, let's fall out and head in." It as a group of tired people that trekked home that evening. George and Terry stayed behind.

"What you think, George?" Terry asked.

"Well, it looks pretty," George shrugged. "Terry, you know, better'n I do, this ain't gonna stop a large, determined force. We can hurt'em, but we'll never be able to stop'em. Not without more people."

"I know," Terry nodded, his voice quiet. "But it's something. We can't just sit here. And this stuff," he nodded to a nearby log wall, "makes them feel more secure. That's worth a lot, right now. They're scared. This will help settle them."

"How you think they're doing?" George asked. He didn't have to explain which 'they' he was referring to.

"No way to know," Terry shrugged. "But Pete's smart. Savy. And don't sell Billy short. The two of'em make a pretty decent team." He paused, looking over the fields nearby. "I hope they're taking it to them," he added. Turning to look at George, he added;

"We can use all the help we can get, right now."

CHAPTER SEVENTY

"My name's Reggie Carroll," the unarmed man spoke. "I was from Nashville, once upon a time. Now, I don't rightly know where I'm from. Nowhere, I guess," he shrugged. "I was tryin' to make do on my own, after things turned bad. Wasn't doin' too bad, but about a month ago I got a little careless. Before I knew it, I was surrounded by this bunch. Been here ever since."

"I'm Dillon. Dillon Branch. Live over near Center Hill Lake. My sister and I were out foraging when they took us. No way to escape. My sister can't shoot, and there were too many of them. It was either let them take us, or get her killed. I ain't so sure I made the right choice, now," he admitted.

"You're alive," Billy shrugged. "So is she, maybe." Branch looked at Billy for a minute, and nodded.

"Who're you guys?" he asked.

"Name's Billy," was all Billy said. "Came here huntin', so to speak."

"I'm Pete," Pete spoke up. "I clean up after him." Branch snorted in dark amusement.

"You two got this whole bunch jumpin' at shadows, I'll tell you that. There ain't a lick o' sense between this whole lot when it comes to facin' real fightin' men with an even chance. But there's a shitload of'em. That's how they get you. Numbers."

"And trickery, according to what I hear," Carroll offered. "Little settlement up the way, Weber I think it is, let a man put up with them for a few days. Next thing they know, few days later, he helps this bunch walk right in on them. Took them all without a shot. Made their way into the day care, and threatened to kill every kid in the place, they didn't surrender. And that snake in the grass had met everyone by then, so there was no way for part of them to stay hidden and see what they could do. He kept a count, and they kept guns on the kids until everyone was accounted for." Pete looked at Billy on hearing this.

"Well, that's one question answered." Billy nodded, saying nothing.

"How many men do they have locked up down there?" Pete asked. "And what for? Are they willing to fight, if we can get them armed?"

"I don't know exactly how many," Branch replied. "They keep it dark in the cells. And separated into small groups. As for what for, all I know is what some of the guards have said. Apparently, we're being sold to someone on a train. No idea what for, though for the women, I can guess."

"This bunch is. . .well, they're crazy!" Carroll blurted. "Did you. . .did you know they *eat* people?"

"We heard the rumor," was all Pete would say.

"It ain't no rumor," Branch said thickly. "At first, from what I've heard, they did it to survive. Now, they got to where they like it. Been several prisoners go missing of late. No one wants to ask what happened to them. Afraid of the answer."

"I 'magine," Billy snorted. "Don't blame'em none, either."

"What are you two doing here, anyway?" Carroll asked. "Are you from the government? Come to rescue us?" Hope filled his face, and Pete almost sighed.

"You oughta know by now, there ain't no government any more," Pete told him gently. "None except what we make. As to what we're doing here, well, we're buying time. And trying to keep this bunch penned in as long as we can." Billy frowned, but said nothing. He wasn't sure they should be telling these guys anything at all. Least of all the truth.

"All two of you?" Carroll asked derisively.

"Been doing okay so far," Pete shrugged.

"You've been doing more than okay," Branch chuckled bitterly. "Like I said, this whole bunch is jumping at shadows. Including their own."

"You handled that rifle like you knew how," Pete noted. Branch nodded.

"I do. Spent six years RA, then went private. Just lucky I was home when things happened. Just as likely to have been in Africa or South America."

"Blackwater?" Pete asked.

"*Hell* no!" Branch looked offended. "I'm a *soldier*. I worked for Black Diamond International."

"That right?" Pete mused. He'd heard of them. Small outfit, but professional, just like Branch said. "Knew a fella with them, once. Named Pasquallie. Ever run into him?"

"You mean Pascal?" Branch smiled. "Nice trick, by the way. Yeah, I worked for him on my first tour in Africa. Working for the government and the Conservation of Wildlife Fund, believe it or not."

"Congo?" Pete asked.

"Yep," Branch nodded. "Helping guard gorillas, and stop illegal charcoal operations."

"Huh?" Billy couldn't help it.

"I know, it sounds nutty," Branch shrugged. "Thing is, the charcoal keeps the rebels there in money. Hell of it is, the people in the refugee camps really need it, but they won't allow anyone to do it. Not only do the rebels use it, but it's destroying the forests. Where the gorilla's live. Hard to care about that when you need to cook, and stay warm, I reckon, but. . . ." he lifted both hands, palms up. "It's a job."

"Look, I hate to break into this professional resume swap, here," Carroll said a bit snidely. "But what are we gonna do now?"

"Well, I'm gonna eat," Billy shrugged. "Ain't but MREs, but you're welcome to share."

"After the swill they've been giving us, I'll take it and treat it like lunch at Tiffany's," Branch nodded.

What's an MRE?" Carroll asked.

"It's a delicious supplemental government meal designed for emergencies and military use," Branch told him straight faced. "Best food you can get outside a kitchen."

-

"You lied to me," Carroll accused, his face making it clear that his MRE, a wonderful selection called Chicken Ala King, was not, in fact, delicious.

"Try some hot sauce," Branch and Pete said at the same time, then laughed. "Look," Branch took the envelope, and pulled forth a tiny bottle of Tabasco Sauce. "This is in almost every pack. You can cover up almost anything with it." Carroll looked suspicious, but applied the sauce and tried again. He nodded after a moment.

"That does help," he admitted.

"You have no idea," Pete laughed.

"Look, I don't want to look a gift horse in the mouth, or anything," Branch spoke up, "but if you guys ain't interested in freeing their prisoners, then I'm gonna need that rifle back. I don't aim to leave my sister in this hell hole for a minute longer than I have to."

"Cool your jets," Pete raised a hand. "We'd thought about that, but like your partner said, there's only two of us. All we've been doing lately is trying to keep them off balance."

"And now?" Carroll looked concerned.

"We'll see," Pete shrugged. "We're gonna have to get a look at the holding area. We're gonna have to scrounge some wheels that'll take everyone away that wants to leave. We'll have to think on freeing the other men first, either to help us free the women, or create a big enough distraction that we can do it. Lot of things we have to plan for."

"Look, I don't want to seem ungrateful," Carroll said, "and I sympathize with the plight of your sister, I do," he said to Branch. "But. . .I'm not a soldier of any kind, and never have been. I've never even fired a gun."

"How you been livin', you ain't able to hunt?" Billy asked.

"What? Hunt?" Carroll stammered. "I. . .I haven't needed to hunt. I was finding plenty of stuff to live on in Nashville. It's pretty much deserted these days. Well, there are people there, but not many. Most people fled."

"You mean there's still stuff in Nashville?" Billy asked, suddenly interested.

"Well, yeah," Carroll answered. "Or there was. I don't know if these idiots took it or not. But. . .almost nothing was touched that I saw. It was almost as if people who had survived were afraid to come into town."

"How 'bout that?" Billy murmured to himself. His mind came to life in a wheel of thinking. Nashville would have a lot of the things they needed. There would be fuel, supplies, clothes, building materials, the list was almost endless.

"Billy," Pete cut into his thinking. "One job at a time, brother," he reminded his friend gently. Billy nodded, his mind back on the here and now.

"Anyway, like I said, I appreciate it and everything," Carroll continued, "but. . .I'm not a fighter. I don't know how. And. . .well, I don't want to, either."

"You ain't gonna last long, like that," Billy told him flatly.

"What?"

"Things ain't like they used ta be," Billy reminded him. "Ain't nobody gonna fight your battles for ya. You better learn to take care o' yaself, cause ain't nobody else gonna do it for ya."

"I don't need anybody to take care of me, if people will just leave me alone!" Carroll almost cried.

"Yeah, about that," Pete smirked. "Case you haven't noticed, that really isn't how things are going these days." Carroll's face flushed at that, and he stood.

"Well, all I need to do is get home, and I'll be fine. No more being careless, that's all. I'll make sure they can't take me again. Can you at least give me a ride home?"

"With what?" Billy asked. He was starting to wish Carroll had run off with the others.

"How did you get here?" Carroll demanded. "If you were planning a rescue, *surely* you made provisions for taking everyone away from here!"

"We *weren't* planning a rescue," Pete rolled his eyes. "Which we told you earlier, had you been listening. We walked here. When we're done, we'll walk back."

"Walk?" Carroll looked aghast. "It's. . .it's *fifty miles* or better back to Nashville!"

"'Bout that," Billy nodded in agreement. "Better get someway to carry ya some water. Maybe some food, too. Doubt there's much 'long the way."

"You. . .you could give me. . . ."

"I ain't a charity, fella," Billy shook his head. "Like I said, ain't nobody gonna do it for ya. You head on out, and good luck to ya."

"I. . .you can't just leave me! It's not *right*!"

"Whole lotta things ain't right these days," Billy shrugged. "I don't recall takin' ya ta raise. Ain't my 'sponsibility. An' I ain't aimin' ta leave off what I'm doin' ta take ya home, neither."

Pete listened as Billy told Carroll what time it was, a slight worry beginning to creep up on him. He'd learned a good deal about Billy over the time they'd worked together. One of the things he'd noticed was that when Billy's drawl and pronunciation began to go downhill, he was getting irritated.

Like right now.

"I *demand* that. . . ." Before Pete could stop him, Billy was at Carroll's throat. Or rather his knife was at Carroll's throat.

"I done heard 'bout all yer whinin' I kin stand fer one night," Billy all but growled. "You need ta stop. Case you ain't noticed, I ain't above killin' somebody."

Carroll's face had gone completely white, and his eyes were wide enough to see the edge of his eyeballs. His lips trembled, but he didn't speak.

"I ain't carin' if you ever get to Nashville, hear?" Billy said more calmly. "I got fam'ly I'm worryin' over, and next ta them, you don't even exist. Now you got that?" Carroll nodded jerkily.

"Mister Carroll, I think you ought to consider sitting down, and maybe being quiet for a while," Pete interjected slowly. "My friend here's kinda on edge, and you're making him worse. Trust me, you don't want to see worse." He looked at Billy.

"Billy, why don't you let Mister Carroll here sit down, and we'll see if he can be quiet, huh?" The fire went out of Billy's eyes, and he removed the knife.

"Just 'member, you ain't the only one got pro'lems," he snarled, and went to sit by the window in the other room.

"That. . . ." Carroll began.

"I wouldn't, was I you," Branch shook his head. "That man ain't playin'. He'll like as not kill you next time. Hell, I can't say I blame'im. You really are a whiny little shit, ain't ya?"

-

Everyone had taken a day off at the Farms, seeing to their work around their own places. Jerry and Jon had made the rounds in the fields, checking the crops, and working out between them how they would run the harvest. Both agreed that there was not enough grain storage available, and headed over to talk with Ben, who was working with Ralph and George to set posts for the first hay barn. He listened to them describe what was needed, and then went to Jerry's to see the older man's corn crib. After looking that over, he confirmed that he could build more storage, but that lumber would be an issue.

"We can use logs, I think," he told them. "But we'll need a safe way to seal around them, or critters will eat us out of house and home. What can we use for that, that won't hurt the grain?"

"Old timer's used mud," Jerry shrugged. "I guess we could too."

"You know, that makes me think of something else," Ben mused. "We could use adobe bricks to build some buildings. I mean, it won't be like the one's they build out west, since we don't get that kind of dry heat here. But we could kiln'em. Dry'em out like with a big oven."

"We need to score some lumber somewhere," Jon sighed. "I know we've got some, but it's pretty good stuff, and we need to hold on to it for building projects down the road. We could use rough lumber for grain storage."

"We need to build us a saw mill," Jerry nodded. "We can cut logs and saw our own boards."

"That'd be good," Ben agreed. "For now, though, I need to get back. I want to have that hay barn ready to roof as soon as possible."

-

The first group of 'trainees' was gathered together in the shade of Billy and Rhonda's yard. By separating into two groups, one would keep working, and keep an eye out, while the other learned to handle the military rifles taken from the National Guard armory in Columbia. Terry and George would be teaching them how to disassemble the rifles, clean and reassemble them, and then how to operate them. Lastly, they would learn to fire them.

George looked at the group in front of him, and sighed ever so slightly. This would be a long day.

-

"That's good work, Toby," Terry patted the boy on the back as he finished putting his rifle back together. "Good job. But then, I expected that from you." Toby flushed with pleasure at that.

Everyone else managed to put their rifles back together as well, though none so quickly or cleanly as Toby. George looked at them.

"Do it again," he ordered, to a symphony of groans.

"Listen, people," he cut their complaints off. "When you get this down, you're going to shoot these rifles. And they had better be put together correctly, since if they aren't, they might just blow up in your face." That sobered everyone, and they went through the process again.

-

George and Terry were fairly pleased with the progress. Everyone had done pretty well. Even the women at the Clifton House had learned to handle the rifles, and operate them satisfactorily. In the event they were forced to defend themselves, or the house, they would be able to do so effectively.

The same could be said for the handguns. Everyone who didn't have a handgun had been issued a Beretta, also taken from the armory. The two had discussed, briefly, having everyone use them, so that mags and ammo could be exchanged, but decided against it. Too many people already had their own, and were not inclined to trade. In the end, all of the women at Clifton House wound up with one, every one doing better than expected at the range.

Neither man allowed himself to think this made the community safe. Safer, yes. But against forty, fifty, or more determined attackers, people who had already crossed a line in the sand, they weren't safe.

"We need to have a fall back position," Terry told George that night, as the two of them mulled over their progress so far.

"Got anywhere in mind?" George asked.

"Well, there's really only two places that will work," Terry sighed. "It's either Billy's place, or the Clifton House. I favor the Clifton Place, because we wouldn't have to move all those kids, and there's a basement to hide them in."

"Wouldn't want to get pinned in there," George observed.

"We'd have to make sure we had a way out," Terry nodded. "And somewhere to go to, if we had to abandon."

"If we have to abandon, I don't think we'd get far, trying to carry everyone," George shook his head. "I think we just have to bite the bullet here, Terry, and make a stand somewhere. Clifton House is as good as any, and better than most. I say we start fortifying the place, and stocking it for a siege if it comes to that."

"Think on it," Terry finally agreed. "I hate the thought of using that place. But. . .we've got to think about so many things. That place meets all of our needs, like it or not."

-

Toby awoke from a dead sleep, sitting straight up in bed. He was wringing wet with sweat, despite the fan running in his room. He rubbed a hand over his face, trying to force his heart to slow down.

He had been in Franklin again, only this time things hadn't gone so well. This was the third time he had been awakened by that dream, and it was starting to scare him. Toby didn't like being scared.

He looked at his watch, noting that it was three in the morning. He sighed, and rolled out of bed. No sense in waiting. He wouldn't be going back to sleep any time soon.

He showered and dressed as quietly as possible, then took his rifle and walked out onto the porch. On an impulse, he decided he'd walk down to the road, and back. There was no real reason why, it just came to him.

As he walked, his mind ran over so many things. A year ago, he'd been just another lazy teenager from his lackluster generation. He didn't like farm life, he didn't like school, he didn't want to do anything much. Never thought about making something of himself.

He realized that the notion of making something of himself had pretty much been taken out of his hands. So had his dislike of farming. If he wanted to eat, he had to farm. He had to grow crops, raise meat, and keep on doing it. He was learning everything he could from his father. It pained him to think that he might not have many more years with his parents. They had been up in years when he and Shelly had come along.

Odd Billy Todd

We must have seemed like a blessing to them, he reflected. *We sure didn't act like it though. Not until the whole world just up and went to hell.*

And that bothered him too. He wanted to go back and fix all that, but he couldn't. He knew that, of course, but it didn't stop his regrets. How often had he left his aging father to take care of things on the farm while he watched television, played video games, and other useless stuff?

What kind of son does that? he wondered. Billy hadn't done that, he'd bet money. And since when had Billy become so important to him? He thought back on that, and realized it was the day Billy had brought that trailer load of stuff over to them. He'd done that even after he and Shelly had been so mean to him. Never said a word about it.

Toby realized that this had been the turning point. Seeing Billy doing that, even when it might not be appreciated, had made Toby stop and think. Not just about Billy, either. It made Toby examine himself. And the teenager hadn't liked what he'd seen.

True, Shelly was just as bad, but he couldn't change that. And she'd done the same thing, anyway. But Toby had decided, about that time, that he could change himself. He could be a good son, a good neighbor, and learn to farm, raise stock, take care of himself, his family, and his home.

From that time forward, he'd set about proving it, too. Not to everyone else, but to himself. If others saw, that was fine. But the only person whose opinion mattered to him was his own. He vowed he would never again look at himself in the mirror, and not like what he saw. Not like the man looking back at him.

He snorted at the thought of a 'man' looking back. He had only just turned eighteen a little while ago. In the society that was, he'd still be considered a kid. Unsuitable for any responsibility. He looked down at the rifle in his hands, and snorted again.

In this new society, so much like that of long ago, he was a man all right. Whether he wanted to be or not. The days of partying, playing, and acting a fool were long gone. In fact, most of the people he'd shared those activities with were gone. No, all of them were gone. As far as he knew, there wasn't a single person left from his old circle of friends.

Sometimes he felt alone, despite being surrounded by others. There were no other boys near his age, anymore. Not around here. Danny was the closest, but even then, there was four years difference. And anyway, there wasn't much to do, anymore, except work, and watch.

He reached the road, and stopped a moment, listening to the early morning air. It would be hot again today. He could feel it already. Air was a little humid, too. Might rain. He sniffed the air, but couldn't smell any moisture. Maybe not.

Abruptly he turned, and started back to the house. It would soon be sunup, and he'd have work to do. There was never shortage of work around here. On the return trip, he finally turned to the problem that had led him outside so early in the morning.

He had to find a way to stop those dreams. Sooner or later he was going to wake up screaming, and that would scare his mother, and maybe his sister. It would concern his father, who would give him the same look he used to give Toby when he was a boy, and Jerry thought he was into something he couldn't handle.

Toby couldn't stand that. He was a man grown, now, and he had to act like it. And that meant no silly ass nightmares about anything he'd seen, heard, or been a part of. He had to get rid of them, and that was that.

So intent on his thinking was Toby, he didn't notice his father sitting on the porch until he was already up the steps.

"Mornin', son," Jerry said softly. To his credit Toby didn't jump, merely looked over to where Jerry was sitting.

"Dad," he nodded, sitting down next to him.

"Up early, ain't ya son?" Jerry asked.

"Couldn't sleep," Toby shrugged. "Was gonna just sit here, and then decided I'd walk down to the road. Quiet." Jerry nodded.

"Best time o' the mornin'," Jerry breathed deep. "Always did think so. Not hot yet, quiet, good time for a man to sit and think on what worries him. Don't you think?"

"Yes, sir," Toby nodded. "Reckon it is."

"Y'know, when I was younger, I'd come out here, and sit, whenever I had nightmares about Vietnam." He pronounced it vee-et-nahm. "Didn't want to wake your mother. She didn't know I'd been to war. I didn't want her to know. She still don't know, by the way."

Toby nodded, but his mind was racing. His father had nightmares? Had been in combat? He realized that his father had just shared something very personal with him. He felt as if a circle had closed, somewhere. He didn't know what to say, so he stayed silent. In years to come, however, Toby would look back on this moment with pride that his father had entrusted something like this to him.

"Don't get me wrong, I love the attention she gives me," Jerry chuckled. "But some things. . .some things a man just don't want his women folk to know about. Ain't proper, that's all. Ain't. . .right." The word was short, and ended the sentence with a power that Toby recognized. Jerry Had Made A Point, he called it.

"Reckon that's true," he mused. Jerry looked at him.

"How long they been botherin' you," he asked calmly. Toby looked at him, then, surprising himself, answered.

"Week, I guess. Three times, so far. Tonight. . .tonight was pretty bad," he admitted, almost ashamed.

"No shame in having bad dreams, son," Jerry told him firmly, but gently. "Ain't somethin' you can have no control over. It's a manifestation of what you've seen."

"What did I see, pa?" Toby shrugged.

"You saw the underbelly o' the beast, boy," Jerry's voice came back firm. "I'd hoped you'd never have to. Made this place, kept it like I did, thinkin' it would protect you. You and your sister." The older man shook his head.

"Ain't no way to protect you from what's happened, Toby. It saddens me you had to grow up like this. If I had my way, you'd still be innocent. Tryin' to get outta work, playin' them games o' yer's, and workin' to get around me and yer ma."

"I don't want that," Toby shook his head. "Not anymore. I'm happy with the way I am now. I'm not lazy no more, and I don't hate what I see when I look in the mirror. I growed up some. And I needed it."

"Maybe so, but not like this," Jerry said sadly. "I been where you are, right now, Toby. It scares you. Don't seem manly enough. Makes you feel weak." He leaned forward.

"But you ain't, boy. Hear me? You ain't weak, and you ain't soft. You're a man, but just a man. No more, no less." He leaned back then.

"And you ain't no less a man for bein' afraid. I wager was you to talk to Pete, Terry, or George they'd tell you the same thing. And, if they was willin' to admit it, they have nightmares too."

The two of them sat together like that, quiet and thoughtful, for a good long time after they fell silent. Dawn was beginning to top the trees to the east, when Toby spoke again.

"Thanks, Pa."

CHAPTER SEVENTY-ONE

Billy woke with a start. Something was wrong. He lay very still, working to keep his breathing steady, as he tried to gather his wits. He could hear Pete breathing softly not too far away. He also recognized Branch's light snoring. What he didn't hear was. . . .

Billy shot up, looking around him. Carroll was gone.

"Pete, wake up!" Billy called urgently. Instantly both Pete and Branch were awake.

"Carroll's gone," Billy informed them both. "Check your gear. Then we need to be movin'."

"Little piss ant," Branch swore softly. "Cowardly little. . . ."

"We can worry over that later," Pete chided softly. "Right now, we got to move. Shoulda never trusted him." The three of them checked things over quickly. It was soon apparent what Carroll had done.

"He took my canteen, and the last of my MRE's," Pete swore.

"Same here," Billy nodded.

"Well, I didn't have anything," Branch shrugged. "He didn't take the rifle I took from the guards."

"He's tryin' ta git home, I reckon," Billy drawled. "But he ain't like to make it, which means he'll wind up back in their hands."

"Hope they eat'im," Branch muttered.

"Ain't the problem I'm lookin' at," Billy shook his head. "He'll try and trade us for his own sorry hide. And he's like to tell'em 'bout your sister, too." Branch's eyes widened at that.

"Son of . . . ."

"We can worry on that later," Pete said again. "It's time we moved. We need to resupply. Site Five, Billy?" he asked. Billy nodded after a moment's pause.

"Yeah, I guess. We need to get him some ammo for that rifle, and there's mags there. He might can wear my clothes we got there too." Billy rose, and gathered his own gear.

"How many places like that you have?" Branch asked, then shook his head. "Never mind. That's need to know, and I don't. Lead on, and I'll follow. I don't want him sellin' out my sister."

"Billy, you ready?"

"Just a minute," Billy called. Pete couldn't see what he was doing. Finally, Billy stood and nodded.

"What'd you do?"

"Left a surprise for our little friend," Billy replied. "You know, sort of a welcome gift," he grinned.

The three of them exited the building quickly and cleanly, moving with caution. It was nearing daylight, but wasn't quite there, making their movement easier to hide. It was a twenty-minute hike to Site Five, a four story building on the very edge of the area of town controlled by the misfits in charge.

Once inside, it was the work of just a few minutes to get Branch cleaned up and into some fresh clothes.

"Little big on me, but I lost some weight of late," he smiled. "Thanks, Billy."

"Welcome," Billy nodded. "Let's go on up to the roof," he suggested. "Might be able to see somethin' o' value." He and Pete replenished their food supply, and provided one for Branch, and each picked up two quarts of water.

"You guys think ahead, I'll give ya that," Branch complimented.

"Well, we planned on bein' here a while," Billy shrugged.

"Yeah, I got that." The three men made their way to the roof. Staying low, they crawled to the edge of the roof, where they could see down into a large part of the area the others made their homes and headquarters in.

"Looks quiet so far," Pete said, after looking things over with the spotting scope. "No guards visible, and no one out that we can see from here." He turned to Billy. "You want to take a shot or two from here later?"

"Might's well," Billy nodded. "Might get a shot at the big bull hisself, this mornin'."

"Might at that," Pete agreed. "If we take him down, there might be a power struggle among those left. That might be a good time to see about freeing the others."

"Works for me," Billy nodded, setting his rifle up.

"Holy shit," Branch *whoofed*. "No wonder you been makin' such a mess!"

"Yeah, it tends ta do that," Billy agreed, settling in. "Reckon we'll try and make one this mornin'."

"I. . .I need to get my sister," Branch said. "But. . .well, I hate to leave anyone in their hands if I can help it. I ain't gonna baby'em any, but we can at least get them free. After that, they can make their own way, I guess."

"'Bout what we figured," Billy agreed.

"We don't have any way to take care of so many," Pete told Branch with a shrug. "You and your sister, though, we could take. We need more guys who can fight."

"You well enough to do that you can take two more mouths to feed?" Branch asked, clearly skeptical. "Food's hard to come by, anymore."

"I imagine we can feed two more," Pete nodded, and saw Billy suppress a grin. "Thing is, we're a small bunch. Lotta work to be done, too. But we eat good. Got plenty of clean water, even some power. Sound like a place you'd want your sister to live?"

"Beats hell outta this place," Branch nodded. "And sounds better than we had it at home, too."

"You were a soldier," Pete reminded him. "Are you willing to soldier for us? To defend the place?"

"Hell yes!" Branch nodded. "So long as my sister has a safe place to live, then I'm your man."

"Then the two of you go with us when we leave," Pete promised. "Meanwhile, we'll need your help to make sure we get to leave. Deal?"

"No doubt," Branch agreed, and took Pete's hand.

"Well, now that that's all worked out," Billy drawled, "guess who's comin' to breakfast?"

Odd Billy Todd

"You killed four o' my men," Big John said grimly.

"No, no I didn't!" Carroll stammered. "I've never killed anyone in my life! I swear! It was. . .it was those others! The Shooter! And his helper! They killed the guards, and made me go with them!"

"Uh huh," John grunted. "And you went with them as a prisoner, right?"

"It was go with them or be shot!" Carroll stammered. "What kind of choice is that? But. . .I escaped as soon as they went to sleep. Them and the other prisoner! When they went to sleep, I took their food and water, and I ran!"

"But you wasn't coming back here, were you?" John grinned, but it wasn't pleasant.

"I was trying to, but I was lost!" Carroll tried to keep up. "I got turned around when they took me with them. I've never been in this town before, and I don't know my way around! They took me a long way out of town!"

"Long way, huh?" John mused.

-

"He's spillin' his guts," Billy muttered. "I'ma take him, right now."

"Wait," Pete said softly, hand on Billy's arm. "He might agree to try and lead them to where we spent the night. If he does, then we might use that time to free the others." Billy paused for a moment, considering. Finally, he nodded.

He would wait.

-

"And I suppose you'd be willin' to take us there, was we to free you, yeah?" John asked. Carroll smiled immediately.

"Why. . .why sure! That sounds fair!"

"Well, why don't you just do that, then," John nodded, motioning to his two remaining Lieutenants. "You show us where the Shooter is, and then you can just be on your merry!" John smiled.

-

"Looks like you called it, Pete," Billy said softly. "He's gonna try to lead'em back to our hole from last night."

"And he's takin' a whole lotta his 'gang' with'im," Branch nodded. "I count twenty-four, five, twenty-seven men, plus old Big John. That's a good helpin' o' what he keeps in town, right there."

"How many do you think are left?" Pete asked, calculating the odds.

"There'll be at least five in the jail, and should be four, plus some women guards, at the hotel," Branch said. "They don't usually keep any sort of lookouts. That might have changed since you two started shootin' the place up, but I haven't noticed."

"Okay, we need to hit the jail first," Pete said decisively. When Branch started to object, Pete cut him off. "We need the diversion they'll create, even if none of them fights a lick." Branch nodded at that, and settled down.

"Billy, I want you to stay put. We may need you to cover us."

"I can do that," Billy agreed. "Watch yourself, Pete. If things get hot, you high tail it with them. I'll catch up somehow, when it cools off."

"That's not happening," Pete shook his head.

"You never know," Billy shrugged. "I'll make out. Just make sure you get clear. Good luck." Billy offered his hand. Pete took it, suddenly worried.

"Billy, don't do anything silly, now," he warned.

"Wouldn't dream of it," Billy shook his head. "Just do like I said. We'll meet up somewhere. Sooner or later," he added, grinning. "Now ya'll better move," he ordered, taking out his radio. "Put your ear bud in. I'll warn ya if I see anything." Pete had already done that, and now switched it on. "And don't use that door, if you come back, without knockin', and waitin' for me to yell okay."

"Let's go," Pete ordered.

Big John had gathered every person he could lay hands on, including most of the women who weren't actually on guard, and started out with the prisoner to where he had left the Shooter behind.

What a dip, John thought to himself. How stupid did this goofball have to be to think that John would let him go? John wondered if maybe his acting skills were the cause. Maybe he really had sold the idiot a bill of goods.

Either way, this was a prime chance to get a line on the man, men he knew now, who had made his life so miserable of late, and cost him so many people and vehicles.

There was a niggling at the back of his neck, though, and Big John didn't like that. No sir, he didn't like that at all. But try as he might, he couldn't figure out what it was. Finally, he wrote it off as concern that they were walking into the scope of a man who could kill from a distance.

Yeah, that was probably it.

Pete affixed the suppressor to his pistol, and handed his rifle to Branch. They had to be as quiet as possible, for as long as possible. Stealth was their only advantage. The two men had worked their way around the large group Carroll was leading to their hiding spot, and made their way to the main entrance of the jail without being seen.

This was going too fast, and Pete didn't like it. He wasn't Terry, or even George. Pete had never thought of himself as a leader, or a planner. He was a soldier. A warrior, descended from warriors. He was out of his league, here, and he knew it. But this was the best chance they were going to get to free these people, and make life even harder for this bunch.

He looked at Branch, who nodded. Pete took a deep breath, and pushed the door open, and the two slipped inside.

Billy had waited for the other two men to exit, then took a grenade from his bag, and some fishing line. He taped the grenade to a mason jar filled with Jerry's moonshine, with some added ingredients of his own. Careful to leave the spoon clear, he then used the tape to fix the jar on a pipe near the door.

Next, he tied the fishing line to the pin of the grenade, and ran the string over to the door knob, where he tied the line off. Whoever opened that door would be in for a surprise.

That done, he looked for a solid place on the roof to tie off to, and lowered a rope to the ground. He had wondered if he was wasting his time lugging that rope around, but now it would allow him to escape, if his position was found. Seeing that the rope would reach the ground, he pulled it back up so no one would happen

Odd Billy Todd

on it, revealing his presence.

Settling back in behind his rifle, he was just in time to see Pete and Branch enter the only jail door he could see from where he was. He wasn't in an ideal position to provide cover, but it was a good position to watch their backs. And if that bunch came running back, then Billy could put a dent in their enthusiasm, he figured.

As he lay there behind his rifle, Billy thought about Rhonda and the kids. He was gambling here, and knew it. If he wasn't able to get to the Hummer, Pete and the others would leave out. He would be on his own. The thought didn't bother him, but his absence would upset Rhonda, and he didn't like that.

Billy didn't like to upset Rhonda. When she was unhappy, he was unhappy. He wanted her to be happy. More than once he wondered if she could really be happy with him in the long run. He hoped she could, because the thought of being without her scared him. Almost as much as the thought of something happening to her.

Which was one reason he was willing to help Branch get his sister, and help release the others. He wanted to believe that if Rhonda was over there in that hotel, that someone would help her, if he couldn't.

Billy hadn't said much to Pete since yesterday, because Pete knew him pretty well, but Billy had felt a long, slow anger building in him over the last two, or three days. Anger that the world was like it was, anger at people like this bunch who were hurting people for their own greed, killing people, even kids, without regard, and. . .well, the *other*. Pete's people had the right idea about *that*, Billy figured. It was too much to allow.

Billy didn't see himself as some kind of righter of wrongs, though. It wasn't his 'job' to do anything like this. And he was honest enough to admit that if he hadn't been convinced that these people were a threat to his home and family, he wouldn't be here. That idea shamed him a little, having seen how many people were suffering at the hands of these. . .people. But it was true.

He didn't like being here. He didn't like being separated from his family. If he had it to do over again, he wasn't sure he'd come, even though it was his idea. Maybe Terry was right. Maybe they could have made sure that this bunch couldn't have found them. Or if they had, that the people on the Farms could fight them off, protect themselves.

But Pete hadn't hesitated. And Pete knew things Billy didn't. Knew military kinds of things. If Pete had thought they could protect the Farms, he probably wouldn't have come. Yeah. Billy settled in a little lower, his mind going still.

Pete wouldn't have come all this way, endured all of this, if he didn't think it had to be done. That meant Billy had been right. And that was all Billy needed. To know that what he was doing was the right thing.

Without that worry, he would do what was needful. Head clear now, he bent to look through his scope again.

-

"Which way?" Pete whispered. Branch nodded to the heavy door off to the left. Pete nodded, and moved to the door.

"Guard usually sits just inside," Branch whispered. Again, Pete nodded. After a minute's thought, he decided to go with the direct approach, and just knocked on the door.

"Who's there?" a muffled voice came through the door.

"Who d'ya think, ya idiot!" Branch called back.

"All right, all right. Ain't no need to get personal!" the voice replied. Pete heard the heavy lock turn, and tensed. The man pushing the door open had time to open his mouth, and draw a breath, before the 9mm hollowpoint tore his throat out. The man's body simply fell back into the chair he'd been using. Pete edged past, with Branch on his tail.

The next door was open, and the man sitting at the chair there looked up, first in surprise, then in shock as he saw the pistol aimed at him. Once more Pete's pistol *burped*, and the guard's cry of alarm was silenced. The pistol wasn't completely quiet, however, and yet another guard came from within the cell blocks, dropping the tray he was carrying and clawing for his own pistol. Branch nailed him with a three-round burst in the legs, and the man cried out, hitting the floor.

"How many more?" Pete growled, disarming the guard, and hovering over him, knife in hand.

"What?" the guard gasped.

"How many more of you are in here?" Pete demanded.

"Just three of us left," the man gasped out. "Everyone else went with Big John. Help me."

"Sure," Pete agreed, and drew the knife across his throat. Ignoring the gurgling sounds the dying man made, Pete looked at Branch.

"Get'em out. We have to move." Branch nodded, grabbed the keys from the guard at the door, and started opening doors. The men who exited were hesitant until some of them recognized Branch.

"Figured you were long gone, man," one man told him. Branch shook his head.

"Not yet. Most of them are out of the area, but they'll be back soon. Better head on out. There's guns on the guards, and probably a few more inside here. Arm yourselves as best you can, but stay in the building for now. I don't want that bunch across the street to know what's happening until everyone can get away."

Surprisingly, the men agreed. Pete figured some of them would head straight for the door and make a run for it.

There were over fifty men locked into the cells, but Pete had no idea how many. He'd stopped counting as he made his way back to the front. He decided to make sure no one cost them their element of surprise.

Branch joined him five minutes later.

"Some of these guys are in bad shape," he whispered. "Been here a lot longer than I have."

"Nothing we can do about that right now," Pete shrugged. "We have to get across the street, and find your sister." Branch nodded, and the two men started across the street. Branch looked back at the man who had recognized him.

"Give us five minutes, and then head out. Those of you who have women folk over yonder wait here. We're gonna set them free, and then we'll all have to beat feet. Get me?" The man nodded, along with several others.

Pete led the way, holding his pistol down by his leg. Branch kept his rifle at port arms, hiding the suppressor behind Pete's back. As they climbed the steps, they were met by a large, unforgiving looking woman.

Odd Billy Todd

"You two know you ain't allowed in here," she started. "Now get before I. . . ." Pete silenced her with a shot to the forehead. He wasn't in the mood to take prisoners, and these people had long since given up any right to mercy. He pushed passed her and into the building.

Several young women were working in the lobby, cleaning and what not. One man and two women were standing guard.

Before any could react, Pete raised his pistol and shot the man three times. Branch gave both women a three-round burst from Pete's rifle, and they all hit the ground without firing a shot.

"Are there any more?" Pete asked the women prisoners. They stared at him blankly.

"Are there anymore guards!" Pete's voice cracked out, harder this time.

"No, that was all," one woman stammered. "Who are you?"

"Doesn't matter," Pete told her. "Where's the rest of you?" The woman pointed toward the conference room. Branch headed that way, while Pete stayed behind.

"The men are already free," Pete told them. "If you've got menfolk over there, they should be waiting on you. Now's the time to make a move, ladies!" The women stared at him for a moment, then moved as one toward the door. Pete walked outside, and took up a spot where he could watch.

So far things were going better than he could have hoped for.

"*Pete, you got comp'ny comin'.*"

"Well, damn."

-

Big John's men surrounded the building that the idiot pointed out to them. Once that was done, John motioned for Carroll to lead the way.

"Okay, buddy, this is where you get yours. Show us where they are, and you're a free man." Carroll swallowed nervously, and went though the door. John motioned for three of him men to follow, and then he followed himself, with others bringing up the rear.

Carroll was regretting his abandonment of the other three. All he had wanted was to go home. That's all. To get out of this nightmare, and make it back to his home, where he was safe.

He hadn't figured on being caught again. He'd readily agreed to sell out the other three, if it meant he would go free. Now, though, he was beginning to see that John wasn't going to release him. Still, there was always hope, and right now that was all he had.

He climbed the stairs carefully, not wanting to alert the others. He hadn't forgotten the crazy one, and that knife. Nor the look in his eyes. That guy wasn't right, somewhere. Remembering that incident, Carroll felt his resolve harden. It was only right, he decided, that he make sure that man payed for what he'd done.

"That's the room," he whispered, arriving at the top of the stairs where the room was located. "They were all asleep in there when I left."

"Well, go ahead and take us in there. If they see you in front, might relax 'em some. We'll be right behind you, don't worry." John's reassuring smile wasn't. Carroll started to protest, but let it die on his lips. He moved to the door, conscious of John's men behind him. He pushed the door open, and walked inside.

To nothing.

He didn't notice the fishing line he kicked as he moved into the room, followed by John's henchmen. No one else did either.

It was a simple thing, the fuse. Meant for firing civil war cannon, it was just a small brass tube filled with accelerate, sparked by the removal of a small twisted brass pin. The fuse would fire a charge into whatever it was placed in. In this case, a small clay ball filled with black powder. The outside of the ball was covered in small nails.

The force of the blast rocked the building slightly, but turned Carroll and the four men with him into pin cushions. The lucky one's died almost at once.

The other two, including Carroll, would die from internal bleeding where the tiny nails had driven deep into their bodies. Carroll would have plenty of time to reflect on his betrayal of two men who had tried to help him.

—

John was furious, but knew he had only himself to blame. He had been so intent on finally getting rid of his nemesis, he'd never thought about a trap. Carroll hadn't known, it was obvious. He wouldn't have gone into the room if he had.

No, this was someone playing him. And they'd won, dammit.

"Let's get back to the jail," he ordered his remaining men. "Somethin' ain't right. Move!"

The men moved, heading back at a fast jog. One thing about the New World, you shaped up pretty quick.

John was near the front of his people, cursing with every step. The Shooter was somewhere waiting for them, he was sure.

—

Billy heard the small explosion, and smiled grimly. Looked like Carroll had pointed them in the right direction. Billy changed positions, so that he could see the road that whoever was still alive would return by. He had to make sure Pete had time to finish, and get clear. He keyed his radio.

"Pete, you got comp'ny comin'."

—

"I copy, Billy. Any idea how many?"

"Looks like twenty or so. I'ma whittle that down a little. Ain't no point in you comin' back this way. I done got me a back way out."

"Copy that. We're about done here. Make sure you're at the truck," he ordered.

"Do my best, but don't wait on me. I'll make out."

"Dammit, Billy, you better be there!"

There was no answer. Pete was about to call again when he heard the enormous *boom* of Billy's rifle.

"He *better* be there," Pete muttered to himself. "Branch, we gotta speed this up!" he called out loud.

"Comin'!" Branch emerged seconds later, dragging a small, pretty but disheveled brunette of about sixteen, or seventeen.

"Let's go," Pete ordered, pointing up the street from the way they had arrived. "We've got a lot of ground to cover, and we don't have all day."

"Where's Billy?" Branch asked, just as the Barrett spoke again.

"Oh."

"Yeah, oh. He's buying time for us to get out. So, let's go!" The three of them took off up the road, running.

Billy looked down through his scope, and selected another target. That's all they were, now. Targets. They had given up any right to be called human beings, in his book.

He sighted in on a man wearing a leather biker jacket who was desperately trying to hide behind a telephone pole.

"Not hardly, buddy," Billy whispered to himself, and squeezed the trigger. The heavy round tore through the pole, and the gunman, cutting both nearly in two. In their fear, three others ran for new cover, all shooting wildly. The people on the ground still hadn't spotted him, but Billy knew that wouldn't last.

"Make hay while the sun shines," he murmured, sighting in on another one.

CHAPTER SEVENTY-TWO

Big John was furious. From where he hid, he could see figures running from the hotel. Too many figures to be his people. His prisoners, the foundation of their future, were escaping. Without them, he had nothing to bargain with when the train arrived. Nothing to keep the people on that train from sweeping him and his few people away like so much trash.

He had made promises of all kinds to secure their freedom. If he couldn't deliver, there would be consequences.

"We need to get them prisoners back!" he ordered. No one moved.

"If we lose them, we can kiss our ass'es good-bye! Now go get'em back!" Three men rose in obedience. The second one in line took three steps before the Shooter cut him in half. The other two hit the ground again, cowering in fear.

"Damn you, get up there and stop them prisoners from escapin'!" He pointed his rifle at the nearest one of his people, a woman. "If you don't move your ass, I'll kill you right here!"

Gulping in fear, the woman rose to her feet, trying to stay out of the Shooter's line of sight. She made it to the next block, encouraging others to move out as well. Which was just what Billy had planned.

He cut loose with his rifle, laying shot after shot just as fast as he could target and pull the trigger. Six rounds, four kills, one maimed, and one miss. No one else was moving after that. That made a total of nine kills, and one wounded.

John swore again.

"Can anybody see him?" he yelled.

"He's on top o' the second building!" a voice answered. "The Markee Office Building, boss!"

"Take four men, and go get him!" John ordered. "Everyone else, open fire on the top of the building!"

-

Billy flinched as stray rounds started impacting around him. He could see three men and two women working their way toward his building, too.

"Well, 'bout time to go, I reckon," he said to himself. "Still, gotta make it look good." With that in mind, he loaded a fresh magazine, and emptied it again, just as fast as he could sight and squeeze. He didn't bother to see if he hit anyone, since all he was working toward was keeping their heads down, and their attention focused on him. Every second that he delayed them here was a second for Pete to get to the Hummer, and the others to make tracks out of town.

He could hear the people inside the building below him, now, and knew it was time to be gone. He cased the heavy rifle and slung it, then checked his M-4. He might need it, and soon. Running to the rope, Billy anchored off, and waited, an unpleasant smile on his face.

Billy had a plan. He was sticking to it.

-

The three men and two women Billy had seen were tramping up the stairs to the roof even as Billy made his preparations to get to the ground. They were mad, and scared. Mad that so many of their fellows were dead, that their hard work was now running away, and that their own future was now in doubt.

They were scared of Big John's reaction, scared of being disintegrated by the Shooter's horrible rifle, and scared of what might happen when they reached him.

Their fear should have made them cautious, but their anger won out. As the group reached the door to the roof, the man in the lead looked at the others, held up his fingers in a count to three, and kicked the door open. As soon as he did, the five rushed onto the roof.

The leader saw Billy step off the roof, roping down to the ground. He yelled to the others, and made a move toward the man he knew only as the Shooter.

In their haste, and anger fueled attack, no one noticed the spoon fly off the grenade. The fuse was cut for five seconds. When the grenade exploded, the shrapnel was only part of the damage, as the explosive ignited the highly volatile home brew inside the mason jar. Moonshine, mixed with washing detergent.

The homemade napalm splashed over all five members of Big John's team, setting them ablaze, clinging to them like jelly. The two closest to the grenade didn't know it, since the shrapnel killed them outright.

The other three screamed in agony as the flames engulfed them, sticking to their clothes and any exposed skin it had managed to hit. All thoughts of getting the Shooter left their mind, as they desperately tried to put out the fire that ate at them.

—

Billy hit the ground, and took one second to orient himself, and another to glance at the roof. The screaming pretty much assured that the people on the roof would be too busy to bother with him, but he needed to be sure.

Then he was running. If he wanted to go home, he needed to get to the truck before Pete had to leave. Added to the distance he had to travel, was the prisoners that had been freed, and were now armed. Billy didn't trust them to know the sheep from the goats, so he had to proceed carefully.

Carefully but quickly.

—

"Where we goin'?" Branch asked, as he practically drug his sister behind him.

"Truck," Pete told him. "Got a Hummer hid about two miles from here. We need to get to it, collect Billy, and get the hell out of here."

"Billy said not to wait for him," Branch pointed out.

"He says a lot o' things," Pete shrugged.

"Didn't seem like it," Branch replied. "Seemed pretty quiet to me. A little on edge maybe, but quiet like."

"He's not a soldier," Pete told Branch. "Never has been."

"Could o' fooled me," Branch observed. "I'd have sworn he was former service."

"Nope. And we ain't about to leave him, either. His wife will kill us both. Probably slowly, too. She's got a little bit of a mean streak."

"I never thought to ask if there were other women at this place."

"Plenty of 'em," Pete nodded. "Good people."

The conversation trailed off as the three of them kept running.

"I'm Barbara, by the way," the sister said.

Odd Billy Todd

"Pete."

"Nice to meet you!" she gasped. "Is it much further? I don't know how much further I can run."

"Stop talking," Pete told her. "That'll help. It's not far, and you can relax."

"Pete, you copy?"

"I hear you Billy. What's your status?"

"Well, I'm runnin' away at the moment," Billy gasped back. "I'm almost to Cache One. You about where you need to be?"

"Another ten minutes, probably," Pete replied.

"Well, I don't think I'll make it 'fore you do," Billy said after thinking for a minute. "Thing is, that lot you guys let loose are runnin' ever where. I don't wanna shoot any of 'em, and I'd soon they don't shoot me, so I'm kinda goin' slow."

"I'll call you when we reach the truck," Pete told him. *"Where ever you are then, we'll come get you."*

"I don't know that's a good plan," Billy replied. "Might not be safe. Lotta these folks liable to be lookin' for a way out o' town. That ole Hummer'd look mighty good to'em."

"Then we'll have to dissuade them," Pete answered. *"As you like to say, we didn't take 'em to raise. We got them free, they're on their own. Dillon and his sister are with me, by the way."*

"Well, that's good," Billy said. "I'll see ya in a bit, I reckon."

With that, Billy kept making his way toward the Hummer. He really, *really*, wanted to go home.

Pete and the others reached the Hummer eight minutes later. Barbara sunk to the ground, gasping for air while Pete and Dillon uncovered the truck.

"Holy shit, a Ma Deuce!" Dillon exclaimed.

"Can you drive one?" Pete asked, as he almost threw the girl into the back seat.

"Sure can," Dillon nodded, also climbing in back.

"Clear it for action, then," Pete ordered, sliding behind the wheel. "We might need it. I'm tired of running from these assholes."

"You and me both, brother!"

"Pete, you copy?"

"We're on the way, Billy. Where are ya?"

"Well, I'm not far fr. . .from Cache One. Thing is, I'm a little s. . .shot. And I got another p. . .passenger for us. Reckon you might wa. . .wanna hurry along, just a bit, you don't mind."

"Billy, are you okay?" Pete asked.

There was no reply. Swearing, Pete put the heavy vehicle in gear, and started on his way to get his friend.

Billy had been doing pretty good. He was almost at his destination when things turned a little sour. He was making his way toward Cache One, their main cache, when he heard a commotion.

"He's one of 'em!" he heard a man shout.

"I am not!" another voice cried out. "I'm as much as prisoner as any of you!"

"That's a lie!" a third voice shouted. "You was with'em!"

"I'm a doctor!" the second voice came again. "I tried to keep all of you healthy!"

"Healthy for them!" the first voice argued back. Billy stepped around the corner to see what was happening. His radar had picked up on the word 'doctor'. He saw a man lying on the ground, blood running freely from a cut on the side of his head. He looked like he'd taken a beating.

"Look out, there's one of'em!" A tall, gaunt man cried, lifting his rifle.

"I ain't one o'. . . ." Billy tried to get out, but both men were beyond reason. Billy felt a tug at his left sleeve, followed by a burning. His rifle lifted of its own volition it seemed, and pumped three rounds into the tall man. He fell, dead.

The second man hadn't been able to get the pistol in his waistband free, and threw his hands up in despair.

"Don't shoot!" he cried.

"Give me a reason not to," Billy growled, angry now. Rather than reply, the man turned and ran. Billy watched him go, then turned to the man on the ground.

"You a doctor?" he asked, then realized he knew the man. Not his name, but his face. When they had arrived in Franklin the day the train had hit, this man had been working hard to treat the wounded.

"I know you," he told the man. "Seen you last year, after the train hit. What happened?"

"The people who took over made me treat the prisoners," the doctor shrugged. "I would have done it anyway, of course, but it made it look like I was part of their outfit." he shrugged again.

"I guess you want outta here,," Billy told him. For some reason he felt light headed. He must be out of shape. Running all that way had probably made him that way, he decided.

"More than anything," the doctor nodded. "I. . .I did what I could for them, you know. I didn't have much left, and John refused to let me treat anyone who was hurt bad, or too sick. He wanted what little was left for his own people. But. . .I did what I could." The man looked near tears.

"You got a name?" Billy asked, and frowned mentally. Why was his voice slurred?

"Collins," the man nodded. "Jake Collins. M.D. If that means anything, anymore."

"You didn't. . .I mean, you ain't. . .well, they was doin' some bad things here," Billy tried to ask. Collins shuddered.

"No!" he said emphatically. "I'd rather starve. I've been existing on deer corn and roots and berries. And lot's of rock soup." Billy nodded, relieved.

"Well, reckon we can use a doctor, and we're a lot better to work for than this bunch. We done set all the prisoners free, but I reckon you done seen that."

"Yes," Collins snorted. "I don't blame them, though," he added. "They've been through hell. Hey, you're bleeding!"

"So are you."

"Well, I'm not as bad as you are. Let me see that arm."

"Hang on a minute. Need to call some friends o' mine."

-

Odd Billy Todd

Pete tore through town, desperate to get to where Billy was. The fact that he wasn't answering was bad.

"Can anyone hear me?" the radio crackled.

"I can, who is this!" Pete demanded.

"My name is Doctor Jake Collins," the voice replied.

"Oh, hey doc!" Pete replied. "This is Peter Two Bears!"

"Pete! Great guns, it's nice to hear your voice! Your friend is out, but I've stopped the bleeding. He said you needed a doctor."

"We could sure use one," Pete agreed.

"Well, I'm looking for a new job, at the moment," Collins told him. *"Your friend offered me a ride, and said job."*

"That's good enough for me," Pete smiled into his radio. "Where are you?" Collins relayed the information, and Pete nodded to himself.

"We'll be there in two minutes. Is the area clear?"

"For the moment. Your friend here saved me from at least a beating. He got shot in the arm for his troubles, though. He's unconscious, but stable. He's weak from loss of blood, more than anything, I think."

"Just hang on to him, Doc. We'll almost there."

Pete made two turns, and in less than a minute, he was sliding to a stop, next to Billy's unconscious form.

"Hey! You're one of them!" Branch shouted, and swiveled the machine gun around to point it at Collins.

"Not again," Collins groaned, raising his hands.

"Point that the other way!" Pete ordered. "He's a good guy!"

"Like hell!" Branch replied. "He was the one they brought to check us over! People who didn't pass muster disappeared!" Pete looked at Collins.

"I treated anyone who was sick, or injured," Collins nodded. "Only, John wouldn't allow me to treat anyone seriously ill, or injured. He kept what medicine there was for his own people."

"You mean you *refused* to treat them!" Branch almost yelled.

"I've never refused to treat anyone!" Collins shot back heatedly.

"I don't have time for this," Pete grated. "I told you to point that somewhere else. Either do it, or get out and take your chances somewhere else. I've known this man a hell of a lot longer than I have you. If he says that's how it was, that's how it was." Branch glared at Pete, and for a minute, Pete thought he was going to have to shoot the man. Just then, Barbara Branch stuck her head out of the window.

"Hi, Doctor Collins!"

"Hello, Barbara," Collins smiled. "How's your foot?"

"It's all better. I ran on it just a little while ago, and it didn't hurt at all!"

"Barbara get back inside the truck!" Dillon snapped.

"I will not!" the teenager huffed indignantly. "This man helped me when I was hurt. In fact, he helped a lot of us. Protected us from. . .from. . .well. . . ."

"It's alright, Barbara," Collins told her. "Do as he says. It's still dangerous out here."

"Why are you pointing that gun at Doctor Collins, Dillon?" she demanded. "He's a nice man." Dillon mumbled something under his breath, and moved the gun away from Collins. Pete sighed, and eased his hand off his rifle grip.

438

"Help me get him loaded," Pete ordered Collins. The two quickly placed Billy into the rear compartment, with Collins electing to ride with him. Pete handed over their first aid kit, then slid behind the wheel again.

"Let's get the hell out of here," he declared to no one in particular. He was tired, dirty, and at the end of his rope.

"This is why I never wanted to be a platoon sergeant," he muttered. He put the Hummer in gear again, and pointed it toward home.

They left a severely damaged, and strategically weakened Franklin behind them.

CHAPTER SEVENTY-THREE

Terry looked at the 'improvements' the group had made over the last two days at the Clifton House, conflicting feelings running through him. He was happy with the work, there was no question of that. If the need arose, he was confident that the few of them would be able to hold this place against almost anything short of a tank. Considering some of the things George had found in the armory in Columbia, they might stand off even that.

But the fact that they would have to resort to using a place that had been dedicated to raising children left orphaned by the plague was gut wrenching. And maddening. He hated the people who would make such a thing needed. Hated the necessity of even having to think of such a thing.

Terry had been all over the world during his Army career. He had seen fighting that left him wondering what the point was to start with. Seen children used in combat, or held hostage to it. Kids who had lost limbs, or lives, in minefields planted and forgotten by those who used them.

Villages lain waste to, with not even the dogs left alive. He had lost count of the times he had cried himself to sleep, in the dark of his tent, or sleeping bag, hoping no one heard him. The times he had crawled into a bottle when he had a short leave, too short to come home.

He had never, ever, in all those years imagined he would see such things in America. Not even once. But then, he'd never imagined a world where ninety-five percent of the population was dead, either.

He sighed, taking his hat off and rubbing his hand across his brow. Despite everything, there was always the chance they would never have to use this place for anything but an orphanage.

But if they did, it would be ready.

"Terry, how copy?" his radio interrupted his thoughts.

"I read you, Howie. What's up?"

"Pete's on his way in, running hard. Billy's been hit. He wants you to have Amy standing by with everything she would need to treat a GSW. Says he has Doctor Collins on board, you'd know who that was. He also has two others, male, and female, friendlies."

Shit.

"I read you Howie. Did he have an ETA?"

"Half hour, with no problems."

"Roger that. We'll be ready." Terry climbed aboard his horse. If he was lucky, he'd have time to. . . .

"Terry, this is Rhonda. Did I hear that right?" Terry was surprised. She sounded calm, and firm.

"Yes, Rhonda, you did," Terry fought off a sigh.

"Bring him here," Rhonda ordered. *"We'll be ready."*

"Copy that," Terry assured her. He was surprised again. She hadn't demanded anything, like information. She knew everything he did, if she'd been monitoring the radio. He spurred his horse down the road. A thought hit him, then, and he keyed his radio again.

"Rhonda, you copy?"

"*Go ahead.*"

"Can you send Danny over to Amy's with the truck? She'll need to move whatever she thinks they'll need."

"*Already on his way.*" Terry shook his head, smiling in spite of himself.

"Roger that."

-

"Anything?" Pete asked.

"Nope. We're clear," Dillon assured him. "I don't think anyone back there's in any shape to follow us, man."

"Don't assume, though," Pete reminded him. "We can't afford to have someone follow us."

"Where is it we're going, anyway?" Barbara asked. She was in the front seat now, looking and acting none the worse for her imprisonment.

"We're going home," Pete smiled at her. "There's no real name I guess. We just call it the Farms."

"So, it's a farm?"

"A great big one," Pete nodded. Talking to the girl kept his mind off the fact that his friend was lying in the back of the Hummer, unconscious, and slowly bleeding to death.

"Are there horses?" she asked.

"Yeah, there are. That's how we get around in fact, for the most part. We don't have much gas, and don't want to waste what we do have."

"I love horses!" she grinned in delight.

"Well, that's good news," Pete nodded. "There's cattle, too. And pigs. And acres and acres of corn, and beans and. . .well, you get the idea."

"So. . .so it's regular food?" she asked, surprised.

"Regular as rain," Pete nodded. "Nothing fancy, mind you, but there's plenty of it. Everyone plants a garden, too."

"I tried to plant a garden for us, but the deer kept eating it. And the birds, and the raccoon's."

"Well, we have that too, but we work at keeping them out. You'll see," he promised. He slowed the truck, looking for the road. He didn't see it.

"Damn, they did a good job," he murmured to himself. He eased off the road carefully. "Doc! We're gonna have to off road a bit. Is that a problem?"

"Just go slow. I've got the bleeding stopped again, but bouncing around might open the wound again."

"Will do," Pete promised. He decided not to use what he thought was the actual road, thinking it might damage the cover. Instead, he picked a trail to the right of where the road lay hidden.

"Might want to take a seat, Dillon," Pete called. "This'll be rough, I'm afraid." Dillon secured the gun, and slide down into the rear seat. Pete started across the field, bumping only slightly as he took it slow. It grated on him to creep along with Billy hurt, but he knew it wouldn't do his friend any favors to bounce across this field.

-

Odd Billy Todd

Rhonda hurriedly made preparations for when Billy arrived. She was scared stiff, but hid it well, letting her work keep her from breaking down. Tears were falling even as she worked, but she was firmly in control.

Pete had mentioned a doctor, so Amy had brought some things she thought a doctor might want to use for a GSW, including IV's, and transfusion equipment. She hoped Billy didn't need any blood, and that if he did, someone knew his blood type. They would have to take blood from someone else. This was a weakness that Amy had known about, but hadn't been able to fix. As she prepped the room that Rhonda had given her, Amy desperately tried to project calm, knowing that Rhonda was at the edge of breaking down.

"Rhonda, there's a doctor with them," she offered. "I'm sure he's been in good hands."

"He'll be fine," Rhonda replied firmly. "He promised." Amy smiled at that, and returned to her work. It was interesting to note Rhonda's confidence, despite her obvious fear.

She was about to say something else when she heard the sound of an approaching vehicle.

-

As soon as Pete reached the road, he hit the gas. It wasn't all that far now, and he had the Hummer going full out. That didn't mean a great deal, of course. The heavily armored truck wasn't meant to be a racer. It was meant to go, and keep going. Tough, dependable, but would never be called fast.

It seemed like an eternity before Billy's drive came into view. He saw Terry standing there, but merely nodded as he roared past, intent on getting Billy inside where Doc and Amy could treat him. Pete was emotionally drained at this point. Between watching their back trail, expecting an attack at any minute, and worrying about his friend bouncing around in the back, Pete was completely spent. He sighed deeply in relief as the house came into view. Toby, George and Ralph were waiting to help unload the still unconscious Billy. Amy was holding the front door open, while Rhonda stood on the porch, arms folded, watching.

Pete slid to a stop at the steps, and leaped out, followed by Dillon Branch and his sister. The hatch raised, Doc slid out as willing hands reached for Billy's still form. As Toby and George took hold, Billy groaned.

"Watch that arm, kiddo," he ordered Toby. "Hurt's enough as it is."

"Billy!" Toby almost shouted in joy.

"Who else was ya 'spectin'?" Billy asked, sitting up on the tail board.

"We need to get him inside," Doc ordered. "He's lost a lot of blood."

"'He' can hear ya, Doc," Billy mumbled. "And 'he' can walk." Billy stood up, cradling his arm. He staggered a bit, and allowed Toby and George to support him on either side.

"Pete, will you clean my rifle?" he asked, and Pete couldn't help but laugh.

"Yeah, I'll take care of it, pal. All your gear, too. Promise."

"Pete can go rest, I'll take care of it," Toby insisted. "Soon's Miss Rhonda don't need me, Billy, I'll come get it all and clean it for ya."

"Thanks, buddy," Billy smiled, albeit a little weakly. He was still smiling drunkenly when he walked around the edge of the Hummer, and saw Rhonda standing on the porch, arms crossed. Now that she saw Billy up and walking she looked. . . . "Uh-oh," Billy murmured. "Looks like I'm in trouble, fellas."

"You have no idea," Rhonda said darkly. "Get him inside," she ordered. None of the men possessed enough courage to argue, let alone disobey. They helped the struggling Billy up the stairs and into the house, guiding him to the only downstairs bedroom, where Amy was set up to treat him.

"Jack, is that you?" Amy was startled. The man was a shell of his former self.

"Hello, Amy!" Collins grinned. "Yes, I'm a bit worse for wear, but it's me. I'm glad to see you here, Amy. What do you have?"

"I have everything you should need," Amy assured him. "We're short on diagnostic equipment, but have plenty of supplies."

"Oh, that's excellent," Collins almost salivated at the room full of supplies. "I. . .I've been doing what I could, but. . . ." he trailed off, then shook his head.

"Well, that can wait. We need to treat this man's arm. Let's take a better look than I've been able to." Billy was seated on the bed, teetering. Doc carefully and quickly cut away Billy's sleeve.

"Hey, that was a good shirt!" Billy slurred.

"Shut *up*, Billy," Rhonda snapped. "I'll make you a new shirt, you idiot! Let them do their job!"

"Nice to see you too, sweetie," Billy grinned slightly. "I came home, though. 'Member, I promised." Rhonda's gaze softened despite her agitated state.

"Yes, you did," she agreed, a few tears falling.

"Hey, it ain't that bad, now," Billy tried to comfort her.

"How about you let me decide that?" Collins ordered. "Amy, I need this irrigated. The bullet is still in there, and likely some of the shirt. I'll have to dig it out. Do you have anything like a local?"

"Yes, Doctor," Amy nodded. "I'll see to it. Could I suggest you take a moment to clean up, and rest, while I see to irrigation and anesthesia?"

"That. . .I could stand to clean up, I'm sure," Collins grinned self consciously. He wasn't filthy, but he was dirty, and had his own wound as well.

"Once we're done, I'll check that scalp wound, and you can get something to eat, and rest," Amy promised.

"You have no idea how wonderful that sounds."

-

"All right, Mister Todd," Collins sighed. "The bullet is out, and we recovered the piece of shirt material as well. The bullet didn't hit the bone, or any vital or major arteries or veins. All in all, it was just a very messy flesh wound. Considering your overall condition, and Peter's, I'd say your momentary unconsciousness was a result of stress, blood loss, and exhaustion."

"So, I'll be all right, then?" Billy asked. He was much more focused now, and not exhibiting any of the 'drunk' signs he had been before.

"Oh, yes," Collins assured him. "You'll be fine. That arm will be sore for a few days, and I don't want you using it much for at least a week or so, but you'll recover completely."

"I really appreciate it, Doc," Billy told him.

"Hey, you did more for me, my friend," Collins smiled. "I'm glad to be able to return the favor."

"Reckon you'll be staying on with us, then?" Billy asked.

"If you've a place for me, and I'm not a burden, I think I'd like that," Collins said seriously.

"We'll make a place, we have to," Billy promised. "And a doctor, in these days and times, sure ain't no burden."

"Well, let's let the doctor go and clean up," Rhonda ordered. "You both need rest. And I want to talk to you, mister," she added, glaring. There was no power behind it, though, and Billy grinned at her.

"Yes'm," he nodded.

"Doctor Collins, why don't you come with me," Amy smiled. "I'll take you to my place, and you can get cleaned up while I fix you something to eat. We'll find some clothes for you, too. I think those might need to be burned."

Collins was still laughing as he and Amy departed. The others had already gone outside, and were waiting for a report. Collins patiently assured them Billy was fine, but needed some rest. Pete nodded dully, relieved and exhausted. He was about to head home when Shelly caught his arm.

"Oh, no you don't, Mister," she ordered sternly. "You come with me." Pete protested half-heartedly, but allowed her to lead him toward the Silvers' home. Jerry and Toby just grinned. Looked like Pete would be staying with them for a few days.

"Well, what about us?" Dillon asked, looking at Terry.

"We'll take you over to my place," Terry smiled. "My wife can help your sister. The two of you can get cleaned up, and we'll get you some clothing. After that, I'd like to hear about how you met our wayward friends."

"Well, they pretty much saved us all three," Dillon shrugged. "And a bunch more, besides."

"I figured it was something like that," Terry nodded.

-

With everyone gone, this was the first time Rhonda had had with Billy since his arrival. She sat beside him on the bed, where he was still reclining.

"Billy, you scared me," she said simply, and he nodded, his eyes showing his sorrow.

"I know, 'n I'm sorry. I didn't mean to. These two guys was beatin' on the doc, and it just didn't seem right to leave'im to'em. And havin' a sure 'nough Doctor round here ain't no bad idea, neither," he added.

"No, I suppose not," Rhonda agreed. "You're filthy," she added, her nose wrinkling.

"Yeah, ain't much in the way o' bathin' facilities where we done been."

"Was it bad, Billy?" she asked, concern in her eyes, and her voice.

"Well, it's okay to visit, but I wouldn't wanna live there," he grinned, then grew serious. "Yeah, it was. But we put a hefty dent in'em, for sure. And freed all them people they was holdin', too. Hope they get away okay."

"Who are the two that you brought back besides the doctor?" she asked. "You can tell me about them while I help you get to the shower," she grinned, helping him up.

"Hey, that sounds like a plan."

-

Two days later, everyone met at Billy's for the 'debrief'. Everyone listened raptly as the two told their tale, leaving out the more gruesome parts. Doctor Collins relayed his story, as well, much longer and more terrifying. The Branches did the same.

"Well, that's quite a story," Terry nodded, when everyone was finished. "I'd say you managed to put our friends back to square one, for now," he added, looking at Pete and Billy. "Doesn't sound like they'll have the manpower or resources to bother looking for us for a while."

"Don't forget that train, though," Billy cautioned. "Could be they'll decide to come lookin' themselves. I don't think they will, but let's don't go forgettin' it."

"We won't," Terry promised. "We've got a lot more work to do, and harvest time will be on us before you know it. We've got plenty to keep us busy. But we'll keep a steady eye out for the train, or anyone else."

"And don't forget what we heard about Weber, either," Pete added. "We need to be really cautious about new people, until we're sure they aren't spotting for some outfit. Present company excepted, of course," he grinned at the Branch siblings, and Collins.

"That makes good sense anyway," George nodded. "Meanwhile, like Terry said, we've got plenty to do. We need to make another mobile home run, I'm thinking. And now that Doc is with us, we can think about getting him some equipment, like an x-ray machine and what not. We need to find a trailer big enough to put a real clinic in."

"I'd love that," Collins admitted. "It would be wonderful to treat people again." He and Dillon Branch had come to a truce the day before, after Terry and George had explained to Branch what Collins had admitted to them that first night. Branch couldn't hold a grudge against a man that had helped his sister anyway. Learning what the man had braved to help those he could had erased his own anger. In hindsight, Dillon could admit to seeing the Doctor do everything he could for the sick and dying men in the cells.

"Well, I think we can plan all that tomorrow," Terry rose. "For now, I think we can call this a day. Billy needs rest, and Pete does too. And I'm sure Dillon and Barbara and Jake are still trying to adjust, and they all need rest as well as good food to get them back on their feet."

"We'll meet tomorrow at my place, and work out a plan. Until then, I'd suggest you all get some rest."

CHAPTER SEVENTY-FOUR

The next two weeks went by in a combination of hard work and idle time. Rain forced a two day delay in their actions, but the rain was welcome, none-the-less. It came at just the right time to help the crops along.

Billy was sidelined during that time, his arm healing. He was allowed to 'putter', as he put it, around his own place, but nothing more, and nothing heavy at all. Amy or the Doc checked him over everyday, making sure the wound stayed clean. Rhonda made sure Billy didn't over do it.

For the most part, Billy didn't argue. He spent time with Danny around the farm, approving of the care the teen had shown while he was away. He took Mary riding around the valley. He spent time just sitting on the front porch with Rhonda, as the two of them discussed the present, and the future.

The others took up the slack. Two more of the double wide homes were brought in. One would be a clinic, outfitted with material and equipment taken from various doctor's offices, hospitals, and clinics. After a lot of discussion, the clinic was placed with it's back to the creek that ran along the Clifton property, so that some of Howie's water bug creations could be used to provide power for the equipment.

Although the train had cleaned most of the bigger stores out, the smaller mom-and-pop operations had largely been ignored. As a result, there was plenty of supplies to outfit the clinic with, and to provide excellent first-aid kits to every home, and piece of regularly used equipment.

Once the harder work was done, the group settled down to preparing for the harvest. All hands were used to get up hay barns, silos, and storage cribs for the coming harvest. Added to this, wood had to be cut, so harvest would have to be done as quickly as possible. After the ferocious winter they had endured, no one wanted to be caught unprepared.

Billy spent his second week, however, sitting in his den, looking at maps. Carroll had said that a lot of Nashville was untouched. And Billy wanted to go.

It was a risk, he knew, and there were multiple problems. First, he wasn't sure he could believe Carroll. Billy couldn't see any way that the train hadn't made a stop there. None. They had the armament and the people to take just about what they wanted.

Second, even if some items they needed where still available, would there be enough to risk the trip? Were there alcoves of people along the way? Had someone set up shop in Nashville since then? How many ambushes would they encounter along the way, and after they were in town?

Finally, there was the problem of protecting the Farms. There was no way that a trip to Nashville wouldn't take at least three to five days. Columbia had taken a week to prepare, and three days of non-stop work to move. And they had been chased out early by the train, even then. Nashville would take much longer.

Despite his desire to try and scavenge in Nashville, especially for books that would help Howie, Billy determined after three days of thinking and planning that it just couldn't be done. Not now. Maybe not ever. Reluctantly he put away all the notes he'd made, and went to sit on the porch.

It was early August, and the heat was on full blast. Even those homes with power from PV cells couldn't stay cool. Windows were open to catch whatever air was moving, which wasn't much.

A small water park outfit was created for the children at the Clifton Home, and all the children used it almost daily. An inflatable pool was the center of attraction, along with a ground water slide, sprinklers, and water guns provided from stores in town.

The adults performed whatever chores needed doing during the morning and evening, taking it easy in the middle of the day whenever possible. It wasn't unusual to see the mercury hover near 100.

On one of those hot afternoons, several men and women gathered at the Todd farm. Under the cooling breeze of a shop fan, they discussed the current situation.

"We do have this," Pete lifted the map taken the past year from the raiders he and Billy had found about the attack their settlement. "According to this map, there's quite a bit left in these smaller towns. Most of them are within fifty miles, or less."

"Been a long time since that bunch passed through, though," George noted idly. "Might not be anything left."

"That's possible, but I think it bears checking on," Jon Kelvey put in. "There's a lot of things we could sure use. Jerry had the idea to create our own saw mill. I want to follow up on that. A lot of smaller operations used gasoline or diesel-powered engines to drive their mills. If we could find an operation like that, and move it, we could saw our own lumber. Plenty of trees around."

"That's one concern," Terry agreed. "What are the others?"

"Medicines, for one," Doc offered. "Whatever is out there, is all we're going to have. We need to get as much of it as we can, and get it into storage. It will lose strength over time, but we can use more of it, to make up for that."

"Can we use antibiotics we find in vet's offices?" Billy asked. "When Rommel got hurt, we didn't know if people meds'd work on him, or was it safe," he shrugged, when others looked at him.

"We can," Doc nodded. "I'd prefer not to, since we might also need them to doctor the animals."

"We're going to divide the big herd this fall, anyway," Jerry mentioned. "There's enough pasture land for that, so long as we can make sure there's water. By having several small herds instead of one big one, we lessen the chance that one sick cow wipes us out. We'll do the same thing with the pigs, too," he added. "Our little swine herd has grown, somewhat."

"Okay, another point," Terry nodded, scribbling again into a small notebook. "What else?"

"Well, canning equipment comes to mind," Rhonda offered, and Emma nodded in support. "If we start using the new building for that, we can accomplish a lot more, if we have more equipment. And there's always a need for jars, rings, and lids."

"Good one," Terry nodded, writing again.

"Books for the *ninios*," Maria noted. She rarely spoke, in fact rarely attended

Odd Billy Todd

these meetings.

"True, and educational supplies as well," Debby supported. "Maybe take textbooks from a school somewhere?"

"Good idea," Terry nodded, scratching in his pad again. Rhonda reached over and gently took the pen and notebook from Terry.

"You may want to be able to read that, someday," she grinned. Terry laughed, and surrendered both. Rhonda quickly caught the list up.

"Books period," Billy said. "Me and Howie was talkin' the other day. . .well, little longer'n that. Anyway, we need to find technical books. We ain't got no one to count on but ourselves, ya know. We gonna have to learn to do all kinds o' stuff. And we gonna have to teach all the young'uns, too. They'll have to know how to take care o' themselves, and build on whatever we can leave'em." Everyone looked at Billy at that.

"Hadn't. . .that's a good note," George agreed. Rhonda added it to the list.

"We need clothing, boots, shoes, material, all kinds of things in that regard," Emma said. "We'll have to make our clothes someday. We need to be laying in the supplies and equipment for that."

"Very true," Amy agreed. "There's no such thing as enough of anything, in this case," she added. Rhonda added that to the list.

"There's always the chance we can find seed, and the like, too," Jerry noted. "If we can get some heirloom type stuff, I'd feel better. Using that hybrid stuff is fine, so long as we got it, but it'll run out eventually. We need to have seed that'll make on itself, and leave us with seed for the next year."

"We need tools and equipment of all kinds," Ben Kelvey spoke for the first time. "I'm talking about tools to build with, repair with, and do plain ole fashioned manual labor with. Tools break. Ain't gon' be no more runnin' to Lowe's or Ace or wherever, no more."

"Excellent point," Terry agreed. "And the same goes for other supplies. We need ammo, reloading supplies, things like that. More than that, we need to start exploring alternate means. Bows for hunting, things like that."

The discussion went on for over an hour. Billy at one point left, returning a few minutes later with a phone book, and a map.

"We can get addresses from here," he told them. "Post them on the map. Places we want to check on. If we send a scouting trip, they can check on all these places, cross off the ones that are useless to us, and report back. Then whoever makes a scavenger run, already knows where they goin', and what's there."

"Great idea," George smiled, taking the book. Billy's arm was still in a sling, though he was using it more and more. He and Debby started looking up stores and addresses, the teacher noting them down.

"How much of this could we get done before harvest?" Terry wanted to know, looking to Jerry and Jon for an answer. The two considered that for a moment.

"I don't see any way we'll be ready to start harvesting before mid-September. After that, it'll be all hands on deck until we're done. If the weather co-operates, we're looking at two weeks or so of continuous work. And you can just assume the weather won't co-operate," Jerry added, grimacing.

"So, we've got six weeks," Terry mused. He looked at George. "Wanna lead the scouting trip? See what's what?" Debby tensed, but said nothing. She had grown accustomed to having George with her almost all the time. But he had to do his part. The others had been very understanding. With Billy down, however, everyone had to do a bit more.

"I can do that," he nodded. "Say, three men?" Terry nodded.

"Yeah. You can rule out March and Williams," he said, a note of disgust in his voice. "They've got their uses, but anything that might approach needing courage is out." Everyone nodded in agreement.

"I can take Dillon, if he's recovered enough," George offered, looking to where Branch sat, having been quiet during the discussion. He nodded.

"I'm good to go," was all he said. George looked next at Toby.

"What about you, sport?" he asked. "Wanna take another trip?" Toby nodded.

"I'm good," he replied firmly. "When?"

"Well, how 'bout day after tomorrow?" George said after a few seconds. "We all need time to gather gear, and we'll need to plan some. We'll leave at four hundred days after tomorrow."

"I'll be ready," Toby nodded. Jerry smiled in pride, but said nothing. Toby hadn't had any more nightmares lately. Jerry hoped his talk had helped.

He still had his.

-

"I'm glad you aren't going," Rhonda said softly, as the group broke apart and headed home. Billy looked at her, puzzled.

"I'm hurt," he said, as if that should explain everything. "Course I ain't goin'."

"I'm still glad you aren't going," she shrugged. "I. . .it's time some of the others did some of this kind of work. That's all."

"They have been," Billy reminded her gently. "We've all been doing as we can. You included!" he added with a smile.

"I know, it's just nice to have you home, that's all."

"It's good to be home, too," Billy assured her, and his voice, and his eyes, told her he meant it. "I don't like bein' away, ya know," his gentle words soothed her. "Don't like bein' off the farm, bein' away from these young'uns, and I 'specially don't like bein' away from *you*," he added emphasis to 'you'. "All I could think about when I was in Franklin was how glad I'd be to get here. Be with you." He looked at her very seriously.

"I love you Rhonda," he told her gently but firmly. "I mean, love you like crazy, girl. I. . .I don't know that I could cope, you wasn't here. Pretty sure I'd go back to bein' a hermit crab. Be a might hard, I reckon, all these new neighbors. I don't wanna be 'thout you, Rhonda. Times I have to go, and take care o' things, all I think about whilst I'm gone is bein' back here with you. Home." Rhonda smiled broadly at that.

"I'm glad to hear you say that," she carefully hugged him. "I know that sometimes you have to go and do things away from here. We've all had to learn that. But this last trip was especially hard. No way to know when you were coming back, or even if. Maybe one day you'd just stop answerin' radio times, and we might never know what happened to ya." A few tears lined her cheeks then.

"That's the most afraid I been since you came to the shop that night."

"Didn't mean to scare ya then, ya know," Billy apologized. "If I had known. . . ." He stopped as Rhonda placed two small fingers against his lips.

Odd Billy Todd

"I don't mean like that. I mean I was scared to death all the time until you came and asked me to come here with you. After that, I stopped bein' scared. Cause I knew if there was somethin' I couldn't handle, you'd be here to take care o' me. I wouldn't be alone. And, I knew you would take care of me. I knew because you did it all through high school." She grinned suddenly.

"You know I had a crush on you the last two years you were in school. Well, longer than that, really, since I still liked on ya even after you graduated."

"Uh, no. No, I didn't," Billy hardly knew what to say.

"My daddy liked you an awful lot, ya know," Rhonda told him teasingly. "Said you was a throwback to a long time ago, when people had to make tough decisions about livin' and dyin'. A time when men kept their word when they give, it, and if they made a promise, you could like to borrow money on it."

"Way my Pa raised me," Billy shrugged. "Ain't no big deal, I reckon."

"Then you *reckon* wrong," Rhonda told him sharply. "World wasn't like that back then, and it sure ain't now. Ever girl wants the man that will stand between her and the monster in the dark, Billy," Rhonda told him softly, love in her eyes making her seem to glow. "A man suitable to make a home, a family with. Don't never think all a girl looks at is the seat of a boy's britches, of the size of the tires on his truck."

"Or how fast she'll go, either," Rhonda added, even as Billy was about to point out that his truck wasn't no mudder.

"Girls are always looking for a man that will take care of them, protect them, just like their daddy did their momma. Or should have, if they didn't. True, some get sidetracked. But not this one. I knew for a long time I wanted you, Billy Todd. You just seemed so. . .out of reach. Hard to figure. But I meant to try, at some point. When the plague hit, I didn't know what to do. I can't tell you how happy I was to find you ransackin' my daddy's store."

"I think ransackin' is a might strong," Billy protested. "I didn't tear up nothin'.'"

"You know what I mean, and quit tryin' to change the subject, Billy Todd," Rhonda huffed. "You know what I'm sayin'." Billy looked at her for a few more seconds, then dropped his gaze.

"I always figured. . .well, I worried you'd never be really happy with a man likes o' me, Rhonda. I ain't smart, like some, and I reckon I ain't 'cute' or 'handsome' like ole Pete."

"Pete's a fine man," Rhonda nodded. "And not anything I'm looking for in a man, Billy Todd. I want a man who holds me when I cry, even if he don't know what to say, and just tries to sooth me 'til I feel better. A man I can cook and clean for, and sew for, a man who hunts and works and provides for me, and the kids, and protects us from whatever wolf is foolish enough to growl at our door."

"A man who keeps his promises, even gettin' shot when he does," she grinned. "A man who loves me like there ain't no tomorrow, and thinks he can't rightly breathe no more without me. That's what I want."

"Well, I reckon I might have the breathin' part down flat, my little honey badger," Billy admitted. "Cause I sure ain't sure I could make it, you was to be gone from me."

"You ain't got to worry 'bout that, Cowboy," Rhonda whispered hotly into his ear. "I ain't goin' no where. This ain't no game to me. I aim to be here with you when we're old and gray, and have made this place an oasis for people who are willin' to work and earn a place here." She kissed him softly, tenderly.

"The rest'll just have to work itself out.".

-

George and his minions set out two days later, with the Hummer ready to roll. Billy, with Toby and Danny doing the labor, had checked the vehicle over thoroughly and found it ready to roll. Extra fuel, and plenty of food and water were onboard.

Dillon was tacked up now, wearing full gear, and ready to get back into the game. He took rear seat, in case he needed to use the Ma Deuce mounted in the gun tub. Toby rode shotgun, and would help navigate.

"Remember, you're a scouting party," Terry warned. "Information is all you're after. We want to know where anything we may can use is at, so keep good records."

"Yes, daddy," George teased. Terry reddened at that, but smiled to show he got the joke. "We're also looking for anything stray that looks interesting. You've got Howie's list, Toby?"

"Yes, sir," he held up his small notebook. "I even know what about half o' this stuff is, was I to see it." Everyone laughed at that a bit.

"All right. Stay in touch, report anything that looks like it could be a problem, or anything that looks like we should get it now."

"We'll be home for curfew," George agreed. "Ready boys?" Toby and Dillon both nodded their agreement.

"Well, then. Let's be off on this grand and glorious adventure, then, shall we?" George put an AC/DC cd into the player they had installed in the Hummer, and the tunes started cranking out '*Who Made Who?*'.

"Good road music for a trip like this, yeah?" George grinned at the pinched look on Terry's face. The former platoon sergeant looked like he'd bitten into a green persimmon. He favored country music.

"*Vaya von Dios, mi amigo!*" George almost shouted as the Hummer pulled away, heading out on it's mission.

"Travel with God, brother," Terry said behind them as the Hummer pulled out of sight. He sighed. As always, he was torn. He wanted to go. He didn't want anyone going. It was dangerous.

Then again, they needed supplies. And they needed to know what was out there.

It really was that simple.

-

The day the scout trip departed, Billy took his new maintenance crew, consisting of Danny and supplemented by Trey, a now thirteen-year-old boy from the Clifton House, and went through all the vehicles the Farm used. Fluids checked, some replaced, with new filters. Tires checked, one replaced. Batteries charged and ready to roll. Fuel full and treated. Brakes, transmissions, checked.

It took all day, but by the end of it, every vehicle they could muster was certified ready. Danny and Trey, only a year or so apart in age, hit it off pretty good, and Trey asked timidly if he could spend the night. Rhonda agreed at once, and sent the two boys to the Clifton House to inform Regina, and secure clean clothing for Trey.

The two were back in less than an hour. After an early supper, and a shower, the two were in front of the TV playing an Xbox game. Trey was suitably impressed.

"I can't believe we're playing Call to Glory!" he exuded. Sounding just like a teenager his age should sound. "We can't play like this at the House." Billy frowned.

"What d'ya mean by that?" he asked, as the two took a break. "I took a pair o' them up there, and one o' them playstations, too. Why ya can't play on them?"

"Oh, we use them all the time," Trey replied. "We just can't play games like this one. Miss Townsend doesn't want us thinking about how things are away from the house. But we play racing games, and stuff like that. And the little kids play the learning games. She says it helps them with their school work."

Billy frowned a little at that, but decided he better let the others deal with it. He didn't want to go up there half-cocked and cause a scene over what might be nothing. Better to just let the two boys have a regular night for once.

Even as he settled back down, he heard a vehicle coming up the drive, and Rommel gave a loud bark from the door.

CHAPTER SEVENTY-FIVE

George looked at the small store in front of them, and sighed.

"Looks like this one was gutted," he said, and Toby nodded. Dillon was on watch.

"Just a thought, Mister Purdy, but if them others came this way, they'd be more likely to have taken stuff from a small place like this, instead o' something they was 'sposed to report to them train people." George nodded absently.

"Good thinking Toby," he replied. "And just call me George. Mister is too formal by a half." Toby nodded, a faint red tinging his ears at the compliment.

"Well, let's load up. Wait," he stopped short. "Let's check the fuel." He looked around and found the stick used to measure the tanks. It took only a few minutes to test all three tanks.

"Well, they didn't take the fuel," George shook his head. "Strange. According to this," he raised the stick, "there's better than a thousand gallons of gas here, and nearly five hundred diesel. Always tell you're in farm or ranch country when a little country store like this carries diesel," he grinned. "Mark it down, Toby. We'll have to bring a pump and a tanker to get this." Toby dutifully made the notation.

"All right, let's head on up the road."

They carefully avoided what had been heavily populated areas. They weren't looking for trouble, or even for other people on this trip. George had decided he wouldn't refuse to speak to someone who seemed okay, but it wasn't their priority.

"Three Way community is next," Toby mentioned. "'Bout three more miles, looks like. There's a small sportin' goods store there, mom and pop grocery, and. . .huh. A motorcycle. . .no, it's a cycle and ATV repair and racing shop."

"Sound interesting," George replied.

"Heck yeah," Dillon agreed from the back. "Be nice to have a buncha four-wheelers and such. Lot easier on what gas is available, too."

"Very true," George agreed. "Billy and Jerry are the only one's who have them right now, but it would be nice to place one at each farm. Get a lot of work done with one."

"And they're fun to ride," Toby pointed out, grinning.

"That they are," George smiled. The community came in sight, and George eased up on the gas.

"Might as well man the gun, Dillon," he ordered. "Never know if there's someone up here or not. Maybe they're friendly, maybe not."

"You got it, Sarge," Dillon answered, and climbed into the turret. George kept the Hummer at about twenty miles per, both he and Toby looking in all directions. Nothing moved, and no one challenged them. The sporting goods store was first, so George eased them into the parking lot. Two vehicles sat there already, one with the hood up.

"Okay, let's do this slow and easy," George ordered. "Dillon, keep us covered. Toby and I will take a peek inside."

"Roger that," Dillon replied. Toby clambered out of the Hummer, his rifle already slung, and waited for George to motion him forward. Toby was proud to be making another trip, but he had learned the hard way that things were ugly. He took his cues from George, and made sure he did as he was told.

George pointed to the right side of the door, and Toby took up the position, while George took hold of the handle and pulled. The door resisted slightly, but came open with only a gentle tug, telling him the store had been abandoned for a while.

Looking inside, he could see signs of a hurried departure, but the store looked orderly for the most part. He motioned to Toby to follow, and stepped inside.

The store was larger than it looked from the outside. It was basically a convenience store with shooting and fishing supplies in a side room that took up most of the front of the store. The store smelled musty, and George was grateful that any rotting meat left behind had lost it's odor. Toby propped the door open without being told, and then followed George inside.

Thankfully there were no dead bodies. George led the way into the gun room, Toby followed, making sure he kept a look behind them. George stopped, a low whistle escaping his lips.

"Looks like the owner took what he wanted, and left the rest," he said, and Toby took a look.

"Wow," was all he could think of to say. A weapons rack covered two walls, with only a few open slots. Cases of ammunition stood along the walls, and in neat stacks in the aisles of the room. Another wall was covered with holsters, belts, and other equipment.

"This is a gold mine," George said softly. He stood there only a moment, before making his decision.

"We can't leave this," he told Toby. "We're loading this stuff, and going back. Today."

"Yes, sir," Toby nodded. "There's a trailer outside. Sittin' long side the buildin'. Maybe we can hook it up?"

"We'll sure try," George nodded, looking at his watch. "We've got about six hours before dark. I want to be on the road home by then. Let's get moving."

-

They took turns on guard, giving each man a chance to rest. It took some creative engineering, a long piece of chain, and not a little swearing, but they managed to get the trailer hooked behind the Hummer. That done, they wasted little time in getting to work.

By George's watch it took them two-and-a-half hours to load the ammunition, firearms and accessories onto the trailer. All three men were tired and sweating with the effort. George examined the trailer, realizing it was just over three-fourths full.

"Let's check out the grocery," he ordered. "If there's a few things we can use in there, we'll add them to the trailer. Dillon, pull the Hummer over there, and then stand watch while we check it out." Dillon nodded, and stepped into the Hummer.

"Let's go Toby," George ordered, and the two walked the short distance to the store. Again, they were fortunate in that there were no bodies. The aisles showed signs of having been hurriedly pilfered, but there was a lot of stock left.

George led the way toward the stockroom, and they entered it carefully. Boxes were sitting everywhere, with flats of canned goods wrapped in shrink wrap dominating one aisle of the back room. Toby wiped the dust from the top of the nearest one.

"Date's still nearly two years off," he said softly.

"We can't get all this," George shook his head. "Let's get on the road. This is going to take more than just us. Mark it down, and let's get going."

Ten minutes later they were on the way home. Not even one day out, they had found a good source of food, weapons, fuel and ammunition. George decided that had to count as a good trip.

-

Billy walked out onto his porch, surprised to see the Hummer pulling into the yard, pulling a trailer. Thinking something was wrong, he was off the porch in a flash.

"What happened?" he asked, as George got out.

"Nothing's wrong," George promised. "We weren't far out when we came across a good little honey hole."

"Three Way, Billy," Toby commented. Billy nodded in recognition. Three Way was about thirty-five miles north of them.

"There was a gun store there, and a small grocery. We took the guns and ammo from the store. We need to take bigger trucks and more people and go back to the store, though. Just no way for us to get it all." George opened the door to the trailer as he finished speaking.

"Wow," Billy said softly. "That's a load."

"Where in the world are we going to put all this?" George asked.

"Well, we can keep it locked in here for a few days," Billy suggested. "We need to build an armory, I guess. Something under ground, maybe? Like a powder magazine?"

"That would be ideal," George agreed. "Somewhere central, maybe? Where we can always keep an eye out. We still got all that stuff I got from the armory, too," he added.

"We need to work on that," Billy nodded. "I got some ideas about how to store this stuff, too. But I guess we need to go and get that food, first."

"I thought we could head back out in the morning," George nodded.

"Guess we better round up some help."

-

The small convoy headed out the next morning. Pete and Billy stayed behind this time, keeping an eye on things with Jerry Silvers and Ben Kelvey. March was pressed into service again as a driver. He wasn't too happy with that, but he really wasn't in a position to argue, and he knew it.

Sooner or later things would come to a head with the new people. Everyone knew it, but no one wanted to say it. Even Ralph didn't much care for them, and he liked almost everyone.

George, Dillon and Toby once more led the way. They would show the rest to the grocery, and then continue with their own mission. Terry, Ralph, Jon, Fred Williams, the Pinson Twins, Amy and Amanda, and Rhonda all went to help load the goods from the grocery and bring them home.

It was a hard day's work, too. The little grocery had apparently just taken a delivery when things hit. Everyone was amazed that it hadn't been ransacked any worse than it had.

"Short sighted people, or people that didn't have any way to carry more than what they could grab from the shelves," Terry shrugged when Rhonda had asked him about it. "Sometimes people in a panic don't think clearly. Sometimes they do, and just don't have a way to carry through."

The crew took only a short rest break for lunch, and then went back to work. In addition to the canned food, there was still some flour and meal the mice hadn't been into, and that was loaded as well. The rule was that if the seal or bag wasn't broken, it went. If the can wasn't dented, or the food a year or more out of date, it went.

Paper goods were loaded as well. The convoy had two trailer trucks, and an empty fuel tanker. Jon and Fred Williams had checked the tanks at the grocery, and found some fuel there, and were busy pumping as much as they could out, and into the tanker. They would stop at the little country store on the way out and empty that tank as well.

The resulting haul was a good one, but it was a tired and dirty crew of workers who arrived at near dark that evening.

Despite their exhaustion, all agreed it had been a lucky find, and one they couldn't have afforded to pass up.

-

George and company had ventured on North after leaving the grocery store. There hadn't been any working ATV's at the race shop, much to Toby, and Dillon's, disappointment.

"We'll find some somewhere, I'm sure," George promised.

Their winding trail took them passed several more places, some of which had been turned upside down by scavengers, and some that didn't seem to have been touched. They found some places had food, others had fuel, and one small place had carried fabrics and sewing goods. Toby made careful notes about what was what as the Hummer crisscrossed the area.

It was nearing dark when George decided to call it a day. He had been watching for a safe place to spend the night, and decided that a house they passed would do nicely, providing no one was there. It was a two-story brick, off the road about two hundred yards, with an attached garage. A perfect place to hide the Hummer.

If it was empty.

"Dillon, you're with me," George ordered. "Toby, I want you behind the wheel. Something happens, I want you ready to head out as soon as we're back." Toby nodded, and slipped into the driver's seat. George and Dillon approached the garage door, and lifted it. The garage was empty.

"Well, that's a good sign, maybe," Dillon noted. The two of them entered the house from the garage, and searched it quickly in the fading light. A light layer of dust covered everything, showing no one had been here in a while. Otherwise, the house showed signs of a hurried but orderly departure. George was moving through the kitchen when he saw the note.

If you're reading this, you're welcome to use the house, and what's in it.
We bugged out, and are hopefully somewhere safe. We ask only that you not trash the place. We might live, and want to come back someday.
The Ellisons.

"Sound like nice people," George spoke aloud. Dillon came down from the upstairs, informing George the house was clear.

Twenty minutes later, the Hummer was in the garage, and the three of them were eating supper, reviewing their notes.

An hour after that, they were sleeping.

-

Billy went to see Ben Kelvey the morning after the short convoy trip to Three Way. The older man was already up, looking over notes he kept in a small hardback notebook.

"Mornin' Billy," he smiled. "How's that arm?"

"Bout as good as it's gonna be, I reckon," Billy replied. Rommel saw a squirrel across the road, and took out after it. Billy shook his head.

"One day he's gonna catch one o' them, and then I'm gonna have to glue his nose back on." Ben laughed at that, finding it hilarious.

"We need to build an armory," Billy said, turning serious. "We need to have a place to store all the ammo and weapons and such. A place kinda like an old-time powder magazine, like from the Civil War. Know what I mean?"

"Yeah," Ben rubbed his chin. "Seen one once, or a reproduction of one, at Fort Pillow State Park, over on the Mississippi River. The park museum was built like a powder magazine. Good design, I always thought," he added. "Half buried, and got a berm around it, too. That would make a good place," he nodded.

"I figure we need it somewhere central, but still far off enough was somethin' to happen. Safe, like," Billy said.

"Well, we'll have to work out how big it needs to be, and then get us a design sketched out. After that, we'll just have to scout around until we find something."

"I was thinkin' we could put it somewhere back o' here," Billy told him. "Out past the pasture, like. That way it's hid, but got houses all around it. Be hard to get to, 'thout one o' us seein' anybody after it. See what I mean?"

"Yeah. Wouldn't want to live that close to it, though," Ben mused.

"Nah, I'm talkin' 'bout half way or so. We'll prob'ly have to fell some trees, but other'n that, we can dig into the hillside between here and my place. Save a lot o' work gettin' it buried that way."

"Now you're thinking like a builder," Ben smiled approvingly. "Let's take a walk, and look things over."

-

"Good idea," Terry agreed, when they approached him for an opinion. "I've worried about it myself, but there's just so much going on, it always takes a back burner. My best idea was to bury one of the trailers and use it. Your idea is a lot better than mine. Plus, whatever trees we cut can be made into firewood."

"We can get started tomorrow, then," Billy decided. "I don't like the idea of all that firepower just sittin' there."

"Works for me," Terry nodded.

-

"I don't see how we ever won a war if this is what ya'll ate," Toby mourned as he finished his breakfast, consisting of a less than ideal MRE.

"You drew the short straw on that one, kid," Dillon laughed. "Them egg meals ain't natural."

"I could o' used that information 'fore I picked it," Toby groused. "That stuff ain't fit for man nor beast."

"That's why we won," George grinned. "Man eats that, he's so mad, ain't nobody gonna stop him." Dillon laughed at the old joke, and Toby managed a rueful grin.

"All right, let's load up," George ordered. "Toby, what's on our agenda today?"

"We're gonna cut over this road and head to Sweet Lips."

"I'm sorry. Did you say. . . ." Dillon looked like he was fighting to keep from laughing.

"Yeah," Toby grinned. "It's a real place. Kind of a map dot, but there's a store there, and a gas station."

Dillon finally lost it. He actually fell over, he was laughing so hard.

"I lived here all my life," he gasped. "How is it I ain't never heard of a town called Sweet Lips?"

"Better than Skunk Holler," George shrugged, and Dillon collapsed again in a gale of laughter.

"You're kiddin'," Toby objected.

"Am not," George shook his head. "Up north and east of Nashville, in Jackson County, I think. My momma had family there."

"Oh, that's rich!" Dillon was wiping tears from his eyes.

"Well, we won't get there standing here," George rolled his eyes. "Let's load up and go."

-

"I think this is the best place," Billy said, waving an arm across the hillside before them. "Dig straight back into the hill side, and there we are."

"Well, not quite," Ben corrected. "We'll have to do some re-enforcing, and frame up a good foundation. Once we do that, we're gonna need some concrete, Billy. And a lot of it. And some re-bar. Something like this, we can't skimp on the steel. The ground we pile on and around it are gonna weight a lot."

"How much concrete?" Billy asked, frowning in thought.

"A lot," Ben repeated. "I'll have to figure it out based on how big we want this place, but I'm telling you now, it's gonna be a bunch." Billy rubbed his chin for a moment, studying the hillside.

"I'ma have to git back to ya on that."

-

"Nothing worth saving here," George sighed. Another place either ransacked, empty, or in this case, burned to ashes.

"We can check the tanks," Toby suggested. George shrugged, and the teen went to look for a measure stick. He came back at a run, seconds later.

"Dogs! Run for it!"

George waited for a split second, watching Toby, then headed for the Hummer. Dillon, on guard as always, swung the fifty around, and flipped the butterfly switch up, ready to fire.

Toby was halfway to the Hummer when they came into view. George stopped counting at twelve, too busy trying to get Toby's door opened. Dillon gave Toby a three count, and fired a short burst at the lead dogs, killing three of them.

To his surprise, the dogs following never slowed down. Shaking off his shock,

Odd Billy Todd

Dillon opened fire again, this time with a sustained burst that swept before the pack, killing two more and showering the rest with pavement and gravel. Toby took advantage of that lull to dive into the Hummer, and slam the door.

"Ain't no gas here," he said flatly. George looked at him in shocked silence for a moment, and then burst out laughing.

"That had to be the last thing I expected you to say," he said between gales of laughter.

"Is this laugh at Toby day or somethin'?" the teen groused good naturedly.

"Nah, kid," Dillon promised, sliding into the back seat. "It's just that your luck really sucks today, that's all." His grin robbed the words of any sting they might have had, and Toby laughed himself.

"Okay, we can check off Dog Town, I guess," George chuckled. They all needed the laugh after Toby's narrow escape. "What's next."

"Dog Town," Toby sighed, looking at the map.

"You're kidding," George looked over at his 'navigator'.

"Don't I wish," Toby sighed again, and held the map up for both the others to read.

"Kid, this really ain't your day, is it?" Dillon was still laughing a mile down the road.

-

"Well, I can't remember. I didn't even bother to look. So, all I can do is go see now." Billy looked at Rhonda who was not happy.

"No." Her voice was flat and final.

"'Scuse me?" Billy responded, his voice calm.

"You are not going off anywhere like that for a *look see* without me. You need supervision. Both of you do." This to Pete, who was already standing at the door of the Ford.

"And just how d'you figure that?" Billy huffed. Rhonda didn't bother to answer, just nodded to where Billy's arm had been wounded.

"So you think if you'd been there, this wouldn't o' happened. Is that it?" Billy challenged.

"Don't matter. I'm goin' or you're stayin'." Rhonda crossed her arms and stood looking at him defiantly.

"And so am I," Shelly Silvers' voice echoed from behind them. Pete whirled around to see her standing there, Mary by her side. It was obvious that the girl had been sent to bring Shelly to the Todd house.

"We talked about it, and decided we're tired of the two of you gallivantin' all over creation and leavin' us here," Shelly informed them, walking to stand beside Rhonda. "You're going into Cedar Bend? Guess what? So are we." She crossed her arms in mimic of Rhonda. Pete looked at her, then looked at Billy, and shrugged.

"I give," he said simply. Billy nodded.

"Me too. Ya'll get your bags and pile in." The two women did so, and soon the four of them were headed into town to see if Cedar Bend Foundations still had usable concrete.

Neither of the women lorded their victory over the men, choosing instead to discuss what they were doing.

"We need concrete, and a lot of it," Pete informed them. "Even Ben isn't sure

459

how much. We have to see if there's anything we can use here, or if we have to go further afield. Hopefully we'll find what we need in town."

"Don't forget re-bar," Billy mentioned. "Ben says we've got to have a lot of re-enforcement if we're gonna pretty much bury the armory." Pete nodded.

"Yeah, he's right about that. Dirt weighs a lot. We'll need the walls to be strong, but especially the roof. If the roof isn't properly re-enforced, then it could bring the walls down."

"It's a good thing we've got Ben," Billy added. "I'd a just built the thing, and shoved the dirt over the top. Never thought about the weight makin' the roof collapse."

"We've been lucky, in the people we've brought here," Shelly agreed, squeezing Pete's hand as she spoke. He smiled at her, returning the gentle pressure.

"Everyone here knows something, or knows how to do something that the others really don't," Rhonda nodded. "When I think about how bad others have it, I try to remember how lucky we are."

"It's not luck, Rhonda," Pete objected. "It's preparedness, hard work, and smart thinking. All those others had the same opportunity that you did. It isn't your fault if they failed to take advantage of it."

"Well, I guess that's true," she agreed. "Still, we had a good head start," she pointed out, patting Billy's leg, and giving him a bright smile.

"Now that, I'll agree with," Pete replied. "Billy has done a remarkable job thinking about the future, and getting ready for it." Billy flushed slightly.

"I ain't done nothin' but what my folks taught me. Been doin' that since this all started. Not for them, I wouldn't be no better off'n nobody else."

"Don't sell yourself short, Billy," Pete shook his head. "I agree, you had a good start on things, thanks to your parents. But a lot of this you've made happen with plain old hard work, and determination. And getting others to see what you see. Trust me, buddy, that ain't always an easy thing to accomplish."

The discussion turned to other things after that, and the two couples found themselves enjoying the trip, for once. For just a little while, things were almost normal.

It was a good feeling.

CHAPTER SEVENTY-SIX

Work on the 'bunker' as everyone had taken to calling it, started the next day. Billy had been pleased to find that what concrete was still in town had been covered, and had weathered the last year fairly well, considering. They had returned for Ben, who had looked at the supply available and smiled.

"That's enough for the bunker, and a good bit besides," he assured Billy. Pete was relieved to hear that, since it meant they wouldn't have to travel afield to look for more.

Franklin was still on everyone's mind, too. Even though Billy and Pete had hurt them, no one knew for sure what they might do next. There were at least twenty people left in the group, and they would now be desperate. As a result, someone was on call all the time, with Howie and Elizabeth working around the clock monitoring every sensor, alarm, and camera they had operating.

But life goes on, regardless of what else is happening. Chickens won't hold off on the eggs for a day because you're worried about the neighbors. Cow's that need milking can't wait. Horses that need shoeing have to be tended to, if you plan on riding the horse.

Animals that are dependent on their owners for feed, have to be fed. Firewood had to be cut, food cooked, crops and gardens checked, the list was never ending.

This morning found Billy, Pete, Jon and Ben working to make room in the hillside for the new armory. Rhonda, Shelly, and Emma were spending the day gathering, cleaning and canning vegetables from their gardens, with Mary assisting, and Danny fetching and toting.

Others around the valley were tending their own chores as well. Regardless of what else was happening where, if they wanted to eat, things had to be done.

-

Dog Town, the real one, hadn't given them anything worth salvaging, but it did provide a decent place to spend the night. As morning dawned, the three talked about their next step.

"Toby, if we follow the map, and the plan, what's our next stop?" George asked. Toby studied for a minute.

"Well, we can probably hit Nixon Springs, Bitter Creek, and Rossville today," he said finally.

"All about the same as what we've seen so far?" George asked. "Small store, maybe a few shells or fishing supplies, and that's about it?"

"Well, prob'ly," Toby nodded. "Honestly, these ain't much more than map dots. Ain't none of'em even big as Cedar Bend, and that ain't exactly a sprawlin' metropolis."

"So, it ain't," Dillon nodded. "What'cha got in mind, Sarge?"

"I'm just thinking we're spinning our wheels, here, and wasting gas," George shrugged. "I think it's time we took a look as some of these larger towns. We don't have to go in, just to have a peek. We can look around, see if anyone's about, and then head on up the road."

"Which town you got in mind?" Toby asked, studying the map.

"You pick, Toby," George said suddenly. "Where should we go?" Toby looked at George for a minute, then turned his attention back to the map.

"I'd say Centerville," he announced finally. "Fair size town, but not huge. Nothin' like big as Franklin, but bigger'n Cedar Bend."

"Centerville it is, then," George nodded. "Let's get loaded up, and get going."

It took them nearly three hours to reach Centerville, due mostly to the fact that they were being careful, and taking their time. They were on a recon mission. Their job was to look. Anything they passed that looked useful was investigated, and noted down.

They saw not one single living soul during that trip.

"Ya know, I thought there'd be at least a few people," Toby sighed.

"Don't forget how that bunch in Franklin's been operatin', kid," Dillon reminded him. "They may well have hit every place along in here. Then again," he shrugged, "they might all have gotten the sickness, too. And some may just be layin' low, like ya'll have been. There just ain't no way o' knowin'." Toby nodded, his eyes having never left his side of the road.

"How much further, Toby?" George asked, scratching his neck. He didn't like it when his neck itched. That usually meant someone was watching him.

"Maybe four, five miles," Toby answered after checking the map, and then studying the road signs.

"Dillon, I. . . ."

"My neck's itchin' too, Sarge," the other man replied. He was sitting where he could watch behind them. "An' I don't like it neither."

"What's that mean?" Toby asked. His own neck was itching, but he'd assumed it was an insect bite. "My neck's been itchin' for two hours. I thought I was bit by somethin'."

"You may have been," Dillon replied. "But after you been in country for a while, your neck starts to itch when someone's lookin' at you. Don't really know why, just does. I learned during my first tour to trust my feelin's, and that includes an itchy neck."

"Same here," George nodded. "We're in Indian country, too. We got no idea what we're headed into. You boys hang on to something. Next little dirt road I see that offers some cover, we're gonna take it." He sped up suddenly.

A mile down the road he found what he was looking for. With a sharp tug on the wheel, he turned the Hummer down a single track dirt road, and then whipped it into the trees at the first opportunity. Dillon was scrambling to man the fifty before George ever said anything. He stopped the Hummer, and killed the engine.

"What now?" Toby asked.

"We wait."

-

"This here's the last of'em, Rhonda," Danny announced, placing one last basket of veggies on the bar.

"Thanks, sweetie," Rhonda smiled.

"I need to go and put ever thing away," he nodded, and went back outside.

"Well, I'll be glad to see this done," Mary sighed, starting on the last tub of beans from the garden.

"Oh, we ain't done," Rhonda chuckled. "This is just the first haul. If we're lucky, the garden will make at least twice more."

"I know, but it'll be a week or two before then," Mary waved the comment aside. "At least tomorrow there won't be anything. We pretty well weeded today, and all the plants look good."

"We've been very fortunate," Rhonda nodded.

"How come we don't go to church, Rhonda?" Mary asked suddenly. Rhonda stopped working.

"Well, Mary, we don't have a church," Rhonda replied. "You know that."

"Well, we ain't got a buildin'," Mary agreed. "But there's all of us. Reckon the Lord wouldn't hear us, if we was singin' and prayin'?"

"You know, I imagine he would," Rhonda nodded. "We don't have a preacher, but. . . ."

"Mister Jerry's a Godly man," Mary pointed out. "He knows the Bible in and out, I reckon. We could ask him to read from the bible if nothin' else, couldn't we?"

"Well, we can ask."

-

"I'd be honored to," Jerry replied, when Mary and Rhonda asked him. "I've thought about doing that more than once, but it seems something always comes up. Where would we meet?"

"Long as the weather's nice, I say we meet outside," Rhonda suggested. "We can have everyone over to our place to start. We've got seats and what have you. Everyone can bring a dish, and we'll have dinner afterward. Just like real folks," she added with a grin.

"Well, guess we need to see if everyone else wants to," Jerry mused.

"Everyone else can, or not. We want to," Rhonda told him. "We've got a lot to be thankful for. And Mary suggested asking you. This was her idea, really."

"I'm flattered, young'un," Jerry grinned at Mary. "Well, then, say about eleven, Sunday morning?"

"It's a date," Rhonda nodded. "See you then."

-

George had almost decided they were being paranoid when they heard a vehicle approaching. A battered truck pulled into view, and eased to a stop, not far from where George and the others sat concealed in the trees. Five men left the cab and the bed, standing in the road. All were rough and dirty looking.

"You lost'em!" one yelled across the hood to the driver. "First vehicle we seen in how long, and you let'em get away!"

"You was the one said not to follow so close!" the driver spat. "I was doin' what you said!"

"Shut up, both of you," a third ordered. "And stop yellin'. Ain't a soul in ten miles can't hear ya screechin' like monkeys." Both men fell silent.

"That was an army truck," the man noted. "We ain't seen no sign o' the army since everything went to hell. I wonder why they're here abouts, now?"

"Maybe they're comin' to take what we got," the driver suggested. "Like ole Willie alus said they would."

"Willie's a crackpot," the man in charge snorted.

"Wasn't for him, where'd we be?" offered one of the men from the back, who had been silent until now. "Willie might be strange, but he knows stuff. Just like he

463

knew we needed to be out here, patrollin'."

"We ain't patrolling so much as we're fishing," the leader reminded him. "Looking for things we can use. And that truck has probably got rifles, ammo, and MRE's to eat, if nothing else."

"Reckon them soldier boys won't be wantin' to share, Josey," the man from the back pointed out to the leader.

"Reckon we'll just have to persuade'em, Jake," Josey grinned. "Can't be more'n four of'em in there. We'll make out just fine. C'mon, load up. They're headed into town. Willie'll have someone out watchin', so if we stay on the road, we'll be able to come up behind. There might be more where they came from. With more stuff we need."

"Hey, reckon they got any women soldiers?" the driver asked hopefully.

"Rodney, do you think about anything else, ever?" The passenger across the hood asked, shaking his head.

Rodney's reply was lost as the old truck fired up again, and continued its way down the road. George counted to fifty before he leaned back, sighing.

"We almost drove straight into a trap," he muttered.

"Sure did," Dillon agreed. "They was all carryin' M4's, too. If I had to guess, they found an armory and raided it. That means they'll have some heavy firepower. Wonder why they didn't take a Hummer?"

"Fuel, probably," George replied. "That old truck is probably burning home made diesel from the sound of it. Did you hear how it was knocking? It's close to going. That stuff made from cooking oil is easy to get, but it fouls an engine something awful. If I had to guess, this 'Willie' they're talking about it saving what real fuel he has, and the best vehicles, for when he needs them. Using beaters with that home-made crap in the meantime."

"Well, whoever they are, they didn't sound the least little bit friendly," Toby put in.

"No, kid, they didn't," Dillon sighed. "Damnation. Why does everyone have to go feral just cause they can?" he shook his head.

"I don't know," George shook his head. "And not everyone has. We've not but really encountered three bad groups o' folks. Most we've spoke to are fairly okay. The one's the train didn't get, or that bunch in Franklin."

"Well, now we got someone else to worry about," Dillon reminded him. "Sarge, I say we head for the barn. This is a game changer."

"So it is," George nodded. "We'll check the rest of Toby's 'map dots' on the way in. No sense in wasting the gas. But we'll need a good group to come salvage anything we find."

The three were feeling a little forlorn as they pointed the Hummer toward home.

-

It took two days of hard work, but by the end of the second day, the new 'armory' was all but finished. There was still work to do inside, but that would have to wait until the concrete dried.

"There's more concrete," Ben noted. "We can pour a floor, somewhere," he suggested. "Got anything, or anywhere, in mind?" he asked Billy.

"Well, several have asked about a community hall," Billy told him. "How big a floor could we pour? And how fast do we have to do it?" Ben studied what was left in the truck, doing a mental calculation.

"We can pour a twenty by thirty floor, four inches thick I'd say," he announced finally. "And we can probably get by with lettin' the truck run over night. I'd rather not, but for just a floor, it'll probably work. Might crack, later on, though," he warned.

"We ain't got the place laid out, yet," Billy replied.

"Well, we can set up a form in just a few minutes, with some help," Ben shrugged. "Get it poured 'fore we go to bed. But we'll need some folks helpin'."

"Well, let's go see about that, then," Billy sighed. One day, he figured, he'd get to rest some. But this wasn't that day, apparently.

-

Twenty minutes later Ben was supervising twelve people laying out a form for the floor. They had picked a spot that was already level, sitting at the intersection not far from Terry's house. At the last minute, Billy had suggested that the floor, and the building, be oriented along the main road, far enough off of it to allow additions to the building over time.

"We can turn it into a blockhouse," he told Terry. "Kinda like in the old days. Big old log house, maybe two walls with sand between'em. Be a good place to hole up if somethin' bad was to happen." Terry had readily agreed with that, thinking this would keep them from having to use the Clifton House for such a thing.

It was well after dark before they were done, working in the glow of several floodlights.

"She'll cure in a couple days, I'd guess," Ben informed them. "Then we'll see about sketchin' out somethin' to start on."

"Sounds good to me," Terry nodded. "You need any help with that truck?"

"You can help me get'er filled with water, to wash out what's left," Ben nodded. "Make's clean-up a lot easier. Might want to use it again." The two left to go do just that. The rest headed home.

"Thank you, Billy. For remembering," Rhonda smiled, as the two walked home.

"Sure," Billy smiled back. "Course, we ain't got nothin' but a floor, yet. Still, it'll happen." Billy stopped suddenly, and drew Rhonda off the road slightly.

"What is it?" she whispered.

"Truck comin'," he told her. "I think it's George," he added a minute later. "Don't sound like they're runnin'."

Two minutes later, the Hummer pulled into view. Billy stepped out as the vehicle stopped.

"Anything wrong?" Billy asked.

"Well, not right at the moment," George sighed. "But we did find another trouble spot. Place called Centerville."

"I know it," Billy nodded, and Rhonda did too.

"Well, they are hostile," George sighed. "We decided to check on some of the larger places, just on the periphery, you know? Skirt the edges and see what was there. Before we made it into town, we all got the feeling that someone was watching us, so we pulled off the road and hid." He went on to describe the scene that had played out in front of them.

"Well, that sucks," Rhonda sighed. "Just when we were hoping things might calm down."

"Well, they don't know we're here," George pointed out. "And, they thought we were Army, because of the Hummer. I think so long as we don't have contact with them, we'll be fine. I hate to say it, but I think our wandering and exploring is about over."

"I suggest we gather what stuff we've already located, and call it a day. There's just too much risk involved."

"Need to know how many of 'em there are," Billy said thoughtfully. "Be great if we could get them interested in that Franklin bunch, wouldn't it."

"That would require more luck than I think we have to spare," George sighed. "But we should make the first priority gathering what we've found. It's mostly fuel, but there are some other odds and ends."

"When you want to try?" Billy asked.

"I'd say tomorrow, to be honest. It may take us two days, or even three."

"I guess we better get it put together, then. Once we're finished, we can settle in I guess, and just take care of what's here."

-

A small but well armed convoy started out the next morning, led by the Hummer. Once again, Pete and Billy stayed behind, along with Toby and Ralph, and Jerry. All the other men made the trip, along with several of the women, including Rhonda and Shelly.

Pete and Billy decided to take their horses and do a ride across of the valley, something they had taken to doing on a frequent but irregular basis. Danny begged and pleaded to come along, and Billy finally relented. Mary was at the Clifton House, along with Amanda, helping replace Ruth Townsend and Megan Johnson, the teen they had rescued in Columbia. She had recovered nicely with good food and safety, and was ready and willing to work, so both had gone along with the convoy.

The three of them rode a wide circuit, checking on any and everything they could think of. They encountered Jerry Silvers along the way, out checking the crops.

"Near to harvest time," he told them, as the four relaxed in the shade of a tree. "I'd say another six weeks, and we'll be full in the field, if the weather cooperates."

"Which it won't," Pete snorted, and Jerry chuckled.

"No, probably not," he admitted. "Still, I like what I see. Wish we could get one more good rain, 'tween now and then, though. Might up the yields some. But we'll have a good crop, Lord willin', rain or no."

"Reckon we'll be some busy gettin' it all put by," Billy noted.

"Not as bad as you might think," Jerry shook his head. "Remember, the corn is mostly for the stock, and the rapeseed is for the bio fuel. All we'll have to do is store that. The wheat we'll need to harvest, and let dry for everyone to be able to grind it for flour, and we set by that one corn field for corn meal. Sure wish we had a little mill," he added wistfully.

"Can't we build one?" Billy asked. Jerry looked at him.

"Well, yeah, comes to that I reckon we can. Hadn't thought about it."

"Talk to Howie," Billy suggested. "Man's a pure redneck genius."

"Ain't he gone with the convoy?"

"No, he ain't," Billy shook his head. "I wouldn't let him. We can't spare him, ever. He gets hurt, or worse, and we're in a world o' trouble. I don't want him away from where we can protect him anytime we can prevent it. And we can prevent it, this time."

"Well, reckon I'll just mosey on over there, then," Jerry nodded. "Be seein' you fellas. You comin' to dinner, Peter?"

"Yes, sir," Pete nodded. "I'll see you this evening."

"Good enough," the older man nodded, and rode off toward Howie's.

"Peter, you comin' to dinner?" Billy asked, teasing his friend.

"Shut up," Pete growled, grinning. "Man's gonna be my father-in-law. Reckon he wants to call me Peter, he can."

"Be callin' you son, next," Billy grinned.

"Can't see that's a bad thing," Pete said thoughtfully. "That's a right fine man, right there."

"He is that," Billy nodded in agreement. "One o' the best. He's another we don't want to let get too far away, comes to that. Him and Miss Em are a gold mine of information. We need them much as we do ole Howie."

"Yeah," Pete nodded. "Jerry ain't no young man, neither."

"Reckon he ain't," Billy agreed. "But he's tougher'n shoe leather, Jerry is. C'mon, let's get finished." He looked at Danny. "Figure you need to head home. Imagine you got work waitin'."

"Okay," Danny nodded. "See ya Pete!" he called before putting his heels to Thor and starting home.

"Take care, kid!" Pete called after him. He looked at Billy.

"What's on your mind?" he asked.

"Obvious, huh?" Billy grunted. Pete just shrugged.

"You notice that our two new friends were 'reluctant' to help with the convoy today?" he asked, speaking of Williams and March.

"Yeah," Pete sighed. "They're always reluctant, seems like."

"They are," Billy nodded. "Don't think our relations with them ain't gonna end too well."

"I figure the same," Pete admitted. "Thing is, what do we do? We can't just throw 'em out. They been doing pretty good on those places they took, and it's comin' on to winter anyway."

"Well, the way I see it is this," Billy started his horse moving. "They can either get with the program, or they can go it alone. I don't mind 'em stayin' on here, but they can forget gettin' any help from us. They ain't gonna help, and do it cheerfully, then we don't need 'em, and we ain't gonna baby 'em. That sit all right with you?"

"I guess," Pete shrugged. "I don't know of anything else that will do. And they have worked," he reminded Billy.

"They have, and as long as they keep at it, I'm pretty okay with their attitude, long as it don't get no worse. But I figure it's gonna get worse. I know that March was mumblin' 'bout how me and you wasn't goin'."

"Someone's got to watch this place," Pete shrugged, riding alongside Billy. "This time it was us. Them two ain't gonna be much use protecting the valley."

"I think it had more to do with the fact that we wasn't workin' on the convoy, than that," Billy shook his head. "Way I took it, he figured we should be goin', stead o' him and Williams. See what I mean?"

"We done our part, and a few others as well, Billy," Pete protested. "You got shot, too."

"I know that, and so do you. So does everyone, 'cept them two. Their women ain't much better, and they don't allow their young'uns to 'associate' with the rest, neither. Times I wish they'd just missed our road altogether. Wasn't for them kids they brought with'em, anyway."

"Yeah," Pete agreed. "That was a good stroke of luck for the kids. Things might not be ideal at the Clifton House, but it's got to be better'n what they had."

"And they're safer, too," Billy nodded. "Well, anyway. Just be thinkin' on it. I don't know what to do with'em either. And it ain't gonna be up to just us, noway. Ever body'll have a say in it."

"So, they will."

CHAPTER SEVENTY-SEVEN

Days turned to weeks. Work was done. Preparations for winter were under way, despite the fact that winter was still some months away. August gave way to September, and some of the leaves began to change. The weather cooled. Jerry got his rain. The armory was finished, and all the weapons and ammunition not issued or stored at the houses was placed there, and the building disguised.

The blockhouse had walls, and a roof, along with openings cut for windows. The roof was constructed to allow for a loft, and plans were already being drawn to add another wing, this one with a basement for long term storage. Water lines were placed, septic tanks buried. Rough but serviceable bathrooms, along with showers, were added. If worse came to worse, then the blockhouse would make a good last stand position.

Everyone hoped that wouldn't happen.

A week of hard work saw to it that everyone had firewood for the winter. A brief discussion with March and Williams saw the two of them and their families being more friendly, and more open to group efforts, since they, too, profited from those efforts.

Jerry announced that harvest would start in the next two weeks, give or take, depending on the weather. That sent a flurry of work at storage, preparations for the wheat to be ground, the corn to be ground, and the rapeseed to be pressed into oil. Ralph and Howie had taken over the bio fuel project now, with help from Jon Kelvey, and they had found an old roller machine that had once been used to bend and roll sheet metal they had 'pressed' into service to press the seed, and collect the oil.

Danny's friend Trey had been helping with preparations, and one night had returned to the house with Danny and Billy, intending to spend the night, as he did every so often. Danny had invited him to play X-Box, but the boy had declined, sadly.

"Miss Regina says I can't play when I'm here. It's not fair to the others, cause I get more time than they do."

"What's that?" Billy sat up a bit straighter.

"It's the rules," Trey shrugged. "I got to follow the rules when I'm here, just like if I was there."

"Reckon I make the rules 'round here," he said flatly. "You want to play, play. Just don't tell'er. You was on your best behavior and did as what you were told. Keep your own business private from now on." Trey considered that for less than a minute before he was down, controller in hand, and ready to help Danny trounce Toby.

Billy lay aside the book he'd been trying to read, thinking on this. Seems like they might need to pay a little more attention to what them kids at the home was being taught.

Facts was, maybe they all needed to take a hand in teaching the kids the lay of things, nowadays. Most of them were of age to start learning at least some things, already. They needed to get an early start. Trey and one other, a girl of fourteen, were already big enough they should be helping with chores away from the Clifton House. They weren't simply because the others thought having the two working at the House would take some of the pressure off the women who were responsible for so many children.

He decided he needed to talk to Rhonda about this. She's know what to do, and just how to handle it.

—

Rhonda listened to Billy relay his conversation with Trey, growing angrier by the second. She did, however, remain silent until Billy finished.

"Well," Billy said, finally. "What do you think?"

"I think I'm going up there and tear that bitch's hair out, that's what!" Rhonda's voice was a growl. "Of all the stupid things I've heard, this just about tops them all. The whole idea of having that stuff was to give the children a little bit of normalcy. What the hell is she doing up there?"

"I think this ain't no place for me to be involved," Billy said quietly. "Reckon you need to gather up the other women, and discuss this amongst yerselves. And I don't want you trottin' off up there alone, hear? Best this not be done in front o' the young'uns. They got enough on their plate as it is. Ya'll get'er down to the common house, and lay into her there. *Together*," he stressed. Rhonda considered that for a moment, then nodded.

"Fair enough. I'm goin' to see Emma. And Trey stays here from now on."

"What?" Billy looked startled. "Now wait a min. . . ."

"No," Rhonda shook her head. "He and Danny are friends, only a year or so apart in age, and they get along well. Danny needs friends his age that can do the things he does. They can bunk together in his room. Trey. Stays. Here."

"What about the girl?" Billy challenged. "Don't Mary need friends her own age, too?"

"She and Amanda get along famously," Rhonda informed him. "Their age difference is less than three years, and Mary is very mature for her age. In fact, the two of them are together right now at Amy's. Baking cookies."

Okay," Billy sighed. He hadn't intended to wind up with yet another child, but Rhonda had that look. The one she got when she meant to have her way, if it meant hell just had to freeze over so she could skate on by. He didn't like that look. He especially didn't like it aimed at him. He decided he'd leave it aimed at Regina Townsend.

"I'm going to see Emma," Rhonda announced, getting to her feet. "I'll be back when I get back. I'm taking Trey with me. Emma will want to talk to him." With that she gathered her things, gathered Trey, and went.

"Oh, boy," Billy murmured. "This might be bad."

—

"What does Regina have to say about all this?" Emma asked, after Trey had told Emma his story. The two women, especially Emma, had questioned the boy rather thoroughly, and once he realized he wasn't going back to Clifton House to stay, he started talking more.

Essentially, the older children took a backseat to the younger. While the older children were allowed access to some of the toys, any punishments included the loss of those privileges. Neither woman objected to that, since both had done so themselves.

But as the tale went on, Emma began to see a disturbing pattern. It sounded to her as if Regina had adopted a two tier system with the children in her care. The younger children, below school age, were her 'favorites'. The older children, especially those into their teen years, were. . .not. She wasn't cruel to them, and Trey was honest about it. She simply wasn't fair with them, in almost any way.

With Trey gone, Emma sat thoughtfully for a few minutes, clearly playing things over in her mind. Rhonda sat silently, waiting.

"Do you know how many children are up there, at the house?" Emma asked suddenly.

"Uh, not exactly," Rhonda admitted.

"Neither do I," Emma agreed. "And that's our first mistake. How big of a burden have we placed on her?"

"She's got five other. . . ." Rhonda started, but Emma held up a hand.

"Hold on, girl," Emma ordered. "She's got two grown women, and that's all. The others are teens. How much work is it for you to keep reign on Danny and Mary?"

"Well, it's not too bad," Rhonda admitted. "They're both very responsible, and do a great deal of work. They don't argue about their chores, or their school work, either."

"But they are exceptions to the rule," Emma nodded. "My point exactly. I think it's time we had a ladies meeting, Rhonda. We've neglected things like this in all the hubbub of getting other things done. It's time we took a hand it what's happening right here at home."

-

"There are fourteen children living there," Debby informed the others as they gathered around the table in the common building. Rhonda had taken the Ford and brought Amy, Debby and Maria to meet with her Shelly, and Emma. They hadn't bothered with the two newcomers, as no one knew them very well, yet. They had, however, included Elizabeth Rickman.

"That's too many," Amy shook her head. "You know, we talked about this when we were in Columbia," she reminded Rhonda.

"Yeah," Rhonda looked slightly red faced. She wasn't angry anymore, now that she could see that maybe Regina and the others were over worked. "We did. And we haven't done a thing about it."

"There's always more than one side to any problem," Emma nodded, grateful for the attitude. "Now, we need a workable solution. Who'd like to go first?"

"Well, I've already decided we'll adopt Trey," Rhonda announced. The others looked at her in surprise. "He and Danny are good friends, and Trey likes to help him and Billy with working on the vehicles. Danny's been teaching him about his chores, too, which includes taking care of our little herd of cows. It just. . .it seemed like the thing to do," she shrugged. "And he's a great kid."

"He is," Debby nodded. "Always respectful in class, and gets very good grades. George and I have been talking about this as well, but didn't know what to do. There's a four-year-old little girl named Bethany we'd like to adopt. Do. . .do you think we could?" she asked hesitantly. Several months back she and Rhonda had butted heads over Mary. Everyone knew, now, that her problem had been caused by withdrawal from a powerful anti-depressant. Debby was fully recovered now, and doing well.

"I don't see why not," Emma nodded. "You've done a wonderful job with Georgie. He's about the sweetest little boy I've ever met!" Debby blushed at this praise, and nodded her thanks to Emma for the compliment.

"My *ninios* are friends with the one called Sam," Maria said next in her heavily accented English. "He is between them in age, and they get along very well. I must discuss this with Terrance, but I think we can take him into our home."

"I've decided I can take at least one child as well," Emma surprised them. "I don't know, just yet, who it will be, but I was thinking about the teenager, Sally. She came here with Regina. She should be fourteen now, if I recall correctly. She's working there, helping with the smaller children. But with the Beal sisters there now, I'd say she could use a break. And someone has to teach these children how to cope."

Shelly smiled at that, her face lighting up. Rhonda noticed, and gave her a questioning look.

"Pete asked me to marry him," she announced softly, and startled gasps erupted around the room. Emma didn't look surprised at all, an hugged her daughter lovingly.

"You knew, didn't you?" Shelly accused.

"Pete did come speak to your father a week or so ago," Emma admitted.

"Oh, that's so sweet!" Amy sighed. "When's the big day?"

"What day?" Shelly shrugged. "There's no preacher here. We've decided that we're simply going to state that we're married, and that's it. Billy. . .believe it or not, Billy had already decided that would happen, and has been working on the George House for us. Pete's already staying there." She looked at her mother.

"I'm going to move in with him at the end of next week. I. . .I was hoping that Daddy would say some words over us, Momma. It won't be like a preacher did it, but it's the best we're going to get, looks like."

"I'm sure he'll be thrilled," Emma smiled. "And this means we'll need to plan a party of some kind, ladies," she added. Elizabeth had a funny look on her face, and Emma noticed.

"Something wrong, dear?" she asked. Elizabeth didn't reply directly, but looked at Shelly.

"Would it. . .would it be stealing any thunder from you if Howie and I. . .if we asked your father to do the same for us?" she asked shyly. "I mean, I don't want to intrude. . . ."

"Don't be silly!" Shelly exclaimed. "Of course! A double wedding!" More squeals of excitement erupted, and the others gathered around the two blushing brides. Finally, after several moments, Emma called their attention back.

"Ladies, as much fun as this is, we need to get back to the matter at hand. We've found homes for four of these children, three of them teens. Anyone else?" Eyes darted around the table at that. Amy held up her hands, palms up.

"I'd love to, but. . .with helping Doc get the clinic ready, and the lack of room we have, I don't see how it's possible."

"We need to be working on getting your two families into separate housing," Rhonda mused. "I mean, unless you want to stay that way."

Odd Billy Todd

"We get along fine," Amy looked at Debby, who nodded, "but I have to admit, it would be great to have a home of our own again."

"I agree," Debby nodded again. "We have no difficulties, but it's sometimes a bit. . .cramped. Especially this last winter." Everyone could agree with that.

"Well, what do we have available?"

"Again, not the discussion for today," Emma reminded them. "Let's talk about that soon, though. I take it we've gotten about as far as we can for the moment?" Heads nodded in agreement.

"Very well, then. Let's see to getting that done today," Emma ordered. "And I'd like to suggest we meet like this at least once a week, weather permitting, from now on. We simply cannot leave these kinds of decisions to the men. They haven't the smarts for them."

Billy swore later that he could hear the laughing from the front porch.

-

"I don't understand," Regina looked at the delegation. "What do you mean?"

"Just what we said, dear," Emma told her. "We're taking some of these children into our homes. There's simply too many here, and it's not right. Not fair for them, nor fair to you. You're practically a slave to this house. We intend to help correct that."

"Maria, Rhonda, Debby and I have all agreed to take in one child. We'll help get them moved this afternoon, so they can begin settling in. If you need help rearranging after this, we'll send someone along see that it's done."

"Also, we'll each be taking a turn here, once a week, to give you all time to have a day to yourselves. Starting next week. Our goal is to make sure that all of you are included in what's going on around here, and made to feel as if you're part of the community."

"We ain't really done a good job o' that, so far," Rhonda admitted, a bit shame faced. "It wasn't personal, or even intentional. Just. . .lotta work to get done. Sorry," she added.

"But I. . .I thought we would be. . .have to. . . ."

"Have to what?" Emma asked. "Raise them all yourself? Heavens no, child. I wouldn't wish a houseful of kids on my worst enemy," the older woman laughed. "And besides, how are you six going to have any kind of life, if you're constantly tied down caring for all these children?"

"Now, let's get this done, and then we need to set up a schedule. All of us have other duties, so it's important that everyone knows when they should be here, and for how long. It may be that we have to divide the day, to ensure that. . . ."

As Rhonda watched Emma deal with everything, she couldn't help but smile. Sometimes there was no substitute for experience.

-

Trey was a bit hesitant at supper, at first. He was trying to take in the fact that he now lived with his friend Danny, and his family.

"Tomorrow I'll show ya my horse!" Danny exuded. "Once ya learn to ride, why we can roam all over the place!"

"I don't know if I'm allowed to ride," Trey replied. "I'll have to ask."

"You're allowed," Billy told him flatly. "Fact is, you'll have to. Lot o' work around here, and you gotta get to it somehow. We'll have to get you fixed up. Might see to cuttin' you a pony out tomorrow."

"Oh, I can't cut a pony!" Trey looked horrified.

"I meant cut'im out o' the herd, boy," Billy smiled. "That's what it's called when ya separate an animal from the rest o' the herd. Cuttin'im out."

"Oh," Trey dropped his eyes, looking embarrassed.

"Don't go gettin' all shy, Trey," Rhonda ordered. "You'll just have to learn, that's all. Same as everyone else does. No one knows anything until they learn."

"Okay," he nodded. "I want to learn."

"And you will," Billy assured him. "But your schoolin' comes first. Then chores. Then, when you're done, you got time to have fun. Includin' ridin'. And Danny, I reckon we need to talk later about this ridin' all over the valley," he added. Danny's face reddened.

"I didn't mean it like that," he promised. "I ain't never rode no further than the Clifton House, or over to Terry's. But if there was two of us. . . ." he started hopefully.

"Then there'll be two o' ya at the Clifton House, or at Terry's," Billy finished for him. "I'll let you know when that changes. Saves you from havin' to ask."

"Thanks," Danny muttered. He was chafing at the restrictions, but he admitted they were for his own good. Danny had filled out nicely with good food, clean water, and medical attention. Working around the farm had put muscles on him in a hurry, and he felt like he was more man than boy.

Billy really didn't mind Danny riding where he was of a mind to, since the boy had lived on his own for so long. But Rhonda didn't want him or Mary, and now Trey, he added, riding too far out on their own. Rhonda had a mother's instinct, and that meant that everyone had to stay where she could see them. Billy didn't tell Danny that. He allowed Danny to think that it was Billy who had placed the restrictions on him.

Rhonda was very thankful for that.

"Eat up, Trey," Billy urged. "You better get it while the gettin's good."

"That's sure the truth," Mary nodded, helping herself to seconds. "Food disappears fast around here, between Danny and Billy."

"Hey, I'm still a growin' boy!" Danny objected.

"And I'm. . .well, I just am," Billy told her, chewing on a strip of bacon.

"Don't talk with your mouthful," Rhonda and Mary said at once to both of them. Trey sat and watched the back and forth quietly.

"Better dig in," Billy warned again. "And you'll get used to us. Same as we'll have to get used to havin' you here all the time."

"Yes, sir," Trey nodded, and returned to his plate.

Rhonda smiled inwardly at how easily Billy took control, and made Trey feel at home. While she wasn't angry anymore with Regina, she was still glad to have the boy out of the house. Trey was a good boy, and he'd make a fine addition to their little family.

-

With four children gone from the Clifton House, things were much calmer, and the women who worked there began to get out more, and socialize more. Trey and Danny now had the 'job' of keeping the heavy work done at the home each day after class, which meant getting firewood up, taking care of the trash (burning all

Odd Billy Todd

the paper goods, and separating cans and bottles for possible re-use later. The women cleaned them, and kept them separate from the trash).

It wasn't long before Regina and Ben Kelvey were spending more and more time together. At first they thought they were being 'smart', but Howie saw everything from the security shack, and the two of them walking and holding hands couldn't get past him and his electronic eyes. Ben just shrugged, saying they would 'see what happened'.

Jon could see the writing on the wall, however, and started thinking about what to do. If his brother moved into Clifton House, there was no way to justify him staying where he was. With Howie and Liz already gone, Jon decided to start looking for a bachelor pad.

Dillon and his sister, Barbara, were still living with Terry, and they didn't want to enter the winter like that. With Pete gone there was room, barely, for them all, but Dillon didn't want to keep crowding the Blaine family. They had been good to the two siblings, and he didn't want to abuse their hospitality.

Realizing that they had the same problem, the two of them decided to put their heads together, and see what came of it. Jon had been ready to give up the Smith house, but if Dillon and his sister made their home there, then he would stay with them, the two decided.

That still left the fact that two families were living in the Franklin place, and something needed to be done about that. Pete and Shelly would soon be newly weds, and Billy was determined that the two of them would have the George house to themselves. He refused to even discuss the matter, even when Pete suggested it.

"No," he had said flatly, and that was that. No one wanted to argue with Billy, since he rarely objected to anything, anyway. He and Danny had worked long and hard, in the little free time they had had, making the place livable. Rhonda, once she realized they had done so, had taken Mary, and gone to help Shelly for an entire day cleaning and organizing.

The trouble was, there was no more nearby housing at all. The nearest home from the intersection that wasn't occupied was two miles back toward Cedar Bend. And that was a long way on foot or horse back. Both Amy and Debby needed to be nearby, due to their impact on the community as a whole, so that wasn't workable. The home was fine, really, but Billy was uneasy with anyone being that far away from the community as whole, thinking it was just too risky.

When Ben had learned of this discussion, he had just shrugged and suggested they build a house.

Build a house?" Billy looked stunned. "How?"

"Uh, nails, lumber, things like that," Ben said, his eyes twinkling at the chance to catch Billy off guard for once. "Billy, I'm a carpenter. We built the blockhouse from logs. We can build a house the same way. We just make it nicer, and more comfortable. It ain't that hard to do. Just takes a little work, and the right materials."

"Do we even have the stuff to do it?" Billy asked, warming to the idea.

"Pretty much," Ben had nodded. "We'll need to split some logs for the floor, or else find some lumber for it. I'm not sure we have enough, depending on what size house we build. We've got furnishings, and fixings, too. The only thing we won't be able to do is power it."

"What if we build it near a creek?" Billy asked, thinking. "Howie can put some o' them waterbugs o' his there. That'll give it some power, anyway."

"There's an idea," Ben nodded. "We just need to get started pretty soon, is all. With all hands on deck, we can probably have it together and finished in less than a week, once we've got everything together."

"Well," Billy breathed a bit. "Guess we need to start gatherin'."

"We're gonna have to cut some wood, too."

-

It was a simple affair. Everyone gathered together at Billy's, his place once more pressed into service as the best place for such things. Rhonda was tickled at that, while Billy endured it with good nature. Pete had asked Toby to be his best man, and the teen had agreed. Howie had asked Ben, who had likewise been tickled.

The brides wore dresses put together by the women on short notice. Both looked lovely. Howie looked at ease, since this was merely a formality. Pete on the other hand looked decidedly nervous. For him this was far from a mere formality.

Billy sat to the side watching the goings on. He had no real part to play, and that was fine by him. It gave him a chance to study everyone else.

Jerry looked proud as a peacock, smiling at everyone. His daughter was marrying as fine a young man as he could ask for. And he would get to say the words that bound them together. Couldn't ask for much more than that.

Emma looked equally pleased. It was evident that she approved of Pete. She cast a glance at Toby every now and then, he noticed. Probably wondering when and where Toby would get the bug. Toby took turns ignoring her and Mary, equally. Billy had to stifle a laugh. Mary was nothing if not determined. But Toby showed no interest. Billy hoped that didn't cause a problem later.

George and Debby were sitting together with their new daughter. Bethany was a pretty little thing, and it was obvious that both were taken with her. They seemed to have placed their difference behind them for good, and Billy was glad. He like George, and Debby was a great help, teaching the children the valley had acquired. Whatever happened, they would all be educated to at least a high school level.

The rest they'd have to learn from doing.

Trey and Danny were helping Mary with the refreshment table. There had been no bachelor party. Everyone had agreed that it was just too risky for them to be off guard at the moment. There were too many threats out there. There had just been a quiet gathering, where they had all had one good, stiff drink, toasting both grooms.

Doctor Collins was fitting in pretty good it seemed. He was a younger man than Billy had first thought, but he admitted that the Doctor hadn't been having his best days either time. He guessed Collins was about forty, maybe a little older, but not much. He was beginning to look healthy again, filling out, his skin losing it's pallor. Billy didn't want to think about the horrors the man had been through in Franklin.

Ralph and Amy were sitting quietly together, and Billy was pretty sure there was a battle of wills going on there, with a double wedding in the offing. Ralph didn't look unhappy, but he did look determined. That might change if the two of them ever got a home of their own.

Ben and Regina had surprised everyone by showing up together. Everyone 'knew' of course, but the two had been very circumspect with their relationship.

Odd Billy Todd

Both looked happy, Billy decided. He guessed they had decided to go 'public' as the saying went.

Seeing all this made Billy think about himself and Rhonda. Did she want to get married like this? So far as Billy was concerned they were already married. He was set on spending the rest of his life with her, and that was that. He didn't need a ceremony for that. He looked to where Rhonda was fussing over the food. As if she sensed his eyes on her, she looked toward him, giving him a dazzling smile. Billy returned it, and Rhonda went back to fussing.

Billy decided to see if this was something Rhonda wanted. If it was, then he'd just have to see she got it, that was all.

Someone had managed to come up with a copy of the Bridal March from somewhere, and it suddenly started playing. Everyone hustled to their seats, Rhonda waving for Billy to join her, which he did.

The two women walked out, Shelly first, escorted by Jerry, and Elizabeth, escorted by Jon. Ben and Toby had taken their places alongside the grooms, grinning.

As they arrived at the podium, Jerry stepped up, and turned to look at the small crowd.

"Friends and neighbors, today is a fine day the Lord has given us. Let us all be thankful for our blessings, for roofs over our heads, and for food in our bellies." He smiled down at the two couples.

"And for the fact that despite all we've been through, life does go on. We're are here today to witness the joining of these two couples in a bond meant to last a lifetime. One that will take them to great highs, and great lows as well. One that will stand the test of time so long as they are true and faithful to one another, and give one another the dignity and respect they deserve."

Billy listened halfheartedly as Jerry went on, his mind still on Rhonda, and their future. By the new standards, Billy was a wealthy man. He was a good provider, and a good protector. Rationally, he knew that. He worked hard, he made sure his house was in order, and that everyone under his roof had any and every thing they needed.

But there was more to it than that, he decided. He admitted what little he *knew* of being in a relationship he had learned *from* being in a relationship. With Rhonda. She was all he knew, and all he wanted to know.

He recognized, however, that there were things he needed to improve on. The only thing he knew to do was start trying things. He'd learn by trial and error. Just like she had told him, nearly a year ago.

He gently placed his arm around Rhonda's shoulders, earning him a quizzing look, followed by another smile, this one softer, and more intimate.

One down.

-

The party was over, and the newly weds were off to their respective homes. Clean up had been a group affair, so that by the time everyone had left, Rhonda had only to make sure that Danny and Trey had the trash in the right place, and she was done.

As a result, she and Billy were sitting on the porch, side by side in the swing. Mary had gone with Amanda, and the boys were out being boys.

"You know, there ain't a single thing 'bout us that's normal," Billy said suddenly.

"What?" Rhonda replied, startled from her thinking.

"Us. We ain't had a single normal thing between us."

"Well, Billy, I think some of what's between us has been normal, at least in form," Rhonda teased with a devilish little grin.

"You know what I mean," Billy chuckled. "We ain't had a single date o' no kind. Ain't never seen a movie, been out ta dinner, nothin'."

"Well, we kinda missed that opportunity, honey," Rhonda shrugged, and snuggled closer to him. "Do you think we're suffering from it? You feel like you've missed out on something?"

"No, but I worry that you do," Billy admitted. "Ever time we've been away from here together, we done been shot at, chased, put upon in some way. Ever time."

"Well, there's no doubt that life with you ain't never boring," Rhonda giggled.

"That's what I mean," Billy told her. "We ain't what you'd call a regular couple." Rhonda's head came up, her face suddenly serious.

"Where is this comin' from?" she demanded.

"Look at us. Here we are, ain't never even had a formal date together, but here we are, keepin' house, with three teen age kids, and the oldest not ten years younger'n either of us."

Is this about the kids? she wondered. *Is that what's brought this on?*

"Billy, does having the kids bother you?" she asked. "I. . .I mean I should have asked about Trey, I know. I made the decision while I was mad, but I don't regret it. He and Danny are as close as brothers, and. . . ."

"This ain't about them," Billy shook his head. "'Bout us. I. . .I got to thinkin' 'bout it today, at the weddin'. Is that somethin' you want for us? A weddin'?"

"Billy, are you askin' me to marry you?" Rhonda's eyes got big suddenly. She hadn't seen this coming.

"I am, if that's what you want," he nodded. "See, I don't care 'bout no ceremony, either way. Far as I'm concerned, we're married. Til death do us part. Some words and a cake won't make that no stronger'n I feel right now, Rhonda. But I want you to have'em, if you want'em. Only. . .I can't figure out if you do or not, so I'm askin'. Do you wanna get married?" He took something out of his pocket, and took her hand.

"My momma had small fingers, just like yours," he said softly, and slipped what had been his mother's engagement ring onto her finger. It was slightly large, but nothing that some tape wouldn't fix. Rhonda looked at it for a moment, then up at Billy, her eyes watering.

"Oh, Billy, it's beautiful," she all but whispered, hugging him tightly. He returned her embrace, smiling into the wall behind her.

"So do you want a weddin' like today?" he asked as they separated.

"I. . .Billy, ever girl want's a weddin'," she admitted. "But. . .I feel the same way you do. As far as I'm concerned, you're it. Lord knows I crushed on you in high school enough. And since. . .since we been together, I ain't had much to be sorry for, even with the world gone to hell. I can't. . .I don't see how anything could be better for me than you." Billy's heart swelled at that. He was pretty sure she felt the same, but hearing it put him at ease.

"So you want the weddin', then," he grinned. She nodded, her lips spreading into a smile.

"I'd like that," she admitted. "To stand up in front of everyone and show them how much I love you."

"Then I reckon we'll have us one."

CHAPTER SEVENTY-EIGHT

The two decided they would wait until after the harvest. There was a lot going on at the moment, and they didn't want to interrupt any of it. There was still a house to be built, and soon crops to gather, which meant corn and wheat to be ground, and the garden hadn't stopped producing, so there was still canning to be done.

Billy had a quiet word with Jerry, who grinned like a Cheshire cat.

"I wondered if that would push you two into it," he admitted. Billy grinned a little, but nodded.

"Reckon it's what a girl wants," he replied.

Meanwhile, work went on. Ben had cut it pretty fine, but they were almost finished with the new house before it was time to think of harvesting the fields. The decision had been made to place the new house in the field near the Clifton House. That would add to the security up there, plus the creek flowing alongside that field would provide much needed power. The clinic rested between the new house and the Clifton House, which would put more people in that area, in case something happened.

Ben had drawn a progressive plan for the house, and in the end, they had to scrounge to find enough finishing materials to get the inside completed. Fortunately, Billy had never cleaned out completely the lumber yard in Cedar Bend, taking only what he had needed at the time, or what he might need in the future. He hadn't ever gone back to get more because he hadn't needed it.

The house was a single-story dwelling. The center rooms were the living area, dining area, and kitchen. From each side of the large open area, were two bedrooms, sharing a common bathroom between them. At some point, if the need arose, additional rooms could be added, he assured them.

Billy had watched Ben notch the logs and fit them together with a craftsman's touch. Ralph had in no way exaggerated Ben's ability. By the time they were finished, Billy was wishing he could get a new barn built that way.

"Why not," Ben shrugged. "Have to wait a while, but I don't see why not. Won't need any finishing stuff, so it's just log work. Be glad to." Billy was thrilled, and started thinking of some way to repay Ben.

The house finished, Dillon and Barbara took their leave of the Blaine's house, and took up residence. Jon and Ben decided to go ahead and move in to the other rooms, so that the Smith house would be empty at last.

On the day before harvest was due to start, George and Debby moved into the house, with everyone pitching in to help. The Purdy's had decided to move because it would be easier than Ralph having to move his shop, and the leather worker was grateful for that. The two families were still neighbors, and good friends, but no longer had the strain of living under the same roof.

The next day, as harvest set in, Megan Johnson moved in with them. The now seventeen-year-old was a friend of Amanda's, and ready to be away from the 'kid farm' as she called it. There were still nine children, and five more or less adults living there, but the house was large, and so many leaving had allowed more room to spread out, for which Regina and the others were grateful.

Slowly but surely, things were becoming settled.

Harvest was back breaking. They had all known it would be, but they hadn't begun to suspect just how much so. In addition to gathering the crops, there was also another cutting of hay to get in. It truly was all hands on deck for this one.

The 'woman's circle' decided to set up shop in the common house, and use it to grind meal and flour. Emma showed everyone how to go about separating the wheat, and tending to the corn. While that was drying out, they lent a hand at keeping chores up all over.

The men divided into two teams. Pete and Billy took Toby, Danny and Trey, and started on the hay. The rest, including Howie, were assisting Jon and Jerry as they tried to make as many rounds as possible each day. They had over a thousand acres planted in one thing or another, and it took time to gather than much.

Corn was stored, hay was stacked and covered, and wheat thrashed. Howie promised that next year he'd have a mill up and running, so that this particular process would be easier the next time. Howie liked to eat, and knew where his bread was buttered.

Two weeks of solid, never ending work later, they were finished for the most part. That was because most of the corn was simply emptied into the cribs and silos they had prepared earlier in the year, and the rapeseed was stored similarly at the Richardson Barn, where Terry lived, and Ralph and Howie kept their bio fuel set up. Neither hazarded a guess as to how much fuel they would get from the rapeseed.

"Just have to see."

By the end of three weeks, they were finished. Equipment was readied for winter, and stored, food was prepped and put away. Everyone took a single day of rest, and then went back to working their own gardens, which were producing one last weak run of veggies.

The great herd was finally separated, with the result being five smaller herds, all driven to new pastures. Three new hay barns ensured adequate storage for the coming winter, and spreading the cattle into other areas let them take advantage of barns still up in the valley. New fencing was needed in a few places, but it was all minor work, requiring a few hours here and there, rather than days.

The hogs were separated as well, into three places for them, with new coverings and food storage on site. The hope was that if any one herd of either developed a problem, then at least some animals would survive.

October was into it's second full week by the time anyone could stop to take a breath.

Everyone was still worried about someone finding them, but the tension had eased somewhat as the weeks passed without incident. Howie had worked almost continuously on upgrading their security, and the motion senors now all pinged softly when activated. A computer screen showed the location of each sensor all the time, while another cycled through their cameras. There weren't that many camera's, but they were all placed in the most likely access points to the valley.

Billy and Rhonda had a surprise, when Dottie was found to be expecting. She had apparently came into season during harvest, when no one was looking. Both hoped that Rommel was the father, and since they hadn't found any dogs bleeding to death on their farm, they assumed he was.

Odd Billy Todd

One of Ralph's Annie's was also expecting, from Reb, which was good news for everyone. She tended to have large litters, Ralph promised, so they might soon have more dogs to protect the herds. Billy's two female donkey's were also expecting, which would allow them to move the jack's into the smaller herds soon. The colts would need a year to develop, at least, but donkeys were good protection against wild dogs.

They hadn't experienced any dog attacks since Billy and Rhonda had killed those responsible for killing the calf the year before, but no one wanted to assume there wouldn't be anymore. Toby's run in with the aggressive dogs during the scouting mission reminded everyone there was always risk.

The group was starting to settle into their new reality, as well. No one went unarmed outside the house, for any reason. The Sunday church gatherings were no exception. Everyone was glad to hear of the small services, and almost every Sunday the service was followed by a group meal. Even the March and Williams families participated. The March children were also now associating with the other kids, at least on occasion.

The common house was finally finished as November approached, and school was moved there. For now the children walked to school, escorted by the older children, including Danny and Trey. Toby usually walked along with them, just for good measure. The children that were armed kept their weapons with them, even in school.

Billy had gotten Trey to the range, but the boy was still hesitant with the shotgun they had selected for him, so he didn't go armed, usually. As he grew more comfortable, that would change, but for now only Mary and Danny carried weapons.

With work slowing, Billy started working on his new barn. He cut the logs, and began to learn how to notch them from Ben. Almost everyday, others would join them, assisting with the work. Billy took the small track hoe they had brought to the farm and added a root cellar to the new barn at Rhonda's request. That added to the time needed to finish the barn, but Billy figured it would be worth it to have the root cellar.

It helped that Billy didn't need or want a floor inside. It was a barn, he reasoned, not a house. A dirt floor would be more than adequate.

A week before Thanksgiving, Ben put the finishing touches on the roof. Billy was very pleased with the new structure.

"Ben, whatever you need or want from me, you got it," he told the older man. "This is great!"

"Well, you did a lot of the work yourself, Billy," Ben pointed out.

"Couldn't o' done it without you," Billy shook his head. "What can I do for you?" Ben looked down at the ground for a minute, then sighed.

"Regina needs some. . .well, some woman stuff," he shrugged finally. "I got no idea where to come by it."

"No problem," Billy assured him. He went straight to his small shop building and returned in just a moment with a large box of the 'stuff' that Regina needed.

"I took this when I was still in town," Billy explained at Ben's look. "I figured someone would need it or want it down the road. Already gave the most of it away, but I still got this here. That work?"

"Billy, you're a miracle," Ben shook his head with a chuckle. "Man, this'll make me her knight in shining armor, sure enough!" Ben's face was lit up like a Christmas tree. Remembering that Ben had lost his first wife to the plague, Billy wondered how long it had been since the man had been truly happy.

"Take it with my thanks," Billy told him. "And anything else you might need and I got some of you just name it."

"Billy, I don't know of a thing I really need, and this will really put me in good with Regina," he grinned. "And it ain't like I don't owe you, ya know."

"Don't owe me nothin'," Billy insisted. "If you think you did, stop thinkin' it. If we ain't even now, it's cause I owe you. Hear?"

"I hear," Ben nodded. "If I think of something I'll holler. Fair enough?"

"More than," Billy agreed. "Thanks again, Ben. And take care."

-

With the weather growing colder, it was decided to have their Thanksgiving dinner in the new 'blockhouse'. The building was finished now, and had amenities, so all that was required was to move the tables and chairs that were normally kept at Billy and Rhonda's down there.

The building had turned out very nice, Billy thought. It was sturdy, and could probably hold off an attack from anything up to a tank or artillery. He hoped they never saw an attack, but the building's presence was a comfort.

Everyone brought favorite foods, music, and games, and the community made a day of it. Everyone finished their chores that morning, so that all that was left to do was enjoy. The weather was pleasant, with the temperature climbing into the low sixties by noon. There was a slight wind blowing wisps of clouds around, and it was just overall a nice day.

Pete and Shelly left after two hours to relieve Howie and Elizabeth at the security station. This let both newlywed couples enjoy both the dinner, and some privacy on their first Thanksgiving as man and wife.

Billy danced with Rhonda, and then with Mary, but then walked outside, as the noise and the press of people started to get to him. Rhonda understood, and smiled when he told her he needed air. She took Billy as he was, flaws and all, just as he did her.

Sitting outside, Billy paused to reflect on the last six months or so. It had been a wild and hectic year, but a productive one all the same. They had added people to their community, stymied a possible threat, at least for the time being, and had a good harvest. They would survive another winter, if nothing bad happened. All of the houses were equipped to deal with the winter weather, since they now had a good idea of what to expect. Roofs had been strengthened on every building, and the new structures built with the weight of deep, heavy snow in mind.

There was hay and to spare, safely tucked away in a total of five barns, and plenty of feed too. All in all, Billy had to believe that this year had been a good one, and they had much to be thankful for.

He was still feeling good about things when Terry found him.

"We got some news, Billy."

-

"Train hit again," Pete said without preamble. "Paid a visit to our friends in Centerville, it seems. We heard radio traffic from both sides this time. Train finally

Odd Billy Todd

pulled out. Their bosses decided there wasn't enough reward for the risk involved."

"They're headed south," he finished, looking at Billy, who suddenly leaned forward.

"Are they now?" Terry looked between the two of them for a moment.

"What?" he demanded finally.

"Well," Billy said slowly, "I got me a plan. . . ."

-

"There is absolutely no reason at all to do this," Terry shook his head. "They aren't coming near us. No tracks near us. Nothing. Let them go."

"Sooner or later, they'll come to call," Billy shrugged. "And this here is a good chance to stop'em for good. Might not get another."

"I'm in," Dillon Branch said at once. "Hell, I like this idea!"

"I'll go," Toby nodded.

"Me too, I guess," George nodded.

"No," Billy shook his head. "Just me, Pete and Dillon. No more. Just in case." He didn't add just in case 'we don't come back', but he didn't have to, either. They were all thinking it.

"Billy, I admit it's a good idea," Terry tried again, "but it's risky, and there's no reason to do it. None."

"I disagree," Jerry surprised them all. "Billy's right. That bunch has been a thorn in our side since the beginning. And sooner or later, we'll see'em come sweepin' though here. If there's a chance to get rid of'em, I say it's worth taking."

"We're goin'," Billy said flatly. "And the sooner the better. We ain't got long. May already be too late. I'm headed home to get my stuff. Ya'll comin' best do the same. We got thirty minutes." With that he was up and gone. He called Rhonda, and spoke to her. She immediately followed him home. Pete stood and went to find Shelly, and soon they, too, were on their way.

Dillon spoke quietly to his sister for just a minute, then kissed her on top of the head, and went home to gear up. Barbara didn't object, but was visibly upset.

The other men watched, saying nothing.

-

"I don't understand," Rhonda argued. "Why now?"

"Best chance we'll ever have to stop'em," Billy told her, hurriedly gathering his things. "They're on the right track, headin' the right way, for this to work. Might never get this good a shot at'em again."

"Billy, there's too many of them!" she protested.

"We ain't gonna fight'em straight up," Billy assured her. "Gonna trap'em nice and neat, and let nature do the work for us, as far as she will. Timin' couldn't really be no better, considerin'."

"Please be careful," Rhonda's voice was soft.

"I promise," Billy nodded. "And I'll be back, and we'll have us a weddin'. I mean it. We ain't goin' to start a war, just ta finish one. We do this right, won't be nothin' left to worry about. Okay?"

Rhonda nodded, not trusting herself to speak. Instead, she hugged him desperately, fighting her tears.

"I gotta go," he said finally. "Ain't got much time."

"I love you, Billy," she said tearfully.

"Love you too, woman," he grinned.

And then he was gone.

-

Pete looked at the gear, and nodded. Dillon looked at the gear and got a hungry gleam in his eye.

"Oh, this will be fun!" he enthused.

"Let's just make sure it's done," Billy shrugged. "We got ever thing?"

"We do," Pete nodded. "Let's get moving. Clock's against us already."

With everything loaded and ready, the three piled into the Hummer and took off, all three silent, drawn into their own thoughts.

CHAPTER SEVENTY-NINE

The track that the Train was using was an old one. Reworked many times since it's original construction, it was still in use because it had never been cost effective to replace. There was one weakness, however, along this track, that Billy felt could be exploited.

A long trestle, crossing the Duck River and it's surrounding flood plain, was rather aged. Recent rains should have left the flooded river high, and the trestle had three weight bearing spans that crossed the river and it's flood plain. The plain was empty save for a few trees, with no one living closer than three miles. The area was desolate, far from anything but back roads, and absent of any immediate assistance for someone who found themselves in a bind.

And that was *before* the fall of the world.

It was perfect for what Billy had in mind.

"Assumin' the Train don't stop nowhere 'fore it gets here, I figure we'll have about a hour, once we get there," Billy explained, indicating the map as Pete pushed the Hummer faster and faster.

"So, what's the plan?" Dillon asked, leaning forward from the back seat.

"I got eight pounds o' C-4, and some det cord, and a radio detonator."

"Where in the hell did you *get* that?" Pete asked.

"Found it," Billy shrugged. "I also got three gallons o' homemade napalm," he added. "What I'm thinkin', we string the 'explosives on the bridge supports on either side o' the river. They're old, and prob'ly not in the best o' shape. We can hang the napalm jars, all in quarts, and once the fireball goes, I think they'll go with it. If not, we can shoot'em, and the napalm'll just shower down on'em."

"You know it won't work that easy, right?" Dillon asked. "I mean, it sounds like you thought it out okay, but I'm just sayin'."

"I know," Billy nodded. "But if any of it works, then we'll hurt'em, at least. Right?"

"Yeah," Dillon nodded. "It'll hurt, no matter what."

"And I think I got something that'll take the engine down, no matter what. Leave'em stranded if nothin' else, on the trestle." He reached into his pocket and pulled out five fifty caliber rounds.

"Is that. . . ."

"Yep," Billy nodded. "Three 211's, and two SLAP's. I think that should hurt the lead engine, and the second one, too, if I can hit'em."

"The Raufoss will do more damage, for sure," Pete commented. "The AP's will likely penetrate the skin, and the bullet will do some damage. No way of knowing how much, though. Depends on where you hit it."

"I thought I'd try to hit the engineer's compartment with them," Billy admitted. "I was hopin' it would do some damage to the instruments and controls."

"Sounds like your best bet," Pete nodded.

"How far away are we?" Dillon asked as Billy loaded the magazine for his rifle.

"Another twenty minutes, I figure."

The water was high all right.

"Well, shit," Dillon muttered. "What now?"

"We'll have to get on the track back there," Pete pointed the way they came. "We'll get as close as we can, and hump the rest of the way."

"This is gonna be tight," Dillon pointed out.

"We can make it," Billy promised. "Let's go."

Pete maneuvered the Hummer as close as possible to the tracks, finding a flat spot along the tracks.

"Ya know," Dillon mused thoughtfully, "this thing could probably make it down the tracks."

"Think so?" Pete asked, judging the track.

"Well, this thing ain't nothin' like as wide as a train engine," Billy shrugged. "We'd have to go all the way on down to get off, or come back this way, in reverse. Ain't no place to turn around. And we sure don't wanna be on that trestle when the train gets here."

"Give us a lot more time, we ain't got to hump all this stuff down there," Dillon said.

"All right, we'll try it," Pete nodded, conscious of the time factor.

He eased up onto the track bed, working to keep the tires on the ties, and off the rails. Soon they were bumping along at the blinding speed of five miles per hour. It was a rugged ride, but in mere minutes they were on the trestle.

"You guys get the C-4?" Billy asked.

"I can," Dillon nodded. "Used it more'n once. Or twice, for that matter," he grinned.

"Then I'm gonna set the napalm. I just got an idea that'll make it more workable, I think. There's twelve jars, and I got some of them cannon fuses. I can use them, hook'em to a treble hook, and let the train set'em off for us."

"Damn, that's a good idea," Pete said approvingly. "Need help?"

"Get the C-4 first," Billy shook his head. "Then you guys can help me finish."

The three of them worked fast, but very carefully. Pete and Dillon worked on the two center supports, packing the weakest points around them with the explosives. After looking at the trestle for a few minutes, Dillon had decreed that there was enough to sabotage two supports, instead of one, and still bring them down.

"Trick is to weaken'em with the blast," he told Pete. "Ain't got to bring'em down. Weight of the train'll do that just fine, I'd say."

"You sure?" Pete asked, worried.

"Did it before," Dillon shrugged. "Three or four times, maybe," he added vaguely. "And at least twice on trestles in better shape than this one."

"Where?" Pete asked, curious.

"Here and there," Dillon shrugged. "Don't matter none, now, I reckon." With that he concentrated on what he was doing. Pete decided he wouldn't ask again.

Billy meanwhile was strapping the jars of napalm to the supports along the bridge. Each one had a hole hastily punched into the lid, and one of his brass cannon fuses taped in place in the hole, pointing straight down into the volatile substance. He staggered the jars from side to side, working his way toward the far end. There wasn't enough to cover everything, so he tried to guess where things would be when the train reached this point, and place the jars accordingly.

To each fuse was tied a piece of green cotton twine. It was the best color that Billy could come up with not to show up enough to give any warning. He pulled the twine from each fuse to the end of the bridge, where a treble hook was attached. Once he was finished, all the treble hooks would be left to drag a few inches above the track, where the engine would catch them, pulling the fuses.

"That's pretty damn ingenious," Dillon observed, and he climbed back onto the tracks. Pete nodded.

"It's just a back up, but it might hurt'em some," Billy shrugged, checking the lines one more time.

"Reckon we better git," Billy said, rising to his feet. "I can feel the tracks vibratin'."

All three men scurried to the truck. Pete hit reverse and started backing the way they had come, not nearly as slow or careful as he had been on the trip down.

"Be careful, buddy, or we'll be stuck here!" Dillon shouted, bouncing in the rear seat as he tried to watch out the back and stay out of Pete's vision at the same time.

"We don't get off this trestle, we go swimming!" Pete shouted back. "Or worse!"

"True," Dillon murmured.

"And we can't go forward, count o' the hooks!" Billy added. "This is our only way out."

It seemed like forever before the track started to level out, or rather that the sharp drop off from the rail bed started to rise. As soon as there was room, Pete slid to a halt, and started looking for a place to get off the tracks. With the engine idling, Billy leaned out of the window.

"I can hear it," he said calmly. "Gettin' close."

"I'm working on it!" Pete replied. He aimed the truck for a low spot, and eased it downward. Suddenly the water drenched bank gave, and the Hummer lurched down and to the left.

The Hummer hung in mid-air on two wheels. Everyone froze, waiting to see what happened.

In the distance, the noise of the train became louder. The vibrations of the approaching locomotive, and it's cars, could be felt through the left rear tire, still hung on the tracks. There was no time to panic, or else all three would have. Instead, they simply waited. Billy clung to the grab bar on his side for all he was worth, knowing if he let go, his shifting weight would send the truck over onto it's side.

Dillon was still in the middle of the rear seat, his eyes wide as he tried to hold his place. One hand on the gun mount above him, another wrapped around the safety harness, locked into a painful fist. He, too, knew that if his grip failed, they would overturn.

Pete took a deep, careful breath, afraid to move more than that. He could hear the train coming just as well as the others, but there was nothing he could do but wait. He strained to hold the wheel against the front left tire that wanted to turn, and follow the impetus of the vehicle that wanted to turn over. His mind went through a dozen calculations in a split second, and all of them ended in failure. No matter what he chose to do, it wouldn't help.

All they could do was wait. And hold on for dear life.

CHAPTER EIGHTY

Billy took a greater hold on the 'oh-shit' bar, and placed his feet firmly against the floor, bracing them against the transmission hump.

"Billy, what, are, you, doing," Pete hissed through clenched teeth.

"Got me an idea," Billy grunted. "We got to fish or cut bait, here, or we gonna get hit by that train." His window was open.

Billy slowly and carefully pulled himself up toward the window, using his feet only when he had to. He reached through the window and grasped the edge of the window, roof side, and continued to pull. His body was half out of the window when the Hummer started to lean back to his side.

"Oh shit, oh shit, oh shit," Dillon repeated over and over, his calm desperately damaged by their predicament. "Billy be careful, we're rockin'!"

"I know," Billy grunted, and leaned further out of the Hummer. Suddenly, the vehicle groaned slightly, and with a heavy thud, landed on all four tires. Pete had barely had time to let out a sigh of relief when the bank gave way again, and the truck started sliding down the embankment.

"Hold on!" he called out. "I can't stop us!" Billy was still scrambling back inside when the Hummer reached the bottom.

Dillon looked forward and saw a tree branch sticking well into the right of way. If Billy didn't get back. . .He reached forward, grabbed Billy's belt, and then threw himself back, Billy coming with him, minus most of the skin on his left ear.

"Ow!" Billy grunted. "That hurt!"

"Sorry, man," Dillon told him, wide eyed. "That branch. . . ." he pointed. Billy looked and saw the branch, now broken, sitting right outside his window.

"Good night," he breathed, rubbing his ear. "Reckon I'll trade an ear for the rest. Thanks Dillon."

"Don't mention it. Really. Now can we make with the 'git the hell outta here' part of the plan?"

"Hell yes," Pete murmured, and hit the gas. They followed the right of way until a break appeared. Pete never slowed, hitting the opening but leaving some paint behind. No one cared. Pete fought the steering wheel as they bumped through the thicket, trying to get back to the road. They were nearly out when Dillon, still glued to the back window, spoke.

"There it is!" Pete instantly moved to hit the breaks, then stopped. The brake lights on this thing weren't disabled. If he hit the pedal, someone would see.

"Get us on the road," Billy ordered. "Even if they see us, they ain't got time to stop, and nowhere to unload. Let's go!" Pete nodded, and kept going. The Hummer clawed its way up onto the levee the road was built on, throwing mud in every imaginable direction.

Now it was a race. They needed to get back to the bridge in time for Billy to take a shot at the engines pulling the train. Pete worked to get every ounce of speed the Hummer had left to give, while Billy and Dillon held on for dear life.

Suddenly the bridge was there, and Pete threw on the brakes. The Hummer fishtailed slightly, but slid to a halt at the edge of the bridge. Billy was out and running for the back while the truck was still in gear. Dillon got up in the turret, and manned the fifty.

Pete grabbed the binoculars, and took a position at the hood, leaving room for Billy's rifle. Billy hustled to the front, dropping the bi-pod on the hood, already deployed as he slammed the magazine home.

"Range?" Billy asked. Pete hit the laser on the binoculars.

"Three hundred fifty-three yards," Pete replied. Billy turned the dials on his scope, already looking into the reticle.

"Wind is. . . ." Pete started, but Billy cut him off.

"Ain't got the time," he said. "Train's on the bridge." Pete nodded. He could see it too.

Billy set the rifle up, and got comfortable. He had staggered the rounds, planning to use the first three on the lead engine, and the last two on the second. If there was a third. . .he tried not to focus on that.

"Who's got the detonator?" he asked. When Pete didn't answer, Billy turned to see Pete frantically patting his pockets.

"Are you shittin' me?" Billy growled. He could hear Dillon scrambling around in the Hummer.

"I got it! I got it!" Dillon called frantically, trying to get out. Pete ran to the window and grabbed the switch, racing back to stand by Billy. Dillon climbed back into the turret, too short of breath to speak.

Billy watched the train move slowly across the trestle. It occurred to him that their luck had held. The train had been slowing for this crossing, or it would have caught them on the tracks.

"Gettin' close," he murmured, and took a site. He led the engine only slightly, getting the motion in his head. When the lead engine was about thirty feet from where he thought the hooks were, he squeezed the trigger.

Pete watched the round impact. The round's explosive charge went through the side of the massive engine as if it were clay. He could see the charge go off, and pieces and parts fly away. The engine immediately started making a terrible screeching sound.

"Don't know what you hit, but that sounds *bad*," Dillon said gleefully.

"Now," Billy said softly, sending the SLAP round into the cabin. Pete raised the detonator, and squeezed. Billy moved his rifle, and sent the next Raufoss round into the trailing engine. This round didn't create quite as much ruckus, but it was immediately obvious that something vital had been struck, when the engine flamed.

The charges went off just as the lead engine hit the treble hooks, and pulled the first fuse. The quart jars on the far side of the train flamed to life, showering the train cars with burning jelly.

Underneath, the charges had done their work. True to Dillon's prediction, they didn't take out the supports, but they did weaken them. And the engine was grinding to a halt, pulling fuses even as it died.

Three of the fuses failed to fire. The rest engulfed a good portion of the train in flames that would not be easily put out. Now immobile, and on fire, the people on the train were bailing out to see what was happening. They emerged only to be showered in the flaming goo, which stuck to everything it touched on both sides of the train.

Odd Billy Todd

Screaming carried across the water as those first off caught the worst of the fire. Those following hesitated, then tried to help their comrades. As the three friends watched, others tried to fight the fires, while still more tried to get forward to check on the engine, and find out why they weren't moving.

When it happened, it was in slow motion. The left side support from where they were viewing began to crumble under a weight it was never meant to bear so directly for so long. As it began to give way, the right side support went with it in a screeching of torn metal and thunk of broken concrete.

As they watched, the cars above the supports began to fall, pulling others with them. A chain reaction started, as the remaining supports began to buckle, unable to hold against the weight and the pull of the falling bridge. First in pieces, and then in whole stretches, the bridge crumbled into the river, and the flooded plain around it. Succeeding cars were simply dragged along into the water or the mire, until only three remained on the tracks, left behind when their coupling had broken.

No one spoke for the first minute, too awestruck by the damage they had caused. Billy was the first one to offer a comment.

"Guess it worked."

They watched for nearly two hours. So far, they had seen only seven people emerge from the water, or the mud. Those seven were in no condition to lend assistance to the others. If there were any others.

"Should shoot'em," Dillon said softly.

"Should, I reckon," Billy nodded.

"Be the smart thing to do," Pete agreed. Yet no one made a move to do so. Finally, in silent agreement, they loaded into the Hummer, and started for home. It was a quiet trip, as each man was alone with his own thoughts.

The Train was finished.

Billy and Rhonda were married a week later. Danny and Trey served as his groomsmen, with Mary and Shelly standing with Rhonda. It was a much quieter affair than the double wedding earlier in the year, with everyone standing in attendance. Because the weather was getting worse, with a snow threatening, the couple had managed to forgo a big celebration, settling for dishes being brought to the house for them to eat over the next few days.

Emma had corralled both Danny and Trey, taking them home with her, while Mary had gone to stay with Amanda. Billy and Rhonda would have three precious days of privacy, something they hadn't enjoyed in a long time.

Once everyone was off, the two departed together, walking the short distance home arm in arm.

"Well, do you feel married?" Billy asked, smiling.

"I do," Rhonda said solemnly, then broke into a giggle. "How 'bout you?"

"I feel like I'm the luckiest man in the world," Billy answered honestly.

"I love you Billy Todd."

"I love you too, Rhonda Todd."

"Looks like winter's early again," Rhonda sighed, as snow began to fall as they reached the steps to the front porch.

"Looks like it's right on time to me," was all Billy said, as he scooped her up into his arms, and carried her into the house.

Outside, across the little valley that so many now called home, snow fell, blanketing the surrounding area with the silence of peace.

THE END

A MESSAGE FROM AUTHOR N.C. REED

This was the first novel I published, whether on Amazon or anywhere else. To say there were problems would be a severe understatement. Now, with more than a dozen titles under the Creative Texts Publishers imprint, we are constantly striving to improve and respond to your feedback.

I hope you enjoy Billy and I want to say "Thank You" to all of my readers and express to you my appreciation for your patronage and your support, and most certainly for your kind words about my work. There has been many a late night when that encouragement was what kept me writing when I was ready to throw in the towel and give up.

If you enjoyed Odd Bily Todd or any of my other works, please let me know with a review on Amazon, or Goodreads, or you can visit my blog at badkarma00.wordpress.com. There are links there to my Facebook page as well.

You'll find a lot of odd and end stuff there that I work on to piddle when I can't get anything else done. Feel free to leave a comment. I know that it doesn't get updated often enough but I do try to post important notices there, and ANY books released by me will always be posted there and on my Facebook page. You can also visit my publisher's web site at www.CreativeTexts.com for more updates, great books, special promotions, and lots of other good stuff.

Again, thank you.

N.C. Reed

THANK YOU FOR READING!

If you enjoyed this book, we would appreciate your customer review on your book seller's website or on Goodreads.

Also, we would like for you to know that you can find more great books like this one at
www.CreativeTexts.com

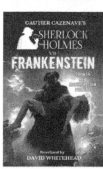

Made in the USA
Las Vegas, NV
18 February 2022